SCHOOL'S OUT
FOREVER

An Abaddon Books™ Publication
www.abaddonbooks.com
abaddon@rebellion.co.uk

This omnibus published in 2012 by Abaddon Books™,
Rebellion Intellectual Property Limited,
Riverside House, Osney Mead, Oxford, OX2 0ES, UK.

10 9 8 7 6 5 4 3 2 1

Editor-in Chief: Jonathan Oliver
Desk Editor: David Moore
Cover Art: Luke Preece
Original Series Cover Art: Mark Harrison
Design: Parr & Preece
Marketing and PR: Michael Molcher
Creative Director and CEO: Jason Kingsley
Chief Technical Officer: Chris Kingsley
The Afterblight Chronicles™ created by Simon Spurrier & Andy Boot

ISBN (UK): 978-1-78108-026-9
ISBN (US): 978-1-78108-027-6

Printed in the US

AN OMNIBUS OF POST-APOCALYPTIC NOVELS

SCHOOL'S OUT
FOREVER

SCOTT K. ANDREWS

WWW.ABADDONBOOKS.COM

The Afterblight Chronicles Series

INTRODUCTION

I'D LIKE TO start by apologising.

See, I love these books. Frickin' *love* 'em. Obviously, we love all our books equally, here at Abaddon Towers, and I know you're not supposed to have favourites, but of all the favourites I don't have, these are among my most illicitly favouritey.

Scott K. Andrews was a happy discovery. When you're starting a new imprint, inevitably you tap into your networks: you talk to agents, approach authors you already know, tap (in our case) into the talent pool already working for our sister imprint, *2000 AD*; try and get some strong titles out there right away. But having sorted out our first couple of commissions, we floated the world bibles for most of our settings out there for people to submit to. Just to see who'd bite.

Scott bit. He gave us a couple of concepts, and his *Afterblight Chronicles* pitch, *School's Out* (which you can see at the back of the book, in the bonus material section), grabbed us. And a future Kitschie nominee was born.

Which makes it sound like he came out of nowhere, but Scott's prouder than anyone I know that he's paid his dues and shown his commitment. If there was work, he's taken it, and given it his all. This is the man who wrote *The Unofficial Guide to* Dawson's Creek, and he's pretty damned proud of that, too.

So why am I apologising?

Scott's an amazing writer, and he captured the feel of Abaddon right away. We need fast-moving and high-action, and he delivered that in spades. We need dark and gritty, and he was all over it. And most of all, we needed really engaging characters. These books weren't going to be long, and the pace was going to be relentless; the reader would have to connect with the heroes quickly.

And you will connect with these characters. Shit, you'll love them. They'll get under your skin, and you'll stand with them every step of the way. When they make questionable decisions, you'll understand, and when they triumph, you'll glory in it.

And you know what? Some of them are going to die.

Not just the bad guys; not just the compromised ones, or the ones that deserve it. Hell, some of the characters who deserve death aren't going anywhere. But some of the guys you love the most, who you'll start mentally planning happy-ever-afters for long before the end of the trilogy, will buy it, messily and alone, and for the cruellest and most arbitrary of reasons. And you'll be totally blind-sided.

So, yeah. Sorry.

There's more than a little of Golding's *Lord of the Flies*, here, but it's a grimier, prouder kind of story. I was always bothered by the way the adults represented such perfect civilisation and restraint in Golding's classic. The adults had to leave the narrative altogether before the kids could really go off the rails; and when the landing party arrives at the end, there's a sense that it's all over now, and the wrongs will be righted.

But Andrews' adults lose their shit roughly five minutes before the kids, when The Cull hits, and it's up to the kids to take care of things for themselves. And when, as the story unfolds and St Mark's School for Boys and Girls becomes something real, a symbol for hope, and sympathetic adults start crossing over from the rest of the *Afterblight* world and try and step in, they get short shrift:

"Don't you fucking dare, Mr High-And-Mighty-Grown-Up-Man, tell me that children have no place in the front line. Because it's you lot who've bloody put us there. And believe me: every adult we meet is going to regret standing by and letting that happen."

It's a big "fuck-you" to authority, a statement of intent from a band of young men and women who have lost every guardian, guideline and moral compass their old lives offered and had to build up from scratch, and I promise you you'll be proud of them.

So again: sorry about what's coming.

David Moore (Editor)
May 2012

SCHOOL'S OUT

Original cover art by Mark Harrison

LESSON ONE
HOW TO BE A KILLER

CHAPTER ONE

I CELEBRATED MY fifteenth birthday by burying my headmaster and emptying my bladder on the freshly turned earth. Best present a boy could have.

I found his corpse on the sofa in the living room of his private quarters. I'd only been in that room once before, when I was among a group of boarders who pretended to play chess on his dining table while he stood behind us beaming benevolently as part of a photo shoot for the school prospectus.

He didn't look so smug now, curled up under a blanket clutching a whisky bottle and a handful of pills. I reckoned he'd been dead for about two weeks; I had become very familiar with the processes of bodily decay in the preceding months.

I opened a window to let out the stink, sat in the armchair opposite and considered the fate of a man I had hated more than I can easily express. At moments like this the novels I had read always portrayed the hero realising that their hatred had vanished and been replaced by pity and sadness at the futility of it all. Bollocks. I still hated him as much as ever, the only thing missing was the fear.

The corridor that ran alongside the head's living room was walled by a thin wooden partition and the dormitory I used to share with three other boys lay on the other side. At night the four of us would lie awake and listen to our headmaster drunkenly arguing with his wife, our matron. We liked her. She was kind.

He had been no nicer to the boys in his care. His mood swings were sudden and unpredictable, his punishments cruel and extreme. I don't mean to make St Mark's sound like something out of Dickens. But our headmaster was a bully, pure and simple. Far worse than any of the prefects he'd appointed, with the possible exception of MacKillick; but he was long gone, thank God.

I was glad the head was dead, even gladder that his death had come at his own hands. I enjoyed imagining his despair. It felt good.

Perhaps I should have worried about my mental state.

I considered pissing on the corpse there and then, but decided it would be crass. Pissing on his grave seemed classier. I was just about to get on with the grisly task of hauling him downstairs when I heard a low growl from the doorway to my right.

Shit. I'd forgotten the dog.

Nasty great brute called Jonah. An Irish wolfhound the size of a pony that liked to shag our legs when Master wasn't around to kick some obedience into it. Always had a hungry look in its eyes, even back then. I didn't want to turn my head and see how it looked after two weeks locked in a flat with a decaying owner.

Two things occurred to me: first, that the dog's fear of its master must have been intense to prevent it from snacking on the corpse, and second, that by the time I was able to rise from my seat it'd be upon me and that would be that.

The headmaster's wife left him in the end. One Saturday morning while he was out taking rugby practice she rounded up all the boys who weren't on the team and together we helped move her stuff out of the flat into the transit van she had waiting downstairs. She'd kissed us all on the cheek and driven off crying. When he returned and found her gone he seemed bewildered, asked us if we'd seen her go. We all said "no, sir."

Perhaps I could roll off the seat to my left, use it as a shield and beat the dog back out of the room. Who was I kidding? It was an armchair; by the time I'd managed to get a useable grip on it I'd be dog food. Despite my probably hopeless position there was an absence of fear. No butterflies in my stomach, I wasn't breathing faster. Could I really be so unconcerned about my own life?

Our new matron had a lot of work to do to win over those of us who'd been so fond of her predecessor. For one thing, she didn't look like a matron. The head's wife had been middle-aged, round, rosy cheeked and, well, matronly. This impostor was in her twenties, slim, with deep green eyes and dyed red hair. She was gorgeous, and that was a problem – she acted more like a cool older sister than the surrogate mum we all wanted. No teenage boy really wants to hang out with his older sister. I liked her immediately, but everyone else kept their distance. They called her

Miss Crowther, refusing to call her Matron, but she won them over eventually.

Two months into spring term we all went down with flu. There were only eight of us in residence that weekend but since the sanatorium had only four beds the headmaster decreed that we should all remain in our dormitories, in our own beds, in total silence until Monday. Miss Crowther wasn't having any of that, and confined us all to sickbay, enlisting our help to carry in chairs and camp beds. Then she set us up with a telly and rented us a load of DVDs.

The headmaster was livid when he found out, and we sat in the San and listened to him bawling at her. *How dare she subvert his authority, who did she think she was? He had half a mind to show her the back of his hand.* It all sounded very familiar. But she stood up to him, told him that the San was her jurisdiction, that if he interfered with her care of sick boys she'd go to the governors so why didn't he just shut up and back off? Astonishingly, he did, and Miss Crowther became Matron, heroine to us all.

The dog's growl changed tenor, shifting into a full snarl. I heard its claws on the floorboards as it inched its way inside the room, manoeuvring itself to attack. I'd foolishly left my rucksack in the hallway; anything I could have used to protect myself was in there. I was defenceless and I couldn't see any way out. There was nothing else for it, I'd just have to take the beast on bare fisted.

When the plague first hit the headlines Matron reassured us that antibiotics and effective quarantine would keep us all safe. The World Health Organisation would ensure that it didn't become a pandemic. Boy, did she ever get that wrong. But to be fair, so did everyone else.

There was a big meeting with the governors, parents and staff, and even the students were allowed a say, or at least the sixth-formers got to choose a representative to speak for them; fifth-formers and juniors didn't get a look in. A vocal minority wanted the school to close its gates and quarantine itself, but in the end the parents insisted that boys should be taken home to their families. One teacher would remain on site and look after those boys whose parents were trapped abroad, or worse, already dead. Matron said she had nowhere else to go, and she remained to tend any boys who got sick. The teacher who stayed alongside her, Mr James, was a popular master, taught Physics, and there had been rumours of a romance between him and Matron in the weeks leading up to the dissolution of the school. One of the boys who stayed behind told me he was secretly looking forward to it. They'd have the school to themselves, and Matron and Mr James were sure to be good fun. It would be just like a big holiday.

I had passed that boy's grave on the way up the school driveway an hour earlier. Mr James's too. In fact almost all the boys I could remember having stayed behind seemed to be buried in the makeshift graveyard that had once been the front lawn. Neat wooden crosses bore their names and dates. Most had died in the space of a single week, two months ago. Presumably the headmaster had returned from wherever he'd been lurking shortly thereafter, had hung around for a while and then topped himself.

My father was overseas when The Cull began, serving with the army in Iraq. Mother took me home and we quarantined ourselves as best we could. Before communications gave out entirely I managed to talk to Dad on the phone and he'd told me that the rumour there was that people with the blood group O-neg were immune. He and I were both O-negs, Mother was not. Ever the practical man, Dad demanded we discuss what would happen if she died, and I reluctantly agreed that I would return to the school and wait for him to come get me. He promised he'd find a way, and I didn't doubt him.

So when Mother finally did die – and, contrary to the reports the last vestiges of the media were peddling, it was not quick, or easy, or peaceful – I buried her in the back garden, packed up a bag of kit and started out for school. After all, where else was there for me? And now, after cycling halfway across the county and surviving three gang attacks *en route*, I was probably about to get savaged and eaten by a dog I'd last seen staring dolefully up at me with its tongue lolling out as it made furry love to my right leg. Terrific.

Jonah had now worked his way into the room and stood directly in front of me. His back was hunched, his rear legs crouched down ready to pounce. Fangs bared, eyes wild, feral and furious. This was a very big, very vicious looking beast. I decided I'd go for the eyes and the throat in the first instance, and try to kick it in the nuts at the same time. I didn't think I could kill it, but with any luck I could disable it enough to force it to retreat and then I could grab my bag, leg it out of the flat and shut the door behind me, trapping it again. The headmaster could bury his own damn self for all I cared. I'd have enough to do tending my bite wounds.

And then the dog was upon me and I was fighting for my life.

I wasn't wearing my biker jacket, but the lighter leather coat I did have on provided some protection to my right forearm as I jammed it into the dog's gaping mouth. Forced back in my chair by the strength of the attack, I tried to raise my feet to kick the beast away, but its hind legs scrabbled on the hard wood floor, claws clattering for purchase, and I couldn't get a clear shot.

I felt the dog's hot, moist breath on my face as it worried my arm, shaking it violently left and right, trying to get past it to the soft flesh of my throat. I brought my left arm up and grabbed it by the throat, squeezing its windpipe as hard as I could; didn't even give the beast pause for thought.

My right forearm was beginning to hurt like hell. The teeth may not have been able to break the skin but the dog's jaws were horribly powerful and I was worried it might succeed in cracking the bone.

We were eye to eye, and the madness in those great black orbs finally gave me the first thrill of fear.

I grappled with the dog, managing to push it back an inch or two, giving me room to bring up both my feet and kick it savagely in the hind legs. Losing its balance, it slipped backwards but refused to relinquish my arm, so I was dragged forward like we were in some ludicrous tug of war.

I kicked again, and this time something cracked and the dog let go of my arm to howl in anguish. But still it didn't retreat. I could see I'd damaged its right leg by the way it now favoured its left. Undaunted, the dog lunged for my throat again.

This time I was ready for it, and instead of using my arm as a shield I punched hard with my right fist, straight on its nose. It yelped and backed off again. Thick gobbets of saliva dropped slowly from its slavering jaws as it panted and snarled, eyeing me hungrily. It couldn't have eaten in two weeks, how could it possibly still be so strong?

Before I had time to move again Jonah tried a different tack, lunging for my left leg and worrying it savagely. This time I screamed. Cycling shorts don't give the best protection, and his teeth sank deep into my calf, giving the animal its first taste of my blood. I leaned forward and rained punches down on his head. I realised that I'd made a fatal mistake about a tenth of a second after Jonah did, but that was enough. He released my leg and sprang upwards towards my exposed throat, ready to deliver the killing bite. I didn't even have time to push myself backwards before a loud report deafened me.

When my hearing faded back in all I could hear was the soft whimpering of Jonah the dog, as he lay dying at my feet. I looked towards the door and there, silhouetted in the light, was the figure of a woman holding a smoking rifle.

"Never did like that bloody animal," she said, as she stepped forward into the room. Grimacing, she lowered the rifle, closed her eyes, and pulled the trigger again, putting the beast out of its misery. She paused there for a moment, eyes closed, shoulders hunched. She looked like the loneliest woman in the whole world. Then she looked up at me and smiled a beautiful, weary smile.

"Hello Lee," said Matron.

I WINCED AS Matron dabbed the bite wound with antiseptic. The sanatorium was just the same as it had been before I left – the shelves a bit emptier and the medicine cabinet more sparsely stocked, but otherwise little had changed. It still smelt of TCP, which I found oddly comforting. Matron had changed though. The white uniform was gone, replaced by combat trousers, t-shirt and jacket. Her hair was unkempt and make-up was a distant memory. There were dark rings under her eyes and she looked bone tired.

"The head turned up here about a month ago and tried to take control," explained Matron. "He started laying down the law, giving orders, bossing around dying children, if you can believe that."

I could.

"He tried to institute quarantine, though it was far too late for that, and burial details made up of boys who were already sick. He seemed quite normal until one day, out of nowhere, he just snapped. No build up, no warning signs. He told Peter… Mr James, to help bury one of the boys, but he was already too ill to leave his bed, and refused. I thought the head was going to hit him. Then he just started crying and couldn't seem to stop. He went and locked himself in his rooms and wouldn't come out. I tried, a few times, to coax him out, but all I ever heard was sobbing. Then, after a few days, not even that. I didn't have the time to see to him, there were boys dying every day and the head was O-neg so I just figured I'd deal with him when it was all over. But when I tried the door all I heard was the dog growling and I, well, I just couldn't be bothered. Plus, really, I didn't want to have to bury a half-eaten corpse. Still can't believe the dog left him alone. Weird.

"Stupid pointless bastard," she added. "What a waste."

I didn't think it was much of a loss, but I didn't say so.

"Did you dig all those graves yourself, then?" I asked.

"No. Mr James helped. At first."

"But you can't have been the only one who survived. Some of the boys must have made it."

I didn't want to ask about Jon. He'd been my best friend since we both started here seven years earlier, and he'd stayed behind when his parents couldn't be located. Mother had offered to take him with us, but the head had forbidden it – what if his parents came looking for him?

"Of the twenty who stayed behind there are three left: Green, Rowles and Norton."

Jon's surname had been Swift. Dead then.

"Oh, and Mr Bates, of course."

"Eh? I thought he'd left?"

"He did." Matron placed a gauze dressing over the wound and reached for the bandage. "But he came back about a week ago. I haven't asked but I assume his wife and children are dead. He's a bit... fragile at the moment."

Bates was our history master. A big, brawny, blokey bloke, all rugby shirts and curry stains; fragile was the last word you'd use to describe him. He was well liked by sporty kids but he had little time for bookish types, and his version of history was all battles and beheadings. He was also the head of the army section of the school's Combined Cadet Force, and he loved bellowing on the parade ground, covering himself in boot polish for night exercises and being pally with the Territorial Army guys they trained with every other month.

My dad didn't think schools had any business dressing fourteen-year-old boys up in army gear, teaching them how to use guns, making war seem like the best possible fun you could have. He had made sure I knew the reality of soldiering – blood, death, squalor. "Don't be like me, son," he'd told me. "Don't be a killer. Don't let your life be all about death. Study hard, pass your exams, get yourself a proper job."

So much for that.

I remember one Friday afternoon Dad stood at the side of the concrete playground we used for parade and watched Bates bluster his way through drill practice. At one point Bates yelled "RIGHT FACE!" especially loud, holding the 'I' for ages and modulating his voice so he sounded like a caricature sergeant from a *Carry On* film. Dad laughed out loud and everyone heard. Bates went red in the face and glared at him until I thought his head was going to explode. Dad just stared him down, a big grin on his face, until Bates dismissed us and stomped off to the staff room.

Anyway, Dad didn't approve of the CCF, but Community Service for three hours every Friday afternoon sounded really dull – helping old ladies with their shopping might be character building but, well, old people smell – so I joined the RAF section. There was a lot less drill and shouting in the RAF section.

My special area of responsibility was weapons training – I taught the fourth-formers how to strip, clean and reassemble the Lee-Enfield .303 rifles that were kept in the weapons store next to the tuck shop; Matron's rifle stood in the corner as she taped up the bandage on my leg, so Bates had obviously opened up the armoury. Made sense. I'd had a few close calls with gangs and vigilante groups on my journey back to school.

"There, all done," said Matron. "You'll be limping for a while, and I want you back here once a day so I can check for infection and change the dressing. Now, you should report for duty! Bates will want to see you. We've all moved into the staff accommodation block, easier to defend, so he reckons." She noticed my curious expression and added, "He's gone a bit... military. Overcompensating a bit. You should go see for yourself while I clean up here. Just remember to call him sir and salute and stuff. Don't worry though, he's harmless enough, I think. He's been very good with young Rowles."

"Okay." I got up, winced again, and sat back down.

"Sorry," said Matron. "No painkillers left. They're on the shopping list for the next expedition, but 'til then I'm afraid you'll just have to grit your teeth. I may be able to rustle up some vodka later, if you're good." She winked and grinned, then handed me a crutch. I hobbled away. *Jesus, my leg hurt.*

As I was turning the corner at the end of the corridor she popped her head out of the sickbay and called after me.

"Oh, and Lee?"

"Yes?"

"It really is very good to see you. We could use some level heads around here."

Trying not to let my level head swell to the size of a football, I blushed and mumbled some thanks.

* * *

THE STAFF ACCOMMODATION was situated in the west wing of the main school building, an old stately home from the 1800s that was turned into a school about a hundred years ago. It was imaginatively referred to as Castle – not The Castle, or Castle House, just Castle. The two towers on either side of the main entrance made it kind of look like a castle, with mock battlements on the roof, but inside it was wood panelling, creaky floorboards and draughty casement windows.

The central heating in our dormitories was provided by huge, old metal radiators that wheezed, groaned and dripped all winter. The paint on them, layers thick, would crack and peel every summer, exposing the scalding hot metal underneath. Some prefects' favourite method of torturing junior boys was to hold their ears to an exposed bit of radiator metal. It'd hurt like hell for days afterwards. MacKillick liked this technique, although he had allegedly once used a softer and more sensitive part of one boy's anatomy, and I don't even want to think about how badly that must've hurt. The radiators were cold now, and the air was chilly and damp.

The school was eerily quiet. I paused in the main assembly hall, breathing in the smell of floor polish and dust. At one end stood the stage, curtains closed. The sixth-formers had performed *A Midsummer Night's Dream* there last term, God knew when it'd see use again. Halfway up the wall, around three sides of the hall, a gallery walkway joined one set of classrooms to the library and staff areas. I limped up the stairs and used it to make my way through into the wing normally reserved for teachers.

I found Bates in the staff room, giving what appeared to be a briefing to the three remaining boys, all in their school uniforms, as if attending a lesson. Bates was stood by a whiteboard, drawing a simple map with arrows showing directions of approach. The central building on the map was labelled 'Tesco'.

The door was open, so I knocked and entered, making Bates jump and reach for his rifle before he recognised me, clocked the crutch, and came over to help me to a seat.

"Kevin isn't it?"

I sighed. "No sir. It's Keegan, sir. Lee Keegan."

"Keegan, right. Well, welcome back Keegan. Been in the wars?"

I've buried my mother, cycled halfway across the county, been attacked three times on the way, eaten ripe roadkill badger for breakfast and then been savaged by the hound of the bloody Baskervilles. I'm covered in mud, blood, bruises and bandages, and I am on crutches. Of course I've been in the damn wars. You prick.

"Little bit, sir."

He had the good grace to look sympathetic for about two seconds.

"Good to have another senior boy back. RAF, weren't you?" He said RAF with a hint of distaste, as if referring to an embarrassing medical complaint.

"Yes sir. Junior Corporal."

"Oh well. You can still fire one of these, though, eh?" He brandished his .303.

"Yes sir."

"Good, good. We'll get you sorted out with one at the billet later. I was just outlining the plan of attack for tomorrow. Take a seat."

Bates looked weird. His hair was slicked back with gel (or grease?) and he was dressed in full army gear. His boots shone but he hadn't shaved in days, his eyes were deep set and bloodshot. His manner was different, too. The blokey jokiness was gone and instead he was acting the brisk military man. Grief, did he really think he was a soldier now? I bet he'd even started using the 24-hour clock. He resumed his briefing.

"We assemble by the minibus at oh-six-hundred." *Knew it.* "The primary objective is the tinned goods aisle at Tesco, but matches, cleaning fluids, firelighters and so forth would come in handy. Yes Green?"

The sixth-former had raised his hand.

"Sir, we've already visited... sorry, raided... Sainsbury's, Asda and Waitrose. They were all empty. Morrisons wasn't even there any more. Why should Tesco be any different?"

For the briefest of instants a look of despair flickered across Bates' face. It was gone in a moment, replaced by a patronising smile. God, he really was in a bad way. It'd been hard enough for me to bury my mother but it was, after all, the natural way of things – children mourn their parents. I couldn't begin to imagine what burying his wife and children had done to him; he seemed broken.

"Got to be thorough, Green. A good commander leaves nothing to chance. Nothing!"

"Right sir!" The boy shot me a glance and rolled his eyes. I grimaced back. I knew Green reasonably well. He was in the year above me, but was in my house and had helped organise our annual drama show last term. He was a high achiever in exams, and always put himself front and centre in any play or performance, but get him near a sports field and he looked like he wanted to run and hide under a bush; smart, but a wimp. Exactly the kind of boy Bates wanted nothing to do with. He was tall and lean, with dark hair and brown eyes, and the lucky bastard had avoided acne completely. No such luck for me.

I had been in the Lower Fifth before The Cull. Rowles was a second-former and Norton, sat next to Green, was Upper Fifth.

I barely knew Rowles. He was so much younger than me I'd never had anything to do with him. Even for his age he was small, and his wide eyes and freckled cheeks made him look like one of those cutesy kids from a Disney film, the kind who contrive to get their divorced parents back together just by being awfully, grotesquely, vomit-inducingly sweet. He was looking up at Bates, eyes full of hero worship. Poor kid. Bad enough losing your parents, but to latch onto Bates as your role model, now that was really unfortunate. I realised he was young enough that the world pre-Cull would soon come to seem like a dream to him, some fantasy childhood too idealised to have really occurred.

Norton, on the other hand, was all swagger, but not in a bad way. He was confident and self assured, a posh kid who affected that sort of loping Liam Gallagher strut. Well into martial arts, he had the confidence of someone who knew he could look after himself, and spent most break times smoking in the backroom of the café over the road, chatting up any girls from the high school who bought his bad boy act. Although he fitted the profile, he wasn't a bully or a bastard, and I was pleased to see him; things could be fun with Norton around.

What a gang to see out the apocalypse with – an aspiring luvvie, a wideboy hardarse and an annoying mascot child, overseen by a world weary nurse and a damaged history master who thought he was Sgt Rock. Still, it could be worse – the head could be alive and MacKillick could be here.

Just as that thought flickered through my brain I heard someone behind me clear their throat. I cursed myself for tempting fate and turned around knowing exactly which particular son of a bitch would be standing behind me.

"Hi, sir," said Sean MacKillick. "Need a hand?"

"Oh, fuck," said Rowles.

CHAPTER TWO

SEAN MACKILLICK WAS Bates' golden boy, and the highest ranking boy in the army section of the CCF. He was Deputy Head Boy and captain of the rugby team – three successive county trophies. He was also a Grade A, platinum-plated bastard.

Because of his sporting achievements the school authorities thought the sun shone out of Mac's jock-strapped arse, but when the teachers weren't around he was the worst kind of bully – sadistic, vicious and totally random. Jon always said it was because he was so short. Even now, at nineteen, he was shorter than everyone in the room, even Rowles, but he was built like a brick shitter and his head was so square it had corners. His thighs were meaty and his legs so stumpy that he kind of waddled – some of the juniors had christened him Donald Duck – but there was no mistaking the raw, squat power of the man.

His eyes were piercing blue under close-cropped blonde hair, and his face was heavily freckled, but there was cruelty in the curl of his mouth, and his eyes were all cold calculation.

Mac was a posh kid. His father was in the House of Lords until they did away with hereditary peers, but he had adopted the persona of an East End gangster. Born into the aristocracy but he acted like Ray Winstone. Pathetic, really.

Most of his classmates worshipped him, but beyond that he'd been almost universally hated, especially in the CCF. He saw the uniform as a licence to do whatever he pleased, and although he was a bully on school grounds, that was nothing to how he behaved when the army section was away on camp or manoeuvres. Army summer camp last year had reportedly turned into an endless round of forced marches, press ups and endurance tests, all overseen by

Mac and ignored by Bates, who seemed to think it was just good, clean fun.

At the last camp, an outward bound week in Wales doing orienteering and stuff, he actually threw a boy into a river and then held his head under the water until he lost consciousness. When they fished him out and revived him Mac made him finish the exercise with them, sodden and disorientated. This was winter, halfway up a mountain, so by the time they made it back to the rendezvous he was literally blue; ended up in hospital with hypothermia. Too scared to tell, he pretended he'd slipped and fallen in. The other boys in the squad kept quiet too – Mac had a little gang of hangers-on and if you didn't want to end up black and blue, you didn't mess.

He and his lackeys would strut (well, they'd strut, he'd waddle) around the school laying down the law, but whenever a teacher appeared Mac would smile and fawn. The head loved him. He was only relegated to Deputy Head Boy because the Head Boy's dad had just donated a new chemistry lab. Matron loathed him. She was always cleaning up the wounds he inflicted, but the head waved away her complaints muttering platitudes about youthful high spirits. Wanker.

There were dark rumours of a death too, a long time ago, back when Mac was a junior. But as far as I knew that's all they were – rumours.

Mac had left school the term before The Cull started, won some big prize on speech day for being king of the brown-nosers, and Jon had keyed his car during the ceremony. Jon who was now dead. We were so relieved to see the back of Mac, so sure he was gone forever.

Basically, Sean MacKillick was the last person on the earth you wanted looking after a group of vulnerable kids in a post-apocalyptic wasteland.

Bates gave an exclamation of joy and – God help us – hugged the bastard.

"Welcome back, Mac," he said. "Now we can really get started."

OVER THE NEXT few weeks we had a steady influx of people taking up residence. There had been over a thousand boys in the school and at 7% survival rate that left about seventy alive. Of these about forty turned up in the weeks following my return. Some brought brothers or sisters, mothers, grandparents, uncles, aunts and friends. Only one boy arrived with his father, but the man died the next day of pneumonia. Bates was especially good with the boy – Thackeray, his name was – and I saw a whole other side to him. He was caring, kind and thoughtful; surprising. All in all we were forty-six by the end of the month and it felt like life was returning to the old buildings.

Everybody who returned brought their stories with them. Wolf-Barry, a skinny sixth-former who was a bit of a computer geek, told of bodies littering the streets of London, rats emerging from the sewers to feast in broad daylight. Rowles had seen mass graves and power stations converted into huge furnaces to burn the dead. 'Horsey' Haycox, imaginatively nicknamed because he was obsessed with horses, had encountered a group of born again fundamentalist Christians who had declared holy war on anyone not of their faith, by which they basically meant anyone non-white. Speight, another sixth-former, told a very similar story, but his local God-bothering nutters were Muslims. There were many other tales of shell-shocked survivors turning to extreme perversions of religion to try and make sense of what had happened, and charismatic leaders building power bases while beheading, hanging or even burning anyone they deemed impure or unclean.

A generator was set up and fuel was collected from a nearby petrol station. We emptied a Blockbuster and most evenings we ran the power for a couple of hours and watched a movie. Television and radio were pretty much dead by this point, although we kept scanning the airwaves for signals. Some satellite stations were still broadcasting as far-off generators slowly ran down, but mostly they all just broadcast muzak and test cards apologising for the interruption in service. An Italian channel played an old dubbed episode of *Fawlty Towers* on a continuous loop for three weeks. One by one all the stations faded away to dead air. The last live station broadcasting came out of Japan, where one guy ran a daily news show. He showed footage of distant explosions and gun battles, empty streets and haunted, echoing city canyons. We watched him every day for a month until one day he just wasn't there any more.

Bates and Mac took charge and organised everyone into work groups, and we started to feather our nest. A spotty little Brummie called Petts prepared a section of land to be a market garden come spring; after all, our supplies of tinned and dehydrated food were running low and soon we'd need to start growing our own.

The main kitchen was a useless modern gas range, but in one of the outbuildings we found a turn of the century kitchen with a long-forgotten wood burning stove. We cleaned it up and had hot food once a day, prepared by one of the boy's aunts, who we started to call the 'Dinner Lady', although her name was Mrs Atkins. Lots of the dorms had old, bricked-up fireplaces, so we took a sledgehammer to those, opened up the chimneys again, harvested some grates from an abandoned hardware store in Sevenoaks, and slept snug every night. The woods in the school grounds provided all the fuel we needed.

We even set up a paddock and rounded up a cow for milking, two pigs and three sheep. Being a posh private school, St Mark's had no shortage of wannabe gentleman farmers and two had survived and returned – Heathcote and Williams took to their tasks like pigs to swill.

The school came to seem like a haven. We organised football and rugby tournaments, started having assembly after breakfast; hell, we even had campfires and sing-alongs. The big stone wall that enclosed the grounds on three sides, and the River Medway which marked the school's southern border, kept the outside world distant and held it at bay. We felt safe and insulated, and Bates and Mac were fine as long as that lasted. Sure the scavenging parties were a little too soldiery to take seriously, but without his cronies Mac seemed almost normal, and Bates gradually settled down. He relied heavily on Mac to organise things, but sorting out the rota for planting spuds and milking the cow doesn't really provide much opportunity for megalomania.

It was surreal. The world had died and here was this tiny, insular community of grieving children carrying on as if everything was fine. And for a while, just for a while, I allowed myself to be lulled by it, allowed myself to think maybe things would be all right, maybe the world hadn't descended into anarchy and chaos and cults and blood and horror, maybe the rest of the world was like we were – hopeful and coping. Maybe this little society we were setting up would work.

What an idiot I was. A community is only as healthy as the people who lead it. And we had Bates and Mac. I should have realised we were fucked before we even began.

We could only keep the madness at bay for so long. We were living in denial, and Mr Hammond's arrival changed everything.

NORTON AND I were in the south quad working on a madcap contraption designed by some fifth-form chemistry 'A' student called Dudley, designed to harvest methane gas from animal shit, when we heard the first gunshots. They echoed off the walls and we couldn't tell where they were coming from. There were sharp repetitive sounds too, which we quickly realised were hooves on tarmac, and distant shouts. *The front drive!*

We ran through the buildings to the front door and looked out at the long driveway that led from the front gate up to the school. An old man was running as fast as he could up the drive towards us, holding hands with two boys. All three were shouting for help. Behind them, just inside the gate but gaining fast, were a man and a woman on horseback. Both carried shotguns. The woman took aim at the fleeing trio. She fired and one of the boys stumbled and fell forwards onto the gravel. The old man hesitated, unsure what to do.

"Run, you idiot, run," whispered Norton.

The old man ushered the other boy towards the school and as the child continued running the man turned back to get the wounded boy. He crouched there protectively, shielding him from the approaching riders as they reined in their steeds and loomed over them. The woman took careful aim at the running boy.

While all this was happening boys had come running up to the door one by one, drawn by the noise. Bates arrived last, carrying his rifle. He pushed to the front and went to open the door just as the woman fired and the running boy threw up his arms and tumbled head over heels onto the cold drive. He lay there for a moment and then started crawling towards us. We all gasped, horrified. The woman started her mount trotting towards him.

I glanced up at Bates but the look on his face said it all; he was frozen, unable to make a decision. We weren't going to get anything useful from him.

"Where's Mac?" he asked.

"Scavenging party, sir," I replied.

"Oh. Right. Ummm…"

Shit. I had to do something.

"Sir, give me the gun sir," I said.

"What?"

"Give me the gun, sir." I didn't shout, that wouldn't have worked. I was just quietly insistent, assuming authority I didn't really feel. He handed me the rifle just as Matron came running. She too was armed.

"Matron," I said. "Get out there and talk to them. Just give me two minutes."

Startled, she looked to Bates for confirmation, but he was just staring out the window, biting his lip. She looked back to me and nodded, then stepped out onto the front steps, rifle ready but not presented for firing.

The horsewoman had dismounted and was standing over the injured child, who continued to crawl away from her, whimpering and crying, leaving a thick red snail trail behind him. Her colleague was still mounted, covering the other two, about twenty metres behind her.

I turned away from the door, pushed through the crowd of boys, and ran up the main stairs. I needed to get to a good vantage point.

I heard a shot behind me and my stomach lurched. Jesus, she'd executed the boy.

I reached the first floor landing and ran into the classroom that looked down over the driveway. Dammit, the bloody windows were closed. I laid the rifle on the window seat and tried to pull up the sash. No use, it was painted shut and wouldn't budge. I looked down, saw Matron, and realised with relief that it was she who had fired, a warning shot. The wounded boy was still crawling. The horsewoman's shotgun was now aimed square at Matron.

I could have shattered one of the small panes of glass, but I didn't want to draw attention to myself, and I needed to be able to hear what was being said. I cursed, grabbed the gun, and ran back to the staircase. I was losing seconds I couldn't afford. I sprinted up the stairs to the second floor. The front room here was a dormitory with beds lying underneath the windows, one of which was already open. I muttered silent thanks and lay down on the bed, brought the rifle up and rested the barrel on the window frame. I nestled the stock deep into the soft tissue of my right shoulder. The .303 kicks like a bastard, and if you don't seat it properly you can give yourself a livid purple bruise to the collarbone that'll leave you hurting for weeks. Believe me, I know.

I lifted the bolt, drew it back and a round popped up from the magazine to fill the void. I then pushed the bolt forward again, smoothly slotting the round into the breach, snapped the bolt back down and slipped off the safety catch. I took careful aim and calmed my breathing, steadied my hands, focused on the woman with the shotgun.

"...looters, plain and simple," she was saying. She stood about five metres in front of Matron. The boy was still crawling, still whimpering, halfway between the two women.

"Looters?" replied Matron, incredulous.

"They were seen taking food from a newsagent's in Hildenborough. An old man with two boys. No doubt. We've been tracking them for the past hour."

"And who the hell says they shouldn't take food where they find it? You may not have noticed, dear, but our debit cards don't work any more."

The boy kept crawling.

"We control Hildenborough now," the woman said. "Our territory, our rules."

"And who's we?"

"The local magistrate, George Baker, took charge. He's the law there, and if he says you're a looter, you're a looter."

"And you shoot looters?"

"The ones who run, yeah."

"And the ones you catch?"

"We hang them."

Matron leant down to the boy, who had now reached her and was clawing at her shoes.

"I know this boy. He's thirteen!" she shouted.

The horsewoman shrugged.

"Looter is a looter. And people who shelter looters are no better."

Matron stood up again, raised her rifle and walked right up to the horsewoman. I thought the rider would fire but she kept her cool, confident that her colleague would deter Matron from firing the first shot.

The two women stood face to face, one raised gun barrel length between them.

"Well this," said Matron, "is my territory. And here I am the law. You leave. Now."

The horsewoman held Matron's gaze for a long minute. I had to shift my aim; Matron's head was blocking my shot. I sighted on the horseman instead.

The horsewoman called Matron's bluff.

"Oh yeah," she sneered. "And who's going to make me? You and whose army?"

She pushed the barrel of Matron's rifle aside, raised her shotgun and, before I could react, clubbed Matron hard on the head with the stock. Matron slumped to the ground, stunned.

This was it, the moment of truth. I'd fired this rifle countless times on the range, blasting away at paper people, but I'd never fired at a real, breathing, living human being. If I could list my unspoken ambitions in life one of them, which I think most people probably share, was to never actually kill someone. I didn't want anybody's blood on my conscience, didn't want to stay awake at night playing and replaying my actions, seeing someone die again and again at my hands.

I'd heard my dad wake up screaming.

I knew what becoming a killer meant.

But there and then hesitation meant that other people, people I cared about, would die. I didn't have time to consider, philosophise or second guess. As the horsewoman lowered her gun to point at Matron's head, I took careful aim at her chest and gently squeezed the trigger.

But before I could shoot, before I could take my first life, someone else opened fire at the man who sat covering the other two 'looters'. The man spun in the air, tumbled off the horse and lay still. The woman turned to see what was happening. Matron, injured but mobile, gathered the wounded boy into her arms and began staggering towards the school. The man's horse took fright and ran left onto the grass, whinnying and rearing, revealing Mac, stood at the school gate with a smoking rifle held firm at his shoulder.

The horsewoman gave a cry of anguish and ran towards Mac. She fired her shotgun once, causing the old man to duck, but the shot went wide, and then she too was felled by a single shot from Mac. Her momentum carried her on a few steps and then she fell in a heap alongside the two looters she'd been pursuing.

Her horse now took fright and bolted, racing, head down, towards Matron, threatening to trample her and the boy she was carrying.

Without a second's thought I re-sighted and fired.

The rifle kicked hard into my shoulder and the explosion deafened me. But the horse went down, clean shot, straight to the head. It was the first time I had ever shot a moving target. The first time I'd ever shot anything alive.

I lay there for a moment, shocked by what I'd done. I could see Mac looking up at my window in surprise.

My hands were shaking.

I wasn't really a killer.

Not yet.

I WALKED BACK down the stairs, unsteady on my feet, wobbly with adrenaline comedown. The entrance hall was in commotion. Matron had already gone; run straight through the crowd on the way to the San, and Norton had taken control of the situation.

"Heathcote, take some boys and get these fucking horses out of sight," he was saying. "Williams, you take care of the bodies. The last thing we need is their friends finding their corpses on our front door."

The two farmboys gathered groups of older boys and hurried outside to begin cleaning up.

I stood there, letting the noise and confusion wash over me. It took me a moment before I realised that Norton was talking to me.

"Lee. Lee!"

I shook my head to clear away the fog. "Yeah?"

He put his hand on my arm, concerned. "You okay?"

"Yeah." I nodded. "Yeah, I think so, yeah."

"Good. Come on, let's get the other wounded boy inside."

"Yeah, sure."

Outside the sky was clear blue, the air crisp and fresh. The gravel crunched underneath my feet as we ran to the fallen boy and the old man who was tending him. All my senses seemed heightened. I could hear my heart pounding, see far off details with crystal clarity. I could smell the blood.

We ran past the dead horse, next to which stood three boys debating the best way to move the great beast. I slowed and stopped. I stepped around the animal and knelt down beside it, reaching out to touch its still warm neck. Its eyes stared, mad and sightless, and its mouth lay open, tongue lolling out, teeth bared in fright. There was a neat hole above its left eye, from which black and grey matter oozed onto the drive.

I felt its fading body heat and tears welled up in my eyes. My stomach felt hollow, my head felt tight, and all I wanted to do was curl up in a dark hole and cry. It was the first real emotion I had felt since my mother died.

I forced the feelings down. Time for that later; things to do now. I muttered "sorry," and then rose and ran after Norton, wiping my eyes as I did so.

As I approached the looters I was shocked to recognise the man. It was Mr Hammond, our art master. I knew the boy too, by sight. He was a third-former, I think, but his name escaped me. Hammond was an old man, seventy-five and long overdue for retirement, but he looked about ninety now. His face was pale and unshaven, his cheeks hollow and shadowed. His clothes, so familiar from countless art classes, were ragged and torn. He had a deep gash across his forehead that streamed blood down one side of his face.

He didn't look like he'd endured the easiest apocalypse.

Williams lifted the dead woman and pushed past me as I approached. Norton was helping Hammond to his feet, Mac was lifting the wounded boy. Bates was standing there too, staring at the pool of blood on the ground, eyes glazed, expression blank. When I reached him he didn't look up.

"Sir," I said. No response. "Sir."

Bates snapped out of his reverie and looked up at me.

"Hmmm?"

"Your rifle, sir," I said, and handed it to him. He looked down at it in horror, as if I'd just offered him a severed human head. Then he reached out and took it.

"Thank you," he murmured.

Norton and Hammond moved off back towards the school, and Mac handed the boy, bleeding but breathing, to a couple of fifth-formers who carried him away.

So there we were; me, Bates and Mac, stood around two pools of blood, all unsure exactly what to say to each other. It was only now that I noticed that Mac had dried blood smeared across his combat jacket. I studied him closely. I had just killed a horse and I was a wreck; he'd just gunned down two people and he didn't seem in the least bit concerned. I may not have been a killer, but he was. And something about his reaction, or lack of it, told me this was not the first time he'd taken a life.

"What happened to you?" I asked. "Where are the others?"

Bates looked at Mac and seemed to regain his senses. Mac was watching him carefully, and his cool appraising stare made me feel deeply uneasy.

"Yes, Mac," said Bates. "You left with McCulloch and Fleming. Where are they?"

He would have answered but he was suddenly surrounded by a crowd of sixth-form boys, eager to congratulate him. Wolf-Barry slapped his back and punched the air, Patel kept saying that it was "so cool", Zayn just looked awed.

Great, he'd got a new fan club.

WE GATHERED THAT evening in the main common room after a subdued dinner of curried horse. I didn't eat.

Bates was first to speak.

"You're all aware of the incident that occurred this afternoon.

Matron is even now working to save the lives of the two boys who were shot. These boys are Grant of 2B and Preston of 4C."

One boy in the second row gave an audible gasp at this news. A classmate, probably.

Bates seemed more sure of himself in this safe, controlled environment. All trace of his earlier loss of composure was gone. He stood erect, in full uniform, with his arms behind his back, like a regimental Sergeant-Major.

"I'm going to hand over to Mr Hammond at this stage, who will tell you what happened. Dennis..."

He gestured to his colleague to take over, and resumed his seat. Hammond stood and surveyed the room, scanning our faces, mentally noting which of us he knew, seeing who had survived and who, by omission, had not.

"Boys, it's good to be back. It's good to see so many of you again. It gives me hope that..." He trailed off, momentarily overcome.

"Preston and Grant lived near me in Sevenoaks, and they both arrived at my house together a few days ago. It was my suggestion that we return here. If we'd stayed where we were, maybe... Anyway, we ran out of petrol just as we entered Hildenborough. But it's only an hour's walk to the school so we weren't worried. Grant was hungry so we stopped at a newsagent's and rummaged around for something to eat. The place had been pretty thoroughly cleaned out, but we found chocolate bars underneath an overturned cupboard. We considered ourselves lucky, and set off again. But within minutes there was a hue and cry. The shout 'looter' went up and we saw a man running towards us, so we just ran for our lives.

"Preston knows the area very well and thanks to him we were able to elude our pursuers, although we never seemed able to completely shake them off. They finally caught up with us at the gate and you know the rest.

"If it hadn't been for Matron and MacKillick here..." Again he trailed off into silence.

You would have expected Hammond to have been grateful to the man who had saved his life, but the look he flashed Mac was one of distaste and suspicion.

Bates stood again, thanked Hammond, and handed the floor to Mac with an alarming degree of deference. Norton and I exchanged worried glances. Mac had cleaned up and changed his uniform, but he still sported combats and camouflage.

"Thank you, sir" he said, with perhaps the tiniest hint of sarcasm.

"I'll be brief. Fleming, McCulloch and me left this morning to scavenge in Hildenborough. As you know the shops have all been cleaned out, so we had to go house to house. Not the prettiest work. Those houses that haven't already been got at have normally still got occupants. You need a strong stomach."

What a smug, self-satisfied, aren't-I-hard sod he was.

"We found one house full of stuff we could use and we started carrying it out to the minibus. I was inside when I heard shouting. I went to the window and saw three men, all carrying guns, coming at McCulloch and Fleming. Our boys weren't armed, they'd been surprised, they didn't stand a chance. I watched as they were led away and then I followed, dodging house to house and keeping out of sight. They took the lads to a big house down a side road, an old manor house I think. I didn't even have time to sneak up and look through a window before they were brought out again. The three men and a new guy, some posh lord of the manor type in tweeds and stuff. They led our boys round the side of the house and I followed, hiding behind the hedges. And there, like it was the most normal thing in the world to have in your garden, was a gallows.

"McCulloch started screaming, so they did him first. It was all over in an instant. Then they did Fleming. He'd wet himself before they even put the noose around his neck."

Bloody hell, Mac. No need for the fucking details. I clenched my fists angrily. He was enjoying this.

"I didn't stick around after that. But as I was leaving town I saw some guys putting up a new fence across the road and a sign saying 'Hildenborough Protectorate. Governor: George Baker. Traders welcomed. Looters hanged.'

"I had to try another way out of town and found guards posted at all the exit points around the perimeter. So I dealt with one of them and came back here. Just in time too, I reckon."

'Dealt with one of them'. That explained the blood on his jacket. So he'd killed three people today and he looked for all the world like he was having the time of his life. I felt sick.

He sat back down and Bates took the floor again.

"Boys, I know this is hard, but we have to accept the reality that we may be, um, at war."

There were murmurs of disbelief.

"I know it sounds ridiculous, but consider the facts. A hostile force has established a base of operations practically on our doorstep. They've killed two of us and wounded two more; we've killed three of them. We know they're armed, entrenched, and determined. We must assume they will attack, and we must be ready."

I raised my hand to ask why he thought they'd attack.

"Put your hand down, Keegan," he barked. "I didn't throw the floor open to questions. And that goes for everyone. If we're to survive this we need to be focused, united, organised. There needs to be a clear chain of command and all orders will need to be followed promptly and without question. Is that clear?"

"Well, really," said the Dinner Lady. "I don't expect to be talked to like that."

"Ma'am," snapped Bates. "You are welcome to remain at St Mark's but I am in charge here and if you accept my protection I'm afraid you accept my rules."

And just like that Bates declared martial law.

I looked over at Mac. His face was solemn but his eyes told a different story. They shone with glee.

Hammond spoke up.

"I say Bates, are you quite sure you need to…"

Bates leaned forward and hissed something peremptory at Hammond, who fell silent.

He went on: "We need to secure our perimeter, post guards, organise patrols and so forth. To this end we are re-establishing the CCF and every boy will be expected to do their bit."

Broadbent raised his hand and began bleating before Bates could stop him.

"But sir, I was excused CCF because of my asthma. My dad wrote a note and everything."

"I said no questions, boy!" Bates yelled. "And no excuses either. If you're old enough to dress yourself you're old enough to carry a gun."

You could feel the shock in the room as everybody's eyes widened and their shoulders stiffened. Bates breathed deeply and visibly calmed himself.

"I know it's not how we want things to be, but it's the way things are," he reasoned. "It's my job, and Mac's, to keep you safe. I failed in that today. Not again.

"As of now you will all refer to me as Colonel and Mac as Major. Is that clear?"

I wanted to laugh in his face. I wanted to stand up and shout "Are you fucking joking? You're a history teacher, you deluded tinpot tosser". But I didn't. It was all too tragic for that. Tragic and – I glanced at Mac – sinister.

"I said is that clear?"

Some boys muttered "yes, Colonel" unenthusiastically. I thought Bates was going to push it, but he must have realised the time wasn't yet right.

"Good," he said. "Now, I want Speight, Pugh, Wylie, Wolf-Barry, Patel, Green, Zayn and Keegan to stay behind. The rest of you are dismissed for the evening."

Norton whispered "Good luck" as he got up to leave. Everybody else shuffled out leaving myself, Bates, Mac and the seven other boys whose names had been called. They were all the remaining sixth-formers; I was the only non sixth-former there.

When everyone else had left, Bates gestured for us all to come and sit together at the front, and sat to address us.

"You're the senior boys here, and a lot of the responsibility of this is going to rest with you. We'll be assigning ranks in the coming days but for now you'll all be acting corporals. Major Mac will be managing you directly and I want you to follow his orders promptly and without question at all times. Is that clear?"

"Yes Colonel."

"Good lads," said Bates. He smiled what he probably thought was a reassuring smile, but he actually looked more like a scared man presenting his teeth to a sadistic dentist. He patted Mac on the shoulder.

"All yours, Major," he said, and left the room.

Mac glared at us and grinned a sly, feral grin. He didn't look impressed by us, but he did look pleased with himself. He pulled his chair around so that he was facing us.

"Right, I've killed three fuckers today and if none of you want to be number four you'll keep your ears open and your mouths shut. Clear?"

Oh yeah. Here he was. This was the Mac I remembered. All these weeks of playing nice and sucking up to Bates, he was just biding his time, waiting for the right moment. Now Bates had shown weakness, there was blood in the water, and Mac was the shark.

Things were going to get ugly.

CHAPTER THREE

I saw Mac with his father once, on speech day. Jon and I walked behind them for a while, fascinated by the way they talked. His father, being a Lord, was all fruity vowels and wot-wot, and the brilliant thing is that Mac was too. He was all 'Gosh Daddy' and 'Super' and 'Cripes'. Once he actually said "Oh, my stars and garters!" Jon and I had to walk away at that point because we were finding it impossible to stifle our giggles.

I looked at the wannabe gangster who sat in front of me now and all I could think was: *what would your father think?* And also: *I know you, fraud. Everybody else may think you're a hard nut but underneath it all you're just a spoiled upper class daddy's boy overcompensating for the silver spoon you've got shoved up your arse.*

"Right," he said, in his broad cockney accent. "From now on, as far as you're concerned I am your fucking God. I am the law. Proper Judge Dredd, that's me. What I say goes and you don't question a fucking word, got it? You are mine."

He paused for effect and graced us with a menacing leer.

"But I'm not unreasonable," he lied. "I'm not unfriendly. Stick with me and you'll be all right. I'll take care of you. I like loyalty. If you're loyal we'll rub along just peachy, clear?"

Again, we nodded.

"Right. So. The Colonel has made me second-in-command and you lot are my officers. You're my go-to guys. You'll be able to give orders to all the other scrotes and you'll carry weapons at all times. I'll be doing some extra training with you over the next few days – leadership, strategy, warcraft, that sort of shit. And you'll be leading scavenging groups, raiding parties and any other kind of operation too fucking menial for me to dirty my lilywhites with.

"Stick with me and you'll be in clover. Fuck with me and you'll be pushing it up.

"Now, most of you were in the CCF under me, so you know how I like things done. Those of you who were fucking flyboys will learn."

I'm sure we will, I thought.

"Keegan!" he bellowed suddenly, making me jump.

"Yeah?" I stammered. He glared at me dangerously. "I mean, yes, sir?"

He nodded, letting it go this once.

"You showed a lot of initiative this afternoon."

"Thank you, sir."

"For a flyboy," he added. "And a fifth-form scrote. Bloody good shooting too. Almost as good as mine, eh?" He laughed at his little joke. Pugh sniggered sycophantically until silenced by a contemptuous look from Mac.

"We're going to need you, Keegan, if things get sticky," he went on.

He turned his attention to the others and I sighed heavily, suddenly aware that I'd been holding my breath.

"The rest of you could learn from this one. Proactive is what he is."

He leaned in close to me, his hot sour breath in my face, and hissed: "But not too proactive, yeah? Don't want to be too smart for your own good, do you, Keegan?"

"No sir," I said, crisply. He leaned back and smiled.

"Right, let's get you lot into patrols."

As the briefing got underway I realised that I was being given an opportunity. If I was to be part of the officer corps then I could get close to Mac, and if I could get close to him perhaps I could influence him, divert him, maybe even, if the need arose, deal with him.

I prepared myself to be Mac's bestest of best mates: reliable, steadfast and sneaky as a bastard.

SPEIGHT AND ZAYN got first watch, the rest of us were dismissed. I'd be reporting for guard duty with Wolf-Barry first thing in the morning so I wanted to get my head down.

The difference between night and day used to be blurred by electricity; streetlights turned the night sky orange and blotted out the stars; electric lights in the home allowed people to keep doing whatever they wanted all night long; car headlights made travel in the darkness a cinch. Things were different now. Battery torches were only used when absolutely necessary, so any light after dark had to come from flame. People were returning to the old rhythms of day and night, rising and retiring with the sun.

Nonetheless, the old term-time routine of lights-out was still being preserved by Bates; juniors in bed at 8, fourth and fifth-formers by 9:30, seniors by 11. So normally I'd need to be tucked up by 9:30, but I'd been told that as an honorary senior – with all the duties that implied – I could observe senior bedtime, so I had some time in hand and there was someone I wanted to see.

The door of the sanatorium was closed, but the candle light flickering through the frosted glass windows revealed Matron moving around inside. I knocked and I saw her freeze. She didn't respond. Perhaps she wanted to be left alone. I knocked again.

"Matron," I said, "It's me, Lee. I just wanted to see how you are."

Her silhouette relaxed.

"Come in Lee," she said.

I pushed open the door and entered to find Matron standing at the side of the padded table she used for examinations. There was a livid purple bruise on her forehead where the horsewoman had clubbed her, and for an instant I was so furious I wished I had shot the bitch after all. Matron was dressed in medical whites and an apron stained with fresh blood. Her sleeves were rolled up and she was wearing thin rubber gloves which she was removing as I entered. Her face was as white as her clothes.

Four bodies lay on the floor, covered with sheets. Both boys had died then.

I stood there in the doorway, unsure what to say. She broke the silence.

"Too many pellets," she said simply. "Not enough anaesthetic."

Next to the table stood a complicated system of tubes suspended from a metal stand. She must have been giving transfusions.

She followed my gaze and nodded.

"Atkins gave blood first, then Broadbent, Dudley and Haycox. They were so brave, but it just wasn't enough." Her voice caught in her throat and she leaned against the table as if light-headed. Then she looked up, remembering.

"Oh Lee, I forgot to thank you. You saved my life, didn't you?"

I nodded, still unsure what to say.

"Bless you. You saved me, but I couldn't save them." She slumped to the floor. "What a fucking waste. To survive the end of the world just to be murdered for a Mars bar." She hid her face in her hands and wept.

I walked over to her, knelt down, and gingerly reached out to touch her shoulder. As I did so she leaned forward and embraced me, burying her face in my neck, soaking it with tears.

We sat there like that for quite some time.

WITH THE BODIES buried, one horse butchered and salted, and the other released ten miles down the road, we removed all evidence of the confrontation on the school drive.

The minibus that had been abandoned in Hildenborough was thankfully not one of those with the school name and crest painted on the side, so no-one could trace it back to us without checking the registration plate with the DVLA, and they weren't taking calls. We just had to hope that McCulloch or Fleming hadn't revealed our location to our neighbours before they were hanged. However, Bates wasn't prepared to take any chances, and the next afternoon he called all the officers to the common room. He got straight to the point.

"We need ordnance," he said simply. "Our armoury holds ten rifles and a few boxes of rounds, but if it came to a shooting war we'd be lucky to last a day. Of course with law and order entirely broken down there are weapons and ammunition there for the taking, if you know where to look. And I do. So we're going on a field trip."

He took out his whiteboard pen and started drawing a map.

PUGH AND WYLIE stayed behind to guard the school. Mr Hammond was planning to teach a class, so most boys would be safe inside. Meanwhile the rest of us hit the road, with Mac and Bates each driving a minibus. In full combats, all armed, and with mud and boot polish rubbed into our face, we were off to get ourselves an arsenal and we were ready to meet resistance.

Giving Hildenborough a wide berth we headed out into darkest Kent. The only cars we passed had been abandoned, and the roads were well on their way to becoming impassable. With no council workers to operate the hedge trimmers or clear fallen trees, the narrow country lanes were rapidly disappearing under the greenery. On some roads the hedgerows scraped along both sides of the bus. A couple of summers and they'd be buried forever.

We passed through picturesque villages with large greens, their cricket squares so neat for so long, now shaggy and unkempt. We saw ancient churches with their stained glass windows smashed and their huge, centuries-old oak doors hanging off thick, bent hinges. We drove past fields of cows, most dead or dying, suffering agonies because they'd been bred to produce milk that nobody was around to extract.

There were some signs of life: a man driving a horse and cart carrying a crop of leeks; the occasional cottage with a column of thin smoke snaking up into the dull grey sky; a village hall ablaze. In one hamlet a gang of feral children heaved bricks at us as we drove past. Mac fired some warning shots over their heads and laughed as they ran for cover.

When we were half a mile from our destination we pulled into a farmyard. Mac and I swept the buildings to ensure they were empty, and then we stashed the buses in a barn. From here we were on foot. We split into two groups. Me, Mac and Green went one way, Bates, Zayn and Wolf-Barry went the other. Speight and Patel stayed to guard the transport. The intention was to approach the target from different directions.

We headed off into thick forest. One startled, honking partridge could reveal our presence, so we trod lightly. We did startle a small family of deer, but they ran away from our objective, so we reckoned we were okay. Off to our right a brace of pigeons noisily took flight and flapped away; Bates' group were clearly less covert than they thought they were.

As we approached the edge of the trees we fell to our stomachs and crawled through the wet, mulchy leaves, rifles held out in front of us. Eventually Mac held up his hand and we stopped. He took out his binoculars and studied the terrain beyond the tree-line for a minute or two before handing them across to me.

"What do you see, Keegan?"

I took the glasses and looked down onto the Kent and Sussex Territorial Army Firing Range and Armoury.

A chain link fence stood between us and the complex. A burnt-out saloon car was wedged into one section directly in front of us, presumably the result of someone's ill-advised attempt to ram their way in. It was riddled with bullet holes. There were plenty of possible entry points; the fence wasn't much of a barrier, it was falling down in various places, but the state of the car implied that the complex had been defended at some point. Was it still?

Off to our right were the firing ranges. A brick trench looked out onto a long stretch of grass with a huge sandbank at the far end.

Propped up in front of the sand stood the fading, tattered shreds of paper soldiers, stapled to wooden boards. Many had fallen to the floor, or hung sideways at crazy angles as if drunk. Both the trench and the sandbank could provide excellent cover for attackers or defenders.

Directly in front of us stood the main building. It was two storeys high, brick built, with an impressive sign hanging across the large double doorway proclaiming its military importance. Many of the windows were smashed, and the far right rooms on the top floor had been on fire in the not too distant past; streaks of black scorching stretched from the cracked windows to the roof.

The car park in front of the building was empty except for one shiny BMW which, bizarrely, appeared untouched, still waiting patiently for its proud owner to return. Beyond the car park, to our left, was the driveway, lined with single storey outbuildings which appeared to continue behind the main building; there was more of the complex out of sight, presumably a parade ground and maybe an assault course.

There were two sandbag emplacements at the entrance to the main building, but there were no men or guns there. They were the remains of a previous attempt at defence, long since abandoned.

If I were defending this place where would I station myself?

I scanned the roof and windows of the main building but could see no signs of life or other, more recent fortifications – no sandbags, barriers or not-so-casually placed obstacles behind which to hide. The firing range appeared empty, as did the outbuildings lining the drive. Perhaps any defenders would be stationed behind the main building, but that would leave them unable to cover the most obvious routes of approach, so that seemed unlikely. So either I was missing something, or the place was deserted.

I was just about to hand the binoculars back to Mac when I caught a glimpse of a brick corner poking out behind the portico entrance to the firing range trench. I shuffled left a bit to get a better view and found myself gazing at a solid, brick and concrete Second World War pillbox. Anyone in there would have a 360° view of pretty much the entire complex, a mostly unimpeded line of fire, and bugger all chance of being killed by some yokel looter with a shotgun.

I pointed to the pillbox and handed the glasses back to Mac, who nodded; he'd seen it already or, more likely, been tipped off by Bates earlier.

"Bit obvious, though, innit," he whispered, handing the glasses to Green, who took his turn scanning the area. "I'd have someone somewhere else too, covering the approach to the pillbox. Now, where would that fucker be, d'you think?"

"Sir," whispered Green. "The car in the fence. Rear right wheel." He passed back the binoculars and Mac took a look. He grinned.

"Not too shabby, Green. Not too shabby at all." He passed the binoculars to me. Sure enough, just visible poking out from behind the rear wheel was a boot. As I watched it moved ever so slightly. There was a man under the car. Between him and the pillbox all the open spaces in the complex were exposed to crossfire.

We didn't have walkie-talkies, so the next thing was for Green and Wolf-Barry to skirt the complex, staying in the woods. They'd meet halfway between our positions and compare notes. Green scurried away while Mac and I shuffled back from the edge of the wood into deep cover and sat up against a couple of trees. Mac took out a battered packet of Marlboros and offered one to me.

"They might see the smoke, sir," I pointed out. Mac glared at me, and for a moment I thought he was going to pitch a fit, but eventually he nodded and put away the packet.

"Fair point," he said. He regarded me coolly. "Yesterday, why didn't you just shoot that bitch?"

Because I'm not a murdering psycho whose first instinct is to open fire.

Breathe. Calm. Play the part. Earn his trust.

"Wasn't sure that I'd be able to get her mate before he shot Hammond and the others. Didn't want to shoot first, I suppose. But I was just about to pop her before you did. So thanks. Saved me the trouble." I grinned, trying to make out I thought it was funny. "Good shooting, by the way."

"Had lots of practice, ain't I."

Oh very good, hard case. Make out that you shoot people all the time. I know where you got your practice – shooting pheasants on Daddy's estate in your plus fours and Barbour jacket.

Then again, not too fast. I didn't know what happened to him during The Cull. I didn't know what he'd been doing for the last year. He could have been on a killing spree. After all, who'd know? He may have been a pampered Grant Mitchell clone, but I knew it would be dangerous to underestimate him.

"Killed many people since The Cull started, have you?" Casual, unconcerned, sound interested not appalled.

"A few." Cagey, giving nothing away. "No-one who didn't have it coming, anyway. First time's the worst. Easier after that."

"So who was first, then?"

Long silence.

Green emerged, limping, from the trees and the moment passed.

"What the bloody 'ell happened to you?" said Mac.

"Slipped, sir. Think I've twisted me ankle."

"Fuck me, Green, I'd have been better off sending my little sister. Right, sit down. What do they reckon?"

"The parade ground round back is deserted and they can't see anyone, so it's probably just the man under the car and the one in the pillbox. The Colonel and his men are going to take up firing positions in the main building, on the top floor left. Our job is to take out the guy under the car without drawing the attention of the pillbox. He said that's your job, sir."

But Mac was already moving. He'd pulled a vicious looking knife from his backpack, placed it between his teeth, and was crawling away on his belly.

"Cover me, Keegan," he whispered as he slithered out of the woods and began inching his way towards the car, which sat about fifty metres away and down a slope. The long grass provided good cover.

I took up position at the tree-line, nestled the rifle into my shoulder and scanned the area for nasty surprises. The place was as quiet as the grave.

And then, just as he made his final approach to the car, Mac burst out of the grass and ran as fast as he could back towards the trees, blowing our cover completely. I thought he'd lost the plot until the car exploded in a sudden blossom of flame and smoke, flinging Mac forward onto his face. He staggered upright again and continued running. No-one opened fire, and he made it back into cover safely. He sat next to me panting hard.

"Fucking tripwire," he gasped. "There wasn't a man under the car at all. Just a fucking leg, attached to a piece of wire that some bastard was tugging. Lured me in and I didn't see the booby trap 'til I crawled right into it. Fucking amateur!" He threw his knife in fury. It thudded into a tree, thrumming with force.

"Where's the puppeteer then?" I asked.

"The wire leads off to the left, so anywhere between the car and the main gate I reckon. But we're blown now. There could be any number of hostiles in there and they know we're here. We need a rethink."

At that moment there was a crackle of static and an ancient tannoy system hissed into life. A man's voice echoed tinnily around the buildings.

"This facility is the property of His Majesty's Armed Forces and is defended. In accordance with emergency measures, and standing orders relating to Operation Motherland, any attempt to infiltrate this facility is an act of treason. Any further incursions will be met with deadly force. This is your first and last warning."

The speakers fell silent, as did we.

"What the sweet holy Christ," said Mac eventually, "is Operation Motherland?"

He bit his lip and surveyed the complex nervously.

"Right. That place is full of ordnance and I'm bloody well having it, standing orders or not."

"We could wait 'til after dark, sir," offered Green.

"And if they've got night goggles we hand them a major advantage, numbnuts. Nah, we need to do this quickly." He pulled out the binoculars again.

"Two wires we need to trace. The tannoy ones and the puppet one. Let's see where they go."

As he tried to trace the tannoy wires back to the mic I caught a glimpse of a flash from the top floor of the main windows. I looked closer and there it was again. I tapped Mac on the shoulder and pointed it out. He took a look.

"It's Bates," he said. Not 'the Colonel' I noticed. Interesting. "Signalling us with a mirror. Bloody idiot, keep your head down." But it was too late. A burst of machine gun fire raked across the face of the building, splintering the window frame and spraying the remaining shards of glass inward at Bates and the others. The pillbox was manned.

"I think someone's hit, can't see who," said Mac. "Fuck, this is a shambles. Right, enough of this." He handed the binoculars to me. "Green."

"Sir?"

"The tannoy wires go to the pillbox and the puppet wire leads down to the main gate. I think there's a man in cover there, probably a sniper in camouflage. You could probably walk right up to him and not see him, if he knows his job. But I want you to keep in the trees and move down to cover the area. He won't risk a shot until he sees a target the pillbox can't deal with, so I need you, Keegan, to draw his fire."

"Sir?" I asked, trying not to sound incredulous.

Mac grinned. "I know you're the better shot, Keegan, but Green's not going to be doing the 100-metre sprint anytime soon, are you, Green?"

"No, sir," he said, abjectly.

"And you can shoot that damn thing, right?"

"Yes, sir."

"Well then. You're the bait, Keegan, and Green shoots the shooter. Sorted."

"And what will you be doing while I'm being shot at, sir?" I asked.

He opened his backpack, pulled out a stick of dynamite and waved it in my face. "Passed a quarry on my way back to Castle, didn't I? I'm going to blow that fucking pillbox wide open."

"And the Colonel?"

"Fuck him, if he's not been shot already he deserves to be. We're dealing with this. With me?"

"Yes, sir!" yelped gung-ho Green.

Oh, yeah, this was going to end well.

We synchronised our watches and then, always staying in the trees, Green and I went left, while Mac went right, towards the pillbox. Green took up position covering the long grass near the main gate and I kept going. I travelled some way past the complex, out of any possible sniper's line of sight, and scurried across the road leading to the gate. I made it safely into the trees on the other side and started to move back towards the fence. It didn't take long to find a breach and I snaked under the chain link and crawled through the grass until I was behind the first outbuilding on the opposite side of the road to Green.

Even higher on my list of Things-I-Never-Want-To-Do than 'shoot somebody' was 'be shot by somebody else'. So I wasn't entirely comfortable with Mac's plan that I should run up and down in plain view of a sniper, presenting a nice juicy target for a thumb-sized piece of supersonic, superheated lead that could push my brains out through my face.

I lay there for a minute, breathing deeply, calming myself, considering. Should I leg it? Just cut my losses and run? Go it alone? Did I need to remain at the school, taking orders from nutters and idiots, getting involved in unnecessary gunfights and risking my life... for what? For the school? For Matron?

But where else could I go? And if I left, how would Dad find me?

No, there was no choice. I'd made my decision to return to the school and I was stuck with it. I just had to stay alive long enough for Dad to come get me, and then I could split and leave Mac and Bates to their stupid army games. Until then I had to play along. After all, there was supposed to be safety in numbers, wasn't there?

I checked my watch. Time to go. I walked forward slowly. The gap between this outbuilding and the next was about ten metres. I had to cover that distance slowly enough to allow the sniper to notice me, sight, and fire, but sufficiently quickly that he didn't quite have time to take aim accurately enough to kill me. I'm sure an experienced SAS man would be able to do some calculation based on distance, running speed and firing time and tell you, to the second, how long he should be visible for. I was just going to have to guess using my vast experience of watching DVDs of *24*.

Fuck it.

I ran.

Three steps, that's all it took. Three bloody steps and I was flat on my face unsure what had hit me, and where. My mouth was full of grass before I even heard the shot.

And then, as I tried to work out if I was bleeding to death, a burst of machine gun fire and a huge explosion from up ahead. Shards of pillbox brick impacted all around me.

And then, before the dust had settled, a series of sharp reports off to my right, as the sniper and Green exchanged fire.

And then a scream.

And then silence.

CHAPTER FOUR

THE PROBLEM WITH being in a battle is that if you get killed you never know whether your side wins or not. Sacrificing your life in a blaze of heroic glory is fine, but only if you're willing to accept that it might not have achieved anything.

Movie battles have a good solid story structure – beginning, middle, end – and the audience gets to see how it all works out, how the actions of certain characters shape events, how their deaths either do or don't have any meaning. But as I lay there in the cool grass, shot, bleeding, going into shock, I realised that the characters in those films, the ones who save the day by charging the machine guns or providing diversions so their mates can escape, the ones who say 'leave me, I'll only slow you down' or 'I can delay them, give you time to escape,' die alone, clinging to the hope that maybe they've made a difference but not really sure if they've just thrown their lives away for no good reason.

I had no idea if Green had shot the sniper or vice-versa. Even if Green had shot him, our 'side' might still not get the weapons. And if we did get the weapons we still might not survive the coming year. In which case what possible point did my slow, silent, blood-soaked death on a patch of scrubland between two prefabs actually have? How had I helped? Would I be remembered as a hero who sacrificed himself for the greater good, or would I just end up a leg attached to a piece of string underneath a car somewhere, luring other poor bastards into an ambush?

Luckily, the thing about shock is that pretty quickly you stop giving a toss about much of anything, so I soon stopped philosophising. I then briefly, dispassionately, considered giving up or going on, and then began crawling towards cover.

The sniper must have been aiming for my upper body. I wasn't sure whether I was lucky that he'd only hit my left thigh, or unlucky that he'd hit me at all. A thigh wound might sound painful but non-threatening – all that muscle to absorb the slug, no major organs to hit – but you've got arteries running through your legs, and if the bullet had hit one of those I wasn't going to be around for much longer, no matter how much cover I found.

I made it into the shade of the next outbuilding without being shot again. I propped myself up against the wall and examined my leg. It was bleeding freely but not spurting. Lucky. I pulled my belt out of my trousers, looped it around my leg just above the wound, and pulled it tight. Up to now there'd been hardly any pain, but as the belt dug in I had to work hard to stifle a scream.

I fastened the belt and tried to stand, using my rifle as a crutch. As soon as I was upright I had a massive headrush and tumbled back onto the ground.

I may have blacked out, I don't know.

Deep breaths. Focus. Get back up.

I hobbled away towards the main building. Dear God my leg hurt. Jonah had taken a chunk out of it and it hadn't hurt half as badly as this. Matron would be pleased, assuming I ever made it back to the sanatorium.

As I approached the gap between the next prefab and the one beyond I heard the unmistakeable snap of a twig. There was someone coming. If I tried to shoulder my rifle I'd topple over, so I propped myself up against the wall and raised the weapon, waiting for my stalker to break cover.

My vision was starting to blur.

Green hobbled from between the two buildings. He had one hand above his head but the other arm hung limp at his side, dripping fresh blood. Score two to the sniper. But the sniper obviously thought I was dead, because he strolled out in front of me, bold as brass, keeping his rifle aimed square at Green's back.

Two things occurred to me. Firstly, they must have marched right across the road in full view of the pillbox, so the sniper didn't think there was any threat to him from that direction, which might mean Mac was dead; secondly, I was once again being offered an opportunity to become a killer.

"Hold it."

The sniper froze, staring straight ahead. Green, on the other hand, jumped out of his skin.

"I could shoot you right here and now," I said. "You'd be dead before you hit the ground." I was lightheaded, all right, please forgive the clichés. "I really don't want to do that, but please believe me when I say that I won't hesitate for an instant if you do anything at all to make me nervous. I've lost a lot of blood and I'm not sure I'm thinking clearly, so you'd better not make me jump."

The sniper was well camouflaged. His face and hands were daubed in black and green paint, and he had webbing hanging off him like a cloak, with pieces of greenery, twigs, leaves and ferns sticking out of it. He was carrying an L96 sniper rifle and had various other pieces of kit in pouches and holsters. He was about 40 and middle aged spread had taken hold. Hardly Hereford material, probably some weekend warrior TA guy who worked in accounts during the week.

"All right," he said, still not moving an inch. "Now calm down, son. I had no idea I was shooting at kids. I'd never have opened fire if I'd realised. There's no need for any more shooting, okay?"

"Not if you drop your gun, there isn't."

"Can't do that, laddie. Orders is orders, y'know."

I raised the rifle, pointed it straight at his head, and shuffled forward until the muzzle gently kissed his temple.

"Last chance. Drop it, or I drop you."

The cocky bastard actually thought about it for a minute, but then he lowered his gun and let it fall to the ground.

Thank you. Still not a killer.

Green staggered sideways and slumped against the wall of the opposite prefab. He was hyperventilating and glassy-eyed.

"On the floor, face down, hands behind your head."

"Now listen, can we not..."

"On the floor!"

The sniper complied.

"Green. Green!"

"Um, yeah? Yeah? Lee? Lee, I'm shot, Lee. He shot me, Lee."

"I know, but you're fine, doesn't look too serious. You're going to be fine."

"But he shot me, Lee. In my arm. He shot my arm. I've been shot. In the arm."

"He's going into shock. Let me help," said the sniper.

"Shut the fuck up," I barked. "Green, I need you to focus on me. Green. Green. Focus on me." His eyes swam around in his head but eventually they locked onto mine. "I want you to go into the main building, head to the top floor and find the Colonel. He's got a med kit. Tell him what's happened. But Green, keep behind these prefabs and enter the main building from the rear, don't expose yourself to the pillbox, understand? Understand?"

He nodded listlessly.

"Okay, off you go. Quickly now."

He lurched away like a zombie in a bad horror film.

Once I was sure he'd gone the right way, I turned my attention back to my captive.

"TA, right?"

"Is this an interrogation?" He sounded amused. I kicked him. Bad idea. My wounded leg buckled underneath me. He was moving before I even realised I was falling. But he was fat and slow, and I was lucky. I fell in such a way that the rifle remained pointing at him, and as my back hit the wall I was left slumped but upright, with my gun pointing square at his chest. He was on his knees, one hand reaching for a holster on his hip, but he knew he'd never make it. He widened his arms, smiled, and shuffled backwards until he was leaning against the opposite wall. I rested my rifle on my good knee, finger still firm on the trigger.

"Mind if I smoke?"

"Be my guest."

He reached slowly into a webbed pocket, took out a kit and began the rollup ritual. As he did so he considered me.

"How old are you, son?"

"Old enough."

"Fourteen, fifteen? What you doing running around playing soldiers, eh?"

I was not in the mood to be interrogated.

"I want you to very slowly take out the handguns and toss them over to me. Slowly."

He put the ciggie in his mouth, lit it, and then casually tossed me two shiny new Browning L9A1 sidearms.

"Here, have the ammo as well. Call it a gift. Plenty more where that came from." He threw me four clips of 13 rounds. I stashed the guns and ammunition in the big pockets on my trousers. No need for anyone else to know I had them. Insurance.

"What's that you've got, old .303? Where d'you get that then?"

I didn't answer.

"Let me guess. CCF, right? You're from one of those posh schools where the kids play dress up. Listen son, I dunno who's giving you orders but they're fucked in the head if they think that storming a military facility is a job for teenagers. You should be holed up somewhere learning to rub sticks together to make fire, not creeping around the countryside shooting at adults."

"Maybe. But adults keep shooting at us and I feel a lot safer knowing I can shoot back."

He thought about this for a moment and then nodded. "Fair enough, I s'pose."

"And anyway, I'm the one holding the gun and it sounded to me like your pillbox got blown to pieces, so I wouldn't underestimate us, mate. We're not playing games here."

He grinned. "Again, fair point."

"So what's Operation Motherland when it's at home?" I asked.

"Exactly what I want to fucking know," said Mac.

THE ARMOURY WAS a room in the main building's basement, one end of which housed a huge vault door. The sniper and two other men were tied to chairs in front of the door. One of the captives from the pillbox had a nasty head wound and was only partially conscious. The other was covered in brick dust but looked fine.

Mac himself was also covered in dust and had a large purple bruise on his forehead. He'd been knocked out by a piece of brick sent sky high by the explosion, but he'd come round first and pulled these two from the wreckage.

"Pillboxes are fucking solid, right," he'd explained. "So I had to use a lot of geli. I managed to lay the charge without them spotting me, but they clocked me as I was crawling away and I had to hit the detonator before I was fully clear otherwise they'd have killed me."

The rest of us were gathered around the door too, sitting on chairs or lounging on the cellar steps. Wolf-Barry was dressing Green's wound, Zayn was seeing to mine. Bates, Zayn and Wolf-Barry's faces were all covered in tiny cuts where the glass from the window had shrapnelled into them, but none had serious injuries. Apparently they'd still been sitting up there trying to formulate a plan when Mac blew the pillbox and all the shooting happened. Nice one Batesy, leading from the front.

"Dave, I'm sorry about this," said Bates, addressing the conscious man from the pillbox. "But we've got a situation and I need those weapons. Didn't think there'd be anyone defending the place. Not my intention to have any shooting, but you shot first and my boys have a right to defend themselves. All you need to do is tell us how to open the vault and no-one else needs to get hurt."

The man didn't even try to hide his contempt.

"What the fuck do you think you're doing, Bates? I mean, you always were a jumped up little tosser who thought he was a soldier, but seriously, what the fuck is this? Colonel? You're a Colonel? Don't make me laugh. All those times we let you come down the boozer with us after manoeuvres so you could tell us all about the SAS stories you used to read. We were laughing *at* you, you moron, not *with* you. Do you really, seriously think that…"

He trailed off as a loud, sickening gurgle came from the semi-conscious man tied up next to him. All heads turned in time to see Mac pull his knife out of the man's neck. Blood gushed out over his hands, and down the man's jacket. We all sat there in stunned silence as the man shook and jerked in his bonds as he frothed, spluttered and wheezed. It took him a horribly long time to die, and none of us said a word.

Again, the hollowness in my stomach and the deep, sick sense that everything was spiralling out of control. But I was weak from blood loss, light-headed and mildly in shock. My reactions were muted. I could do nothing but watch.

"You're next," said Mac, simply. He then wiped the knife blade on his sleeve and sat back down, staring straight into Dave's terrified eyes with something that looked awfully like lust.

Zayn ran up the stairs. The sounds of him retching echoed back down to us.

Bates was white as a sheet. He hadn't ordered Mac to do that. Even through layers of shock I realised that if he let it go unremarked then Bates' authority would be gone forever and it would only be a matter of time before Mac made his move. I willed Bates to shout at him, to demand his weapon, to dress him down and seize control. But he didn't have it in him. Bates so desperately wanted to be a strong military leader but he was weak, indecisive and vulnerable. And with his next words he doomed all of us.

"Well, Dave?" he whispered, unable to conceal his shock but trying to play along and follow Mac's lead. "What's it to be?"

Dave held Mac's gaze, his eyes full of disbelief and horror. And, I noticed with surprise, tears. He told us the combination.

Mac smiled. "Thanks, mate," he said. He looked up at Bates. "Want to do the honours, sir?"

Bates seemed to be looking right through Mac at something

terrible in the distance, but he nodded and mumbled "Yes, thank you Major." Now he was thanking his subordinate for giving him permission to open a door.

He stepped forward and entered the combination, swung the huge lever handle and pulled the heavy door open to reveal racks upon racks of armaments and stacked boxes of ammunition. Mac gave a low whistle of appreciation.

"Lovely jubbly," he said.

WE BROUGHT THE minibuses up to the front door and started loading the weapons into the back. Green and I sat in the front seats watching the others do all the heavy lifting. There were about fifty SA80 Light Machine Guns, ten boxes of grenades, three more Browning sidearms and four 7.62mm General Purpose Machine Guns, the kind you would mount on a jeep or in a pillbox. There was also more ammunition than we could carry, so there would have to be a second trip. With this amount of firepower, properly used, we'd be a pretty formidable opposition.

"We could even go on the offensive," said Wolf-Barry. "Take the fight to those Hildenborough fuckers. Mac'll see us right, he'll make sure we do what's necessary to protect ourselves."

In his mind Mac had replaced Bates already. I wondered how many of the others felt the same way. And I wondered how long it would be before Mac's assumption of power became official. What would that would mean for poor usurped Mr Bates?

When the buses were loaded Patel opened the driver's door, excited. "You're going to want to see this," he said. "Mac's doing an interrogation."

In fact this was pretty much the last thing I wanted to see, but somehow I felt I should. I was responsible for capturing the sniper, whatever happened to him would be, to some degree, on my conscience. I hopped out of the bus and continued hopping 'til I was back at the vault door.

Mac had the two surviving TA men sitting facing each other, with himself circling around them.

"...got what we came for," he was saying. "But we want to be sure we haven't missed anything, and the only thing more useful than guns is intel, right?"

Neither man moved a muscle, but they were rigid with fear and determination.

"So what I need to know, sorry, what *we* need to know," he gestured at Bates, who was sitting on the steps, reduced to the role of bystander, "is what Operation Motherland is and what it could mean for my merry little band. So who wants to tell me? Dave? Derek?"

So the sniper was called Derek. I almost wished I hadn't known that.

Neither said a word.

Mac started twirling his hunting knife around in his right hand.

"If no-one tells me then I'm going to have get a little cut happy. Now, I must admit, I'm looking forward to that, so I'd encourage you to hold out for a while. Been some time since I gave any fucker a really good cutting."

"Fuck you," whispered Dave.

"Oh, goody, here I come a-cutting," said Mac, with the most malevolent grin I'd ever seen. He advanced towards the captive, knife raised.

"All right, all right," said Derek. "Just leave him alone, okay. There's no need for any of this."

Mac stopped and turned to face Derek.

"Says you," he replied. He stood for a moment, considering, and then decided to give Derek a chance. "Okay then, spill."

But Derek had got the measure of the man, and he cocked his head to one side as he regarded his would-be torturer. I saw all hope go out of his eyes and resignation and defeat set in. He'd realised what I'd long ago worked out – Mac was never going to let him get out of here alive, no matter what he said. He stared into the face of the man who he knew would soon be his murderer and found a depth of resolve that no amount of threats could break.

"Operation Motherland," he said, "is your death, little man. It's your big, hairy, motherfucking slaughter. It's coming for you and you won't even know it's arrived until you're dangling from a rope, kicking in the air and shitting yourself as your eyes pop out and your tongue turns black and you realise in your final moments that all you ever were was a sad, frightened child who wants his mummy. Operation Motherland is our justice and our justification and our vengeance. And that's all you're getting from either of us, cunt, so cut away."

Mac stood there staring at Derek, looking sort of impressed.

"Oh, well," he said. "It was worth a try."

And he pulled out a handgun and shot both men in the head.

"Right then, back to Castle with the booty," he said, and walked up the stairs past us, whistling, leaving behind the corpses of three more soldiers who'd never know how the story ended.

CHAPTER FIVE

NOBODY SPOKE MUCH on the drive home, all of us trying to process what had happened. I would soon come to learn that the lesson the others took from the day was as simple as it was stupid: Mac is the boss, he is hard and cool and if you stick by him you'll be fine. That day Green, Zayn, Wolf-Barry, Patel and Speight all became, to a greater or lesser degree, Mac's devoted disciples, his power base, and everybody else's biggest problem.

What lesson Bates took away with him I'll never know, but it was a different man travelling back to school with us from the one who'd set out that morning. He'd appeared broken before, now he seemed to be a shadow.

When we got back to the school I was ferried up to the sanatorium with Green, and Matron swabbed and stitched and bandaged us. Green was allowed to go, he only had a flesh wound, but my injury was sufficiently severe that I was confined to a bed in the San. Matron warned me that as it healed it would hurt much more, and that if I wanted to recover fully then I must at all costs avoid splitting the stitches. I was prescribed bed rest for a week and a wheelchair for a fortnight thereafter.

It was my second day in the San when Mac came to visit.

"I tried to buy you some grapes, but they'd sold out." He laughed at his own joke, and I cracked a grin. He pulled a chair up next to my bed.

"Listen, Lee, what you did back there – risking your life, getting shot, saving Green, capturing that bastard sniper – that was hardcore shit. I reckon you're probably the hardest person here. Next to me, obviously. And you can really shoot."

Flattery now?

"The rest of my lads are loyal and all that, but, y'know, they ain't exactly Einsteins. If I'm to run this place..." and just like that he admitted he was planning to do away with Bates, "... then I need a lieutenant, a second-in-command, someone I can trust to watch my back when things get nasty. Someone with initiative. And I reckon that's you, mate."

Bloody hellfire. Okay, careful, think this through. Mac's not stupid. He knows to keep his enemies closest so maybe he realises I'm a threat and just wants to keep an eye on me. At the same time, I want to keep him close too, precisely because I am a threat. Then again, if I'm his trustworthy right hand man then it should make it easier for me to keep secrets from him, subvert him and bring him down. Easier and far more dangerous.

My head hurt just trying to work out all the wheels within wheels this conversation was setting in motion. But really, I had no choice whatsoever.

"Wow, Mac, I dunno what to say. I mean, I'm only a fifth year and the others are sixth-formers. I don't think they'd like me lording it over them."

"Let me worry about them. They'll do as I say."

"Okay, well, wow. Um, yeah, I'm flattered you think I'm the man for the job and I'll try not to let you down."

"So you'll do it?"

"Yeah, bring it on." Just the right mix of reticence and gung-ho. I should be on the stage.

Mac held out his hand and I shook it. I waited for the warning, the lean-in and hiss, the 'but if you...' It didn't come. Maybe he was sincere. He smiled.

"That's that then. Now all we need is for you to get better and we can really start sorting this fucking place out."

"What you got in mind?"

"Oh you'll see, you'll see."

Yeah, I thought. *I'm sure I will.*

AFTER BEING IN the thick of things for a few days it was odd to be cocooned in the San while the school went about turning itself into an armed camp, and Mac and his newly acquired groupies started to swagger and strut around Castle like they owned the place. Which, given that they were the only ones allowed to carry guns at all times, they did. They soon started dishing out punishments for supposed transgressions – lines, canings, laps before breakfast. It wouldn't be long before more inventive, sadistic punishments. The bullying was beginning.

Norton visited me regularly and kept me up to date with what was going on, and I was able to pass him my handguns and ammo to be stashed somewhere safe. Through him I learned that a new armoury had been set up in the cellar of Castle, with an armed guard on duty at all times. Bates and Mac carried handguns, but the rest of the senior officers carried rifles.

"Hammond's started giving lessons, if you can believe that," Norton told me. "Survivalist stuff, like water purification, how to trap and skin a rabbit, firemaking, that sort of thing. It's like being in the bloody Boy Scouts again. Oh and he's got these DVDs of this awful old telly show about survivors after a plague and he makes us watch it and 'discuss the issues'." He mock yawned.

"But that's not the best thing," he went on. "He's making a memorial. He won't let any of us see it, but knowing him it'll be some daft modern art sculpture. A ball with a hole it or something. Anyway, he's planning a big ceremony to unveil it the day after tomorrow, so we'll get you down in the wheelchair for that."

"I can hardly contain my excitement," I said.

I had told Norton all about events at the TA centre and he agreed with me that Mac was becoming a serious problem. If it had only been Mac then we might have used our guns to drive him out, or worse. But now he had a new gang of acolytes it was going to be much harder to unseat him. We would have to be cunning, bide our time, wait for the right moment, recruit other boys who would help us when the time came.

"Wylie is the biggest problem right now," said Norton. "He's taken a fancy to Unwin's little sister and he's not taking no for an answer. There've been a few slanging matches, but so far he's not threatened Unwin with his gun, but I reckon it's only a matter of time." He paused and looked at me worriedly. "She's 13, Lee."

"And what's Mac's reaction to this?"

"Seems to think it's funny."

"Look, do you think you'd be comfortable carrying a gun yourself?"

Norton looked surprised. "Me? Yeah, I suppose."

"Good, then find a way of carrying one of the Brownings with you, out of sight, and keep an eye on Unwin and his sister. You may have to intervene if things get nasty. But listen – only if there's no-one else around. If you can get away with doing something then do it, but if you run the risk of getting caught then do nothing."

I was appalled at what I was saying, but if Norton was shocked by the suggestion he didn't show it. Maybe the desperation of our situation hadn't quite sunk in yet, or maybe he was just a cooler customer than I had realised.

"God knows what Mac'd do to you if he found you threatening one of his officers," I went on, "and we have to keep an eye on the big picture here. Mac's our prime target, we can't do anything that jeopardises our plans to take him down."

"We have plans?"

"Um, no, not yet. But we will have. Wait and see. Big, clever plans. Schemes, maybe even plots."

"I like a good plot."

"There you go then."

As Norton and I cemented our friendship with conspiracy, Matron and I also grew closer. I would sit in the San with her as she did her morning surgeries, and she began teaching me the rudiments of first aid and medicine.

We hadn't only found weapons at the TA HQ. On the trip to collect the remaining ammunition Bates had ordered a full sweep of the facility and had found a well stocked medical centre, the contents of which had been brought back and given to Matron. She was ecstatic that now she had some proper painkillers, antibiotics, dressings and stuff. It wouldn't last long, but it provided temporary relief at least.

So in the afternoons I helped her catalogue the haul and she talked me through each drug and what it did. I carefully noted any drugs that could be used as sedatives or stimulants, just in case.

And as we did this she talked to me about books, films and music. She never mentioned her family or her life outside the school, but then I'd never known her to leave the grounds, even on her days off. Maybe she didn't have a life outside the school.

Somehow we managed to do a lot of laughing.

MR HAMMOND HAD been a popular teacher. He expected the class to rise to their feet when he entered the room, wore a long black gown to teach lessons, and you got the sense that there were times he longed to pull a boy up to the front of the class by their sideburns and give them six of the best like he was allowed to do when he was a younger man. But we respected and liked him because you always knew where you stood with him. The rules of his classroom were clear and simple, he never lost his temper, and never gave out punishments just because he was having a bad day – if you did cop it from him he always made sure you knew why.

His lessons were interesting if not exactly thrilling, and his obsessive passion for all things Modern in art meant that anyone seeking enlightenment about mundane stuff like life drawing or sculpture could feel his frustration at having to teach what he considered backward and irrelevant skills. Cubism and Henry Moore's abstracts were all he lived for. I thought it was all meaningless, pretentious crap, if I'm honest, but it's hard not to warm to someone who's so genuinely enthusiastic.

He studied here as a boy and had returned to teach here immediately he qualified, so apart from his first five years, and three years at art college, he'd been ensconced in Castle for his entire life. He was an old man who should have retired years ago but he was such a fixture of the place that no-one could imagine him leaving. At the age of seventy-five he was still teaching art and had looked likely to do so until he dropped.

Although he was the senior master there had never been any question of his challenging Bates' authority, he just wasn't the type. Teaching lessons in post-apocalyptic survivalism sounded like just the kind of thing he'd come up with, and I wished I could have sat in on just one. Norton told me that there were a large group of younger boys who adored him utterly. He was playing granddad to them and they were lapping it up. After all, Mac wasn't exactly the approachable type, and Bates, despite his initial rapport with the younger boys, was increasingly isolated and distant.

In some ways you could say that, in a very short time, Hammond had cemented himself into the position he had held for so many decades before The Cull – the heart of the school, its conscience and kindness.

And of course, there was no room for such things in our brave new world.

THE FIRST SNOW of the winter fell the night before the great unveiling ceremony, making the school and its grounds shine and glitter. Norton turned up to collect me in his CCF uniform, which was unusual, but I didn't say anything. He and Matron lifted me out of my bed and into a wheelchair. My leg was in constant pain, a low dull throb that flared into sharp agony with the slightest movement, but in the absence of the proper hospital kit some of the boys had used cushions and planks to rig up a horizontal shelf for my leg to rest on, so once I was safely aboard I could be wheeled about without screaming all the time. Which was a plus.

With Norton as my driver we crunched through the snow to the front lawn where the school had assembled. I couldn't believe my eyes. Instead of the rag-tag gaggle of boys in what remained of their uniforms, I was confronted by fifty or so boys of all ages in full army kit. On the younger boys it looked comically large, but their trousers had been turned up and the huge jumpers tied with belts. Obviously the berets were a problem, so the younger boys either went bareheaded or wore baseball caps that had been painted green.

Not only were they dressed like soldiers, they were standing at ease in a nice square little cadre. And – my already cold blood ran ice – all of them held SA80s.

"What the fuck is this?" I whispered to Norton.

"I was going to warn you, but I figured you needed to see it for yourself. I can see it and I still don't believe it."

"So he actually did it, all the kids are in the army now?"

"Uh huh. As of this afternoon there's going to be compulsory drill and weapons training for all boys, as well as lessons on tactics, camouflage, all that shit. They've even tapped me to teach martial arts."

In front of the assembled troops was an object, about head height, draped in a sheet. Bates and Hammond stood either side of it, with Matron and the four remaining grown-ups – an old aunt and three grandparents – sitting on a row of chairs to the left; Green, his arm still in a sling, sat with them. To the right stood the remaining officers in two rows, like an honour guard, all holding .303 rifles.

Norton wheeled me up the row of chairs and positioned me on the end, next to Green. He then marched to the ranks and took up his position in the troops. As he stood at ease he winked at me and gave the smallest of shrugs as if to say 'I know, what a farce.'

Once Norton was in place, Bates stood. He looked even worse than he had when I'd last seen him. Although he was clean shaven his face was a mess of red spots and slashes where he'd cut himself. It wasn't hard to see why – his hands, which gripped a swagger stick behind his back so hard that his knuckles had turned white, were shaking. His eyes lacked focus; as he spoke he never seemed to be looking directly at anything or anyone, but to a point slightly to their left or right, or somewhere through and behind them.

Mac stood to attention in front of the troops, facing Bates. He stared straight into Bates' eyes, unwavering. Bates never met his gaze.

The boys stood to shambolic attention at Mac's instruction, and Bates began to speak.

"At ease, men. Stand easy." The boys, many unsure what this meant, shuffled nervously in the cold. "When I was a boy my grandfather used to tell me tales of the Second World War. Stories of heroes and derring-do, secret missions, cunning generals, evil Nazis. It all seemed so simple. Good against bad, good wins, bad loses, everyone's happy..."

He lapsed into silence and stared off into space. As the seconds ticked past it became clear that this was more than just a dramatic pause. It soon became a very awkward silence, and then people started looking at each other out of the corners of their eyes and grimacing. Embarrassment set in, and then genuine discomfort. It must have been about a minute before he started again and everyone's shoulders relaxed.

"But the world isn't like that, is it men?" His voice was harder now, more assured. He started to increase his volume until he was on the verge of shouting. "Now it's just survival. Kill or be killed. It's hard and cruel and violent and wrong, but it's the world we have to live in and we have to be as hard as it is if we're to survive.

"We've all lost people, I know that. But they won't be forgotten. As we build our perfect home here in the grounds of our beloved school we carry with us the memories of those who have fallen before us, to the plague or the madness that followed it."

He paused again, but this time, thank God, it was a dramatic flourish.

"My colleague Mr Hammond, who has given his life to this school, has constructed a monument to our fallen dead. Mr Hammond..." He gestured for Hammond to take his place, and sat down.

Hammond rose and walked to the same spot Bates had spoken from.

"Um, thanks Bates." He paused a second to collect his thoughts and then, to my surprise, he looked up at the crowd with a strong, clear gaze. There was a sense of purpose in his eyes and his jaw was set with determination. The feeble pensioner we'd rescued on the driveway had been replaced by the firm disciplinarian of old. "But I'm afraid I can't agree with your sentiments.

"You see, I remember the war. I was only a boy at school but even I could see that it wasn't glorious. When my parents were burned alive in their house they weren't heroes, they were victims of indiscriminate slaughter. Hundreds of thousands of people died in England during the Blitz, died in their beds, died at their breakfast tables, died on their way to work or in the pub or in the arms of their lovers. And that was hard and cruel and violent and wrong. But do you know how we fought it, hmm? By rising above it! We chose decency and kindness and community, we cared for each other. We refused to become the thing we were fighting and *that's* why we triumphed."

This was rousing stuff. Blitz Spirit! Triumph through adversity! Battle of Britain! Never in the field, etc. I was sitting there thinking of all the bombs we dropped on German cities – what can I say, I'm a cynical sod sometimes – but I was more interested in the reaction of Bates and Mac to this diatribe. Mac's face gave nothing away, but Bates' eyes were finally focused, and he looked furious.

"But you, Bates, what are you offering these children in the face of all this horror? More death! You can't meet violence with violence; you can't fight plague, fear, panic and desperation with a gun! If you want to build an army you need to arm them with knowledge that can help them rebuild, that can help them to help others to rebuild. Then maybe you can hold back the tide. But what you're offering us here, with your uniforms, guns and marching is nothing but an opportunity to die for no reason when we should be looking for a way to live!

"And that's why I made this."

He turned and pulled the sheet off the sculpture to reveal a figure made of white plaster that shone in the reflected snowlight. It was a boy of about twelve, dressed in school uniform. Under one arm he carried a pile of books, and in the other hand he held a satchel with a vivid red cross on it. Beneath the figure was a plinth bearing the inscription 'Through wisdom and compassion, out of the darkness', and underneath that a list of the dead.

We all stared at this gleaming statue, amazed. It was beautiful and awful. I didn't think Hammond had it in him to produce something so good. And judging by the expressions on everyone's faces, nobody else did either.

"This school has been a home to me all my life," said Hammond. "It represents everything I believe in and cherish – kindness, duty, learning and respect. Turning it into an armed camp cheapens everything it stands for, and I will not allow that to stand."

Someone started to clap. It was Matron. She rose to her feet and applauded. Then the four other grown-ups followed suit, and then the Dinner Lady.

Bates was crimson with fury, staring at these insubordinate ingrates, but he was frozen by the moment, shocked into inaction by the open defiance of what he was trying to achieve.

And then one, then two, then ten, then most, then all of the boys began clapping as well. This could be it, I realised. This could be the moment when we pulled back from the brink, abandoned the army game and reclaimed a little bit of sanity and humanity; the moment we pulled the rug out from under the feet of Bates and Mac and took charge. Everything depended upon how our glorious leaders responded to this insurrection.

Bates rose to his feet and strutted towards Hammond, who stood his ground.

"Oh shit," I whispered. "Here we go."

"I should shoot you here and now for insubordination," he hissed. The applause died away as people noticed that Bates' hand was wrapped tightly around the handle of his still-holstered sidearm.

"Insubordination?" mocked Hammond. "I'm not subordinate to you. I don't take orders from anyone, let alone a deluded history teacher who thinks he's Field Marshal Montgomery."

I could have hugged him for that. It was all I could do not to cheer. Still Mac was unmoving, at attention, staring straight ahead. The officers, who had not clapped, also stood still, but I could see they were nervous, uncertain what to do. They looked to Mac for a lead, but he was giving them nothing, letting the scene before him play out uninterrupted. The situation, and the school's future, was balanced on a knife edge.

"These boys need a strong hand, they need to be protected." Bates was trying not to shout, but even so his words carried clearly in the sudden silence.

"Yes they do. From you, and that psychopath there!" He pointed at Mac, who didn't move a muscle. "Look at what you've achieved since you've been in charge, eh? Two boys hanged in Hildenborough, two more shot and wounded in a stupid act of military adventurism. Your second-in-command has murdered four people that I know of in the last two weeks. And this school, which is supposed to be a haven of safety and learning, which could be offering sanctuary and succour to all the lost children wandering around out there in the chaos, has been turned into a bloody fortress. We should be sending out expeditions to retrieve children not armaments. Can't you see that?"

Bates had drawn his gun. It was hard to tell whether he'd done it consciously or not, but he stood there face to face with Hammond, his pistol held tight, shaking with barely contained fury and madness.

I saw Green take a step forward, as if to intervene, but Mac caught his eye and flashed him a look of warning. Green, cowed, stepped back into line.

"Mr Hammond, I am afraid that you are no longer welcome at this institution. You are ordered to leave."

Hammond laughed in Bates' face.

"You can't order me to leave. This is my home far more than it's ever been yours. I was here when your father was in nappies, young man. This is my school, not yours, and you'll have to kill me to get rid of me."

"No, I won't," said Bates.

Bates turned to Mac.

"Major, you and your men escort Mr Hammond from the premises immediately," he said.

"Yes sir!" barked Mac, and nodded to his officers, who raised their rifles and walked forward.

At this point Matron stepped forward to intervene, but Mac blocked her way and hissed into her face "Sit down, bitch, or else". She sat down, ashen-faced.

Seeing Mac advancing towards him, Hammond straightened his back and stuck out his chest. He wasn't going to be intimidated.

"You can't hand me over to this man, Bates," he cried. "We both know I'll be dead within the hour. And these boys won't let it happen, will you boys?"

Oh, what a misjudgement that was. Because the boys didn't make a sound. They were too afraid of the raised guns of the officers, too cowed by the horrors that had overtaken their lives in the last year, too conditioned to fear Mac. They'd enjoyed a mad moment of rebellion but once they'd stopped applauding their own terror had crept in to fill the silence.

Norton looked over at me desperately, seeking guidance. If I gave the nod he'd speak up.

Should I have given the signal? I still wonder about that. If I had, if Norton had stepped forward and rallied the boys, maybe things would have been different. Maybe all the blood and death could have been prevented. But I was unsure. It seemed too risky. I shook my head, and Norton clenched his jaw and remained silent. In that moment of uncertainty and cowardice he and I condemned us to all that followed.

Faced by Mac's slow, menacing approach, and the silent acquiescence of the boys, Hammond began to appreciate the gravity of his situation.

"You can't do this, Bates. For God's sake man, look at yourself, look at what you're doing!" There was a desperate, pleading note in his voice now.

"Mac's orders are to expel you," said Bates, "and that is what he'll do, isn't it Major?"

"Yes sir!"

Mac, approaching from behind Bates, bared his teeth at Hammond, and winked. Bates stepped forward, his pistol raised to cover Hammond and deter him from running. Hammond contemptuously batted the pistol aside. Bates brought it to bear again. Hammond batted it aside again. Bates raised the pistol to hit Hammond with it, but the old man grabbed Bates' arm to counter the blow.

You've seen the movies. You know what comes next. The two men grapple for possession of the weapon, they huddle in tight, almost embracing, as they strain and clutch and struggle for leverage. Then a shot – shocking, sudden, echoing off the buildings and trees, repeating again and again and fading away as the two men stand stock still, frozen, the horrified spectators waiting to see which one of them will topple.

Hammond backed away from Bates, his face full of confusion and fear. Then he fell sideways into the snow, and twitched and shook and died.

Bates stood there, the smoking gun in his hand. He stared at Hammond's body and seemed frozen, rooted to the spot.

Rowles broke ranks and ran towards the school, crying. Without a moment's hesitation Mac drew his sidearm and fired into the air.

"One more inch, Rowles, and I'll have you up on a charge of desertion!" he yelled.

Rowles turned back, his face streaked with tears and snot, utterly terrified. His lower lip trembled.

"Back in line, boy, now!"

Rowles shuffled back, wide-eyed, and rejoined the serried ranks of boys, all of whom mirrored his fear and uncertainty.

"You are on parade. You do not leave until you are dismissed. Understand?"

The boys stood in silence.

"I said," bellowed Mac, "do you understand?"

A half-hearted "yes sir".

"I bloody well hope so."

Mac turned to his officers. Patel and Wolf-Barry were restraining Matron, who had attempted to run to Hammond when he had been shot.

"Zayn, Pugh, take Hammond's body to the San." They did so.

Bates was still standing there.

Mac addressed the troops.

"The Colonel is right. There's no room here for charity, no food for freeloaders, no beds for fucking whingers. We stay tight, we stay hard, we stay alive. Hammond thought otherwise and look where it fucking got him."

"That's Mr Hammond to you, MacKillick," shouted Matron, straining against the boys who were holding her back. Mac turned and walked slowly towards her. He had still not holstered his gun. He leaned forward so there was only an inch at most between their faces.

"Now you listen to me and you listen well, bitch," he whispered. "I run this place now. My gaff, my rules. And if you don't like that you can piss off. But while you stay here you do exactly as I say or so help me God I will fucking gut you. I *own* you, bitch, and don't you fucking forget it."

He leered at her and then raised his free hand and ever so softly caressed her cheek.

And for the first time ever I genuinely wanted to kill someone.

Matron spat in his face. There was an audible intake of breath from the boys.

Mac smiled.

"Take her away boys," he said. "Find somewhere safe and lock the cow up. I'm sure we can find a use for her."

"Sir?" Pugh, having a moment of conscience.

"Yes Corporal?" The danger in Mac's voice was unmistakeable.

"Nothing sir."

"Good, then carry on."

The two boys marched Matron away towards the school.

Bates still hadn't moved.

Mac walked over to Hammond's statue and kicked it hard. It slowly toppled over and fell into the bloodstained snow. Another failed attempt at decency and compassion, white on red.

CHAPTER SIX

THE COURT MARTIAL of Mr Bates began the next morning.

Most of the officers were present, including myself, in my wheelchair, sitting at Mac's right hand. Only Green and Wylie were absent, running exercises with the boys. Mac, sporting a huge bruise on his left cheek which he made no reference to, took the chair. We were to be Bates' judges and jury.

Bates sat before us, hands bound. He was deep in shock and hadn't said a word since the shooting the previous day.

I don't think I've ever felt as powerless as I did in that room. Officially I was now one of the three most powerful people in the school, but this was a pantomime of Mac's devising and we all knew what was expected of us. Step out of line, challenge Mac in this context, and I had no doubt I'd share whatever fate he had in store for Bates. This was to be the culmination of Mac's ascent to power and we had to rubber stamp it, no matter what. Our lives depended upon it.

"Colonel Michael Bates, you are arraigned here today to answer the charge of murder."

Mac was even putting on a plummy voice, pretending to be a High Court judge. Actually, not 'putting on' at all; 'reverting to', more like.

Bates mumbled something inaudible in response.

"Speak up, Colonel," said Mac.

Bates looked up at Mac. The depth of despair in those eyes was like a physical blow.

"I said sorry," he muttered.

Mac snorted. "I'm afraid sorry just isn't going to do. You are accused of a criminal offence of the most heinous type and you must answer for it before the court."

"So sorry," he whispered again, and his head slumped forward as his shoulders began to heave. He began to sob.

Mac was unmoved.

"Do I take it to understand that you are throwing yourself upon the mercy of this court, Colonel?"

But the only sound that came from Bates was a deep, hoarse moan.

"In which case we shall retire to consider our verdict."

As Mac rose Bates looked up and began to speak.

"All I wanted," he sobbed, "was to help."

"Well I think that…"

"All I wanted," Bates interrupted, "was to look after them. To make them safe, to protect and care for them, that's all I ever wanted, even before. But it was always so hard. They never understood what I was doing, never understood that it was all for their own good. Never understood. Nobody ever understood."

He started to speak more loudly now, passionately pleading with us to understand his choices and failures.

"Do you know what it's like to try and help someone who doesn't want to be helped? Do you? To try and persuade them that you know best? It's impossible. But it was my job, my duty, I couldn't just give up, could I? I had to make them see. I had to keep them safe. 'Arm ourselves', I said. 'The school will be safe', I said. 'Sanctuary', I said. But they wouldn't believe me. Wouldn't do things my way. Had to challenge me, always had to challenge me. Undermine, countermand, mock and ignore. All I wanted, all I ever wanted, was to be a hero, their hero."

Mac started to giggle. A man was falling to pieces in front of him and the sick bastard actually thought it was funny.

"And now I never will be, will I?" Bates looked up at Mac again, suddenly clear-eyed and focused. "Because you're going to kill me, aren't you, Mac?"

Mac met his gaze, but said nothing.

"Yeah, of course you are," said Bates. "You've been building up to this from the moment you arrived. Just biding your time, waiting for me to make a mistake. Well, good for you. Good for you. Made it easy for you really, didn't I? Got it wrong every step of the way and you just let me get deeper and deeper into the shit until it was time to make your move. And now you've got your lackeys and your weapons and your army. But what are you going to do with it all? What's the point of all the power? Do you even have a point, or is it just for its own sake, just because you can? You don't care for these boys, you don't care for their wellbeing or safety. You just want to be in control of them. And now you are. My fault, again. My fault."

He took a deep breath and calmed the final sobs that had interspersed his little speech. He raised his bound hands and wiped his eyes and nose on his sleeve, sat upright and stared straight ahead, trying to find some final shreds of dignity.

"Before you pass sentence I want to make a final request." He turned his gaze to me. "I don't know why you're allying yourself with this bastard, Keegan, but I've been watching you and I think you're better than this." *Oh shit, thanks. Blow my cover, why don't you?* "I want you to do something for me, if you can."

"What's that then?" I tried to sound casual and unconcerned. Mustn't let Mac know how much I was hating this.

"I want you to find my sons and tell them what's happened."

"What?" I couldn't keep the surprise out of my voice. "They're alive?"

"Oh yes, they're alive. What, you thought I'd buried them? No, they were both O-neg. But they weren't mine. Carol and I adopted. Pure chance they had the same blood type. All I ever wanted... sorry. Anyway, find them. Apologise for me. They're with their mother at a farm just north of Leeds. Ranmore Farm, it's on the maps."

"So why did you come back here? What happened?" asked Mac, intrigued, in spite of himself.

"They left me." He gave a bitter laugh. "I was the luckiest man in the world, you see. Only child, so no brothers or sisters to lose. Both my parents already dead. My wife and kids all immune. My whole family, everyone I loved, survived The Cull. Luckiest man in the world. But then... they just left me. No reason left to pretend, she said. Not our real dad anyway, they said. And gone. All I ever wanted was to make them safe, be a hero to them, to my boys. But they hated me. All that love and now... just... nothing."

Suddenly Bates was transformed, suddenly he made sense. I felt desperately, achingly sorry for him.

"Wow," laughed Mac. "You're an even bigger loser than I thought!"

"Yes," said Bates, thoroughly broken. "I suppose I am."

"Well, the sentence is death, obviously. But I need a bit of time to consider how, so we'll just bung you back in a locked room for a bit while I work it out, yeah?"

*　　*　　*

WHILE BATES LANGUISHED under lock and key and Mac worked out
which form of painful death most took his fancy, the day proceeded
as normal. Norton wheeled me back to the San where I was still
sleeping, despite Matron's incarceration.

"She's in one of the rooms upstairs," Norton said. He'd been
snooping around for me, trying to find out where she was being
kept. "Mac's old room, actually. The door's not locked as far as I
can tell, but he's got Wolf-Barry on guard outside."

"Has she... has anything..." I couldn't quite bring myself to put
my fears into words.

"I only found out where she was this morning, and as far as I
know no-one's been in to see her since. But I don't know about last
night, Lee."

I didn't want to think about what Mac might have done to her. I
recalled the mysterious bruise on Mac's cheek.

Norton handed me the two Brownings that he'd hidden for me
and I pocketed them both.

"Right, we need to get Wolf-Barry away from that door. I need
to get in there."

"I might have an idea how we can do that," said Norton. "You
might even call it a plot. But how are you going to manage? You
can barely walk."

I lifted my good leg off the wheelchair rest and placed it on the
floor, levering myself upright. I gingerly put my bad leg down and
allowed it to take the tiniest fraction of my weight. Not so bad. A
bit more. Bearable. I tried a step and it was like someone had shoved
a hot metal bar straight through my calf. I grunted in pain and
clenched my jaw. But I could do it. I had to.

Norton looked at me doubtfully.

"Piece of cake," I lied.

WITH THE ARRIVAL of winter the school had become bitterly cold,
and fires were kept burning in most grates throughout the day.
Norton snuck into the dorm along the corridor from where
Matron was being kept and nudged one of the logs out of the
grate and onto the floor where it began to smoulder on the old
waxed floorboard. The dorm door was open so we were counting
on Wolf-Barry smelling the fire and raising the alarm before it

really took hold. Last thing we wanted was to burn the school down.

Norton wafted the fumes towards the door then nipped out the dorm's back door and down the fire escape. It didn't take long for Wolf-Barry to cotton on, and he ran off shouting. I had managed to hop my way up the back stairs and as soon as he was out of sight I pushed open the stairwell door and hopped to Matron's room. I tried to ignore the blood that was beginning to trickle down my wounded leg, and the spots that were appearing at the edge of my vision.

I pushed the door – not locked, thank Christ – and lurched into the room. It was only my unsteady footing that saved me from receiving a floorboard to the face.

"Hey, hey, it's me, Lee," I whispered urgently.

Matron was stood just inside the door holding her improvised weapon. Her face was one big bruise. One eye was swollen shut, her lips were blue and bulbous. There was blood underneath her nose, which bulged where I think it had been broken. Her clothes were torn, too. She was breathing hard and her teeth were bared and bloody.

"What kept you, Lee? Come to take your turn?"

No time to dwell on what that implies. Focus. Concentrate. Things to do.

"Matron, we need to get you out of here now."

"And why should I trust you? They told me, you're his loyal second-in-command now!" She was fighting back tears, her words coming out in a furious mix of anger and pain.

There was no time to explain myself. The corridor would be swarming in seconds. I pulled one of the handguns from my pocket and held it out to her.

"Take it."

She looked down at it, confused.

"Take it!"

She dropped the floorboard, grabbed the gun and then looked up at me. I couldn't read the expression on her wrecked face.

"Now come on!" I grabbed her hand and turned, gently pushing the door open as I did so. But we'd lingered too long. There was already a crowd of boys arguing over which colour of fire extinguisher they should use. Norton was nearest the door, bathed in a dim orange light, trying to take control but also keeping an eye out for our escape. Not only was he providing a distraction for us, he wanted to be closest to the danger, didn't want anyone else getting burnt because of his actions. My admiration for him grew hugely.

I pulled Matron behind me and dashed for the stairwell. We feel through the door and it closed behind us. We'd made it unseen.

It was only when I stopped inside the door that I realised I had run along the landing. Adrenaline is a great painkiller, but I knew I'd pay for that later. I could hear footsteps coming up the stairs below us; someone taking the back route to the fire. Matron and I flew down the flight of stairs and flung ourselves through the door of the next floor down, just in time to avoid being seen.

My leg buckled underneath me, and Matron helped me along the corridor to the San, which was almost directly beneath the burning dormitory. Smoke was beginning to seep through the ceiling from above.

"We don't have much time," I said. "Someone will be coming to get me to safety soon. They can't find you here and they mustn't suspect that I can walk yet. Help me into bed." Matron did so, and her hands came away from my leg covered in blood. She gasped.

"Lee, you must let me see to this, you could be crippled."

"No time. Now take the gun and go. Run. Find somewhere and hole up. This school isn't safe for you any more and I can't deal with Mac if he has you hostage. So go, please."

She hefted the Browning. Then she popped out the clip, checked it was loaded, slammed it home, cocked the gun, chambered a round and slipped off the safety catch. She knew exactly what she was doing. How the hell was a boarding school matron so familiar with a firearm?

"I'm not going anywhere." She was breathing hard and even through the bruises there was no mistaking the look of fury and determination on her face.

"And what are you going to do?" I demanded. "Shoot them all? You don't stand a chance. There are seven of them, not to mention Mac, and after what they've done do you think they'll hesitate to shoot you? This school needs you – I need you – to be safe, so that when we finally get rid of that fucker you're there to help us pick up the pieces."

Her eyes burned with hatred, but I could see she was beginning to hesitate. I pressed my advantage.

"If you go after him now you'll be dead within the hour. Or worse – locked up again. Please, just run."

She hesitated, her hand upon my arm. If I'd been in her shoes I don't know if I'd have been able to beat down the desire for vengeance, but somehow I got through to her. I looked up at her ruined face and saw tears of frustration welling out of her swollen eyes.

I had so much I wanted to say to her but this was not the time.

"Please, Jane, just run. Be safe."

She leaned down and kissed me gently on the lips.

"You too," she said, and ran out the door.

I thought she'd make straight for freedom, but once again I'd underestimated her determination. In fact she took refuge in a deserted classroom until the early hours of the morning and then crept out to implement her plan.

The boys were sleeping in five dorms of about ten each, and each dorm had one officer sleeping there as well, as a deterrent against night-time escape attempts. But the four girls who had taken shelter at the school slept in their own dorm, along with the old aunt and one grandmother. They were unguarded and in a different part of Castle to the boys.

Under cover of darkness Matron snuck in, woke them, got their bags packed and provided armed escort as they slipped silently out of the school and into the night. Although prepared to forgo her revenge, she nonetheless ensured that no other girl or woman would have to endure what she had.

When I found out about Matron's night raid I couldn't help but smile. She was certainly audacious. I didn't want to think about where she and the girls were going or how they'd fare. All I knew was that they were safer elsewhere, and were one less factor I had to consider when it came to planning Mac's downfall.

However, I needed Matron's medical skills more than ever; my leg was wrecked. The stitches had split, the wound was oozing blood and the pain was unspeakable. I started to worry about things like gangrene and amputation. I did the best I could to sort myself out with antiseptic, fresh stitches and dressings.

Have you ever stitched your own wound? I don't recommend it. Once I was finished I lay back and hoped for the best. With any luck I'd be able to stay off it for a while now, and would be able to let it heal.

THE BIG QUESTION now was what would happen to Bates. We got our answer the next morning, and it was worse than anything I could have imagined.

Behind the main school building were two sports pitches and a cricket square, all ringed by woods. The school had favoured rugby over football, and there were huge H-shaped rugby posts at either end of each pitch. Mac had a detail of boys cut down one of the rugby goals, dismantle it and reassemble it in the shape of a cross, which lay flat, ready to be re-erected using one of the vacated postholes.

He was going to crucify Bates.

"We can't let this happen," said Norton, urgently, when the truth became apparent. We were sitting in the San staring out of the window at the ghastly construction and all it represented. "If we let him do this then... I don't know what. But it ain't good."

"And how do you suggest we stop him?" I replied. "He has a cadre of permanently armed boys who are fiercely loyal. At first through stupidity and now, after what they did to Matron, they're as guilty as he is and they know it. He owns them and I don't think they'll hesitate to shoot any one of us dead if Mac orders it. Not now."

Norton nodded. "I've asked around, as discreetly as I can, but no-one saw anything that night. I can't find out which boys went into that room."

Alone in the San, my mind focused by the pain, I'd had plenty of time to dwell on what had happened to Matron. "Come to take your turn?" she'd asked. At first the implication of that question made me sick with horror, but then, as the long night wore on that disgust turned into a deep burning pit of anger, a fury I didn't know I had it in me to feel. It changed me. It made things simple.

"Then we assume they all did," I said. "Every one of those bastards is responsible for what happened to Matron, and every single one of them will pay for it. They crossed a line when they went into that room. He initiated them."

I was actually grateful for being bedridden, and that gratitude made me guilty. Had I been expected to participate I would have either gotten myself killed trying to prevent it, or been forced to take part at the point of a gun. I knew this, but still I felt that I should have been there to protect her, that I could have done something, anything.

"They're like him now," I went on. "He's made them that way, and we mustn't underestimate any one of them. They're loyal and stupid and, we now know, capable of pretty much anything. We have to be so careful. Play the long game."

"Bates won't be around that long."

"No," I admitted, matter of fact. "He probably won't be."

Norton looked at me askance.

"So we do nothing? We just let them do this?"

I looked at the cross and considered my options.

"No. No, we don't. But I can only see one course of action that doesn't get us crucified too. I don't like it, and neither will you."

All the blood drained from Norton's face as I told him what I wanted him to do.

"COMING TO JOIN the party?" asked Mac, as he pushed the wheelchair to my bedside. "I promise you, son, it's gonna be massive!"

"Wouldn't miss it for the world, sir." I smiled my most feral smile and for the first time it didn't feel forced or fake. I felt like a hunter, felt that ruthlessness, that focus, that calm.

"Attaboy, Lee." He playfully punched me on the arm and then helped me into the chair. I didn't bother disguising my discomfort and pain; if my plan didn't work and I had to resort to plan B, I would need Mac to know just how bad my leg really was.

"Still bad, eh?"

"Yeah. Little bit. Wish Matron was here, I don't want it going gangrenous."

"That bitch is long gone, but we'll find her. Just for you Lee, we'll find her."

He pushed me out the door and down the corridor to the stairs, where Patel was waiting to help carry me down.

"Actually, Lee, you missed some fun the other night, y'know."

Staying calm in the face of moments like this was becoming easier; the anger gave me more control.

"Really? What was that then?"

We reached the top of the stairs and Patel took the front wheels.

"What do you say, Patel? The other night. Quality times, yeah?"

Patel looked momentarily uncomfortable, but it might just have been the weight of the chair.

"Yes sir. Top quality," he replied.

"We taught that bitch a lesson all right. Let her know who's in charge around here. You should've been there, Lee. I reckon you always fancied her, am I right? Shame you missed your chance to take a pop, yeah?"

I fantasised about taking a knife, driving it deep into his beating heart and smiling into his dying eyes.

"Now that," I said enthusiastically, "would have been worth getting gangrene for!"

Mac and Patel laughed. All three of us, partners in crime.

We reached the bottom of the stairs and I was wheeled out through the courtyard to the back field.

"The girls legged it during the night, by the way. Don't worry, we'll find 'em. And we've got night patrols now, and sentry boxes. No-one else is getting out of here. Isn't that right, fat lady?" This last to the Dinner Lady, who stood to one side, arms folded, trying defiance on for size, but unable to disguise her uncertainty and fear. She slept alone, above the kitchen, directly opposite the windows of the boys' dorms. Matron must have considered it too risky to wake her.

"She tried to leg it this morning," said Mac, "but she's too big to be proper stealthy. Anyway, what'd we eat if she vanished? You're precious to me, Mrs Dinner Lady, you are. Got to keep you close to home."

He leaned down and whispered to me. "Plus, you know, with Matron gone, we gotta have options for entertainment, yeah."

Norton was stood on the edge of the ranks closest to me. He glanced at me as I was wheeled past and nodded almost imperceptibly. I sighed with relief. Mission accomplished.

Mac parked me and took his place in front of the troops, the cross looming above him.

"It gives me no pleasure, what I'm about to do," he said.

Oh fuck off, I thought.

"But a strong leader must be ruthless in the pursuit of justice and safety. Anyone who harms one of mine will suffer the consequences, and they must know that I will be unswerving in their pursuit. There is no room here for mercy or forgiveness. The only sacred thing here is justice. If you kill one of the people under my protection you kill a part of me. And so help me God, you will do penance for your sins."

This was a new line, this holy righteousness bollocks. I hoped he wasn't going to get a messiah complex. On cue, Mac took out a Bible and began to read aloud as Zayn and Green emerged from the building escorting Bates.

"The path of the righteous man is beset on all sides by the iniquities of the selfish and the tyranny of evil men," read Mac, channelling Samuel L. Jackson. "Blessed is he, who in the name of charity and goodwill, shepherds the weak through the valley of darkness, for he is truly his brother's keeper and the finder of lost children. And I will strike down upon thee with great vengeance and furious anger those who would attempt to poison and destroy my brothers. And you will know my name is the Lord when I lay my vengeance upon thee."

Mac was really hamming it up. This was taking a turn for the weird. Whatever, I had to compliment him on his choice of reading; it was at least appropriate.

The boys led Bates up to the cross and he didn't struggle at all. Even when he saw the construction upon which he was to be mounted, he didn't show the least surprise or concern. I didn't think there was much left of Bates to kill.

Mac walked over to him and forced him down onto his knees, and then his back. He tied his wrists and feet to the improvised crucifix in silence. Then he got the hammer and nails. He looked disappointed when Bates didn't cry out in pain as they pierced his flesh.

He stood back and seized one of the ropes that were attached to the cross. Zayn and Pugh took the others, and together they heaved the construction upright. It was difficult. The heavy structure swayed and warped as they manhandled the post into the hole. They stood back and looked up at their handiwork.

It's a potent image, a man on a cross, possibly the most iconic there is. It's full of associations and meanings, mythic resonances of sacrifice and martyrdom. I looked up at Bates, whose head lolled drunkenly onto his shoulders, glassy eyed. Here was no sacrifice. He was no martyr. He was just a weak man who'd tried to be strong and had failed. No great tragedy, just another failed hero.

Mac seemed unsatisfied by the spectacle. I think he'd expected some wailing and moaning, begging and pleading. He'd been looking forward to this moment and now it had arrived his subject wasn't delivering the goods. Where was the catharsis? Where was the triumph? How could he gloat over a man so rag-doll limp that he was barely even present at his own execution?

I felt a tiny glow of satisfaction. The sedative that I'd taken from the San was doing its work. Norton had ensured that he was chosen to take the condemned man his final meal. He'd relayed my promise to find Bates' family and inform them of his death, before offering him a syringe. Bates had obviously accepted the escape route we'd offered him, and had injected himself. If I'd judged the dosage right he would lapse into a coma and die within a couple of hours and no-one would be any the wiser. Mac would think the crucifixion had been quicker than expected, probably assuming heart failure and shock, while Bates surfed out of this life on a warm wave of drug-induced bliss.

It was the only mercy we could offer him.

The boys were dismissed and they marched away in silence.

Mac took one last look at Bates and then walked over to me and began to wheel me towards Castle, leaving his one-time mentor to what he believed would be a slow and agonising death.

I took some satisfaction in knowing that I'd cheated Mac of that, at least. It was not much of a victory, but it was something, some small scintilla of compassion.

Now that I was his second-in-command I needed to find a way of talking to Mac, of being his mate. It was difficult to know which tack to take but I decided to brazen it out and be chummy and sarcastic and hope he went with it and didn't take offence. I gulped and took the plunge.

"You," I said witheringly, "have seen *Pulp Fiction* way too many times."

He chuckled and replied "I got pre-mediaeval on his ass."

And then Bates began to scream.

"At last," said Mac, with satisfaction. But he kept wheeling me onwards and he never looked back.

THE SCREAM OF a dying man is a terrible thing to hear. It cuts right through you, strips you of all your illusions of immortality, removes any comfort you take in your own existence and reminds you, in the starkest way possible, that we all survive the day at the merest whim of fate and happenstance. It's humbling and horrifying and once you've heard it you never forget it. But at least it's normally over quite quickly.

I lay in the San listening to Bates scream for about an hour before I decided that I could stand it no longer. Either I'd got the dosage wrong and he had come around, or he was suffering the worst trip imaginable. Whatever. I'd either not helped or, perhaps, had made things worse. I wasn't prepared to live with that. Time for Plan B.

I levered myself off the bed and hopped across to the medicine cabinet. My leg was so bad now that even hopping was almost unbearable. But what did my pain compare with that of the man outside screaming into the face of inevitable death? I opened the cabinet and sorted through the little bottles until I found the right one. I grabbed a syringe, filled it, and jammed it straight into my wound. For a moment there were two men screaming, but then the sweet morphine did its work and my leg felt warm and clumsy and twice its normal size. But at least it bore my weight. I had no idea how long it would take for the drug to affect my senses, but I knew I had to be fast. I limped to the door and checked the corridor. Empty. Thank heaven for small blessings. My rifle stood against the wall in one of the corners, untouched since I'd put it there when I was brought into the San wounded, what seemed like a lifetime ago.

I picked it up and limped to the back stairwell. Again, no-one around. I hit the stairs and climbed. I was starting to get dizzy. I held tight to the railing as I made my way up to the locked door that gave out onto the roof. Two hard blows from my rifle butt took care of the lock, and I was out, underneath the low grey clouds.

I made my way to the edge of the roof, which felt springy underneath me, like I was walking on a duvet. The sky above me began to spin and I felt a hot flush rise up my body and face, like a cartoon character who's just eaten a hot chilli. I walked right to the edge and looked down, swayed unsteadily and leapt back. Carefully.

I lay down, assumed firing position and sighted my rifle on the chest of the man so far below me, who screamed and screamed and screamed.

I tried to focus on my task but the roof felt as if it was swallowing me up, engulfing me like quicksand. My head felt tight, my vision swam, my hands shook.

I grasped the rifle tight and closed my eyes. I steadied my breathing and opened them again. The madness scampered around the periphery of my vision, but I found that I had, for a moment at least, clarity.

Maybe it was the recklessness of drugged-up mania, or perhaps I was simply so far gone that I had ceased to worry about the consequences of my actions; whichever it was, I didn't hesitate for an instant. In a heartbeat I did the one thing I had been trying so hard to avoid these long months since The Cull had made each man, woman and child the sole guardian of their own morality; the one thing I had feared the most because of what it would say about where my choices had brought me and what I was truly capable of.

I squeezed the trigger and ended a man's life.

Finally, I was a killer.

LESSON TWO
HOW TO BE A TRAITOR

CHAPTER SEVEN

BEFORE THE CULL, back when St Mark's was just another boys' school and I was just a fourth-former trying to pass my exams, I got on the wrong side of Mac once.

It was Friday lunchtime and I had cycled into town to buy myself a bag of chips and pick up a magazine. Popping out at lunchtime wasn't forbidden but it was tight, time-wise, and if you dawdled you ran the risk of missing the start of afternoon lessons.

That day I bumped into a girl from the high school who I had met at one of the formal social events that the two schools collaborated on every now and then. I was awkward around girls. I had been in single-sex education since I was barely able to walk, and I didn't have sisters. It wasn't that I didn't know what to talk to girls about; I didn't know how to talk to them at all.

So while I was browsing the shelves in the newsagents this girl came up, said "hi" and we chatted for a few minutes. Her name was Michelle and I liked her. I can't really remember what I said; it's a bit of a blur. I was just concentrating on not spitting, swearing or belching. But it seemed to go off okay and she smiled as she said goodbye. She was pretty, I was blushing beetroot red, and I dawdled and daydreamed all the way back to school where I cycled straight into Mac, lying in wait at the school gates for waifs and strays.

"What the fuck time do you call this?" he asked.

"Sorry, I just, um…" Nope, no way out, caught bang to rights.

He grabbed the magazine.

"Hey, hey, what's this? *SEX*?"

"Um, no, it's *SFX*. It just looks like that 'cause the picture's covering the bottom of the F."

"So you say. But all I can see is a magazine with a woman in a bikini on the cover and SEX written across the top of it."

"It's Princess Leia."

He rolled up the magazine and whacked me round the head with it as hard as he could.

"I don't care if it's Princess bloody Diana, it's confiscated."

There was no point protesting.

"So you a geek then, eh? Little spoddy sci-fi fan? Wank off over pictures of Daleks do you?"

So many cutting responses came to mind but I wasn't stupid enough to deliver any of them. I just stood there, head down, silent.

His punishment was typically creative. I had to stand in a corridor and hold the magazine against the wall with my nose. Simple enough, you might think. But he made me keep my feet a metre away from the wall, with my hands behind my back. I was leaning forward at an angle of about 45 degrees, and all my weight was pushed down onto my nose. Within a minute the pain was excruciating. He made me stand like that for half an hour. I never crossed him again, and he soon forgot who I was.

I was still in junior school when I learnt the secret to dealing with bullies: hit them as hard as you possibly can and make their noses bleed. Always worked for me. But when the bullies were officially sanctioned, when they were prefects (or teachers, come to think of it), then the more you protested, challenged them, fought back, or answered their rhetorical questions, the worse things got. They had authority on their side and any argument, reason or excuse you offered could just be ignored.

So I learned to swallow my pride, to bite back the retorts, to clench my fists but not let them fly. Keep your head down, don't draw attention to yourself, fly under the radar. Secret to a quiet life; secret to survival.

That instinct was deep ingrained in me by the time The Cull came around. I suppose that's why I didn't challenge Mac at the start, why I motioned to Norton to keep quiet when Hammond needed our help, why I decided to try and bring Mac down by infiltration and subterfuge. A lifetime of learning how to survive institutional bullying had taught me how to be sneaky, but I no longer understood the rules of open confrontation.

Mac still had the authority, although now it came from the muzzle of a gun and a cadre of lackeys rather than a fancy blue blazer braid, and I was still locked into the role of submissive victim, seething with resentment but staying silent, fighting the injustice indirectly, with plots and schemes.

But I still remembered the satisfaction of bloodying a bully's nose, and longed to feel Mac's cartilage crack beneath my fists.

MY MOUTH FELT dry and sandy, my eyes were gummed shut, and my leg was just a distant ache. I could hear someone moving around in the room, but I couldn't speak or move for a minute or so. Eventually I was able to manage a croak, and I heard a squeal and what sounded like a glass hitting the floor. I'd made somebody jump.

Then the sound of someone filling a glass of water from a jug, and a hand behind my head lifting it and putting the glass to my lips. I gulped down the liquid gratefully.

"Thanks," I rasped.

"You're welcome." The Dinner Lady.

"What's... where..."

"Don't try and speak, just rest your head a minute."

I heard her dabbing something in water and then a cool flannel wiped my eyes clear of sleep and I cracked them open, wincing at the bright sunlight streaming through the windows. I was still in the San.

"How long?"

"You've been unconscious for a week. We weren't sure you were going to survive, to be honest. Your leg was pretty bad. But your fever broke last night, and the infection seems to have burnt itself out. You are a very, very lucky boy."

I squinted up at her. My head felt like it was full of rocks.

The San door opened and Green poked his head inside.

"He awake?" he asked.

"Just about."

"Great, I'll go get Mac." He closed the door and I heard him walk off down the corridor.

The Dinner Lady leaned in closer, conspiratorially.

"Now listen, before he gets here, I've got a message for you from Matron."

She saw my agitation and shushed me.

"I stayed behind deliberately that night. What, you thought she'd left me behind? Someone needs to be here to keep an eye on you boys and I thought it might as well be me. But we've got a little system and we leave notes for each other. I'm not telling you where; she trusts you but I'm not so sure. Anyway, she's been telling me what drugs to give you, so it's thanks to her that you're still breathing. She wants you to know that she and the girls are all right. They're not too far away but the place they're hiding has already been searched by one of Mac's hunting parties, and they didn't find them. They're unlikely to search it again so we think they're safe for now."

I breathed a sigh of relief, which probably sounded more like the gasp of a dying man, because she offered me more water. I drank thirstily.

"Mac? Bates?"

She hesitated and looked at me with deep suspicion.

"Mr Bates is dead and buried, God rest his soul. Mac's spent most of the time searching the area for the girls, and training the boys in drill. He's had an assault course built down by the river and he makes them do it every day for an hour. You should see the way he treats them. Scandalous. Says he's preparing them for war. Mad fool will get us all killed, mark my words.

"He's been very interested in you, though. Thinks highly of you, he does. Wants you fighting fit. Says he doesn't want to start a fight without you there. So you just take your time getting better. The longer you laze around here feeling sorry for yourself the better off we are."

She fell silent as we heard Mac and Green arriving outside.

"All right, thank you Limpdick, stay on guard, there's a good boy," said Mac, as he entered. He dismissed Mrs Atkins with a glance. She made her exit and Mac took her vacated seat.

"Hi," I said weakly.

"Hi yourself." He sniffed and considered my leg. "How's it feel?"

"Throbbing."

He nodded.

"Well, I'm told you're a lucky laddie and you're gonna be fine. You rest up 'til you're fit, but don't take too long coz I'm gonna need you."

"Why, what's been going on?" I was barely conscious, disorientated, croaking like a frog, and I was being bombarded with information my brain wasn't quite ready to process. But I needed to know how things stood.

"We've got a traitor. Some fucker shot Batesy. Put him out of his misery and spoiled all our fun. I would've had you down for it, but you was semi-conscious and raving here in the San when I came to see where you were. So don't worry, we know it wasn't you. But we dunno who it was and that makes me... jumpy. Either one of my officers is going behind my back, or some junior's got a gun hidden away that we don't know about. I don't like either of those possibilities.

"Anyway, the fat lady'll get you some nosh and we can start sorting you out. I'll fill you in on my plans when you're more with it."

I was grateful; I was having trouble keeping my eyes open.

"You rest up, mate," said Mac. But I was already half asleep.

DURING MY CONVALESCENCE I had plenty of time to assess the situation.

The school was now a fortified camp. There were patrols of the perimeter twenty-four hours a day, and permanent manned guard posts at the main gate and the school's front door. As a rule there was one officer in each patrol or guard detail, to keep the boys in line.

The day began with parade and inspection at 8am, followed by breakfast, then drill and exercises all morning. The afternoons were taken up with sports and scavenging hunts. Mac had kept the evening movies going for as long as there was fuel, but it was all gone now, so we had to live without electricity. The only technological toys we had left were battery-powered stereos and torches; we'd scavenged enough batteries to keep us going for a while, so we could at least listen to music. When Mac wasn't running a night exercise the evenings were free time. Boys played board games; Green organised a theatre group and started rehearsing a production of *Our Town*; a third-former called Lill started up a band.

Heathcote and Williams had expanded their farm and we now had a few fields of livestock. Petts' market garden was coming along well. Everywhere there was business, activity and purpose.

But there was no disguising the tension that hung in the air at all times. The officers, united by their shared crime, had become a coherent unit, a tight, loyal gang who held absolute power and weren't afraid to use it. We were lucky that only one of them, Wylie, was an outright bastard. The others bossed and bullied and threw their weight around but things never threatened to get as violent as I had feared they would. Mac seemed to be restraining himself a bit, and I didn't know why. I had expected that by now he'd be using thumbscrews on a daily basis, but he mostly just shouted and threw the occasional punch. His punishment of choice was getting miscreants to run laps of the pitches before breakfast.

I think maybe he'd shocked even himself with how he'd behaved towards Bates.

He had stopped searching for Matron and the girls. With all the fuel gone our minibuses were now useless and so our search area was limited to a few miles in every direction. Horses were collected when and wherever they could be found, and Haycox was running riding classes for the officers. I could already ride but it was not until very late in my healing that I could bear the pain of being bounced up and down on top of a galloping quadraped.

All Mac's efforts seemed to be going into securing our position and training the boys. But training them for what? I asked him and all the cryptic bastard would say was "You'll see". I was supposed to be his second-in-command but he wasn't taking me into his confidence.

And as he made his plans and preparations, so I made mine.

Norton's attitude towards me changed after I shot Bates. Although he was still jokey and conspiratorial I could sense a wariness about him. He didn't quite know what to make of me any more. I think my actions had surprised him almost as much as they'd surprised me. I didn't blame him. I was wary of myself.

My father used to wake screaming at night sometimes. I know something awful happened to him during a tour of duty in Bosnia, but he would never tell me what it was. Now I too was waking up sweating and shouting. In my nightmares Bates would scream into my face from his crucifix and Mac would stand by, applauding, as I carved our old teacher into tiny pieces, all of which grew mouths and joined the chorus of agony.

I had never had nightmares before. All the horror and death I had witnessed during The Cull, all the violence that had been done to me physically and psychologically, had never caused me a single night's sleeplessness. But the violence I had visited upon others was tormenting me. I had always believed that something awful had been done to my father; now I knew it was something awful that he had done to someone else. I realised that I hardly knew my father at all, or what he was capable of.

I was starting to realise what I was capable of, though. And it terrified me.

Nonetheless I remained focused on my objectives – gain Mac's trust, find an opportunity to betray him, find Matron and the girls, make the school the sanctuary it should always have been. I was willing to do almost anything to achieve my goals, but I couldn't do it alone.

* * *

"YOU'VE GOT A gun, so why don't you just shoot the bastard?" asked Norton one day as he was wheeling me around the pitches for my morning constitutional.

"What, you mean just walk up and shoot him dead in cold blood?"

"Well, duh. Yeah, that's exactly what I mean. Why not? Seriously, why not?"

"Not exactly ethical, is it?"

He burst out laughing.

"Ethical? Are you fucking joking? This from the man who shot our history teacher, the man who's accepted a position as second-in-command to a psychopath, the man who, in any court of law, would be held an accessory in the murder of those TA men? Ethical? Don't make me laugh. Is it any more ethical to plot his downfall from your hospital bed? At least if you went up and shot him you'd be being honest and direct. There's some ethics there."

"I'm not a cold-blooded murderer," was the only answer I could give him.

"Sorry, mate, but you are."

We moved past the assault course. It was a collection of netting, rope and wood constructions, and a little bit of barbed wire. There was climbing, crawling, jumping, swinging and all that sort of stuff. A group of the youngest juniors were racing through it under the supervision of Wylie, who was hounding poor Rowles, throwing clods of earth at him, firing his gun off close to the boy's head to simulate being under fire, screaming at him all the time. The poor boy looked utterly terrified.

"If I shot Mac there's no telling what the other officers would do," I said. "They certainly wouldn't take orders from me. I'm just a fifth-former, remember. I may be second-in-command but I've not given a single order yet and when I do it'll only be because of Mac that they obey it. I need to get to know them, earn their respect and trust before I make a move. Divide and conquer, that's what we have to do here. I'm just trying to get through this with the fewest possible deaths."

He didn't pursue the argument, but I could feel that he and I were on tricky ground. We were still friends and allies, but I'd need to be careful not to alienate him any further. Mac tolerated my friendship with Norton, and I needed him to be my eyes and ears amongst the regular boys.

He wheeled me back to Castle in silence, but despite his reservations the next day we sat down to compare notes.

"Wylie is our biggest problem," Norton explained. "It's like he's trying to out-Mac Mac. The others are mostly content with handing out laps, the occasional slap or chores. But Wylie likes to humiliate people. He made Thackaray do ten rounds of the assault course naked the other day. The kid was a mess of cuts and bruises by the end. And he's got Vaughan sleeping in the cow shed just 'cause he didn't finish his breakfast."

"Okay, so if Mac goes then Wylie is most likely to try and take his place, you think?"

"For sure. The rest of them are much of a muchness except Green, who sits at the other end of the spectrum. He's the whipping boy, the runt of the litter. They've started giving him nicknames."

"Like?"

"Gayboy. Bender. You know the kind of thing. Limpdick is a popular one."

He looked at me significantly until the penny dropped.

"Oh man," I whispered. "You think that…"

He nodded. "Couldn't get it up is my guess."

"And that makes him vulnerable. They'll resent the fact that he's not as guilty as they are and they'll hate him for it. Plus, you know, he is kind of a poof."

"You should see him directing *Our Town*. I think he wants to play Emily himself. He's got Petts doing it. Says if boys dressed as girls were good enough for Shakespeare, then it's good enough for us."

I considered this intelligence.

"Right then, we attack on two fronts," I said. "I try and get Mac to see Wylie as a threat, and foster Green's resentment of the others until he's ready to turn."

"And while you're doing that what do I do?"

"You need to sound out the others, but do it subtly. We need to identify those boys who are coming off worst and use that to get them on side. We need officers of our own who can be ready to move when an opportunity presents itself."

Norton grinned. "Finally we have a scheme."

"And a plot."

We shook hands.

"Marvellous," said Norton. "I think we just increased our chances of being crucified by about four hundred per cent."

AFTER THREE WEEKS of rest I finally took to my pins and started walking with a stick. I would always have a pronounced limp, but I began a programme of exercise designed to help build the leg back up to strength.

On the day I walked again Mac asked me to join him in his quarters. He had moved into the headmaster's old flat. As I knocked on the door and waited for him to let me in I noticed that he'd added a lot of locks to the door. Just like a leader – caution takes the place of ease and soon, inevitably, paranoia takes the place of caution. I hoped I'd be able to hurry that process along a little.

He opened the door and gestured me inside with a smile.

"Take a seat," he said. I looked around the living room where I'd fought Jonah and was relieved to see that Mac had replaced the furniture; I didn't fancy sitting on the stain of half-dissolved headmaster. I slumped into the plush upholstery gratefully. I couldn't remember when I'd last sat on a sofa; it felt like the height of luxury.

I was expecting to be offered a cup of tea or something, but instead he opened the drinks cabinet and poured a couple of large whiskies. He handed one to me and then sat opposite, regarding me thoughtfully.

"I don't think you like me very much, Lee," he said eventually.

Oh.

Fuck.

Play innocent? He'd never buy it.

Make a joke out of it? He'd see straight through that.

Okay. Play it straight. Be serious but not confrontational.

I met his gaze. "What makes you think that?"

He shrugged. "Instinct and observation."

He sipped his drink. I did the same. I felt like I was playing poker. I don't know how to play poker.

"I think Bates was right, you see," he continued. "I think you think you're better than this. I catch you, sometimes, looking at me and I think I can see you changing your expression, trying to hide the look of contempt before I notice it."

"Don't be daft." I laughed, all matey. He didn't smile.

"I'm many things, right? But I'm not daft." There was an edge of warning in his voice, but he didn't seem like he was about to get angry. Not unless I said something really stupid. I held up my hands and mimed innocence.

Mac leaned forward. "Thing is, you're right not to like me. I'm a cunt. A total and utter bastard and I don't care who knows it. I'm a murderer and a rapist, and that's just for starters. I shoot first and ask questions later. I'll fucking slaughter anyone who gets between me and what I want, I don't care who they are. And I enjoy being in control of things. I like bossing people around, giving orders, laying down the law, playing the big man.

"But the thing is, Lee, it's the only thing I'm good at. I have a talent for it, see. Ask me to do maths or English, paint a picture or play the piano and I'm a fucking retard. But give me a situation that needs some muscle, a bit of ruthlessness, and I'm your man.

"And the one thing The Cull did, the one great, beautiful, brilliant thing that The Cull did, is it handed people like me the keys to the fucking world.

"There's no rozzer to haul me in for GBH, no magistrate to hand me an ASBO, no judge to send me to the Scrubs. There's only one law now, and it's not who's got the biggest gun – it's who's bastard enough to use it first. And I am.

"And so are you, I reckon."

All I could manage was "Eh?"

"Oh, don't embarrass yourself by playing innocent. You shot Batesy."

I tried to keep a stoney face, give nothing away. But there was no point.

"Yeah," he said, studying me, "I thought so."

This was not going well.

"Now you might think I'd be angry at you for that. And I was for a bit. But then I got to thinking. You probably did it coz you wanted to put him out of his misery, right?"

I didn't make a sound.

"Right?" There was that note of danger again.

I nodded, never breaking eye contact.

"Merciful. Heroic, even. But that doesn't change the fact that you killed him. Shot him dead in cold blood. However you dress it up, you're a killer now. Just like me. And I like me, so I like people like me, yeah?"

Again, I nodded.

"The others are just followers, thugs, pussies who feel hard when they're around a big man like me. But I reckon you've got a bit more spine than that. I reckon you've got a bit of backbone. You went behind my back, deliberately did something that undermined what I was trying to do. That took guts, especially with that leg of yours. I like guts. But I do not like people who fuck with me.

"So that leaves me with a choice to make."

We stared at each other.

"Let me guess," I said eventually. "Kill me or promote me."

He inclined his head in agreement, leaned back in his chair and took another sip of whisky. Then he reached out his right hand, placed the drink on the side table and lifted the Browning that had sat there throughout our conversation, a silent threat. He placed the gun in his lap but kept hold of it, his finger resting gently on the trigger.

"What do you think I should do, Lee?"

I said nothing.

He lifted the gun, put it back on the table, and lifted his drink again.

"See, you took a risk and made a difficult decision because you thought it was the right thing to do. If I can convince you that helping me is the right thing to do then I reckon you and I will be quite a team. But I have to convince you, not threaten you into it. If I threaten you then you'll just say what I want to hear and I won't know if I can really trust you.

"So let me give you my sales pitch. After all, I was supposed to be going into advertising. If you don't like it you can walk – sorry, limp – straight out the main gate. I won't stop you."

He leaned back in his chair, took another sip of whisky and settled down to give me the hard sell.

"When I first arrived back here Batesy took me into his office and he gave me a little lecture. All about history, it was, which was his thing. He said to me that if you look at the history of primitive civilisations, then the same patterns keep appearing again and again. Farms clump together into villages. Then these villages get to know other villages and gradually they clump together and you get tribes. But tribes ain't democracies. No-one votes for the leader. The person who's in charge is the hardest bastard around and that's that.

"Now, if you don't like your tribal leader then you can challenge him, and there'll be a fight, and the winner is leader. It's a simple system. Everyone understands the rules. And it works. It works fucking beautifully. That's why it was the same all over the world.

"Democracy is a luxury. You can only manage it if your society is fucking loaded, well off, organised, stable, got a good infrastructure. But until your society has got that stuff, tribalism is the best way to run things coz it gives the most people the best chance of survival. And that is the only thing that matters – survival. The leader is chosen on merit, on strength. People like strength. They understand it.

"Now Batesy reckoned, and I happen to agree with him, that The Cull has left us in situation where we have to go back to tribes. We haven't got electricity, running water, gas. Fuck, we haven't even got much agriculture to speak of. Small, strong groups is the only way for people to rebuild. And strong groups need strong leaders. And that's me.

"You see Batesy's problem is that he convinced me he was right. And of course once he did that I realised I had to replace him. I knew he wasn't hard enough to lead. A tribe led by him would never be strong enough to keep everyone alive.

"So I replaced him. I crucified the poor sod coz it was the most dramatic thing I could think of. I sent a strong message by doing that:

"I am the leader.

"I am strong and ruthless.

"Fuck with me and I'll kill you.

"And that, Batesy said, is how you establish yourself as the leader of a strong tribe. He knew that was the truth, he knew that kind of demonstration was necessary, but didn't have the stomach for it.

"I did, and I do.

"But it's because I do that I'm the right man to lead this tribe. A tribe led by me has a good chance of survival when it meets other tribes that might want to take us on. I'm these boys' best chance of staying alive. I'm convinced of that.

"Are you?"

Maybe I was.

Dear God, the mad bastard had a point.

It hadn't occurred to me for a second that he'd have anything so evolved as an ideology. I'd just assumed he was a power-mad psychopath. But here he was talking what sounded horribly like sense. Brutal, nasty and dangerous, but logical.

"No," I said. "Not entirely."

He leaned back and took another sip. He gestured with his head for me to continue. I took a deep breath and plunged in.

"Bates may have been right about the tribe thing. I dunno, I was never really into history myself. But it sounds plausible. And if he was right then, yeah, strong leaders are probably a necessary evil, for a while anyway.

"I didn't think much of Bates as a leader. He was bloody useless, frankly. He froze whenever anything difficult happened, and that was dangerous for everyone. He was a liability.

"I don't think crucifying the poor bastard was the answer. But all right, that's done now, and you're leader. Let's ignore what you did to get the job, the question is what are you going to do now you've got it?"

I paused; I needed to phrase this right.

"What I want to know is this," I said. "Do you intend to use the same level of cruelty to hold onto your position as you did to get it?"

"If I need to, yeah," he admitted. "But I don't think I will. I only need to get nasty if there's anyone who looks likely to challenge me. And I don't think there is. I can lay off a bit. Already have done."

"Yeah, I've noticed. I must admit I was expecting things to get really bad when you took control but that's not happened."

It was so weird talking openly to him like this. I was still half sure that this conversation was going to end with a gunshot, but he'd left me with no choice but honesty and I was committed now. Still, I didn't need to be completely honest.

"Look, Lee, I've got the job now," he said. "I'm going to toughen these boys up, and my officers are going to help with that. But I have to get the balance right, make sure I don't piss them off so much that I lose them. I've got their obedience, but I need their loyalty and their respect. And I know that's going to be difficult for me. Not my strong suit.

"With you at my side I reckon I've got a shot at winning them over. I watch you; you get on with the juniors and stuff. They just annoy me, and I fucking terrify them. Which is good, don't get me wrong, I want them scared of me. But only scared enough. I need a bit of niceness in the mix. Carrot and stick, yeah? And that's why I need you."

"I can see it now," I laughed. "Lee Keegan, the caring face of crucifixion. So what, you want me to be your conscience? To keep you in line?"

"If you wanna put it that way, yeah. Let me know if I'm going too far. Keep your ear to the ground with the boys. Keep me up to date with how they're feeling. Watch the officers and find out which ones might be a problem."

"Wylie," I said briskly.

"Really? I like him. He's cruel," he said with relish.

I gave Mac my best 'well, duh' expression.

"Yeah, okay," he said. "Well, that's my point, innit. You notice this stuff. We make a good team. Plus, I can rely on you in a fight. And that's important. Coz we've got a lot of fighting to do, I reckon."

"So I'm your second-in-command. I can give orders to the officers, and my job is to back you up and let you know when I think you're going too far. And I'm doing this because a strong ruthless leader is our best chance of survival in a tribal world. That about right?"

"Yeah."

I made a show of considering my response and then I leaned forward and held out my hand.

"All right, I'm in."

But as he took my hand in his all I could think about was what he'd done to Matron and Bates, and how badly I could make him suffer before I ended him.

CHAPTER EIGHT

THE GUARD LOOKED us up and down with an expression of distaste.

"What do you want?"

Petts held out a battered Sainsbury's bag.

"We've got vegetables, cheese and milk to trade at the market," he said.

The guard peered into the bag.

"Got any Cheshire?"

"Um, no, sorry. It's just home made stuff. It's kind of soft, like Philadelphia."

The guard sniffed. "Filthy stuff. My wife used to eat that. Shame," he said wistfully. "I did love a bit of Cheshire."

We stood there looking expectant as he drifted away into a soft, crumbly reverie. Williams cleared his throat.

"What? Oh, yeah, well, you'd better come in, then. Bill will pat you down." He nodded to his colleague, who stepped forward and searched us for weapons. When he was done he pushed the barbed wire and wood barrier aside and nodded for us to go through.

"Curfew's at seven," said Bill. "If you plan on staying you'd best find yourself a bolthole before then. There's rooms at the pub, if you can pay."

Petts, Williams and I walked through the barricade and into Hildenborough.

As far as Mac was concerned this small town, three miles down the road from the school, was our first problem. It was these guys he was preparing us to fight.

To borrow Mac's terminology, their strong tribal leader was George Baker, local magistrate. The man who'd so ruthlessly hanged

McCulloch and Fleming was a zero tolerance kind of guy who, like Mac, believed in public demonstrations of authority.

Petts and Williams visited Hildenborough once a week to attend a market at which they would trade the vegetables, meat and cheese they produced. Petts hadn't managed to convince anyone to eat the snails he collected, though.

Markets are a good place for gossip, and Hildenborough boasted what must have been the only working pub for a hundred miles, so it was good place to gather intelligence. The plan was for the others to trade as usual – for some reason Williams was desperate to find a good homebrew kit – while I mingled and got the lie of the land.

The town was well defended. Although it is ringed by open country on three sides, it kind of bleeds into Tonbridge on the fourth, making this the hardest front to defend against attack. To address this they had bulldozed a whole tranche of houses to create an exposed approach, then erected a bloody great fence and put in impressive gun towers. All it needed was a few spotlights and some German Shepherds and it would have been Berlin in the fifties.

Consequently the sides facing open country, where the guards were mostly posted on obvious routes like pathways and roads, were slightly more exposed and would be easier to infiltrate, especially after dark. Knowing this, Baker had imposed a strict curfew. Petts had discovered that the guards patrolled in pairs, with torches, and all wore high visibility jackets to prevent friendly fire incidents.

Before The Cull this part of Kent used to resound with the noise of shotguns blasting away at birds, so the Hildenborough survivors had no shortage of guns and ammunition. But our armoury was far more impressive, so if it came to a shooting match we'd have the advantage. In terms of numbers, Williams thought there were about forty men who acted as guards, and about two hundred residents in total.

Mac wanted me to establish some details about Baker himself, and find out whether he was likely to try and expand his territory.

Petts, Williams and I, all dressed in mufti so as not to attract attention, made our way through town to the market, which was held in front of the large stately home that Baker had adopted as his HQ. It was strange to see streets free of debris and burnt cars. As we approached the big house the cottages increasingly showed signs of occupation; the gardens were well tended, the curtains neatly draped. One thing about the new reality was that everyone who was still alive, no matter what they did before The Cull, got to live in the very best houses in the nicest parts of town. It seemed that in Hildenborough they were proud to show off their newly acquired properties.

Williams told me that the big house used to be some sort of medical centre before The Cull. It had impressive dormitory buildings in the grounds and a big swimming pool. The market, such as it was, was held on the forecourt. A collection of trestle tables had been erected and people were milling about trying to exchange jams, batteries, useless technology, clothes and so forth. There was a barbecue selling burgers and sausages, if you could provide the chef with something he wanted. There was even music from a folkie band, and the pub had laid on a tent and a few barrels of local brew.

The whole thing felt more like a village fete than a post-apocalyptic shambles. A little old lady sat knitting behind a pile of jars containing bramble jam, while a vicar stood proprietorially next to a table piled high with old books. There was an old wooden message board by the entrance to the beer tent and a handwritten note stated that the tug of war would start at two sharp, after the bail tossing and the egg and spoon race, but before the Main Event, whatever that was.

The world may have ended in plague and horror, but Middle England was doing very nicely, thanks for asking, would you like a bun Vicar?

And what could be more Middle England, more 'Outraged of Tunbridge Wells', than stringing people up? Off to one side, clearly visible but mercifully unused at the moment, stood a gallows. I shuddered as I imagined how McCulloch and Fleming must have felt in their final moments, as they stood on the trapdoor waiting for the lever to be pulled.

I let the other two go about their business and made a beeline for the beer tent. I don't like beer much, I'm more a whisky and coke kid, but I had a bagful of leeks to trade so I figured I could swig a few pints and make small talk with some locals. Infiltrate and inebriate, that was the plan.

In the end I didn't need to, because Baker himself was in the tent, jug of beer in hand, holding forth to an appreciative audience. I swapped a handful of leeks for a mug of mild, sat down on a bendy white plastic garden seat, and got an earful of the man himself.

He was tall but round, early fifties, dressed in 'Countryside Alliance' tweeds. His eyebrows were bushy, his cheeks were ruddy and his eyes were piercing blue. His jowls wobbled as he spoke.

"What you've got to understand, John," he said, "is that expansion is our only option."

Wow, ten seconds, job done. I can go home now, thanks. I never knew being a spy was this easy! At least I wouldn't have to drink any more of this foul brew; one sip was more than enough.

"But that doesn't have to mean confrontation," he continued.

Really?

"I see Hildenborough as the centre of an alliance. Some kind of loose affiliation of trading partners. Tribes, villages, maybe even city states, who knows. But we've got a safe, secure position here. We've got all the food we can use thanks to our farming programme, we're well armed and crime is virtually zero."

Interesting.

"Virtually," laughed one of his fellow drinkers. "It'll be zero after you hang that bastard later on." The group of men shared a convivial chuckle. You'd have thought he'd just told a joke about golf or something. That confirmed what the main event was.

"True, true," said Baker. "Anyway, we have stability here and I believe we can export that. Help other communities organise and sort themselves out."

He took a long draught of ale.

"Obviously it won't be easy," he continued. "I dare say we'll have to knock a few heads together along the way, deal with a few thugs and nasties, line some of 'em up against a wall and put them out of our misery. But really, one doesn't have a choice, does one. Got to have rule of law otherwise it'll be back to the bad old days of muggers and rapists and, God help us, niggers with attitude."

Oh no, hang on, I was right to start with – just another racist law and order nut with a passion for execution. Not that I minded anyone stringing Mac up and watching him dangle. But I didn't particularly want to become a citizen of Daily Mailonia. I'd rather take my chances with Mac.

A little alarm bell at the back of my head said 'so who's choosing their strong leader now then? Who's putting faith in the hardest bastard around to protect them? Who's starting to think that maybe Mac is right?'

I ignored it.

I was just about to get up and leave when Baker said something that brought me up short. One of the others had asked something about local communities.

"The nearest thing to a community in the area is a school up the road," said Baker. "A proper school, mind; fee-paying, uniforms, teachers in gowns, army cadets, pupils from good families. There's a whole collection of boys there playing soldiers."

"So are you going to approach them? Bring them into your alliance?" asked another.

"Hard to say. We've been keeping them under surveillance for a while now..." Shit! "...and there have been some pretty unpleasant goings on there recently. About six weeks ago they actually crucified one of their teachers."

Various exclamations of disbelief.

"No, really. And they're very heavily armed. They raided the armoury of a Territorial Army HQ, so they've got machine guns and grenades. They've not threatened us at all but I have a suspicion that they may be behind my niece's disappearance. She left in pursuit of three looters a few months ago, and two of them were boys, so..."

As he momentarily lost the thread of his conversation in a choke of emotion I had a familiar sinking sensation. Here was the biggest player in the area and Mac had only gone and shot his bloody niece. A confrontation would be inevitable if this ever came to light.

"Anyway," he continued, "I've been considering our first move and I think we have to let them know who's boss. After all, they're only boys, they should fall into line if they're shown a firm enough hand. No need for a shooting war. I think a strong demonstration of authority should sort them out."

This was all starting to sound familiar. Mac's idea of a strong display of authority involved crucifixion. I imagined Baker's would involve some poor sod swinging at the end of a noose. Anxious that it shouldn't be me, I lustily knocked back the remains of my pint, forced myself not to gag, and rose to leave. But as I made for the exit Baker stepped into my path and said:

"My dear Lee, where do you think you're going?"

"I APOLOGISE, LEE – it is Lee isn't it?"

I nodded.

"I apologise, Lee, for misleading you back there. I am well aware that your glorious commander-in-chief executed my niece."

Baker was sat at a huge desk in what I took to be his office. I could see the business of market day proceeding normally through the huge arched window behind him. A tall woman had just taken the lead in the egg and spoon race.

I was tied to a chair, facing Baker across the desk and wondering how I'd ended up here.

"My source passed on that tidbit of information a few weeks ago," he said.

"Your source?"

"Steven Williams. I believe he helps run your little farm. He's out there now, trading vegetables. Nice young man. He thought rather highly of Mr Bates and didn't take his death well. He came to us one market day and asked for sanctuary, but we were able to persuade him to return to the school and draw us a few maps, detail your defences, provide us with profiles of the key players, that kind of thing. He's been most helpful."

I took a moment to digest this. Williams had betrayed us. I didn't know how to feel about that. On one hand, I couldn't really blame him; but on the other he'd thrown in his lot with a bunch of tweed-clad fascists who probably thought The Cull was all the fault of immigrants.

"He told us about you, too, Lee. The loyal second-in-command, wounded in action, accessory to at least three murders that we know about."

There was no point explaining that I was planning to betray Mac too. I was going to have to stay in character; play the part I'd created for myself and hope I could find a way out of this.

How ironic if I ended up hanging for Mac's crimes before I had a chance to hang Mac for them myself.

"You killed two boys who were just scavenging for food. Don't you dare talk to me about murder," I spat.

Baker rose from his seat, walked around the desk and backhanded me hard across the face. A large signet ring cut a groove across my cheek and I felt blood begin to trickle down it.

"Don't answer me back, boy," he growled, his façade of civility momentarily stripped away. "I killed looters. Plain and simple. We need law and order, especially now. There can be no exceptions to the rule of law, not for sex or age. Wrongdoing must be punished. Justice must be seen to be done and it must be swift and merciless."

I lifted my head and stared at him.

"What about the right to a fair trial? What about mitigating circumstances?"

"A fair trial? Like the one you gave your teacher before you killed him? Don't be naive."

Dammit, why did all the nutters I found myself talking to always have to keep making such fair bloody points? Anyway we'd killed his niece. There was nothing at all that I could say that would change that. There was no talking myself out of this.

"Okay, I'm your hostage, you've got a plan to take the school and you're probably going to kill me. So let's get it over with. Why don't you tell me what you've got up your sleeve and then I can escape and foil your evil scheme. What do you say?"

Even as I said the words I cringed inwardly; I've seen too many bad movies. Perhaps it was because this was a scenario I'd seen played out so many times that I couldn't quite bring myself to feel I was really in jeopardy. The hero always ends up talking to somebody who's about to kill them, and they always manage a last-minute escape. It's a rule.

"My dear boy," replied Baker, his façade back in place. "I won't have time to explain my plans. Sorry."

Baker was working from the script of a different film.

"Why? Got an appointment to keep?"

"No. But you do."

ONLY A FEW months ago I had found it hard to conjure up any real concern when faced with imminent death. Reeling from the carnage of The Cull, emotionally shut down after burying my mother, I was barely interested in my own survival. Now, after being savaged and shot, I was keenly aware of how easy it was to die, and more determined than ever not to do so until I was old, feeble and surrounded by fat grandchildren.

But as I was marched up to the gallows I couldn't see any way to stay alive beyond the next five minutes. My nerve was only barely holding. By the time the rope was slipped around my neck I felt like shitting myself and I wanted to cry.

I stood on the raised wooden platform looking down at the assembled faces of the Hildenborough market crowd, eagerly awaiting the 'Main Event' – my death. Some looked excited, others looked bored. They munched on hot dogs or sipped their beers as if it were just another day. Williams avoided my gaze.

I tried to work out how a simple trip to market and a little light gossip had led so quickly and inescapably to my imminent death. This hadn't been the plan. I wasn't supposed to die here, not now. What about Mac? What about Matron? What about my dad? This was supposed to be an ordinary day, nothing too risky, nothing spectacular. This wasn't supposed to be the second date on my tombstone.

It seemed that death had caught me unawares.

Which, of course, is what it always does.

Baker stood beside me and addressed the throng as I tried to prevent my knees from buckling. The rope itched and scratched at the soft flesh of my neck.

"Citizens of Hildenborough, and honoured guests, today marks a new beginning for this town."

There was a smattering of enthusiastic applause and a few cheers.

"Ever since The Cull descended upon us I have striven to make this town safe – safe for mothers and children; for families and old people. In this town I have made it my business to preserve the values and ideals that made this country great. And I believe I have done so, with your help. Hildenborough is a haven, a sanctuary in a violent and depraved world. But no longer. Today we shall begin to take the message to the country. Today we shall start the process of civilisation anew. From this town, from this very spot upon which I stand, we shall spread peace and safety throughout the land and we, *I*, shall be its saviour.

"And that process begins with an enclave of violence and sickness that sits on our front doorstep. Yes, friends, in a small village not far from here is the school of St Mark's. I know that some of you had children that attended that school, and you remember it as a centre of excellence, fostering values like duty, respect, obedience and independence.

"It is my sad duty to inform you that those values have become perverted. Under the leadership of a cruel, vicious man, the surviving children have armed themselves, overthrown their teachers, and declared themselves an anarchist state.

"Their lawlessness threatens us all. If we allow them to go unchecked then it won't be long before we are overrun by thugs and bullies, muggers and hoodies; feral children who know only the instinct to smash and destroy the homes and lives of their elders and betters.

"I am here to tell you that this shall not be allowed!"

Cheers and applause again. But, I noticed, not from everyone. A group of about fifteen men stood at the rear of the audience and they appeared to be watching not Baker, but the crowd. The hysteria Baker was whipping up with his well judged oratory was not reaching them.

When the cheering had died down Baker gestured to me.

"This young man had a bright future. He's not from a good family, his parents own no land and possess no great wealth. But his father served in Her Majesty's forces and they helped pay for his son's education at one of the finest schools in the land. They offered him an opportunity to better himself, to rise above his humble origins and excel. And what has he done with that chance? He has put on a uniform to which he has no right, picked up a gun, and embarked on a campaign of slaughter that is too horrific to relate to you good people here today."

I wanted to point out that it was Mac he wanted. But that was beside the point. Baker had to demonise me before killing me, only then would his point be made and his lesson handed down.

"One could say that he has simply reverted to type. That he was never of good stock and had no place at a school such as St Mark's. I leave such judgements up to you. What I can do, however, is dispense justice for the men and women he has slaughtered. One of whom, friends, was my own, dear niece, Lucy."

A gasp from the crowd.

"The execution of this murderous animal signals the start of my campaign to clean up this county, *this* country! Even as we stand here a force of men is taking control of the school that harboured his vile criminal urges. By tonight we shall have expanded our territory to include this great institution for education and civilisation which I shall personally see is restored to its rightful place at the heart of a nation ruled by respect!"

Huge applause. And the group of men at the back of the crowd sloughed off their long coats and stood waiting for... what?

Baker turned to me.

"Lee Keegan, I find you guilty of the crime of murder and I hereby sentence you to hang by the neck until dead."

And he pulled the lever.

CHAPTER NINE

JON USED TO have this battered old hardback book called *The Hangman's Art*. He was sick like that. It was the memoirs of an executioner but also a manual for a good hanging. Amongst all the factors the author considered important – a black canvas hood, the binding of hands and feet, the fluid motion of the trapdoor – the most crucial detail was the length of the rope.

If you hang a man with a rope that's too long the drop will decapitate the condemned, and nobody wants that. Conversely, if the rope is too short then the condemned person's neck will not break and they will swing there, choking to death. This outcome was not considered merciful.

The book contained a graph charting the ratio between the weight of the condemned and the correct length of rope required for a clean, clinical snap of the neck and a swift, essentially painless dispatch.

Thank Christ nobody on Baker's staff had a copy.

I DON'T THINK there's any shame in admitting that as I fell into space I lost all control of my bodily functions and shat myself. As I reached the full extent of the rope's length it snapped tight and dug hard into my windpipe.

I heard a sharp crack and knew that I was dead.

The brain takes a fairly long time to die once deprived of oxygen. I remember Bates telling us once that during the French Revolution the severed heads of guillotine victims could blink on command for up to four minutes after the chop. I wonder what they were thinking, how conscious they were of their situation. Were they screaming silently or were their final, bodiless minutes strangely serene?

As I swung there, knowing that my neck had snapped and that I was beginning the irreversible process of brain death, my vision swam and my lungs cried out for breath that I couldn't force into them. I didn't feel serene at all. I wanted to kick and fight and bite and scream my way out of the noose. But my hands were tied and my feet kicked helplessly at thin air. All I could see was the sky rotating above me.

I've no idea how long I hung there, it felt like a lifetime. Eventually, just as my vision was starting to fade and the roaring in my ears reached the pitch of a jet plane taking off, I felt someone grab my feet and push upwards. The pressure on my windpipe briefly abated and I gasped down the tiniest of breaths before the grip loosened and I swung free once more.

Then my weight was taken again, but this time it felt like I was standing on someone's shoulders. I was pushed upwards until I flopped onto the wooden platform like a landed fish. I felt hands loosening the noose and I breathed deep. Before I had time to get my bearings, while my hearing and vision were still blurred and faded, I was pulled to my feet and two people took my weight. I staggered between them, powerless to control where I was being led.

My senses began to re-establish themselves as we hurried down off the scaffold and across grass, around the side of the main building and away from the market. I could hear screams and gunshots. After a short run we stopped and my two rescuers started arguing.

"Where?" Petts.

"Um…" Williams.

"Quickly! We won't get far with him like this."

"Okay, inside."

"Are you fucking nuts?"

"Inside!"

They dragged me through a side door into the main building and then up three flights of stairs. When we finally stopped we were inside a tiny attic room, probably an old servants' quarters. A small window looked down onto the square below. There was a bed in the corner and my two schoolmates dropped me onto it. Williams closed the door and pushed a chest of drawers across it before slumping onto the floor.

"Who are they?" asked Petts.

"How the fuck should I know?" shouted Williams, on the edge of hysteria.

Resting on the bed I felt the adrenaline surging through me. I was shaking like a leaf, but I could breathe!

"My... my neck. I heard it break," I gasped. "Why am I still alive?"

"If your neck was broken you'd be dead. Your neck's fine," said Petts. "I mean, you've got a hell of a bruise, and rope burns and shit, but no broken bones."

"But I heard it! I heard it break!" I protested.

"That wasn't your neck, that was a gunshot," said Williams. "They opened fire the second you dropped."

I levered myself upright and felt the awful slickness in my pants as I did so.

"Who opened fire?"

"Take a look," said Petts, gesturing to the window.

I shuffled sideways on the bed and peered down onto the market square. It was a scene of total chaos. The first thing I noticed was Baker, lying next to the lever, half his head missing, sprayed across the gallows platform.

At least that was one less mad bastard to worry about.

The forecourt was still full of people, but they were surrounded by the men I had seen at the back of the crowd. Some of these men carried guns; all brandished what looked like homemade machetes. There were some bodies lying around the place, a few villagers, and two of the attackers.

I could hear sporadic gunfire in the distance.

"They shot Baker just as he pulled the lever, and the crowd panicked," explained Petts. "There was a stampede but they were ready for it and they herded everyone back towards the building's entrance. Some of the men had guns and there was a fight, and during the confusion we were able to get to you. But it looks like these new guys, whoever they are, have got things under control now. By the way, Lee, you stink."

"Yeah, sorry about that."

At that moment a strange figure appeared, walking down the driveway towards the house. He was tall and lean and dressed in an immaculate three-piece pinstripe suit, complete with stripy tie and bowler hat. He carried an umbrella and his face was daubed with watery brown paint. He was flanked by two huge bodybuilder types, stripped naked and entirely daubed with the same brown stain. Both men carried machine guns.

Obviously an unknown force had stormed the town. I reasoned that one or two of them must have made it over the wire under cover of darkness and hidden a cache of weapons, probably in one of the abandoned houses. Then the main force had arrived one by one, ostensibly for market day, collected the weapons and waited for the appointed time – my execution. The gunshots in the distance indicated that another force had attacked the guard posts once they'd heard the shooting from inside the town. It seemed like a well organised and effective attack. Now here, in his finest suit, came their leader.

Much as I wanted to see what transpired I was conscious that a force of men from Hildenborough was about to storm the school. We couldn't hang around here, we needed to get back and warn them. I turned to Williams.

"When do they attack?"

He looked up at me, wide-eyed. "What?"

"Look, I know you sold us out to Baker so don't waste my fucking time. Do you know when they are planning to attack?"

Williams stared at me like a rabbit in headlights.

"Williams, listen to me. I don't give a damn about what you've done, all right. I just need…"

"I don't know," he muttered. "He didn't tell me."

"Hang on," said Petts. "Are you saying…"

"No time, Petts, not now. Got to get back to school and warn them. Stay here. I'll be back."

I rose to my feet. My knees felt like jelly but I forced myself to walk to the door. I listened but could hear no-one outside, so I shoved the chest aside and pushed the door ajar. No-one. I edged out into the corridor and worked my way along the rooms until I found one with a wardrobe full of clothes. I stripped my lower half and used a towel to clean myself up as best I could. I put on a clean pair of trousers and went back to the room, where I found Petts beating the living crap out of Williams.

I pulled them apart.

"Leave it Petts. Later!"

He was breathing hard and his fists were raw; Williams' nose was broken and his lip was bloodied. He was terrified.

"Oh God, he's going to crucify me. He's going to crucify me," was all he could say.

"I fucking hope so!" said Petts. I glared at him and told him to back off. He reluctantly sat on the bed. I knelt down and looked straight into Williams' eyes.

"Nobody is going to crucify anyone, Williams. I give you my word."

He looked at me for a moment and then nodded.

"Right now I need you to keep it together and help us get out of here without running into any of these guys with the machetes. Can you help us do that?"

He nodded again. "I know a way," he said.

"Good man. Right, we're going to try and get out of town as quickly and as quietly as we can, all right?"

Petts and Williams nodded. I sighed. I had just been bloody hanged. Why, oh why, did I have to take the lead yet again? The shit on my shorts wasn't even dry. All I wanted was a long bath and a stiff drink. And maybe a massage.

I led them out onto the landing and let Williams take point. We descended to the second floor but then we heard voices coming up the stairs from below. They were searching the house. I ushered the boys through the nearest door.

We had taken refuge in a bathroom.

"Dammit," I cursed. "Why couldn't it have been an armoury?"

There was precious little to use in the way of weapons. Petts cracked the door open and peered out while I unscrewed the shower hose and handed it to Williams – at least he could use that to choke someone with. Not that I had any intention of killing anyone, I just wanted to get back to the school as quickly as possible. For all I knew this new group could be the good guys, and I didn't want to go slaughtering them willy-nilly until I at least knew who or what I was dealing with.

I picked up the heavy porcelain slab that sat on top of the toilet cistern and held it ready to use a bludgeon. The only other potential weapon was a bottle of bleach. I pressed it into Petts' hand.

"Only if we need to," I whispered. "And try not to kill anyone, okay?"

They nodded.

The voices came nearer and two young men appeared at the top of the stairs. Both were wearing jeans and T-shirts. Their arms were daubed with the brown stain but their hands and faces were clean; left that way so they could blend in with the normal market crowd without arousing suspicion.

They began to work their way along the corridor towards us, checking the rooms as they went. I steadied myself and got a firm grip on the cistern lid; if I swung it right I should be able to take one of them out of the picture.

Two doors along from us they found someone hiding and both vanished into the room, where a struggle ensued. I was just about to try and use the distraction to slip past them when they dragged an old man of about eighty out into the corridor, threw him to the floor and kicked him hard in the ribs. He lay there, gasping, clutching his chest.

One of the men looked guiltily up and down the corridor, and then said to his mate: "Lets bleed 'im."

His colleague looked uncertain.

"What, here?" he asked.

"Of course here, you berk. Where else?"

"David won't like that."

"David doesn't have to know." He gestured to his face and hands. "I feel naked like this. Don't you? We're not safe, mate. Gotta be safe."

"Yeah, I s'pose."

"So let's bleed the cattle and then we can relax, yeah?"

"Yeah, all right, then. Bleed him."

The old man who was the subject of this banal, macabre exchange, whimpered helplessly. The first man grabbed him by the arms and lifted him upright, while the other advanced towards him with his machete. It was only then that I realised exactly what they were talking about.

The brown stain wasn't paint at all. It was blood.

Human blood.

Right. So. Not the good guys.

I felt a familiar sinking feeling as I realised that I was going to have to get involved. I turned to the others and whispered "Follow my lead". Then I pushed open the door, bellowed as loudly as I could, and ran at the man with the raised machete.

On the whole I try to avoid picking fights with people, especially people who are clearly insane, daubed in blood, and carrying a fucking huge knife, but I was now doing exactly that, armed with only a detachable piece of flushing toilet.

I had surprise on my side and my target had little time to react. I swung the cistern lid with all the momentum of my short run up, and smacked him under the chin as hard as I could. There was a shattering crunch as he was lifted off his feet and his head smacked satisfyingly into the corridor wall. He slumped to the floor, unconscious, his jaw a bloody mess.

His mate shouted out in anger and threw the old man aside, raising his machete and moving towards me menacingly. At which point Williams snuck up behind him, wrapped the shower hose around his neck and tugged him off his feet. They collapsed backwards in a tangle of limbs. Then Petts ran forward and squirted bleach into the man's face.

Williams scrambled clear as the man clawed at his eyes and screamed loud enough to raise the dead. Before I could knock him out with my trusty cistern lid, the old man stood up and drop-kicked his would-be murderer into the middle of next week.

There was a brief moment of calm as all four of us stood there breathing heavily, contemplating the two unconscious men.

"Thanks, lads," said the old guy, cheerily, "but I had it all under control."

We all gaped.

"Know a bit of unarmed combat from my army days," he went on. "I was just waiting for him to get a little closer then I'd have kicked him in the goolies, tossed this chappy over my head and done a runner."

"You were whimpering!" I said.

"All part of my act, dontchaknow."

We didn't have time for this.

"Right," I said. "Good. Fine. Um, we're running away now, if that's okay with you. So you ain't seen us, right?"

He tapped his nose and winked. "You hotfoot it, lads. I'll take care of these two." He bent down and picked up a machete. "Haven't used one of these since Burma," he said with relish.

We legged it.

We made it to the ground floor without encountering anyone else. We could hear someone giving some sort of speech from the forecourt, but I didn't want to hang around so Williams led us through the kitchens to the back door.

"We go out here and around the side of the house," he told us. "Then there's a garden hidden from the driveway by a tall hedge. Then it's over the road, across a field and into woodland. We should be safe from then."

I pushed open the door. No guard. We ran as fast as we could, Williams in the lead, until we came to the sheltered garden that ran alongside the forecourt. Still no sign of anyone. They were all on the other side of the hedge listening to whoever was ranting. We were halfway down the garden when we heard a truly bloodcurdling scream. It was no use; I had to see what was going on. I ran to the end of the garden and peered around the edge of the hedge.

I wish I hadn't.

The men with machetes were still encircling the captured citizens of the town, but all attention was focused on the scaffold. The noose was lying on the platform, the rope slack. A middle-aged woman was struggling in the grip of the two heavyset, naked guards, but she was tied hand and foot and had no chance of escape. One of the naked men looped her feet though the noose and then a third pulled the rope. She swung into the air, suspended upside down.

The man in the pinstripe suit, who was also standing on the platform – I assumed he was this group's leader, David – stepped forward and began to undress, meticulously piling his folded clothes to one side. The last thing he removed was his bowler hat, which he placed on top of the pile. He stood there naked, his body caked in crumbly dried blood. He spread his arms and addressed the crowd.

"In the fountain of life I shall be reborn," he intoned.

All the machete men chanted back in unison: "Make us safe."

From then on it was call and answer, like some kind of Catholic Mass gone horribly wrong.

"With the blood of the lamb I wash myself clean."

"Make us safe."

"From the source of pestilence comes our salvation."

"Make us safe."

"Life for life. Blood for blood."

"Make us safe."

He turned, tenderly cradled the woman's head and kissed her lips.

"I thank you for your gift," he said.

Then she was hauled as high as the rope would go. David stood directly beneath her. One of his acolytes stepped forward and smoothly, emotionlessly, drew his machete across the trussed woman's neck.

And David showered in her fresh blood as the crowd screamed and his acolytes chanted together:

"Safe now. Safe now. Safe now."

Suddenly Mac didn't seem like such a bad guy after all.

I turned away in disgust to find Petts, white-faced in shock, Williams, throwing up, and a very big man with a machete standing behind me.

Without hesitation I threw a punch, but he rocked backwards and I swung into thin air. He snapped upright and brought his machete scything down at my shoulder. I followed my fist and spun left as the metal blade sliced within a millimetre of my ear. I stumbled, my weak leg momentarily betraying me. I hit the ground and tried to roll with it.

I'm not a martial arts specialist. That's Norton's thing. I can do guns, no problem. I can even do toilets, in a pinch. But straightforward fighting, especially when I'm unarmed and the guy I'm fighting has a piece of metal specifically designed to split me in two, is not something I'm very good at.

My cack-handed attempt at a forward roll probably saved my life. The man brought the machete around with lightning speed and chopped at the space where I would have been had my hand not slipped in some mud, pitching me face first. I scrambled forward on my hands and knees as he raised the knife again.

Petts barrelled into the guy's side, classic rugby tackle. The man staggered sideways but didn't fall, and he brought the machete handle down on the back of Petts' neck, hard. He went down like a sack of spuds.

I had regained my feet by now, and the man and I circled each other warily. I caught a glimpse of Williams, running for the safety of the trees in the distance. Cowardly bastard. Maybe I would crucify him, if I ever saw him again.

I considered letting myself be captured, escaping later. But after what I'd just witnessed I didn't want to spend any more time in the company of these lunatics than I had to. No point taking a chance of being bled. But I was hopelessly outmatched here. This guy was faster, older, stronger and armed. I was limping, breathless and my neck hurt like hell.

He lunged forward, sweeping the machete sideways, trying to gut me. I sucked in my stomach and bent myself like a bow. The knife missed its mark. He then stepped towards me, and in one fluid movement the knife swept up and across, slicing down at my neck. I took a single step forward, ducked under the swing, and raised both hands to grab his forearm. I spun and shoved my back into his belly, tried to use his weight against him, throw him off balance. But, dammit, he was too solid on his legs and I hadn't practised this move before; I was just aping what I'd seen on TV, and he obviously knew what he was doing. He pulled in his arms, kept me cradled to him and squeezed, lifting me off my feet and tossing me aside.

I got to my feet and ran. Of course I say 'ran', I was still limping so there was no point my making for the tree-line; I'd just never make it. Instead I ran back to the house, making it inside just seconds before my pursuer. I flung myself through the kitchen door and scanned left and right for some kind of weapon with which to defend myself.

When the man came pelting through the door in pursuit, his face met the business end of a frying pan and his feet went out from under him. He crashed down onto the hard tiled floor with a rush of expelled breath. But still he kept a tight grip on his machete. I aimed a kick at his nuts but he rolled away. Nonetheless I connected with his thigh and he grunted. Finally a stroke of luck – I'd given him a dead leg.

He pulled himself up on a table as I swung at his head with the frying pan again. He swatted it away with the machete and it went flying from my grip, clattering to the floor. His nose was bleeding freely and one side of his face was vivid red where the pan had caught him on the cheekbone.

He snarled at me, wiped his hand in the blood from his nose, licked it, smacked his lips, and then smeared the fresh blood all over his face, mixing the new blood with the old.

"Safer now," he chuckled as he advanced, limping, towards me.

Jesus, was this guy for real?

I backed away, looking all the time for another means of defence. There was a rack of knives to my left, and I snatched a short one which I brandished menacingly. A voice in my head mocked: "Call that a knife? That's not a knife. That thing he's got, *that's* a knife!"

I continued backing away, trod on my discarded flying pan, and went flying like a character in a bad slapstick comedy. To add insult to injury I somehow contrived to land on my own knife, stabbing myself in the side. I yelled in pain as I pulled the blade out and felt hot blood seep down my hip. I looked up and there he was, looming over me, grinning.

"Good cattle. Bleed yourself. Save me the trouble."

"Oh, fuck off," I said wearily. And then I sat up, leaned forward and buried the knife hilt-deep into his thigh. Now it was his turn to yell. I flung myself backwards to avoid the answering swipe of his machete. I scrambled to my feet again and staggered away from him.

He resumed his advance without even pausing to remove the knife. I started grabbing things off the work surfaces and hurling them at him without taking time to see what they were. A colander, a kettle, a bottle of oil, a box of teabags; nothing slowed him down. This was futile.

I turned and scurried to the door.

It was locked. I looked left and right frantically. This wasn't the door Williams, Petts and I had entered from, that was on the other side of the room. This was – oh fuck, it was the door to a walk-in freezer.

I was trapped.

Long metal work surfaces stretched forward on either side of me, hemming me in. Behind me was a locked door, and in front of me stood some kind of Home Counties Jason Voorhees, dripping with blood, and grinning.

"Time to bleed, boy."

There was nowhere to run, nothing to hand offered any chance of defence or offence. It was just me, him and a very big knife.

Fuck it.

I put my head down, and charged the bastard. I slammed into his midriff and this time, with both legs damaged, he lost his balance and fell backwards. We tumbled to the floor and slid across the tiles and – hallelujah! – I saw his machete go sliding away underneath the tables. We wrestled, each trying to gain some purchase, but both of us were slick with blood and our hands kept slipping off each other. I tried to reach up and grab his throat but he was way too strong for me. He forced my arms down and somehow spun me, taking a firm grip on my clothes and pinioning me, face down on the floor. He folded his arm around my neck, nestling the soft inside of his elbow on my already bruised and battered windpipe, and squeezed.

For the second time in an hour I was being choked to death and I couldn't see any way of escape. I writhed and kicked, tried a reverse head butt, scratched and gasped and thrashed, but he was solid as stone, bearing down on me. I couldn't move him an inch.

Again my vision began to cloud, my ears began to roar.

And then my thrashing hands brushed against something hard. The knife – it was still in his thigh! I grasped it, twisted and pulled. He grunted and tightened his grip. I couldn't move my arm up to hit anything vital so I resorted to stabbing him in the thigh again.

And then again.

And again.

And again.

I kept the knife pumping in and out of his thigh with all the force I could muster, but as my body failed, my thrusts got weaker and weaker.

Eventually the blade fell out of my blood-slicked hands and I felt myself blacking out.

I REGAINED CONSCIOUSNESS what must have been a minute or two later. The dead weight of my assailant was still on top of me, but his grip on my neck had loosened. I lay there for a second as my head cleared. He wasn't breathing. I roared with the exertion of throwing him off of me, and I slipped and slid in the blood pool that surrounded us both before finally standing upright. Pausing only to pick up the machete, I staggered away, back towards the garden.

My windpipe was so badly swollen that I could only breathe in short ragged bursts. My side was on fire where the knife had speared me. I was a mass of bruises, my head felt light, my hearing was muffled and I was covered, absolutely covered from head to toe, in blood – both mine and that of the man I had killed.

No, don't think about that. Don't think about the killing, about the intimacy of it, the penetration and the spurting and the tactile slickness of his dead skin. Don't think about his breath on my neck, his hands on my throat, his knee in my back. Don't think about how awfully, sickeningly different it was to the clinical dissociation of a gunshot. Don't think about it. Save it for later. There's time for the nightmares later. Things to do.

I limped outside into the sunlight and listened. The chanting had stopped but I could still hear the noises of a large group of people. My route to freedom was still the same, so I started walking towards where Petts should have been lying unconscious. But he wasn't there. Had he regained consciousness and fled, or had he been found and captured? I peered around the corner of the hedge again and saw the machete men herding the townspeople into canvas-topped troop trucks, which had pulled up at the edge of the forecourt. They were shipping them off, presumably to their base of operations.

One man carried the dead body of the woman from the scaffold and tossed it into a truck amongst the living cattle.

Oh, God, they had a use for corpses as well. Could they be cannibals too?

With a jolt I saw Petts, holding his head, clearly disorientated, being shoved into one of the trucks. There was no hope of a rescue. He'd have to take his chances.

There was nothing I could do here. I had to get back to the school and warn them about the imminent attack by all that was left of Hildenborough's militia, assuming it hadn't already taken place.

I made my way as fast as I could across the small section of exposed ground and then back into cover on the road, behind the hedgerows and up to a stile. Even the simple act of climbing over a stile felt like an achievement given what I'd been through. And then into the field and safe to the trees.

Apart from the young woman, daubed in blood, carrying a gun, barring my way and looking at me quizzically.

We stood and stared at each other for a moment, and then I smiled and said:

"Safe now."

She regarded my blood-soaked self and nodded.

"Safe now," she replied.

And I was free to go.

CHAPTER TEN

I HAD NO idea what awaited me back at the school, but that three-mile journey felt like one of the longest of my life. I wanted to run but I just wasn't capable. A shambling half-jog was the best I could muster.

I wondered how good David's intelligence had been. Had he chosen this afternoon to attack Hildenborough because he'd known that some of their forces would be busy elsewhere? And if so, did that mean he knew about the school? Could we be his next target? All this, of course, assuming the school wasn't already occupied.

I decided my best approach was to head along the river and come at the school from the rear, through the woods. That way I could get a sense of what had happened before showing myself.

The River Medway was part of the Ironside Line, the premier inland line of defence against the expected German invasion during the Second World War. As a result there are pillboxes all along the river, five of which mark the rear border of the school grounds. Under Mac's defence plan only two were manned at any one time, and never the same two on consecutive days.

I approached the first, but it was empty, as was the second. But the third had finally seen combat, many decades after its construction. There were four men, all of whom had been carrying shotguns, lying spread-eagled on the ground; victims of the General Purpose Machine Gun that had been housed in the pillbox. When I entered the pillbox I found one of our boys – a third-former called Guerrier, who I don't think I'd ever even spoken to – dead from a shotgun blast to the face. There was no sign of the GPMG, so I assumed the remainder of the Hildenborough attackers had commandeered it to use against further resistance. That would have evened the odds slightly.

I picked up one of the shotguns, emptied the cartridges from the pockets of the dead men, loaded the gun and moved on.

The fourth pillbox was empty but the fifth was pebble-dashed with shotgun pellets, and there was an abandoned GPMG inside, surrounded by spent casings. There were no bodies anywhere. Whoever had been manning this pillbox must have done a runner.

I moved cautiously through the woods to the edge of the playing fields and the assault course, which provided me with cover. I crawled through the netting and under the barbed wire and took up position by a wooden climbing structure.

There was no-one to be seen and no gunshots or screams to be heard; the school was silent and still. The fields offered no cover, but I had to keep going. I ran to the edge of the playing fields and made my way towards the school keeping myself close to the hedge. I made it to the outbuildings, where the walls were freshly chipped by what looked like GPMG rounds. One of the minibuses was aflame. The GPMG that had been taken from the pillbox was beside it, still resting upright on its tripod. There'd been a hell of a fight here, but it had moved on. There were two more Hildenborough attackers lying dead on the gravel path at the back of the building. All the windows on the ground floor were broken and one had a dead boy lying across it, half in and half out. I walked over and lifted his head. It was a junior called Belcher. I'd known him; nice kid, cried himself to sleep at night because he missed his mum.

Then I heard shots. But they weren't the sporadic shoot and return of a fire-fight; it was a series of measured single shots, about ten in all. I had a horrible suspicion I knew what that meant.

I made my way carefully through the corridors of Castle, passing bodies and bullet casings, splintered wood panelling and blood-soaked floorboards, until I came to the front door. I looked out across the driveway and lawn.

The guard post at the front gate was smoking and I could see the body of a boy lying across the sandbags; it was Zayn.

One less officer to worry about.

One less rapist for me to deal with.

The fight at the front didn't look like it had been as fierce as the one out back, which had obviously ended in a running battle indoors. I figured they'd sent a small force to the gate as a distraction, while the main force had attacked from the river. It's probably what I would have done. Fat lot of good it did them. Because standing in front of the school, before the assembled body of surviving pupils, stood Mac, smoking Browning still in hand. To his left lay a row of eleven men, all with their hands tied behind their backs, all with neat bullet holes in their heads. Six more men were kneeling to his right.

As I watched, Mac popped the clip out of his Browning. Empty. He nodded to Wylie, who raised his rifle and executed the next man. Then Wolf-Barry, Pugh, Speight and Patel each took a life. Green protested but he had a gun forced into his hands by Wylie. Mac barked an order and stood beside him, menacingly. Given no choice, Green closed his eyes, turned his head, and pulled the trigger. Mac patted him on the back.

One more team-building exercise.

One more crime to unite them.

I pushed open the front door and walked outside. The gasps of the boys alerted the officers, who turned, guns raised, and then stood there, amazed. Mac came running up to me, his face a mask of astonishment. He looked me up and down and said:

"What the hell happened to you?"

I told him.

"So what you're saying is that I've just executed a whole bunch of potential allies who could have helped us take on a far nastier bunch of heavily armed psychotic fuckers who like bathing in human blood and are probably cannibals?"

"That about covers it, yeah."

"Fuck."

Mac ordered the officers to hang the corpses from the lamp-posts that lined the school drive in the hope that they'd deter any attackers for a while.

AFTER FILLING MAC in on my escapades I went to the San and attended to my own wounds, dosing myself with antibiotics and rubbing antiseptic and arnica on bruise after bruise. The wound in my side was excruciatingly painful, but I'd managed to miss all my vital organs and I didn't think I'd punctured my guts. I stitched it up and hoped for the best; it would make strenuous physical exercise even more awkward and painful for a while. By the time I was done a hot bath had been prepared for me, one of the privileges of rank. Lowering myself into it was sweet agony, but I lay there, boiling myself for about an hour, letting all the tension seep away, trying to work out my next move.

We had been training for a potential war with Hildenborough, but after a brief, bloody skirmish they were out of the picture, replaced by a far more menacing enemy. This new force was highly organised, armed with machine guns and machetes, driven by religious fanaticism and pre-emptively attacking communities in our area. We had no idea what, if any, strategy they were using, where they were based, or when, if at all, they planned to attack. We were vulnerable and uninformed; what we needed more than anything else was good intelligence.

When I was cleaned up I briefed all the officers on the events in Hildenborough. I was relieved to find that there was no sign of the resentment I had been expecting from them; I had been blooded once again and it seemed I had earned their respect without even having to try. Mac made it clear that all information regarding the new threat remained amongst officers only; he didn't want to scare the boys.

"Give 'em a day or so to mourn the dead and celebrate our victory," he said. "We've seen off an attacking army of adults – twenty-eight of them – with only five boys dead. We can use this to increase morale a bit, coz if what Lee is telling us is correct then this was just a warm-up. I won't leave one of my men in enemy hands so we've got to go and rescue Petts. That means picking a serious fight."

Once the briefing was over the officers went back to the grisly task of hanging out the Hildenborough dead, and burying our own. Mac and I pored over an OS map of the local area and picked out the most likely bases of operation for the group that Wylie had colourfully christened the Blood Hunters. We mainly focused on places that would have good defences, which meant stately homes and old manor houses. There were a lot of them, but we prioritised and drew up a search plan.

While Mac pondered the offence that we would adopt as our best defence, I sent a note to Matron via Mrs Atkins, warning her of the new threat and telling her to be on guard.

"I HAVE NEVER been so bloody scared in my entire life," said Norton. "There were bullets everywhere, the windows were exploding, the minibus blew up. I just closed my eyes and fired blind. Fat lot of use I was. Give me hand-to-hand and I know what I'm doing, but this was mental. Just fucking mental. And what I don't understand, right, is why they picked a fight with us in the first place? I mean, what've we done?"

"They were watching us," I said. "They saw Bates' crucifixion, thought we were a threat. You can see their point, I suppose."

"Still, couldn't they have just, y'know, knocked on the door and said 'hi, we're the neighbours, we baked you a cake?' I mean, there was no reason to come in guns blazing, no reason at all."

"Look where it got them."

"Look where it got Guerrier, Belcher, Griffiths and Zayn."

I had no answer to that.

"I don't want to die like that," he said eventually.

"If it's choice of being shot or being bled and eaten, then I'll take a bullet every time, thanks. After all, been there, done that."

"Yeah, yeah, stop boasting," he teased, sarcastically. "By my reckoning you've been shot, stabbed, strangled, hanged and savaged by a mad dog since you came back to school, three of those in the last twenty-four hours."

"I also shat myself."

"All right. You win. You are both vastly harder and far more pathetic than any of us."

"And don't you forget it."

"So, oh great unkillable smelly one, do you want to know how I've been doing?"

I nodded eagerly.

"Things in the ranks are confused. Some boys are really pumped up about the fight, gung-ho, ready for more. They reckon Mac's leadership saved our bacon and they're willing to fight for him now."

"Mac's fucking leadership provoked the bloody attack in the first place."

"But they don't know that."

"Which boys are we talking about?"

"Most of the fourth- and fifth-formers. They're the ones who cop it least from the officers, so they've got a less highly developed sense of grievance. But I've had a quiet natter with Haycox, the horsey one, and filled him in on what happened to Matron, and he's with us. He's trying to spread the word, subtle like."

"And the juniors?"

"They're more interesting. Rowles is a sneaky little sod when he's not sniffling, and he's got pretty much all of them on side. They loved Matron and Bates, and they fucking hate Mac. Plus the officers pick on them all the time and they're feeling pretty pissed off."

"So we've got basically all the seniors led by Mac, against all the

juniors, led by us," I said, morosely. "Not going to be much of a
fight is it."

"Do we have a better plan?"

I shook my head. "We'll just have to choose our moment carefully,
won't we?" I said.

AFTER BREAKFAST THE next morning – a surprisingly good Kedgeree
made with fish from the river – everyone gathered in the briefing
room. Without explicitly detailing the situation, Mac told the
boys that there was a new threat abroad and that we were going
to be searching for their HQ. A group of five search teams was
assembled, each comprising one officer and two other boys, and
they were allocated specific targets to recce. The rest of us were
to concentrate on repairing the damage of yesterday's attack and
bolstering our defence perimeter.

As walking wounded I was excused any actual work. Instead I
spent a quiet day with three boys who had been wounded in the
fight. The youngest of these, Jenkins, had been shot in his left hand,
which was shattered and unlikely to be fully useable ever again. He
was only eleven but he had already made it to grade six on piano; he
was having a hard time coming to terms with the fact that he'd never
make grade seven. Vaughan had a nasty head wound, although this
was from crashing into a table as he dived for cover. He was a bit
concussed but he'd be fine. Feschuk had taken a splinter of glass to
his left eye, and it was likely that depth perception was a thing of the
past for him. We spent the day rummaging through the dusty library
for any useful books and sharing stories of life before The Cull.

I casually manoeuvred the conversation around to the subject of
Mac and was horrified to learn that, despite the wounds, despite
what his actions had cost them, despite how he'd treated Bates and
Matron, they were starting to like the bastard.

"If it weren't for him we'd have been captured and hung yesterday,"
said Feschuk. He related how Mac had taken his place in the defences
when he'd been hit and had rallied the boys in the heat of battle to
regroup and ambush the attackers inside Castle itself.

"The officers are a pain, but at least we're safe here," said
Jenkins. His best mate Griffiths had died in the fight but he seemed
detached and unconcerned by this. In shock or just accustomed to
losing people?

"I never liked Matron anyways," said Vaughan. Who was a prick.

*   *   *

THE NEXT MORNING I swapped dusty books for damp leaves and beetles, as I crawled through mulchy undergrowth on a reconnaissance mission. My side stung every time I moved, but the stitches held and the painkillers I was taking helped a bit. When I reached the edge of the forest I brought out my binoculars and looked down a long sweeping lawn at the headquarters of the Blood Hunters.

"I don't fancy trying to storm that," said Mac, who was lying beside me.

Neither did I.

Ightham Mote was a solid wood and stone 14th century manor house that sat in the middle of a deep wide moat. This house was specifically designed to withstand siege and attack. The main entrance was a stone bridge that led underneath a tower flanked by stone buildings. The other three sides of the house comprised a half-timbered upper storey sitting on a solid stone lower level. There was another, smaller stone bridge at the rear. There were sandbagged gun emplacements on both bridges. There used to be a wooden bridge on one side, but that had obviously been pulled down by the building's new occupants; the National Trust would have had a fit.

One of the teachers used to take junior boys on trips to Ightham and had produced photocopied floor plans for the lessons he gave before the trip. Earlier we had turned Castle upside down and found a pile of these sheets in a store cupboard. The building was a maze, not somewhere you wanted to get involved in close quarters combat.

"This is suicide," I said. "There is no way we are getting in and out of there without getting shot to pieces."

"What this? Nine Lives Keegan walking away from a fight?"

That was his new nickname for me, Nine Lives. Funny guy.

"Yes," I replied. "Always. Whenever humanly possible I walk away from a fight. I don't like fights. They hurt."

"Petts is in there. He's one of our boys. We never leave one of our boys behind."

Grief, he was starting to speak 'Tabloid'.

"Mac, mate, we're schoolboys not Royal Marines. He's probably already dead. And I know it's callous, but chances are some, if not all of us, will die getting him out. Surely one dead, however regrettable, is better than twenty?"

Mac favoured me with a look of total disgust.

"You'd really leave him in there?"

"Considering the odds, yes."

"Then you're not the man I thought you were."

Hang on, I wanted to say, since when did the murdering rapist have any claim to the moral high ground?

"Look," I said. "I agree with you in principle, of course I do. But for fuck's sake, look at that place. What good does it do anyone getting ourselves slaughtered?"

He just ignored me and crawled away. Clearly I was beneath his contempt.

The more I thought about attacking that place the less I liked it. I could see Mac's point about rescuing Petts, it was the only honourable sentiment I'd ever heard him utter, but it was going to get us killed. The power base that Norton was trying to build for a coup was just not strong enough yet, so there was no way of seizing power before the attack. And Mac was riding a wave of post-victory loyalty, so even our progress so far was looking wobbly. The boys had seen Mac's strategy win them a battle, and he'd been in the thick of the fighting, leading from the front. He'd proved himself both clever and brave. Which is, let's face it, what you want in a leader.

Not for the first time I wondered if maybe Mac was the best choice to lead us after all. And not for the first time I recalled Matron's face and Bates' screams, and felt my resolve harden.

Time was of the essence. We needed to devise a plan of attack quickly and efficiently and for that we needed more intelligence. We were clear on the approaches to the house and its internal layout, but we needed to know more about the routines and behaviour of the people who lived there. After all, attacking in force during their daily weapons training drill, the only time of the day when every single person inside is armed to the teeth, would not be a good thing. We needed to know stuff, and the simplest way to find stuff out is to ask. Rather than knock politely on the door and ask the insane cannibals to fill in a survey we decided to wait until someone left and then capture them. We didn't have to wait long.

A group of three young men left the house around midday, armed with machetes and guns, and headed off in the direction of a nearby village. Speight led an ambush in which two of the men were killed, and then rode back to school with the survivor strapped across the back of his horse.

*   *   *

"YOU'LL BLEED FOR this, cattle fucker!"

The man was in his early twenties. His blond hair was slicked back with dried blood and his face, torso and arms were similarly daubed. He stank like a butcher's shop and his breath reeked. Mac had tied him to a chair in an old classroom and was sitting facing him, turning his hunting knife over and over in his hands, saying nothing.

"David will come for me and when he does you'll pay. You'll all pay." This last directed at me and Speight.

"Let me guess," said Mac, impersonating The Count from Sesame Street. "We'll pay... in blood! Mwahahaha!"

Speight chuckled. I rolled my eyes.

"You'll help make us safe. We're chosen. You're nothing."

"This whole 'safe' thing, let me see if I've got this straight," said Mac. "You smear yourself in human blood to protect you against what exactly... the plague?"

"The chosen shall bathe in the blood of the cattle, and they shall eat of their flesh, and they shall be spared the pestilence."

"But you've already survived the pestilence, yeah? I mean, you're O-neg, right? David's O-neg, your blood brothers are all O-neg, your victims are O-neg. You're all immune anyway otherwise you'd be dead, wouldn't you? So what's the fucking point?"

"The pestilence was sent by God to cleanse the Earth. It was The Rapture, don't you see? The worthy were taken up to The Lord and we have been left behind. We are the cursed ones and we must prove ourselves worthy in his sight before the Second Coming. We are living through the seven years of The Tribulation. We must not fail the trials before us or we shall burn in hell forever. David is the prophet of the Second Coming and he shall lead the chosen into Heaven. He anoints us with the blood of the unworthy so that when the pestilence returns to carry off those who have failed in the sight of The Lord we shall be protected from the mutation. We shall live forever, don't you see? When David takes the blood of the cattle and blesses it then it becomes the blood of The Christ and we are cleansed. Hallelujah!"

We just stared. None of us really had an answer for that.

"Um, right," said Mac, for once rendered almost speechless. "Okay. Look, mate, I don't want to get into a philosophical discussion with you and stuff. I just want to know the routine in your little manor house, yeah? What times you eat, what time you put the lights out, guard changes, that sort of stuff. Oh yeah, and where you keep the cattle from Hildenborough locked up. You know, just the basics. Think you can help me out?"

The prisoner appeared to think about this for a moment and then replied: "Piss off."

Mac turned to me and Speight, and beamed. "Finally, fucking finally, I get to torture somebody!"

He turned back and brandished the knife. "Right, you smelly little toerag, I am going to cut you into tiny chunks and feed you to the pigs!"

"Mac, a word," I said. I was still in Mac's bad books but he hadn't demoted me or anything, so I figured I was still persona grata.

"What is it, Nine Lives? I'm busy." He advanced towards the captive.

"Mac, a moment please," I insisted. "Outside."

He turned to look at me. He did not look happy. "This had better be good."

In the corridor I explained my idea to Mac, who thought about it for a moment and then nodded. Speight scurried off to get the necessary torture implements.

"Does this mean I don't get to cut him?" said Mac, disappointed.

"You can, yeah, but not now, eh? Just let me do this, we'll get the info we need, then you can do what you want with him. Fair?"

"All right. This better work though."

"Trust me."

Speight returned and handed the tools over to me. I re-entered the room, with Mac and Speight behind me, and I advanced on the bound prisoner. I placed the torture devices on the bedside cabinet, pulled up a chair, and leaned forward to whisper conspiratorially in the captive's ear.

I told him what I was going to do.

He begged for mercy, but I refused to relent.

I reached into the bowl, pulled out the wet flannel, wrung it out and began to wash the blood from his face.

He screamed.

Not so safe now.

By the time I reached for the shampoo he was telling us everything we wanted to know.

EVERYONE ASSEMBLED IN the briefing room later that evening, in full combats, camouflage on their faces. Guns had already been issued.

The thirty-eight remaining boys, remaining officers, myself and Mac gathered together to plan an attack that I felt sure many of us would not survive.

Mac talked us through his plan and I watched as it dawned on the boys exactly how dangerous this night was going to be for them. Rowles looked terrified, Norton was ashen-faced. Defensive fighting is one thing, but to deliberately pick a fight with a heavily armed force entrenched in a near impregnable fortress is quite another. Mac gave it the hard sell, and nobody refused to participate. And to be fair, the plan could work, with a huge truckload of luck.

As the sun fell we marched out the front door and began the three mile yomp to Ightham Mote, determined to rescue our schoolmate and neutralise a threat that could destroy us.

St Mark's school for boys was going to war.

CHAPTER ELEVEN

THE MAIN ASSEMBLY hall in Castle is full of names. On the wall that used to face the massed school each morning are six large black wooden boards, all hand decorated in blue and gold. The first three list, in chronological order, the Head Boys of the school going back 150 years. The next two list those pupils and teachers from St Mark's who died in The Great War, and the final one lists the Second World War dead.

But these aren't the only names in the main hall. The wooden panelling which clads the walls, deep polished and ancient, has been carved on by generations of boys. From the modern graffiti, simple scratches with a compass, to the old, ornate graffiti, with serifed fonts and punctuation, which must have taken hours of patient work with a penknife, boys have left their mark on St Mark's.

These names tell stories, and one name always fascinated me. James B. Grant carved his name into the wood panel beneath the farthest rear window. It's a beautiful piece of work, one of the most elaborate signatures in the hall. It must have taken him ages. It reads 'James B. Grant, 1913.'

His name also appears on the middle board of Head Boys, which tells us that he was Head Boy for the school year 1912-13; he must have carved his name on the wall in his final week at school, unafraid of punishment.

Finally, his is the last name on the board listing the dead of The Great War. He died in 1918.

A whole life story in three names.

There are pictures of the boys St Mark's sent to war, all dressed up in their corps uniforms. The faded, sepia photographs hang in the corridor that leads to the headmaster's study, each one with a list of names beneath, telling us who these boys were. There is one photograph, of the school corps from 1912, in which every single one of those names is to be found on the list of war dead. Every single one. Even given the slaughter of those years that's a remarkable and tragic clean sweep.

James B. Grant sits front and centre in that photograph. He's wearing puttees and a peaked cap, and he's got a swagger stick lying across his lap. He looks confident but not serious; there's a twinkle in his eye and a slight hint of amusement about the lips. He looks like a man who doesn't take himself too seriously, and I like that about him. He was an officer in the school corps and was doubtless an officer at the front.

When I was much younger I told my dad about this boy, whose name recurred through the fabric of my school. I remember asking him if I'd ever have to go to war, and he said no. He promised me there'd never be another war of conscription, not in my lifetime. The only people who'd go soldiering, he said, were those who'd chosen that life for themselves, like him. I was reassured.

When I had to do a special project for my history GCSE I took Grant as my subject, and I researched his war record. What I discovered horrified me and reinforced my determination that I would never become a soldier, like Grant or my father.

Now I was marching to war like so many boys before me and all I could think about was the tragic fate of James B. Grant.

Because Grant wasn't killed in action.

He was executed.

THE SUN WAS just edging over the horizon as I ran to cover and peered around the corner of the hedge. The two guards on the west bridge hadn't seen me. I gestured to the others and, one by one, Mac, Norton, Wolf-Barry, Speight and Patel hurried across to join me. If we could make it across the five metres of open space in front of us then we'd be out of the guards' line of sight and safe. One of the Blood Hunters' biggest mistakes was trusting the moat to keep them safe – there were no perimeter patrols at all, just the two sets of guards on the east and west bridges.

Dressed only in a pair of shorts, but daubed all over with shoe polish and carrying a plastic bag with clothes and weapons in it, Mac crawled forward across the lawn until the corner of the building shielded him from the bridge. Then he ran to the stone wall that ringed the moat on the north side. We followed quietly and without incident. There had been a wooden bridge entrance on this side of the house, but it had been knocked down by the Blood Hunters. They thought this side of the house was safe from attack.

Mac clambered over the wall and then climbed down the rough stone. He slid into the moat silently, but we heard him give a tiny gasp at the shock of the cold. He trod water until he was acclimatised and then he turned and swam slowly across the moat to the tiny set of stone steps that led down to the water's edge from a small door. He climbed out of the water and stood in the doorway. Once there he opened the plastic bag he'd been carrying and popped on a dry shirt and trousers. He also pulled out his gun and machete.

We watched him climb the three narrow steps and peer through the leaded window into what had been the house's billiard room. There were no lights on, so we couldn't be sure if anyone was in there or not. He used the machete to force the fragile door until it opened with a splintering crack that I felt sure must have been heard. We all crouched there, frozen, listening for sounds of alarm. Nothing. He pushed the door open and stepped into the room, then turned and waved us across. We were in.

A few minutes later all six of us were assembled inside, each of us armed with a gun and a knife that we were hoping we wouldn't have to use. So far we hadn't heard a single sound. Patel, Wolf-Barry and Speight hurried away. Mac, Norton and I waited but we heard no-one raise the alarm. Two minutes later the old longcase clock behind me whirred and chimed six. We heard footsteps overhead.

The Blood Hunters were waking up. Right on time.

Stage one accomplished.

"First in is me, Nine Lives here, Wolf-Barry, Speight, Patel and Norton, coz I'm told he's good in a fist fight, right Norton?"

"Yes sir."

"The two stone bridges on the east and west sides are guarded, but there's another way in they don't have covered. On the north side, out of the sightline of both sets of guards, there's a door in the billiard room that opens onto some steps down to the moat. Nine Lives reckons that when the posh blokes were smoking pipes and playing snooker then the ladies went out this door to a little boat so they could have a row on the moat. Charming, innit? That's our way in.

"Now, the building is square, with all four sides looking down into a big central courtyard. The Blood Hunters get up at six sharp, so we've got to be inside and in place before then, coz that courtyard won't be safe once they're awake. Once inside we split up. Patel and Speight go through the billiard room to the west bridge. There's two men on guard there but they won't be expecting anyone to come at them from inside. It's got to be a knife kill, quick and silent. Think you can manage that?

"Wolf-Barry, you take the east bridge. Same drill, but there's only one man there. Once you've dealt with the guards shove the bodies out of sight behind the sandbags and take their places. In the half light there's a good chance you won't be rumbled. Then signal to Wylie and Pugh in the woods and they'll get to work laying the charges."

THE THREE OF us went left through a large oak door into a stone-floored ante-room. At the end of this room was another door, which led to a small passageway. We had to cross this passageway and enter the door directly opposite us, which would take us into a room once used by visiting school groups. Unfortunately the passageway was open to the courtyard. Although we'd be in shadow we'd be visible to anyone in the courtyard as we made our dash from room to room. Norton looked out the window and indicated that there was no-one around, so Mac cracked open the door and jumped across. Norton followed suit and I went last. As I stepped out into the passageway I heard a noise to my right and froze, flattening myself against the wall, trying to force myself into the shadows.

A group of men and women were making their way across the courtyard. All were dressed casually in jeans and t-shirts. They were gossiping sleepily, rubbing their eyes, off to morning worship in the chapel. If it hadn't been for the dried blood in their hair and on their faces you'd have thought they were students. They entered the building on the far side of the courtyard and I hurried after my comrades. We made our way through an old pantry and then we stopped at the far door. Beyond this door lay a small room and beyond that lay the crypt, where the captives were kept. We were expecting at least one guard on the door.

Mac and Norton drew their knives, stood side by side at the door and, on a silent count of three, opened the door and stepped inside. I heard a brief scuffle and a muffled groan, then nothing. Mac's face appeared at the door, grinning.

I followed them, past the dead body of a young woman, slumped in a corner with her eyes staring into space and her throat slit open. Mac was wiping his knife clean on her shirt.

The next door would lead us into the crypt. With luck there'd be no guards inside, only prisoners. My heart was pumping for all it was worth as I turned the handle and pushed open the door. The crypt was a low-ceilinged room of white stone with a brick floor. Huddled together in this space were around forty people, crammed in tightly, most of them asleep, curled up against each other for warmth.

Stage two accomplished.

"ME, KEEGAN AND Norton will make our way to the crypt. There's two doors to the crypt but only one of them locks, so there's a guard on the one that doesn't. Luckily that's the door closest to our entrance point, so we should be able to take out the guard easy.

"By this point the Blood Hunters should all be safely settled into the big chapel for morning worship, which starts at 6:15 and lasts about half an hour. We should have woken the prisoners and taken control of both bridges by half-past. They'll still be singing hymns and getting ready for the morning sacrifice, which happens at half-past, sharp.

"Now, the sacrifice is chosen the night before and spends the night locked up in the bedroom of the cult leader, David. And yes, before you ask, both boys and girls receive his personal attentions. They're drugged and then brought to the chapel for the morning show. They're blessed as part of the ceremony and then the whole shebang moves from the chapel to the top of the main tower above the west bridge. It's the most important ritual of their day, apparently, and they like to do lots of shouting; y'know, 'hallelujah,' 'praise be,' that sort of cobblers. Point is, they'll be making lots of noise and, apart from the guards on the bridges, who are excused, everyone will be there."

WE CLOSED THE door behind us and scanned the room for Petts. The few captives who were not asleep sat up to take a look at us. I put my finger to my lips and they nodded, becoming alert as they realised what was going on. I recognised most of them from the market at Hildenborough.

"Very quietly, wake the person next to you," I whispered, and the room gradually came to life in a frenzy of shushing. I tiptoed through the half-asleep bodies to the far door and put my ear to it, but could hear no sound outside. I checked my watch. 6:20. Loads of time.

The chapel was on the north side of the house and one floor up, so there was little chance of us being heard, but there was no point taking risks. All three of us moved through the mass of captives whispering for quiet until everyone was awake. We found Petts, alive and well, huddled up with a young girl in the corner. Held prisoner by a blood cult, with nothing to look forward to but a gruesome death, and he had managed to pull. I was impressed. I don't think anyone has ever been so glad to see me in my life. He hugged me, which made me wince as he pressed on my tender stab wound.

"Williams is here, too," he told me.

Shit. I turned to try and find him but I was too late. Mac had him up against the far wall with a knife to his throat. I tried to push my way through the tightly packed crowd to intervene. Williams' eyes were popping out in terror; he must have thought we'd come all this way for revenge.

"You sold us out," Mac hissed.

Williams couldn't say a thing, he just shook with fear.

"Mac, leave him," I said urgently, fighting my way forward. "We don't have time for this."

"You're right," he said. "We don't."

Before I could reach them he drew his knife across Williams' throat. As the boy slid down the wall with a wet, gargled scream, his hands grasping at the gaping wound, trying to push the raw red gash together, trying to push his blood back in, Mac hissed into his face: "That's what we do to traitors."

Before I could react a woman behind me, half awake, unsure what was going on, saw the blood and began to scream.

"They've come for us, they've come for us! Oh God, oh God, I don't want to die."

The man next to her slapped her hard across the face.

"Shut up you stupid cow, we're being rescued." It was the guard from Hildenborough, Mr Cheshire Cheese. He looked up at me, desperate. "We are being rescued, right?"

"Yeah," said Mac. "Just taking care of a little unfinished business. Nothing for you to worry about."

There was a sad, feeble gasp from Mac's feet as Williams breathed his last.

Norton found my gaze and held it. I saw his jaw clench and his eyes widen. His knuckles went white on the grip of his knife.

Now?

Oh, how I wanted to shoot Mac there and then. But there were too many people around; the plan was going too well. It could derail everything and get us killed if I took him out now.

I gave a single, almost imperceptible shake of the head.

Not yet.

Cheshire Cheese stood up, electing himself spokesman for the prisoners.

"You're from the school right?" he said to me. "I remember you."

"I should hope so," I replied. "My execution was the big draw, after all."

"I suppose I should be grateful you survived, then, huh."

"I suppose you should."

"So what's the plan?"

Mac took his small waterproof backpack off, opened it up and started handing out the guns.

While the ten most capable prisoners were selected and armed, Norton got to work on the locked door. That's when things started to go wrong.

"ONCE WE'VE ARMED the prisoners, we get through the locked door, go through one more room, and all we've got to do then is walk out across the east bridge. Then, once we're clear, we blow the bridges, trap the fuckers in their little moated manor house, and burn the place to the ground. Take care of these blood suckers once and for all. Piece of cake."

PLAN A – FORCING the lock – didn't work.

"I can't pick it. This lock is ancient."

Plan B – shoulder charging it – didn't work.

"It's no use, it's too solid, even three of us charging at once can't budge it."

Plan C – shooting out the lock – didn't work.

"Fuck it, they might have heard that. Time to move."

Plan D – blowing the thing open with a grenade and running like hell before the Blood Hunters had time to mobilise – was abandoned when it was pointed out that the crypt was tiny and the explosion would deafen those it didn't kill.

We'd lost five minutes by now, and time was running out.

"Okay, fuck! We'll have to go out across the west bridge," said Mac. "The east bridge is inaccessible. That means we go back the way we came, through the pantry and across the courtyard. We'll be exposed to the chapel, and the top of the tower, so wherever they are by now they'll see us or hear us, but if everyone runs like fuck then we should make it across the courtyard before they can open fire. Once you're across the bridge just run for the tree-line. We've got boys there and you'll get covering fire. Everyone clear?"

People nodded and mumbled nervously.

"Okay, Petts you take point," said Mac, and he opened the door we'd entered through.

Petts went first with Norton, Mac and I ushered the prisoners out after him as swiftly as we could. Not all the prisoners were out of the crypt before we heard gunfire from the courtyard.

Fuck, they weren't wasting any time.

We didn't let the remaining prisoners hesitate, though, we kept pushing them out until the crypt was empty, and then we followed.

About half the prisoners had made it across the courtyard, under the tower and across the bridge. We could see them through the gate, hurrying into the trees. Patel and Speight were stood underneath the tower, at the entrance to the bridge, firing up at the chapel windows directly above us. The Blood Hunters were returning fire.

We stood in the pantry with about twenty terrified people and looked out across the twenty-metre space. There were two people lying dead on the cobbles.

One of them was Petts.

"They'll be fanning out across the building," I shouted. "If we don't move now we'll be caught in a crossfire. So run!" I shoved the prisoners as hard as I could and they stumbled out into the courtyard and ran, heads down, for safety. Mac and Norton helped me shove, as did Cheshire Cheese, and eventually they all made the dash across the exposed space. Two more were shot, the rest made it out.

We four followed hard on the heels of the last man out, but the second we set foot outside, the man in front of us shook and jerked under the impact of a stream of bullets from the billiard room door in the corner on the ground floor. The Blood Hunters had cut us off. We'd never make it to the bridge alive.

We were trapped.

*   *   *

"Now if things go tits up and we get stuck in there I want the fucking ninth cavalry to come storming in and sort it out. You'll be split into two teams and you'll wait under cover by the bridges. If we yell for help you are to come pelting across those bridges and shoot anything that moves. Got it?"

"We're trapped! Move in!" shouted Mac at Speight and Patel. But they turned and ran across the bridge to safety.

"Oi!" called Mac, but they kept running.

We had no choice but to turn and run back the way we'd come. We heard a huge explosion behind us as we ran. They'd blown the bridge.

"Bastards! This way," yelled Mac, and we hared back through the pantry to the doorway of the crypt. Mac yanked a grenade from his pocket, pulled the pin and rolled it to the far door. He closed the door in front of us, waited for the *crump* of the explosion, then ran back into the crypt and through the splintered oak door on the far side. As soon as we ran out of the crypt, bullets began smashing into the thick oak-panelled walls around us. In the time it would have taken us to cross the stairwell we'd have been cut to pieces, so instead of dodging right, past the stairs and into the room that housed the door to the east bridge, we rode our momentum up the flight of stairs that lay directly in front of us.

This was the worst possible thing we could have done. The east bridge was our only possible escape route now, plus the enemy were mostly upstairs – we were being herded right towards them. We made it to the first floor without being cut to pieces, but as we gathered on the landing we heard a shout from our left. I ducked behind the balustrade, Cheshire and Norton took cover in the doorway to the left of the stairs, and Mac crouched down on the bottom of a small flight of stairs that led up to the second floor. Almost as one, we opened fire at a gang of men and women who came running towards us. Two of them fell straight away but the remaining three took cover and returned fire.

When you're fighting outside you can hide behind walls, cars, trees and things, all of which will easily stop a bullet. But wattle and daub walls with a bit of lime plaster, doorframes and balustrades made up of wooden struts with great big gaps between them, don't provide the best cover.

The sound was deafening. Bullets were flying everywhere and splinters of wood and chunks of plaster smacked into my face and head. The smoke and dust soon filled the hallway with a fog that made accurate shooting impossible. Everyone was firing blind.

Then I heard a yell from behind me and I turned to find Cheshire and Norton struggling with a pair of men. I grabbed my machete and rose to my feet, heedless of the ordnance whizzing past me. One attacker had Cheshire by the throat and was throttling him. I hacked at the man's head and felt a sickening crunch as the blade embedded itself in his cranium. He fell backwards. Norton bucked and rolled and his attacker was suddenly on the floor. Norton shot him in the face and then twisted in the air as a bullet smashed into his right shoulder. He spun straight into Cheshire's arms.

"Mac," I shouted. "We need to go up!"

There were running footsteps approaching from both left and right, so we legged it up the small flight of stairs to the second floor, Cheshire helping Norton. This was the part of the house that had been closed to the public, devoted to private apartments by the National Trust, so we had no map to guide us. We were running blind, but at least we were above our pursuers. With luck there'd be nobody up here.

We were on a landing with four doors leading off it, so we opened the first door and ran inside. We found ourselves in a living room; plush sofas, deep pile carpet, old TV in the corner. There were three mullioned windows along the far wall and Cheshire dumped Norton on the floor and ran to open one of them. Mac and I pushed the sofa across one door and a sideboard across another. We heard the clatter of pursuit up the stairs and the sound of bullets hitting the door.

"Those doors are solid oak," I said. "Bullet-proof unless they've got a heavy machine gun. They won't blow them either, 'cause this floor is all wood and they won't risk burning the place down."

"Great," said Mac. "So they can't get in, but we can't get out."

"Oi!" Cheshire was shouting out the window, across the moat. "We could use some help here."

Mac and I ran to join him. We could just make out a group of boys and prisoners in the trees, milling around. There seemed to be an argument going on but we couldn't hear. A burst of gunfire came from the floor below us, and they ducked. That obviously made their minds up, because a few seconds later the East Bridge, below us and to the left, exploded in a shower of stone and mortar.

"We are so fucked," said Norton, who had joined us at the window, his shoulder a bloody mess and his face white as a sheet.

He was right, we were fucked. And it was all Mac's fault.

I stood and looked at the man who'd led us to this place. I thought about Matron and Bates; I remembered the twitching corpses of the TA guys, Dave, Derek and the one whose name I'd never know; I saw Williams clutching his gushing throat.

I felt the weight of the gun in my hand.

ON THE MORNING of March 24th 1918, James B. Grant was part of a group of men leading an assault on a copse somewhere in Belgium. There was a German machine gun emplacement in this small group of trees and it was holding up some advance or other. Grant and his men were instructed to remove this obstacle.

Although Grant was a Lieutenant he was not in charge of that particular assault. A new officer, William Snead, fresh from Oxford and Sandhurst, was in command. It was his first week at the front and he was eager to prove himself a hero, keen to win his first medal. His naiveté and reckless enthusiasm made him dangerous.

Grant had been serving with that group of men for years. They had seen terrible things; survived the battle of the Somme, lost friends and comrades by the score, trudged through mud and blood 'til they were more exhausted than I can imagine. But they trusted each other, even loved each other, in the way that men who've risked their lives together do.

So when Snead ordered them to make a frontal assault on an entrenched machine gun nest, a strategy that offered both the greatest chance of glory and the near certainty of pointless death, Grant tried to talk him out of it. They should circle around the gun, he said, approach under cover of darkness, and lob a grenade in. Simple, effective, risk-free.

Snead was having none of it. He accused Grant of cowardice. A shouting match ensued, the privates got involved and Snead, suddenly fearful, drew his Webley revolver and threatened to execute Grant on the spot for desertion in the face of the enemy. Confronted by the muzzle of an officer's gun, Grant backed down. He apologised, prepared to mount the assault as ordered.

And then, as the men readied themselves to attack, Grant shot Snead in the back.

The German position was taken and Snead was listed as the only casualty of the engagement. Grant had saved the lives of his men in the only way available to him. It was an act of heroism in the face of leadership so stupid that it beggared belief.

But Grant couldn't live with himself and the knowledge of what he'd done. He surrendered to his commanding officer, made a full confession, and was executed at dawn the next morning.

As was the custom for cowards and traitors, Grant's name was left off the roll of honour. He was only added to the list of war dead in St Mark's main hall after one of Grant's surviving men pleaded his case with the headmaster of the time.

I wonder how many other St Mark's boys died in the war whose names were not listed. How many were shot at dawn for cowardice as they twitched and shuddered from shell shock; how many were gunned down where they stood because they refused to go over the top to certain, pointless death; how many were executed for refusing to take orders from upper class idiots who were trying to fight entrenched armies with machine guns as if they were Zulus with spears.

Hammond had tried to commemorate those boys who had died in The Cull, but who would paint and hang a roll of honour for those who had survived? Who would paint Petts' name onto black board, or Belcher's, or Williams', or the rest of those boys killed in yet another pointless war they had little choice but to fight?

Who would paint Mac's name?

Who would paint mine?

As I raised my gun and brought it to bear on the man who had appointed himself my leader, I knew exactly how Grant had felt, nearly a century before me. I knew the anger and resentment of someone forced to follow orders that are cruel, cowardly and wrong. I felt the righteous hatred of a man who believed in justice and honour slaved to a ruler who cared only for power. I felt the despair of a man who longed for peace forced to resort to violence because of the madness of others.

I realised that my days of following orders were done.

So I pulled the trigger and shot the bastard.

CHAPTER TWELVE

HE DIDN'T FALL down. The bullet hit him in the left forearm. Not where I was aiming, but my hands were shaking so much it's lucky I hit him at all. Why couldn't I be like Grant; cool under pressure, calmly ruthless?

We looked at each other, neither of us knowing what to do next. The hole in his arm started to leak. He raised his gun to fire back so I shot him again. I hit him in the right shoulder. This time he fell down.

"Drop it!" shouted Cheshire, raising his gun to cover me.

I stood there, staring at Mac, who had fallen backwards and was sitting on the floor with his back against the sofa. He'd dropped his gun and was trying to put pressure on the wounds to stop the bleeding, but neither of his arms was working properly.

Norton walked over to Cheshire, reached out and gently pushed the gun down.

"Leave him," he said.

I'd killed three people in the last few months. One I could justify to myself as a mercy killing. The other was kill or be killed. The third had been in the heat of battle. But shooting Mac without warning, without any immediate threat to myself, in cold blood... that was different. I wasn't sure of my own motives any more. Had I shot him to save the school? Was I taking revenge for Matron and Bates? Or was I punishing him for what he'd done to me, what he'd made me into?

I looked down at the smoking Browning in my right hand. I couldn't work out what it was doing there. I used to hate guns, I thought. How is it that this thing feels so natural? When did I become someone who always carries a gun? I relaxed my fingers and it fell to the floor.

Mac was fumbling, trying to find some way of repairing the damage. His arms flapped and spasmed uselessly.

I crouched down so I was on the same level as Mac.

"It doesn't hurt yet, but it will," I said. "At the moment you've got so much adrenaline going through you that your body's not letting you feel the pain. I don't know for sure, but I suppose that if you die you might never feel it. It's only if you survive and heal that it hurts."

He looked up at me. If I was expecting confusion or fear I was disappointed. There was only fury.

"You fucking coward," he said. "You pathetic, weak, stupid fucking coward."

The noise from outside had stopped the instant I'd pulled the trigger. I could hear people running back down the stairs. They must have left a guard on the door, but for now they'd stopped trying to get in.

"What is going on here?" demanded Cheshire.

"Call it a coup," said Norton as he sat down in an armchair. "Can you pass me that tablecloth, please."

Cheshire pulled the cloth off the table and began helping Norton to dress his wound.

"Why now?" asked Mac. "Why wait until we're alone and trapped and probably going to die anyway? What is the fucking point of doing it now?"

I didn't have an answer to that.

"I'll tell you, shall I," he went on. "I reckon..." he broke off as a violent coughing fit seized him. "I reckon you were hoping they'd do your job for you."

"Perhaps," I conceded.

"Coward," he said again. "I told you the rules. I explained how this works. You want me out the way you fucking challenge me like a man."

"Like you challenged Bates?"

"Bates was weak. He didn't understand, didn't deserve the respect. I thought you understood. I thought you got it."

"I get it, I just don't accept it. If I played it your way, by your rules I'd be buying into your bullshit, accepting this strong tribal leader bollocks," I said. "If I challenged you and proved myself the harder bastard then all I'd be doing was extending an invitation to some other hard fucker to come along and knock me off."

"That's how it works."

"I don't accept that. And you know what, the rest of the boys don't either. You might not have noticed, but they've left us – you – here to die. First chance they got, they cut you loose."

"So what's your alternative, eh?" he sneered. "You gonna run the school as a democracy? Student councils? Tea and scones and cricket on the green? Fucking fantasist."

His face was white as chalk. His ruined shoulder made an awful grinding sound as he tried to lever himself into a more comfortable sitting position.

"I don't know what it'll be like, but it's got to be better than rapes and crucifixions. There won't be executions. Boys won't be bullied and tormented."

"And my officers? You gonna deal with them?"

"If I need to."

He laughed bitterly. "Brilliant. Lee Keegan's brave new world kicks off with a group execution. You fucking hypocrite."

He was right. I knew that. But I was in no mood to argue any more.

"Your problem," I said, "is that you thought you were only vulnerable to someone stronger than you. But you never thought you might be vulnerable to someone smarter."

He gave a bitter laugh, which turned into another fit of coughing. His left sleeve was soaked with blood. It ran down his fingers and soaked into the carpet.

"The smart thing to do would have been to shoot me before we even attacked."

There was that tone of contempt again. I thought of James B. Grant and I knew that Mac was right.

Norton tried to interrupt but I waved for silence.

"I know that," I said. "But unlike you I try to avoid killing people."

He laughed again. "Tell that to the guy at the foot of the stairs with half a head. You're a killer, kid. Stone cold. You just don't want to admit it. Your problem, Nine Lives, is that you never want to do anything. You wanted to leave Petts here to die..."

"He's dead anyway."

"Not the fucking point and you know it," he shouted. "You want me out of the way but you can't pluck up the courage to challenge me like a man so you wait for someone else to take me out of the picture. And when that doesn't happen you figure, screw it, what've I got to lose, and you just fucking shoot me. And then, to add insult to fucking injury, you shoot me in the bloody arms! What's the matter, bullet to the head too fucking easy?"

"Don't tempt me."

"Oh, piss off. Like you've got the guts to finish me off." He leaned forward. "Come on then," he whispered. "Pick up the gun. It's right there. Still loaded. One bullet and it's all over. Come on. Finish what you started. Show me you've got the backbone to be leader. Prove it to me. Come on. Look me in the eye when you pull the trigger. Come on!"

Without thinking about it I reached behind me, picked up the gun and pressed the muzzle against his forehead. I pressed hard. God, I wanted to kill him. I mean really, *really* wanted to kill him. I wanted to watch him die screaming. I wanted to laugh in his dying eyes and spit on his corpse. I actually smiled as I began to squeeze the trigger.

And then I saw the look of triumph in his eyes.

"Maybe you're right," I said. "Maybe I am a coward, maybe I was afraid. But I wasn't afraid of you, Mac. Not really. I was afraid of becoming like you."

I threw the gun aside. Mac laughed in my face, soundlessly.

"Face it Lee, you'll never be like me. You haven't got the balls."

I heard a tiny metallic ping.

"Lee!" shouted Norton in alarm.

I felt something pressing itself against my stomach. I looked down and saw Mac's left hand holding a grenade. The pin was on the floor beside us.

I looked up. Mac was smiling.

"I'm holding down the lever, Lee. When I let go the chemical fuse starts and then nothing can stop it exploding seven seconds later. Reckon you can wrestle the grenade off me and throw it out the window in that time?"

I stared into his eyes as I reached down and wrapped my hand around his. There was little strength in his fingers; his shattered shoulder saw to that. As long as I kept squeezing he couldn't release the lever. We were at an impasse.

"You don't have to die here, you know," I said. "We can still get out of this, take you back to school, try and patch you up."

"And then what?"

"You leave. Just go."

Again with the laughing.

"Spineless wanker. You shot me in cold blood and there's no fixing that. At least have the integrity to live with it. I'm never leaving this room and you know it. But I can make sure you never do either."

I don't know how long we'd have sat there if Cheshire hadn't intervened.

He walked over to us, casual as can be, and then rammed his rifle butt into Mac's shoulder wound. He screamed and jerked in agony, and I slipped the grenade from his grasp. I picked up the pin and re-inserted it.

I think I'd been hyperventilating because I had a huge head rush as I stood up. Cheshire reached out to steady me until the world stopped spinning.

When Mac stopped screaming he looked up at me and sneered.

"What did I ever do to you, Nine Lives? What do you hate me so fucking much?"

"You made me a killer, Mac."

"Oh, I see. So basically, I shot myself, yeah?" He shook his head in disbelief. "Jesus, you are fucked in the head."

"Can we focus, please," said Norton, who had tied his arm tight into a sling and appeared to have stopped the bleeding. "Does anyone actually have a plan to get us out of here?"

"Maybe," I replied. "But the silence is bothering me. What can you see out the window?

Cheshire poked his head outside and leapt backwards as bullets ripped into the glass.

"Missed!" he shouted. He turned to me. "They're covering the window from the tower."

I walked to the door and knocked on it.

"Anyone out there?" I asked.

There was a pause.

"Um, yeah. Hi," came the tentative reply. It was a young man's voice.

Norton sniggered and started me giggling. Borderline hysteria.

"Hi yourself. So, you guarding this door to stop us escaping then, yeah?"

"There's three of us and we've got guns."

"Good to know. The others gone off to the morning sacrifice have they?"

"Got to purify the moat."

"Great." I turned back to Norton and Cheshire. "They're all going to be on the tower for a while, so we've got some time to prepare."

"Any chance of a cuppa while I'm waiting to die?" said Mac, witheringly.

The morning sacrifice was one of the Blood Hunters' more disturbing rituals. The selected victim was brought to morning worship and blessed by David, then everybody processed up to the tower. David then slit the victim's throat and two acolytes dangled the poor sod over the battlements so they bled into the moat. Fresh blood in the water every morning kept them safe, they reckoned.

Serenaded by singing and screams from the tower I opened Mac's backpack and we got to work. It took about ten minutes or so, but by the time the ritual was finished we were ready. Cheshire had picked Mac up and put him on the sofa. He was still conscious.

"You haven't got a cat in hell's chance," he said.

I ignored him.

"Hey, Norton," he went on. "How long you been planning this little takeover?"

"Since day one."

"Traitor."

"What you gonna do, slit my throat, like you did to Williams?"

"Come over here and I'll show you."

"Enough, already," I said. "Does everyone know what they're doing?"

Norton and Cheshire nodded.

"What shall I do, Nine Lives?" gasped Mac, sarcastically.

"Fuck off and die."

We heard footsteps on the stairs. A group of people coming to talk. Then a voice I recognised.

"Hello in there." It was their leader, David.

"Morning," I replied, cheerily. "Lovely day for a blood sacrifice."

"Are any of you hurt?"

"Why do you care?"

"We have first class medical facilities. If you open the door I give you my word your wounded will be given the proper treatment."

"What, no bleeding?"

He laughed. "Of course there'll be bleeding. Got to be made safe. But we need fresh, clean, healthy blood. So we'll make you better first. While there's life there's hope, isn't that what they say?"

"I've got a better idea. We want to convert. We want you to make us safe."

"Sorry. No initiations today."

"They've got a bomb," yelled Mac. I punched him in the face as hard as I could. I felt the cartilage in his nose shatter. Felt good.

"One more word and I'll finish you now," I hissed.

"Like you've got the guts," he replied, and spat in my face.

So I took my Browning and I smashed him over the back of the head, knocking him out.

"Everything all right in there?"

"Fine. We're just, um, conferring."

I gathered up the strings we had taken from the window blinds and backed towards the open windows, where Norton and Cheshire were already waiting.

"Ready?"

They nodded.

"All right, we agree. Come and get us," I shouted. Then we all three turned and leapt out through the windows.

The gunmen on the tower opened fire. As I fell I took the string with me. I felt a slight resistance at the other end and then it came free and sailed out the window after me, with the pins of all our remaining grenades attached to it.

We hit the bloodied water before any of the bullets could find their mark, and the room above us exploded while we were still submerged. Stone, glass, wood and furniture crashed into the water all around us as we swam for safety.

The fire, smoke and confusion that reigned in the building behind us masked our clumsy emergence from the water, using the rubble from the exploded bridge as a ramp. We made it to the tree-line safely. The other boys and the Hildenborough captives were long gone. I stood in the shadow of the trees and watched the conflagration take hold of the fragile wooden house.

Mac was in there. The explosion had probably killed him, and if he'd miraculously survived the blast then his wounds would probably finish him off. Either way, he was gone for good. Everything had gone according to plan. I'd gained his trust, lulled him into a false sense of security, and betrayed him. I was a traitor, pure and simple. I hated myself for it. Mac had been right, I was a coward. I'd opposed him because I'd never accepted that the ends justified the means, and yet look at what I'd done. In order to get rid of Mac I'd betrayed every principle I'd ever held dear. I'd lied and cheated, betrayed trust and committed murder.

But the school was free of him now, and with the Blood Hunters burning in front of me, and Hildenborough ravaged and leaderless, there was no-one around to threaten us. At least for a while.

The means had been despicable, but the end had been achieved. Still, I wondered whether I hadn't failed in one crucial thing: preventing myself from becoming the thing I hated. After everything I'd done I couldn't help but feel that I was that little bit more like Mac than I'd ever wanted to be. I didn't know how I was ever going to come to terms with any of this.

I'd killed two people today and seen many more die. As I watched the fire I prayed that this was the last I would see of killing.

Should've known better, really.

LESSON THREE
HOW TO BE A LEADER

CHAPTER THIRTEEN

"WASN'T MY FAULT. They were bigger than we were."

Wylie was making excuses, but his heart wasn't in it. Like all the best bullies he was a coward at heart. It turns out the boys hadn't blown the bridges to get rid of Mac and me. The adults from Hildenborough, scared out of their wits, some of them armed (by us), had demanded that the boys blow the bridges immediately. Wylie, who'd been in charge of that part of the operation, had agreed.

I was wet through, cold, tired and very, very pissed off.

"You left us to die," I said, through gritted teeth.

"You look fine to me." Cocky little shit.

I raised the Browning and pointed it at his face. He hadn't expected that.

"Give me your gun," I said.

"You what?"

I twitched the gun sideways an inch and fired a shot past his right ear. He jumped, yelled and backed away.

"What the fuck are you doing, man?"

"I won't ask again."

He threw the rifle at me. I let it fall to the floor.

"Here, have it you fucking psycho." His shout was half whine, like a spoiled brat being told to give back the car keys.

I didn't lower my gun.

"How old are you, Wylie?"

He glanced left and right looking for support or a way of escape. I had him cornered.

"Seventeen. Why?" he said. Half petulance, half defiance.

"And how many men have you killed?"

His eyes widened as he felt a jolt of genuine fear.

"Just the one."

"One kneeling man with his hands tied. What, you didn't off a few more when the Hildenborough men attacked?"

"My... my gun jammed."

I laughed.

"Not what I heard."

Rowles had found him cowering in the art room. He hadn't told anyone but me because he was too afraid of what Wylie would do to him if he blabbed.

"Fuck you! I'm a sixth-former! And a prefect!" He was starting to cry.

"That's right. And I'm only fifteen. But I've killed four people, two of them this morning. So who do you think is the scariest person in this room?"

He sniffled.

I chambered another round.

"Who do you think is the scariest person in this room?"

I fired a shot past his left ear.

"You. You are, all right. You." His lower lip was trembling.

I nodded.

"Right again. I am. I am the scariest person in this room."

I was having fun. I'd have been worried by that if I'd stopped to think about it. But I didn't. I was enjoying myself too much.

"You're a bully, Wylie. And a coward. I don't like cowards much. But I hate bullies."

His nose started to run.

"But do you know what I hate even more than bullies, Wylie? Do you?"

He shook his head. Mingled snot and tears dripped off his wobbling chin.

I walked right up to him and pressed the gun against his temple. He let out a low moan of fear.

"The one thing I hate more than bullies," I said. "Is anyone who was in the room when Matron was raped."

He looked like he was about to shit himself.

"It... it... it wasn't my idea. It was Mac... he made us... he had a gun and everything."

"Don't. Care."

"I had to! I didn't enjoy it. Honest. I didn't enjoy it all. Really."

"Not an excuse."

"What... what are you going to do to me?"

"Haven't decided yet. I reckon it's a choice between shooting you in the back of the head or crucifying you. Do you have a preference?"

His knees buckled and he fell to the floor, snivelling and moaning. I knelt down beside him and whispered in his ear.

"I'm inclined to crucify you myself, but it's time-consuming and a bit of a drag. Probably easier to just shoot you. What do you think?"

"I'm sorry, all right?" he cried. "I'm sorry, I'm sorry!"

I yelled into his ear as loud as I could: "I don't care!"

He cowered against the wall.

"Choose!"

"Oh God."

"Choose!"

"Please, no, I'm sorry, please." He buried his face in his hands and curled up into a foetal ball, wracked with sobs.

"Fine," I said. "A bullet it is."

I grabbed him by the shoulder and hauled him to his feet. He made a half-hearted attempt to resist, so I kneed him in the balls. Then I herded him down the corridor and out the front door. He could barely walk for pain and terror.

I kicked him down the steps and he sprawled in the gravel, clawing for purchase. He tried to get up, but the best he could manage was to crawl away on all fours. I sauntered after him. When he reached the grass I planted a foot in the small of his back and he collapsed onto the turf.

"Kneel," I said.

He let out a cry of anguish and scratched at the dirt.

"Kneel!"

I bent down and grabbed him, pulling him up until he was kneeling in front of me. The second I let go he toppled sideways. I kicked him in the ribs as hard as I could.

"Kneel, you pathetic little shit."

I pulled him up again and this time he stayed in position. He shuddered and shook, gasped and wept.

"This is pretty much the spot where you executed that helpless, unarmed man, isn't it? Kind of fitting you should die here too."

He started to beg.

"Please, oh, God please don't. Please don't."

"Is that what she said, huh? Is that what Matron said?"

I pressed the hot muzzle of the gun against the nape of his neck. He screamed.

"Is it?"

I let him sweat for a good minute or two before I pulled the trigger. After all, he didn't know I'd used all my bullets.

"Was that necessary?" asked Norton, as we watched Wylie limp out of the school gates. I gestured to the faces pressed against the windows of the school behind us.

"Yes."

I LOOKED AT the faces of the boys before me. They looked so tired. They hadn't slept all night and they'd marched three miles expecting to go into battle. In the end they'd only been shot at from a distance before being threatened by a bunch of fear-crazed adults, but it must have been terrifying for them, especially the little ones.

It wasn't just the events of the past twenty-four hours, though. These were boys whose lives had been calm and orderly before The Cull. They'd lived every day according to a rigid timetable set down for them by distant, unapproachable grown-ups. They'd played games and sat in lessons, pretended to be soldiers on Fridays and occasional weekends. They'd eaten set meals at set times and known months in advance exactly what they'd be doing at any given day and time.

Of course there had been bullies, beatings and detentions, but unless Mac was the bully in question it never went too far. And Matron had always been there to give them a hug and put a plaster on whatever cut or bruise they'd received.

But for the past few months things had been very different. They'd seen their parents die and had run back to the one refuge they could think of. They'd hoped to find safety in the familiar routine of St Mark's. Instead they'd killed men in combat, seen their teachers and friends die before them, been bullied and abused, subject to the whims of a gang of armed thugs who'd ordered them about day and night. They'd been trained for war and had learnt to live with the expectation of their own imminent deaths.

I was looking at an entire room of young boys with post-traumatic stress disorder. And I was supposed to lead them.

I didn't have a clue where to begin.

"Mac's dead," I told them. I had expected some response; a few cheers, perhaps. But all I could see were dead eyes and dull faces.

"As his second-in-command I'm in charge and things are going to be different around here. Right now I want you all to get some sleep. Leave your guns at the door and go to bed. There'll be cold food available in the dining room for anyone who wants it, but your time is your own until tomorrow morning. Just... relax, yeah?"

I waited for them to leave, but they just sat there. I looked at Norton, confused.

"Dismissed," he said.

"Sorry. Dismissed."

As the boys got up I added: "Oh, and no more army kit, all right? You can wear your own clothes from now on. We'll collect the uniforms tomorrow and they can go back in the stores."

The boys shuffled out in silence.

When they'd gone I was left alone with Norton, Mrs Atkins and the remaining officers: Wolf-Barry, Pugh, Speight, Patel and Green.

"Gather round everyone," I said.

They all came and took chairs at the front. I sat down too.

"You all saw what happened to Wylie earlier, yes?"

The officers nodded.

"Good. You were meant to. Mac would have shot him, but I let him go. That's the difference between me and Mac; I'm not so keen on killing. But I want to make it perfectly clear to you that I will see you dead and buried if you disobey a direct order from me. Understood?"

The boys mumbled and nodded.

"In which case I want you all to pile your guns in the corner and sit back down."

They did so.

"Good. Rowles!"

The door opened and Rowles entered, holding a rifle. The officers flashed me confused glances.

"What's going on?" asked Wolf-Barry, suddenly nervous.

"You're leaving," I said. "All of you. Right now."

"You what?" said Patel.

"I said you are leaving. *Now*. Out the gate and don't look back. I don't ever want to see any of your faces on these grounds again. *Ever*. 'Cause if I or any of the other boys see you inside these walls again we will shoot to kill without hesitation. Understand? And count yourselves lucky. I've fantasised about killing each and every one of you in all sorts of creative ways. But there's been enough death for one day, I don't think I could stomach any more."

"Now look here..." Speight rose to protest.

There was the unmistakable sound of a gun being shouldered ready for firing. He turned and saw Rowles taking aim.

"Permission to shoot, sir?" asked the junior boy.

Speight froze as I made a play of considering the request.

"Escort these men from the grounds, Rowles. If any of them resist you have permission to shoot."

Nobody moved. The officers looked confused and scared.

"But where will we go?" said Pugh.

"Somewhere else. Anywhere else. Just not here," I replied.

"You're not going to fire that gun are you, Rowles?" said Patel. He rose to his feet and started walking towards the boy, his hand outstretched. Rowles smiled one of the scariest smiles I've ever seen. I wondered what had happened to the quiet, scared little boy who'd hung on Bates' every word.

"Try me," he said.

Patel, wisely, thought again.

"Enough," I barked. "I want you all out of here immediately. You are expelled."

I was relieved when they made to leave. I hadn't wanted any more violence today.

"Green, stay behind a minute," I said, as he reached the door. The other officers made their way outside. I gestured for Green to sit down. He looked petrified as he did so. I regarded him for a moment before asking: "Why do they call you Limpdick, Green?"

"I don't know, sir," he mumbled.

"Please don't waste my time. I'm tired and I want to have a cup of tea and go to bed. The sooner I can finish here the sooner I can relax. So, I ask you again, why do they call you Limpdick?"

He stared at his feet and mumbled a reply.

"'Cause of Matron."

"You were there when she was attacked?"

He nodded.

I swallowed hard. I didn't want to know the details, but I had to ask.

"Did they all take a turn?"

He nodded.

"But you couldn't, yes?"

He nodded again.

"Are you gay, Green, or just a fucking wimp?"

That got a reaction.

"Fuck you!" he shouted, suddenly defiant. "Just 'cause I don't get off on raping somebody doesn't make me gay, all right?! I liked Matron. What happened in that room wasn't right. It just... wasn't right. I told Mac I wouldn't do it, I argued with him, but they teased me and… they had guns. They made me take off my trousers and lie on top of her. And she was just staring at the ceiling. I kept apologising to her but she wouldn't look at me. I couldn't do it. I just couldn't do it."

Tears welled in his eyes.

"And the man you killed?"

He broke down.

"Mac said he'd shoot me," he sobbed.

I sighed heavily. Good.

"Okay. That's what I thought. I just needed to be sure."

I got up and went to sit next to him. I put my hand on his shoulder. He shrugged it off resentfully and stared back down at his shoes.

"Will you stay here, with us?" I asked.

He looked up at me, confused, and wiped away the tears.

"But I thought…"

"We're going to get Matron tomorrow. If she corroborates your story, and I'm sure she will, then we'd be glad to have you. We need people like you here. Petts is dead, so you'll have to recast, but God knows we could use some entertainment to take our minds off everything. So stay, put on your play. Yeah?"

I held out my hand. He took it and we shook.

When he was gone Mrs Atkins smiled at me.

"Not a bad start," said Norton. "Not bad at all. Now can I please go and sort out this fucking bullet wound before my arm falls off."

WHILE NORTON GOT himself patched up I went to my room and changed out of my wet clothes. Peeling off the muddy, half-dried uniform was like uncovering a map of my recent escapades.

I had a scar on my left calf where Jonah had bitten me; a puckered red hole in my right thigh where I'd been shot; a bandage around my waist where I'd stabbed myself; a deep purple welt across my throat where the rope had cut into me; my torso and arms were covered in bruises; my right eye was blackened, my left cheekbone was blue and I had long scab on my cheek from Baker's signet ring, which would probably scar as well.

I was a complete mess.

I collapsed onto my bed. I was so tired I felt like I could sleep for a week, but my mind was racing. I had done it. Mac was gone, our enemies were defeated. Before Cheshire (his name, it turned out, was Bob) had gone back to Hildenborough he'd assured me that the two communities would be allies from now on. My job now was to find a way to mend the school. Tomorrow I'd go to the farm where Matron and the girls had sought refuge and see about bringing them back to Castle. Mrs Atkins had told me that there were twenty girls there now, under Matron's protection. We could use the fresh blood; this place was altogether too male.

Not that I wanted to do away with everything Mac had achieved. The school had withstood an attack from a force that had been well prepared for our defences, and in all the time he'd been in charge there'd been very little dissent or division. I had to try and use community building and reconstruction to maintain the unity that he had achieved through fear and force.

I would need my own officers, but I wasn't going to keep the military structure. There would have to be guard patrols and so forth, and they'd have to wear combats and carry guns, but for everyone else we'd go back to normal clothes and activities. We'd start lessons again, organise some round robin sports tournaments, foster a sense of structure and order that didn't come from a strict military outlook. St Mark's should start to feel like a school again, not an army camp.

Norton would be my right hand man, and Rowles would be the spokesman for the junior boys. I'd divvy up jobs to those boys that wanted them, delegate responsibilities. The deaths of Petts and Williams had left the garden and livestock with only Heathcote to tend them; he would need help. Riding was going to be our main form of transport now, so we needed to try and round up some more horses for Haycox to look after. We should try and find some glass to re-glaze the windows broken in the attack, too. Couldn't have the rain getting into the building.

And there was the Blood Hunter we'd taken prisoner. By the time I'd finished washing him he was gibbering and hysterical. He was still locked in a store cupboard, raving about the Second Coming.

There was so much to do.

Maybe, if I kept myself busy enough, I could prevent myself dwelling on the things I'd seen and done. Maybe I'd go to bed so tired each night that I'd be able to sleep without nightmares.

Maybe.

THE NEXT MORNING I put on a pair of old Levis and a t-shirt. It felt odd to be back in normal clothes. Comforting, though. I ignored my tough leather boots and put on a battered old pair of trainers. Luxury.

I went downstairs to the refectory and helped myself to some water and a slice of fresh bread. We hadn't got any yeast, so it was flat bread, but it was still warm and delicious. I walked across the courtyard to the old kitchen, where Mrs Atkins was already baking the second batch of the day.

"Mrs Atkins, that smells wonderful and you are a marvel," I said. I cleared away a pile of cookbooks and perched on the work surface.

"You sound chipper," she said.

"I can't remember the last time I woke up feeling good about the day," I replied. "But the sun's shining, we've got fresh bread and eggs for breakfast, and as far as I can tell nobody's trying to kill us. There'll be no drill today, no weapons training or marching, no assault course ordeals, gun battles, executions or fights. I think tomorrow I may spend the whole day just sitting in the sun reading a book. Can you imagine? Actually sitting and reading a book in the sun. In jeans! Today is going to be a good day, mark my words, Mrs Atkins. It's a new start. I warn you, I may even get down off this table and give you a hug."

"Don't you dare," she said, but she was laughing in spite of herself. "If you leave me alone to finish this batch of bread and get the breakfast done I'll see you later and tell you where Matron and the girls are. Deal?"

"Done!"

I jumped down, ran over and gave her a big kiss on the cheek. She threw a wooden spoon at me so I left. I might have been whistling.

The boys wandered down to breakfast in ones and twos over the course of the next hour. With everyone dressed in normal clothes again the refectory looked welcoming and normal. Mrs Atkins' scrambled eggs, collected from our chicken enclosure, were delicious. With no drill scheduled or battles to fight, the boys were all at a loose end, and they hung around the refectory when they'd finished eating, waiting to see what would happen.

I stood on the table at the top of the room and cleared my throat.

"Morning everyone. Looks a lot nicer in here without all the camouflage gear! Now, I know we should have a timetable and stuff, and I'll be sorting one out soon, but I think we should have a day off, yeah? I don't want anyone leaving the school grounds, and Norton is going to organise a few of you into guard patrols, but for today let's just relax and enjoy ourselves. Go play football, swim in the river, go fishing, read a book, whatever you want to do is fine. Dinner and supper will be at the usual time and I'd like everyone to gather here at six this evening. We should have Matron back by then and I'm sure she'll want to say hello to you all. But until then bugger off and have some fun. You've earned it."

"You should have been a red coat," muttered Norton when I sat down again. "Let's go have tea and scones on the lawn and play croquet. And maybe we can have lashings of ginger beer and get into some scrapes."

"Piss off."

"Yes sir, three bags full sir."

"How's your arm?"

"Unbelievably painful, but I don't think there's any major damage. I've stitched and sterilised it. Not going to be playing rugby any time soon, though."

"Fancy coming with me to get Matron?"

"Nah. Bouncing up and down on a horse doesn't really appeal. I'll be here, taking many, many painkillers and bestowing the gift of my withering sarcasm on the juniors."

"Just be careful Rowles doesn't shoot you."

"I know! When did he get scary?"

"I think he killed someone in the fight with Hildenborough. I have a horrible feeling he kind of enjoyed it."

That grim thought stopped our banter dead.

As I walked out to the paddock there was a football match kicking off on the rear playing field; one boy was walking off to the river carrying a fishing rod; and the third formers had a beatbox on, using up precious battery power playing music as loud as they possibly could. It was just like an ordinary Saturday in term-time. But with fewer children, and no teachers to spoil the fun.

Haycox was tending the horses. We had five now, all of which were happy to be ridden. He'd had converted one of the old stables back to its original use, and all the animals had warm quarters for when the weather changed. Each had its own saddle and bridle set, too, which Haycox polished and oiled. As long as he was left alone to look after the horses he was a very contented boy indeed. I'd been riding since I was ten, it was one of the extra activities the school offered on weekends, but with my wounded side and tender leg I found it hard going. The ride to Ightham and back for reconnaissance the day before yesterday had been agony; I'd been happier when we'd walked there *en masse*.

Nonetheless, I asked Haycox to saddle three of the horses for a short trip. He gathered up their reins and led them back to the courtyard.

There was one task I'd been putting off all morning, and I couldn't delay it any longer. I walked across Castle to the headmaster's old quarters. The door was locked. I suddenly saw an image of the keys, in Mac's pocket, burnt into the dead flesh of his thigh in the smouldering ruins of Ightham Mote.

It's surprising the different and creative ways your imagination can find to torment you when you've got a guilty conscience.

I kicked the door open.

Mac hadn't tidied up before leaving, and the flat revealed details about his private life I didn't really want to know. A half-finished whisky bottle sat on the coffee table, next to a tatty copy of *Barely Legal* and a box of mansize tissues. There was a CD player on the sideboard, and the bookcase had a huge pile of batteries on it. The kitchen was a stinking mess. There was a small calor gas ring with a saucepan on it and a collection of tinned food sitting next to it; baked beans and macaroni cheese, mostly. A huge pile of empty tins and Pot Noodles lay in a pile in the corner, a beacon for rats and 'roaches.

In the bedroom the quilt lay half-off the bed, exposing crumpled, stained sheets. We hadn't got the best laundry system worked out. I made a mental note to prioritise that.

Above the bed was a collage of photographs, blu-tacked to the wall. There must have been a hundred pictures. Most were of his family, but some were of friends, and there was one corner reserved for pictures of a pretty blonde girl I didn't recognise. It'd never occurred to me that he'd had a girlfriend.

I didn't want to linger here, to look at his pictures and see his crumpled bed sheets. I didn't want these things making me think of him as an ordinary person, giving my imagination any more details to torture me with. But it was already too late for that. I knew that somewhere in my nightmares that blonde girl would appear, accusing me of murder, weeping over Mac's chargrilled corpse.

Angrily I flung open every drawer and cupboard I could find. I rummaged through underwear and socks, spot cream, CDs, books and t-shirts until I found what I was looking for: the spare set of keys to the cellar. I left that room as quickly as I could and slammed the door behind me. I didn't look back.

Rowles was already waiting for me when I got to the armoury. The small door that led down to the cellar was underneath the rear staircase in what had originally been the servants' quarters. Mac had kept it padlocked and guarded at all times; I didn't think we needed the guard.

I opened the door and switched on the light. The cellar smelt damp and musty. We went down the stone steps and found ourselves in a corridor with vaulted rooms lying off it to the left and right. There were six chambers down here; all but two were full of guns, ammunition and explosives.

Without being asked, Rowles selected a rifle for himself, picked up a magazine, and snapped it into place. He seemed completely at ease, as if operating a semi-automatic machine gun was the most normal thing in the world. I reminded myself that he was only ten and wondered if I'd be able to restrict guns to older boys. Would that weaken our defences too much? One more thing to worry about.

I was appalled by how comfortable I'd become with guns, how naturally the Browning nestled into my palm like an extension of my hand, as it was designed to. I didn't want to be someone who always carried a weapon. I worried that I would come to rely on it to solve all my problems. After all, as Mac had pointed out, there was no-one to haul me off to prison for murder. The only thing stopping me ruling at the muzzle of a gun was my own determination not to let it happen.

But we were riding out of the school into unknown territory. Who knew what we'd encounter? Reluctantly I picked up the cold metal pistol and checked that it was loaded.

I promised myself that I'd return it to the cellar as soon as I got back.

WE SAW THE smoke long before we saw the farm.

Rowles, Haycox and I approached on horseback from the west, but we tethered the horses to a fence and made our final approach more stealthily. At first I thought it was probably a domestic fire, maybe someone burning rubbish or leaves, but as we got closer I could see that it was the dying embers of a much larger blaze.

Panicking, I started to run. My reluctance to carry a gun was forgotten as I drew my weapon, but I knew before I arrived at the farmhouse that there was nobody to shoot or save. This place was abandoned.

The main building was a shell. It could have been smouldering for days. There was a discarded petrol canister on the grass in front of the house. Someone had deliberately burnt this place down. Dispatching the others to check the outbuildings and oast houses, I peered in through the front door.

The floorboards had been burnt through and all that remained of the crossbeams were thin charcoal sticks. The ground floor was gone and the cellar was exposed to the sunlight for the first time in two hundred years. There was no way in here. I circled the building, looking in through the empty, warped window frames. All I could see was blackened furniture and collapsed walls. I didn't see any bodies.

Rowles reported that the oast houses were empty, but we heard Haycox yell and we hurried to the stables. When I first saw the body of the young boy lying there, half his chest blown away by a shotgun, I didn't realise the significance of it; after all, there was a lot of blood. It told me was that there'd been a fight, and the body was long cold. I reckoned he'd been dead about three or four days, which must have been when the farm was atacked. But then my stomach lurched as I saw that his hair was matted with blood. It wasn't his own.

Matron and the girls had been taken by the Blood Hunters.

CHAPTER FOURTEEN

WE HAD RIDDEN to the farm at a gentle canter, but we left galloping as fast as our horses could carry us. I felt the stitches in my side split. I ignored it.

Rowles rode back to the school to let Norton know what was happening. Haycox and I made straight for Ightham. The farm had been attacked three days ago, which meant the Blood Hunters had taken Matron and the girls captive before we'd stormed their HQ. My imagination started finding new ways to torture me. Perhaps they'd been held prisoner in a different part of the building and they'd burnt to death as a result of our attack.

I remembered the screams of the morning sacrifice. I'd been so grateful for the respite that had offered us. But maybe it had been Matron hanging from those battlements bleeding out in the moat. Maybe I'd swum to safety through her diluted blood.

I kicked the horse hard. Faster. Must go faster.

It took about an hour to reach Ightham. My horse and I were exhausted by that point. Haycox looked like he'd enjoyed the ride. We couldn't just go storming in; the surviving Blood Hunters could still be here. We tethered the horses in the woods and approached through the trees, weapons drawn, on the lookout for sentries or stragglers. There was nobody around.

The building was still on fire. All the wooden parts of the house had collapsed into the stone ground floor, where they were burning up all the remaining fuel. The house was a shell, completely abandoned, but there were about twenty bodies in the moat. I really didn't want to do this, but I had to be sure, so I found the wheel that controlled the level of water and turned it all the way. The water slowly began to drain away through the sluice gate. When it was down to knee height we jumped in and began to work our way around the building, turning over the bodies. Most were badly burnt. It was a tiring and grisly task, one of the most distressing things I've ever had to do. None of the dead were Mac or David, but the final body I turned over was Unwin's little sister.

So they'd been here all the time we were rescuing the people from Hildenborough. I looked up at the burning building. They might still be inside, charred and lifeless. I could be directly responsible for their deaths. There was no way of knowing.

Haycox and I climbed out of the moat and searched the grounds for evidence of escape. The canvas-covered trucks I'd seen them driving at Hildenborough were nowhere to be found, but there were fresh tyre tracks in the gravel of the car park. At least some of them had escaped the fire and moved on.

They could be miles away by now.

But had they retired to lick their wounds and start again somewhere else, or were they planning their revenge?

When we got back to the school we were met by guards at the gate. Norton had beefed up security upon Rowles' return. I left Haycox to tend to our exhausted steeds and I went straight to the store cupboard and flung open the door. Our captured Blood Hunter was curled up into a little ball, rocking back and forth muttering in the dark. I grabbed him and hauled him out.

"The other prisoners," I yelled. "Why didn't you tell us about the other prisoners?" I shook him and kicked him, slapped him round the head and yelled into his face but I could get no reaction. He was oblivious.

An hour later, after we'd given him some food and something to drink, he started to talk.

"But you only asked about the prisoners from Hildenborough," he said. And there was that urge again, the one I was trying to resist. The urge to shoot someone in the head.

When the girls and Matron had been captured the crypt had been full so they'd been imprisoned in the library, on the south side of the house. As far as he knew they were still there when we attacked. There was nothing more he could tell us, so we escorted him to the main gate and turned him loose.

Then I went to find Unwin. I had to tell him that his sister was dead.

* * *

167

IN THE MONTHS that followed we searched far and wide. We collected six more horses, Haycox trained all the boys in riding, and we sent out three-man search parties every day. After a month we'd searched everywhere within a day's ride and we had to start sending out teams that slept under canvas. Two-day searches gradually evolved into three-day searches, and still no sign of the Blood Hunters.

Eventually we had to abandon the hunt. It was likely that Matron and the girls were dead, that David died in the explosion, and that the trucks were taken by the remnants of a leaderless cult which had now scattered far and wide. We were probably searching for a group that no longer even existed. It was a hard reality to accept but eventually we had to move on.

As spring turned into summer the school slowly started to become what it should always have been. We cultivated a huge vegetable garden, and erected a couple of polytunnels for fruit and salad. The herds of sheep, pigs and cows grew steadily, and all the boys helped when it was time for lambing and calving. Heathcote's careful husbandry made sure we never went without meat, milk, butter or cheese. The river gave us plenty of fish, and the re-established Hildenborough market grew to the point where we could trade for sauces, jams and cakes.

Hildenborough elected Bob as their new leader. We developed close ties with them, and even played them at cricket once a month. A few of their adults came to live with us, mostly those with surviving children. I made it clear to the parents that I was in charge and any adults were here strictly by the permission of the children.

One market day Mrs Atkins came back to school with a tubby, red faced, middle-aged man, and she moved him into her room without ceremony or hesitation. His name was Justin, and the two of them made the kitchen into the hub of the school. They were always in there cooking something up, and all the boys loved to hang out there. It felt homely, which was something none of us had felt for a long, long time.

Our searches had found no trace of the Blood Hunters, but they had allowed us to compile a very good map of the area's settlements and farms. We made contact with as many as would allow us to approach, and although it was early days I could sense the beginning of a trading network.

Once I was sure that the school was secure and running smoothly, we began to look for new recruits. There were plenty of orphaned kids in the area, running in packs, or living with surrogate families.

Seventeen new children joined us, ten of whom were girls. A few tentative romances blossomed. Two women from Hildenborough volunteered to teach classes, and so each morning for two hours there were lessons. We didn't have a curriculum to follow, so they just taught whatever took their fancy. Both of them were naturals, so although attendance wasn't compulsory they always had a full house.

Green's theatre troupe was a roaring success, too. They abandoned *Our Town* in the end, and produced a revue that they took to Hildenborough and some other nearby settlements. They were our finest ambassadors.

In spite of the sunshine and goodwill we didn't neglect the military side of things. We maintained a strict defence plan, with patrols and guard posts, and every Friday we did weapons training and exercises. I devised a series of defensive postures for possible attacks, and we drilled the boys thoroughly in all the permutations; if someone came looking for a fight they'd find us ready and waiting.

Every now and then we'd catch a whiff of something happening in the wider world, rumours of television broadcasts and an Abbot performing miracles, but our fuel was long gone so we couldn't tune in. Whatever was brewing in the cities couldn't reach us out here in the countryside. Not yet, anyway. So we carried on building our little haven and prepared for the day when either madness or order would come knocking on our door again.

I flatter myself that I was a pretty good leader. The boys would come and talk to me when things were bothering them, and I did my best to resolve disputes and sort out any issues. I think I was approachable and fair. You could hear laughter in the corridors of Castle again, something I never heard when Mac was in charge. I relied on Norton and Rowles to let me know when and if I got things wrong, and they weren't shy about knocking me down a peg or two when necessary.

As my wounds healed I continued exercising my leg and found that my limp became much less marked. My cheek did scar slightly from Baker's ring, and Norton joked that it made me look like an Action Man. Within a couple of months I felt as fit and healthy as I'd ever done.

None of this stopped the nightly visitations of the dead keeping me awake, of course.

And there was still no sign of my dad.

*   *   *

I WENT THREE whole months without picking up a gun.

Felt good.

Couldn't last.

THE WOODHAMS FARM was about two miles south-west of the school. A collection of outbuildings and oast houses around a Georgian farmhouse, it was inhabited by ten people who'd moved down from London after The Cull. They'd found the place empty, moved in and started running the farm, which boasted a huge orchard and fields devoted to fruit production, including grapes and strawberries. Mrs Atkins met them at Hildenborough market and they'd extended an invitation for Green and the theatre group to visit their farm for the weekend. The boys would put on their show and in return they would put the boys up, feed them, and let them bring back some fruit for the rest of us. Lovely. What could possibly go wrong?

Jones was one of our new recruits. His parents were dead but he'd been living in Hildenborough ever since The Cull. He was a good pianist, so Green had recruited him for the revue, and he'd fitted in well. Green's troupe had left for the Woodhams place in a horse-drawn cart, so when Jones came staggering through the front gate after midnight the duty guards raised the alarm.

"I'd just played the opening chords of *After Fallout* when there was a knock on the door," he told us. "Ben Woodhams got up to answer it, we heard a struggle at the door and then a gang of men burst in wearing balaclavas and waving guns around. Green put up a fight and he got hurt pretty badly. I managed to slip out in the confusion and I've been running ever since. It's about two hours or so now. You need to hurry!"

Me, Norton, Jones, Rowles, Haycox and a new kid called Neate, who fancied himself a soldier boy, were dressed, armed and saddled up within ten minutes. There was no moon and we rode blind to the edge of the farm, but we could see flickering candle light around the edges of the curtains.

"There are seven boys and ten adults in there," I said. "Jones reckons there were four or five gunmen, that right Jones?"

He nodded.

"We've got no idea what's going on in there," I continued. "They might just be looting the place, they might have decided they like the look of it and want to move in, they might be doing any number of things. Our advantage is that they don't know we're coming, so we should have surprise on our side. The hostiles are dressed all in black and had balaclavas on."

"Why?" asked Norton.

"What?"

"Why were they wearing balaclavas? Were they afraid of CCTV or what? Doesn't make sense."

"I don't know. Probably just for effect."

Norton didn't look convinced.

"Haycox and Neate, you cover the front door," I said. "I don't want you to shoot any of the hostiles unless necessary. If they make a run for it let them go. But if they try to leave with hostages I want you to fire off some warning shots and force them back indoors. We need to try and contain them.

"The rest of you are coming with me. Everyone was in the living room when they were attacked, and that's at the front of the house so we're going in the kitchen door at the back. We go in quietly and cleanly, and we keep an eye out for sentries. We use knives until such time as they become aware of us, after that you can fire at will. Don't take any chances, but only kill if you have to. Jones knows the house so he and I will take point. Questions?"

"Just... be careful everyone, all right?" said Norton. "I don't like this at all. Something doesn't feel right to me."

I smirked. "Corny line!"

"I'm serious."

We left the horses a safe distance away and approached on foot, knives drawn. There were candles burning in the kitchen but there was no-one inside. The door wasn't locked and it didn't creak. So far so good. The room still smelt of roast beef. I looked greedily at the pile of dirty plates as I tiptoed around the large wooden table. The interior door was open a crack. It led into a corridor that ran to the front door. A number of rooms opened out of it to the left and right, and at the far end there was a staircase on the left.

I couldn't hear any voices and I couldn't see anyone. Gesturing for the others to stay in the kitchen I pushed the door gently and got lucky again: no creak. The hallway was carpeted so I took a chance and walked to the living room door, which was ajar. I leaned in and listened. Total silence. I was just about to try the other doors when I heard a small cough from inside and then someone shushing the cougher.

They were in a remote farmhouse, after dark, no-one expected or likely to arrive. Why would they be trying to keep so quiet?

I heard a small creak behind me and to the left. There was someone on the stairs. Suddenly I felt the world shift around me and I realised that I wasn't the hunter at all. I was the prey.

This was a trap.

There was a slim chance whoever was waiting on the stairs hadn't seen me. Without looking up at them I backed away towards the kitchen as slowly and quietly as I could.

And then another noise, this time behind me. Someone opened a door between me and the kitchen and stepped out into the hallway. I spun to see a black-clad man looking straight at me. He was wearing a balaclava and carrying a sawn-off shotgun.

He opened his mouth to shout a warning as I lunged forward. Normally I would have drawn my gun, told him to freeze. But something odd was going on here and I felt cornered and threatened. I wasn't inclined to take any chances. I led with my knife. I slapped my left hand over his mouth and shoved the blade up between his ribs as hard as I could, lifting him onto his toes with the force of the thrust.

I felt hot blood spurt out across my hand as I stared into the eyes of the man I was in the process of killing.

It wasn't a man, it was a boy. I recognised him. It was Wolf-Barry.

There was no wall behind him and he toppled backwards. I tried to follow him down, to maintain the silence, but I was overbalanced. We fell backwards together and as we hit the floor his shotgun went off, blowing two big holes in the plaster ceiling.

Dammit, this always looked so easy in the movies. I felt reassured that I wasn't a practised and professional killer – I didn't ever want to be that – but *fucking hell*, it would have been nice not to screw it up just this once.

I saw the eyes of the boy I had just killed begin to glaze over. I had a sudden memory of the first time I'd met him, in IT lab three years earlier. I remembered he'd made some joke about the headmaster, but I couldn't recall what it was. It was funny, though. I thought he was funny. And now I'd stabbed him through the heart without a second's hesitation.

I felt everything I'd achieved in the last three months evaporate in an instant. Who had I been kidding? This was my life now. Not cricket and plays and lessons, but killing and bleeding and dying. I was a fool to ever hope otherwise.

With both barrels fired and a knife in his chest, Wolf-Barry was no longer a threat, and since our cover was well and truly blown there was no longer any need for stealth. I rolled off him, trying to draw my gun as I did so, but I was tangled up and couldn't pull it free. A man came down the stairs swearing loudly, and as he turned the corner into the hallway someone behind me fired twice. Both bullets found their mark and he jerked backwards, two holes in his chest.

There were shouts from the living room; Green shouting "In here!" and a woman screaming. But no-one came out of the door.

Without rising to my feet I crabbed backwards towards the kitchen door and safety. The door was wide open and Norton and Rowles were stood there, smoking guns aimed down the corridor over my head, covering my retreat.

"You were right, it's a trap!" I shouted.

I reached the door and sprang upright. As I did so there was gunfire from outside, at the front of the house. Someone was attacking Haycox and Neate, someone who'd been waiting for us to get inside the house before revealing their presence.

I pointed to the boy on the floor in front of me, the one with the pink froth bubbling out of his mouth.

"That's Wolf-Barry," I said.

"I fucking knew it," replied Norton.

"And I think that's Patel," I said, indicating the corpse at the foot of the stairs.

"Green," I shouted. "Are you alone in there?"

"What do you fucking think?" came the reply. It was Wylie.

This was not good. Not good at all.

"I've got a gun to Limpdick's head, Keegan. If any of your men offer the slightest resistance I'll splash his brains all over the walls, got me?"

"What do you want, Wylie?"

"Want? I've got what I want: you. You're surrounded. My men were waiting outside in the dark. There's ten of us, how many of you?"

Fuck fuck fuck.

I heard the sound of a gun hitting the floor behind me and I turned to see Jones standing stock still at the back door, his eyes wide as saucers. Pugh had a knife to his throat.

"Drop the guns," he said.

Nobody moved.

"I said, drop the guns!"

Pugh pressed the knife into Jones' throat and a small trickle of blood escaped.

We dropped our guns.

"Now on the floor," he shouted. "Hands behind your heads."

We complied. The kitchen tiles were hard and cold.

"All right, chief, we've got them," he said.

TEN MINUTES LATER I was tied to a chair in the dining room. The other prisoners were being kept next door. I'd caught a glimpse of them through the door when I was being trussed up; Green had a huge purple bruise on his forehead, and Neate had been shot and killed out front, but everyone else was okay. All ten of the farm family were there, as were the six kids from Green's troupe, Norton, Jones and Rowles.

I'd obviously been set aside for special treatment. I didn't want to dwell on what Wylie was likely to do to me. My hands and feet were firmly bound, and there was no give in the ropes at all. I wasn't going anywhere.

Wylie pulled over a chair, reversed it, and sat facing me, resting his arms on the seat back. He had removed his balaclava, no need for it now. He looked very pleased with himself. And so he should. I'd walked obediently into his trap like the amateur I was. I would've kicked myself if my feet hadn't been tied. I figured that the best I could hope for was a bloody good kicking and I saw no reason to prolong the agony.

"Patel and Wolf-Barry are dead," I said. "That just leaves you, Pugh and Speight. So who are the other guys, Wylie?"

"They're old friends of yours, Lee," he said. "Wanted a chance for a bit of payback. Actually I'm working for them, sort of sub-contracting. They wanted me to deliver you to them. Piece of piss, really."

"Wolf-Barry didn't look like he thought much of your plan as I shoved a knife into his heart."

Wylie looked annoyed. "He shouldn't have broken cover. He was supposed to stay in there 'til I gave the signal. Prick."

"No wonder you command such loyalty, you're just so compassionate."

He smiled the smile of a man who knew he was in total control. "No point trying to piss me off, Lee. I've got my orders and I'm going to stick to them. You're not going to annoy me into making mistakes. I'm supposed to deliver you in one piece and that's what I'm going to do."

He stood up and walked over to me, leaning down so we were face to face.

"Doesn't mean I can't hurt you just a little bit first, though, does it?"
He leaned back, raised his right leg and stamped on my balls.

There's no point describing the pain. If you're a woman you've got
no idea, and if you're a guy you know only too well. Suffice to say I
screamed for a bit, whimpered for a while, and then passed out.

Unconsciousness passed into sleep. Wylie woke me in the morning
by kicking me in both shins. The first thing I heard, apart from
my own curses, was a chorus of screams from outside the house.
He untied my feet and led me out the front door, where a familiar
canvas-top truck was parked. The engine was running and the rest
of the captives were already in the back. All except Mr Woodhams,
who was lying on the grass, sliced open from pubis to throat, with a
group of young men stood around him, dabbling their hands in the
gore and wiping it all over themselves.

Blood Hunters.

Pugh and Speight were standing at the back of the truck, machine
guns slung across their chests. They were trying not to watch the
gruesome ritual occurring right in front of them. Pugh looked sick.

Wylie forced me into the truck, and then the six Blood Hunters
climbed in and sat at the back. They sat silently, staring into space.
Each carried a machete and a gun. They stank like an abattoir. Pugh
closed the tailgate, the three sixth-formers went to sit in the cab, and
we pulled out of the driveway onto the road.

The nine remaining residents of the Woodhams farm were
cowering in the far end of the truck, in various states of hysteria.
The eleven St Mark's boys were all there too, hands bound, all
looking to me for ideas or hope as we were bounced about by
potholed roads. I shrugged helplessly. But Norton found my gaze
and winked. Good to know somebody had a plan.

We rumbled along for about five minutes until I felt a nudge from
Jones, who was sitting next to me. I felt something cold touch my
fingers. A knife! Where the hell had he got a bloody knife? I glanced
up and saw Norton grinning at me. He nodded subtly downwards
and wiggled his right foot. He'd had a knife in his boot. I could have
kissed him. I scanned the faces of all the other boys. All of them still
had their hands behind their backs as if still tied up, but they all
looked at me, excited and nervous. Christ. They were all free!

I grabbed the knife and set about cutting the rope that bound me.
It didn't take long; it was razor sharp. I felt my hands come free and
I squeezed the knife handle firmly in my right hand. I looked up. All
eleven boys were looking at me.

I mouthed silently: "One, two, three."

As one, we leapt up from our seats and shoved towards the six Blood Hunters. One of them went over the tailgate and smacked onto the road before he even knew what was happening. I buried the knife in the eye socket of another, and grabbed his machete as he tumbled backwards towards the tarmac. The other four were no match for the combined shoving weight of twelve boys, but the tailgate was still closed, and they braced themselves against it. One of them tried to grab his gun, but the crush of bodies was so tight that he couldn't bring it to bear, and his hands got stuck down on his chest so he couldn't defend himself. Rowles hit him repeatedly, over and over again, both hands working the man's face like a punchbag. Jones wrestled for control of another man's machete, which was suspended over his head. But he was too weak to prevent it coming down and splitting him open. As the Blood Hunter tried to wrench the blade free, Haycox, who had somehow got hold of a machete in the struggle, returned the favour, striking his head from his shoulders with one powerful swipe. Norton grabbed the decapitated man's feet and tipped him over the tailgate onto the road.

The Blood Hunter being hit by Rowles was unconscious by this point, and only remaining upright because of the mêlée surrounding him. Rowles kept punching him anyway. The other two Blood Hunters were backed right up against the tailgate now. One was hacking and slashing wildly, and as I watched he sliced open the throat of a young boy called Russell, who sang comic songs in Green's revue. The boy tumbled backwards with a terrible screech. The other Blood Hunter was struggling with Norton for possession of his gun until his mate's wild swinging blade smacked into the side of his head with a soft crunch. Norton shoved him back over the tailgate and onto the road, the machete still embedded in his head.

The one remaining Blood Hunter, bladeless, tried to reach for this gun. But suddenly he jerked and wretched as his eyes went wide and a torrent of blood gushed from his mouth. Haycox pulled his dripping machete free of the man's ribcage and pushed him back over the tailgate.

Job done.

I reached down past Rowles, who was still punching, and grabbed the machine gun from the unconscious Blood Hunter beneath him. I pushed my way through the crowd to the front of the truck.

"Everyone brace yourselves," I shouted.

"Lee, hang on, do you think..." said Norton.

But I didn't let him finish. I popped the catch and emptied the entire clip through the canvas in front of me, riddling the driver's cab with bullets and killing Wylie, Pugh and Speight instantly.

"Should have done that in the first place," I said, as the lorry swerved violently off the road. I was flung off my feet in a tumbled tangle of limbs as the lorry hit a ditch and rolled over onto its side. There was a monstrous crash, a chorus of cries and then stillness and silence.

I'd come to rest under a pile of bodies, my nose buried in somebody's armpit. It took a few minutes for everyone to untangle themselves and climb out of the lorry onto the road. We took stock.

Russell and Jones were dead, and a young girl from the Woodhams farm had broken her neck in the crash. Otherwise it was all just scrapes and strains. I pulled the clip out of the machine gun. It was taped to another, which was still full, so I reversed it and slammed it home.

Norton was incandescent.

"What the fuck was that, Lee?" he yelled. "Why the fuck did you shoot them up? That was the most insane thing I've ever seen you do."

I grasped the gun tightly, my finger itching at the trigger.

Calm down. Things to do.

"Look at where we are," I said patiently.

Norton glanced down the road.

"So?" he said, confused.

"The school is about a mile down the road. We'd have been there in two minutes. They were taking us to the school."

"Oh." He realised what I was getting at. "Oh shit."

I turned to address the other boys, who were sitting in the road, catching their breath. "Listen everyone. Wylie was taking orders from the Blood Hunters. His job was to lure me away from the school and then deliver me to them. But they were taking us back to the school."

"So?" said Rowles. "They were going to let us go?"

"Don't you see? While we've been gone the Blood Hunters have attacked St Mark's."

CHAPTER FIFTEEN

I GAVE A machine gun to the Woodhams party, so they had some means of defence on their journey home, and they carried away the dead girl. One of them, a young man, had to be restrained from attacking me. He was still shouting after me as he was pulled away: "Murderer! Psychopath!" I couldn't blame him. I'd caused the crash that killed her. But what choice did I have? I could have shot above the officers' heads and told them to pull over, but in moments we'd have been within earshot of the school. If I'd had to fire again then the Blood Hunters would probably have heard the shots and come running. Assuming I was right, and they were at St Mark's.

It was one more death on my conscience, but I could worry about it later. Things to do.

I walked around to the front of the crashed truck and peered into the shattered cab. I could see that there were three bodies inside, but I didn't look too closely. They weren't moving, so I was satisfied they were dead. (When had I started taking satisfaction in killing?)

I was starting to appreciate Mac's point of view; perhaps I wasn't ruthless enough to be a leader. My decision to let the officers go had led directly to four deaths. Wouldn't executing them have been better?

Three months ago I was unable to contemplate such a thing, but now I found that I could. Perhaps it was because of what we'd achieved in the last three months. When I was planning to topple Mac and take control it was in the hope of building something good, but my aims had been intangible and distant. Now it was a reality. We'd achieved so much, built something so valuable. I felt as if I was willing to go to any lengths to protect it.

* * *

178

I DISPATCHED HAYCOX and Rowles back down the road to collect the guns from the bodies of the dead Blood Hunters. When they returned we had five machine guns and six machetes, and enough ammunition to pick a fight. Green, Norton, Haycox and Rowles each took a gun; we shared the big knives out amongst the remaining members of Green's troupe.

"We have to assume they've taken control of the school," I said. "And they probably have lookouts and sentries posted. We need to know what's going on inside, and we can't approach mob-handed. So Norton, you're with me. We'll cut across country and come at the school from the river. Haycox and Green, I want you to get behind these hedgerows and follow the road, out of sight, until you can see the school gates. Only approach if you're absolutely certain there's nothing wrong. This is just a recce, right? We don't get involved, we don't show our faces. Rowles, take the rest of the boys to Hildenborough and wait for us. We'll rendezvous back there when we're done. Everyone clear?"

Nods all round.

"Good luck everyone."

It took thirty minutes to reach the edge of the school grounds, but the sight that greeted us was not what we expected at all. We crawled through the undergrowth until we could just make out the first pillbox. We could see the muzzle of the GPMG poking out, but it was trained towards the school. I couldn't work out why that would be. We needed a closer look.

Leaving Norton to cover the pillbox, I crawled back out of sight and stripped to my boxers. I discarded my gun but kept the machete, then I ran to the river's edge and slipped into the water. I let the current take me slowly downstream, along the edge of the school grounds. As I drifted past the first pillbox I could see the body of a boy lying against one wall. He'd had his throat slit. I was right, the Blood Hunters had attacked, and they'd taken this pillbox. But why train the gun on the school... unless they hadn't succeeded in capturing it!

I drifted further. I couldn't see anything at the second pillbox, but two Blood Hunters were sitting outside the third, looking towards the school, smoking. There was no sign of a corpse anywhere, but their hair shone slick with fresh blood. I grabbed the bank of the river and hung there for a moment, considering my options: sneaky or direct? I could return to Norton, head to Hildenborough with what I'd learned; or I could choose to kill without mercy. Three months ago I wouldn't even have had to think about it. But I thought again about where my reluctance to kill had brought us and my resolve hardened. There was no longer any point pretending that I wasn't a stone cold killer.

Time to start acting like one.

I climbed out of the water as quietly as I could, and crept towards them, knife in hand. The secret to stealth in woodland is to tread straight down, not to roll your feet with each step as you do normally. That way you avoid snapping any twigs you stand on. Barefoot, I stalked my prey.

As I approached I could hear them gossiping. They were trying to decide whether a girl called Carol fancied the one on the right. He thought she didn't, but his mate was sure she did, and was urging him to 'get in there'. Murderous religious fanatics, coated in human blood, wittering about dating. They were so engrossed in their debate that they didn't become aware of me until I pressed my cold wet blade against the throat of the one on the right.

"Hi," I whispered in his ear, as he stiffened in fear.

His mate exclaimed loudly and jumped up. He brought his gun to bear on both of us.

"Now, now," I said conversationally. "Don't be hasty. Pull that trigger and your friend dies." *Plus, every Blood Hunter in the area comes running.* "So put it down, eh?"

He hesitated, unsure what to do. I pressed the knife harder into the throat of the man in front of me, and he moaned. His mate cocked his gun, chambering a round. "So?" he said, trying to sound more confident than he was. "He gets his eternal reward a little early. He'll thank me when I see him again."

"Um, Rob," said the man in front of me. "He's gonna slit my throat, man."

"He's right, you know," I said. "I am. So if you don't want to break poor Carol's heart, best drop the weapon."

Rob stared at me, trying to maintain his cool. But eventually he bent down and placed the gun on the ground.

"Thanks," I said, and smiled at him. "Now kick it away." He did so.

A minute later I had them both on the ground, face down, hands behind their heads. It didn't take much to persuade them to talk, but it took me a lot longer to believe what they were telling me. When I'd learned all I could, I had a choice to make. I'd been quite prepared to kill one of them to make the other one tell me what I needed to know, but to kill them now would be murder, plain and simple.

Nonetheless, the best course of action was clear. Kill them, bleed them, cover myself in their blood, dump the bodies in the river, then saunter up to the next pillbox and kill the occupants before they realise I'm not really a Blood Hunter. Repeat for all remaining pillboxes. Even the odds while I had the chance. It was the safest thing to do.

I tightened my grip on the knife, gritted my teeth and prepared to strike, but I had a sudden flash of the confusion and fear in Wolf-Barry's eyes as I'd plunged my knife into his chest. I choked. I couldn't do it. Even now, after everything I'd done, I couldn't conceive of embarking on that kind of killing spree, no matter how necessary it was.

I felt like I'd failed some kind of test.

I made them undress, cut their clothes into strips, and bound them tight. Then I swam upstream and rejoined Norton.

I had a lot to tell him.

I COULDN'T SLEEP at all that night. In the pub at Hildenborough we'd talked ourselves hoarse trying to come up with a plan of action that didn't leave us all hanging upside down with our throats slit. By the time we finally agreed on a plan of attack it was dark and everyone was exhausted. Norton accepted his role without complaint and walked out into the night to do his part. Bob had prepared beds for us in the big house where three months ago I'd fought for my life. Strange to be sleeping there as a guest of honour.

But of course I couldn't sleep. I ran the day over and over again in my mind. Killing Wolf-Barry, shooting the others, the head of the dead woman hanging limp as she was carried away, the stench of the Blood Hunters, the sense that I should have killed them there and then, the nagging feeling that I still wasn't as ruthless as I needed to be. The knowledge that, had Mac been in charge of us, things would have been a lot simpler. Not to mention my anxieties about the coming day, the probability of battle, the anticipation of more killing, the possibility of my own imminent death and those of my friends. I was afraid of the nightmares sleep would bring.

Plus, it felt wrong to be sleeping safe and sound while Norton was risking his life out there in the darkness.

So I lay there, listening to the owls and the foxes, wishing that my father were here to take charge on my behalf. I wished I could go back to being a boy again, that I could retreat to a world where my only worries were acne, BO and whether that girl from the high school would laugh at me if I asked her to meet me at lunchtime for a bag of chips at the bus stop. That was what my life should be like. I was fifteen, for God's sake. Whoever heard of a fifteen-year-old general? Well, Alexander the Great, perhaps. Whatever happened, things would be settled once and for all by the end of the day. Either I'd be dead and the school would be destroyed, or the Blood Hunters would be wiped from the face of the earth like the plague they were. When dawn finally broke I greeted it with a kind of relief; waiting to fight is far worse than actually fighting.

Breakfast was a sombre affair. Green hadn't spoken a word since we'd rescued him, and he sat at the end of the table, picking at his bacon and eggs. Haycox was in shock, coming to terms with the fact that yesterday his life had changed from horse grooming to disembowelling and decapitation. I hardly knew any of the boys who made up Green's theatre troupe, but they were artsy types, uncomfortable in a fight, reeling from the deaths of their friends Russell and Jones. Bob was subdued because he'd had a very hard time convincing some of the men in Hildenborough to provide support for our plans; after all, they'd lost friends in an attack on the school once before. But the opportunity to revenge themselves on the Blood Hunters was enough to sway them in the end.

The only person who ate well was Rowles. He cleaned his plate, and then went back for more. He didn't seem worried at all. But if you looked closely you could see that he was dead behind the eyes. I worried about that boy.

When we were finished we washed up and got dressed. Rowles, Haycox and I had our combats, the others had to make do with green and brown clothes that Bob had begged and borrowed the day before. We met the new Hildenborough militia on the forecourt of the house and went over the plan once again. Weapons were distributed and goodbyes said. Then we walked down the drive towards the rising sun.

We were going to pick a fight.

THERE'S SOMETHING MEDIAEVAL about pitching a tent outside a fortified castle and laying siege to it. But since the Blood Hunters had to do without smart bombs, air strikes or fuel, it seemed logical to re-adopt the neglected arts of war.

The marquee sat to one side of the school's main gate, outside the walls, on the grass between the road and the school wall. The gate itself lay on the ground in pieces, run down by a truck. The truck in question lay on its side about twenty metres inside the gates. There was a corpse hanging out of the driver's side window. The sandbagged machine gun emplacement at the main gate had been scattered by the impact, I had no idea of the fate of the boys who'd been manning it. The Blood Hunters had collected the sandbags and rebuilt it, remounting the GPMG and pointing it down the drive at the school.

With the drive covered, and the pillboxes manned at the rear, all approaches to the school were pinned down. But the long driveway in front, the playing fields at the back, and the paddocks and gardens on either side provided no cover for attackers who made it over the wall, which meant that a straightforward attack would be suicide. Stalemate.

The Blood Hunters were going to have to starve the school into submission. And I wasn't going to allow them that much time.

I turned my binoculars towards Castle and was relieved to see a Union Jack flag dangling from a window. That was the signal; Norton had made it past the guards and was inside. There was nothing left to do now. Time to begin.

I broke cover about half a mile down the road and strolled as nonchalantly as I could towards the school. I tried whistling but my mouth was too dry. It took them a minute to spot me. Three of the biggest guys I've ever seen ran towards me, weapons raised for firing.

I grinned at them. I was going for confidence but I probably looked unhinged.

"Take me to your leader," I said. So they did.

There was a crowd milling around outside the entrance to the marquee as we approached. A whole tribe of people in jeans and t-shirts, wearing flip flops and trainers, carrying machetes and guns, their faces, arms and hair soaked in human blood. The meeting of mundane and surreal was hard to accept. So was the smell.

I've never been religious. It just never made any sense to me. But I sang the hymns and intoned the prayers at school assemblies and the compulsory Sunday morning service in the chapel. The kind of religion I was exposed to always seemed harmless enough. Either the vicars were pompous bores or young men who tried to be cool by playing guitar or something embarrassing like that. One of the boys in my dorm had attended a thing called the Alpha Course one summer holiday, and the subsequent term he'd stopped smoking and joined the school's Christian Fellowship. But that was about as sinister as it got. And I sort of got it. It was about feeling part of a community, taking comfort in a belief that there was some point to everything. I didn't feel the need of it myself, but I kind of understood why some people did.

But this... I couldn't begin to wrap my head around this. How fucked in the head did you have to be to think that human sacrifice was going to save your immortal soul? How desperate for certainty did you need to be to imagine that smearing yourself in human blood was a good idea? I wondered whether the Blood Hunters were just a collection of weak, scared people in thrall to a charismatic nutter, or were they some expression of something deeper, more fundamental? The Aztec part of us, if you like.

I might as well have been walking through a crowd of Martians. I couldn't comprehend these people on any level. And suddenly I realised I'd made a terrible mistake strolling in here. Because how can you talk to someone when you don't even know their language?

The tent flap was held open for me and I walked into the marquee. The air inside was fetid and humid, and smelt of grass, sweat and blood. Blankets lay on the floor, surrounded by bags and collections of random objects and piles of clothes; lots of little Blood Hunter nests. Running down the middle of the tent was a long red carpet, and at the far end, raised on a wooden dais, was a throne. I say throne, but it was really just a big wooden chair with a gold lame blanket tossed over it and a red velvet cushion. Sat on this throne was David, wearing his immaculate pinstripe suit and bowler hat. His umbrella rested on one of the arms. Two armed guards stood either side of the throne.

I was shoved onto the red carpet and marched down it to meet the Blood Hunters' leader. I had no idea what to expect. I certainly didn't expect him to get up, walk down to meet me, shake my hand and offer me a cup of tea and a slice of cake.

But that's what he did.

"We've spoken before, haven't we?" he asked as he poured Earl Grey into a china cup.

"Yes, we have." He handed me the cup and saucer and I thanked him. "At Ightham."

"I thought so. You were one of the boys who attacked us."

I took a sip. "Yeah."

We sat on canvas chairs facing each other across a wrought iron table. There was a plate on the table with lemon drizzle cake on it. I didn't ask where they'd managed to find lemons, I just helped myself. It was delicious.

Imagine a clown performing for children, his face covered in make-up. Then try to imagine what he looks like when all the slap's taken away. Is he old or young? Ugly or attractive? It's impossible to say. All you can see is the clown face. It was the same with David. I found it very hard to get a sense of what he looked like, because all I could see was the cracked and crumbling patina of blood that caked his face. It made him difficult to read.

Obviously I was taking tea with a madman. But was he personally dangerous? Was he likely to kill me himself, with no warning, on a whim or because of something I might say? Or did his threat lie solely in his power over others? I could find no clue at all in his expression or his cold grey eyes.

"So what can I do for you this fine sunny day, young man?" he said. "Do you wish to join us, perhaps? We always have room for penitent souls." He smiled insincerely.

"I've come to ask you to leave." Even though I'd been rehearsing this in my head all night I still couldn't believe I'd just said that.

"I'm sorry?"

"I want you to leave St Mark's alone. Just leave. Please."

He put down his tea carefully, then he placed his elbows on the table and rested his face in his hands.

"Why would I want to do that? There are young, innocent souls in there, in need of salvation. I can provide them with that. I'm only here to help."

"And if they don't want your salvation?"

"Then they can aid in the salvation of others."

"As bleeders."

"Or food. Or both. Their blood and flesh is a holy sacrament."

"Is that all they are to you, a resource?"

"If they will not accept the word of God then yes." He leaned back and shrugged as if to say 'what can you do?'

I decided to try a different tack.

"When we blew up that room you were outside the door," I said. "How did you survive?"

"I am watched over," he replied.

I thought: *you ran down the stairs when you heard the window break, more like*. "But if your little cult is so blessed, why were we able to burn your house to the ground?"

He laughed, as if indulging a child who's just asked a particularly stupid question. "You were merely the messenger of God's wrath. He wishes me to bring His word to the world. I was betraying my calling by situating myself in one location." He gestured around him, at the marquee. "Now, you see, we are mobile! And we save more souls every day of our never ending journey. All thanks to you."

"You're welcome. So why not move on. Why lay siege to a school when there are so many other places to save?"

"I may be a holy man, but I am not above a little vengeance. You killed my disciples, you oppose me and my followers. That cannot go unpunished."

"People are going to die here today. Lots of people. Yours and mine. Men, women, boys, girls. And there's no need for it all. You can just walk away."

"Shan't."

Strike One.

"All right then, let the people in the school leave and take the building as your new base. Rent free. All yours."

"Didn't you listen to what I said? We are mobile now. That is how it is meant to be."

Strike Two.

"Then take me."

"Excuse me?"

"Take me. Bleed me, eat me, do whatever you want. I won't resist. But leave the school alone."

"My dear young man, I have you already. Where's my incentive to make a deal?"

Strike Three.

Okay then. I'd given him every chance; done everything I could to avoid bloodshed. No choice now but to fight. Only problem was that my plan relied on my being outside. And I was stuck in this bloody great tent. I needed to be creative.

"How many men and guns have you got here anyway?" I asked.

He smiled. It was not pleasant. "Lots and lots."

I made a play of considering this.

"Can I, perhaps, join you, then?"

Finally, I'd managed to surprise him. "You wish to join the flock of the saved?"

"I don't want to die, so on balance, yeah. Please."

"Do you understand what joining the ranks of the saved entails?"

"I've heard about the ritual blood letting. Correct me if I make a mistake. A victim is selected from amongst the prisoners or, if the person joining is considered particularly valuable, from the ranks of the already saved. The victim is held down by two men, and the supplicant, who has been stripped naked, slits the victim's throat and collects the blood in a bowl. When the bowl is full they drink the blood. Then the body is turned over and sliced open. You then dab your hands in the gore and make the sign of the cross, in blood, on the supplicant's chest. The supplicant takes the knife, cuts their palm, and drips their blood into your outstretched hands, and you wash your face with it. That about right?"

"And you'd be happy to take the ritual of salvation?"

"If it means staying alive, then yes, I would."

"Can I tell you a secret?"

"Please."

He leaned forward and whispered conspiratorially: "You're not a very good liar."

"I'm not lying. I swear I'll join you if you let me."

"If you wish to join us why did you kill the acolytes I dispatched to bring you to me? We found their bodies on the road yesterday. And why attack and tie up the two men by the river? No, I think it's more likely that you've developed some kind of plan and this conversation is the start of it. Did you really think we would just leave if you asked me nicely?"

He spat the word 'nicely' at me like a curse, and there was a sudden flash of furious madness in his eyes.

"I hoped so. I had to try, didn't I?"

The fury was replaced by contempt.

"You believe yourself to be in a story, don't you?" he sneered. "I think you imagine yourself as the hero who strolls into the enemy camp, baits the villain and then runs away to fight another day. Yes? But you're so wrong. My crusade is holy and righteous and you are nothing but a clueless heathen. I have bound my followers together in faith and blood through the power of my will. I lead them to glory and salvation. You have no idea of the trials I have undergone, the opposition I have overcome, the demons I have banished. I am the hero of this tale, boy, not you. You're just a footnote. Nothing more."

He was impressive when he got going.

"I don't know what you and your boy scouts have planned, but I can assure you it's utterly futile," he ranted. "You have no forces to call upon. We have the school surrounded and all your boys and their weapons are contained inside. They can't attack us for the same reason we can't attack them – they'd be cut down before they reached the walls. And even if it does come to a fight, which I think unlikely, my men outnumber you two to one and are not afraid to die. You should see them fight. It's a glorious thing. They fling themselves into danger without a second thought. They are magnificent!"

David's messianic fervour was impressive but I wasn't completely convinced by it. I thought about the two men I'd interrogated on the river bank the day before. Magnificent wasn't the word I'd use to describe them; they were just scared idiots happy to have a tribe to belong to. Obviously there would be a hard core of men, like the one I'd killed in Hildenborough, who'd fight to the last, but I was sure that if David were taken out of the equation then the majority of Blood Hunters would fall apart. I hoped so, anyway. My whole plan relied upon it.

"You're... you're right," I said, trying not to overplay it. "I know we don't stand a chance. I was bluffing. There's no way we can fight you, not like this."

"Don't believe a word he says, David," said a familiar voice behind me. "He's got a plan, all right."

I turned to face the new arrival. The guys I'd interrogated at the pillbox had told me Mac was here, so I'd expected to come face to face with him again. But nothing could have prepared me for how he looked. I recoiled involuntarily at the sight of him.

His hair was all burnt away, his bald head blackened and scarred. The left side of his face was also a mass of scar tissue, and it sagged downwards, indicating that he had no muscle control there. The left side of his lips had been burnt away too, leaving half his teeth exposed and giving him a permanent sneer of loathing and contempt. His left ear was a ragged tatter and his left eye socket gaped, black and empty. His left arm ended abruptly just above what used to be his elbow, but the right hand held a machine gun with measured confidence. He looked like some kind of zombie.

But it wasn't the sight of Mac that froze my blood and stopped my heart.

Because standing next to him was Matron.

And her face and hair were smeared with human blood.

CHAPTER SIXTEEN

"Look," I said, "It's a pretty simple plan."

"Too simple if you ask me," said Bob.

"Can your man shoot as well as you say… yes or no?" I asked.

"He's bloody brilliant," he replied.

"And does he have a problem with shooting people?"

"No," he replied darkly.

"Then I reckon it's our best shot. Um, sorry. Not intended."

"But are you sure it'll work?" asked Rowles.

"The Blood Hunters are a cult of personality. It stands to reason that if we eliminate their leader then they won't know what to do. There's every chance they may just wander off."

"I can't believe this is our best plan. Hope they wander off. Jesus," muttered Norton.

"You said he never comes out of the tent, so how are you going to get him out in the open?" asked Bob.

"I'll improvise. Just make sure your man's ready. The second David steps outside, I want him dead. Then while they're running around flapping their hands and wailing you lot come out onto the road and line up, weapons raised. But don't fire unless you have to. And Norton, you lead the boys out of the school and do the same. With their leader dead, and us sandwiching them between two rows of guns and making a show of force, I think there's the possibility of a surrender."

"And Mac?" said Norton. "We don't expect him to just walk away, do we?"

"No. I don't really know what he's going to do. He's the wild card."

*　　*　　*

MATRON HELD A gun on me as Mac and David walked to one side and talked quietly, glancing over at me every now and then. I stayed seated. I looked up at Matron, trying to get some indication that she was under duress. Nothing.

Eventually David returned to the table. Mac stood behind him, his twisted mouth lolling into a dangerous smile. His face was as hard to read as David's, probably because half of it wasn't really there. But he was up to something, and I didn't like it.

"At the urgings of Brother Sean, I have reconsidered your request to join us," said David.

What the fuck?

"Oh. Um… thanks."

"If you wish to retire to prepare yourself, Sister Jane will sit vigil with you in seclusion until the appointed hour."

"Great, thank you," I said, confused and suspicious. "I promise you won't regret this."

And so Matron and I found ourselves sitting on the grass in a corner of the tent, shielded from view by an improvised partition made of blankets draped over wooden stands.

I had so much I wanted to say. Jane Crowther was funny and vivacious; she stood up for herself and didn't take any shit from anyone. Could this blank-eyed acolyte really be her?

"I'm sorry," I said eventually.

She looked up at me. It was hard to tell, but I thought she looked confused.

"If I'd just got rid of Mac earlier then I could have brought you back to the school sooner. They'd never have found you."

"Thank heaven they did," she replied. "For I am saved!"

Please, God, no. I felt tears starting to well up.

"Nah," she said eventually. "Only kidding."

I had never been so relieved in my life. Except for that time when I didn't die on the scaffold. On reflection, that probably trumps it. But I was pretty bloody relieved. I went to hug her but she pushed me away.

"Better not. I kind of stink. The blood, y'know," she whispered, careful that we shouldn't be overheard by anyone lurking on the other side of the blanket.

"Yeah, about that. I meant to ask, why exactly are you covered in blood, carrying a gun and hanging out with psychotic religious cannibals?

"I'm a loyal disciple now, Lee. Have to be."

"Why?"

"They have the girls. There are about a hundred people travelling with David now, and many of them have medical conditions that need to be managed. They need a doctor, so they need me alive. But I made it clear when they took me that if they harmed any of my girls I'd kill myself. The girls stay alive and untouched as long as I co-operate. They keep them in a caravan but they park it about a mile away from the main tent each night, just so I'm not tempted to try and find them."

"But you're not a doctor."

"You don't know everything about me, Lee," she snapped impatiently. I'd touched a nerve. "I went to medical school for three years."

"So why…"

She interrupted me. "Not important right now. That was another life."

I looked at her blood-caked face.

"You had to convert?"

"Yes. It was a condition."

"So you performed the ritual?"

She nodded. "They chose a Blood Hunter as the victim. Made it a little bit easier. I couldn't have done it to a prisoner. God knows what would have happened to us then, but I couldn't have done it. Even so, it was…" she broke off, unable to continue.

"So the girls are safe and you're the cult doctor, yeah?"

"Yeah."

"I don't really want to ask this, but Mac…?"

"Yes, I patched him up. Not the prettiest job, and he died on the table twice, but I managed it in the end. I think it was sheer force of will that kept him alive. He's very, very angry at you, Lee."

"No shit, Sherlock. But why the fuck would you help him?"

"It's my job. I save people. It's what I do. I don't… I try not to kill."

"But after what he did, how could you?"

"How could I not?" she replied furiously.

I didn't know what to say to that. "And he's David's right-hand man?"

She groaned. "Yes. After I patched him up he asked to convert and David let him. Said he had brought a message from God and deserved to be saved. They chose a child for his initiation. A young girl, no more than fifteen. He didn't hesitate for a second. And then he started doing it again."

"Doing what?"

"Worming his way in. Showing off, seizing the initiative, getting things done. He brought back more prisoners in the first month than they'd had in the previous three. Their strategist died in the attack on Hildenborough. Mac sussed that there was a vacancy, and filled it. David relies on him a lot now."

"He should watch his back then. He'll be crucified before he knows it."

"Not that easy. Mac doesn't have the same power base here. He's not been able to gather a little gang of followers. Everyone's first loyalty is to David. It was Mac who persuaded David to come here, and he devised the plan of attack. I think he stumbled across the, let's call them officers for want of a better word, a few weeks back, and they hatched the plan together. Lure you away, attack while you're off-site. He was incandescent when the attack on the school failed. He didn't anticipate such an organised resistance. And when he found the bodies of the boys in the truck yesterday evening, my God. Did you do that?"

I explained what had happened to us at the farm and subsequently. As I told her about killing Wolf-Barry she did the strangest thing. She reached out and stroked my hair.

"You poor boy," she said, her voice full of compassion and sorrow. I suddenly felt very uncomfortable.

"It was necessary," I said awkwardly. "I'm just doing what has to be done."

She nodded, wordlessly. But she left her hand resting on mine.

"So what's with persuading David to let me convert?" I asked.

"I have no idea. Whatever he's got planned it can't be good."

"But the ritual takes place outside, yes?"

"Normally."

"Good. When we get outside things are going to kick off. With any luck there won't be a proper fire-fight, but if the shooting starts I need you to run, as fast as you can, across the road. There's a stile in the hedgerow a few metres to the left of the school gate. They'll be waiting for you and they'll give you covering fire if need be."

She nodded.

At that moment a blanket was flung aside and Mac leered down at us.

"How's the reunion going?" he croaked.

"Sorry?" I replied. "Couldn't quite catch that. Could you enunciate a little better, please."

He looked down at me, furious. It's hard to talk when your lips have been partially burnt away.

I stood up and held out my hand.

"Hey Mac, you look great. No hard feelings, yeah?" I glanced down and pretended to be surprised that there was no hand for me to shake. "Oh. Sorry." Mock embarrassed.

"Come with me," he said, with what looked like an attempt at a smile.

A crowd had gathered outside the tent, and Matron and I were led through them to a clear space in the centre where David was standing. This crowd was no good at all. The sniper wouldn't be able to get a good shot at David in amongst all these people. I was thinking as fast as I could but I had nothing. I might have to go through with this foul ritual after all.

"Have you selected a victim for today, David?" asked Mac. And something in his tone of voice made me even more uneasy.

"I have decided to take your advice, Brother Sean," David replied.

The crowd parted and two men walked forwards, herding a boy between them. It was Heathcote. So now I knew what had happened to the boy manning the GPMG at the school gates. His face was streaked with tears and snot, and he was snivelling. He looked utterly petrified. He saw me and a moment of hope flashed across his face, but he swiftly realised what was going on, and he let out a low moan of animal terror. He started muttering: "Oh God, oh God, oh God no, please God no."

His escorts walked him into the centre of the space and forced him onto his knees. Once he was kneeling I could see that his hands were tied behind his back. One man grabbed his hair and pulled his head back, exposing the soft flesh of his throat. Heathcote fell silent, too terrified to even whimper. He knew he was about to die. As he looked over at me I saw the mingled pleading and fear in his eyes and I felt like I wanted to be sick.

I was so transfixed that I didn't even notice Mac walk up beside me. I only registered his presence when he whispered in my ear.

"You weren't there when we taught this bitch a lesson. You weren't there when we executed the men from Hildenborough. I made you my second-in-command but you never really earned it, did you? You never got your hands wet. Or your dick, for that matter."

I clenched my fists. Mustn't let him provoke me. I had to think of a way out of this.

"It was too easy for you," he continued. "I wonder, would you have shot one of the prisoners that day if you'd been there?"

I turned to face him, defiant and angry.

"No, I wouldn't have. I'm not a murderer."

He chuckled. "You keep saying that, Lee. Who are you trying to convince? I should warn you, I'm a hard sell. I'm the one you betrayed, shot in cold blood and left to die, remember. Bates might disagree with you too. And I imagine you killed at least one of my officers yesterday. So what's the difference between a killer and a murderer, hmm? Coz you're definitely a killer."

I just stared into his eye.

"No answer to that? Well, let's put it to the test. You have a choice. If you want to live you have to kill Heathcote. Take a knife, slit his throat, watch him die. And then you have to drink his blood. You want to be in my gang you have to earn it this time. If you refuse I'll put a bullet in both your kneecaps and hang you upside down to bleed."

David was smiling indulgently at the pair of us. He couldn't hear what Mac was hissing in my ear, but he was allowing his favourite acolyte a little fun.

"And what's this lesson supposed to teach me?" I asked.

"That you aren't capable of doing what needs to be done," replied Mac. "If you kill Heathcote and join us, then I won't be able to touch you. You'll be protected as one of the brethren. Then you can plot and scheme to your heart's content. Try and bring him down the way you did me. You may even pull it off. God knows you're a devious little fuck. There's a chance that you might be able to save the school. And Matron, and the girls. But only if you stay alive. And you only stay alive if you kill Heathcote. Sacrifice him to save the others, or sacrifice yourself to save your conscience. Your choice."

He pressed a hunting knife into my hand.

"You've cheated your way into leadership without ever having to make the tough choices. This is what leadership is, Lee: the willingness to send men to their deaths when necessary, the ability to kill without compunction or hesitation when you need to. Show me what you're made of."

He stepped back, his hand resting on the butt of his holstered pistol.

The knife felt heavy as lead in my hand. I stared at Heathcote's wide, terrified eyes as he shook his head imperceptibly, in denial of what was happening. I looked around me, at a sea of blood-smeared faces, expectant and excited. And David, amused but curious at my hesitation.

"Come, come young man," he said briskly. "If you wish to join us you know what you must do. Bleed the cattle. Earn your salvation. Make yourself safe."

I thought of the two men at the pillbox who I had spared. If I'd killed them and taken care of the river defences, we'd have been able to evacuate the school unseen by the forces at the gate.

I thought of the officers I had released. If I hadn't let them go then Ben Woodhams, that young woman, Russell and Jones would all still be alive.

I thought of Mac. If I'd killed him before he'd seized power then Matron would have been spared her ordeal, and countless lives would have been saved.

If I had done what was necessary, so many people need not have died.

Every time I'd spared a life I'd made things worse. Mac was right. And Heathcote was a dead man anyway.

So I stepped forward, bent over the quivering boy, leant into him, whispered 'I'm so sorry' into his ear, and slit his throat open. All the while, looking straight into Mac's face. Even half ravaged as it was, his look of triumph was unmistakeable. It was the most terrible thing I have ever seen.

He mimed applause as the crowd began shouting hallelujahs.

As I stood up I saw Matron standing in the crowd. She was crying. Her tears ran red as they streamed down her cheeks. It was only then that I realised I was crying too.

The two men held Heathcote as he writhed and kicked his way to death, collecting the blood that flowed from his throat in an ordinary breakfast bowl. When his feeble struggles finally ceased, and the bowl was brimming with fresh blood, David stepped forward, lifted the bowl and brought it to me. He raised it to my lips. My nostrils filled with the metallic tang of slaughter.

"Drink of the blood of the lamb, and be transformed to your very soul," he said.

He didn't realise that I was transformed already.

I took two short, deep breaths, and leaned forward to take a sip.

As I did so I gripped the knife tightly, and brought it up as hard as I could into David's chest, aiming for his heart.

The blade bounced off the bullet-proof vest that David was wearing beneath his jacket, and fell to the grass.

And all hell broke loose.

CHAPTER SEVENTEEN

I DIDN'T EXPECT to survive. If it had been a straight choice – kill Heathcote or die – I like to think I would have chosen death.

Thing is, I had a knife, but David was ten feet away. If I moved towards him I'd be shot down before I got halfway. The only way to kill him was to get him to come to me. And the only way to do that was to kill Heathcote and continue with the ritual. I knew, when I slit that poor boy's throat, that his death was buying me the chance to kill David. That was the deal. I also expected to be shot in the head a second after the knife slid into the bastard's heart. I was fine with that.

But he didn't die. Nor did I. And so I have to live with the knowledge that I killed a friend in cold blood. The other nightmares keep me awake, but Heathcote's hopeless pleadings whisper in my ears every waking second.

"OOPS," SAID DAVID, grinning. Then he kneed me in the balls. I doubled over and he brought his knee up again, into my face, smashing my nose and sending me reeling backwards. I stumbled and fell to the ground. A huge cry went up from the crowd, and they fell upon me. Everything was a blur of kicks and punches, shouts and screams. Boots slammed into every inch of my body, I managed to raise my arms to try and protect my head, but it was of little use.

I heard a dreadful crack as my left arm snapped in two. I screamed in agony, and my head began to swim. It felt like I'd come adrift from the ground, weightless. I was starting to pass out.

Then the shooting started. The beating stopped almost instantly and I heard the screams of bloodlust change to cries of fear. I heard feet running left and right, the loud, insistent stutter of machine gun fire, and shouted orders from Mac and David. I lay there, unable to move. Every part of my body hurt, and my arm was agony. My head felt twice its normal size. I tried to calm my breathing. Couldn't lie here in the open like this. Then I felt hands reaching underneath my arms and lifting me. I opened my eyes but all I could see was swirls of colour; nothing made sense. I'd taken so many blows to the head it felt like my brain was bouncing back and forth inside my skull. Whoever was helping me managed to get me upright and I took a few shuffling steps.

"Down!" Matron.

She pushed me forwards and I sprawled back onto the grass. I landed on my broken arm and passed out.

When I came round I was moving again, staggering forward with Matron holding me up. I could hear the sounds of battle but I couldn't tell where they were coming from. Were we in the thick of the fighting or had we left it behind? Then I felt canvas on my face as we pushed through the flap into the tent. My vision started to clear slightly, and I could make out vague shapes and colours.

"Sit here," she said as she lowered me onto a chair.

My vision and hearing continued to improve. There was a hell of a battle going on outside. Matron came running up with a medical kit.

"You're holding your arm, is it broken?" She was breathless, and kept glancing over her shoulder at the tent door.

"Think so."

"This is going to hurt," she warned, and then she took hold of the arm and wiggled it a bit, trying to find the break and set the bone.

I passed out again.

When my senses returned my arm was in a sling, bound tight across my chest. I looked up and saw Matron struggling with an attacker. My vision was still blurred, and I couldn't make out the details, but I could see she was being overpowered. I looked around for a weapon and saw the med kit case lying at my feet. I leant down and picked it up with my good right arm. I tried to stand but my legs were like jelly. I managed to rise off the chair and then I toppled sideways and crashed to the ground. Luckily I fell onto my good arm this time.

Deep breaths. Focus. Things to do.

This time I managed to get upright and I lurched towards the struggling couple. I brought the corner of the med kit case down as hard as I could on the head of the man who had his hands around Matron's throat. He grunted and slumped to the ground. Hang on, he wasn't a Blood Hunter. Fuck.

Matron greedily sucked in some air with a hoarse yelp.

"Thank you," she gasped.

"We need to get out of here," I said. "Our guys are going to think you're the enemy, and any Blood Hunters who see you helping me will cut you down. You need to go."

"I know. Need to find the girls. One last thing, though."

She grabbed the med kit, opened it, pulled out a syringe and bottle. She filled the syringe and jabbed it into my good arm before I had a chance to ask what she was doing.

"What the fuck is that?" I asked.

"Home brew," she said. "Should help you stay on your feet for a bit. Take this." She pressed a machine gun into my good hand. Then she leaned forward and kissed me hard on the lips. "Good luck!" And she was gone, machine gun held ready, out the rear tent flap.

The spot where she'd injected me felt red hot. The heat spread out from my arm, creeping through my veins until my entire body felt like it was full of lava.

It felt fantastic!

A stream of bullets ripped through the tent fabric right in front of me, cutting a horizontal line. I dived for cover. The bullets stopped for an instant, hitting something between shooter and tent, and then continued. A body slammed into the canvas, and slid down to the grass. Then a Blood Hunter backed into the tent, firing wildly. Once inside he turned and made to run for the other exit, but he saw me. He screamed furiously and raised his gun. I was quicker. Two bullets to the chest took care of him.

The man lying beside me groaned and rubbed his head, coming around. I vaguely recognised him as one of the men from Hildenborough.

"Wake up," I yelled at him. He looked up at me, shaking his head to clear his vision.

"You all right?" he asked.

"Will be. You?" He nodded.

We got to our feet.

"Come on then," I said. And we ran out of the tent into the battle.

I'd never seen anything like it. It was a free for all. Everywhere I looked there were people fighting hand-to-hand; everywhere the glint of sunlight on machete blades, the smell of blood and cordite. People were being stabbed and shot, strangled and beaten. It was a mêlée and it was impossible to get a sense of who was winning. The force we had brought from Hildenborough was only forty strong, so they were hopelessly outnumbered.

I raised my gun and took a few potshots, killing two Blood Hunters outright and wounding at least one more. I was shooting one-handed, from the hip, with my other arm useless on my chest, but I was still shooting better than I'd ever done before. All my senses felt crystal clear. Whatever it was Matron had injected me with, it made me feel invincible.

The guy next to me staggered backwards as his head exploded in two, cleaved by a machete. I spun, firing, and the stream of bullets ripped into a Blood Hunter who jerked backwards and collapsed like a puppet with its strings cut. Suddenly I was in the thick of the fighting.

People crashed into me, locked in life and death struggles. Bullets whistled past my head. One Blood Hunter came for me, machete raised. I tried to bring my gun to bear, but it was grabbed by another Blood Hunter. I wrestled for control of the weapon, saw the raised machete out of the corner of my eye and let go of the gun. The Blood Hunter who'd grabbed it fell backwards with a shout of surprise and let off a burst of bullets, which cut down the one with the blade. As he fell I grabbed the blade and whipped around, throwing it as accurately as I could. It found its mark in the chest of the man who'd shot its owner. I grabbed my gun back from the lifeless hands of the Blood Hunter and tried to get some sense of what was going on around me. I couldn't see any boys. Where the hell was Norton?

Through the mass of fighting I caught a glimpse of the sandbagged machine gun nest at the gate. Inside, a Blood Hunter was firing the GPMG down the drive towards the school. A group of Blood Hunters were kneeling next to him, firing back into the mêlée, picking off Hildenborough fighters. If nothing changed it was only a matter of time before the Blood Hunters got the upper hand. We had to shut that gun down, allow Norton to bring reinforcements. Someone crashed into me from behind, knocking me to my knees. I turned to find a young blood-daubed woman staring at me, a neat hole above her left eye. She fell sideways revealing Rowles, smoking pistol in one hand, machete dripping blood in the other.

"Orders, sir?" he shouted above the din.

"We need to..." He raised his gun and I ducked. A bullet whipped over my head and I heard a strangled cry. I looked up at him again.

Definitely the scariest ten year-old I've ever met. I was glad he was on my side.

"GPMG!" I shouted, pointing towards the gate. He leant down and helped me to my feet. I was only halfway up when I had to shoot through his legs, kneecapping a woman who was coming at him with a machete. He turned and finished her off with a single shot.

Once I was upright I took the lead. We shoved our way through the fight, firing and hacking our way to the edge of the scrum. Then we skirted around the outside, collecting two Hildenborough men on the way. We found a clear space near the wall, and Rowles said "Let me, sir." He raised his gun and took careful aim.

As he took shots at the men behind the sandbags we stood guard around him, picking off any Blood Hunters we could get a clear shot at. The man next to me took a bullet to the thigh and then, as he bent down to put pressure on the wound, another round took him in the top of the head. He collapsed in a heap, instantly dead.

Rowles took a step forward each time he fired and the remaining man and I paced him, keeping him covered. He'd picked two of them off before they worked out who was shooting at them. By that point we were within a couple of metres of the sandbags. Rowles' gun clicked empty and he tossed it aside without a second's hesitation. I dropped to my knees and sprayed the sandbags with bullets as he ran towards them, machete raised, shouting some sort of battle cry. My bullets took one Blood Hunter across the chest and he fell backwards out of sight. The other fired wildly at Rowles but somehow the bullets kept missing, and soon the shooter was missing his left arm.

I heard a fleshy impact above me and the head of the man who'd been fighting beside me dropped at my feet. I dived forward and spun so I landed on my back, firing as I did so. But the gun didn't fire. Empty.

I rolled sideways to avoid the blade that curved down towards my head. In doing so I rolled over my broken arm. Didn't hurt a bit. The blade slammed into the grass next to my ear. I reached across with my good arm, grabbing the Blood Hunter's wrist, but it was drenched in fresh blood from the battle, and my hand slid off as he pulled the blade free of the ground. He raised the machete again as I lay there on the ground, nowhere to go. Then a blur above my head as someone literally dived over the top of me, their shoulder hitting the Blood Hunter in the stomach and taking him down. Haycox.

Even over the din of battle I heard the dreadful crunch as they hit the ground. Haycox sprang backwards, his opponent's neck snapped. He turned and reached down to offer me a hand up. But before I could take it his head snapped sideways as it shattered in a spray of blood and brain matter. Bullet to the head. He fell, stone dead. I scrambled backwards and tried to get to my feet. I was spending far too much of this fight flat on my bloody back. I saw two Blood Hunters come running towards me, lowering their guns as they came. Then they lurched backwards as an arc of heavy GPMG rounds picked them up and flung them, lifeless, to the grass. I looked across at the sandbags and there was Rowles, God love him, unleashing the GPMG at any Blood Hunter foolish enough to offer him a target.

I got to my feet and ran, crouching as I weaved through the fight, to the sandbags. I dived over them, landing smack on the fresh corpse of one of Rowles' victims. I pulled his gun free and took my place at Rowles' side, sheltering behind the wall of sandbags, picking off Blood Hunters.

A quick glance to my right revealed a stream of armed boys, running down the drive towards us; Norton and reinforcements. But looking at the scene in front of me I realised that it was already too late. The Blood Hunters were overwhelming the opposition. We were losing.

The heavy machine gun next to me chattered once more and then fell silent.

"All gone," said Rowles simply. "What now?"

"Back to Castle. Run!"

As Rowles legged it down the drive, waving for Norton and his troops to fall back, I stood and yelled into the mêlée as loud as I could: "Retreat! Back to the school! Retreat!"

Bullets from a host of Blood Hunters smacked into the sandbags, and I dived for cover again. This time I crawled across corpses and flung myself behind the school wall, out of the line of fire. Then I got up and ran for Castle as fast as I possibly could.

I could hear the sounds of pursuit behind me, cries and crashes and weapon fire. Running is bloody difficult with only one arm; you get unbalanced and wobble all over the place. I got halfway to the school, with bullets whistling past me all the way, and then my torso somehow outpaced my legs. I ploughed, head-first, into the grass. I tried to roll with it, and get back up on my feet, but my useless arm threw me again and I ended up in a heap.

I regained my feet and chanced a look behind me. Twenty or so Hildenborough men, Green, and a few of his surviving actors, were racing towards me, a horde of screaming Blood Hunters in their wake. Mac was leading the pursuit. He was bellowing encouragement to his cohorts, waving a bloodied machete above his head.

As the human tide caught up with me I turned and was swept along with them. Ahead of us I could see Norton lining the boys up into ranks. They shouldered arms and took careful aim right at us. What the bloody hell was he doing?

When we were within ten metres of him he shouted: "Get down!"

We didn't need telling twice. All of us dived to the ground. There was the most tremendous noise as all the boys fired at once, sending a wall of lead into the massed Blood Hunters.

"Positions!" yelled Norton.

We scrambled to our feet and ran forward. Then Norton shouted: "Down!" We dived again. A second volley thundered over our heads.

"Inside!"

We leapt up and piled in through the large double doors. As I stood at the doorway, herding people inside, I could see the results of Norton's volleys. They had wiped out the first rank of approaching Blood Hunters, maybe thirty or more, who lay twitching and groaning on the blood-soaked grass. Once those behind them had realised no third volley was likely, they'd kept running, trampling their dead and wounded underfoot in their eagerness to slice us open. They were nearly upon us. I couldn't see Mac. Had he fallen?

I ushered the last man through the doors and then followed him inside. Norton was there amongst the boys, manhandling an enormous barricade. Constructed from bookcases and table tops, it sat on two wheeled trolleys. They pushed this up against the flimsy main doors. A group of boys at each side took the strain, the trolleys were whipped away, and then the edifice was lowered to the floor. It was buttressed with thick wooden beams at 45 degrees, and once it was down it covered the main doors entirely. Almost the instant it hit the ground a huge body of men slammed into the doors and began pushing. The barricade didn't move an inch.

"Positions!" yelled Norton. Two groups of boys ran left and right out of the entrance hall and into the rooms that faced the lawn on the ground floor. These each boasted huge windows through which the Blood Hunters could pour. But each had thick wooden shutters inside, with metal crossbars to secure them. Through the doors I could see that these were all closed, and had been buttressed and reinforced with anything the boys could lay their hands on. Norton had done his job well. Another group ran upstairs to take up sniping positions at the windows on the first floor. A few moments later I heard the first shots from above as they rained fire down on the attackers. The final group ran backwards to take up defensive positions at the rear of the house.

The group of men and boys who'd survived the battle at the gate milled around, tending their wounds and catching their breath. Mrs Atkins moved amongst them, selecting those who needed the most urgent care.

Norton came running up to me and pressed a Browning into my hand.

"What happened?" he asked

"The wild card got creative," I replied. "Are all the defences in place as discussed?"

"Yeah, we're ready for them."

I turned and shouted at the people in the hall with us. "All those of you too wounded to fight make your way to the top floor. We've collected all the medicines and stuff in a dorm up there. Go patch yourselves up."

Mrs Atkins led about ten wounded men and boys up the stairs.

Green was standing right in front of me. He had a nasty gash across his forehead and his hair was matted with blood. He was gripping his machine gun tightly, but his lower lip was trembling. He looked like he was about to curl up in a ball and start weeping.

"Green, take these guys to the armoury and issue them with new weapons and ammunition."

He nodded wordlessly, and ran back into Castle, towards the cellar. The others followed.

Suddenly the banging on the door stopped, and the Blood Hunters' guns fell silent. Norton and I exchanged worried looks and ran up the stairs and into one of the rooms overlooking the lawn.

"What's going on?" I shouted.

"Dunno sir," replied one of the boys who'd been shooting down at them. "They all just ran around the side of the building."

At that moment there was a terrible scream in the distance.

"That came from the back," said Norton, and we ran out of the room and across the landing. We pushed through the double doors and ran across the main hall balcony to the rear stairs. Norton was in the lead as we crashed through the door and jumped down the stairs three at a time. We came out next to the cellar entrance, and found ourselves in the middle of a pitched battle. Green and the men he'd been arming were fighting hand-to-hand with a group of about ten Blood Hunters, but I could see more pouring into the courtyard outside.

How the hell had they gotten in?

Norton and I opened fire from the stairs. I could see Green, both hands raised, trying to slow the descent of a machete that a big, muscled Blood Hunter was forcing down towards his head. The Blood Hunter was grinning as his biceps flexed and the blade inched down. I couldn't get a clear shot through the crowd, so I lowered my head and shoulder charged the fighting men, barrelling through them until I was next to Green. I shoved my pistol into the Blood Hunter's perfectly sculpted six pack and squeezed the trigger twice. The man staggered back and slid down the wall, clutching his guts.

Green fell backwards too, into a corner. He curled up, buried his head in his hands and began to sob. I couldn't worry about him now. Someone banged into my left side and sent me staggering against a door. Which was open. I tottered for a moment in the doorway but I couldn't regain my balance. I reached out with my left arm to steady myself. But my left arm was in a sling. I fell headfirst down the hard stone steps into the musty cellar.

While I sprawled on the damp brick I heard someone slam the door against the wall and come running down the stairs behind me. Still on the ground I turned and saw a Blood Hunter woman charging towards me. I shot her twice but her momentum carried her forward and she collapsed on top of me. Her lolling head cracked into mine and the force smashed the back of my skull against the brick floor.

Bright spots danced in front of my eyes, and felt myself starting to pass out. I closed my eyes, steadied my breathing and tried to focus, but it was hard. God knows how many blows to the head I'd taken in the last twenty minutes. I was pretty sure the only thing keeping me conscious was Matron's home brew. I wasn't looking forward to the comedown.

I managed to stave off unconsciousness, and rolled the wounded woman off me. She was still alive, but she was out for the count. I decided the time for taking prisoners had long passed. I put one in her head to finish her off.

I had just got to my feet when I heard a tremendous explosion and a sustained volley of gunfire. It sounded like it came from the front of the school.

They'd blown the doors.

The sounds of battle overhead grew more intense. We were being overrun. I turned and ran into one of the side chambers. I picked up a box of grenades and a kit bag. I shoved as many of the bombs inside as I could, then I nipped into the next chamber along. I strapped two machine guns across my shoulders, put another pistol in my belt, and shoved as many clips of ammunition as I could carry into my pockets. I was carrying more hardware than Rambo.

A Rambo with bugger all muscle tone, gangly arms – one of which was useless – a mild case of acne, a broken nose, a head that felt like a punching bag and a system full of unknown drugs. Still, I had lots and lots of guns.

"Rock n' Roll!" I yelled, cocked my machine gun, and went running up the stairs. Straight into somebody's fist. My nose cracked once more and I went tumbling back down the stairs to the bricks.

"This," I said wearily as I lay there, "is getting repetitive."

"Don't worry," said a familiar voice. "It'll all be over soon." Mac was standing at the top of the stairs, shaking the fingers of his good hand. At least hitting me had hurt. He looked down at me and sneered.

I tried to bring my gun to bear but Mac was too fast for me. He was down the stairs before I could gather myself and he kicked the pistol from my grip. Then he stamped on my good hand. Even above the sound of the battle overhead, and my own shout of anger, I heard yet another bone crack.

Didn't feel it though. Really, *really* good drugs.

There was a stutter of machine gun fire from the top of the stairs. A Blood Hunter stood there, shooting back into the corridor, guarding the cellar door. At all costs I had to stop them taking possession of the armoury. I wanted to reach for a grenade, but even if my free hand had been working and I could pull a pin I'd only succeed in blowing the entire school sky high, taking everyone with it. Not an option.

Mac stood above me, gun pointed straight at my face.

"I really want to shoot you in the head, Nine Lives," he snarled. "You have no idea how much I want to shoot you in the fucking head."

"Be my guest." I screwed my eyes closed, waiting for the impact.

"But that would be no fun," he said. "I mean, orgasms are great, but they're so much better after a little foreplay, don't you think?"

"Shoot me or shag me, Mac... make your mind up."

He ground his foot on my hand. I could feel jagged edges of bone scraping against each other in my little finger.

The screams and gunfire from above were intense now. I imagined the Blood Hunters pouring through the front door, slicing and shooting the boys, smearing themselves in fresh blood and bellowing their victory.

"It's all over, Lee. There are too many of us. I'll be back in charge of the school within the hour. Maybe I'll celebrate with another crucifixion. What do you think?"

"Not very original," I replied. "You want to supersize it. How about a flaying, perhaps? Or maybe a dismemberment? Surprise me."

He squatted down on top of me, and leaned forward until my broken nose was almost touching his stubby little burnt wreck of one.

"I will, Lee. I promise you that. Now get up and dump the hardware."

He stood up and let me rise, keeping his gun on me as I let the weapons and ammunition drop to the floor.

"Now we wait for the commotion to die down so I can go claim my prize," he said.

"What about David?" I asked. "Won't he have something to say about you taking control?"

"David's my problem. Let me worry about him. You worry about me, Lee. Worry about what I'm going to do to you, Norton and that little shit Rowles, and anyone else who survives the fight. There's gonna be a bleeding tonight."

There was something different about Mac, and it wasn't just the injuries and the missing hand. He was taking real joy in the destruction happening above. He seemed more feral, less in control. His one good eye sparkled with barely concealed madness, very different from the power hungry thug I'd known before. He used to be unpredictable; now he was just plain scary.

"Mind if I sit while we wait?"

Mac opened his mouth to reply, but a burst of gunfire from the doorway silenced him. I saw the Blood Hunter by the door struggling with someone, heard a bone-crunching snap, and a man's lifeless body tumbled down the stairs to land at our feet.

"Yeah, why not," said Mac, ignoring the corpse. "Pull up a box of grenades. Let's bond."

I turned into one of the side rooms, looking for something to sit on.

"On second thoughts," said Mac. "Let's not and say we did."

Something hit me on the back of the neck, hard, and the world went black.

As I lost my grip on my senses the last thing I heard was Mac laughing. It was the insane cackle of a triumphant madman.

CHAPTER EIGHTEEN

I SPLUTTERED AS the water poured down my face. Ice cold, it brought me round instantly. I was lying flat on my back on wooden boards. I wiped my eyes and looked up to see Mac standing above me. I could see cloths and pulleys suspended high above him; I was lying on the stage in the school assembly hall. I could hear lots of other people moving around, the hall sounded full.

"Wakey, wakey, Nine Lives," he said. "Shake a leg. Rise and shine."

I put my hand to the floorboards to lift myself and found that my little finger was twice its normal size. It had a sharp point of bone sticking out of it above the knuckle. The drugs were wearing off, so when I put pressure on that hand it hurt. A lot. I gasped and gritted my teeth. Wouldn't give him the satisfaction of seeing how much pain I was in. I suspected the drugs were still dulling a great deal of it; my broken arm still felt okay. As long as I didn't do anything stupid, like throw a punch, I'd be fine for a while. I used my elbow to lever myself up into a sitting position.

The hall was to my left. Along one side all the surviving boys and girls, and the men who'd been fighting with us, were lined up. They were kneeling with their hands on their heads. I scanned the crowd and breathed a sigh of relief when I spotted Rowles, Norton and Mrs Atkins, all safe and sound. Green was there too. There were about thirty surviving children and ten men. Bob was not among them, but Mrs Atkins' new man, Justin, was. Guards stood over them with guns and machetes, making sure they didn't try anything. The wooden balcony that ringed the hall on three sides was empty. There were roughly sixty Blood Hunters in the room, each and every one of them glistening with the very freshest blood. They were all staring at the stage. At me. Nobody was speaking.

"Show time," said Mac, with a grin.

I had two options. Stay silent and risk letting them know how terrified I was, or take the piss and try to appear confident.

"Go on then," I replied. "Do us a dance. Show us your jazz hands. Oh, sorry, forgot. Jazz *hand*."

His grin didn't waver. "Get up."

As I did so I saw that David was sitting behind us on the stage, on his throne. He looked as immaculate and unruffled as ever, apart from where my knife had ripped the fabric of his suit.

"Welcome back, Lee," he said. "As you can see we have taken control of your school. It amused me to organise a little assembly. We might sing a few hymns later, would you like that?"

"Fine by me, as long as we don't have to sing *Morning Has Broken*. I fucking hate that song."

I was thinking fast, trying to work out the angles. There were guards in the wings at both sides. Behind David the stage stretched back into darkness. There was a fire exit door back there, but I'd never make it. There were three entrances to the hall itself: two sets of double doors on either side of the room and a fire exit at the back. All were guarded. There was no way out of here. Whatever Mac and David had planned I was stuck with it.

"I was going to bleed you in public," David said when I had gained my feet. "Make an example of you to others. But Brother Sean persuaded me otherwise. He has big plans for this place. He wants me to allow him to create a religious retreat here for our brethren. New recruits will be sent here for study and contemplation. Our wounded and old can find shelter here. He would run this endeavour for me. He even wishes to create a blood bank. The children you've watched over would be kept under lock and key, bled regularly but kept alive; a resource for the faithful. I and my chosen acolytes would continue our travels, taking the word to the world outside. I like the idea. What do you think?"

"Sounds lovely," I replied enthusiastically. "You could even have a cricket team, play the locals. Hildenborough are quite good, although you may have just slaughtered their first eleven."

David chuckled indulgently. "I thought you'd like it. But Brother Sean has some strange ideas." *Here we go*, I thought. "Even though we have taken your school by force, subdued your army and seized your weapons he feels bad for you."

"I'm sure his heart bleeds," I said, looking at Mac. His face gave nothing away.

David continued. "He has this quaint notion that he needs to prove he's better suited to run this place than you are. I can't imagine why."

"He's always had inadequacy issues," I said. "It all goes back to his childhood. Bed wetter, you see."

"I see. That explains a lot," said David, winking at Mac.

"I told you how it works, Lee," said Mac. "You want to be boss you've got to challenge the leader and beat him. Prove you're better. You never learned that lesson. But you will now. You're the leader of this place now, so I challenge you."

I laughed incredulously. "What, to a fight? You and me? Are you joking? I've got a broken arm and a broken hand. I fall down if I try to run and I can't even make a fist. What kind of victory would that be? You might as well wrestle a puppy, you fucking idiot."

He stepped forward and hissed furiously in my face: "Better than stabbing you in the back, you traitorous son of a bitch."

I turned to David and shrugged. "Your boy has issues, Mr David, sir."

"Can I say something?" All heads turned to the crowd of captives. It was Norton.

"No! Shut the fuck up!" yelled Mac, incensed at being interrupted, spittle flying through the gash where half his lips used to be.

"It's just that I remember something you said once about delegating responsibility," continued Norton.

Mac turned to the crowd. "Bring that little fucker up here."

A Blood Hunter walked over to Norton and hauled him to his feet by his hair, then marched him up the steps onto the stage. Mac was on him instantly, holding a gun to his face. "Explain," he growled.

Norton flashed a nervous glance at me and made his pitch.

"Let me see if I understand this. You want to fight Lee for control of the school. Winner takes all, yeah?"

Mac nodded.

"And what happens to the loser?"

"The fight's to the death. If he wants the school he's got to kill me with his own bare hands. He's learned that lesson well. Ask Heathcote."

Norton looked at David. "And you agree to this? If Lee wins then you leave?"

"I'll leave anyway," said David. "It's just a question of who's in charge when I do. Whoever wins, this will be a holy place for us. But I would allow Lee to complete the ritual and take charge for me.

He'd have a large group of helpers, of course" – David indicated the crowd of Blood Hunters below us – "to keep him on the path of righteousness."

"Okay," said Norton, turning his attention to me. "Lee, you're the leader round here, Mac – sorry, Brother Sean – acknowledges that, don't you?"

Mac nodded, suspicious.

"Then delegate to me, Lee. Let me fight him for you. For all of us."

"No fucking way," snarled Mac.

"Hang on, you're changing your bloody tune," I said. "Only half an hour ago you were telling me that I had to be able to send men to fight and die for me. One of the things real leaders have to do, you said. So why can't I delegate? Norton, you willing to die for me?"

"Sir, yes sir!" barked Norton. He even gave a cheeky salute to go with the grin.

"Good man," I said cheerily. I liked this plan. Norton was a black belt. He'd kick Mac's one-armed arse all the way to next Christmas. "So Mac, this lesson you've been wanting to teach me. Looks like I've learned it. Willing to put your money where your mouth is? Gonna take on my loyal deputy? Or are you only willing to fight if you've got to fight me? I mean, yeah, if I only had a broken arm we'd be evenly matched. But you broke the little finger on my other hand. So unless you're going to give me a gun the best I can do is slap you. Not going to be a very satisfying fight, is it? Your victory won't be worth shit. But beat Norton, well, that'd be something. You'd have earned it then. That's what you said, isn't it... it's all about earning it?"

Silence fell. Everyone in the room was transfixed, waiting to see what Mac would do. If he went for this then we had a chance

I walked up to Mac, who still stood with his gun aimed at Norton. I whispered in his ear.

"All this time you've been pointing out to me the ways in which I'm a failure. The things I can't do that a leader needs to. Not forgetting the rules of challenge and succession you keep banging on about. You want to do this right, yeah? According to the rules? Then here's your chance. Follow your own logic, Mac. Fight the man I delegate to represent me. Prove you're better than the best I can field."

"And what if I delegate too? What if I ask Gareth to fight for me?" He indicated one of David's giant guards.

"Brother Sean, I think you're forgetting who's in charge here," said David, with steel in his voice. "I do the delegating, not you. I'm indulging your whim. Take care that my indulgence doesn't run out. The young man's logic is sound. I suggest you accept the challenge. Otherwise I may decide you're not the man you profess to be. I might decide you're cattle."

Mac looked rattled. But he had no option now. He'd engineered this situation, he'd have to see it through.

"Fine," he snarled as he let the gun fall from his grip, and charged.

Before Norton could react Mac took him in the midriff and barrelled forward, propelling him off the stage. They sailed through the air, crashing five feet to the floor of the main hall. Norton fell flat on his back, with all Mac's weight on top of him. There was a dreadful crack of bone as his spine hit the hard wood floor, then a hollow thump as his skull bounced. Lying on top of Norton, Mac reached his one good arm up, grabbed Norton's hair and slammed the back of his head onto the floor. Once, twice, three times. Then he leaned back, folded his arm and brought the sharp end of his elbow smashing down with all his might on Norton's throat. There was an awful soft crunch as his windpipe collapsed.

The whole fight had lasted about five seconds.

Mac rolled off and got to his feet. Norton lay there, clutching at his collapsed throat, gasping for air. The assembled Blood Hunters roared in triumph.

It's a measure of how used to this kind of thing I'd become that while everyone was watching my best friend die, I took the chance to get to Mac's discarded gun. I dived forward, landing on my broken arm, reaching for the gun with my semi-good hand. Yep, the drugs were wearing off. That hurt.

Gareth the guard stepped forward and kicked me under the chin before I could reach the weapon. I was flung backwards off the stage. I fell hard and lay on the hall floor, winded, next to Norton. We looked into each other's eyes. I could see all the fear and panic and horror in his, as they widened, dilated, and died. The crowd kept cheering.

Mac's leering zombie face appeared over mine.

"Well done," he said, shouting over the din. "One more corpse for the cause. Hope you're proud."

At that moment I finally accepted it. We were finished. We'd lost. I had no clever plan to fall back on, no trap to spring, no argument to put forward. I felt the darkest, blackest despair. I was beyond weeping or begging for mercy. There were no more sarcastic comebacks or flippant putdowns. My friends were dead or captured. I was a broken wreck. Everything I'd tried to achieve had been destroyed. I'd failed my friends, my father, myself. All I had to look forward to was a creatively stage-managed death. And I was okay with that. It'd be kind of a relief.

I got my breath back and slowly rose to my feet. Mac faced me across Norton's cooling body, one mad eye gleaming with triumph. I spat in it. He just laughed.

I looked over his shoulder at the kneeling captives. Rowles' face a mask of cold fury, Green weeping, Mrs Atkins staring blankly into space. I wanted to tell them how sorry I was, but it wouldn't have meant a damn.

"Loser," said Mac, taunting me. I didn't reply.

David called for silence and the noise died away. The cult leader rose to his feet and addressed us.

"Brother Sean has brought great credit to our crusade. He led us out of our hermitage and set us on the true path. And now, brothers and sisters, he has brought us to a place of refuge and sanctuary, where the chosen can abide in peace through the Tribulation. This place, once a school, will become a beacon of hope for all the world. Children will study here under our guidance, learning of the one true faith. Here we shall train acolytes and pilgrims, preachers and reapers. The good word shall spill from this hallowed place like a flood and it shall sweep away all the cattle from our lands and make us safe. Hallelujah!"

The Blood Hunters howled their hallelujahs in response. David pointed at me. "Bring that child to me." I didn't wait to be grabbed and herded. I walked to the steps and mounted the stage again.

"No!" shouted Mac. "You promised me! You said I could do it!"

David silenced Mac with a look before turning to me.

"Young man," said David. "You were given an opportunity to join us, but you rejected it. Instead you tried to silence my holy voice. This cannot go unpunished." He gestured to the men in the wings. "Fetch rope," he said. They didn't even have to move, they just reached out and grabbed a rope that dangled from the gods. One of the guards walked out onto the stage holding the rope, which came easily, because it was only anchored to a wheeled pulley way up high. David took the rope and bent down, tying it around my feet.

He motioned to the guard, who walked back into the wings and unlaced the other end of the rope from the metal peg that secured it. Then he hauled on it, and my feet went out from under me. I crashed to the stage, face first. I felt one of my front teeth shatter. I was pulled upwards until I dangled in the air, suspended so my head was level with David's.

I could see Mac in the crowd. He looked agitated.

Slowly, meticulously, David stripped naked. Then he took a knife from one of the guards and walked centre stage. He spread his arms and addressed the crowd.

"In the fountain of life I shall be reborn," he intoned.

The Blood Hunters replied: "Make us safe."

"With the blood of the lamb I wash myself clean."

"Make us safe."

"From the source of pestilence comes our salvation."

"Make us safe."

"Life for life. Blood for blood."

"Make us safe."

He turned towards me, cradled my head and moved to kiss me.

"I'll bite your fucking lips off," I growled. He backed away.

"I thank you for your gift," he said.

Then, suddenly, the right side of his head wasn't there anymore. He reached up to feel his face, as if he were confused at what was trickling down his cheek. Someone in the crowd started to scream. David's hand came away from the gaping wound and he held the bloodied fingers up in front of his face, trying to focus on them. He emitted a bark of laughter and said: "As if by magic!" Then he collapsed in a heap.

Mac stood on the right side of the stage, smoking pistol in his hand.

"You promised!" he shouted at David's crumpled form. "You fucking promised! He's *mine*. I told you that and you promised."

The fallen cult leader craned his head to look at Mac. He gave a sick, gargling laugh and blood bubbled up out of his mouth. "Safe now," he gasped. And then his head fell backwards, lifeless.

While all this was going on my eye caught a flash of movement as the door to the balcony swung open. I couldn't see anybody emerge. It didn't swing shut, but it was pushed further open, as if someone else was entering. Then again and again it swung a little shut but was pushed back open. There were people crawling onto the walkway overlooking the hall, hidden from view by the waist-high wooden guard rail. Who the hell was up there?

The crack of David's head on the wood jolted the guards out of their shock and they ran at Mac, machetes raised. He gunned them down. While they were still falling, he turned to the screaming crowd and fired over their heads. "Shut the fuck up!" he yelled. Silence fell. "I'm in charge now, right? You!" He pointed at one of the Blood Hunters in the wings. "Cut him down." The Blood Hunter didn't move. Mac waved the gun at him. "Now!" Still he didn't move. Mac paused, seemingly unsure what to do in the face of this refusal to comply.

It was as if his head suddenly cleared and he realised the position his unthinking rage had placed him in. He'd just killed the religious leader of a group of insane cannibals, all of whom were armed. And they were all looking at him.

"Nice one, Mac," I said. "Good move."

There was a collective roar, a guttural explosion of fury from every Blood Hunter in the hall. Then they rushed him. They could have shot him, but I guess there was something about wanting to inflict the pain personally, needing to feel the kicks and punches landing. Some of them even threw their guns aside as they ran. Like a tide, the cultists swept left and right to the stairs and streamed up them onto the stage. I was ignored, forgotten. Mac fired, mowing some of them down as they approached, but it was no use. They fell upon him and he screamed as he vanished beneath a flurry of fists.

Two things happened at once. The boys and men who'd been held prisoner ran forward and grabbed all the discarded weapons they could; and an army of girls appeared on the balcony above us.

Matron stood directly opposite and above me on the balcony, machine gun pointed down. To her left and right, flanking the room on all three sides, were fifteen young girls, all similarly armed.

I saw Rowles look up in astonishment. Then he looked at the stage and he smiled broadly.

"Fire!" he yelled.

All the girls opened up at once, pouring fire down into the throng of Blood Hunters. Those boys and men who'd grabbed discarded guns did the same.

The Blood Hunters didn't stand a chance. It was a massacre. Some of them realised what had happened and tried to bring their weapons to bear, but the onslaught was too fierce, the fire too concentrated. The gunfire seemed to go on forever, a cacophony of stuttering weapons with a staccato accompaniment of spent cartridges hitting the floor. The noise reached a crescendo and then gradually died away as magazine after magazine clicked empty and the guns fell silent. As the smoke rose, and the smell of cordite swamped everything, silence fell.

The stage was piled head-high with twitching, bleeding Blood Hunters; dead, dying and wounded. And me, upside down, swinging gently above the slaughter, splashed with blood and gore, laughing hysterically.

MATRON WAS APPALLED at what had occurred, but she took control with assured, businesslike calm. She sorted out the youngest children, both boys and girls, and sent them outside to collect weapons from the battlefield. The men and older boys set to work pulling the Blood Hunters off the stage and sorting them into three piles: dead, mortally wounded, and those who could perhaps be saved. Matron co-ordinated the triage.

There was a brief argument between Rowles and Matron, with Rowles arguing that they should all be shot in the head. Matron wouldn't hear of it. Rowles surprised me by accepting her authority.

After I was cut down I sat at the far end of the hall and nursed my wounds, unable to believe that I was still alive. After a while Matron came and sat next to me, resting her hand on my knee.

"You all right?" she asked. I didn't need to answer that. "No, of course you're not. Sorry. Stupid question."

I smiled to indicate I didn't mind and she grimaced. "Ouch," she said, as she leant forward, took hold of my jaw and opened my mouth to reveal my missing front tooth. It had snapped in two, leaving a jagged, serrated edge that I couldn't stop probing with my tongue. "That must really hurt."

"Not yet," I lisped. "Your drugs are still taking the edge off. But I wouldn't mind another hit before you pull the root out."

"No problem. Hold still." She took hold of my re-broken nose and wrenched it into place again, making me yell. "You need a splint on that. I'm not sure it'll set quite right, though."

"Great," I laughed. "I'm a limping, lisping, gap-toothed scarface with a broken nose. What a catch."

She placed her hand on my cheek. "Oh, I don't know." She flashed me a cheeky, girlish grin that made me feel all sorts of interesting things. I actually blushed.

"Are all the girls okay?" I asked, changing the subject.

She nodded. "David kept his side of the bargain. They didn't touch them. Which isn't to say they enjoyed being locked in a caravan for so long." She surveyed the makeshift morgue in front of her. "I was hoping they wouldn't have to open fire; that just the threat would

215

be enough to get the Blood Hunters to disarm. It seems that these days everyone has to end up killing somebody."

I looked at her and suddenly I realised where we'd gone wrong, all those months ago.

"It should have been you," I said to her.

"Sorry?"

"In charge. It should have been you, not Bates."

"Don't be ridiculous," she scoffed.

"Think about it. Every time things went wrong you were the one who did the right thing. You stood up to that woman on the drive; you stood up to Bates and Mac when Hammond was killed. While I was making plots, pretending to be something I wasn't, you were always the honest one. Of all the lessons Mac was trying to teach me about leadership, that's the one he never understood: you can only be a proper leader if you're willing to stand up for what you believe in and be counted when it matters. I never was. You always were. It should have been you, Jane. Not Bates, not Mac, not me. You. Maybe then none of this would have happened."

"Oh fuck off, Nine Lives" said a voice from the stage. There was Mac, fished out from the very bottom of the pile of bodies. He was covered in cuts and bruises, but not a single bullet had made its way through the crowd to him, curled up on the floor at the epicentre of the lynch mob. "The last thing we need right now is a fucking moral, yeah? Spare us, please."

Two of the boys who'd been sorting through the bodies stood beside him, keeping him covered. I stood up and walked towards him across the hall floor, skirting the wounded and dying.

"What does it take to kill you, eh?" I said, incredulous. "I mean, I shot you, I blew you up, you just got beaten and shot at. What does it fucking take to get rid of you?"

"Back at you, Nine Lives," he replied, with a sneer.

I reached the stage and leant on it, resting my arms on the footlights and looking up at him. I sniffed and shook my head. I didn't understand it, but I was almost glad to see him. "Shooting David wasn't the cleverest thing you've ever done, was it?"

He shrugged, then he limped over to the front of the stage and sat down, dangling his legs over the side next to me.

"Fair point." He chuckled. "Snatched defeat out of the jaws of victory there, didn't I?"

"Kind of, yeah. You do realise you're insane. Really, genuinely psychopathic."

"Probably," he replied. He paused and then said: "I blame society."

I couldn't help it; that made me laugh. After a second he joined in and before I knew it we were holding our sides, tears streaming down our faces, in the grips of the most terrible giggles. When they subsided I reached down and picked up a discarded Browning. I checked it was loaded and chambered a round.

"Still," I said. "I'm going to have to kill you now, Sean. I hope you understand that."

He looked at me and nodded.

"It's what I'd do," he said evenly.

"I just want you to know, it's completely personal. I really hate your guts and I want you to die."

"I understand," he said.

I took a step back, raised the gun and aimed at his heart. I looked straight into his face, at his one remaining eye, as I squeezed the trigger to the biting point.

"Lee, put it down," said Matron, behind me.

I didn't move a muscle.

"Lee, please, put it down. Enough now. You don't need to kill him. I worked too bloody hard to put him back together."

Mac held my gaze. His face gave nothing away. He seemed more curious than scared, interested to see which way I'd jump. Was I finally the cold blooded killer he'd always told me I needed to be? The answer was yes, and I was going to prove it. I wanted to kill him. I was sure it was the right and necessary thing to do.

I felt Matron's hand on my arm. "Put it down, Lee. It's over."

I turned my head to look at her. Somehow I'd not noticed before now, but she'd washed her face clean of blood. I could really see her for the first time in months. Her eyes held such compassion and warmth. My stomach felt hollow and empty, but I couldn't be sure whether it was because of the drugs wearing off, the sight of her face, or the certain knowledge that I was going to pull the trigger whatever she said.

"Sorry, Jane. But I'm a killer now." I turned back to face Mac. "It's what he made me." I steadied my arm to fire. I would have done it too, but Mac wasn't looking at me any more. He was looking over my shoulder. He smiled. "Finally," he said. "Someone with balls."

The first bullet took him in the jaw, ripping away half his face. The second got him right between the eyes. The third and fourth hit him in the right shoulder. The fifth went wide, and the sixth ripped open his throat. The seventh and eight took away his nose and one remaining eye. The ninth, tenth and eleventh hit his chest, exploding his heart and lungs. Then the hammer hit metal. Mac fell backwards, a dead weight.

Green, by this point standing beside me, dropped the smoking gun to the floor, wiped his eyes, and walked away without a word.

EPILOGUE

I REMEMBER THE first time I met Lee. He was fourteen and it was my first day as Matron at St Mark's, my first day as Jane Crowther. I wasn't sure if it was an identity I'd be comfortable with. I'd trained to be a doctor, not nursemaid to a bunch of spoiled upper-class brats. I was nervous and uncertain.

The police had taken care of all the details, and Inspector Cooper assured me that my cover was absolutely water tight. A few years hidden away in this anonymous little school and then maybe I could resume my medical studies somewhere else. Somewhere they'd never find me.

The last words Cooper said to me were: "I promise you, Kate, it's over. You'll never have to pick up a gun again."

What a joke.

Anyway, there I was, hair freshly dyed, first day at my new school. And the first boy into the San that morning was Lee. He was awkward and gangly, with arms that seemed too long for his body, and a smattering of spots across his forehead. His hair was wild and scruffy, and his uniform was a mess. He'd hit a pothole and fallen off his bike, he said, as he showed me the nasty graze on his arm. I swabbed it clean, smeared it with germolene and slapped on a bandage. *Three years of medical training for this*, I thought, totally depressed.

But then Lee did the sweetest thing, I've never forgotten it.

"You've got a hell of a job here, you know," he said. "Your predecessor was quite something."

I remember thinking 'Predecessor'? What kind of fourteen-year-old uses a word like 'predecessor?' Certainly not the kind of kids I grew up with.

"Really? How's that, then?" I asked.

So he told me all about the headmaster and his wife, and explained why the boys might resent me; he gave me tips on how to defuse the head's rages, and schooled me in the tactics needed to manage the particularly difficult boys, who he named and shamed so I wouldn't get caught by surprise. He was shy but friendly, presenting himself as a willing conspirator and helpmate. By the time he left I felt much better about things.

It was such a thoughtful, welcoming thing to do. I had a soft spot for him from that moment on, I suppose.

I think back to the year after The Cull, and the broken, hard-faced wreck that he became, and I want to weep. You see, he was never cut out for leadership, not under those circumstances, anyway. He was sweet and slightly bookish, a bit of a dreamer really. Young, yes, but mature for his age and with a strong sense of right and wrong.

Even now, years later, he hasn't got over the choices he made that year. I try to tell him that he shouldn't feel bad, that what he achieved was flat out heroic. But he doesn't see it that way. He still has the nightmares. I like to think that I'm a help to him, but sometimes he suffers from deep depressions that can last up to a month, and I'm powerless then. Still, I think writing this account has been therapeutic for him.

However, he can't bring himself to write the final chapter of the St Mark's story, so he's asked me to do it for him. I'm not much of a writer, so I'll keep it brief.

We were still clearing out the main hall when we heard shouts and running feet in the corridors. Then Rowles appeared on the balcony and shouted: "Bomb!"

Everyone was very calm about it, no one panicked. I suppose after what we'd just been through this seemed kind of tame. We walked outside and made our way to the playing fields at the back. Rowles had been putting the guns back into the armoury when he'd discovered a cluster of dynamite sticks, booby trapped and wired up to a clock.

MacKillick must have left them there, as an insurance policy. If he'd survived he'd have gone down and cut whichever wire he needed to cut. But he was dead, and neither Rowles nor Lee wanted to take the gamble of choosing red, yellow or black. As we stood there debating what to do there was the biggest explosion I've ever seen. All the grenades and bullets in the armoury went up with the dynamite, practically demolishing Castle in one horrendous bang.

Sean had the last laugh in the end. If he couldn't rule St Mark's then no-one could.

The wreckage burnt long into the night, warming us as we tried to decide what to do next. Lee just sat there, silent, staring at the fire, tears streaming down his face as he watched all his dreams, everything he'd fought for, burn away to ashes.

In the morning we packed up the Blood Hunters' marquee and walked to Hildenborough, where we moved into empty houses and slept all day.

I had been thinking about what Lee had said, about me being the natural leader. Those three months at the farm with the girls had been wonderful, and yes, I had enjoyed being in charge. Lee made it very clear that he didn't want the job any more.

So I called a meeting and we put it to the vote. Should we stay and become part of the Hildenborough community, or should I take charge of the search for a new home, a new school? The vote was unanimous.

Weeks later, when we were having our final meeting to choose between two likely places, Lee took me to one side.

"I'm leaving, Jane," he said.

I told him to stop being silly. His arm and hand were healing but he still had limited movement. He needed more physiotherapy and time to recover. But he was determined.

"I have to go find my father," he explained. "I know he survived the plague, but he should have been back here by now. Something's gone wrong and he might need my help."

"But where will you look?" I asked, unable to believe this.

"Iraq," he said simply.

I begged him to reconsider, told him to wait for us to finish our meeting and then we'd discuss it. He promised he would. But when we wrapped up half an hour later, he was gone.

I only spent two years as the matron of St Mark's School for Boys. I'd gone there looking for a refuge from violence, and instead I'd found more death than I could have imagined. And more kindness, too. We took the sign from the front gate with us when we moved into Groombridge, establishing some sense of continuity. "St Mark's is dead, long live St Mark's," as Rowles put it.

I was in control and I swore this time it would work, this time everyone would be safe.

I'd make sure of it.

THE END

OPERATION MOTHERLAND

Original cover art by Mark Harrison

PART ONE
LEE

CHAPTER ONE

I CELEBRATED MY sixteenth birthday by crashing a plane, fighting for my life, and facing execution. Again.

I'd rather have just blown out some candles and got pissed.

"HELLO? IS ANYBODY there? Hello?"

"Lee? Oh, thank God."

"Dad? Dad, is that you? I can hardly hear you. Where are you?"

"Still in Basra, but we're shipping out soon. Listen, I don't know how much time I have. Is your mother there?"

"Er, yeah."

"Put her on, son."

I'D BEEN SCANNING the terrain for about ten minutes, looking for a decent place to land, when small-arms fire raked the fuselage.

Stupid, careless idiot; I'd been flying in circles, just asking to be shot at.

The problem was that I couldn't find the airport. I could see the river snaking to the sea, the city straddling it and blending into desert at the edges. I could see the columns of smoke rising high off to the north, and the boats bobbing in the long abandoned harbour. But I couldn't see the bloody airport. So I had to get closer and look for somewhere to land.

I'd managed to fly thousands of miles, refuel twice without incident (if you didn't count that psycho in Cyprus, but he wasn't that much trouble) and make it to my destination unscathed.

Then, on arrival, I descend to within shooting distance and wave my wings at anyone who fancies a potshot.

I bloody deserved to be shot down.

I pulled hard on the control column, trying to raise the plane's nose and climb out of range, but it didn't respond.

"Oh shit," I said.

I was at 500 feet and descending, nose first, towards a suburban street littered with abandoned cars and a single burned-out tank. I tried to shimmy the plane left or right, pumped the pedals, heaved and wrenched the control column, anything to get some fraction of control.

Nothing.

Too low to bail out, nothing to do but ride the plane into the ground and hope I was able to walk away.

My arrival in Iraq was going to be bumpy.

"JESUS DAD, WHAT did you say to her? Dad, you still there?"

"Yeah, just... I, um... listen, Lee, there's something I have to tell you."

"Ok."

"The plague, from what we've been hearing here, it's sort of specific."

"Eh?"

"You only get it if you've got a particular blood type. No, that's not right. You don't get it if you've got a particular blood type. Everyone who's O-Negative is immune, that's what the doc here told us."

"And everyone else..."

"Is going to die."

I WAS COMING in clean towards the road, lined up by pure chance. If the road had been clear, and if I could've got the nose up, I'd maybe have had a chance. But I was heading straight for the fucking tank, and no matter what I did the plane was just a hunk of unresponsive metal.

There was another burst of gunfire, and this time I could see the muzzle flash of the machine gun on a rooftop to my left. His aim was true and the plane shuddered as the bullets hit the tail, sending fragments of ailerons flying into the tailwind. I yelled something obscene, furious, defiant, then pulled the control column again, more in frustration than hope.

And, *hallelujah*, it responded. That second burst of fire must have knocked something loose. I never thought I'd be grateful that someone was shooting at me.

Of course, at twenty feet and however many knots, there wasn't that much I could actually do.

The nose came up a fraction, just enough to change the angle of attack from suicidal to survivable. Not enough to actually stop my descent, though.

I'm pretty sure I was yelling when the tail of the plane slammed into the turret of the tank, snapped off, and pitched the plane nose first into the hard-packed earth.

The world spun and tumbled as I screamed in tune with the crash and wrench of twisting metal. The plane somersaulted, over and over, down the road, bouncing off cars and buildings, losing its wings, being whittled away with every revolution, until it seemed there was just a ball of warped metal and shattered plastic cocooning me as it gouged the ground, ricocheting like some kind of fucked-up pinball.

Eventually, just as the darkness crept into my vision and I felt myself starting to black out, the world stopped spinning.

My head was swimming, there was blood in my mouth, I was upside down, the straps of my harness digging into my knotted shoulders, but I was alive.

"One more life used up, Nine Lives," whispered a familiar, sarcastic voice in my head. I told it to piss off.

Then I realised that I was wet. I reached up and wiped the slick liquid from my face. When my eyes could focus and my dizzy brain began to accept input, I realised that I was soaked from head to toe in fuel.

I heard gunfire in the distance, as someone started taking shots at what was left of my plane.

And I couldn't move.

"ALL OF THEM?"

"All. Lee, you're O-Neg. So am I."

"And mum? Dad, you there? I said, what about Mum?"

"No."

"Oh. Right."

"Now listen, she might be safe if you can just quarantine yourselves. Don't leave the house, at all. For any reason."

"But what about food? The water's been switched off, we've got no power. There's these gangs going around attacking houses, Dad, they've got guns and knives and..."

"Lee, calm down. Calm down. You mustn't panic, son. Breathe... You okay now?"

"Not really."

"I know. But you're going to be strong, Lee. For your mum."

"She's going to die isn't she... Dad?"

"Yes. Yes, she probably is."

"But there's no doctors, you know that right? The hospital's been closed for a week. They put these signs up saying to wait for the army to set up field hospitals, but they haven't shown up. They're not going to, are they?"

"No, I don't think so, not now. I know it's hard, but it's all up to you, son. You're going to have to nurse her. Until I can get there. I'm coming home, Lee. As fast as I can. You've got to hang on, understand?"

"But what if you're not fast enough? What if something goes wrong? What if I'm left here, alone, with... with... Oh God."

I REACHED ACROSS and unclasped my harness. It snapped free and I slumped, shoulder first, into a mess of tangled metal. I screamed as my left shoulder ground into a sharp metal edge. Something felt wrong about the way it was lying. I tried to move my left arm but all I felt was an awful grinding of flesh and bone.

It was dislocated.

Add that to the disorientation, which would probably give way to concussion, and the numerous possible wounds that I'd yet to discover, not to mention the chunk of my lower lip that I'd bitten out with what remained of my teeth...

Actually, I'd got off pretty lightly all things considered. If I could just avoid getting burned to death, this might even qualify as a good day. I squirmed in the wreckage, trying to find a gap through which I could wriggle, some way to gain purchase. It was agony; every move ground my shoulder joint against the slack, useless muscles, causing shooting pains so intense that they made my vision blur.

I could hear cries from nearby streets, and more gunfire, as men closed in on my position. I really needed to move.

Finding nothing that offered any chance of escape, I braced myself as best I could and pushed hard, using my full body strength to try and force my way out, like a bird kicking its way out of a metal egg. My spine cracked like a rifle, and my legs burned with effort. My shoulder joint minced the flesh that surrounded it, and I screamed in impotent fury until finally I felt something near my feet give ever so slightly. I redoubled my efforts, taking every ounce of strength I had in my small, wiry frame, and concentrating it in my feet. Oh so slowly, I forced a metal strut backwards and it groaned in protest.

Eventually it bent far enough to let in a small circle of sunlight. I squirmed again, rotating inside my shell, until my head and shoulder were positioned beneath the opening.

I gritted my teeth. This was really going to hurt. I closed my eyes, and pushed myself upwards, squeezing my agonised shoulder through the tiny gap. I felt something rip inside my arm and I screamed again. Once my shoulders were clear I was able to pull my right arm through and use it to push myself free.

Just as my feet emerged, the mass of wreckage beneath me shifted under my redistributed weight, pitching me forward. I lost my balance and tumbled to the ground.

I lay there on the hot, baked earth and I smiled through the pain.

This dirt was Basra.

I'd made it.

"Lee, focus, you've got things to do."

"Right. Yes. Okay."

"Now we're shipping out of here before the week's out."

"Back to England."

"Yeah."

"So, what, I should see you in ten days or so?"

"I'm afraid it's not quite that simple. They're not just letting us go home. I'm still a soldier and I still have to obey orders. If I try to just come home, I'll be shot as a deserter. They executed one of my mates yesterday. He wanted to stay here, got a local girlfriend, kid on the way. Tried to slip away, got caught. They shot him at dawn."

"Bloody hell."

"Apparently there's some big thing planned for when we all get home, but nobody's saying what."

"So what do I do?"

"You go back to school, to St Mark's."

* * *

BEFORE I COULD gather my wits and rise to my feet, someone started kicking the crap out of me.

I tried to roll away from the kicks, raise my good arm to protect my head, find some space in between the blows to reach down and grab my Browning, which was tucked into my waistband. But with one arm useless, and my head woozy with shock and pain, I ended up just curling into a ball and letting the blows come. My attacker was shouting and firing his gun in the air, laughing as he kicked me to death. Luckily he was wearing trainers, not hobnail boots. So it was going to take him a while.

Then, what was left of the plane exploded. The shockwave actually rolled me along the ground a bit, like a balled-up hedgehog. My mouth and eyes filled with dust and sand. The kicking stopped. I cautiously removed my arm and saw my assailant sprawled on the floor beside me. There was a short metal stanchion protruding from his forehead. I uncurled myself, lurched upright, reached down and took the AK-47 from his still twitching hands.

He looked younger than me. Dreadful acne, dark skin, khaki combats, plain white t-shirt. He lay there on the sandy ground, staring sightlessly into the sky. My first victim of the day. I hoped he would be the last, but I didn't think it likely.

A yell from the far end of the street reminded me that he had friends. I had to move. I staggered as fast as I could in the opposite direction. I had no idea of the layout of this town, but it was their home turf. I was one wounded boy with a useless arm, a half-empty machine gun and pistol with a couple of clips; there were probably loads of them, armed to the teeth. I had salvaged no water from the crash, the midday sun was beating down on me hotter than anything I'd ever experienced before, I was losing blood, sweating as I ran, and had no idea how to come by safe drinking water.

I was so screwed.

I wished I had some of Matron's homebrew drugs on me. Just a shot of that had kept me fighting in the battle for St Mark's despite shattered teeth, a broken arm and more blows to the head than I could count. But I'd left without saying goodbye. I regretted that now; I'd almost certainly never see her again. Still, it seemed like the right thing to do at the time. I'd probably have ended up blubbing or, worse, trying to snog her, and that would have been excruciating.

A bullet pinged off a brittle brick wall next to my head as I dodged down an alleyway, weaving in between burned-out cars and abandoned barricades. This was pointless. If I could get far enough ahead of them I had a chance, but I just wasn't capable of any kind of speed. I'd never outrun them.

I had to go to ground.

"BACK TO SCHOOL, seriously?"

"Listen, some of the teachers stayed behind didn't they? And some of the boys?"

"Yeah, but..."

"No buts. It's the only safe place I can think of. They've got weapons there, in that bloody armoury, haven't they?"

"Uh huh."

"Then get back there, join up with anyone who's left, arm yourselves and wait for me."

"You promise you'll come?"

"No matter what happens, Lee, I'll be there. It may take a while, that's all. If you're at St Mark's you'll be as safe as houses and I'll know where to find you. Promise me."

"I promise."

I EMERGED FROM the alleyway into a housing estate. Residential tower blocks rose up in front of me, some burnt out, some with great gaping holes punched in them by depleted uranium shells, one reduced to nothing but rubble. Their balconies were festooned with clothes, bedding and the occasional skeleton. This desolate, abandoned maze of passages, flats and stairwells was my best chance of eluding my pursuers.

I stumbled across the churned up paving stones, heading for the doorway of the block that seemed most intact. The sound of pursuit echoed eerily around the empty estate, making it impossible for me to know how many pursuers there were, or how close.

The blue metal door to the block lay half open. I shoved it, using my good shoulder. Something inside was blocking my way, so I had to shimmy through the narrow gap into the musty, foetid darkness of the stairwell. My foot sank into something soft and yielding. I felt something pop beneath my boot, and a pocket of evil smelling gas was released that made me gag and choke. I tried to free my foot, but it was caught on something hard. I looked down to find that I was ankle deep in a bloated corpse, my lace end snagged on a protruding edge of fractured ribcage.

After I'd dry heaved for a minute or two I slung the machine gun over my shoulder, reached down and gingerly unsnagged the lace, smearing my fingers in vile black ichor as I did so. I limped away from the unfortunate wretch, wiping my fingers on the wall as I went.

That man (had it been a man? I couldn't be sure) had been dead for some time, but he'd outlived the plague. He still had a gun in his hand, so I assumed he'd died fighting. On the evidence so far, it looked like Basra was still as violent and deadly a place as it had been before The Cull.

And I'd come here by choice. Bloody moron, Keegan.

The stairs were littered with junk. It was all the stuff I'd have expected: toys, prams, CDs, DVDs, clothes, a bike, some chairs, computers, TV sets. But the CDs and DVDs had Arabic titles and lurid cover pictures; the computer keyboard had a strange alphabet; the TV sets were old square cathode ray boxes, not widescreen or flat. The big picture was the same, but the details were different. It was disorientating.

This place had been taken to pieces, but it seemed like most of the stuff had just been thrown around for a laugh rather than salvaged and squirreled away.

I negotiated the wreckage and made it to the third floor without stumbling across any other recent casualties. I risked a glance through a shattered windowpane, and could see a group of three young men, machine guns at the ready, cautiously moving through the car park below. It wouldn't take much for them to realise I'd come into this block; one whiff of the doorway should do it.

I needed a hiding place, fast. I ran down the corridor, trying to decide which flat to hide in. Some still had their armour plated doors firmly locked shut from the inside, entombing anyone who'd sheltered there.

One door was decorated with a collection of human skulls, hanging from hooks in the shape of a love heart. I gave that one a miss. Eventually I just ducked inside a random door and pushed it closed behind me. I was about to slide the large metal bolts home when I realised that the bolt housings had been ripped from the wall when someone had kicked their way inside.

I turned to explore the flat, and found two long-dead bodies lying sprawled on the sofa. The one in the dress, with the long red hair, had a bullet hole in the middle of its skull. The other, presumably her boyfriend or husband, still held a pistol in his bony fingers, the muzzle clasped between yellow teeth. The flesh was long gone; all that remained were tattered clothes and bones, picked clean by rats that had long since moved elsewhere in search of food. I imagined that most of the locked doors in this block concealed similar tableaux.

It was the kind of thing I'd seen many times before, but again, the details were different. The sofa was a bright orange with the kind of swirling patterns that my gran used to like, and it was hard to tell which was more grotesque: the corpses or the wallpaper pattern. It was like some awful seventies throwback. But in the corner there was the first widescreen telly I'd seen here. New technology, old furniture; it was plain that Iraq had been changing when The Cull hit, caught between a brutal past and an uncertain future that at least promised shinier toys.

But Iraq hadn't moved forward into a bright new day of flat-screen HD tellies, democratic freedom and plush modern furnishings. It had bled out in a slow parade of mercy killings and suicide pacts.

Just like everywhere else.

"AND LEE, LISTEN, your mother..."

"Yes?"

"I've seen what this disease does. And I want..."

"No."

"Lee, I wouldn't ask..."

"Dad, no. Please. Don't ask me to do that."

"But..."

"No. I'm not like you. I couldn't do something like that. I just couldn't. I won't give up hope."

RIGHT. FIRST THINGS first. I needed to sort out my shoulder. I took a quick walk through the flat but found only the abandoned fragments of other people's lives. I looked out the bedroom window at an expanse of sandy scrubland. It took me a minute to realise what I was looking at, but when I did it was all I could do to stop myself throwing up.

Lined up on the ground were three rows of impaled corpses. Maybe fifteen or more people, all with their hands tied behind their backs, lying with their faces skywards, sharpened wooden stakes protruding from their shattered ribcages. The stakes had been dug into the ground and then the victims must have been flung on to them. And pushed down. Recently, too; the flies were still buzzing.

I'd seen some pretty horrible deaths in recent months. I'd been responsible for a few of them. But this was far and away the most awful thing I'd seen.

I stood at the window for a minute or two, feeling the first stirrings of panic.

After all that had happened to me in the last hour, it took a field of impaled sacrifices to make me start panicking. That's a good indication of how fucked in the head I was at this point. Running, hiding, fighting for my life, killing people who were trying to kill me; all this had become part of an ordinary day. A year ago I'd have been a shuddering, stammering wreck. But now that stuff barely even touched the sides. I just got on with it.

A few weeks previously I'd stopped looking at myself in mirrors, started actively avoiding my own reflection, scared of what I'd see. I just kept telling myself to get on with it. Things to do. Sort it all out later. I think I imagined some sort of quiet solitude, a retreat or something, where I'd go and try to get my head straight once I'd got everything done, ticked the final item on my list of jobs (take out milk bottles, finish geography homework, defeat army of cannibals, iron shirts, fly to war zone and rescue Dad from enemy combatants who like impaling people).

I suspected that if I allowed myself too many moments of introspection I'd go mad.

I shook my head, impatient with myself.

Stop being maudlin.

Things to do.

Fix my shoulder. I was pretty sure it was only dislocated, not broken, and I knew how to sort that. You just grit your teeth and shove your shoulder really, really hard against a wall or something and it just snaps back in. Simple. I'd seen it in countless films.

It'd most likely hurt a lot, so I picked up a piece of wood from the floor, part of a smashed doorframe, and shoved it into my mouth. I didn't want any screams bringing my pursuers right to me. Then I stood before the bathroom wall and calmed my breathing, focused, and slammed my dislocated shoulder into the wall as hard as I possibly could.

The pain blinded me and I was unconscious before I hit the floor.

"ALL RIGHT, LEE. Look, I gotta go. Look after your mother. I love you."

"I love you too. And make sure you come find me, 'cause if you're not back in a year I'm going to come find you!"

"Don't joke. If I'm not back in a year, I'm–"

Click.

"Dad? Dad, you there? Dad?"

WHEN YOU'VE BEEN unconscious as many times as I have, you learn a few tricks. The most important is not to open your eyes until you're fully awake and have learned all you can about where you are and who's there with you.

I was bleeding, hungry and thirsty, and I ached all over from the crash and the kicking, but I was still alive.

The most obvious thing was that I wasn't lying on a tiled bathroom floor. I was sitting up, with cold metal cuffs binding my hands to the chair back. Someone had captured me, then. I'd probably screamed as I passed out and they found me where I dropped.

The second thing was that my shoulder hurt like hell and I still couldn't move my arm, so I hadn't managed to relocate it. Thanks a bunch, Hollywood.

The air was still and dry and there was no wind, so I was indoors. I listened carefully, but I couldn't hear anybody talking or breathing. I risked opening my eyes and found myself staring down the lens of a handy cam.

It took a minute for me to realise the implications. I craned around to look behind me, and saw that I was sitting in front of a blue sheet backdrop with Arabic script on it. That's when I really started to panic. Could I really have flown halfway round the world just to end up in a snuff video?

It took a lot of effort to regain my composure, but I calmed myself down, got my breathing under control, forced down the panic and concentrated on the details of the room. Dun, mud brick walls, sand floor. Single window, shuttered. Old, tatty blue sofa to my left, sideboard to my right. Lying on the sideboard was a big hunting knife, its razor sharp edge glinting at me like a promise. The handy cam was shiny and new, like it was fresh out of the box. Behind it there was a metal frame chair with canvas seat and back, the same as the one I now occupied. Next to that was an old coffee table on which were piled small video tapes. The last thing I noticed, which made the panic rise again, was the dark red stain on the floor, which formed a semi-circle around my feet. There was a splash of the same stain across the floor in a straight line and on to the wall beside the sofa. That would be the first gush of arterial blood from the last poor bastard who'd sat in this chair.

I remembered the siege of St Mark's, two months earlier; walking into the Blood Hunters' camp, all cocky bravado, baiting the madman in his lair. I remembered the plan going horribly wrong, and the moment when they forced me to kill one of my own men. I remembered holding the knife as I slit Heathcote's throat, and felt the blood bubble and gush over my hands as I whispered pleas for forgiveness into the ear of my dying friend. I remembered the hollow ache that had sat in my stomach as I'd done that awful thing, the ache that had never left me, which still jolted me awake most nights, sweating and crying, reliving his murder over and over. He had not died easily or well. When the siege was over, and the school was a smoking ruin, I had found Heathcote's body in amongst the mass of slaughtered, and dug his grave myself. I had broken my arm so it took me two days, but I wouldn't let anyone else lift a shovel to help me.

It was as I placed the plain white cross on his grave that I realised I could not stay. All my decisions, all my plots and schemes and plans had just brought the school to ruin. It would be better for everyone if I left Matron in charge and gave the school a fresh start. I was cursed. I stayed long enough to heal the arm, and then I just walked away.

Dad hadn't shown up, and it had been nearly a year. Time for me to come good on my promise. Time to fly to Iraq and find out what had become of him. I had little expectation that he was still alive, but I had to try. I had to have something to keep going for, to stop me just ending it all. So I found myself a little Grob Tutor plane, the one I'd been taught to fly by the RAF contingent of the school's County Cadet Force, plotted a route via various RAF bases where I thought I'd be able to find fuel, and set off.

All that distance from Heathcote's grave, all that effort just to put myself in a place where I could suffer exactly the same fate. It seemed only fair. Inevitable, even.

"Poetic justice, Nine Lives," said the voice in my head. I couldn't really argue with that.

I heard footsteps approaching and low, murmuring voices. The door opened and two men stepped inside. They wore khaki jackets and trousers with tatty, worn out trainers. Both had their faces swathed in cloth, with only their dark eyes visible. They stopped talking and stood in the doorway for a moment, just staring at me. Not long ago I'd have wracked my brain for a quip or putdown, but there'd come a point some months back where I'd heard myself saying something flippant to a psychopath and I'd realised that it didn't make me cool; it just made me sound like an immature dick who'd seen too many bad action movies. So I just told the truth.

"I have no idea who you think I am," I said, trying to keep my voice level. "But I'm not your enemy."

They ignored me. The taller one moved to the handy cam and hunched over it, preparing to record. I wondered how he'd charged the battery. The shorter one checked the sheet behind me before picking up the knife and taking his place at my side, still and silent like a sentry.

"I'm just a boy from England looking for my dad," I went on hopelessly. "Just let me find him and I'll fuck off out of it, back home. I promise."

No response, just a red light on the handy cam, and the whirr of tiny motors as it opened to receive the tape.

Of course, it could be that they didn't even speak English.

"Look, there's no media any more anyway. There's no Internet or telly. So what's the point of cutting my head off on video? Who's going to see it?" I thought this was a pretty good point, but they didn't seem to care.

The cameraman slid the tape into place and snapped the handy cam closed. A moment's pause, then he nodded to his companion.

I tried to calm my nerves, tell myself that I'd been in situations like this before, that there was still a way out. But no-one knew I was here. There were no friends looking for me, no Matron to come riding to my rescue. I was thousands of miles from home, in a country where I couldn't make myself understood, and I was about to be executed as part of a war that was long since over.

I supposed it made as much sense as any other violent death.

I felt a tear trickle down my cheek, but I refused to give them the satisfaction of sobbing. The weird thing is, I wasn't sad for myself. I'd faced death many times, and I'd got to know this feeling pretty well. I was ready for it. I just felt guilty about my dad. He'd never know what had happened to me after that phone call. I'd been looking forward to that conversation. I missed him.

The man standing beside me began to talk to the camera in Arabic. I made out occasional words (Yankee, martyr) but that was all. At one point I gabbled an explanation to the camera, drowning out his monologue. At least that way anyone watching it would know who I was. I had no idea where this video would end up so it was worth a shot, I supposed. Nothing else I could do.

"My name is Lee Keegan," I shouted. "It's my sixteenth birthday today, and I'm English. I flew here to find my dad, a Sergeant in the British Army, but my plane crashed and these guys found me. If anyone sees this, please let Jane Crowther know what happened to me. You can find her at Groombridge Place, in Kent, southern England. It's a school now. Tell her I'm sorry."

The guy with the knife punched me hard in the side of the head to shut me up. He finished his little speech and then there was silence, except for the soft whirr of tiny motors.

I stared straight into the camera lens, tears streaming down my face. I clenched my jaw, tried to look defiant. I probably looked like what I was: a weeping, terrified child.

I felt cold, sharp metal at my throat.

Then the guy behind the camera stood up straight, unwrapped his face and took off his jacket, revealing a t-shirt that read 'Code Monkey like you!'

"Hang on," he said. "Did you say your name was Keegan?"

And that's how I met Tariq.

CHAPTER TWO

I DIDN'T FOLLOW the war in Iraq as closely as I should have.

You'd think that, with my dad on the front line, I'd have been watching and reading everything I could. But there was never any good news. It was all doom and gloom; insurgents, roadside bombs and body counts. It gave me nightmares to think of my dad in the middle of all that. So I stopped reading, listening and watching. I didn't want to know.

I knew the general details – Dad was in Basra, a coastal town important to oil supplies; things there weren't as bad as they were further north, where the Americans were in charge; the British troops didn't have the right equipment, or enough equipment, or any equipment at all, depending upon whether you watched the BBC, Sky News or Al Jazeera.

The only thing I knew for sure was that he was somewhere dangerous and there were people who wanted to kill him. Beyond that, I didn't ask.

But then, as Mum pointed out, that was his job. He was a soldier. He put himself in harm's way to pay for our food and clothes, the roof over our heads and the education that would ensure I never had to risk my life the way he did.

I knew that her family paid for my schooling, not Dad, but I understood what she meant, so I just nodded. She knew how I felt, anyway; she was the daughter of a military man herself.

"JOHN KEEGAN'S SON?"

He knew my dad. Oh, God, maybe he'd already sat in this chair. Maybe that was his blood on the floor. My eyes went wide and I couldn't speak.

The young man stepped out from behind the camera. "Answer the question will you. Oh shit, he's going to..."

I leaned forward and threw up all over his sneakers. I retched and retched until I was dry heaving, snot and tears and puke sliming my face. He jumped backwards, but it was too late.

"Bloody hell, man," he said, grimacing at his vomit-coated sneakers. "Do you know how hard it is to get Chuck Jones out here? Fuck."

The guy with the knife laughed and said something to him in Arabic (is that what they spoke here? Or was it Iraqi? I'm ashamed to admit I didn't know). Sneaker man flipped him the bird, annoyed and sarcastic.

I sat back in the chair, feeling about as wretched and pathetic as it's possible to feel. I couldn't think of anything to say. My mind just kept replaying the image of my father sitting here, straining at his bonds as his throat was cut.

Sneaker man stepped forward, avoiding the puddle of puke. He reached into the back pocket of his jeans and pulled out a photo, which he held in front of me.

"My name is Tariq," he said. "Please, is this your father?"

It was Dad, in desert combats, smiling at the camera, holding a bottle of coke.

I nodded.

I wanted to scream "Where did you get that? What have you done with him?" but experience back home taught me that people who enjoy slitting throats don't normally feel the need to explain themselves.

"Shit!" he said. "I thought you were one of the Yanks." Tariq shoved the knife man aside, grabbing his blade as he did so. He knelt down and began sawing at the rope that bound my wrists.

"If I'd known you were John's son, I'd never have done this."

The rope gave way and my hands were free. He shuffled around the front and began working on the rope that bound my feet.

"It's not like we were actually going to kill you. It's just a trick we use to make them talk. They think we're all Islamist nutters, so we play up to it. Works a treat."

Where the hell did his guy learn his English?

My feet came free and I sprang up, reached behind me and grabbed the chair with my good arm. In a moment I was standing in the corner, chair held up in front of me like a lion tamer.

"Honest, we weren't going to hurt you," he said, still crouching on the floor, discarded rope all around him. Then he rose to his feet, dropped the knife to the floor and kicked it over to me.

"We were just going to shit you up and make you talk."

"About what?"

He laughed. "You're going to love this."

"Try me."

"Well, we thought you could tell us where your father is."

Before I could answer, a young woman ran in. She was also wearing jeans and a t-shirt. What kind of radical Islamists were these? She spoke to Tariq quietly and with urgency, he replied briefly, then she ran from the room. Tariq reached around to the back of his trousers and pulled out an automatic, chambering a round. Another rush of adrenaline and fear; was he just going to shoot me?

"Your arrival attracted attention," he said. "We have to move. I do not have time to explain exactly what is happening here, but we are allies, you and I, and should be friends."

My disbelief must have been plain to see, because he sighed, stood up, ran his fingers through his thick black hair and said: "Yes, I wouldn't believe me either. Okay, listen to me, Lee. We have to get away from this building quickly and quietly. If you make a noise or shout for help, then you will be killed. Do you understand? And later, when we are safe, I will explain everything and we will laugh about this."

"Right," I said. "If you say so."

He shook his head wearily and threw me the cloth that had bound his face. "Clean yourself."

I used my good arm to wipe my face clean. I finished with the cloth and dropped it to the floor. Jesus, I ached everywhere.

"We should fix your arm." Tariq reached forward and grabbed my useless limb. "Ready?" I nodded. "Don't scream."

He lifted, twisted and pushed, all at once. I felt the bone rotate and then snap back into its socket. I grunted, and my vision clouded for a moment, but I managed not to scream or pass out. He let go and I lifted my arm up. I could use it again, but it hurt like hell.

"Toseef is going to lead, you will go after him, I will follow you. Please, I beg you, don't do anything stupid. If you do, we will all die."

Then we were moving. We left that awful room and entered a living area with doorless frames and open windows. The girl was standing by the main door, rifle in hand, scanning the street outside. My three captors shared an urgent, whispered conference. It seemed the girl wanted to go out the front door and down the road; Tariq disagreed. Eventually he ended the discussion with a curt word of command, and we climbed out one of the side windows into a narrow, dusty alleyway that ran behind the houses on this street.

The sky was deep blue, not a cloud in sight, and the air was heavy and wet. I had expected Iraq to be dry, but Basra was a coastal town, humid and damp. It smelt different, the sandy tang of desert mixed with a dash of salt air from the sea. And something else, a hint of something thick and cloying; I would later learn that it was the smell of burning oil. As soon as I stepped out into that glaring sun I began sweating from every pore all at once. My t-shirt was patched with sweat before we'd even gone a hundred metres. I needed water. A whole great bathful, preferably, to wallow in for a week.

When we reached the end of the alley the girl motioned for us to flatten ourselves against the wall as she peered cautiously round the corner to see if the street was clear. She leaned back into cover and held up her hands to signal that there were two of whoever it was we were hiding from, to the right. She indicated that they were not looking our way.

Again there was a disagreement. The girl wanted to risk running across the road to the alley opposite; Tariq wanted to go back the way we had come. This time, she won the toss. She counted down from three with her fingers, and we broke cover. It was only a few metres to a burnt-out car, and we made it without the alarm being raised. We huddled behind it. She glanced down the road on my right, Tariq on my left. Stuck between them, with Toseef, I was unable to see who or what we were hiding from. All I could see was a tiny lizard, sunning itself on the rear bumper of the car, an inch from my nose. Lying there, frying itself alive on that scalding metal, it radiated warm contentment.

Toseef grabbed my bad arm to get my attention and I winced. He let go and gave me a look that said sorry. Tariq gave us a silent countdown and we all turned to face the other side of the road as the girl moved to my side, ready to run. There was no-one behind me. They all broke cover, scurrying for the other side of the road. But in the heat of the moment none of them tried to drag me with them; they were so focused on their own predicament they must have just assumed I'd follow suit. But I didn't. I let them run away and I stayed, crouched behind the car with my small, cold-blooded friend. They didn't realise I wasn't with them until they reached the safety of the opposite alleyway. Tariq turned, alarmed. I waved at him and smiled. He slapped Toseef around the head, annoyed, then urgently beckoned for me to follow them. I pretended to consider this for a moment, then shook my head, grinning. I didn't trust him an inch.

Of course, I hadn't exactly escaped, but I'd bought myself an opportunity. I turned away from his frantic gesticulations, and peered around the side of the car. About thirty metres down the road stood a humvee. Result! Through the heat haze I could just make out two soldiers standing either side of the vehicle, backs to me. I looked back at Tariq and I could tell he was about to come running back for me. Now or never.

I stood up and began walking towards the vehicle. I saw Tariq grasp the air in fury and frustration, so I gave him a jaunty wave and sauntered towards the soldiers. I was safe.

"Hey guys," I shouted when I was halfway between the burnt-out car and them. I had stopped walking and had my arms raised high and wide. Didn't want to give them an excuse to shoot.

They spun around, rifles raised to their shoulders, but they didn't fire. They hesitated, obviously surprised and suspicious.

"I'm British," I yelled. "I just arrived here. I'm looking for my dad. He's a squaddie like you."

That sounded as lame as it did unlikely, but it was the truth so it was all I had. I expected them to tell me to lie on the ground, hands behind my head, that sort of thing. But they didn't move. One of them reached for his radio and muttered something to someone, then his colleague shouted: "Take off your shirt. Slowly."

It took me a second to work out what he'd said, and then another to work out why.

"Okay," I said. "But my shoulder's pretty torn up, so bear with me." Both rifles were sighted on my chest as I struggled out of my shirt. I let it drop to the ground. "All right? See, no bomb vest."

"Now your pants."

"Seriously?"

"Do it!"

So I unbuckled my belt and let my combats fall around my ankles. I considered making an inappropriate quip, something like "If you want me to take my boxers off, you'll have to buy me lunch first," but I thought better of it.

"On the ground, hands behind your head."

I sank to my knees and lay down on the ground as he'd instructed. The gritty dirt burnt my skin, and a sharp stone jammed itself between my ribs, but I didn't wriggle. I heard them walking towards me slowly, their heavy boots grinding the dust beneath them.

"Lie completely still," said the talkative one. "If you move a muscle my friend here will shoot you dead."

"Understood. Just be careful please, I dislocated my shoulder earlier and it hurts like fuck."

I heard him fumbling with something, and then a thin strip of cold plastic was looped around my wrists and pulled tight. Then he grabbed my bound wrists and hauled me upright, grinding my damaged shoulder horribly. I yelled in pain and anger.

"Sorry," he said sarcastically.

The talkative one pushed me ahead of him, back to the humvee, while his mate scanned the surrounding buildings for danger. I had so many questions I wanted to ask them, but I decided it would be best to keep quiet for now. These were frightened, frightening soldiers; anything could happen. Best wait 'til I was safe in their HQ talking to a senior officer. Shouldn't take long to sort everything out then.

And yet... I didn't tell them about Tariq and his friends, hiding in an alleyway behind us. I was probably concussed, certainly dehydrated, definitely scared, and it was only as they marched me back to the car with brisk military efficiency that it occurred to me, belatedly, that perhaps my judgement wasn't the finest right now. So I kept quiet about the Islamists who had nearly beheaded me, the ones who could even now be taking up positions in nearby buildings and sighting their rifles on us. I think that maybe, through all my confusion and adrenaline, I'd started to have an inkling that I'd jumped out of the frying pan into the fire.

They shoved me into the humvee roughly. My shin banged painfully against the metal lip of the door, making me curse. The quiet one stayed outside on guard, while the one who'd bound my wrists sat opposite me. He was a young man, about twenty; Hispanic, with a wispy, bumfluff moustache. But despite his youth he seemed confident, in control, self contained. His face was hard and cold, and gave nothing away. I suppose his accent could have told me which part of the States he was from, but apart from New York and the deep south I don't know my American accents well.

"Name, rank, serial number," barked Bumfluff.

"I'm not a soldier."

"You're British, right?"

"Yeah."

"Name, rank and serial number. That's all you Brits ever tell us."

"If we're soldiers. And it's the Second World War. And you're Nazis. But I'm not a soldier and you're not wearing jackboots."

So the Yanks and the Brits weren't working together. Maybe they were even enemies. Suddenly all my preconceptions came tumbling down. I'd assumed that the army would have retained some order and discipline in the face of The Cull, but sitting here, facing an American soldier who thought I was an enemy, that idea seemed wilfully naïve. They could have splintered into all sorts of warring factions. This led straight to the idea that maybe Tariq and his gang had not been all they seemed either, and I cursed my prejudices and my stupidity.

From the second I'd hit dirt I'd been reacting instinctively and without thought. I knew too well that that kind of thing gets you killed.

Engage your brain, Keegan.

"Tourist?" he asked.

"I flew here from England."

"Economy?"

"You must have seen my plane coming down, light aircraft, two seater. I've been unconscious but I think it was yesterday."

"Maybe."

"I was shot down."

"Not by us."

So should I tell him about Dad? I couldn't see why not. I had to ask someone, after all.

"Listen, I'm just looking for my father. He's a sergeant in the British Army. He never came home after The Cull. I flew here to find him."

"On your own?"

"Yes."

"And you're, what, fifteen?"

"Sixteen. Yesterday."

"Happy fucking birthday."

"Thanks. Do I get a cake?"

"I don't have time for your bull, kid. It'll be better for you if you just tell us the truth."

"My name is Lee Keegan, my father's name is John, he's a Sergeant in the British army and I just want to find out if he's okay. If you radio your base I'm sure they can just check their records and it'll all be sorted out in no time."

His eyes went wide with surprise and recognition. Obviously he knew my dad, or knew of him. So I'd been captured by two groups since touching down and both knew my dad. What were the odds? What the hell was going on here? Bumfluff was thinking hard. It looked like it hurt.

"John Keegan? Your father's name is John Keegan?"

"Yes. Know him?"

"Oh, yeah. I know him. Our General is going to be very happy to see you."

Something in the way he said that convinced me that I wouldn't be so happy to be seen.

"Great," I said, cheerily. "But look, I'm not whoever you thought I was, right? I'm obviously not a threat, and I want to come with you. So can I please put my clothes on? I mean, I'm getting grit in places you don't want grit to get, know what I'm saying? And I don't want to see my dad for the first time in two years just dressed in my boxers."

He considered me carefully and I gave him my most innocent, pleading grin.

"Please?"

He nodded slowly. "Reckon it can't hurt. Hey, Shane, go get the kid's clothes. We'll get him dressed then head back. We're going to get so much kudos for this." His friend looked at him quizzically. "This is Keegan's son." Shane gave a small whistle.

"Fuck me," he said, nodding in appreciation. "Score!" Then he walked off to get my clothes, gun raised, scanning the buildings as he went.

"My dad popular then, huh?" I asked, playing dumb.

"Oh yeah, kid. Everyone wants a piece of your dad." He chuckled. I chuckled with him. Good joke. He was now completely convinced that he had outsmarted me in some undefined way. If it came to a battle of wits, I didn't think this guy would be too much trouble. But the body armour, knife and guns did kind of give him the edge. I was going to need help whatever happened. Time to jump out of the fire and back into the frying pan; I just hoped Tariq and his crew were still watching, because despite what they'd put me through I felt they were more likely to be my allies than the musclebrain sitting before me.

Shane got back and threw my trousers and shirt on the ground outside the vehicle. Bumfluff indicated that I should step down, and I did so. I turned, holding out my bound hands for him to untie me.

"Don't try anything stupid," he said.

"Look, I just want to see my dad. You're going to take me to him. Why would I cause trouble?"

He grunted and sliced open the plastic tie with his knife. "I'm gonna be standing right here. You so much as twitch and I'll stick you. Understand?"

I nodded. I shook the sand off my clothes and pulled them on. No point trying anything now; they were expecting me to. Once I was dressed I meekly turned around, put my wrists together behind my back, and let Bumfluff put on another wrist tie. Then he relaxed. Silly boy.

I struggled into the humvee and managed to sit back in my seat. Shane and Bumfluff took the opportunity to have a whispered conversation outside, and I undid my wrist tie.

Yes, I know, what kind of person travels around with a tiny scalpel blade gaffer taped to the inside of the back of their trouser waist band? All I can say is, when you've been tied up as often as I have you learn to take precautions, and it's the kind of little detail that a cursory pat down isn't going to uncover. I had one inside my right front pocket as well, just in case they tied my hands in front. And one in each of my shoes. And sewn into the hem of each trouser leg, in case they went for a hog tie approach. Back before The Cull it would have been crazy, now it was just part of life. Of surviving.

My life had brought me to the point where I took routine precautions against being hog tied. Jesus.

Now what to do? I could wait for them to get back in. One of them would sit in front of me and I could probably liberate his knife and improvise from there. But I'd be trapped in an enclosed space with two strong, armed men. Not an attractive proposition. Then an obvious approach occurred to me.

I reached forward, grabbed the door handle, and slammed it shut before they could react. I pressed down the lock and voila, I was safe inside an armoured cage.

I scrambled into the front as the two soldiers rattled the door handles, shouting and threatening me. I ignored them. The keys weren't in the ignition. I couldn't drive, but I figured I'd have been able to at least get the damn thing moving, but no luck. I needed another plan; assuming the glass wasn't bullet-proof it wouldn't be long before they just shot me. I scanned the controls for inspiration as I rifled through the glove compartments hoping to find a spare firearm. Nothing. I saw a radio clipped on to the dashboard, but who would I call? Then I noticed a tiny button next to it that said 'loudspeaker'.

I grabbed the radio, flipped the switch and shouted "Okay Tariq, I trust you. Come get me."

The two soldiers immediately shifted their attention from me to the surrounding buildings, raising their rifles to their shoulders, eyes going wide with sudden fear. It didn't help them. There was a single crisp rifle shot and Shane's back slammed against the side of the car. He left a red stain on the window as he slid down to the ground. Bumfluff started running for the street corner. I thought he was going to make it, and I was almost rooting for him, but then there was another crack and his head jerked sideways and blossomed with red. He fell to the ground and didn't move again.

Two more deaths on my conscience. And what would happen when I opened the door? What if they decided to just shoot me too? I didn't fancy the odds, but I'd made my choice and I had to live with it. What option did I have?

So I unlocked the door, jumped down, grabbed the rifle from Shane's cooling corpse, and stood there waiting.

Tariq burst out of the side alley on his own and came haring towards me, shouting.

"Keys, get the keys."

I didn't move, keeping my rifle trained on him as he ran.

His face was a mix of frustration and fury as he skidded to a halt beside me.

"Fine, I'll do it." He fell to his knees and rummaged through Shane's pockets until he found the keys then he ran around to the driver's side and leapt in. "Coming?"

I heard the sound of an engine echoing down the street; someone was coming, probably more soldiers. I jumped into the passenger seat and slammed the door. Tariq didn't hesitate. He turned the ignition, revved the humvee, and we took off at full speed in a cloud of sand and dust.

"Where are the others?" I asked.

"Lying low. We've got to draw the soldiers away from them. We'll meet up with them later."

"If we escape."

"If we escape." He wrenched the wheel and we careened around a corner. "What changed your mind?"

"Call it a hunch," I said

"Good call."

"I'm still not so sure about that. Did you really need to kill them? You couldn't have just fired some warning shots or something?"

He cursed in Arabic; obviously my stupidity was annoying him. "You told them your name, yeah?"

"Yeah."

"But they didn't radio it in, did they?"

"No."

"If they had, we'd be in a lot of trouble."

An armoured car appeared in the distance ahead of us. I was flung sideways as Tariq swerved into an alleyway littered with abandoned cars. We smashed our way through the obstacles, sending the hollow metal wrecks spinning and rolling as we slalomed our way between them.

"More trouble than this?"

"Fuck yeah."

One car braced itself against another and they dug into the ground as we hit them. The humvee's nose wrenched itself upwards and we rolled over the vehicles, bouncing madly, my head crashing against the roof. Tariq was yelling, but it was hard to tell whether it was in excitement or terror. Then we hit dirt again and the alley cleared ahead of us. Left on to another main road and that was that, we didn't see another car until we pulled up at the dock ten minutes later.

Tariq hit the brakes and the humvee skidded to a halt just inches from the water.

"Out," he barked.

I didn't need telling twice. I clambered down, bruised and shaken, holding the rifle tight.

"Now help me," he said, leaning forward and pushing with all his strength. I didn't bother asking why, I just took up the strain on my side. Together we pushed the humvee into the water and watched it sink. Then Tariq turned and walked away. I stood and watched him for a minute then I shouted after him.

"Should I come with you, or what?"

"I don't really care," he replied, without glancing back or slowing down. "If Toseef or Anna are dead because of your fucking stupidity, I'll kill you myself when we get back to base. But if they're fine, you're better off with me. Your call."

He rounded a corner and was gone.

I thought about it for a moment, then I shrugged and ran after him.

AT THE NEAR-derelict building that Tariq's group used as an HQ, an American deserter called Brett gave me anti-inflammatories for my shoulder, and patched and dressed my various wounds.

When he'd finished, Tariq apologised for being so harsh by referring to yet another online personality I'd never heard of –

"Sorry, I was a dick. Wil Wheaton would not be impressed" – then spent a couple of hours telling me his story. We sat on a flat, warm roof looking out over the city as the dusk turned to darkness and he laid it all out for me. It was a lot to take in, and it raised almost as many questions as it gave answers, but I mostly let him talk without interruption. When he had finished we sat in silence for a while, and then I told him my story in return. By the time I finished I felt that we had reached an understanding; after all, our experiences weren't that different when you got to the root of it.

Then he told me his plan and my role in it.

Then he gave me food and water and showed me where I could bed down for the night. I slept well, woke with the dawn and went looking for Tariq. I found him on the roof, exactly where I'd left him the night before.

"Well?" he asked.

"Your plan is insane."

He shrugged as if to say 'what can you do?' I laughed and shook my head ruefully.

"Our chances of success are..." I didn't have a word for that amount of small.

Again he shrugged and smiled.

I looked out over Basra. The squat white buildings of the centre, the tower blocks in the distance, the docks full of abandoned boats. And on the horizon the columns of rising smoke as the oil burned out of the wells. I was so very far from home. I'd come here on a very personal mission, tired of having the weight of everybody's expectations hanging on me, weary of making decisions that determined which of my friends would live and die. I'd figured that either I'd find my dad or I'd die trying. Either way, the only person paying for my mistakes would be me.

Now here I was, in Basra only a day, and a guy I barely knew was asking me to take on a huge responsibility. It almost seemed like fate was laughing at me. No matter how far I flew, I seemed to end up at the centre of things. I might as well just get used to it. I shrugged and held out my hand.

"It's a stupid plan, but okay," I said. "I'm in."

So an hour later, unarmed and on my own, I walked up the main gate of Saddam's palace and surrendered myself to the American Army.

CHAPTER THREE

IT TOOK MY eyes a minute to adjust to the darkness.

The cell, deep underneath the palace complex, smelt of sweat and bad breath, fear and urine. The silence was absolute once the footsteps of the American soldier who'd thrown me in here had faded away; no whirr of air conditioning, no echoes from the long corridor outside, no snatches of distant conversation. Which is how I could hear the soft breath of the cell's other occupant.

I stayed just inside the door until I began to make out shapes.

Thin chinks of light filtered in through the square holes in the metal window shutter, picking out the concrete walls, the bucket in the corner beside me with the cloth over it to mask the stench, the filthy mattress on the floor and the man lying upon it, knees pulled up, arms around his legs, foetal. It was hard to make out details but he seemed wounded; something about the hunch of his shoulders, the way his head was buried in his lap, spoke of pain and endurance.

My stomach felt empty and hollow, my head swam. I think I was more scared at that moment than I had ever been. It wasn't the fear of combat or imminent death; that fear was half adrenaline. This was deeper, stronger; the fear of loss, fear born of love.

My mouth was dry as chalk so my first attempt to speak came out as a strangled croak. I bit my cheeks, squeezed out a drop of saliva to moisten my tongue and tried again.

"Dad?"

I REMEMBER THE excitement I always felt when I knew Dad was coming home. I'd run to meet him in the driveway where he'd pick me up, swing me around and hug me so tight I couldn't catch my breath.

The house smelt different when he was home, of Lynx deodorant and shaving cream, boot polish and Brasso (which, trust me, doesn't really make pigeons explode). We'd go see football matches, take trips to the cinema, he'd teach me to swim or ride my bike and it would be glorious. And then he'd be gone again, for months at a time, just phone calls and letters and Mum putting a brave face on it.

We never lived on station, in barracks or Army housing. Mum's family had money, and Dad insisted that I shouldn't grow up an Army brat. He'd always been so determined to keep me as far away from the trappings of the military as possible, absolutely insisted that I should never pick up a gun.

I wondered how he'd react when I finally found him, when he saw what The Cull had made of me. But it never occurred to me to wonder what The Cull would have made of him. He'd become this fixed point in my mind. My dad. Solid, reliable, capable, wounded inside but getting on with things as if he weren't. He couldn't change.

How naïve of me.

THE FOETAL FIGURE didn't stir. I spoke again.

"Dad, is that you?"

He let out a low mumble. I couldn't make it out.

"Dad, it's me. It's Lee." I took a step forward, tentatively.

Again he mumbled, this time a little louder.

"Go away," he growled.

ONCE, WHEN DAD was home on leave from his Kosovo posting, I came running into the bedroom to find him fast asleep, taking a crafty afternoon nap. I had something I wanted to show him. I can't remember what it was any more, but I was five and it was super mega important that I show my dad this amazingly cool thing.

Anyway, I ran in, grabbed his arm and shook him awake.

One of the stupidest things I've ever done.

I don't remember the movement clearly, but he was instantly in motion. Before I could utter another syllable I was in a headlock and he was squeezing my windpipe tightly. I remember that his right hand went to my temple and braced. I realise now that he was about to snap my neck.

He came to just in time, got his bearings, woke up properly. Then he sprang back across the bed, pushing me away from him with a cry of terror and alarm. He curled up into a ball then, too, shaking, the horror of what he'd almost done sending him into a near catatonic state of shock. I sat on the floor, mouth open, stunned. I definitely remember thinking that my dad really needed me not to cry, so I tried very hard and managed to stop my lower lip trembling.

After a minute or so I calmed myself down and I climbed on to the bed, where I put my arms around him and gave him a cuddle. We stayed like that for a long time as he muttered, over and over again "I'm so sorry, so sorry", and I said it was okay, everything was okay.

From that day on, if I ever had to wake Dad for any reason, I always talked to him at a normal volume from beyond arm's reach until he awoke. Nothing like that ever happened again, but I had learned, at five years old, that my dad, my brilliant, wonderful, funny, teach me cycling, football kicking, fish and chip supper Dad was in some fundamental way broken. And he never told me why.

I SAT IN the corner of the cell, opposite the bucket, at the foot of the mattress, and just started to talk.

"I waited for you. At school. I waited a whole year for you to come and get me. But you didn't show up, so I figured I'd better keep my promise and come get you. I stole a plane, mapped out a route, selected RAF bases for refuelling and here I am.

"Remember how annoyed you were when I joined the cadets? Even though it wasn't the army cadets, you were still furious. 'I don't care if you get to fly, you still have to handle a gun and I won't allow it,' you said. But I argued and argued, and Mum backed me up. Wow, I remember that row. But hey, they taught me to fly, which is all I really wanted. I didn't care about the guns and the uniform and the drill. It was just an excuse for the really crappy teachers to shout at us a bit more and make themselves feel important. Anyway, I hate guns. Always have. Still do. But I can't deny that training came in useful.

"So here I am and it's all the RAF's fault. So I'm glad I stood my ground, 'cause otherwise I might never have found you. And that would have been terrible.

"I got shot down on approach though. I couldn't find the airport and I was circling the city trying to make it out, navigating by the river. I flew God knows how many thousand miles in a straight line, found and landed at three different RAF bases, then I get to my destination without a hitch and can't find an international bloody airport! Pathetic, really.

"Anyway, I crash landed, threw out my shoulder, and got chased halfway across town by a bunch of local nutjobs who kept taking pot shots at me. But eventually I got lucky, found this place. I thought I was safe.

"So much for that."

The man on the mattress slowly began to unfold himself as I wittered. I caught my breath and my monologue petered out. Gradually he levered himself upright and I could see his face.

He was unshaven, his hairline had receded a bit and there was a lot more grey there. His eyes were deep pools of black. But it was Dad.

"Lee?" His voice was little more than a whisper.

"Yes."

"Oh God, Lee?"

He raised his hands to his face and a flash of white bandage caught the scarce light. His right arm ended in a mass of bandages. Someone had cut off two of his fingers.

I GULPED THE coke gratefully but soon remembered why it was a drink for sipping; the bubbles burned my parched throat and I let out a mighty belch.

"I'm sorry," said Brett after he'd massaged my damaged shoulder more securely back into its socket. "We've got no painkillers left. It's just going to have to heal at its own pace. You'll have restricted movement for a while."

I laughed. "I broke my other arm about six weeks ago and I still can't quite use it one hundred per cent. I'm going to look like Frankenstein's monster." I tried to lift both my arms straight in front of me, but it hurt too much. "Maybe not."

Brett smiled and went back downstairs. I remained on the roof with Tariq, sprawled on a tatty old sofa that had been dumped up here, enjoying the soft, shapeless, smelly cushions; after a week in the cockpit of a light aircraft it felt like the Ritz.

Tariq looked at me thoughtfully. Nineteen or twenty, the Iraqi was about five seven, with short black hair, dark skin and brown eyes. His geeky T-shirt ("What, you don't know Jonathan Coulton?" he said, amazed, when I asked about it), Converse sneakers and jeans, not to mention his improbably white teeth, brilliant colloquial English, and the shoulder holster with sidearm nestled snugly beneath his left arm, sent out a confusing mass of signals that I couldn't quite decipher.

"So Brett's a Yank," I said, "but you and your friends are fighting the Yanks?"

He nodded.

"And even though the Yanks and the Brits were allies, my dad has been fighting with you?"

Tariq nodded again.

"And you're not Islamic fundamentalists?"

Tariq shook his head, grinning.

"What are you then?"

Tariq thought about this for a moment then he shrugged and said: "Brett is a hockey fan from Iowa, Toseef has a thing for thrash metal, and I'm a celebrity blogger." My confusion must have been obvious. Tariq laughed. "We're a family," he said simply.

I thought of Norton and Rowles, the dinner lady and Matron, and all my friends back at the school. I nodded. I understood that. "And the guy who attacked me? The one who died?"

He shook his head sadly. "Jamail. Good kid but hotheaded. A shoot first, ask questions later kind of boy. He was hard to control, and he made me crazy. But he would have grown into a fine man. He was the one who shot you down, even though I ordered him not to."

"I didn't kill him, you know. The plane exploded, there was shrapnel." It suddenly occurred to me that word was way too obscure, so I added: "that's metal that goes flying around after a big bang."

He looked at me like I was an idiot. "I know what shrapnel is."

"Sorry. Of course you do."

"I've lived in a fucking war zone the last eight years."

"Of course, I'm sorry. It's just that it's not a word we use every day in England." I suddenly felt very embarrassed. "Your English is really good," I added, lamely.

He beamed, his face transformed into a mask of boyish glee. "I know. I studied very hard. I wanted to go to university in England. Your father was going to help me with my applications."

"You knew him before The Cull, then?"

"Everyone knew your dad. Most people kept their distance. It was not wise to be too friendly with the occupying forces. But it was his job to make friends with local people, and I decided to become his friend. I was a liaison. I got good books and DVDs that way. And these sneakers which you fucking well threw up on."

"Sorry. But you did tie me to a chair and threaten to decapitate me."

"It's a traditional Iraqi greeting." He was so stony faced as he said this that, for a moment, I didn't realise he was joking.

"Very funny," I said. Only the tiniest twinkle in his eye betrayed his amusement. A big, gun-carrying geek with a desert-dry sense of humour.

"My name's Lee," I said, holding out my hand. "I think we're going to be friends."

"I would like that," he replied, taking my hand.

"I don't have any DVDs though."

"Oh. Sod off then."

IN THE FETID darkness of the cell, I looked at him. And he looked at me. And neither of us knew who we were looking at.

"But..." Dad shook his head and blinked his eyes as if he couldn't believe what was happening.

"Your time was up," I said. "I told you I'd come and get you if you didn't come home within a year. So here I am." I laughed and gestured at the dry concrete walls. "I've come to rescue you."

His shoulders hunched and he gritted his teeth.

"You think this is funny?"

"No, I..."

"You think this is a fucking joke?"

"Dad, listen..."

"You were safe! I told you to go to school and stay there. You were safe! Christ. Everything I've been through, everything I've done here, the one thing, the one thing I held on to as my friends were dying, was that at least you were out of it, at least you were safe. What the hell are you doing here, Lee? Why couldn't you just do as you were told, eh? Just this fucking once, why couldn't you do what I told you?"

My stomach tied itself in knots as he shouted at me, just as it always had. When you hero worship your dad, the last thing you want to do is let him down, make him angry, give him a reason to shout at you.

It had been a long time since I'd felt the shame of a child who's let down a parent, and it took me by surprise.

"Safe? Jesus, Dad, I'm safer here!" I protested.

"Do you have any idea what's going on here?" He shouted. "What you've come running in to the middle of?" Then suddenly the anger just drained out of him. His shoulders slumped as he closed his eyes and bowed his head. "Oh, God, Lee," he whispered. "What have you done? What have you done?"

I felt the shame slowly change and build into the kind of self-righteous anger unique to teenage boys having a fight with their dads.

"What have I done?" I hissed. "I'll tell you what I've done. I've shot and killed my history teacher, shoved a knife into the heart of a prefect, shot three others, slit the throat of one of my friends, watched my best friend murdered right in front of me. I've been complicit in torture, executions and gang rape. I've been shot, stabbed, strangled, blown up and hanged. I've seen battles and massacres and all of it's on me. My fault, my doing. All the bloodshed, all the death, all of it on me. And through all of it, all the shit, all the killing, all I kept telling myself, over and over again, was 'Dad'll be here soon, he'll sort this out'. But you never came. You left me on my own in a fucking nightmare and you promised, you swore you'd come and find me. Where were you, Dad? Where the fuck were you?"

Hot, furious tears were streaming down my cheeks as I shouted terrible things at the person I loved most in the world.

"You left me, you bastard!" I shouted. "You fucking left me!"

My anger gave way to impotent sobbing. And then he was holding me, like I'd held him on the bed all those years before, and he was saying softly: "It's okay, I'm here, everything's okay now."

And despite everything, it was. It really was.

"Your dad was on the last plane out," Tariq explained. "Part of his job was to liaise with local people, and he stayed as long as he could, trying to see that everyone he knew was taken care of. I lost count of how many people he helped when things got bad; bringing food and medicine, persuading the army doctors to visit the sick, even looking after some people himself when the withdrawal began.

"That's why he was on the last plane out, because he stayed to help. But someone shot the plane down. We don't know who or why. Cowardly thing to do, shooting down the last retreating plane. It was a Hercules, full of troops. It crashed over by the river and only your father and two other men survived. He is very lucky to be alive. Assuming he is still alive."

"He's alive," I said, trying to persuade myself.

Tariq looked at me curiously. "What was it like in England?"

I sighed. "I heard it was chaos in the cities. Fires and mobs and mass graves. But where I was, in the countryside, it was kind of civilised. Lots of old ladies locking themselves away, desperate not to be a bother to anybody. The odd farmer started shooting anyone they saw on their land, but that was about as bad as it got. The trouble only really started after the plague burnt itself out."

"It was not like that here," said Tariq, shaking his head wearily. "Exactly the opposite. The British got orders to pull out and leave us to die. There was talk of a big operation back home."

That triggered a memory: a dead man, tied to a chair screaming.

"Operation Motherland?"

"Yes, that was it. Your father never told me what it was, but the army just packed up and left. The Mahdi army tried to take control for a while. There were some massacres, lots of fighting. It was horrible. But then Sadr died of the plague and eventually there weren't enough of them left and it just sort of dribbled away.

"For us, the plague ended the fighting. The big armies were gone and there was more than enough room for all the religious and racial groups to stay out of each other's way. The Kurds have their own homeland now, in the north. The Shi'ites and the Sunnis have their own towns and holy places and they leave each other alone. And although there are only a few hundred of them left, it's the first time in living memory that no-one's been trying to wipe out the Marsh Arabs up in Maysan.

"The Cull was the best thing that ever happened to Iraq. It achieved what no army ever could: it brought peace."

I couldn't help but laugh. The irony that so much death could end the killing.

"So what went wrong?" I asked.

"After the British had gone, the Americans came to Basra."

"What was so bad about that?"

Tariq looked at me in amazement, as if I'd just asked the stupidest question of all time.

"Did you not see the pictures from Abu Ghraib? Hear about the murders in Haditha?"

"Of course, but you're not going to tell me that all American soldiers are like that. I mean, those were isolated incidents. Bad apples."

Tariq inclined his head, as if to say "maybe".

"You may be right. We have Brett with us, and there were others who deserted rather than follow the orders they were given. Brett is American and he has saved my life more than once."

"Well then."

"But what they did here, Lee. It was awful."

"Then tell me."

He thought for a second and then shook his head.

"No," he said. "I will show you."

"START AT THE beginning," said Dad. "And tell me everything."

So I did. From the moment I arrived at the school gates, to the explosion that levelled the place. I left nothing out. All the decisions I'd made, the consequences of those choices, the lives I'd ended or destroyed. The blood and the guilt. When I finished he just sat there and stared at me, tears rolling down his face. It took him a long time to find his voice.

"I don't..." he whispered. "I'm so sorry."

I shrugged. "Not your fault."

We sat there in silence for a few moments, neither of us knowing what to say.

"Remember all those arguments you and Mum used to have about Grandad?" I asked, forcing a grin, changing the subject.

He smiled and nodded, wiping his eyes.

"He thought the army was the only place for a young man," he said.

"'Just look at your father,'" I said, imitating Grandad's round, fruity, upper class vowels. "'It made a man out of him.'"

"And the way he said that, so you knew that he meant 'and he was just a bloody guttersnipe'."

"Never liked you much, did he?"

"Oh, he was all right I s'pose. He could have been a lot worse, believe me. It's just, well, he was a bloody General and he thought his little girl married beneath her. She should have married an officer, but he ended up with a Black Country grunt for a son-in-law and he didn't really know how to talk to me. He had this idea that if you joined up you'd go straight to Sandhurst and the Officer's Club, and at least the next generation would sort of get things back on track. He could pull some strings, make sure you'd never end up a squaddie. Not like me."

"You used to get so angry when he started banging on about me joining the army, especially when Mum didn't tell him to stop."

"I never wanted you to become a soldier," said Dad, seriously.

"Well, look at me. That's what I am now, Dad. Sorry. At least Grandad would be proud of me."

He started, looked surprised, made to say something, but I cut him off.

"He died early," I said. "Him and Gran. First wave."

"I know, your Mum told me on the phone."

There was an awkward silence, then he said: "About your mother."

"I don't really want to talk about it."

"But it must have been..."

"It was what it was."

I avoided his eyes as he searched my face for clues. Eventually he nodded, accepting my refusal to talk about her death. I was grateful for that.

"So the school was destroyed and you just, what, stole a plane and flew here on your own?"

I nodded. He whistled through his teeth.

"Nowhere else for me to go," I said.

"You could have stayed there. Gone with them to the new place. They're your friends, surely you'd have been welcome?"

I didn't feel like explaining myself any more, so I just shrugged.

He gestured to the cell walls. "And how...?"

"I surrendered. Thought they'd know where you were. Which, as it turns out, they did."

"Oh Lee, you shouldn't have come here. You really shouldn't."

"Why are you a prisoner?" I asked.

But I knew damn well why.

THERE WERE SKELETONS everywhere, picked clean by predators and bleached by the sun. Charred, tattered clothing still hung off most of them.

The low stands of the rickety football stadium were mostly free of bodies. A few people who'd tried to escape were sprawled across the wooden benches, but the majority of the dead lay in piles on the pitch itself. They were grouped in tens and twenties, as if neighbours and families had huddled together when the shooting started.

"The adults tried to protect the children," said Tariq, following my gaze. "Used their bodies to shield them from the bullets. Told them to play dead. Didn't work. The soldiers went through the bodies, finishing off survivors. Then they poured petrol over them and set them alight. One man had been missed by the sweep but he ran, screaming and burning out of the bodies and was shot. That's him, there." He pointed to a small heap of disarticulated bones.

In the face of such a sight all I could manage was the obvious question.

"Why?"

"Orders. Secure the town, evict the survivors, kill anyone who wouldn't leave willingly. All these people wanted was to be left alone, to rebuild their town."

But in spite of the evidence I still couldn't believe that the Americans had done this. Dad used to call them cowboys, insisted their army wasn't as well disciplined or trained as ours, but they were still the good guys. No matter how bad things got I couldn't believe that the American army would do such a thing. A few loose cannons losing the plot at a checkpoint and killing some civilians, yes. But cold-bloodedly massacring a hundred people? Surely not.

Then I remembered something Grandad told me once: "An army is only as good as the orders it receives."

So who was giving the orders?

"IT WAS A SAM that brought us down," said Dad. God knows who fired it. We never found out. There were about seventy of us on board. I've never been so certain I was going to die. But somehow I walked away. I was sitting right at the back, just got lucky. I wasn't the only one, mind. There were two others, Jonno and Jim. Good lads. Quite a double act, they were."

"What happened to them?" I asked.

"They're dead now. It took us two days to get back to HQ. We figured it was the safest place. But when we got here we found the Yanks had moved in. I tell you, I'd never been so happy to see a white star in my life. So we come rolling up to them, waving and smiling, and they welcome us with open arms. Then they throw us in here and start interrogating us."

"About what?"

"About home. England. The army. Something called Operation Motherland."

"What's that?"

He shrugged. "Search me. I know it's what we were supposed to be doing when we got back to England. But no-one briefed us before we left. And fuck knows why the Yanks here are so bothered what we're doing back home. Makes no sense."

I started to ask Dad how he got free but I was just able to stop myself. I remembered what Tariq had told me; the Yanks would be listening to us and they mustn't know I'd had contact with them. Which meant I had to mislead Dad as well, at least for now.

"So how did you... cope with being tortured then? I mean, you must have been locked up for, what, eight or nine months?"

It was lame. My hesitation was too obvious, the substituted question too stupid. Dad looked at me askance for a second but I just about carried it off. I hoped whoever was listening to us was as easily fooled.

"Nah, we broke out," he said. "Well, we were helped. The guy in charge here, General Blythe, he started doing some strange things; running the survivors out of town, harassing the ones who wanted to stay. Quite a lot of the lads here started to get antsy about the orders he was giving. So they decided to do a bunk. And they broke us out on the way. There was a fight, Jonno didn't make it, but Jim and I did, and eight Yank kids. And we were on our own then."

"What did you do?"

Now it was Dad's turn to play his cards close to his chest. He knew we were being overheard as well.

"Met some locals, formed a resistance movement, did a bit of asymmetric warfare."

"What's that?"

"We blew stuff up a lot."

"Oh."

"And then I got captured again a few days back."

"What happened?"

"WE WERE BETRAYED." Tariq shrugged. "Blythe wanted your father. Badly. It was only when he took charge of us that we became a proper resistance. A little army. Your dad is a good soldier, he led us well. You should be proud of him.

"There were more of them, and they had better equipment; night goggles, heat sensors, helicopters. And they hunted us. But we know this town, where to hide, how to move unseen. We fought well. Killed many of them. But we could not prevent what happened at the football ground. And after that we were more visible. There were no local people to shelter us, no market crowds for us to hide in. Things became more difficult. And there was nobody left for us to fight for. So we decided to leave, find somewhere else to go. I thought maybe I would like to grow vegetables and tend goats. Something simple, you know? I mean, there's no-one left to read my blog even if there was an Internet to post it on!

"But then they attacked us at night, as we slept. Only six of us escaped and they captured the rest. Fifteen of them."

It took me a minute to realise, and then I gasped.

"Oh, Jesus," I said. "The people on stakes."

Tariq nodded.

"Blythe wanted your father to surrender. He sent out humvees with loudspeakers, telling him to give himself up. But of course your dad was planning a rescue.

"Anyway, Blythe gathered his prisoners in that courtyard and had his men fix big wooden stakes into the ground. Then he tied them up, stood each one in front of a stake, and told your father to surrender or they would be impaled.

"We just didn't believe he would do it. But Blythe killed Jim himself. Grabbed his shoulders and pushed him down, looking into his eyes as he did it. When he stood up his face was splashed with blood. Your dad immediately put down his gun and walked out there, hands in the air.

"The Yanks tied him up, forced him to sit on the ground and made him watch as they impaled the rest of the prisoners anyway. Just because they could. The one who betrayed us, an American called Matt – barely nineteen, always scared – he begged and screamed. But Blythe showed him no mercy. Then they left. That was two days ago."

"THEY'VE BEEN QUESTIONING me ever since. Nothing I can't handle."

Dad shrugged, trying to make light of it, not going into detail so he wouldn't terrify me. But I looked at his sunken, haunted eyes and I felt more anger than I've ever felt. It was amazing; I didn't know I could want to hurt someone so much. I hadn't even wanted to kill Mac as much as I wanted to take a knife and shove it into the hearts of the men who'd tortured my dad.

"They want me to betray my friends," he said. "The ones who are still free. I won't do that. They can't make me. I'll die first."

I let that lie there for a moment and then I said what we were both thinking.

"But now they have me."

The look on his face said it all.

We heard footsteps in the corridor outside, then the cell door slammed open.

"Get up, kid," said the soldier silhouetted in the doorway. "General Blythe wants a word."

CHAPTER FOUR

"Have a seat, son."

The general's voice was deep and warm, and his tone was friendly. He sat in a plush, red leather chair, the kind you expect to see in front of roaring fires in the libraries of grand houses. It looked out of place behind the huge black marble desk. But then, this whole place was absurd.

I'd been brought out of the filthy underground cells, up into the great entrance hall with its amber mosaics, gold lined ceiling dome and intricate pine balconies. It seemed like something Disney would have built. I was marched up the sweeping staircase, where the enormous windows gave stunning views of the Shatt-Al-Arab waterway as it meandered through the various mansions and gardens that made up Saddam's old palace complex. White stone bridges arched across the slow flowing water. It looked like paradise outside, and all I wanted was to lie in the shade beside the cool water and feel the wind on my face.

Matron would have loved it here, I thought. She liked lying on the soft earth and closing her eyes. But I was glad she wasn't with me in this cold stone building; it wasn't a friendly place.

The general had set up camp in a cavernous, empty ballroom on the first floor. His desk sat in front of double doors that led out to a balcony. The doors stood open, and white gauze curtains billowed into the room, bringing the scents of jasmine and orange blossom from the gardens below. Beside the desk was a huge flatscreen telly on a big stand, hooked up to some sort of computer equipment with wires snaking out the back of it; they ran outside through the balcony doors, presumably to a generator.

He was about 50, at a guess. His black skin was lined and

weathered, and his close cut hair almost entirely grey. Barrel-chested and broad shouldered he gave an impression of contained physical power, and his voice reflected that. He was exactly what I would have expected an American general to be; all he needed was to start chomping on a cigar and the picture would be complete.

I shuddered as I imagined that weighty frame leaning into me, pushing me down on to a sharp wooden stake.

He gestured to a metal and canvas chair on my side of the desk, and I sat down.

"Dismissed," he said. My escort saluted crisply, turned on his heels with a squeak of rubber, and stomped away. The tall doors, made of elaborately carved dark wood, slowly swung shut behind him. We were alone.

General Blythe regarded me curiously and I could see the muscles in his jaw clenching and unclenching as he did so. I met his gaze and held it. Not too defiant, but trying to seem confident. I'd looked into the eyes of madmen before. There's a feral quality they have which, once seen, is impossible to forget. I searched the general's eyes for signs of madness.

He narrowed his eyes and smiled.

"Yes, I think I believe you, son," he said.

"I'm not your son."

"Well, we'll come to that in a minute. I believe your story, though. That you flew here from the UK looking for your dad. Gutsy thing to do."

"Didn't have a choice."

"We always have a choice, son. You could have left him behind, grown up on your own, become your own man."

"Is that what you did?"

He laughed. "I'm asking the questions." There was a flash of warning in his eyes that hinted at all sorts of unpleasantness. "Drink?"

He reached across the desk and poured me a beaker of water from a tall glass jug that was frosted with condensation. I took it and swallowed it at once.

"Thank you," I gasped, wanting more but not willing to ask.

"You're welcome. So what's it like in Britain now?"

"Chaos, what else?"

He considered this and then said: "But you've got the arms, right? I mean to say, when our British allies pulled out of Iraq they had a plan to restore law and order. Must have started to work by now."

"Not in my part of the country."

"Fancy that. And what part of the country would that be?"

I don't know why I lied, it was just instinct I suppose. But I didn't want to tell this guy a single true thing.

"East Anglia. Ipswich."

He nodded. I couldn't decide which was odder: his interest in British internal affairs, or the fact that he'd heard of Ipswich.

"And that's where you flew from?"

"Yes."

"Hell of a thing, kid your age. But you've got plenty of scars, I can see that. Fresh too. You ever killed anybody, son?"

"If you were listening to my conversation with my dad, then you already know the answer to that question."

He nodded, conceding the point.

"You knew I was listening from the start, didn't you?" he said with a smile.

"No."

"Liar. Otherwise you'd have told your old man about meeting up with his buddies."

"I don't know what you're talking about."

The playful smile vanished from his face and he became impassive, his eyes dead and cold.

"Let me put you straight on a few things," he said. "Prisoners have rights. Many checks and balances exist to ensure those rights are protected. You are not a prisoner because you don't exist. Ain't nobody looking out for you. I could kill you now with my bare hands and nobody but your daddy would give a damn."

"You forgot to say 'In this place, I am the law!'"

"It goes without saying."

"Why?"

He seemed surprised by the question. "Excuse me?"

"Why? To what end? For what purpose?"

"There has to be law, son. Chain of command is the only way I know of running anything, and this place needs running."

"But why?" I pressed him. "I mean, shouldn't you be back in the US, shooting looters on Capitol Hill or something? Why are you here?"

"Capitol Hill ain't there anymore. Nuked."

"Okay, so New York, LA, Boston, Buttfuck Idaho, I dunno. Since The Cull the world's been full of tinpot dictators throwing their weight around. I've met a couple of them. You're not like that. I'm looking you in the eye and you're not insane, and you don't strike me as power crazy. So why are you still here?"

"I got my orders."

"From whom? Who can possibly..."

I didn't get any further because this huge granite man sitting opposite me suddenly moved faster than I've ever seen anybody move in my life, pulling a gun out of nowhere and firing a round over my head so close it ruffled my hair.

"Next one goes between your eyes. Understand?"

Fuck, yeah.

"I have no beef with you, boy. Your daddy's a dead man, but if you tell me what I want to know you can still walk out of here. Hell, I'll give you a lift back to Ipswich myself. But if you don't answer my questions now, while I'm still of a mind to be civil, I'll start asking a lot less nicely. Clear?"

"Crystal."

I gritted my teeth. This was my last chance to back out of Tariq's plan. If I said the wrong thing now, I was dead.

"Good. Question one, and make sure I like your answer: two of my men were shot and killed yesterday. Before they were shot they radioed that they had captured a British deserter. Was that you?"

"No," I replied. "It was Captain Britain."

He didn't like that answer.

I HATE BULLIES.

They're worse than madmen, psychopaths, dictators or power mad religious cultists; at least they all have either an excuse or an objective. Bullies are just cruel to make themselves feel cool.

I was bullied when I started school. Once.

I was six years old and had only just started at St Mark's prep. The bully in question, Jasper Jason, was a year older than me. He was a snotty-nosed prick with a little coterie of fawning acolytes who laughed at his cruelty. They tortured cats, that sort of thing.

Anyway, one day, who knows why, he decided that I was going to be his victim. He came over to me in the playground, grabbed my Gameboy and started taunting me with it, threatening to break it, promising to make me cry and so on.

I punched him as hard as I could and broke his nose.

I was suspended from school for a week. Dad was at home that summer, and I remember him coming to collect me. I was terrified of his reaction, but when the circumstances were explained to him he just laughed at the teachers. Then he took me out for McDonalds and told me he was proud of me.

Nobody ever bullied me again.

As the hood was pulled over my face, I tried to remember how I felt in that playground.

As the ties were fastened around my wrists and ankles, I tried to find that sense of mocking superiority I felt when I realised that Jason was just an insecure little shit who could only feel good about himself by picking on weaker kids.

As I was laid on the thin wooden board and trussed like a chicken so that the board and I moved as one unit, I recalled the satisfaction of feeling his nose crunch and the realisation that I wasn't scared of him.

As the towels were laid gently across my hooded face, I drew on all the anger, resentment and hatred I felt for bullies and I projected it on to the men who were about to drown me. How insecure they must be to torture a child. I laughed at them.

As they began to pour the water on to the towels, I felt myself tilt backwards. The liquid dribbled up my nose and I felt the hard pressure of a finger in my solar plexus, testing whether I was timing my breaths to coincide with the dowsings. I felt the purest resolve I had ever felt in my life.

I was stronger than this. I was The Boy Who Was Never Bullied. I knew they weren't going to kill me, so all I needed to do was be strong. I could do this.

And then I had to exhale, unable to hold my breath for another second.

And then I was drowning, the thick cotton towels moulding themselves to my mouth and nostrils, gagging me, choking me, sealing me in a dark, wet, airless nightmare.

I felt the board tip up, a momentary respite, the towels loosened, I dragged in a ragged gasp of air, and then tilted again, more water, more choking, flooding, drowning in the unstoppable water as it probed every orifice, relentless, drawn by simple gravity, pushing its way inside me.

There was liquid somewhere else, but I couldn't tell where, my senses were so scrambled. Only later did I realise that I'd wet myself.

And my resolve vanished, my strength disappeared, time elongated and claustrophobic terror took its place. Before I knew I was doing it, I was begging for release, promising to tell them everything they needed to know. Anything to make it stop.

So they did it once more, just to be sure. This time I lost my mind. I may have screamed and begged, I don't know. But in my head I was with Matron. She was at Groombridge, I was in the gardens outside the room where I was dying, yet we still lay side by side, holding hands with our eyes closed, feeling the Earth turn beneath us, breathing slow, steady meditative breaths as the darkness closed in.

It seemed like a lifetime, but the whole ordeal probably only lasted thirty seconds.

WHEN I REGAINED consciousness I was lying on the floor in a puddle. It was better than being tied to a chair, I supposed.

They had untied me and dumped me on the hard marble floor

I was foetal, with my hands, now untied, near my ankles. I kept my breathing shallow, pretending to still be asleep, and I listened, trying to work out how many of the men who had waterboarded me were still in the room. I heard someone clear their throat, but that was it. Just the one, then.

The question was: where was he looking? I cracked one eye ever so slightly and I saw him standing near a window with his back to me. Either he was a rank amateur, which I doubted, or he had underestimated me.

"Oh yeah," said the sarcastic voice in my head. "Can't imagine why he underestimated you. You proved how gnarly you are with all the begging and pissing."

I forced myself not to think about what I'd just gone through. Banished it to the back of my mind; something to deal with later. There was no lasting physical damage, and a resumption of torture didn't seem imminent. Any psychological wounds could be cauterised later.

I had things to do.

I slowly moved my right hand to the hem of my left trouser leg and searched along it until I felt a tiny bit of resistance. Then I grasped it with my finger and thumb and pushed the thin metal down, slicing open the bottom of my trousers and slipping the razor blade out and into my palm.

I was not in the dungeon, as I'd assumed. Instead I was in a large empty room, perhaps an antechamber of the ballroom the general was using. It seemed incongruous that somewhere so light and opulent could be used as a place of torture. But with the bag over my head I hadn't known where I was, so it hadn't made any difference to me. I supposed the guys here just liked doing their job in the nicest available office.

I decided my best bet was to pick up where I'd left off.

I pretended to jerk awake with a yell. I breathed as hard and fast as I could, widened my eyes in panic, then sat up and scrambled backwards 'til my back was against a wall. I pulled my knees up tight to my chest, buried my face in my lap, and began begging for them not to hurt me any more, rocking slightly as I did so.

The torturer turned away from the window and walked over to me. He crouched down, reached forward and grabbed my chin, forcing my head up, getting right in my face.

"Start at the begin..."

The word lapsed into a strangled gargle, half rasp, half choke. I swiped the blade across his windpipe again, harder. And again, and again, feeling my fingers slip into the slick wet wound as they sliced deeper and deeper into his neck. I had grabbed his head with my left hand, holding him in place, preventing him from tumbling backwards and escaping. By the time he twitched free of my grasp he was unable to cry for help. He clawed across the floor leaving a thick red smear behind him.

I got to my feet, stepped over him, turned and looked down at one of the men who had tortured me. I looked into his despairing eyes as he gazed up at me, grasping at the air, and I felt not one shred of pity or remorse.

"I hate bullies," I said. Then I jumped and landed with both feet on the back of his neck. There was a sharp crack and I felt his body crumple and grind beneath my heels.

Strangely, it still wasn't quite as satisfying as breaking Jason's nose all those years ago. I suppose you just feel things that bit more intensely when you're a child.

I rolled the cooling corpse on to its back, intending to take his trousers, but he'd wet himself too, and more besides, so I left them.

I frisked him, looking for a gun or knife, but he wasn't armed; probably hadn't thought it necessary. There was bound to be a man on guard outside, but the thick wooden doors had masked any noise, so I reckoned I had a few minutes at least. I ran to the window, but there was no balcony or convenient ledge I could climb out onto. The door it was. I looked around the room for some kind of weapon.

In the centre of the room stood two wooden chairs with the board laid across them. The hood, towels, bucket and ties were lying discarded on the floor beside it. I walked over to the apparatus, lifted the board and placed it on the floor. Then I picked up one of the chairs and smashed it into the wall as hard as I could, snapping one of the legs off. Voila: one genuine vampire-slaying stake.

I ran over to the door and banged on it, and then I crouched down, holding the stake in both hands against my chest, pointing out and up. The door cracked open. In normal circumstances a well trained soldier would have drawn his weapon and pushed the door open at arm's length, but these doors were so weighty that the soldier outside had to lean his full weight against it, and even then they moved slowly.

He was so focused on pushing the door open that he didn't notice me, crouched down below his eyeline, until it was too late.

I sprang up and drove the stake with all my strength into his belly and up under his ribcage into his heart, lifting him off the ground with the force of my attack, pushing a spout of blood out through his mouth. I couldn't hold his weight, and he fell backwards, crashing to the floor in a dead heap.

Was a time I would have felt bad about doing something like that, but I thought of all those people left to rot in the town with huge shafts of wood sticking out of their shattered ribcages, and any remorse I might have felt evaporated.

The general's desk stood alone at the centre of the vast room, but there was no-one else there. I grabbed a gun and some magazines from the impaled soldier and ran to the main doors, familiarising myself with the weapon as I ran. It was some variant of an M16; not a weapon I was familiar with. All I knew is that you load it by pulling the charging handle back and letting it go. Simplicity itself. Other than that I'd have to hope it wasn't too different to the guns I knew. I found the safety and switched it off.

The problem with these huge bloody doors was that you couldn't hear a thing through them. Probably useful if you wanted to stage a little private torturing, or a discreet orgy, but fuck all use if you wanted to sneak around the place undetected. I pressed my ear to one of the doors but there was no way of knowing what was happening on the other side. I was about to climb out the balcony when I noticed something slightly askew in one of the wall patterns in the far corner; a tiny line that didn't quite fit the design. I ran across to it and found a concealed door with a metal ring flush to the wall. I popped it out and pulled, revealing a narrow, gloomy back staircase, presumably installed for the servants.

I stepped inside, pulled the door closed behind me and made my way downstairs, gun at the ready.

I passed one exit, which I gently cracked open. It led into a large kitchen on the ground floor. There was no-one inside, so I took the opportunity to slip out and find a couple of good knives which I slipped into my waistband. I then returned to the staircase and continued my descent. Eventually the stairs ended at another door, beyond which lay the damp concrete corridor and the cells. I crept along the corridor to the point where it met the cell block at a kind of T-junction. Back to the wall, I risked a quick glimpse into the prison run and saw only one guard, sitting reading near the main entrance. He was facing me, about fifty metres away. No way to take him out silently. I was just going to have to hope for the best.

I shouldered the M16, took a deep breath, and steeped into his line of sight. He didn't look up; too engrossed in Tom Clancy. I walked towards him, gun sighted square on his chest as I did so. I was half way to him when he turned the page, and in that instant he registered my presence. He looked up at me in surprise and opened his mouth to challenge me. I squeezed the trigger softly and sent a round spinning straight at his chest.

And missed.

I'm not accustomed to missing, but I'd never fired an M16 before so I was unfamiliar with its quirks. The gun pulled upwards much more than I'd expected. The bullet hit the wall beside his shoulder, sending out a puff of white plaster. My surprise at missing caused me to hesitate, and in the instant before I could resight and fire again my target said: "Jesus, Lee, what the hell are you doing?"

Which was unexpected.

TEN MINUTES LATER, with a knife at my throat and my right arm pinioned behind my back, I was led out of the palace into the dark orange of sunset. The palace looked oddly unimpressive from outside. Partly this was because it had been shot to shit more than once, partly it was that all the opulence inside wasn't reflected in the blocky, uninspired exterior. The effect was that of walking out of a cinema into the street; glamour and colour replaced by dullness and dust.

The man with the knife – the man who I'd failed to shoot – marched me straight ahead, past the wonderful gardens and on to a paved path that led from the main palace building to a smaller, but still very large outbuilding (a palacette, perhaps, or a palacini?) There were a few of them dotted around inside the thick stone walls that ringed the enormous compound. There were fields too, scrubby and untended with a few lonely trees, probably once intended as orchards but never irrigated properly and now ignored.

It was a grim place. Badly planned, hardly finished, abandoned, fought over and now occupied, baking in the relentless heat. But that garden somehow seemed to have survived. Perhaps it was because I was so nervous, but I fixated on the garden as I walked away from it, daydreaming about its pools and arches. But I wasn't going to somewhere calm and cool and green. I was going to be executed.

There were two other soldiers escorting me, and two more at the open doors of the building ahead. We entered a large reception hall, lit by the amber light that flooded through an enormous lattice window. Blythe was there, seated on a seventies style sofa; polyester covered foam squares on a basic metal frame, all in a garish swirling pattern of green and brown. My father sat beside him, hands cuffed to the frame. In front of them stood something that came up to my shoulders, covered in a white sheet out of which snaked thick cables that coiled across the mosaic floor and out of the door we had just entered by.

"Thank you, Major," said Blythe. "You can release the prisoner."

The knife was removed and my arm freed. The man who'd been steering me stepped back into the lengthening shadows.

"You all right, Lee?"

"Yeah Dad, I'm fine."

"You are anything but fine, son," said Blythe.

"He's not your son," spat my father.

"I told him that, Dad, but he wouldn't listen. Maybe he wants to adopt me."

"I already have a son, Sergeant Keegan," replied Blythe. "One more than you, in a few minutes."

"If you touch one hair..."

"Soldier," barked Blythe.

The nearest of his troops yelled "Sir!" in reponse.

"If Sergeant Keegan utters another threat you will shoot him dead."

"Sir, yes, Sir!" The soldier raised his rifle and stepped forward, keeping the muzzle a few inches from my dad's head. Blythe glanced at the soldier and said witheringly: "Not there, you'll cover me in brains. Stand behind him."

"Sir, yes, Sir!"

I looked into Dad's eyes and I could see him willing me to be strong and calm. I could also see his panic. I smiled at him.

"Lee, you surprise me, you really do," said the general, turning his attention back to me. "I thought you were going to be the answer to my prayers. Instead you kill two of my men in what I can only call very creative ways, and you almost manage to make it three. I'm impressed."

The look on Dad's face was a picture; a mixture of horror, disbelief and pride. He mouthed 'really?' and I nodded, matter of fact.

"I don't like being bullied, General," I said.

"I can tell. Anyway, here's what we're going to do. You're going to tell me where your father's band of merry men is hiding or I am going to kill you."

"You're going to kill me anyway."

He laughed at that, a rich, warm laugh that contained no humour whatsoever.

"I surely am," he said. "But I can make it quick or slow, and given how long you lasted on the waterboard I'm thinking you don't have the stomach for slow."

He wasn't wrong.

I considered my options and the general waited for my response, studying my face closely as I did so.

"What constitutes quick?" I asked.

"I like to give people a choice."

"A choice?"

"Yes. You can be shot, hanged, electrocuted or given a lethal injection. Your call."

Again I considered. Again he watched me do so.

"Well, I've been shot, and I've been hanged, and I really don't like needles, so I reckon I'll go for the electric chair please."

As soon as I said it I realised I'd made a mistake – he hadn't mentioned a chair. Dad noticed too, and his eyes narrowed as he cocked his head at me curiously, trying to work out what was going on.

Blythe, however, missed it.

"All right, the chair it is. It is a classic, after all. But first..."

"They're in the souk. It's a courtyard behind a carpet shop with a green sign with red letters on it. I know they're planning to stay there until tomorrow night. That's the best I can tell you."

Blythe nodded, satisfied.

"And why did you give yourself up?" he asked. "They must have told you about me, you must have known what would happen. Did you really think you could rescue your dad single handed? Can you possibly be that naïve?"

I shrugged. "What can I say? I have this thing about walking into the compounds of my enemies and baiting them. It worked once before, I figured why not try it again."

Blythe stood up and walked over to me, leaning close into my face and studying me.

"I know you're lying," he said softly. "You're not that stupid. And I'm curious, but not that curious. You are a footnote, son, and I don't have time to waste on you. I've got a major operation to stage and this sideshow is holding me up."

He turned back to face my dad.

"I had intended to torture your boy, make you beg me to stop, break you, force you to tell me everything you knew and then kill him in front of you," said the general. "But events have moved more quickly than I'd anticipated. I have new orders, and that's no longer necessary."

Then he stepped to his left, reached out, and pulled the sheet away with a theatrical flourish to reveal an electric chair.

"So I'm going to skip to the end."

The sun was half hidden by the horizon now. In a few minutes darkness would fall. The shadow of the electric chair stretched long across the marble. It was a curious thing, home made and jerry rigged. It was an ornate, tall backed ebony chair that probably once sat at the head of a grand dining table. Who knows, it may have been Saddam's. Thick metal wire had been wrapped around the arms and legs, leading to a plain metal bowl, once intended for eating out of, now pressed into service as the head contact. The four other contacts – two for the feet, two for the hands – were made of gold, some relic of Ba'athist luxury beaten with hammers and flattened into something far less elegant. It made sense, though; gold's the best conductor there is. Thick straps festooned the framework, ready to secure my body and limbs and ensure that contact was not lost when I thrashed and jerked as the current hit me.

"Please, I beg you, don't do this," cried Dad. "He's my son. Please, God, no."

I tried to catch Dad's eye, tell him to stay calm, but it was getting too dark, and anyway it sounded like his eyes would be too full of tears to see clearly. The sound of my father begging for my life was the purest despair I'd ever heard. I wanted so much to tell him everything was all right, but I couldn't. The truth was, I was probably about to die, and he was going to have to watch it happen.

"Power up the generator," shouted the general, and the man who'd brought me here emerged from the shadows and stepped outside. A moment later there was the sound of a large engine spluttering into life, faltering momentarily, then finding its rhythm and settling into its work.

"Strap him in."

I felt strong hands grab me and force me towards the chair. I tried to resist, I screamed my furious defiance, but they were too strong and too many. One of them punched me hard across the face and my senses reeled. Then I was sitting in the chair, and my arms were forced down and strapped in place. My shirt was cut off and my boots removed. Then the straps were fastened across my chest, forehead and legs. My hands and feet rested on solid gold as I felt someone taking an electric shaver to my head, shaving off all my hair and smearing my raw scalp with conducting gel.

The sun was gone now, and twilight was fading fast. I heard someone pull a switch, and arc lights burst into life, flooding the room with cold white brilliance. My father, able to see me again, let out a feral cry of agony and screamed his fury into the echoing dome above us, where it reverberated and rebounded, briefly amplifying his defiance before fading away into hopeless, beaten sobbing.

The general stepped in front of me and said: "Any last words, son?"

"I am not your fucking son."

"So be it."

Then he crouched down beside a junction box and pulled a big red lever, releasing the current to fry me alive.

CHAPTER FIVE

"He gives them a choice," Tariq had said, as we sat on the roof the night before.

"A choice?"

"Of execution."

"You have got to be kidding me."

"No. You can be shot, hung..."

"Hanged."

"What?"

"Sorry, it's hanged, not hung."

"Oh. Your father said hung."

"Yeah, well. Hanged. I got this scar on my neck when I was hanged. I like to be grammatically correct about the forms of execution I survive. I'm a pedant. Sue me."

"Okay," said Tariq, rolling his eyes. "Anyway, you can be shot, hanged, injected, or he's got this electric chair he's made."

"Made?"

"Yeah, out of a big generator, a dining chair, some wires and a lot of gold."

"Shit."

"Your dad is going to be executed tomorrow. Blythe has decided he won't break, so he gave him the choice."

"Shot," I said immediately.

"Um, yeah. How did you know?"

"Dunno, just seems like the one he'd choose."

"But we have a plan to rescue him and it depends on him changing his mind and sitting in the chair. Unfortunately our inside man can't get a message to him and tell him to change his mind."

"So your plan is, what, I get captured and tell Dad to change his mind?"

"Perhaps. But I think it will not be so easy. Blythe will try and use you to get your father to break. So you may have to improvise."

"Okay. No, wait, hang on. Your plan is that I get captured and then give Blythe an excuse to kill me – but not there and then, later, at his leisure – and I choose the chair?"

"Yes." He saw the look on my face. "I know."

"That is a fucking useless plan."

"I know, I know."

"And who is your inside man?"

"Oh, that's the best bit..."

AS THE LEVER slammed home, the arc lights dimmed and flickered.

My back went rigid, I gritted my teeth as my eyes bulged out of my head. The veins in my temples strained to bursting point and the muscles in my neck stood out like ropes. I shook uncontrollably in the grip of the current.

Then I turned my head to General Blythe, smiled, winked, and said "gotcha!"

The lights went out and darkness fell, but not for long.

The chain of high explosives that ringed the walls of the compound exploded one by one, like a string of enormous firecrackers, lighting the room with a blinding orange strobe.

I saw the man who'd turned on the generator run into the room, pistol raised. In his early twenties, dark skinned, of medium height and build, he was nothing to look at. Just another shaven haired grunt made anonymous by the shapeless uniform and regimented body language. But his face was a terrible mixture of fury and pain.

He picked off the guards one by one, calm and efficient, his gunshots timed exactly with the explosions, so it took the guards – those not already dead – a few moments to realise what was happening. And a few moments was all it took.

When the explosions finally ended, he and Blythe were the only men standing in the room, cast into sharp relief by the flickering fires that now raged outside.

"Put down the gun, son," said the general.

"I'm not your son," said the man with the gun.

"Yes, David, you are and you will do as I say."

"Screw you, Dad."

* * *

"AND WHO THE fuck are you?" I asked the guard with the book.

"David Blythe," he said. "I'm the one..."

"I know who you are. I thought you couldn't get a message to my dad, so what are you doing here guarding him?"

"He's been moved. My dad's taking one last pop at him."

"Where?"

"It wouldn't do any good. Too many of them. You'd just get yourself killed."

"I thought that was the whole idea," I said drily.

"How the heck did you get down here?"

"Scratch two of your dad's goons."

"Holy... well, at least that should have sealed the deal. If you let me take you in, I reckon Dad'll give you the choice."

"Why should I trust you?"

"Tariq trusts me."

"I'm still not entirely sure I trust Tariq."

"Look, I've spent three days setting this up, at great risk," he told me. "Sooner or later someone's going to notice that I've been rewiring things. We get one shot at this. And Dad's been talking about new orders, hinting that we're moving out soon. If we wait too long, he may be too busy to waste time with games; he might just shoot you both in the head. We have to do this now."

"I do not like this plan."

"Complain about it if you survive. Now give me the gun. Thank you."

THE CRISP CHATTER of automatic weapons fire drifted across the darkened compound as Tariq and the others fought their way in. All they had to do was create a diversion for a few minutes and allow Dad, David and myself time to escape.

"Sar'nt Keegan, untie him," yelled David.

Dad was already working at the straps that bound me, but it was slow going with only one useable hand.

"What is going on, son?" Blythe sounded calm and reasonable, even indulgent, as if this was all just some little misunderstanding that could be sorted out with milk, cookies and a moral homily from Papa.

"You're not my father. Not any more."

"I assure you, I am."

"My dad's a soldier, not a butcher. The man who raised me doesn't massacre civilians, impale people for fun, strap kids into electric chairs. My father was a man of honour and principle, proud to serve his country. You're just a madman."

My head and chest were free.

"David, I'm just following orders," said the general. "Same as I've ever done."

"Bullcrap. What orders? Who the heck is there left to give you orders? And even if there were, these orders are illegal."

The general shook his head. "That's not my judgement to make." Was that regret I could detect in his voice?

"You told me once that a soldier's greatest duty is to protect the people from their rulers," shouted his son. "Refusing to obey an illegal order is a soldier's highest duty. That's what you told me. Remember that, Dad?"

My right hand came free and I started loosening the strap on my left.

"I surely do," said the general. "But the world has changed, son. New laws, new rules."

"I don't accept that."

"That would make you a fool, and I didn't raise a fool."

With both hands free I got to work on my feet.

"Weapons," I said, and Dad nodded, moving away to salvage guns and knives from the corpses of the guards.

There was a huge explosion somewhere nearby. The room shook and my eyes were dazzled by a flash of pure white light. When my vision returned, the general had gone.

"Shit, where'd he go?" I yelled.

David just stood there, gun still raised, dazed by the enormity of his betrayal.

"He just vanished," shouted the young man, surprised. But I'd seen how fast his father could move. I was amazed he'd chosen to run rather than fight.

We urgently needed to be anywhere else.

As the last strap came free I leapt out of that awful chair. I held out my hands for a gun, but Dad dropped the weapons to the floor and grabbed me, holding me in a tight, choking embrace and kissing my head.

He muttered over and over: "Thank God, thank God."

I squirmed free, embarrassed and annoyed by his show of emotion; we didn't have time for this. I held his good hand in both of mine.

"We have to go," I said.

"So you're giving the orders now, huh?" he said, shaking his head in wonder.

I wanted to say "Can we bond later, yeah? When there's less chance of sudden, bloody death? That okay with you?" But I decided to go with the more laconic "Looks that way."

I bent down and picked up an M16, cocking it as I stood. I handed a sidearm to Dad.

"You still able..."

"Oh yes."

"Then let's get the fuck out of here."

At that moment Tariq came haring through the door, bullets churning the ground behind him, and yelled: "RUN!"

He ran right through us and kept going, so we turned and followed him, scattering the chunks of plaster that had been knocked free from the ceiling and walls by the earth shattering explosions. At the rear of the entrance hall was a sweeping marble staircase and Tariq made to climb it. David shouted at him not to, and he took the lead, dodging right and taking us to ornate double doors behind the stairs. These led into a kind of sitting room, empty except for one painting of Saddam on to which someone had felt-tipped a noose, and a large cock and balls squirting into the dead dictator's face.

David held one door open as we all ran through it, and then raked the hall behind us with fire to discourage pursuit.

"Where?" shouted Dad.

"This way," replied David breathlessly, and ran to the corner of the room. In the half light I would never have noticed the door ring, but David had planned this well, and he went straight to the hidden door, pulled it open and ushered us through into a dark passage.

I was last through, and as I passed the threshold I heard a metallic clatter from behind me which, although new to me, I instantly realised was the sound of grenades bouncing across marble. I grabbed the door and pulled it closed just in time. A deafening roar, amplified by the cold stone acoustics of the enormous, empty room, filled my senses and flung me backwards.

The door held.

David reached across me and slid a bolt home, locking it behind us. Then he leant down, helped me to my feet, and dragged me away into the depths of the unlit passageway.

"Lee!" hissed Dad urgently.

"I'm all right," I replied.

"Ahead thirty metres, then turn left and up the stairs," said David loudly. I dimly heard Tariq give a grunt of acknowledgement somewhere ahead of us.

We made our way forward in the pitch darkness as quickly as we could.

"Thank you," I said. "You saved my life."

David said nothing. I wondered which he was regretting most – betraying his father, or not shooting him when he had the chance.

We soon reached a door, and huddled together, lit by the chink of light that gleamed through the tiny crack that outlined its frame.

"This leads into a private bedchamber," whispered David. "Uday would bring his whores here in secret. It should be unoccupied, but you never know. Once I open the door we run to the balcony. It looks out over the river, and over the wall. There's a ladder under the bed. I'll get it; we lay it across the gap, walk over the wall and drop down. Clear?"

"And if the room is occupied?"

"Then, Sergeant, we have a fight on our hands. Everyone ready?"

There was the sound of four guns being cocked and then David counted down from three. We burst into the room, guns waving.

"Clear," said Dad. I got to the balcony first, and looked out into the night. I couldn't see much because the balcony looked out of the compound across the waterway. There was less gunfire than before. It was coming in sporadic bursts now, somewhere off to my right, from a building that stood close to where one of the bombs had exploded. I could see the riverside wall was ablaze, flames licking out of the empty window frames. Tariq had only a few people left to him after last week's massacre. The plan was that they would stay outside and lay down covering fire at the points where the wall was breached, that way the Yanks wouldn't know which breach we planned to exit by. We would go across the wall here and then we and the rest of the gang would simply melt away into the darkness. It was a good plan, but it had one fatal flaw.

"Where is it?" hissed Tariq urgently, behind me. I turned to see the three of them standing by the bed. No ladder.

"I don't know," said David. "It was here this morning. Someone must have taken it."

"Fuck," said Tariq, succinctly. "Fuck, fuck, fuck, fuck, fuck. What now?"

"Can we jump it?" asked Dad.

I shook my head. "It would be suicide. Options? David, you know the layout of this place. Where's the nearest breach in the wall and how do we get there?"

"Two hundred metres east. I set a charge near the swimming pool."

"Okay then," said Dad, looking for the door. "Hang on. Where's the door?"

"There isn't one," replied David. "Secret bedroom, remember? The passage is the only way in or out."

"Jesus," I said. "Who the fuck builds a secret chamber with only one entrance?"

"The Ba'ath party," said Tariq, "never could do a damn thing properly."

"So you mean we're trapped?" asked Dad, incredulous.

"Yeah," said David.

"And how long before someone figures out where we are?" I asked.

"Not long."

"Then we have to go out the window."

"You said it was too high," protested the Iraqi.

"He didn't say anything about jumping," said Dad, smiling. Weird, but that moment, when he read my mind before the others, made me feel closer to him than all the hugging and wailing a few minutes earlier.

"We climb," I said.

One of the good things about the palace compound was that the buildings were as ornate as they could possibly be. It wasn't hard to climb up on to the roof using all the elaborate cornices, cupolas and jutty-out bits. Tariq went first, then me. Then David gave Dad a boost while Tariq and I pulled him up. David was still outside on the wall, perched on the ledge above the balcony, reaching for the lip of the roof when Uday Hussein's secret fuck pad was blown to shit by grenades.

The shockwave dislodged him and he began to topple backwards. I leaned out and grabbed his flailing right hand, pulling him back in. He scrambled up, flinging himself on to the roof. Almost immediately we heard someone run out on to the balcony and shout "clear!" I silently mouthed "close". David nodded and mimed back "thank you". I smiled and patted his shoulder.

The flat roof was littered with discarded bits of stone, half cut rolls of waterproof tar stuff and other assorted junk left behind by the builders responsible for this architectural abortion. We moved away from the edge so we couldn't be seen from below.

"Now they're going to be confused," whispered Tariq grinning.

"I hope so," replied Dad. "Because if they figure out where we are, they'll just blow up the building, or worse, set a fire and leave us up here to burn."

That shut us all up for a moment, and in the silence we all realised the same thing; the gunfire had stopped. Tariq's forces had fled, been captured or killed.

We were on our own, trapped on a roof in the middle of a compound swarming with people who wanted to kill us.

"I told you I hated this plan," I said.

THERE WAS LITTLE we could do but wait.

From our vantage point we could see that the area was heavily patrolled, plus there was a team sorting out David's creative rewiring of the backup generator, so the building was a hive of activity. Come daylight, things would start to return to normal. This part of the compound was usually pretty quiet, said David; the main activity was all focused on the barracks, supply dump and vehicle store, about half a mile away on the compound's northern side.

"It may sound counter-intuitive," he said, "but we've got a better chance of sneaking out in broad daylight tomorrow than we do now."

And so we decided to get some sleep. I was just clearing a space to lie down when Dad came over to me and sat beside me.

"I'll take first watch, keep an eye out," he said.

"Okay," I replied.

There was an awkward silence. I don't think either of us knew what to say to each other.

"When I last saw you, you were a just a schoolboy. It was all *Doctor Who*, *Grand Theft Auto* and wondering if you were going to snog that girl from the high school, Michelle, wasn't it?"

"Yeah," I muttered.

"Did you?"

I looked at him, incredulous. This is what he wanted to talk about?

"She's dead, Dad."

He looked down at his feet. "Yeah, of course she is."

Another silence.

"So you're going to take watch, yeah?"

"Um, yeah," he said, lifting his eyes and regarding me curiously, as if he had no idea who I was. "You get some sleep."

"Wake me when it's my turn."

"Will do."

I lay down and turned away from him, resting my head on my folded arms and closing my eyes.

"And Lee, thank you," he said softly.

I said nothing. A moment later I heard him moving away.

Of course he didn't wake me. A distant secondary explosion jolted me awake; the fires must have reached an old fuel tank or gas cylinder in one of the other buildings. It was still dark, but I checked my watch and saw I'd been asleep for four hours. I lay there for a moment looking up at the stars, so clear and bright now, without electric light bleeding into the sky to hide them. I pulled my jacket tighter around me as protection from the cold, even though I knew it was still hot by English standards.

I looked around and saw that Tariq was on watch now; my dad was asleep over to my left, and David was sitting balled up in the middle of the roof, head rested on his knees, staring blankly into space. I didn't think he'd welcome it if I approached him.

I could tell I wasn't going to get any more rest, so I got up and went to sit next to Tariq.

"Anything happening?" I asked.

"Not really. They've fixed the generator and gone away, but they are still searching all the buildings. It's the third sweep they've done, but Blythe must think we're still here so he's getting them to do it over and over. Just pray he gives up soon. I don't want to starve to death up here." He gave a quiet, sardonic laugh.

"Back when I first met you, you told me you were a celebrity blogger," I said.

Tariq nodded. "I used to blog about life in Basra under the occupation. I had two hundred thousand readers. Some of it was printed in a British paper and a publishing company wanted to do a book. A few other bloggers did it, made big bucks. I'd just signed the bloody deal when everyone started dying. Just my luck."

"So how..."

"Did I become a soldier? My knowledge of covert stuff made me a natural, I suppose."

I was confused. "But how does a blogger become an expert in covert stuff? I mean, why would you need it?"

"You really know nothing about what life here was like, do you?" he said, shaking his head in wonder. He wasn't annoyed at my ignorance, merely resigned, as if he expected the rest of the world to be blind, stupid and uninterested.

"Enlighten me."

"Bloggers were targets. If I dared to criticise one of the militias, there was a very good chance they would find me and kill me. And that's just for writing about how hard it was to buy bread in their district."

"People would try and kill you just for blogging?"

"And I did more than that. I investigated. I chased stories, played the journalist, tried to find the truth about certain things."

"Like?"

"Kidnappings, massacres, bombings. It wasn't hard. Basra was not a huge city, the grapevine was very good. And all the time I had to keep my identity secret. If anyone ever connected me with my blog, I was dead."

"And did anybody ever realise it was you?"

"No, but they laid a trap for me. I thought I was so careful, but they threatened the family of one of my contacts and lured me into an ambush. I was looking into the looting of the stores outside town. My contact told me he knew a British soldier who was helping the looters. But the militia was waiting for me at the rendezvous. Luckily a routine patrol came past, and I was able to just walk away. One in a million chance.

"But after that they knew who I was, so I could never go home again. I had to go into hiding, which is why I ended up working with your dad. I was lucky. Some of my friends, fellow bloggers here and in Baghdad, they were not so lucky."

"And now you lead the resistance."

"What's left of it. Anyway, I've got nothing better to do; my laptop's run out of batteries. If only I had an XO, with wireless mesh networking and some good cantennas we could have a local network up and running in no time."

"Stop," I laughed. "I have no idea what you're saying. I can use computers but I have no idea how they work"

"So what were you going to be, huh?" asked Tariq. "Before The Cull turned you into soldier boy. You were going to university to study?"

"I have no idea. I wasn't a failure at school, but I didn't exactly get the greatest grades either. I'd probably have ended up doing English at some crappy university, assuming I got in. After that, God knows.

"All my life I've had my dad telling me what he didn't want me to be – a soldier. I never had a clue what I wanted to be. Rich, I suppose. Irresistibly attractive to women. I dunno. I was fourteen when The Cull hit. I hadn't even chosen my GCSEs yet, although I had one meeting with a careers advisor to help me choose."

"Careers advisor? Someone who tells you what jobs you'd be good at, yeah?"

"Yeah, something like that."

"What did they recommend for you?"

"Promise not to laugh?"

"I swear on the grave of Warren Ellis."

"They said I should go into banking."

"Ha!"

"Yeah, that was my reaction too."

He fell silent, and I could see he was trying to frame a question.

"What you did," he said eventually, "was insane. You know that, right?"

"Which bit? Flying here, giving myself up to Blythe, trying to escape, letting him strap me into an electric chair?"

"All of it. Fucking insane. I mean, I know a lot of it was my idea, but honestly, if someone had tried to persuade me to do what you did I'd have told them to go fuck themselves."

"He's my dad."

"Is that all, though? I wonder if maybe you do not have a death wish."

"Don't be daft," I said, but he didn't seem convinced.

He pressed on. "You would not be the first. Many of the people who survived The Cull took their own lives. Those who could not do that looked for people to do it for them."

I felt a sudden surge of anger. "Well that's not me, right?"

He just looked at me, head cocked slightly to one side, his face asking silently "are you sure?"

"Fuck you, Tariq," I hissed and made to rise. He grabbed my arm and I shook it off angrily before walking back to my clear patch of roof and lying back down.

I lay there seething. How fucking dare he!

"Why so angry, Nine Lives?" said the voice in my head. "Touch a nerve, did he?"

I LAY THERE a long time watching the night turn to grey twilight before the soft glow of morning bled across the skyline. David didn't move a muscle in all that time. Tariq, on the other hand, was restless and unsettled. He moved from one side of the roof to another, checking the area, keeping his head low to avoid being spotted. He must have been worried sick about his friends.

Dad slept like a log, proving that he was the only real soldier amongst us; he once told me that the ability to fall asleep anywhere, at any time, is one of the best tricks a combat soldier can learn.

He woke with the sun and we gathered in the centre of the roof. No-one would make eye contact with me.

"Sitrep?" asked Dad.

"They've stopped searching, and the generator's fixed," said Tariq. "I think we can go now."

No sooner had he said that than there was a hum of power, a screech of feedback, and Blythe's voice echoed across the compound.

"Good morning," he said.

"Oh crap," said David.

None of us moved, waiting to hear what the general had to say.

"I hope you slept well," said the echoey tannoy voice. "I know you're still inside the walls. Your chances of getting out of here alive are not that great."

"How the fuck..." began Tariq, but David shushed him urgently and ran to the edge of the roof, looking north. He gestured us to come and see. Blythe was standing on a clear patch of ground off in the distance, with a small group of men. It was too far to make out details, but I assumed he had a mic headset on, patched into the speakers which I now saw were hanging from every lamppost. But we were close enough to make out the detail that mattered. Five stakes driven into the ground, each with a person kneeling beside them, their hands bound behind their back.

I heard Tariq gasp in horror. My dad put his arm around him and hugged him tightly. It was a comradely, even paternal gesture and I felt an unexpected pang of jealousy.

"Is that all of them?" I asked.

Tariq nodded.

"I have with me," the general continued, "five of your friends. I am going to kill them whether you give yourselves up or not. But you have a choice."

"Always a bloody choice," said Dad.

"If you surrender now," said the general, "I will kill you all quickly and painlessly. You have my word."

"And if we don't?" muttered Dad.

"If you don't surrender now," Blythe went on, as if he could hear us, "I will impale your friends one by one and leave them to die slow, painful deaths. My soldiers will then lay fires in every building in this compound and burn them to the ground. All the gun towers are manned, there's no way to escape. Wherever you're hiding, we'll smoke you out. And if you survive the fire, then you'll join your friends on a stake. Quick and easy; slow and painful. Your choice. You have two minutes to make your position known."

We moved back from the edge. Tariq was in shock, David looked furious, Dad's face gave nothing away; he was busy calculating the odds.

"Okay," said Dad, "here's what we do..."

"Pardon me Sar'nt, but I think I'd better handle this," interrupted David. "I can get us out of here."

Dad looked skeptical.

"How?" I asked.

"I'm Special Forces, Mr Keegan. I'm trained for this kind of thing. Just before deployment I completed a SERE course."

"Seriously?" asked Dad. "You're like, what, twenty?"

"When you've got a father like mine, Sir, you don't have much choice but to be the best. He started preparing me for Special Forces the day I finished potty training. I'm the youngest soldier ever recruited to my unit, and trust me, I did it all on my own."

"Your father must have been very proud," I said, sarcastically.

"I no longer have a father," he replied, matter of fact.

"What's SERE?" Tariq asked.

"Survival, evasion, resistance, escape," he replied. "I can get in and out of anywhere."

"Then we have to stop him," said Tariq, finally. "I can't watch this happen again."

He looked at us desperately, but none of us could meet his gaze.

"We can't leave them! We can't!" he said urgently. "If you won't help me, I'll do it myself."

"Sit down, T," said Dad.

"John, I won't let this happen," said Tariq, almost shouting now. "They're going to die because they followed my orders. Orders I gave trying to save your life. We can't abandon them."

But his face, the tears in his eyes, betrayed the truth. Tariq knew it was hopeless.

Dad put his arm on Tariq's shoulder and gripped it tightly, leaning forward and resting his forehead against the distraught Iraqi's. "They're dead already, T. It's over."

"So what, we just run?" said Tariq, crying now. "We let him kill our friends and we walk away? Then what the fuck has this all been for? What's it all been for?"

"Oh no, we don't walk away," said Dad. "Not now. Not after all this." He turned his attention to David. "You know this camp, right?"

David nodded.

"You can help us move through it undetected?"

"If you do exactly as I say and keep your heads, I believe I can, Sir."

"Then here's what we're going to do," said Dad, and I could see the resolve harden in his eyes as he spoke, seeing my father the soldier fully apparent in front of me for the first time. Suddenly I could see why he'd commanded the respect of the resistance. When he turned to us and outlined his plan, the force of his determination was impossible to resist.

Ever since I'd arrived in Iraq he'd been on the back foot, imprisoned, reacting to events, frightened for me. But now he was in a position to take direct action again. I realised there was a whole side to my father I'd never seen before. And it echoed in me. I learned as much about myself as I did about him in that moment, and I felt proud.

"We're going to hunt and kill General Blythe before the hour is out," said Dad, calmly. "And anyone who gets in our way dies. Everyone with me?"

All eyes were on the son of the man we were proposing to kill.

An awful, gut wrenching scream of pure terror and agony erupted from a hundred tiny speakers.

"I believe that is an achievable objective, Sir," said David.

CHAPTER SIX

D<small>AD TOOK ME</small> to one side as we prepared to leave.

"I want you to stay here, Lee."

"What? Why?"

"We're going to into combat against a vastly superior force of men who want to kill us. It's no place for a boy. I couldn't live with myself if I got you killed. You sit tight, wait 'til dark and then try to slip out on your own. You'll have more of a chance that way. We'll rendezvous at the football ground tomorrow morning. Okay?"

I didn't know where to start, but I felt the anger welling up in me and tried to choose my words carefully. I failed.

"Fuck that. And fuck you," I spat. "I'm the one who rescued you, remember? No place for a boy, my arse." I clenched my jaw and stared him down, full of defiance.

I could tell he wanted to get into it, shout me down, ground me, even give me a slap. But I could see the uncertainty in his eyes, no longer sure which, if any, approach would work with me. He was right to hesitate.

Eventually he just nodded.

A<small>S THE DYING</small> screams of Brett, Toseef and Anna echoed around the buildings and gardens, we moved through the compound like ghosts.

We stole the uniforms off the first four soldiers we encountered, and took their weapons too. Viewed from a distance we would now look like a normal patrol. But we only broke cover when needed, preferring to move through the buildings and shadows.

David was terrifying; silent, focused, seemingly without fear, and totally in control. My dad and Tariq followed his every move and gesture like the practised guerrilla fighters they were. I just tagged along behind them, trying not to give the game away with a careless move.

When we encountered guards or patrols David would take the lead, sidling up to them with the grace of a dancer, silencing them so quietly he almost seemed gentle. He would wrap his arm around their throat, compress their carotid artery and squeeze until they passed out. Then he would lay them on the floor, take hold of their hair and slit their throats.

When two or more stumbled across our path Dad would take the second, and Tariq would take the third. Although neither of them were as poised and fluid as David, they each held their own.

Tariq favoured a slow, delicate, tiptoe approach until just out of striking range, and then he would suddenly leap forward with his arms raised and snap the neck of his prey with a flourish, and let them collapse to the ground at his feet as his arms went wide as if to take a bow.

My father, on the other hand, was more straightforward. I was shocked by the calm precision with which he killed.

He would walk casually up behind his intended victim with his knife drawn, looking like he was going to pat the guy cheerily on the back and suggest a quick beer. He would then wrap one arm around the man's mouth as he slid the knife in between their ribs, as matter of fact as slicing open an envelope.

We hid the bodies as best we could, but we knew we had to move quickly. Sooner or later someone's absence would be noted, or a patrol would not radio in on time, and they would begin to zero in on us.

It probably only took us fifteen minutes to make our way to the main palace, but it felt like a lifetime. I didn't need to kill anyone during the journey, and I was grateful. I didn't want Dad to see me get blood on my hands. Not yet, anyway.

I was worried that he'd see my face as I took a life and he'd realise the truth about me.

The first time I murdered someone – not the first time I took a life, that was earlier – I was out of my head on drugs. I remember the actions but not how it felt.

The second time I took a life it was more by luck than judgement, scrabbling around on the floor, slick with blood, struggling to free myself from a man who was throttling me. I was stabbing his leg as I passed out; he died before I woke up. But I remember how sickeningly tactile it was. Here I was sharing – causing! – the most important moment in this person's life, more intimate even than sex, and I didn't know anything about him. Not his name, his sexual orientation, footy team, nothing at all. His entire existence culminated in a meeting with me, and yet we were strangers.

After that my killing became more focused and deliberate, even clinical. I saw the confusion and pain on my next victim's face as my knife penetrated his heart. I knew him, so his death was more than just meaningless slaughter; I was aware who and what I was snuffing out. It made me feel unbearably sad and guilty.

And powerful.

Then there were those that I killed in the heat of battle, gone in a flash. They were barely even people, just objects, like cars, which I had to stop in order to prevent collision. Yet each of them was unique, identifiable, and known to someone, just not to me, their killer. I had complete power over them, but they never even saw my face.

That feeling of power grew in me with each death, like a sickness I couldn't control and wasn't sure I wanted to. Until Mac, who I didn't even kill.

It shames me more than I can say, but when I stood in front of Mac, preparing to put a bullet in his head, I felt a thrill of anticipation and excitement that transported me. It was only because I lingered in order to savour the moment that Green was able to shoot him instead.

Let me be clear: I didn't hesitate because I wanted to be merciful; I hesitated because I wanted the moment to last. I even got a hard on. I can't stand to think what that says about me.

And now I was watching another killer, one I had thought I knew better than anybody still living, plying his trade with cool efficiency, and I thought: "Is that what I look like? Is that what I've become?"

Even with all that blood on my hands, the smooth, practised ease of my father's emotionless murdering shocked me. It shouldn't have. He was a soldier, after all. I knew he'd been in combat, I knew he'd killed people, just as he'd been trained to do. I knew who he was and what he did.

But seeing those hands, the ones that used to tickle me, throw me up in the air, lift me on to his shoulders on sunny country walks, coolly sliding a blade into the back of a man whose face he'd never seen, was a revelation. I realised three things in quick succession.

He was much better at this than me.

I had no idea who he really was.

And finally, if I got to know my murderous father, maybe it would help me understand his murderous son.

*   *   *

OUR POINT OF entry to the palace was the cell block. There were no prisoners in there any more, so it was unguarded. Then we were into the servants' passageway and safe in the dark, forgotten staircase. We soon came to the hidden door I had used to escape from my torturers the day before. On the other side was the vast room the general had taken as his office. The only problem was that we had no way of knowing who was in there.

There was nothing for it but to take the plunge, so David gently cracked the door open and peered through the tiny opening. There was nobody there, so he pushed the door open and ran, soft footed, to the main doors of the room. They stood ajar, and he looked through the gap then waved us out; there was nobody around. Everyone was too busy scouring the compound for us. This was the last place they'd be looking.

He gestured for me to watch the stairs, and waved Dad and Tariq across to search the room where I'd been tortured. There was a pool of congealed blood by the door, a memento of my most recent kill. There was a wide smear running to the balcony where the body had been dragged away and tossed over the railing to the ground below.

Tariq indicated that the room was clear. Dad went to the balcony to scan the area. David was already at the desk, hard at work placing the small block of C4 that he'd appropriated from stores on our journey here. I heard footsteps echoing through the hallway below and hissed at them to hurry. But David continued to work. The footsteps reached the stairs, and I hissed again, but David still stayed put. I ran across to him and grabbed his shoulder but he shrugged me off. I looked up at Dad, frantic, *What do we do?*

Dad ran around, grabbed my shoulder and dragged me towards the torture room. We ran inside and Tariq pushed the door almost closed behind us. Through the crack we could see David finish his handiwork and stand up, turning as if to leave. But then the main doors opened and there was his father, framed in the doorway.

"Ha," said the general. "You got balls, son."

David said nothing. I could see he held the detonator in his left hand, his thumb on the small, shiny switch.

The general turned, said "stay outside" to the men who had been escorting him, and closed the main doors behind him.

Father and son stood face to face for a minute before the elder man spoke.

"Bet you ten bucks I can put a bullet in your head before you press that button," he said in a pally way, as if referring to an old shared joke.

"Bet you ten bucks you can't," said David, with a wry smile.

But neither of them moved a muscle.

I went to push the door open, but my dad's hand on my shoulder stopped me.

"Let it play out," he whispered. "David can handle himself."

I nodded, but Dad kept his hand on my shoulder as a gentle reminder of who was in charge.

"I remember the day you were born..." began the general.

"No," interrupted David, shaking his head.

The general considered for a moment and then nodded, abandoning that approach.

"I agree," he said. "It's gone too far for that, hasn't it?"

"Yes, it has."

The general shook his head in weary disbelief.

"Was it always going to end like this, do you think?"

"No. If things had stayed the way they were, we'd be eating Thanksgiving dinner with Mom and Sarah, fighting over the gravy."

"But things didn't stay the same, did they?"

"No, they didn't. They never do."

"I reckon that's true. I love you, son."

I expected David to respond with "I'm not your son" again, but this time he replied: "I love you too, Dad."

There was a brief pause, and then a blur of movement and sudden violence that I couldn't even process. There was a single shot and David was lying on the floor, his head at a terrible angle, glassy eyed, his limbs in spasm, a thick pool of blood spreading out from the back of his shattered skull.

My dad gasped, his fingers crushing my shoulder (thankfully not the one I'd recently dislocated, or I'd have yelped). I placed my hand over his and squeezed back.

General Blythe stood over the body of his dead son for a minute, silent, shoulders hunched. But there were no tears, not even a single sob. Eventually he drew himself back up to his full height and walked to the doors, pulling them open and gesturing wordlessly for a soldier to remove David's corpse.

When the mess was cleared away, the general was once again alone in his room with the doors closed. He sat heavily in his chair and swiveled to stare out at the rising sun.

Tariq and I both looked at Dad, guns tight in our grips. Dad nodded and we began to push open the door. Suddenly there was a shrill alarm. I felt a rush of adrenaline. Had we triggered it somehow?

But the general spun his chair so he had his back to us and the large flatscreen telly buzzed into life. That was where the sound had come from. Dad grabbed my shoulder and dragged me back, pulling the door almost closed again. I shrugged his hand off me, full of resentment, but resumed my previous position, watching the general as he began to talk to the man who had appeared on screen.

It was clearly a live feed, so some satellites must still be functioning up there somewhere. The man on the screen was old; seventy at least, with a liver spotted face, pallid, ghostly skin and a thin ring of white hair around his shiny bald pate. He was wearing a black suit, white shirt and dark blue tie, all immaculately pressed, and he was sitting in front of the stars and stripes. He was obviously indoors, but well lit, as if in a TV studio about to present the news. Wherever he was he had lots of power to burn.

"Good evening, General," said the man. His voice was thin and reedy.

Even with all the clues the screen offered me, nothing prepared me for what the general said next.

"Good evening, Mr President."

"Fuck," whispered Dad under his breath.

"Progress report?" wheezed the old man.

"We've eliminated all local resistance, as ordered."

"And the English soldier, Keegan?"

"Dead." So the general wasn't above lying to his Commander-in-Chief. Interesting.

The old man smiled a little at this news. It was not a pleasant sight. "Good. About time. Did he give you anything useful before he died?"

"No. He didn't break."

The old man gave a harrumph of displeasure. "Pity. We'll just have to make do with the satellite images. Did you receive them?"

"Yes, Sir. Are you sure about the choice of target, Sir? I still believe that it might be better to take out the Tsar now, before his power base grows even more."

"We considered it, General, but we've decided that a strong Russia is actually to our advantage at this point. Let the Tsar continue his rise to power. He cannot threaten us. We predict that he will control most of Russia within two or three years, and that suits us. We have long term plans in that respect."

"In that case, Sir, we've prepared flight plans and fuelled the planes. We're ready to go whenever you give the order."

"Good, good. No time like the present, General. In your own time, proceed with the plan. Destroy Operation Motherland and take control of their arsenal at your earliest convenience. Establish martial law in as wide an area as you can. Put the techniques you've honed in Basra to good use. Terrorise the population, bring them to heel, by any means necessary. They shouldn't be too much trouble now they've been disarmed."

The main doors cracked open and a soldier poked his head in. The general waved him to enter, and a group of four heavily armed men silently filed into the room and stood waiting. It looked like there was now no chance for us to kill the general without sacrificing ourselves.

"I'd like to initiate a secondary operation, if you'll permit it, Sir," said the general.

"Explain."

"I've received intelligence about an armed camp. It's outside our target area, but I believe that a show of force there could send a strong message that our operations are not confined inside our perimeter."

"Where is this camp?"

"Somewhere called Groombridge Place, Mr President. I believe it's the base of operation for a group of Special Forces, a training school for new recruits. One of them came here to retrieve Keegan and killed some good men. We dealt with him, but I think it would be wise to shut the facility down."

"Do I detect a lust for revenge, General?"

"Just doing my job, Mr President."

"Very well, proceed as you see fit."

"You can count on me, Mr President. By this time next week, England will be in American hands and we can proceed to the next phase."

"Don't let me down, General."

The screen went black, there was a momentary burst of static, and then silence.

The general rose and barked "follow me" at the soldiers who'd waited patiently during his teleconference. They filed out of the room and we were alone again.

My mind was whirling with the implications of everything I'd just heard. But one awful image was inescapable: me on a video screen, tied up in front of a blue sheet, yelling for someone to find the school and tell Matron about my death.

They must have found the tape.

Oh, God, what had I done?

Jane.

PART TWO
JANE

JANE

CHAPTER SEVEN

WORK HARD, KEEP your nose clean, own your house. That was the advice Kate's gran always gave her.

"It's not difficult, dear," she'd say. "Just follow those simple rules and you can end up like me and your granddad." Of course, when Kate was seventeen that was the last thing in the world she wanted. But she loved her gran, so she'd nod and smile, and say "Yes, Gran."

On one hand I was glad that her gran died before The Cull, as it spared her all this horror. On the other, she'd have been magnificent, riding out the apocalypse on a wave of warm, milky tea and allotment carrots. It was at moments like this that I missed her most.

But Kate and her gran were gone now.

Rowles strained at his leash, trying to pull away from me. I cuffed him around the head.

"Don't mess me about," I growled.

He whimpered.

The guard in front of us smiled a gruesome, black-toothed grin.

"Can I come in and trade these kids or what?" I said. "Olly's expecting me."

The guard ran his slimy tongue along his lower lip, considering us carefully, then sucked his disgusting teeth and nodded. Lee once told me he used to give people descriptive names to help him keep track of them in his head. It was something that helped him focus when he was under pressure. So I christened the door guard.

"S'pose," said Blackteeth. "Come on in, love."

He turned and waved to the man on the wall behind him, who shouted something to someone in the courtyard. The huge doors swung inwards with a shriek of rusty metal. The guard leered at me and mock-bowed, sweeping his right arm towards the doors, inviting us to enter.

I remembered Kate willingly walking into danger – a heavy, steel-reinforced door, a cold, dark warehouse, and a man standing there with a machine gun strapped across his chest, saying exactly the same thing to her. "Come on in, love." And Cooper's voice in her ear had whispered: "We're right here, don't be afraid."

Eight years ago.

I shook my head and dismissed the memory. If Lee were here he'd tell me to stay focused on my objective.

I so wished Lee were here.

I flashed the guard a disgusted look. "About time."

Drawing myself up to my full height – I'm 5'3" and I was wearing flats, but it's all about posture – I strolled through those gates with all the dignity and attitude I could manage. As I passed the guard he goosed me.

I stopped dead, turned towards him slowly, gave him my most seductive smile and slapped him hard across the face.

"Touch me again, sunshine, and I'll rip your balls off and feed them to you."

I heard Kate's gran saying "Now, now dear, don't be a potty mouth." I had to bite back the urge to giggle. It's something I do when I'm scared.

The guard laughed.

Caroline sobbed involuntarily. I tugged her chain hard and aimed a half-hearted kick at her shin. She looked up at me, chin wobbling, wide eyes full of tears.

"Button it, you," I said.

"Third stable on the right, darlin'," said Blackteeth. "Tell you what, when you're done you come find me. I've got a bottle of real wine in my bunk. Been saving it for a special occasion."

I turned my back on him and walked towards the stables, tugging the kids behind me. Rowles slipped and fell on his face. I didn't look back or break my stride; I just dragged him through the mud until he regained his footing and staggered after me. I imagined his collar was really chafing by now.

The courtyard ahead of me was deserted. I knew there were at least three guards behind me at the gates, but I didn't turn to see if there were more. The main farmhouse stood at the far end, three storeys high. Tattered curtains hung from dusty windows, some of which were shattered. The kitchen door was open and I got an impression of movement inside. To my left was a large derelict barn, its roof fallen in; to my right stood a row of brick stables. A large truck was parked awkwardly in the far left corner, its engine idling, the exhaust fumes misting in the chill morning air. That was a statement in itself – who had enough fuel to waste it warming up a lorry cab, even on a morning this cold? I knew exactly what its cargo would be, but after long weeks of investigation I still had no idea where it was going.

I thought about knocking but decided I'd make an entrance, so I walked into the stable, dragging the children behind me. The man behind the desk jumped slightly and reached for the pistol that lay in front of him, but relaxed when he saw that it was only me. He leaned back in his chair, his great blubbery weight threatening to topple him backwards at any second. This was Olly.

"What bloody kept you?" he asked as he returned his attention to the thick rare steak he was eating, held in a piece of old newspaper.

"Ask your guards. More interested in flirting than doing business." I looped the chain and the rope around a hook on the wall, and shoved the two children to the floor. I sat in the chair facing Olly and put my feet up on his desk.

Careful, I thought. Don't overdo it.

"The reason I want to do business with you, Olly, is 'cause you're such a class act," I said.

It took him a moment to realise what I meant, and then he laughed, his thick lips parting in a strangled wheeze, revealing half-chewed raw meat. He thrust the steak towards me.

"Want some?" he offered. "Fresh kill."

"Thanks, but no thanks."

"Suit yourself. Talking of fresh meat, what do we have here?" He levered himself out of his chair and waddled around the desk towards Rowles and Caroline. Both of them cowered against the wall, a pathetic sight in their tattered, muddy rags.

"The boy's eleven, been living rough," I said. "Girl's twelve. Untouched, if you can believe that. They're a bit scrawny but they're healthy as far as I can tell."

Rowles put his arm around Caroline's shoulder as Olly leered at them.

"Don't worry, C," Rowles whispered. "I won't let him hurt you."

Olly leaned down and grabbed Rowles' chin in his greasy fingers. He got very close indeed and hissed into the boy's face: "Of course I'm not going to hurt her. I'm most gentle, me. Break her in all carefully, I will. You too, if you're good."

Rowles spat in Olly's eye as Caroline sobbed and buried her face in his shoulder. Olly snarled and raised his ugly paw, ready to strike the boy, but I leapt up and grabbed the man's wrist. It was so thick I couldn't even get my fingers around it.

"You don't lay a finger on either of them till I get my payment, fat man," I said.

He turned to me, teeth bared. But his raw meat snarl changed into a grin, he wheezed his laugh again and lowered his hand.

"There's no hurry, is there?" He looked down at the pair. "I'll have plenty of quality time with these two when you've gone, won't I? No need to rush."

I let go of his arm and he moved back to his side of the desk and sat down again. I followed suit. He took another bite of steak, tearing the flesh off and chewing sloppily.

"Price is fixed, as discussed," he said. "Go see Jonny in the big house, he'll sort you out. If you make a habit of bringing me good stock like this I'll make it worth your while. Any more where these came from?"

"Plenty, but I can only take them one or two at a time. Don't want to get caught. The villagers might not take kindly to me pinching their kiddies."

"Can't imagine why, little runts."

"But you'll be moving them soon, won't you? 'Cause they might come looking for these two." I tried to sound conversational, barely interested, but I knew immediately that I'd made a mistake. He looked across at me, suspicious and threatening.

"What do you care?" he demanded.

I pretended to think about this, then shrugged and rose to my feet. "I don't. Just curious. Jonny, yeah?"

"Jonny. Yeah."

"See you around, Olly." I didn't look back at the two children as I left.

I crossed to the farmhouse door, which was still hanging open, and casually glanced back at the gates. The high brick wall was solid, so they felt secure in here. Apart from Blackteeth who was outside the metal doors, now closed, there was a guy on a ramshackle scaffold inside, looking out over the flood plain to the south. He had a shotgun over his shoulder. A third man lounged on a damp sofa inside the doors reading *Oliver Twist*. He also had a shotgun, but his was sawn off.

Two inside the doors, one outside. Then Olly in the stable and Jonny in the house. Might be more, though. But where?

I walked into the farmhouse kitchen. The smell was appalling. In the centre of the large flagstone floor was a wooden table, around it six children of varying ages. All of them had ropes looped around their necks, binding them together in one long chain. They sat there, eyes dead, faces white, most with black eyes or thick lips, dressed in clothes either too big or small, mechanically eating porridge from bowls. I doubted any of them had seen soap and water for at least a month.

Again, Kate's gran came to mind. I had a sudden flash of her cooing "Poor dears", spitting on to her hankie, and wiping all their faces clean with saliva. Kate used to hate it when she did that. God, she used to squirm. Looking back, it seems like the gentlest act of kindness imaginable. Small acts of kindness, that was what the world was missing these days.

I forced my attention back to my situation. I was distancing myself from it, retreating into my head, rambling. It's a trick I learned the first time things got bad, back before The Cull. It had come in handy once or twice since.

But I couldn't afford to absent myself now. I needed to stay sharp. Anyway, I wasn't the one in danger, not really. I wondered where these children had gone to in their heads. I was pretty certain none of them were entirely present any more. I looked into their eyes and I thought that this was how I must look when I zone out. Like a victim. That made me sad and angry to my core. I held on to the anger, focused it, concentrated, brought myself back.

I am nobody's victim. Not any more.

An interior door swung open and a scrawny teenage boy walked in. His face was a battlefield of acne and bum fluff and he dragged a young blonde girl behind him on a rope. Thirteen at the oldest, her face was streaked with tears and snot. His belt was still unbuckled.

I didn't give him time to react to my presence. I was around the table and my arm was around his neck so quickly he didn't know what was happening. He was unconscious before he had a chance to open his mouth. It took all my willpower to relax my grip – it was so tempting to squeeze the life out of the sorry bastard. I wanted to kill him, I felt justified in killing him, even righteous.

But I hadn't let the horror overwhelm me, so I wouldn't let the fury take me either. If I succumbed to either I'd lose myself, and there were children here who needed me.

The boy stopped struggling and his eyes rolled back in their sockets. I relaxed my grip and gently laid his head on the floor. I ran back around the crowded table and closed the door into the courtyard. No-one had raised the alarm, so the struggle hadn't been seen.

I turned back and found six pairs of eyes staring at me with distant curiosity. One boy was still eating, so far gone that he didn't even register what was happening around him. The young girl who had just entered was staring down at the boy who lay unconscious at her feet. I opened my mouth to speak but before I could utter a sound the girl raised her foot and stamped it down, as hard as she could, on the boy's neck. There was a dreadful crunch, the boy spasmed and twitched, gasped, sighed, then lay still. A trickle of blood leaked from his mouth. The girl looked up at me and wiped the back of her hand across her face, smearing away the tears and snot. Then she cocked her head to one side, and said: "Now what?" She spoke primly, with the self-possession of monied privilege.

It took me a few seconds to respond.

"Is there anybody else in here with you?" I asked.

"Just Tim," said the girl. "He's upstairs. He's sick."

"No more guards?"

She shook her head.

"All right. Can you open the front door for me? Walk outside and wave. My friends will see you."

She looped the rope over her neck and let it drop to the floor, then she nodded, turned and left.

I looked down at the seated children. One boy seemed more present than the others. He looked about ten. I leant down so we were eye to eye.

"When my friends arrive can you show them where Tim is and help them get everyone out the front door?"

He nodded solemnly.

"Thank you. Now, could you all just keep quiet for a moment? I have one more thing to do then we can get you out of here."

A few small nods. One girl went back to her porridge.

I avoided looking at the dead teenager, closed my eyes, took a deep breath, fixed a smile on my face and opened the door to the courtyard again. I strode out confidently, but I was painfully aware that I was unarmed. It wouldn't have helped anyway; my hands were shaking too much to use a gun even if I'd had one. I couldn't tell you whether they shook from fear or fury – probably an equal measure of both. I took a deep breath and tried to relax; I'd need steady hands for the next bit.

As I walked past the stables, I saw Rowles and Caroline, still sitting on the floor in Olly's office. I caught Rowles' eye and inclined my head. He nodded back and rose to his feet. I kept walking past the doorway, towards the bookworm. He lay his book aside as I approached, carefully inserting a bookmark to keep his place.

"I thought you were getting paid?" he asked as he swung his legs over the side of the sofa.

The plan had been to find a bag and fill it with stuff, make it look like I'd been paid. I'd been distracted, lost my concentration, and forgotten. Stupid mistake.

"Nothing left," I improvised. "Jonny told me to come back tomorrow. He reckons you'll be flush once you've offloaded this consignment."

The man looked confused.

"Yeah, we will be. But we won't be back for a week."

So wherever they took the children was much further away than I'd thought.

The guard smiled. "Jonny probably just wants you to come and visit him while we're away. Dirty bastard."

The gun was on the sofa beside him. Bookworm stood up and walked past me to yell at the farmhouse. "Oi! Jonny! You dirty fucker. Your dick making you tell porkies again?"

He obviously expected a comeback. But Jonny wasn't saying anything. He stood there, smiling, waiting for a sarcastic reply. Then the smile gradually changed to puzzlement. "Oi! Jonny! You in there?" He took another step forwards. Suddenly he realised something was wrong, and he spun around to face me. I couldn't go for his gun because the guard at the top of the scaffolding was watching us. He'd have picked me off if I'd made a move. But I was standing between the bookworm and his sofa, blocking access to his gun. I silently urged everyone to get a move on.

"Last I saw Jonny, he was dragging some girl upstairs by a rope," I said, shrugging.

Bookworm eyed me suspiciously.

"Probably can't hear you for her groans of ecstasy," I added. Then I flashed my eyes at him knowingly, pretending to be one of the lads, laughing at the teenage rapist.

I felt sick.

"So not tomorrow, next week, yeah?" I asked.

"Yeah," he said thoughtfully.

We stood there facing each other as he see-sawed between amusement and suspicion. Amusement eventually won.

"He's a dirty little bastard, Jonny," he laughed. "You want to watch him."

"Will do. See you next week then?"

He nodded and walked to the gate, unshackling the chains and pulling hard. The guard on the tower returned his attention to the flood plain as the door swung open. I leaned down and grabbed the sawn-off shotgun from the sofa, and walked up behind Bookworm. I buried the muzzle in the small of his back. He stiffened and froze. I pushed him forward so that the metal door shielded us from the man on the scaffolding.

The guard outside the door looked puzzled for an instant and then raised his gun to his hip.

"Drop it," I whispered to the black-toothed lech. "Or the bookworm dies."

He considered this for a moment.

"I don't really like him that much," he replied.

"Fred!" protested Bookworm.

"Shut up, you speccy twat," said Blackteeth. "Always got your nose buried in a book. Think you're better than the rest of us. Threatening him ain't gonna stop me, love. Oi, Mike, we've got a situation down here. Wanna lend a hand or you just gonna sit up there staring into space all afternoon?"

I heard the metal clang of the other guard climbing down the scaffolding.

All the plan required was that I disarm the door guards. It should have been easy. Instead I had two barrels ready to fire, two armed men coming at me from two sides, and one unarmed but still dangerous guy stuck in the middle with me. Lee would have known what to do.

I just had to stall. What was keeping everyone?

"What about you, Mike?" I shouted. "You want to see your mate's guts blown out?" I had my free hand on Bookworm's shoulder, and I began backing us away from Blackteeth, back inside the courtyard, towards the sofa. When Mike finally hit the ground and rounded the gate we were far enough back that I could see him and Blackteeth without dividing my attention. At least I'd avoided being caught between the two of them – now they were all in front of me.

"Not really," said Mike. He was tall and lean, bald, about forty. He wore a Barbour jacket, blue jeans and green wellies, and he had the shotgun held up to his shoulder, aimed steadily at us. Something about his poise made me very nervous. He wasn't a thug like Blackteeth, or a novice like Bookworm – he was experienced and deliberate. He was the real threat here.

I remembered the briefing that morning. "Nobody gets hurt," I'd insisted. "Whatever happens, no-one gets killed. All right?" I looked pointedly at Rowles as I said this. He smirked, then nodded. "Yes, Matron."

One dumb teenage bastard was already going cold twenty metres to my right. I didn't want anyone else to join him. Not even these guys.

"Olly!" Mike shouted. "Get out here, boss."

"Olly's not available right now," came the reply. "Can I help at all?" It was Rowles; all five foot nothing of him. He was standing outside the stables, muddy and bedraggled, legs apart, arms raised, with a pistol in his hands. His face and hair dripped fresh blood.

"Dammit Rowles," I shouted. "I told you not to kill him."

"He's not dead, Matron," replied the boy quietly. "I can't guarantee he'll ever be the same again, but he's not dead."

Mike's aim didn't waver for a second, but his eyes widened as he calculated the odds. He was square in Rowles' sights.

"Fuck me," said Blackteeth.

"It's just a kid, Fred," said Mike. "Get a grip."

"Caroline, you got a minute?" said Rowles.

Caroline walked out of the stable to join him. Taller than Rowles, one year older, solidly built, her ginger hair cut brutally short, Caroline also held a pistol. She bit her lip thoughtfully, concentrating, as she took careful aim at Blackteeth.

"Actually, he is dead," she said, quite matter of fact. Rowles looked at her, surprised.

"Really?"

"You hit him over the head with an iron bar. Twice. Of course he's dead. Idiot." She said 'idiot' indulgently, with love, as if talking to a silly toddler or sullen boyfriend. My very own pre-pubescent Bonnie and Clyde.

"Oh," said Rowles, nonplussed. "Sorry, Matron." He blinked back his surprise and refocused his attention on Mike.

"Shall we shoot them, Jane?" asked Caroline.

Mike looked into my eyes as I pretended to consider Caroline's question. That made his mind up. He began backing away slowly, heading for the gate.

"I think we'll be leaving," he said. "Coming, Fred?"

Blackteeth nodded and joined his mate, walking backwards, gun raised. As soon as they were clear of the wall they ran left, out of sight.

The farm was ours.

The children were safe.

WE WERE TOO late to help Tim. He had pneumonia and didn't survive the day.

I had Rowles bury Olly, Jonny and Tim as punishment for his overzealous retribution. He didn't complain. He might go overboard at times, but he had never once questioned any order I'd given him, which is partly why I relied on him so much.

A team of older boys and girls from the school joined us, and we loaded the rescued children into the back of the lorry then set out for home. We left Rowles burying the dead. He could walk back to the school. That was another part of his punishment. It was only ten miles, and I wasn't worried about him. I was far more afraid for anyone that tried to cross him.

Bookworm came with us, too. I reassured him that no harm would come to him, but I still tied him up and put a sack over his head. I had questions I wanted to ask.

Half an hour later I swung the lorry into the driveway of the school and hit the brakes as hard as I could. The lorry skidded and ended up diagonally across the tarmac. I heard protests from the cabin behind me, but I couldn't worry about that now.

There was a roadblock ahead of us, flanked by armed men in combat uniforms.

I reached down, grasped the sidearm that I'd taken from Caroline, and considered what to do. One of the men was approaching the lorry, rifle raised. He didn't look like the usual rabble. None of the local wannabe soldiers wore uniform that convincing.

I thought about throwing the lorry into reverse and running, but it would require a three-point turn, and he'd be here long before we could escape. If he opened fire the children could be hit. I wouldn't put them at risk.

Charge the checkpoint, then? I seriously considered it for a moment, but eventually decided against it. I had to follow the rules I'd set down for myself: never shoot first and prepare for the worst but assume friendly intent until proven wrong.

I kept the engine running and the lorry in first, with my foot on the clutch. I had no idea who this guy was or which group he represented. They could be friendlies. I forced myself to stay calm and wait for him to show his hand.

But he and his mates had obviously taken control of the school. My school. That made me angry. I tried not to imagine what could be going on in there right now.

I cocked the pistol and rested it on my lap, then I rolled down the window.

The man stopped about ten metres from me, rifle raised.

"Are you armed?" he shouted.

"Yes, thanks," I replied, politely.

"Throw down your weapon and step out of the cab. Keep your hands where I can see them."

"Why?"

"Because I'm asking nicely, ma'am. I don't want to shoot you."

"That's good. I don't want you to shoot me either. We have something in common. Now do you mind telling me who the fuck you are and what you're doing in my school?"

"Not your school any more, ma'am, I'm afraid. You'd be Jane Crowther, yes?"

"That's right."

"Then it's my duty to inform you that in accordance with emergency provisions, and Royal decree, this estate is now under the control of the British Army. And you are under arrest for looting, kidnap and suspected murder."

CHAPTER EIGHT

KATE'S BROTHER HAD a thing for soldiers.

If I close my eyes and concentrate I can almost see those bright eyes, that cheeky grin, and hear him saying: "Imagine, all that time in uniform, being butch, sharing showers and never even copping a snog. I mean, talk about repressed. I tell you, Sis, a closeted soldier on a night out is my idea of heaven. So gloriously dirty!" Then he'd tell that unrepeatable anecdote about a captain from Aldershot, a rubber hose and a camcorder, and Kate and her friends would all be wetting themselves by the time he got to the bit where the lube tube exploded.

"Something funny, miss?"

I put my hand over my mouth and forced myself to concentrate. "No, Captain, nothing at all. Just... wind."

I was sitting in my office on the ground floor at Groombridge Place, but I was on the wrong side of the old mahogany desk. I loved that desk. It's amazing the sense of power and confidence just sitting behind a big desk can give you. Props like that help when you're making it all up as you go along, like I'd been. But today I was sat on a hard plastic chair with my hands cuffed behind my back while the man who had introduced himself as Captain Jim Jones sat in my comfy leather swivel chair, facing me across my desk. He pouted sourly and rubbed the back of his neck. He kept doing that. As nervous tics go it wasn't the worst, but it was starting to irritate me.

The captain was thirtyish, six feet tall, slightly built, with thin sandy hair and big teeth that looked like they were trying to escape from his face. Pretty rather than attractive. He seemed comfortable in his uniform, though, and when I'd been brought in here his men had followed his orders efficiently and without question. Command came easily to him, it seemed. Whoever these guys were, they were well disciplined.

He narrowed his blue eyes warily, as if daring me to give my assessment out loud.

"Well then Miss, as I was saying before your breakfast interrupted me, we've taken control of this establishment following a report that you were involved in the trafficking of children."

There was something about the way he said 'Miss' that made me want to kick him in the shins. I suppose I should have stayed calm and pliant, played the innocent, but he was in my chair and he was patronising me. I wasn't in the mood to be patient.

"Okay," I replied. "Let's deal with that first, before we get to the question of who you are and by what authority you've taken control of my school. What report? From who?"

"We have certain assets in play, Miss," he said. Smug git.

"Right," I snapped, irritably. "In English we say 'spies.' You've got a spy or spies in the trafficking network that I've been negotiating with."

I paused for a second and ran through everyone I'd come into contact with since I'd started negotiations with Olly a few weeks ago.

"There was only one person in that organisation who knew where I came from, except Olly," I said. "The spotty one, Smith. He wasn't there this morning. Reporting in, was he?"

Jones was wrong-footed by that and almost stammered.

"I can't discuss ongoing operations," he said curtly.

"Right, so Smith told you I was selling children to Olly, and instead of shutting that scumbag down you waited 'til I'd gone to do business, seized the school, presumably to protect the kids, and then waited for me to get back. That way you leave Smith in place, which means you don't know where the kids end up yet. That about it?"

The captain rubbed his neck.

"Thought so," I said. "Only two problems there, Captain.

"One: I'm not trafficking children, I'm rescuing them. If you talk to the kids from the back of the truck I was driving when you arrested me – kids, by the way, who need medical attention, which is what I should be doing now rather than explaining myself to you – if you talk to them, they'll confirm what I'm saying.

"Two: Olly is dead, as is one of his goons. The other two ran away and the final one is the sod with the bag over his head. I was going to interrogate him and find out where the kids end up, but if you really are the British Army and not just a bunch of roleplaying inadequates, then I'm sure your interrogation techniques will be far more effective than mine. I don't enjoy inflicting pain."

Captain Jim was not used to people talking back to him. I could see that it was taking a lot of effort for him to stay calm. He was used to unquestioning obedience; maybe I could use that.

"If what you say is true, we'll have it sorted out in no time, Miss."

This was not the reasonable, measured answer I wanted. And he'd called me Miss again.

"And while we're at it," I said, "who the sweet holy fuck do you think you are to come walking into my school at gunpoint and start tossing orders about?"

"As I've explained, Miss, we are the British Army." He was getting testy. I wondered what would happen if I really pushed him.

"My big fat arse you are."

"I can assure you..."

"If you're the army then where were you after The Cull burnt itself out? Where were you when martial law fell to pieces? Where were you when the rape gangs and cannibals and the England-for-the-English death squads started running things? Where were you when I had to lead an army of children into battle, for fuck's sake? We could've used you! What, were you too busy putting 'assets' in place to actually fucking help? And how many of you are there, eh? Seriously, are there even enough of you to be an army? Even if you are all soldiers you're just another militia now. And as for that Royal Decree bollocks, Christ, don't make me laugh. That bunch of parasites bled out and died just like everyone else. Who's left? Fergie? Is that it? Are you Fergie's Forces? God help us. Or is it Harry? He likes a good uniform, that one; just make sure it's not got a swastika on it."

I was red in the face, breathing hard, and I'd stood up half way through my rant, trying to assert some measure of control over the situation, impose myself on him a bit.

The captain just sat there, placid, letting me get it out of my system.

"Finished?" he asked.

I'd misjudged him. He'd been annoyed by my niggling jibes and insubordination, but a full temper tantrum just brought back his sense of superiority and condescension.

I nodded and sat back down. So much for that idea.

"Well?" I asked.

He spoke calmly and with control. If he was angry he was determined not to let me see it.

"I can assure you, Miss, that I am a member of His Majesty's Armed Forces. At present the UK has no civilian administration, but the emergency provisions laid down by the government at the start of the crisis still hold. Martial law remains in effect. However, we do not have enough troops to enforce it. Instead, we are engaged in an operation designed to restore some level of order and security."

I waited for more information, but he said nothing else. "Is that it?"

"I am not authorised to tell you more," he said smugly. "We are not in the habit of revealing top secret plans to school teachers."

"I'm a matron, not a teacher, and if you think you're going to restore order by wearing a uniform, looking pleased with yourself and being vague at people then the best of luck to you."

He smiled thinly and for the first time I suspected that Captain Jim could be quite ruthless if the circumstances demanded it.

"You misunderstand, Miss. I have more than a uniform." He reached down and I heard the soft metallic click of a button being undone, then he laid a Browning semi-automatic pistol on the desk in front of him. "I have my standard issue Browning sidearm."

I was about to make some sarcastic rejoinder when he reached down and produced the handgun I'd been carrying when I was detained. He gently placed it alongside his own.

"The curious thing," he said, "is that you do, too. And you're no soldier. Which raises some interesting questions, don't you think?"

Before I could reply there was a sharp knock at the door and the captain barked "Come!"

A young female soldier entered, snapped to attention and saluted.

"We found what we were looking for, Sir."

"Thank you, Private," replied the captain, getting to his feet and holstering his gun. "Bring her," he said, and left without giving me a second glance.

I felt the squaddie grip my shoulder, so I stood up and was led out of the room and into the main reception hall of the old house. The double front doors were to my right, the main staircase with its plush red carpet was to my left, and a series of doors led to rooms off the hall. Normally this space would be full of life – running kids, play fights, all sorts of wonderful commotion. Now there was just a young man in uniform with a machine gun nestled in the crook of his arm, indicating to the captain that he should walk past the staircase and into what would once have been the servants' area. I followed, receiving a sneer of contempt from him as I passed. Like I cared.

We went through a small door beside the staircase into a narrow corridor that led to the scullery, pantry and kitchen. But it turned out that our destination was the cellar. As I got to the cellar door I caught a glimpse of the courtyard through a small window. I saw all the children and staff of my school, lined up, stood to attention, being watched by three soldiers whose guns were trained on them. My first instinct was to raise hell, but I'd realised what was coming, so I bit back my anger and followed Captain Jones down the stairs into the armoury. The female squaddie remained in the corridor above.

A single naked bulb lit the cool, damp, barrel-vaulted chamber where we kept our guns and ammunition. It was not that different to the armoury back at St Mark's, out of which we'd hauled as many boxes as possible while Mac's time bomb counted down. The captain was standing by a box of SA80 machine guns, inspecting them closely. He lifted one out, felt its heft, and assured himself it was the genuine article and not a replica or a toy. Then he scanned the room, found the ammunition, checked that too, and slammed the magazine into place. Satisfied, he shoved the muzzle hard into my abdomen and looked me in the eye.

"I'm authorised to shoot looters," he said quietly. "In fact my C.O. positively encourages it. But lucky for you I like to get my facts straight before I start shooting. So I'm going to give you one chance to explain to me how a young nurse and a house full of children happen to be in possession of enough army property to wage a small war. And you'd better make it good, Miss Crowther, because the serial number on that box tells me that this ordnance came from a Territorial installation about ten miles from here, and the men who were guarding it were found tied up and murdered last month. As you can imagine, we take a dim view of people who kill our colleagues."

I took a deep breath and maintained eye contact. Such pretty blue eyes, but they were hard and cold. I didn't doubt he'd shoot me if I said the wrong thing.

"I thought," I said, "that you were here to stop me trafficking children?"

"I am. And I'll do as you ask – talk to the children from the truck, interrogate your prisoner, check on Olly and see if he's as dead as you say. It's easy to check a few facts and find out if you're lying. But this," he gestured to the crates, "is another matter. And I'm still waiting."

There was nothing to do but tell the truth.

"I took control of this school a few months ago," I explained. "Before that it was briefly run by a man called Sean MacKillick – a ruthless, violent psychopath. He was setting himself up as some kind of tribal leader until he was betrayed and killed by the children he was attempting to lead. Then I stepped in and took his place. These children were – are – horribly traumatised. I'm trying to look after them and keep them safe. It was MacKillick who raided your base, killed those men and took the guns. I just sort of inherited them."

His eyes were sharp and calculating as he considered what I'd just said. I stood there underneath the light bulb, with my back to the staircase, waiting for his decision, knowing that I might only find out what it was when a bullet hit my spine.

Looking back at that moment, I think he believed me. I fancy that I saw the change in his eyes, the instant he chose trust over fear. But I may be wrong. I'll never know. Because at that precise moment the young woman soldier from upstairs was thrown down the cellar stairs. I looked down and to my left and saw her eyes blink once in surprise before she died. Her throat had been slit and there was arterial blood still pumping from the gash.

"Drop the gun," said a familiar voice behind me.

Oh no.

Captain Jim still had the machine gun jammed into my stomach but he was looking over my shoulder at the boy coming down the stairs. Then he looked back to me and held my gaze. I suppose that's one of the things about soldiers – they're trained to stay cool even when awful things happen out of the blue. I could see the captain calculating the odds, weighing his chances, not sparing a second thought for the poor dead girl lying next to me on the floor.

"I said drop it," barked Rowles as he came down the stairs. I couldn't see him, but I presumed he had a gun aimed at the captain's head.

I needed to try and defuse this situation.

"I thought you were walking back, Rowles," I said, maintaining eye contact with the captain, telling him with my eyes that he shouldn't do anything hasty.

"They had horses. I nicked one. Who are these bastards?" asked the boy.

"They say they're the British Army."

"Ha. And who are they really? More traffickers? Militia? What?"

"Thing is Rowles, I think they might be telling the truth. I think they may actually be the army."

The captain inclined his head slightly, acknowledging what I was doing, giving me leave to continue

"So why have they got everyone lined up outside like they're about to start shooting?" asked Rowles.

"He's got a point, you know," I said to the captain. "You go around kidnapping people at gunpoint with no explanation, they're going to assume you're just another bunch of thugs. They're not going to think 'hang on, maybe they're here to help, maybe they're lining us up against a wall for our own good'. They're going to think 'oh look, another shower of bastards with big guns', and they're going to start a fight. You can't blame them for that. After a year of fighting for our lives against all sorts of gun toting, uniform wearing bully boys, why would anyone give you the benefit of the doubt if this is the way you do business?"

Don't do anything stupid, Captain, please don't shoot the boy.

He considered what I'd said, his gun muzzle still nestled in my tummy, Rowles' gun still pointing at his head.

"We're the army, Miss," he said. "We don't have to explain ourselves."

"And that's the kind of arrogant bullshit that gets people killed," I replied angrily. "Of course you have to explain yourselves. Anyone can get army guns and uniforms these days, they're just lying there. The point of the army is to be better than that. You're supposed to protect us from the thugs, not act like them. That girl on the floor, what was her name?"

"Julie, Julie Noble."

"Well Julie Noble would still be alive if you'd just knocked on the door and introduced yourselves instead of waving guns around and lining up children like cattle."

"These days people have a tendency to shoot first and ask questions later," he said. "We've lost a lot of good soldiers trying your approach. It's proven more efficient to seize control and then explain later. Saves lives."

"Army lives. But how many innocent people have been killed resisting you before they knew what was going on?"

He shrugged. "A few."

"Even one is too many. Your job is to risk your lives to keep them safe, but you're risking their lives to keep yourselves safe. And if you do that you lose what little authority that uniform gives you. The boy behind me is eleven. Look what this world has driven him to. Look what you're driving him to. Someone is going to die here in a moment – you, me or an eleven-year-old boy – if you don't start acting like a proper soldier. And I'd really, really like it if no-one else died today. So be a dear, Jim, and put the bloody gun down."

"Him first," he said.

I rolled my eyes. It was hard to know who was the bigger child, the soldier or the schoolboy.

I glared at him and said: "Rowles, lower your gun please."

"But what if he shoots you, Matron?"

"He won't."

"I can take him, Matron. Just say the word."

A momentary flash of disbelief crossed the captain's face.

"Oh, he's not lying, Captain," I said.

"Listen, son," said the soldier.

"No no no!" I interrupted, frantically signalling him to stop. "Don't do that. Don't."

There was a long pause and then Rowles said: "I don't like people in uniforms telling me what to do." The emotionless calm in his voice told the captain everything he needed to know about Rowles' state of mind and why it would be a really bad idea to patronise him.

"Rowles," I said firmly. "you've never disobeyed a direct order from me, or moaned once if you don't like an order I've given. As long as I let you say your piece before I make up my mind you let me make the call. Right?"

"You listen and you're fair. I trust you."

"Trust me now and put down the gun. That's an order."

After a moment's hesitation I heard the sound of his gun being uncocked. That was half the battle. Now which way would the captain jump?

"He's eleven years old," I said quietly. "You've invaded his home and kidnapped his friends at gunpoint. He's done nothing wrong, nothing you wouldn't have done in the same situation. This is your fault, Captain. Your actions led us here. And your actions will determine whether this ends peacefully or not. I don't think you want the blood of children on your hands, do you?"

The captain was staring at the floor, at poor dead Julie, his jaw clenched, furious and armed and eager to avenge the death of a soldier under his command.

"No, I don't," he said eventually. But it was an effort, I could tell.

"Good," I said. "Then here's what we're going to do. Rowles, throw your gun over here."

He did so.

"Captain, lower your gun and uncuff me. Then we'll walk out of here, brew up a nice cup of tea, have some of Mrs Atkins' flapjack and sort this out like civilised adults."

The captain half laughed, a mixture of amusement and warning. Then he nodded.

I breathed a sigh of relief as he withdrew his gun from my stomach.

But I was a fool.

Quick as a flash he stepped sideways and opened fire at the staircase behind me. The noise was unbearably loud in that enclosed chamber. I whirled to see what was happening and felt something hot and sharp hit my left ear. I caught a glimpse of Rowles diving to his right, gun in hand, muzzle flaring. The light bulb was shot out and we were plunged into darkness, lit only by strobe flashes of gunfire.

I should have dived for cover, but I was frozen in place. I should have shouted for them to stop, but my teeth were too tightly clenched.

I don't know how many rounds were fired, but I heard the captain give a low grunt and the gunfire stopped. All that was left was the ringing in my ears and the soft thud as someone hit the floor.

"Matron!" shouted Rowles in the darkness. It wasn't a cry for help, he was desperate to know that I was okay, which meant that it was the captain lying on the ground.

"I'm here, I'm fine. Quick, find the keys to the cuffs, they're in his top right breast pocket."

"Okay." I heard him fumbling about in the dark. There was no point shouting at him now, but something was going to have to be done about that boy. He was leaving far too many corpses in his wake. I worried what he'd be like without me to keep him in check.

I heard the jingle of keys and Rowles began feeling around for my wrists.

"Oi! Hands!"

"Sorry Matron."

"Do you always carry two guns?" I asked as he unlocked the cuffs.

"Three. One for show, one in my boot, one in my trousers."

I crouched, found the captain, and took his pulse. He was alive, just about. I grabbed his gun and stood up.

"How many?" I asked.

"Two in the courtyard, one at the front door."

"I meant, how many did you kill?"

"Oh, um." There was silence as he did a little bit of mental arithmetic. "Five, including this one."

"Jesus, five!? How the hell did you manage that?"

"There were three of them on the perimeter, in the woods." He sounded confused. Why was I asking such a pointless question? "I did them one at a time. Quietly. Then the girl, then him."

"We're going to have a very long, very serious talk about this when we're done, young man."

"Yes, Matron."

"But for now, options?"

"You've got one option," said a voice from the hall upstairs. "And that's to walk up these stairs with your hands above your heads and surrender. Or I toss a grenade down there and blow you to pieces."

I HELD THE scalpel in my hand and looked at the mess in front of me.

The captain had taken two bullets to the chest and there was massive damage. His breath was just a soft, raspy whisper, laboured and painful. I knew there was nothing I could do to save this man's life. He was dead already.

I didn't have any of the equipment I needed to try and stabilise him, but at least I had a blood donor – Green, the school's senior boy and an avowed pacifist who never touched a gun, had volunteered.

I stood in the enormous kitchen and looked across the operating table, which was really just a big wooden kitchen table that I'd washed with alcohol and spread a clean sheet over. The sharp tang of the alcohol mixed with the iron smell of the captain's blood and burnt my nostrils. The only light came from the window but the sun had come out and was streaming through the old mottled glass.

Green was lying on a couch that we'd dragged to the far side of the table, a tube coming out of his arm snaking its way into the captain's. Beyond him, in front of the Aga, stood the young soldier who'd assumed command after his C.O. had been shot. His eyes were wild with shock, and his face was pale. He was only a kid, barely in his twenties, and he was nervous and twitchy. But he had Rowles kneeling on the cold floor tiles, with his hands handcuffed to a radiator, and a gun aimed at the back of his head. Rowles seemed only mildly concerned, as if this was a minor inconvenience rather than the last minute of his life.

"I mean it," shouted the soldier, barely in control of himself, his thick Bradford accent sounding strangely out of place. "You said you were a doctor. You save the captain or I execute the boy right here. Then you. If he dies, you die."

There was nothing I could do. I needed to buy some time, think of a way out of this. So I raised the scalpel and made the first incision.

And with a low groan, the captain died.

CHAPTER NINE

I REMEMBER THE day Kate decided to become a doctor. She was nine years old.

It was a cold, wet Sunday morning and her gran had taken her to the local swimming pool. It was a grotty, run down place with cracked tiles and graffiti on the doors of the changing cubicles, but she loved it there. There was a girl from her school called April, and they would meet there and splash around every week. I remember that they were always giggling. Their shrill little voices must have echoed around that pool and driven all the adults nuts, but they didn't know or care. Kate's gran just sat there watching them with an indulgent smile.

The pool attendant was supposed to stop anyone running on the slick, wet tiles, but he couldn't be bothered. He was too busy chatting up bored mums. That morning he was nowhere to be seen.

Anyway, that Sunday, April and Kate were having a splash fight in the shallow end. It wasn't that busy, there were about ten or fifteen people in the pool and a collection of parents reading the Sunday papers on the hard wooden benches. There was one guy swimming lengths. He was fast and energetic, obviously there for exercise rather than fun. He was bald and slightly pudgy, and he was red in the face as he swam past them, gasping for air.

I remember Kate doing an impression of him – rolling her eyes up, pouting like a guppy and turning her face puce – and making April laugh. Then suddenly the man was thrashing about in the water, gurgling and trying to shout for help. Kate didn't know what was going on, but April surprised her by shouting loudly: "Help! Someone get a doctor!"

Kate's GP was Doctor Cox, a small sweaty man who smelt of

boiled sweets. She neither liked nor disliked him, he was just a fact of life – the guy who gave her injections and took her temperature when she had flu. Kate couldn't imagine how he'd be able help a drowning man.

Then this mumsy woman with short blonde hair came running out of the pool attendant's changing room wearing only her bra and pants, and dived cleanly into the water. She swam to the man and wrestled him to the side, keeping his head above water. By the time she'd got him to the edge the attendant had joined her, pulling on his t-shirt as he ran. Together they heaved the man on to the side and the woman knelt down beside him. A little gaggle of curious bystanders gathered to watch.

"Give me room," shouted the woman. "I'm a doctor."

The man was blue by now, but she was calm and efficient as she took his pulse, massaged his chest and administered CPR.

"Call 999, this man's having a heart attack," she said. The attendant hurried away.

As she worked, the colour gradually returned to the man's face and he seemed to stabilise. By the time the ambulance arrived it looked like he was going to be okay. The doctor kept working on him until he was stretchered away. And then, when they were gone, she was just a bedraggled middle-aged woman standing by a grotty pool in soggy, see-through undies.

But she was the coolest, most heroic person Kate ever seen.

April sniggered and said: "Her tits are all saggy."

"I want to be just like her," Kate said. Then she turned her back on April and swam away.

"HE'S HAVING A heart attack," I shouted, dropping the scalpel on to the table.

The squaddie snarled at me through gritted teeth: "Fix it or the boy dies."

He was serious, but Rowles didn't look worried as he knelt there with a gun to his head, waiting to die. He just looked bored.

"I need help," I said desperately.

"Get him to do it," replied the squaddie, gesturing to Green, who sat beside the captain, auto transfusing to try and maintain his blood pressure.

"If I disconnect him, the captain will die. Now come here!" My tone of command worked.

Stressed and panicky, the soldier stepped to the opposite side of the table and laid his gun alongside his stricken C.O.

"All right, what do I do?"

Over his shoulder I saw Rowles, handcuffed to a radiator, miming to Green that he should tackle our captor. But Green just shook his head and stayed where he was. Rowles cast his eyes skywards, looked at me and shrugged. Green also looked at me, apologetically.

Green was a gentle boy, sensitive and artistic, but during MacKillick's reign at the school he had been forced to do the most awful things. In the end he'd snapped and shot his tormentor to death, emptying an entire clip into him. Since then he'd been passive and withdrawn, totally refusing to take part in any of the patrols that defended the school. He looked at the gun on the table, within easy reach, but I knew he'd never make a grab for it.

So it was down to me.

But the soldier was on the opposite side of the table.

I started to massage the captain's chest, pushing down rhythmically, one two three, making it look good. I considered the young man in the uniform. He couldn't be more than twenty, so he'd probably only just joined the army when The Cull hit. His manner didn't exactly scream high intellect. He was an uneducated, inexperienced, scared young man. Just the kind of person my school was intended to help. But he had a gun, a twitchy trigger finger and he was threatening my children. I didn't think I could talk him down or overpower him. Which didn't leave me many options.

"We need to shock him," I gasped.

"With what?"

"I dunno, Sherlock. Improvise!"

"But there's no fucking power, is there!" He looked around the room, frantic.

I pointed at a large battery-powered torch on the sideboard. "Get that," I said.

He reached over and got it. If only it had been a little further away I'd have made a grab for the gun, but there wasn't time.

"Now smash the bulb," I instructed, "switch it on and when I say so, shove it into his chest."

"But it'll cut him."

"For fuck's sake," I yelled, "do you want him to die or not?"

"Okay, okay."

He cracked the glass on the table side and stood there, poised, with the torch in his hands, ready to save his captain's life.

"No," I said, leaning across the table and moving his hands so that the torch was over the captains's left breast. "There."

He nodded as I leant back over to my side of the table.

It took him a second to realise that I'd stopped working on the captain. Another half a second to notice the sticky wetness at his throat. Then he saw the scalpel in my hand.

"Torches don't work like that," I said softly. "I'm sorry."

"But..."

"You left me no choice."

He stepped back and dropped the torch to the floor.

"But..."

"He's already dead, I'm afraid."

The young soldier reached up to his throat and his hands came away covered in blood.

"Benefits of medical training," I said sadly. "It only takes the tiniest cut in the right place."

He looked confused and upset, as if I'd said something that had really hurt his feelings. His face crumpled.

"I couldn't let you hurt my children," I explained.

His legs gave way and he crashed to the floor.

I walked around the table, knelt down, lifted his head and cradled it in my lap, stroking his hair.

"It's all right," I said. "Everything's ok now. Don't be afraid. You're fine."

"Really?" He sounded hopeful and relieved. "That's good."

His eyes glazed over, he wheezed, and he was gone.

There I was in my surgery, the place where I was supposed to mend broken people, with blood on my hands for all the wrong reasons.

And I wasn't finished yet.

I STEPPED INTO the courtyard with my hands in my pockets.

It sits on the west, with the house on one side, stables on another, mews buildings on the third, and a wall with large wooden gates on the fourth. The floor was cobbled and muddy. In the centre of the courtyard stood all the children and staff of my school, lined up and standing to attention with their hands on their heads, watched over by two soldiers who kept their machine guns trained on them at all times.

There was Mrs Atkins, the dinner lady. With her florid face, ample bosom and floury apron she looked like a character from a *Carry On* film, but she was cunning and determined when she needed to be. The boys adored her unconditionally.

Beside her stood her husband Justin, a tall, stick-thin man with thick grey hair and a hawk-like nose. Quiet and soft spoken, I didn't know much about him except that he used to be a customer service manager for BT, had lost a wife and two children in The Cull, and he made Mrs Atkins' hair curl (her words).

Then there was Caroline, Rowles' partner in crime. I'd never seen them hold hands or kiss, so I wasn't sure if they were what you'd call boyfriend and girlfriend, but they were inseparable and she was almost as scary as he was. Almost.

There were also twenty-one surviving boys from the original St Mark's, fifteen girls who'd joined me when I'd been hiding from MacKillick, the strays we'd rescued that morning, plus three teaching staff who'd joined us from the nearby community of Hildenborough.

These were my people, my responsibility, my family. I'd killed to protect them before and I'd do it again.

The two soldiers guarding them were young – a man about the same age as the one lying dead on the surgery floor, and an older woman, about twenty-five. I'd describe them, but in their uniforms and helmets, in that gloomy brick-lined square, I'm ashamed to say that nothing leapt out at me. They were just soldiers, that's all.

Maybe I deliberately didn't look too closely.

Mrs Atkins smiled at me as I entered, but her smile quickly faded when she saw how much blood had soaked into my clothes.

The female soldier saw me then and brought her gun to bear. She was to my left, about eight or nine metres away, at eleven o'clock. Her male colleague was hidden behind the hostages but I knew he was to my right at about one o'clock, in the far corner.

"Don't move," yelled the woman.

I stopped moving.

"Where's Rich?" she asked.

"Do you mean the young man who took charge?"

"Where is he?"

"Dead. Your C.O. too. Sorry." I meant the apology, but I can see how that wouldn't have mattered to her.

"Why you..." She took one step forward. There was a sharp echoing crack and one of the cobbles at her feet splintered into flying shards. She froze.

Nice shot, Rowles.

There was another shot and I heard a cry of "Fuck!" from the other soldier. Green making his presence felt – under the circumstances he'd agreed to use the gun, but had sworn he wouldn't shoot anybody. I hoped it wouldn't come to that.

"Do I have your attention?" I asked.

The woman nodded.

"Yeah," came the nervous reply from one o'clock.

"Would everybody except the soldiers please sit down."

Silently, all the children and adults sank to the floor. Not much protection if bullets started flying, but it was something. I could see both soldiers clearly now, above everyone's heads. Time for my big speech.

"I woke up this morning feeling nervous," I began. "I planned to take two of these children into a hostile, dangerous situation and put their lives at risk. Mine too. I had a plan and I was determined that no-one would get killed. But I should know by now that plans rarely work. As soon as you start waving guns around somebody dies. Somebody always dies.

"But I thought I was doing the right thing. There were children who needed rescuing from bad people, and I decided it was my job to do that. You might think that was arrogant and reckless of me, but no-one else was going to rescue them. Not the police, not the army.

"Anyway, the decision to take action was mine alone. And we rescued those kids. But two people died. Two vicious, evil bastards, but people all the same. And I'm a doctor. It's my job to save lives, not take them. But you two are the sixth and seventh people today to aim guns at me and I'm sick to the back fucking teeth of it. So here's where things stand.

"Your C.O. is dead. His second-in-command is dead. Every one of your colleagues is dead. You two are the only surviving members of your team and both of you are in the crosshairs of the telescopic sights of sniper rifles. If I give the word your heads will be blown off. Then we'll take your corpses to the farm we raided this morning, pile you up outside it, pour petrol over you and set you on fire.

"When your friends come looking for you they'll find evidence of a firefight and they'll think you died fighting vicious child traffickers. And when they come here we'll be ready for them. With tea and cake. Then maybe second time round things will go a little better for everyone.

"To be honest, we'd probably be better off if I killed you now. But I'm sick of killing and I'd really like to go to bed tonight without any more blood on my hands.

"So put your guns down and I promise that you won't be hurt."

I had the guy at "I woke up", his face told me that. But the woman was a different story. Even as she laid her gun on the ground I knew what was coming. I opened my mouth to tell Rowles to shoot, but I was too late. She crouched to lay the gun down and then sprang forward like a sprinter off a starting block, a large knife suddenly in her hand.

Rowles managed a shot but she was too fast. She was on me before I could get out of her way. She led with the knife, going straight for my heart. I managed to turn just in time and the blade nicked one of my ribs and bounced off again. I was wearing a green t-shirt and the blade didn't snag at all, which told me how sharp it was. I didn't feel the pain of the cut for a few seconds, just the glancing impact, and by the time I felt the sting I was too busy to scream.

As the knife carried on past me she lowered her shoulder and took me in the midriff, winding me and sending me flying backwards on to the cold, hard cobbles. I went down hard, with her on top of me. My right shoulder smashed into the stones and I was unable to stop my head bouncing off a cobble, which left me briefly dazed.

Some of my old training was still in there, even all these years later, and I heard Cooper telling me to rush a gun and flee a knife. Which was perhaps not the best advice for my subconscious to offer me at that precise moment. The other thing I remembered Coop teaching me was that if you find yourself in a knife fight, the most important thing is to never, ever lose track of your opponent's blade.

I must have reacted automatically, because when my head stopped spinning I was lying flat on my back with the soldier astride me, both my hands wrapped around her wrist, trying to stop the knife coming down. She was snarling and furious, but controlled. I'd been in fights before, but if this woman really was army trained then I was in serious trouble; she'd know moves I'd never even heard of, and she wouldn't hesitate to kill me.

I saw Caroline out of the corner of my eye, moving to get up and come to my aid. I shouted at her to stay where she was as I suddenly stopped blocking the knife and instead pushed left with all my strength, shoving the knife aside for a split second and bringing the soldier's head and shoulders closer. Then I sat bolt upright and smashed my forehead into the bridge of her nose. There was a sharp crack and a crunch then she reeled backwards, blood spurting everywhere, still with her knees keeping me on the ground.

I let go of her wrist and hit her as hard as I could, pushing her broken nose into her face with the heel of my hand, releasing a small explosion of blood and making her scream.

Before I could press my advantage her left elbow slammed into the side of my head and then I felt something swipe past my face. The knife. As it swung out on its arc, trailing blood from my cheek, I brought both arms to my chest and shoved up and forwards with all my strength, knocking her backwards. Then I pulled my legs in, toppling her on to the cobbles.

There was a shot and I felt something tug my shirt. My attacker grunted as Rowles' bullet hit the ground an inch from her head.

"That nearly hit me!" I yelled.

"Sorry," he shouted back from the roof of the main building where he was lying safely at the roof's edge. "Just trying to help."

"Do me a favour and don't."

But the distraction had enabled the soldier to regain her footing as well.

The shining blade formed the centre of a circle as we sidled around each other looking for an opening. Then she took me by surprise, darting sideways to grab a girl by the hair, pushing the point of the knife into her throat.

The girl's name was Lucy. She was ten and had long red hair and freckles. She wore thick specs and had buck teeth, but she sang like an angel and was nobody's fool. She went rigid with fear as the soldier threatened to slit her throat.

"Up," said the soldier. Nervously, Lucy rose to her feet. The soldier wrapped herself around the girl, keeping her as a human shield between herself and Rowles.

"Anybody follows us, the girl dies," she snarled.

I nodded.

"Barker, get your gun, we're leaving," she said.

The male soldier slowly took his hands off his head.

"Don't move, Barker," I said. He stopped, unsure which way to jump.

The woman pressed the knife just a bit harder and Lucy yelped.

"I fucking mean it, bitch," growled the woman.

"The second she dies my boy on the roof will end you," I said, then I walked, as casually as I could given that I was shaking like a leaf, over to Barker the squaddie. Our eyes locked as I reached out and removed his sidearm. The look on my face must have been convincing, because he didn't resist. I felt the cold metal thing nestle itself into my hand as I turned back to face the girl I'd sworn to protect, and the woman who was threatening her life.

I was through with talking.

Without even thinking I raised the gun and fired a single shot, taking the soldier right between the eyes and spraying her brains all over Mrs Atkins' best floral pinny.

The soldier's legs crumpled and she fell in a heap on the floor as Lucy screamed and screamed and screamed.

It was the first time in my life I'd ever killed someone and enjoyed it. I felt a glow of satisfaction. It felt good.

The vomiting quickly put an end to that.

When I'd finished spraying my lunch all over the cobbles I turned and walked back to Barker, wiping my mouth with my sleeve and noticing that it came away covered in blood from the gash on my cheek.

"On your fucking knees," I said.

Barker knelt down and begged for his life.

He fell silent when I pressed the gun barrel into his forehead.

"It's in the best interests of everyone here for me to shoot you. You know that, right?"

NEXT MORNING, I sat in front of the school and waited.

It was so silent. All the kids had left, the staff too. I lay on a glorious lawn, in the warm spring sunshine, listening to the birds and the first crickets. There were rabbits nibbling the grass not twenty metres from where I sat, and sometimes the breeze carried the distant cry of a peacock from the gardens behind the house.

I lay back on the grass and closed my eyes, rested my hands on the cool ground. I tried to visualise how fast I was moving – around the sun, around the Earth's core. It sounds strange but it's the closest I've ever come to meditation. Lying on grass and trying to feel the Earth move calms me down.

I needed a lot of calming down.

I thought back on my decision and I knew in my heart that I'd done the right thing. With everyone relocated and in hiding, all the blame for the slaughter would fall on me. It was the only way to make sure everyone was safe. The buck stopped here, and that was only fair. But that didn't mean I wasn't scared to death.

So as I lay there, a row of bodies draped in sheets beside me, waiting for the rumble of army vehicles, I felt okay with my choice. I was ready to accept the consequences.

My thoughts went back to that day at the swimming pool, all the ideals Kate had when she'd started medical training. The Hippocratic Oath seemed like a sick joke to me now. I wondered what the woman at the swimming pool would have thought of me, lying here surrounded by bodies. The thought caused a sharp pang of loss.

"Your cheek looks a lot better. I don't think it's going to be a bad scar," said the man sitting to my right. "You stitched it really well."

"Thanks, Barker," I said. "But I don't really think I'm going to have to worry about my good looks much longer, do you?"

He didn't answer and I didn't open my eyes to see the look on his face.

"I'll tell them what really happened," he said.

"But you weren't there, were you? Not in the cellar, not in the surgery. I appreciate the thought, but your word's not going to carry much weight when you stack it up against all these corpses."

He didn't say anything else, so we sat and listened to the birds.

"Do you ever think things will get back to normal?" he asked eventually. "I mean, telly and buses and elections and stuff?"

"Not in our lifetimes," I said.

"The king says it will."

"The what?"

But before he could answer I heard the sound of tyres on gravel.

"You're on," I said.

I heard him get to his feet and begin walking away, towards the fellow soldiers he'd radioed yesterday. I just lay there, eyes closed. I caught snatches of conversation, and the sound of boots on gravel, then someone walking towards me.

I sighed. Time to face the music.

"Miss Jane Crowther?" The man's voice was deep and strong, the voice of someone accustomed to being listened to and obeyed. I'd tried to develop a voice like that over the last few months, but my efforts in the courtyard suggested I'd probably failed.

The voice was also oddly familiar.

"That's me," I said, and I opened my eyes. The soldier was standing over me, and the sun behind his head made a halo and shadowed his face. I winced at the brightness.

"No, it's not." The voice had changed. It was softer, surprised, almost friendly. And definitely familiar.

"Pardon?" I said, as I sat up. I rested my weight on one arm and raised a hand to shield my eyes so I could get a look at the man who'd come to serve justice on me. It took a second for my eyes to adjust.

"Hello, Miss Booker," he said. "What have you got yourself into this time?"

CHAPTER TEN

KATHERINE LUCY BOOKER – Kit to her family, Kate to everyone else – died five years ago in a warehouse on Moss Side.

Then she gave herself a bit of a makeover. She dyed her hair, got that nose ring she'd always secretly craved, dumped the Jigsaw wardrobe and went a bit more casual. She even started listening to different kinds of music – out with Kylie, in with Dresden Dolls – and stopped watching thrillers and horror films altogether, preferring inoffensive romcoms and bodice rippers. She walked differently too, but only because she stopped wearing heels.

Her sleep patterns altered. She used to sleep like a log for eight hours straight, preferring early nights and cosy jim jams. Now she was more likely to crawl to bed in the early hours in her knickers and t-shirt, cuddling a bottle of chianti, before waking, sweating and alarmed after four hours fitful rest.

She moved to a different part of the country, broke contact with all her friends and family, abandoned her career as a doctor and became a far less illustrious type of medic, ministering to spotty boys and institutionalised teachers with bad breath and nicotine fingers.

Kate Booker became Jane Crowther.

Then, one day, lying on the grass surrounded by corpses, Jane was visited by the ghost of Kate.

And I couldn't think what to say to her.

"I'M SORRY, DO I... do I know you?" I stuttered as the ground, which had been so solid beneath me only a moment ago, began to spin.

"Lieutenant Sanders, Miss," he said cheerily. "I was part of the team that oversaw your training."

I wracked my brains. Sanders? I didn't remember any Sanders.

He reached down a great paw. I took it and he pulled me up without the slightest effort. The man radiated strength.

Once I was upright the spinning was even more pronounced and I stumbled a bit. He caught me in his arms like I was some kind of swooning schoolgirl. I blushed red with embarrassment. This, of course, made it even worse. I shook him off firmly and regained my composure with a brisk cough.

"It's been a long time since a man's made me dizzy, Lieutenant," I joked.

He laughed awkwardly as I took a closer look at him. He had the tanned skin of a man who spends time outdoors; thick black eyebrows topped deep-set brown eyes that sat either side of a classic Roman nose. His large chin jutted out slightly, making him look like a weird mixture of toff and bruiser. It was a striking face rather than a handsome one.

"Wait a minute," I said, as realisation dawned. "I do remember you! You were one of the soldiers Cooper took me to train with out in Hereford. You were the judo guy, weren't you? Spent a whole day throwing me round a gym like I was a, oh, I don't know what."

"That's me, Miss. I was part of the assault team at the warehouse as well. Nasty business. I'm sorry about... you know."

"Yeah, right. Wow. It's, um, it's been a really long time since anyone's called me Miss Booker. You threw me there for a minute."

He nodded. "What exactly is the reason for the name change, Miss?" The shift from friendly reminiscence to polite officialdom almost went past me. Almost.

"Witness protection," I replied. "They made me into a boarding school matron, would you believe. I was only supposed to be here 'til they caught up with The Spider, but I never heard anything. And then, The Cull, obviously."

"Kept the name though."

"Kate's a distant memory now. It's Jane who looks after the kids. I'm not sure Kate would have been up to this kind of thing."

He was looking at me oddly, trying to suss out whether I was delusional or just weird.

"I know," I said. "It just helps me if I keep them separate in my mind, lets me focus on the here and now. And it would only confuse the kids if I introduced them to Kate after everything we've been through. They trust Jane, they might not be so sure about Kate."

He nodded again. "I've been undercover, Miss, I get it. So, Lance

Corporal Barker says you've evacuated the school and he doesn't know where they've gone. That right?"

"Yes."

He looked at the row of bodies and his cheeriness faded. Our surprising reunion lost its novelty and the reality of his job reasserted itself.

"It was just an awful misunderstanding," I said.

He regarded me coolly. "I'm sure it was, Miss. But it's not me you've got to convince, it's Major General Kennet."

More soldiers had arrived now, and Sanders set them to carrying the bodies into one of the three trucks they'd brought, expecting to have to transport all the children and staff to safety.

"What's he like?" I asked as we walked away.

"I've served under worse," he replied.

"But you've served under better?"

"Oh, yes."

We reached the first truck and he took a pair of handcuffs from his pocket.

"I don't want to cuff you, Miss," he said. "So if you promise that..."

"I promise."

"And I'll keep an eye on her, Lieutenant," added Barker, who was already sitting on one of the hard wooden benches that lined the metal-bottomed, canvas-topped transit vehicle.

"All right then," said Sanders briskly. "We've got a long journey ahead of us. A lot of the road has been cleared but not all, and there are some unswept areas on the way. We took some fire on our trip here, but nothing too serious. Of course they could be waiting for us on the return journey, but we'll vary our route, just in case. If we do run into trouble, then Barker, your job is to look after Kate here. I spent a lot of effort keeping her alive once upon a time. I'd hate all that work to be wasted."

"Sir," replied Barker, resting his rifle on his lap.

"What do you mean, unswept areas?" I asked.

"I'll let the C.O. answer that, Miss," replied Sanders. "Now if you'll excuse me."

Sanders left and I could see him poring over a map with the three drivers, plotting a route.

"Where are you lot based, Barker?"

"Operation Motherland HQ is at Salisbury Plain," he replied.

"Operation Motherland? What's that?" I asked.

"Top secret," he replied, tapping the side of his nose. "Look, I was expecting you to get some pretty rough treatment, but the Lieutenant was all pally. You got really lucky, knowing him, otherwise you'd be on the floor, in shackles with a sack over your head."

"I know. I can't quite believe it myself."

"My point is that it isn't always going to be like this. The C.O. is not a very flexible boss, if you know what I mean. Me and the Lieutenant speaking up for you might not make a lot of difference."

And with that happy thought, the engine sputtered into life and we rumbled away.

I looked out the back of the truck at my beloved school. I'd worked so hard to build something special, to make it a safe, happy place. It was my home and the people who lived there were my family.

I wondered if I'd ever see it again. Probably not. I shed a tear as it receded into the distance. Not for myself, but for the loss of a dream. Nowadays it seemed like every good, clean thing had to end up covered in blood.

As we slowed to turn the corner at the end of the drive I saw two small figures burst from the bushes by the side of the road and leap quickly over the duckboard of the third and final truck.

I didn't know whether to curse or smile. It seemed like I still had two psychotic guardian angels looking after me.

IN THE EIGHTEEN months since The Cull had burned itself out I'd not moved outside a twenty mile radius. With one notable exception, who was now God knew where, people just stayed put. The days of travelling long distances for work or pleasure were long gone. This was a parochial world of small, paranoid communities. Apart from some mad American religious broadcasts, which I wouldn't allow anyone at school to watch, there was no TV, no newspapers to keep people up to date with events taking place outside their immediate circle of family, friends and neighbours. Horizons had narrowed, and life had focused on the local and familiar. So it felt weird to pass a battered metal sign at the side of the road which read 'You are now leaving Kent'.

It might as well have said 'Here Be Monsters!'

We moved down quiet country roads, deserted for the most part, until we came to the A272. Barker told me this had been cleared about a month ago, which was why the soldiers had only just shown up at my school. Their sphere of influence was expanding along reclaimed A-roads and motorways. But this road still ran through large unswept areas, which I took to mean places not yet brought under military control. This, it turned out, was not entirely correct.

The A272 had once been a nice wide road, but now there was only a narrow path through the thousands of abandoned vehicles. Londoners had fled the capital as The Cull took hold, hoping to hide away in the country until things calmed down. Soon all the main roads and motorways were gridlocked. Of course many of those fleeing were already infected, and they began dying in their cars. It soon became clear that the traffic was never going to move again, so those still alive just got out of their cars, vans and trucks, and walked away.

The path through the debris, which Barker told me had been cleared by huge diggers salvaged from a quarry, was wide enough that we could get up to a reasonable speed, but with so much raw material available for use as obstacles, the risk of ambush was great.

We travelled this graveyard highway for about an hour until we pulled off the road and into a small market town, empty and forgotten, slowly decaying. The convoy stopped in the middle of the narrow high street, littered with abandoned cars, and Sanders gathered everyone together at the bonnet of the lead truck.

"Change of orders," he told us. "Since we've got more room than expected, the Colonel wants us to recce a site near here and sweep it if possible."

Barker sighed softly and shook his head, but when I tried to ask him why he just rolled his eyes.

"The site is half a mile south-east of here," continued Sanders. "I'm going to take Patel here and we'll scout around. The rest of you stay here and stay alert. If we're not back by oh-two-hundred hours, I want you to radio for support and then come looking for us."

"Sir, isn't this Midhurst?" asked one of the squaddies.

Sanders nodded.

"But we swept here. Remember, the gang war we sorted out? Bossy bloke with red hair running things."

"I remember," said Sanders. "But this new site was top secret, apparently. All hush hush. HQ have only just identified it. We went right past it last time."

The squaddie shook his head. "That's not my point, Sir. This town's inhabited and we made it safe. So where is everyone?"

Sanders shrugged. "I dunno," he said. "Moved on somewhere better? It's not our problem. Just stay close to the trucks and keep an eye out for trouble, all right?"

Sanders and his colleague checked their weapons and left, leaving me with Barker and five soldiers whose idea of staying alert turned out to be lighting up and playing cards. Barker was not invited to join them.

"They don't trust me," he explained.

"Well I need to pee, and I trust you not to peek, so that's something, eh?" I said, and I linked my arm through his and led him towards Woolies in search of privacy.

"Ooh," said Barker as we approached the ruined store. "I wonder if they still have any Stephen Kings."

We heard a jeer from behind us.

"Great," moaned Barker. "Now they think we're shagging."

Woolies had been comprehensively looted, and there was crap all over the place. Literally – someone had smeared their own shit on the windows.

"Euw, that's gross," I said, looking around for a quiet spot. "I'm going over there." I pointed to a brick flower bed that housed a large ugly bush. Barker nodded and walked into the shop while I scurried behind the bush.

Sometimes, when I'm feeling especially morbid, I wonder what my last words might be. I picture myself lying in some grand four-poster bed, surrounded by fat, happy grandchildren as I fade away, elegant to the last, imparting pearls of wisdom gleaned from a long, fulfilling life. I bet that Barker, if he ever gave it a second's thought, never considered "great, now they think we're shagging," as particularly likely or desirable last words.

But we don't get to choose, do we?

As I started to unbuckle my belt I heard a tiny metallic 'sprang' and a soft grunt. I assumed Barker had trodden on a toy car or something, and I sighed gratefully as I emptied my bladder.

When I emerged a minute later I went towards the shattered doors of Woolies and peered into the gloom.

"Find anything good?" I shouted.

No reply.

My eyes adjusted to the darkness of the shop interior and it became clear why that was.

The metallic twang had been poor old Barker stepping on a tripwire. The grunt, the only sound he'd managed to make as the six foot long spring-loaded metal spike had leapt free of its housing and swung down from the ceiling, skewering him and lifting him off his feet. And there he remained, dangling in mid-air, a huge sharpened girder sticking out of his back, blood everywhere.

Dammit, I liked him.

I staggered back with an involuntary scream and the next thing I knew someone slammed into my back, shoving me hard up against the store window, pushing my right arm up behind my back, and grazing my stitched cheek on a streak of hard, dried shit.

"You fucking do, cunt?" yelled a squaddie in my ear.

It would have been impossible to reply with my face pressed against the glass, so I didn't even try to respond.

"Easy, Col," said one of his mates. "It's a booby trap."

Col wasn't inclined to let me go, though, and he kept me pinned there for another few seconds, pressed up against me. He let me go by pushing himself away from me with his groin, so I could feel his erection, snorting his disgust as he did so.

The wise thing to do would have been to let it go. But I turned like a flash and slapped him as hard as I could.

He snarled and raised his hand to hit me, but his mate intervened, grabbing his wrist and staring him down.

"Fuck's sake, Col, get a grip," he said. My assailant gave a sick laugh, pulled his arm free and walked away backwards, giving me the evil eye.

"Thanks," I said as I spat on my sleeve and wiped the shit and blood off my face.

"Shut the fuck up," replied my rescuer, "and get back in the fucking truck before I shoot you myself. And don't even think of doing a runner."

Leaving the squaddies to their grim task I stepped away and walked back to the trucks. Before stepping out into the road I instinctively looked left and right for oncoming traffic, then paused, realised what I'd done, and laughed at my own stupidity. Then something registered, and I looked right again.

At the far end of the street stood a figure. I think it was a man but it was hard to be sure because they were dressed in a bright yellow hazmat suit, their glass visor glinting in the sun, hiding their face. The figure just stood there looking at us, seemingly content just to watch.

I looked back at the soldiers. Two of them had taken up positions in cover and were scanning the opposite buildings. I was pleased to notice that Col had chosen the bush to hide behind, which meant he was kneeling in my piss. Ha. The other three were inside the shop attempting to pull Barker down. None of them had seen our visitor. I looked back and now there were two of them, both in the bright yellow suits. And I could see that they both carried shotguns.

"Um, guys," I said quietly, but they didn't hear me. Snatches of their conversation floated across to where I stood.

"No, not that arm, dipshit..."

"Jesus, now I'm covered in guts..."

"Oi, careful I just washed this bloody uniform..."

I spoke more clearly. "Guys, we have company."

The nearest man on watch heard me and called the others. They dropped what they were doing and I heard Barker hit the floor with a thud. Weapons raised, they scattered to positions of cover and vantage, all the while keeping their eyes on our two – no, three, now – visitors.

I turned to see where the soldiers were taking up positions, about to move myself, and over their shoulders I saw four more of the yellow-clad figures standing motionless outside a ruined hardware store at the other end of the road. Before I could shout a warning, one of them raised a megaphone to his visor and a tinny voice echoed up the wrecked street.

"You shall be cleansed," he said flatly, his voice altered by a distorter that made him sound like a Dalek. "All shall be cleansed."

"Ah shit, cleaners," yelled the squaddie nearest to me. "Masks!"

"They're in the bloody trucks," yelled someone else.

Then there was a dull pop, I heard something metal hit the tarmac, and then a soft hiss.

There was a second's silence before I heard Col shout "gas!" and then I ran like hell for the truck where Rowles and Caroline were hiding. A cloud of thick yellow smoke billowed out from the area where the soldiers had taken up positions. I heard screams and then indiscriminate gunfire. A burst of rounds whipped past my head, punching holes in the nearest truck's canvas covering.

The hazmat guys just remained where they were.

Staying just ahead of the drifting cloud, I reached the truck and looked inside. Empty. They must have slipped away. No time to look any closer, the thick yellow cloud was nearly at me. I ran for the opposite side of the road and straight through the shattered doors of a branch of Lloyd's Bank. I was so panicked that it was only once I was inside that it occurred to me to look for tripwires. And there one was, about a centimetre from my right toe. Unfortunately I was still moving and my left foot was just about to hit the thin metal strip. I dived forward, clipping the wire as I did so. I hit the damp, mouldy carpet hard and heard the clang of something big and metal above my head. I rolled on to my back and saw enormous metal jaws, cut from what looked like car bonnets. It was a sort of huge, upside down mantrap and it would have taken my head clean off.

"They really don't like giving overdrafts," said a boy's voice to my right.

"You armed?" I asked.

"Natch," said a girl's voice to my left.

"Spare?"

"Catch."

I caught the Browning semi-automatic handgun, chambered a round and sprang to my feet.

"There a back way out of here?"

"Nope," replied Rowles. "Already checked. How d'you know we were in here?"

"I didn't."

"Cool, woman's intuition," said Caroline.

"Yeah, right," Rowles laughed.

"Enough," I snapped. "Quiet."

We listened but could hear no noise at all from the street outside. The shooting was over. Through the door I could see the cloud of gas had nearly dispersed and was being blown towards the other side of the road. As the mist cleared a figure emerged. It was Col, with his hands over his face, staggering like a blind man. He walked into a car and his hands came away from his face. taking most of the flesh with them. His cheekbones shone white in the sunlight as he slumped forward across the car and lay still.

"I think I'm gonna puke," said Caroline.

"Are they all dead?" asked Rowles.

"Looks like it," I replied. "But Sanders and another one, Patel, they're off doing a recce. They should have heard the gunfire. They'll be back any minute."

"And do they have gasmasks?" asked Caroline. "'Cause if not..."

"Sanders is SAS. He'll sort it. We just have to sit tight and wait for..."

A yellow suited figure stepped into the doorway holding a gas grenade in his left hand.

"You shall be cleansed," he said.

And he pulled the pin.

CHAPTER ELEVEN

THE MEN IN yellow suits had come to the school during The Culling Year, a month after we closed the gates and instituted quarantine.

They pulled up to the gate in their trucks and got out, sealed inside their protective shells, eyes hidden in shadow beneath Perspex visors, mouths covered by bulbous gas masks. There were four of them, and two had cylinders strapped to their backs. Long tubes snaked out of the cylinders to metal spray guns with tiny pilot lights flickering beneath the nozzles. Flamethrowers.

We'd heard reports of their activities. They were roaming the country in teams, burning any houses that contained dead bodies, carting away anyone they found alive. We'd been waiting for them. Bates was still running the school then, so he and I went down to the gate to talk to them. We took guns.

"We hear you've got kids cooped up in there. Any of them blood type O-Neg?" asked the spokesman, his voice distorted by the mask.

"A couple, why?" I replied.

"They'll need to come with us, Miss. Government orders. All O-Neg citizens are to be taken to special hospitals. They're immune, you see."

"These children are under our protection," said Bates. "They're going nowhere."

"Look, don't make us get rough, mate," said the weary official. "They won't be harmed, they're immune, ain't they? We just need to take some blood samples and then take them to a special camp where all the O-Negs we round up are being looked after. We keep 'em safe, okay? Either of you O-Neg?"

Neither of us replied.

"If you're not, then you're going to die unless you got one of these," he gestured to his suit. "Simple as that. It's airborne. Animals carry it, birds carry it, it's in the water, and it's in the rain. There's no escape. Quarantine won't work. And who'll look after the kids then, eh? Best thing for everyone if you just hand 'em over to us."

"And if we don't?" said Bates, nervously levelling his rifle at the quartet.

"We have the authority to take them by force."

"There are two of us with guns, and there are more back in the main building," I said. "There are only four of you and two flamethrowers, which don't reach as far as bullets. I don't fancy your chances."

We stood there, facing each other.

"You really don't want to pick a fight with us," said the spokesman eventually. His voice was quiet, the threat clear.

"I think we just did," I replied.

"I'm sorry you feel that way, Miss."

I gripped my gun harder, waiting for the inevitable fight. But it never came.

"We'll be back," said the spokesman. "You can count on it."

And they got back in the truck and drove away.

We spent that night and the whole of the next day erecting defences at the main gate, breaking the weapons out of the armoury and rallying the few boys still not sick.

But they never returned. They were the final representatives of bureaucracy and government we ever encountered. When they left, they took the last traces of the old order with them. Or so we thought.

We weren't sure whether they encountered some other group who gunned them down, or they succumbed to the virus.

But as I stood in that bank another possibility occurred to me.

Maybe they just went mad.

THE CLEANER WHO stood in the doorway had seen one unarmed woman run into the building. He wasn't prepared for three of us, with guns. We all opened fire at once. The blood flowed slickly down his yellow protective suit as he jerked and shook, then he collapsed in a heap. The grenade rolled forward a few inches then stopped on the threshold.

Without thinking I jumped up, ran forward, and kicked it as hard as I could. I was always more of a netball girl, but Johnny Wilkinson would have been proud of me. The grenade soared away across the street and landed in a bin. It popped and a column of evil poison smoke rose up, only for the wind to take it and blow it away from us.

I ducked back inside the bank, knowing that our victory was temporary.

"We need to get out of here now," I shouted.

"This is a bank," said Rowles, exasperated. "The back door is armoured, we can't kick it down."

"Shit."

"There is the vault," offered Caroline, sounding scared for the first time since I'd met her.

"The what?" I asked.

"There's a vault, a walk-in thing," she explained. "It's not huge, but it's probably airtight."

"And once we're in there how do we get out? Or breathe?" said Rowles.

"Fine," she shouted resentfully. "So what's your plan, genius?"

I didn't have time to waste watching a lover's tiff. "No, that's a good idea, Caroline," I said. "And it might work as a last resort, but..."

"Look!" screamed the girl.

I turned to see a yellow arm withdrawing from the doorway and a gas grenade rolling towards us, making a nasty squelching noise on the sodden carpet.

"Up!" I shouted. We ran through the door that said 'No Entry' and headed for the stairs. Even as we scrambled up that narrow staircase I knew that all I'd done was buy us a few minutes. We were trapped. Where the hell was Sanders?

This building was one of the few new ones on the main street of town, and it only had two storeys. We came to a landing and a series of non-descript offices so dull that nobody had even bothered to trash them.

"There has to be a fire escape," I said. "Check all the rooms."

None of the windows had been shattered, so cracking open these doors was like walking into a time capsule, breathing pre-Cull air, still with the faint tang of PVC chairs, air conditioning and carpet fumes. One of the desks had a framed picture of two blonde toddlers on it, next to a desk tidy full of neatly arranged pens. I didn't know which was creepier – booby trapped Woolies or this strange museum.

"Here," shouted Rowles. Caroline and I ran to the office he was in, which had a fire exit with a push-bar in the wall facing away from the street. Caroline and I stepped back and raised our weapons then I nodded to Rowles, who crouched down and shoved the door open.

The exit led on to a metal staircase in a dim courtyard. So dim, that the figure standing outside was just a silhouette. I held my fire, unsure, but Caroline panicked and squeezed off two rounds. I yelled at her to hold her fire but it was too late.

The figure grunted, staggered back against the metal railing and toppled backwards into space. We heard him hit the concrete below with an awful thud.

"Dammit Caroline," I yelled. "We have no idea who that was."

"But..."

I ushered her and Rowles out of the door and they clattered down the fire escape. As I turned to pull the door closed behind me I caught a flash of yellow on the landing and fired through the plasterboard walls at where I thought the cleaner was standing. I didn't wait to see if I'd hit him.

I pelted down the loud metal steps and found Rowles and Caroline standing, appalled, over the body of Patel, the squaddie Sanders had taken with him. Caroline had got him clean in the chest. He was stone dead.

In the dank concrete-floored courtyard, with the interior walls of buildings rising all around us, their small staircase windows looking out on this joyless scene, I could see her face was ashen white. Rowles was holding her hand tightly.

"He must have been coming to help us," she said softly.

"No time," I barked as I reached down and grabbed Patel's machine gun.

Then there was a loud clang. And another, and another, as something metal bounced down the fire escape behind us.

At the same time we heard the distant echo of gunfire from the main street. That had to be Sanders.

I threw my arms wide and herded the children towards a small brick alley that led beneath one of the buildings and out of the courtyard. As they ran I turned, slipped the safety off the machine gun, and sprayed the fire escape with bullets, hoping to discourage pursuit. Then I ran after the kids as I heard the loud hiss of escaping gas behind me.

We emerged into a car park littered with wrecked vehicles and shopping trolleys. But no cleaners, thank God. I strained to hear the gunfire and tried to identify where it was coming from. As soon as I was sure that it was coming from our left I turned and ran right, urging the children ahead of me as we ran behind the row of buildings.

"I think we're parallel to the main street," I explained as we ran. "If we can get to the opposite end of the street to Sanders we might be able to trap the cleaners in a crossfire."

The buildings ended at the car park entrance road, which turned right to rejoin the main street. I flattened my back against the wall and indicated for the kids to do the same, then I risked a quick glimpse around the corner. Nothing but a burned-out bus.

I turned to the children.

"Rowles, you stay here and make sure we aren't followed. Caroline, with me."

Why did I do that? I've asked myself a hundred times since then. Why didn't I take Rowles? But at that instant I was sure that it was safer to come with me, to approach the cleaners from behind with the element of surprise. I was certain that Rowles would be in more danger than she would be, and I knew he could cope with that.

So I ran around the corner, waving the traumatised girl along behind me. Guns raised, we moved slowly along the side of what had once been a small branch of Boots. There were sporadic bursts of gunfire ahead and to our right, so it sounded as if Sanders was still in the fight at the far end of the street.

I reached the next corner and again flattened my back against the wall and glanced around. The trucks were about thirty metres away. The gas had cleared and the bodies of the dead soldiers lay on the pavement and in the road.

Beyond the trucks were three cleaners, crouched behind available cover – a car, a brick flower bed, a phone booth. All were now armed with machine guns taken from the squaddies. They leaned out, took their shots, and then ducked back under cover, obviously involved in a firefight. But none of them spared a glance behind them.

I turned to Caroline.

"Okay," I said. "We go quickly and quietly. Move from car to car, stay in cover as much as possible. When we're close I'll give the signal and you take out the one on the right. I've got the machine gun, so I'll take the other two. OK?"

She nodded but I could tell she was having to work very hard to keep herself under control.

"It wasn't your fault, Caroline," I said gently. "But we can talk about it later. Right now I need you to focus on what we have to do. Can you do that?"

She nodded. "Yes, Miss."

I put my arm around her shoulder squeezed. "Good girl. Now come on."

We moved out of cover and ran into the road. It took us only a minute or so to get close to the cleaners. They were so preoccupied, and the noise of gunfire was so loud, that they had no idea they were being stalked. Both Caroline and I, on opposite sides of the road, took up firing positions behind cars.

I was just about to give the signal when it all went wrong.

There was a burst of gunfire from behind us and to our right. I ducked instinctively before I realised it was echoing across from the car park. A cleaner must have bumped into Rowles. One of the men in front of us heard the exchange of fire and turned to look back. He saw Caroline. I turned to the girl and yelled at her to get down and as I did so I saw, over her shoulder, another cleaner emerging from the bank.

And then there were bullets everywhere. The one in the bank doorway raised his shotgun as the man in front of us turned and raised his machine gun. Caroline, unaware of the cleaner to her right, opened fire as I dived sideways and shot around Caroline at the man in the bank.

Caroline hit her man. He missed her and fell backwards, shot in the arm. I hit the man with the shotgun and his arms flew up as his gun went off. This saved Caroline's life; only the edge of the shotgun's pellet spray hit her, and those pellets were slowed by the glass in the car behind which she was standing.

But it was enough. She fell, screaming.

I continued firing and the cleaner in the bank disappeared back into the gloom, full of bullets.

The two remaining cleaners turned to see what was going on. One of them foolishly allowed his head to pop ever so slightly out of cover. A single shot from Sanders, still out of sight down the street, took the top of his skull off. I rolled on to my back, brought the gun up to my tummy and turned the middle cleaner's chest into mincemeat before he could get a shot off.

That left the wounded one. I stood to see where he was, but he was out of it – the bullet had hit an artery and he was lying in a widening pool of blood, not long to live, no threat to anyone.

I ran to Caroline. She was lying in the road, breathing hard, teeth gritted, whimpering.

Before I could bend down I heard pounding boots approaching

and I spun, gun at the ready. A yellow suit passed in front of my eyes but the helmet was hanging down. It was Sanders. He casually put a bullet in the wounded cleaner's head as he ran past, without even slowing down.

"Easy, Kate, easy."

I lowered my weapon.

"First aid kit?" I asked.

"Truck," he replied, and ran to get it while I knelt down to tend to Caroline.

She was barely conscious.

She had been lucky. When I rolled her over I could see that pellets had hit her from the waist up, including five that were embedded in her right cheek, one that looked like it had damaged her right eye socket, and a couple above the hairline. If I could treat her quickly, and if I could prevent any of the wounds from becoming infected, she should survive.

"Hold on, sweetheart," I said, grasping her hand tightly. "Hold on."

WE SET UP camp in a house near the centre of town. It had been lived in until very recently so it was clean and had everything we needed. I set up a workspace in the living room and did my best to patch Caroline up. Once I'd finished, I went into the kitchen and gratefully accepted the mug of hot tea that Sanders offered me. The kitchen had been installed some time in the seventies and had escaped renovation. The table had a chipped Formica top, like a greasy spoon café, and the chair was cheap moulded plastic.

"Well?" he asked.

"I got all the pellets out, sterilised the wounds, stitched the ones that needed it, dressed them, put her to bed. She should really have some antibiotics, but there's nothing I can do about that. The vodka you found helped, thanks."

"Any left?"

"No, sorry. I wish."

"You lush," he smiled.

"I couldn't save her eye," I said quietly, "and her face will be horribly scarred. Rowles refuses to leave her side. He's just sitting there, holding her hand and stroking her hair. I never really thought he had a tender side. Funny how people can surprise you."

"He's not people," said Sanders. "He's an eleven-year-old boy. Who you took into combat."

I laughed bitterly. "Like I could have stopped him! Trust me, Sanders, the boy's a law unto himself. I'm just trying to keep him contained and alive."

"And Caroline?"

"Goes where he goes. Always."

"And which of them shot Patel?"

Shit, that took me by surprise.

"Sorry?"

"I found his body where you told me," he said. "He wasn't killed with a shotgun, he was shot with a sidearm, and you three had the only ones in play."

"There was a fight upstairs at the bank," I lied. "One of the cleaners got my gun off me. Patel burst in and got shot. Then Rowles hit the cleaner over the head with a chair and in the confusion I snatched back my gun and ran."

Sanders shook his head slowly. "Nice try. If I thought you shot him trying to escape custody..." He left the threat unspoken. "But no, I think one of you shot him by accident. Caroline, at a guess."

I stared intently at the swirling patterns on the surface of my tea.

"He was a good lad," continued Sanders. "Would have made a good officer."

"Look, she just panicked, that's all."

"And that's why you don't take children into combat."

I looked up at him angrily. "What, like we seek it out? Are you joking? I just want to keep them alive and teach them to read. But people keep pointing guns at us. People like the cleaners and you." I jabbed him in the chest with my index finger. "We have no fucking choice. Do you think I like seeing what it does to them? You know, Rowles used to be the sweetest kid in the world. I mean Disney sweet, saccharine, cutesy. Now look at him! He's terrifying. But he's alive, and one day, maybe, if I can keep him alive long enough, he can stop fighting and grow into a man. That's all I want, to see him grow up safe, to see all my kids grow up safe. But as long as there are nutters with guns strolling around telling everyone what to do, that's not going to be possible. And now Caroline. I was supposed to keep her safe."

I stood up and threw my mug across the room, full of fury that had nowhere to go. It smashed against the wall and then, before I knew what I was doing, I was crying my eyes out and Sanders was holding me tightly as I pounded my fists against his chest and wept for the girl lying shattered in the bed upstairs.

Then there was kissing.

Then there was sex.
Then there was sleep.

WHEN MORNING CAME I woke refreshed, warm and mortified.

Not because I'd slept with a guy who was about as far from my type as it's possible to get, but because as I lay there feeling him breathe, I replayed the night's events in my mind and realised something awful.

I felt guilty.

Which was, of course, ridiculous. I wasn't seeing anyone.

(Do people still 'see' each other after an apocalypse? 'Seeing' someone makes me think of flirty text messages, bottles of wine, dinner in fancy restaurants, making your date suffer through a romcom as a test of their forbearance. None of those things were possible any more. I found myself drowsily wondering what *Sex and the City* would say about the rules of dating in a post-viral warzone. Of course, with society entirely gone away, every woman who wanted Jimmy Choos could have them, as long as they were prepared to fight their way to a lootable store. And then I had a vision of Sarah Jessica Parker in a sequined dress, with an AK47, mowing down hoards of Blood Hunters, screaming "if you want the strappy sandals you'll have to go through me, motherfuckers!" That was Kate thinking. Jane told her to shut up and focus.)

I had no ties. Since that thing with Mac and the sixth-formers last year I'd not been within arm's length of a man I felt like getting to know better. Still, there was nothing to prevent me bedding the entire male population of the UK if the mood struck me.

But as I replayed the night's exertions I realised that at a very particular moment I was thinking of a very particular person. It wasn't as if I was thinking of Sanders at any point. It was a comfort fuck at the end of an awful day; it wasn't about Sanders at all. Neither was I fantasising about anyone else. It was all about me, about being alive while people were dying around me, about wanting to feel something other than pain for a moment.

Yet at one moment, as I arched my back and dug in my fingernails, I had a crystal clear picture of Lee in my mind, just for a second. And I lay there in the morning with a sinking feeling. I knew what it meant, but I refused to accept it. I banished it from my mind. As Lee was so fond of saying: "No time, things to do."

But, really, damn.

*   *   *

WHEN HE WOKE, Sanders was brisk, businesslike, unsentimental. He didn't want to cuddle or talk or any of that, which suited me fine.

Kate had never had a one night stand, but Jane had had plenty. Of course, Jane had never bedded a guy who knew Kate and that collision did strange things to my head. He was detached come daylight, the kind of behaviour that would have thrown Kate into despair and angst but which was a blessed relief to Jane.

He wasn't cold, though. He smiled and cracked a few lame jokes. Don't worry, his behavior said, I don't expect or require anything else. Ironically, that made me like him a whole lot more than I had the day before.

I checked on Caroline and Rowles. They were curled up on the double bed in the main room, spooning, fast asleep. They looked so peaceful and innocent lying there that I decided to let them sleep. Sanders found some tinned spaghetti and a calor stove, and we sat down to breakfast. We ate our food out of china bowls with old, dull forks and listened to the harsh wind battering the open doors and windows of this deserted little suburban cul-de-sac.

"You said you swept this town," I asked as I wiped tomato sauce off my chin with my sleeve. "What does that mean? What is exactly is Operation Motherland?"

"Our orders are pretty simple," he replied. "We're emptying every armed forces base in the country, gathering all the weapons and ordnance in a series of huge depots on Salisbury plain. The idea is to disarm the population, take guns out of the equation. Then, when we've got all the hardware, we can start to re-impose law and order, raise a new army, take back London, put the king on the throne, get back to some sort of normality."

I gaped. "You're just collecting weapons? That's it? That's your masterplan?"

He nodded. "Yeah, for now. We've got more kit than we know what to do with, to be honest. Take this town, for instance. There was a TA base nearby and a gang of kids had broken in, got themselves all tooled up, and they were running this place. It was ugly, what they were doing. So we rolled in, executed the worst of them, took all their guns away so it couldn't happen again. Job well done."

"And where is everyone now?"

He shrugged. Not his problem.

"Jesus, Sanders," I said. "Didn't it occur to you that it would have been better to arm the people here? The sane ones, the adults?"

"Our orders are to disarm everyone, Kate."

"It's Jane, and those are stupid orders. Obviously these cleaners came to town, found the people here defenceless and either drove them out of their homes or massacred them. And that's your fault. If they'd been armed, they'd have been able to defend themselves."

Sanders put down his bowl and stood up suddenly. "Time to ship out," he said brusquely, and he left the room.

KATE WAS ALWAYS a good girl at school. She studied hard, got good grades, excelled at science, biology especially, and made her parents proud.

She only got in trouble once, and that wasn't her fault. Her friend April had started a fight – she never really understood what about – and Kate had tried to break it up. But in the struggle to keep the peace she ended up getting thumped, hard, by a nasty little bitch called Mandy Jennings. So Kate thumped her back – the first and only time she ever threw a punch. Well, until Moss Side. Unfortunately, her aim was true and Mandy wore glasses. So when the screaming and hair pulling finally ended, Kate was marched off to see the headmaster, who gave her all that guff about letting herself down. And Kate bought it, 'cause she was a good girl, and she felt ashamed and she cried and said, "Sorry, Sir."

As Sanders drove the truck through the gates of Salisbury HQ I felt an echo of what Kate had felt when she was about to be brought up before a figure of authority – a sick, hollow, butterfly ache in the stomach. The only difference was that Jane would have told the headmaster to go stuff himself. And the headmaster was unlikely to have Kate lined up in front of a firing squad.

Salisbury had been the centre of British Army maneouvres for decades, and all the facilities had recently been given a 21st century facelift, so the main base at Tidworth was modern and sprawling, with barracks aplenty and facilities for the maintenance of all sorts of vehicles. But there was so much stuff gathered here that it had spilled out of the base perimeter and on to the plain itself. Row upon row of trucks, tanks, armoured vehicles, jeeps, fire engines, both Green Goddesses and the conventional red ones, ambulances and police vans. Not to mention the hundreds of oil tankers, lined up in rows stretching off to the horizon.

Sanders had undersold the operation's ambitions. They weren't just hoarding weapons, they were collecting all the resources they could lay their hands on. After all, resources meant power. If they had all the service vehicles and all the fuel, married to a well drilled force in possession of weaponry vastly superior to anything else out there, they would be unstoppable.

As I looked out of the truck window and saw all that hardware I felt both excited and scared. All that power, just waiting for someone to give the order to move from preparation to implementation. Operation Motherland was a sleeping giant. When it awoke nothing and nobody would be able to stand in its way.

We drove past a parade ground where at least 400 men were doing drills, and groups of soldiers in full kit marched past us at regular intervals, heading for trucks or armoured vehicles, off to round up more guns, fuel, Pot Noodles or whatever. The place was buzzing, full of organised, purposeful activity.

So as we drove into that awe inspiring place I felt insignificant and afraid, and I wondered what the headmaster would be like. Because with all this at his command, he could do pretty much anything he wanted with me.

Sanders pulled up outside the medical centre and carried Caroline inside. We'd made her a little bed in the back and Rowles had sat with her during the journey. He'd not said a word to me since she'd been shot. I think he blamed me for letting it happen, and an angry Rowles was not someone I wanted to confront, so I left him alone to brood. Caroline herself was conscious and cogent, but complaining of sharp pains in her head, which worried me. There was a possibility that she was bleeding into her skull, and I wanted her x-rayed as quickly as possible. I let Sanders sort out the formalities and I sat in the truck feeling guilty, useless and scared.

I caught myself wishing Lee were here, but I banished that thought as quickly as it appeared.

Sanders emerged five minutes later and opened the cab door for me, indicating that I should get out.

"They think she'll be fine, but they're going to give her a full work up. Rowles is staying with her," he said as I clambered down. There was an awkward moment as he put his hands around my waist to lift me down. I stared at him, not unkindly, and he removed his hands and apologised with a smile.

He led the way to the regimental HQ.

"The doctors here have lots of practice treating injuries like hers," he explained. "The one I saw said to tell you that you'd done an excellent job on her."

I nodded, trying to take pride in the compliment, but I felt nothing but shame.

We came to the steps of the main building and Sanders put one of his huge hands on my shoulder. I stopped.

"Let me do the talking, okay?" he said.

I looked at him curiously.

"I think I can sort this out," he explained. "But you'll have to trust me."

"Sure," I said, allowing myself a flicker of hope.

We walked up the steps and through the double doors. There was a notice board on our left as we entered, plastered with timetables, orders, a poster for a karaoke night. It was so normal, it reminded me of school. Down the long corridor which stretched ahead of us men and women in uniform were bustling from room to room carrying clipboards and folders. A drink machine, actually powered up and working, was frothing a coffee for a bored looking army clerk. That corridor was the closest thing I'd seen to pre-Cull England in two years. Nobody was scared, nobody was hungry. There was an air of ordered, peaceful activity, like any office, really. I wondered if this was the way forward for us survivors, or whether the military machine was just hiding itself away inside a secure compound where they could pretend nothing had happened, that routine military life was just the same as it had always been, running like clockwork, all hierarchy and structure.

We walked down the corridor and Sanders knocked on the door at the far end. The nameplate read Maj. Gen. J. G. Kennett. This was the big man. I braced myself, but when a stern voice barked "Enter!" Sanders turned and pointed to a chair in the corner.

"Stay there," he said. "I'll only be a minute."

I nodded, aware that my life, and the lives of my kids, rested entirely upon what this man, who I hardly knew, was going to say next.

As Sanders opened the door, I sat down to wait. I'd only been there for a minute, twiddling my thumbs and staring at the patterns on the carpet, when a young woman brought me a cup of tea in a saucer, with biscuits.

"There you go, Miss," she said with a smile.

Cup and saucer, tea and biscuits. I shook my head in wonder.

About ten minutes later, long after I'd exhausted all the entertainment possibilities of sitting on a chair in a corridor, the door to Kennett's office opened and Sanders popped his head out.

"Jane," was all he said by way of summons.

I felt a pang of butterflies in my tummy as I rose and entered the office of probably the most powerful man in the country. The room was plush but not opulent. Regimental photos lined the walls, and there were even a few paintings – Waterloo, the trenches of the Somme. The floor was polished wood with a huge, deep rug laid across most of it. There were old wooden filing cabinets, upholstered wooden armchairs, a sideboard with decanter and glasses. The room was old school privilege and power; comfort, security and authority embodied in the trappings of tradition and duty.

Major General Kennett was standing in front of his desk, leaning back against it, his arms folded across his chest. He was about forty, plump, red cheeked and bald, with a strong square jaw, and was dressed plainly in green trousers and jumper. He regarded me with calculating green eyes. I was unsure whether his air of easy authority was innate or whether it was bestowed upon him by the room itself and all the cultural and social respect it represented.

Sanders stood to one side, hands clasped behind his back. He wasn't at attention, but he was formal. I think they call it 'standing easy.'

"Miss Crowther, welcome to Operation Motherland," said Kennett, leaning forward and offering me his hand. His voice was high and nasal, with a strong southern accent, kind of like Ken Livingstone. It didn't suit him at all.

I took his hand and he shook it once, firmly.

He didn't offer me a seat, so I stood there, unsure what was required of me.

"The lieutenant has been telling me what happened at your school and on the journey here. There'll have to be an investigation, of course." He folded his arms and pursed his lips, assessing me.

I couldn't think of anything to say, so I just said, "Right."

There was a long pause.

"I'm not entirely sure I believe everything he told me," added Kennett.

"Sir..." began Sanders, but Kennett silenced him with a look.

"But I've known him a long time, Miss Crowther. He's one of my most trusted officers. So I choose to believe him. And I feel sure that everything the investigation discovers will corroborate his story. Won't it, Sanders?"

"Sir."

"Yes," mused Kennett. "Thorough. I like that in a soldier. So I shall continue to believe him, and by extension to trust you, unless you give me reason to do otherwise. Do you think you're likely to do that, Miss Crowther?"

"No, Sir," I said, surprised by my instinctive deference.

"Good. In which case you are welcome to remain here while the girl in your care recuperates. After that you will be escorted safely back to your school. We will, I'm afraid, have to disarm your merry band, but I'm sure you understand that's for the best."

"Actually, Sir..." I began. But the warning in his eyes was clear and unambiguous. I fell silent again and nodded. Jesus, this really was like talking to my old headmaster.

"Excellent." Kennett clapped his hands and smiled. Business concluded. "Sanders will find you a billet, and maybe we'll see you at our karaoke night tonight. Sanders does a very good Lemmy, I'm told." With that he turned his back on us, picked up a file and began to read.

A second later, almost as an afterthought, he said, "Dismissed."

Sanders saluted, said "Sir" and ushered me out of the door.

"What the hell did you tell him?" I asked incredulously as we walked out of the building into the crisp air of a spring evening.

"What I needed to. I'll brief you properly later, so we can get our stories straight for the investigators. Essentially, the child traffickers killed our guys, and you killed the traffickers."

At the bottom of the steps I stopped, took his hand, leant up and kissed him on the cheek.

"Thank you," I said.

He squeezed my hand and smiled. "You're welcome. Now let's get you billeted, then you can start thinking about what you're going to sing tonight!"

"You wish! I've got a voice like a strangled cat."

The billet was a room on the first floor of a simple barrack building. It had a single bed, wardrobe, wash basin with clean running water, a TV with DVD player and plug sockets that had power. Plus, central heating! I leant my bum against the radiator, enjoying that slightly too hot feeling that I'd almost forgotten. Log fires are nice, but give me a boiling hot radiator any day of the week.

After Sanders left me alone I went to the communal bathroom at the end of the landing, drew myself a hot bath and soaked all the aches away. Sanders had scraped together some toiletries from somewhere, so I washed my hair, soaped myself clean, shaved my legs, plucked my eyebrows, waxed my top lip, and did all those things I used to take so completely for granted. When I was all done, I lay back in the water and watched the steam rise and curl as the stitches in my cheek throbbed in the heat.

I closed my eyes and imagined I was at home, that Gran was downstairs making tea, and that after I'd dried my hair I'd go downstairs and eat her corned beef pie with mash and we'd watch trashy telly.

It was a nice, warm daydream.

I felt safe for the first time in two years.

When I woke, the water was tepid and night had fallen. The light was off so the bathroom was dark. I suppose that's why Sanders hadn't found me and dragged me off to karaoke. I looped the plug chain around my big toe and pulled it out, then I rose, pulled my towel off the hot radiator and wrapped it around me. Back in my billet I found that Sanders had left me some clean clothes, bless him, and although the short black dress he'd chosen for me was perhaps not quite what I'd have opted for, I decided to indulge him, and myself. There was fancy underwear as well – nothing crass, just good quality – and the shoes were nice. He'd almost guessed my size right in all respects.

When I was all dolled up, I put on some slap and looked at myself in a mirror. Bathed, well dressed, made-up. Nothing out of the ordinary a few years ago, but the woman staring back at me seemed like an old stranger, someone I'd known very well once upon a time but had lost touch with. I was glad to see her again, but I knew she was only visiting briefly.

I looked like Kate.

Well, no matter. I was about to walk into a room full of soldiers, looking pretty damn good, if I said so myself. It had been a long time since I'd turned any heads, and I was looking forward to it.

Pulling a coat around my shoulders, I left the room, turned off the light and walked downstairs, listening to my heels clicking on the lino. Again, a sound from the past – high heels on a staircase. One small detail of a forgotten life, once commonplace, now extraordinary to me.

I opened the door and stepped outside. The camp was dark, but the roads were lit with orange sodium lights. I stopped and listened. From somewhere off in the distance I could hear a chorus of drunken voices singing *Delilah*. I followed the sound, enjoying the sensation of once again being able to walk alone at night without fear.

Which is why it was such a surprise when the man dropped out of the sky on a parachute and landed on the path in front of me, and hands grabbed me from behind, muffling my shouts, dragging me into the shadows.

CHAPTER TWELVE

I KICKED AND struggled, but the man holding me was too strong. I'd have bitten his fingers off if he hadn't been wearing heavy leather gloves.

I was pulled off the path and into the bushes, where I was pushed down on to my knees and held firm.

"If you do exactly as I say, you won't be harmed," said a soft voice in my ear. The accent was unmistakeably American, an exotic twang after two years of Kentish brogue. I felt cold metal at my throat.

"If you cry out, I'll slit your throat, Limey bitch. Understand?"

Limey? Who the hell called Brits 'Limeys' anymore?

I nodded gently. He removed his hand from my mouth.

I've been in worse spots before, but I was completely unprepared for this. I was in the safest place in Britain, in my bloody party dress! So unfair. Anyway, I was more scared than I'd been in a long time and I momentarily lost my cool. My terror, I'm embarrassed to admit, made me compliant. I didn't make a sound.

"Good girl," said my captor. "Now, which way to the main gate?"

"I only got here today, I'm not sure. I can't direct you. I could probably walk you there, though."

He tightened his grip. "Not good enough."

He fell silent, thinking it over. As he did so the bushes rustled and another man, the parachutist, joined us. He was dressed entirely in black, almost invisible. It was only when I saw his thick leather gloves that I realised that both men had fallen out of the sky. My captors shared a brief, whispered conference.

"All right," said the new guy, also a Yank. "Here's what we're going to do. You're gonna walk us to the gate. We'll stay in the shadows, but we'll be watching you. If you try to shout out or run, you're dead."

To illustrate the point he pulled out a handgun and slowly screwed a silencer into the barrel.

"Joe's a really good shot," added the man holding the knife to my throat, and I could hear the smile in his voice. "You should remember that. Now go."

He withdrew the knife and released me. I knelt there for a moment, composing myself, then I got up and walked back to the path, brushing the dirt from my knees. So much for karaoke, I thought, as I stood in a pool of orange light, rearranging my dress and getting my bearings. I didn't doubt the ruthlessness or ability of the men who were threatening me. Plus, they'd bloody parachuted here. I'd not seen a contrail in two years, so that implied all sorts of things. I decided to play along until something clever occurred to me or an opportunity presented itself. Which it did almost immediately.

"There you are," boomed a voice to my left. I turned to see Sanders striding towards me wearing shirt and jeans, a bottle of lager in his hand. "I wondered what was keeping you. Lost?"

I nodded. Shit, would they just kill him? Sanders walked up to me and held out his arm. I slipped mine through his and said, "Let's take a walk."

He seemed unsure, eager to get back to the singing, but his guard was down, he wasn't expecting trouble, and a woman wanted to spend time with him. He smiled. "All right," he said. "But there is no escape, sooner or later you get to hear my *Ace of Spades*."

"I've already seen your ace in the hole, Sanders. It wasn't all that."

"Hey!"

As we began walking, I caught a tiny flash of movement out of the corner of my eye, a shift in the shadows, black on black. We were being stalked.

I gripped his arm way too tightly and increased the pace. He gave me a curious look and I tried to signal with my eyes that something was up. But it was dark and he was slightly drunk. Sanders the soldier was off duty, this was Sanders the boozed-up Motörhead fan. I wondered how long the two Yanks would allow this to continue before they got trigger happy. I needed to stall.

"Let's take a walk to the medical centre," I said. "I want to look in on Caroline."

"Okay," he replied, giving my arm a squeeze of sympathy.

"It's by the main gate, isn't it?" I asked, slightly too loud.

"Um yeah, it's this way," he answered.

He led the way and we walked in silence for a minute or two.

I caught no hint of our pursuers. They were good, whoever they were.

"You look beautiful," said Sanders as we passed a row of silent tanks.

"Well, thanks for the clothes and stuff," I said, lamely.

"You're welcome. You wear them well."

For the love of Mike, Sanders, you dope.

We ambled on a bit more, then I had an idea. If I pulled him into an embrace the gunmen would know I was up to something. But if he pulled me close they wouldn't be sure, and I could whisper in his ear.

"Well," I said, as if suddenly shy, "I'm only wearing them for you." I moved my hand along his forearm and laced my fingers through his. He looked down at me, surprised, as I stroked his thumb gently with my index finger.

"I'm honoured," he said, smiling but a little awkward.

"You should be. It's not every day I make such an effort." Oh this was painful. I was spouting bad dialogue from a Meg Ryan movie.

"You don't need to make an effort, Jane." Now he was at it.

I moved fractionally closer, so our thighs brushed together as we walked.

"Look, I can't keep calling you Sanders. What's your proper name?"

"Neil."

"Neil, I want to make an effort for you. Last night was... special."

"That's a relief. It's been a while. I was, um, married. Y'know, before. My Chrissie."

No, this is supposed to be a seduction, you twit. Don't get drunk and maudlin.

"Kiss me," I whispered urgently as we walked around a corner into the road that led to the medical centre. He kept walking. He hadn't heard me. Oh, fuck this. I never was much of a femme fatale. I dug my fingernail into his palm, hard, and he stopped, baffled.

"Kiss me," I whispered again. Finally the great lunk wrapped me in his arms and stuck his tongue down my throat. We were lucky – the men following us must have thought he'd done it on the spur of the moment. They held their fire. Sanders tasted of Grolsch and Marlboro, which brought back hazy memories of another life.

As soon as I was able, I broke the liplock and hugged him hard. Then I whispered in his ear: "Two men. Silencers. Bushes. Main gate." He stiffened and then relaxed, on duty again. He disengaged, wrapped his arm around my waist, and we continued walking. He didn't seem to be looking around, but I was sure he was trying to get a bead on our stalkers.

"Y'know, Jane, you're a piece of work," he said, slightly too loud. His acting was pitiful, I only hoped the darkness would compensate.

"Really?"

"Yeah. Once you turned the corner, after you left the school, I really thought you'd fall in with a bad lot."

Ah-ha, I thought, so that's why he was never recruited by MI5. I rolled my eyes.

"Yes, but I had you to keep me on the straight and narrow, didn't I?" I improvised. Then, as we turned the corner on to the road that led to the main gate, I fell to my left, rolling off the pavement and on to the grass verge. Sanders turned and ran to his right. I heard the soft *phutt phutt* of a silenced automatic, and saw a tiny muzzle flare from the spot Sanders was running towards ("rush a gun, flee a knife" said Cooper, in my head). He held out his hand as he ran, smashing his lager bottle on a lamppost and then bringing it up to use as a weapon. The gun fired once more, then Sanders vanished into the undergrowth, which rustled and shook.

I heard a cry of "stitch this!" and a grunt.

I leapt to my feet and ran for the main gate, forgetting that I was wearing heels. My right ankle went from under me and I sprawled on to the concrete, scraping my knees and hands. I reached down to undo the straps and as I did so the other Yank was on me, straddling me, rolling me over on to my back and bringing his knife down to my chest. I grabbed his descending arm with my right hand as my left continued to fumble with the strap on my shoe and pulled, releasing the catch. Then I grabbed the sole, brought my arm up and plunged the heel of my shoe into my attacker's ear as hard as I could.

He toppled slowly to his right, falling into the road. I got up, reached down, and pulled the shoe. It came out with a wet sucking sound. Waste of a perfectly good pair of shoes.

The camp was quiet, no-one aware of the struggle that had taken place. I needed to raise the alarm. I looked over my shoulder, and saw that the bushes Sanders had run into were still and silent. I got my bearings – I was right outside the medical centre. There were bound to be people in there, I was about to run and start banging on the door when I felt a hand on my shoulder. I yelped and spun around, swinging my shoe as a weapon. Sanders caught it in his great paw and I sighed.

"Sorry," I gasped.

He shook his head as if to say *it's nothing*. His other hand was holding his side, and I could see a red stain spreading through his fingers.

"You've been shot," I exclaimed. "Let's get you inside." I wrapped my arm around his waist and tried to drag him towards the medical centre, but he resisted.

"No," he said firmly. "It's just a flesh wound. First we search the body and find out who these guys are and how they got in here."

He shrugged my arm away and knelt down beside the body, grunting as he did so from the pain of his wound. I knelt down beside him.

"They're both Americans and they parachuted in," I said.

He looked up at me sharply. "You sure?" I nodded.

He reached down and pulled open the dead man's jacket, searching his pockets. His hand was on the man's chest when he mumbled "oh fuck" and ripped open his undershirt. Strapped to the man's bare flesh was a little metallic gizmo.

"What's that?" I asked, but Sanders was already up and running for the main gate. I pelted after him.

"Life sensor," he yelled back to me as he ran. "It means whoever sent them knows they're..." His final word was lost in the scream of an approaching missile. We were caught in the shockwave of an enormous explosion, which picked us both up and flung us backwards on to the hard tarmac, knocking the air out of us and singing our eyebrows. The main gate and the guard post beside it vanished in a huge fireball and I felt the scorching air blast across me and cook my lungs as I gasped for air.

The perimeter was breached. Operation Motherland was under attack.

My senses were scrambled. I didn't know which way was up, my eyes couldn't focus, my ears were ringing and I felt like I was going to be sick. As I tried to clear my head I felt the world lurch and start bouncing. It took me a moment to realise that Sanders had actually picked me up, slung me under his arm, and was running away with me. I heard sharp cracks all round us, which must have been gunshots, but they sounded distant and dull. Then I landed on soft grass with a thud and felt large hands running themselves up and down my body. Odd time to cop a feel, I thought, feeling disconnected and out of body. Then he slapped my face and the world got sharp, hot and focused.

"Oi!" I shouted, and slapped him back.

"You're not hit." He was leaning over me, black smears on his face, his carefully combed hair wild and frizzy. "Can you run?"

I nodded. "Come on then." And he was off. I shook my head, rose to my feet with a groan of protest, and staggered after him. Even after being shot and blown up he was making good speed. But he was running away from the sounds of gunfire and explosions. Shouldn't he be in the thick of the fighting? We ran through the base, which was suddenly full of shouted orders and running men, all heading in the opposite direction. Sanders grabbed one man as he ran past and relieved him of his weapons, sending him back to get re-equipped. I caught up with him and he handed me a sidearm.

"What the hell are we doing?" I asked, shouting to be heard over the sirens that were now ringing out. "What's going on?"

"In situations like this, I've got standing orders. Now come on." And he was off again, his wound not even meriting a wince. He wasn't even breathing hard as he ran past the mustering troops. I was gasping for air and trying to ignore the stitch in my side.

"But don't you want to know what's happening?" I bellowed as I chased after him.

"I'm a soldier, Kate... sorry, Jane. I never know what's bloody going on. I just do what I'm told."

It seemed pointless to argue, but I couldn't really wrap my head around it. I never followed orders, never did what anyone told me without being given an explanation first, always made sure I knew the big picture before making a decision. But I was a free agent, always had been. Sanders was a soldier, conditioned and trained to be a cog in a machine. He didn't need to know the whys and wherefores, he just did as he was told, immediately, without question, confident that by following orders he was doing the right thing. I couldn't imagine allowing anyone to have that control over me, or allowing myself to trust someone so much that I'd take their word for anything without being given proofs and reasons.

That said, I was running after him, so I suppose I trusted him that much. I really wanted to be running back to the medical centre. Rowles and Caroline were there, and they were my responsibility. But I knew the fight would already be at their front door, and it would be suicide to head back there now. I just had to hope they'd be safe. After all, no-one would attack a hospital. Would they? I told myself not to worry about it. Rowles could look after himself and Caroline, and as soon as I was able I'd be back for them. For now, I kept following Sanders, hoping he had a plan.

We ran across the base to a barracks that sat at the heart of the compound. It was a low building, brick built, with two guards on the door, one of whom greeted Sanders.

"Lieutenant," he said, businesslike in the face of sudden chaos. "What's going on?"

"He in there?" asked Sanders as he slowed and stopped.

"Yeah."

"Okay, stay here, no-one comes past. Understand?"

"Sir!"

"Come on," he said to me, and I followed him through the doors and into the barracks.

We came to a door and Sanders knocked and entered.

It was a simple bedroom, nothing too fancy. A single bed, a desk, a cupboard and a wardrobe. A bookcase full of *Alex Rider*, *Young James Bond* and Robert Muchamore. There were posters, too, of the Pussycat Dolls and Slipknot.

Kneeling on the bed was a young boy, fourteen or thereabouts, oblivious to our presence, listening to a CD player with his headphones on, the volume so loud it was drowning out all noise. His face was ravaged by acne, his hair was greasy and unkempt, and he was wanking over a porn mag. He looked up in horrified alarm as Sanders tapped him lightly on the shoulder.

"What the...?" spluttered the boy, his face turning red as he realised he was not alone. He pulled his headphones off and dragged the quilt over his erection.

"You need to get dressed and come with me right now," said Sanders.

"What do you mean? What's going on?" the boy whined, spluttering in embarrassment and fear.

"The base is under attack. We need to get you to the safe house. Get dressed. Quickly, Your Majesty."

The boy didn't move, he just stared at Sanders and nodded his head sideways at me, indicating that Sanders should remove me. I grabbed Sanders' arm and pulled him towards the door.

"We'll, um, wait outside," I said, trying to keep a straight face. "Sire," I added, and snigered as Sanders pulled me out the door and slammed it shut.

"That's him?" I giggled. "That's the king?"

But Sanders wasn't laughing. His face was white and he was leaning against the wall. I glanced down and saw that the blood from the wound in his side had soaked his clothes right down to his knees. Suddenly things didn't seem quite so amusing.

"I need to get you stitched up."

"No time," he said, forcing himself to stand upright. "We need to get the king to safety."

"I'm the doctor," I said firmly. "Is there a med kit or anything in this building?"

He glared at me and then reluctantly said: "Try the kitchen."

I ran off down the corridor, looking in all the rooms until I found a small kitchen with a fridge, microwave and a Baby Belling cooker. There was a red plastic med kit on the wall, so I pulled it open and rummaged inside. I pulled out sterile dressing, elastoplast, alcohol and a needle and thread, then I ran back to Sanders, dragged him into the room opposite the king's and set to work.

"So this is your job, huh?" I asked as I worked. "You look after the king?"

"Yeah. Ow!"

"Big baby."

The bullet had gone clean through him, just missing a kidney, but I couldn't be sure whether his guts were punctured or not. I thought they probably were, and if so he'd need proper surgery sooner rather than later or there'd be a great risk of infection. In the meantime I did the best I could. I sterilised the wound, stitched him up, slapped a dressing over it and gave him a huge dose of painkillers.

"I train him, keep him safe," explained my patient. "I don't get out much. They only let me come to the school to get you because I begged and it seemed like a milk run. If the perimeter is ever breached, I'm to get him to a safe house we've set up about ten miles away. He's my only priority."

"But shouldn't he have, like, a whole team of men guarding him?"

"Just me. That's the best way. Keep it low profile, don't draw attention to ourselves. Chances are that whoever is attacking us doesn't even know he exists. We've not exactly gone public with him yet. He's not ready."

"He seemed to have things well in hand a moment ago."

"Jesus, Jane," he said, exasperated. "He's fourteen, all right? Cut him some slack. You know what teenagers are like."

"Of course I do. I run a school, remember."

"He's all right, he's a good kid."

"As long as he doesn't expect me to curtsey, I'm sure we'll get along fine."

Sanders and I grabbed uniforms from the cupboard and quickly changed into combats. My uniform was ridiculously oversized, and the only way I could get the boots to fit me was to wear four pairs of socks, but at least it was better than my party dress and heels. All the time we could hear the sounds of battle outside, steadily getting closer. There were explosions, constant gunfire, the rumbling of tanks and, just as we finished getting ready, the roar of a fighter jet swooping low overhead, and the whooshing sound of a missile being released. Sanders was agog.

"F-16?" he said, incredulously. "We really have to go."

At that moment the door to the king's room opened and he stepped out. He was dressed head to toe in black and his face was smeared with boot polish. He handed the tin to Sanders and as we blacked up, he interrogated us.

"Attackers?"

"Americans," I answered. "Trained soldiers, I think."

"And you are?" His air of authority was impressive, but I thought it was an act. I'd seen a fifteen-year-old boy really take control, and there was a quality of certainty that Lee possessed that the king lacked. He was trying hard, though, I gave him that. And it must have been difficult for him to try and regain any dignity in front of me after what I'd just witnessed.

"Jane Crowther, I run a boys' school, Your Majesty."

"She's with me, Jack," said Sanders, passing the boot polish to me and checking his SA80.

"Good enough for me, and please call me Jack, Miss Crowther," said the boy, drawing his sidearm. "Shall we go?"

"Both of you follow me," said Sanders. "Stay low, we keep to the shadows, we don't engage the enemy unless forced to. We make straight for the exfil and leave. Is that clear?"

The king and I both nodded. (No, I needed to stop thinking of him as the king. It was ridiculous and it made me think of Elvis. I would follow Sanders' example and call him Jack.)

"All right then," said Sanders. "Come on."

Without another word, we ran out into a battlefield.

CHAPTER THIRTEEN

I ALWAYS SEEM to be running away from fights.

The last time I was in a proper pitched battle – on the day St Mark's was blown sky-high – I grabbed a gun and ran like hell. In my defence, I was going to locate the girls who were in my care, and we did come back later and save the day. But my experience of being in a proper battle was of running as fast as I possibly could in the opposite direction. As we ran out of the barracks I was reminded of why that had seemed such a good idea last time.

The two men guarding the door were still there, and we all stood for a moment, getting our bearings and identifying where the heaviest fighting seemed to be.

The night sky was bright with orange flames and the blinding flashes of explosions. The noise was deafening, like a hundred fireworks displays going off at once all around us. The fighting, which had begun at the main gate, had moved quickly, and I could see a group of British soldiers using the buildings in front of us as cover. They were firing around the corners at the attacking forces.

One man readied a fearsome looking missile launcher, which he hoisted on his shoulder, and then he ran out between the buildings, straight into the line of fire. He knelt down and took careful aim at what I presumed must be a tank. It was an act of such bravery and madness that I stood riveted to the spot, trying to understand what would make someone risk their lives so foolishly. The only answer was training and necessity. It was the kind of thing that would be unthinkable in a skirmish, but in the heat of war it was almost commonplace. This was true soldiering. It was awe inspiring, actually. And doomed.

A swarm of bullets thudded into the soldier, and he toppled backwards, arms flailing. The rocket launcher flipped over his fragmenting head, still held in his right hand, until it was pointed straight at us. Then his dying fingers twitched and the rocket screamed free of its housing.

Someone must have shouted for us to run. We scattered and kept moving. Sanders, Jack and I ran one way; the two squaddies ran the other. They drew the short straw. The rocket slammed into the far corner of the barracks, hitting an oil tank used for heating. I was much closer to this explosion than I had been to the one at the main gate and it was stronger than anything I'd ever felt before. I lost consciousness in mid-air.

WHEN I CAME to, I was lying on a hard metal surface, being bounced up and down. My head felt like someone had filled it with nails, and every bone in my body ached.

"Where..." I started to say, but my voice was drowned out by the sounds of a revving engine and a machine gun. I looked up and saw that I was in the back of a jeep. Next to me crouched Jack, SA80 at his shoulder, firing out the back at a similar vehicle which was pursuing us. The enemy jeep had a white star painted on its bonnet, and a bloody great machine gun mounted above the driver's cab. A soldier was standing in the back, firing at us as we drove far too fast along a muddy track on Salisbury Plain.

I was about to reach for my gun and join the fight when our tyres exploded. The jeep lurched to one side then another as the driver – Sanders? – struggled to keep control. But it was hopeless. The jeep swayed from side to side with increasing velocity, then we hit a rock in the road and we rolled and spun. Everything around me whirled and crashed as I was flung up and down, smashing every part of me into the four sides of the jeep's cab as the vehicle tumbled down a slope. We were still falling when my head met Jack's with an enormous crack.

I slipped into the darkness again.

THE NEXT TIME I woke I felt like I'd never move again. My head was beyond painful. I couldn't focus my eyes, which were as full of blood as my mouth and ears. I was lying on my face in thick wet mud.

It was like that moment when you get home from the pub, drunk. Your head hits the pillow and you realise that even though you're lying down, your senses think you're still moving and you feel the first inklings of the nausea and awfulness that's going to take up the next day or so of your pathetic drink-sodden excuse for a life. The only sense that was working properly was my sense of smell. And all I could smell was petrol and blood.

I could hear an engine idling nearby, footsteps approaching, and two American voices shouting: "Show us your hands! Get down on the ground!" That kind of thing. So that told me at least one of us was alive and moving.

I blinked and concentrated until I began to make out shapes. I wiggled my fingers and toes, trying to work out if anything was broken. My limbs felt okay, but every movement sent shooting pains across my ribs, at least three of which were definitely fractured. The pain was excruciating and all I could think about was that I'd be lucky if I'd only punctured a lung.

When the world stopped spinning again and the pain receded slightly, I gently lifted my face clear of the mud and saw that I was lying in a ditch. I must have been flung clear as the jeep rolled. It also meant that the bad guys probably didn't know I was here. Slowly, agonisingly, I got to my knees and lifted my splitting head over the edge of the ditch. Our jeep was lying on its back about twenty metres away from me, directly ahead. Its lights were still on but the engine was dead. The American jeep was parked on a ridge above it, and the man in the back had a spotlight, and his huge machine gun, trained on the scene below him. Sanders was on his knees with his hands behind his head, an American soldier standing over him. Another soldier was pulling Jack out the back of the jeep by his boots. The boy was a dead weight and he left a deep groove in the mud behind him.

That galvanised me – an injured child needed my help.

I reached down and cursed. My sidearm had been lost in all the confusion. I was unarmed and concussed, with broken ribs, dull hearing, blurred vision and nausea, and I was wearing a uniform too big for me and boots that dangled off my ankles like weights. Yet somehow I had to take out three armed American soldiers.

I'd have been better off in the heat of battle.

The obvious target was the man in the jeep. With the spotlight shining down, I couldn't tell if there was a driver in the cab. If there was only the gunman, I maybe had a chance, but if there was a driver then I was screwed. To my left the ditch led around a small hillock, so I crawled through the cold mud on my hands and knees, sure that at any moment the squelching noises would bring a soldier running. But I was lucky, and I rounded the hillock safely. Now I could move. I dragged myself out of the ditch, grinding my ribs together and groaning with pain in spite of myself. I couldn't run, so I shambled as best I could down a small depression and into a copse of trees which provided cover as I climbed the ridge down which our jeep had tumbled.

When I got to the top I collapsed in a heap, crying in agony, unable to make myself take another step. But I had to. I gritted my teeth and breathed short and fast, hyperventilating to help ease the pain – after all, the world was already spinning, a little extra lightheadedness couldn't make much difference, could it? Then I pulled myself up and staggered on. I approached the American jeep from behind and saw, to my relief, that there was nobody in the driver's compartment.

With no gun, I would have to get very close in order to put this guy out of commission. There was no point walking up to the jeep, he'd shoot me down. I couldn't vault up on to the flatbed and struggle with him – I wasn't capable. I had to get him down somehow, and I needed a weapon. I cast around until I found a large piece of jagged flint which I grasped in my hand tightly. Then I just improvised.

"Help," I muttered, shuffling towards the jeep with my hands to my head. "Someone help me, please!" I didn't look up at the gunman. Instead I gazed vacantly left and right, as if blind. "I can't... I can't see. Oh God, someone please help me."

It didn't need much acting to sell the guy; I was barely functional. I made sure not to look straight at him, but as I gazed around, pretending to be sightless and confused, I saw him get down from the jeep and walk towards me, machine gun levelled. If he decided to shoot me, there was nothing I could do. As he got within a few metres of me I slipped and fell. I wish I could say that was part of my plan, but I genuinely lost my footing and went sprawling on the stony track, crying out as I hit the ground. I lay there and cried. "Oh, God, please help me, someone, please, God." But I kept hold of my stone.

The gunman, completely convinced by my impression of a concussed, bleeding wreck who could barely stand, did the damnedest thing. He took pity on me. He swung his gun over his shoulder so it rested with the muzzle pointed skywards and he reached down to help me up.

"Take my hand, ma'am," he said.

I reached up with my left hand. "Oh, thank you, thank you. Who's that? Where am I?"

He grabbed my hand and kneeled down to put his arm round my chest and lift me up. As he did so I swung my right hand as hard as I could and smashed the rock into the side of his head. He grunted and fell sideways, dragging me with him. We splashed down into a puddle in a tumbling heap. I was weak, though, and the blow didn't knock him out, it merely stunned him. He tried to crawl away from me but I held on to his belt and pulled myself up his body, each movement causing awful pains in my chest. He tried to roll over and fight back, but he was too badly hurt. After what seemed like an age but was probably mere seconds, I managed to get myself into a position where I could grab his head. I pushed hard on the buzz cut hair, pressed his face into the puddle, and then collapsed on top of him, holding his face under the water with the weight of my whole body as he writhed and bucked and struggled to throw me off. But I just lay on top of him, crying with pain and anger and horror at what I was doing, until his struggles weakened and, eventually, stopped. I lay there for another minute, just to be sure, and then I rolled off him, lying flat on my back in the mud, breathing hard.

There was no time for rest, though. I bent double, levered myself upright and walked to the jeep. I couldn't climb into the flatbed, I was just too weak, so I flopped on to it and then lifted one leg over the edge and dragged myself on to the hard metal surface. Then I used the machine gun's column to pull myself upright, and I looked down the ridge. Sanders was still kneeling, and Jack was lying beside him. I could see his chest rise and fall, so I knew he wasn't dead, but he was unconscious. The two soldiers were still standing over them. Which certainly made things easier from my perspective.

The gun was not unlike the GPMGs we had at St Mark's, so I checked that the safety was off, sighted carefully, held my breath, tried not to worry about the fact that I was starting to see double, squeezed the trigger and held on for dear life. It took a few seconds for the vibrations of the gun to throw me off; I was so weak I couldn't cope with the recoil. I collapsed to the floor.

If that hadn't done it, then so be it. I had nothing left in me.

I heard shouting, the crack of small-arms fire, but it was distant and not my concern. I felt as if I was falling into cotton wool. The world stopped spinning, which was nice. Then Sanders' face appeared above mine. His mouth moved but I couldn't hear what he was saying.

Then he faded away, and I was warm and safe and gone.

*   *   *

THE NEXT THING I was became aware of was a distant voice. It was deep and rich, male, unfamiliar. American. It was saying my name.

"Miss Crowther. Jane. Wake up, Miss Crowther."

I struggled to open my eyes and, when I did, I immediately scrunched them shut again. The light hurt. My hands felt soft cotton sheets beneath me and everything was soft and warm. I was lying in a bed.

"Welcome back," said the voice. "You've been away for quite a while."

The ache in my limbs was gone, my chest felt sore but not agonising, and my head was fuzzy and muddled, but not painful. I knew this feeling; I had been drugged.

I opened my eyes again and winced. Things slowly came into focus through the glare. The first thing I saw was the man sitting beside my bed. He was African-American, with a lined faced and short grey hair. He wore an army uniform. The room swam into view and I saw familiar cream walls. I was at Groombridge. This was my sick bay. I was home. I tried to speak, to ask him what was going on, but I couldn't form the words.

"Don't," he said. "You've been drugged for some time. You took quite a knock and there was severe swelling of the brain. My medics put you in a drug-induced coma and nursed you back to health. But you've had three lots of surgery, you died on the table twice and I'm sorry to say you don't have any hair right now."

I felt my scalp, shocked by the smoothness of it.

"They tell me you're going to be okay," the general said. "They called me this morning and I flew down so I could be here when they woke you."

It took all my effort and concentration to croak: "How long?"

"Three weeks."

"Who...?"

"General Jonas Blythe, at your service, ma'am. I command the US forces here. I gave the order to attack the British Army on Salisbury Plain, and I gave the order to take control of your school. Sit her up."

I heard someone walk across the wooden floor in heavy boots and felt strong arms lift me into a sitting position. I was propped up on some pillows so that I could see out of the window. It was a bright, sunny day, cold but clear. Next to the window stood a TV set with a camcorder plugged into it. The general nodded to the soldier who'd propped me up, and the young man went to the camcorder and fiddled with it until it began playing. The screen crackled with white noise and then solidified into a picture.

Lee. Bruised, bloodstained and terrified, sitting tied to a chair in front of a blue sheet with Arabic writing on it. A man in a black hood stood behind him holding a sharp knife. I gasped in horror. I knew what this video was. Everyone did.

The sound kicked in and there was Lee. Kind, lonely, brave, broken Lee, sobbing into the lens. "My name is Lee Keegan. It's my sixteenth birthday today, and I'm English. I flew here to find my dad, a Sergeant in the British Army, but my plane crashed and these guys found me. If anyone sees this, please let Jane Crowther know what happened to me. You can find her at Groombridge Place, in Kent, southern England. It's a school now. Tell her I'm sorry."

And the screen went blank. Tears streamed down my face and my stomach felt empty and hollow. Oh God, Lee. Poor, sweet Lee.

"He's dead, Miss Crowther," said the general.

Now I found my voice. Dry throated, I croaked between sobs: "How did you get this?"

"Recovered it from an insurgent hideout in Basra about a month ago."

"Did they...?" I couldn't say it.

"Not them. Believe it or not your boy made friends with them. They let him go."

"I don't understand."

"He joined them, Miss Crowther. To fight me."

I stared at him. "You killed Lee?"

The general nodded. I screamed and tried to fling myself at him, reaching out to scratch his eyes and bite his face. I wanted to pull him apart. But I was too weak, and my limbs wouldn't obey the instructions I was sending them. I just fell forwards and slid off the bed on to the floor, collapsing in a heap at his feet, a pathetic, tear-stained, wailing, wreck.

The young soldier lifted me up. I tried to shake him off, but I was helpless. Instead of placing me back in the bed, he sat me in a wheelchair and pushed me so I was face to face with the general. I stared into his pitiless eyes, summoning all the defiance and fury I could muster.

"Why are you so important?" he asked. "What is it about this school?"

I didn't understand what he meant, but my face betrayed nothing but anger.

"A young soldier from this school flies to Iraq and almost succeeds in destroying my operations," he explained. "The one name he gives us is yours. Then, when we attack British Army HQ you're there in the thick of it, with your very own SAS bodyguard, whose sole purpose, as far as I can tell, is to ensure your safety and bring you here. Why? Why are you so important? What's your game, Miss Crowther?"

Sanders had brought me here. So where was he? And what had become of Jack?

"Shall I tell you what I think?" continued the general. "I think you're a spook. MI5 or 6, back before The Cull. I think this school is a front for all that remains of your British Secret Service."

I started to laugh silently. It hurt my healing ribs but I couldn't help it. I held my sides and laughed and laughed till more tears flowed.

"You fool," I said. "You stupid, pathetic, paranoid fuckwit. I'm not a spy. I'm just a boarding school matron." I could hear the hysterical edge to my laughter but I couldn't stop. "If you want spies, you're barking up the wrong tree, General. All I've got is TCP and sticking plasters."

He sat there and let me laugh for a while, then he stood, grasped the handles of my wheelchair and pushed me to the window.

"Let me show you what I do to people who waste my time, Miss Crowther," he said quietly.

I looked out of the window at the lawn below. It seemed like only yesterday that I'd lain on that grass with Barker, feeling the Earth move beneath me. Now, in the exact spot where I'd passed that quiet moment of contemplation, was one of the most awful things I've ever seen. It was Sanders - strong, gentle, musclebrained Sanders, my sometime lover. He lay facing the sky, impaled on a huge wooden stake which jutted, bloodied and obscene, from his shattered chest. A crow pecked hungrily at a gaping eye socket and then flapped away, as if ashamed of being seen.

Had I anything in my stomach, I would have been sick.

"Now, Miss Crowther," said the soft, menacing voice behind me. "Let's start again, shall we?"

PART THREE
LEE AND JANE

CHAPTER FOURTEEN

LEE

"DOES THIS THING have a loo?" I asked eventually.

"No," said Dad.

"Well, I'm sorry guys," I said, "but I really, really have to pee and unless you want to sit in here and breathe ammonia all the way home, I'm going to have to get out to do it."

"Don't we have a bottle or something?" asked Tariq.

"All full of water, which we'll need," replied Dad. "Lee, you can't hold it any more?"

"You remember when I was little and we went on that road trip to Rhyll? How much did it cost to get the car seats cleaned?"

Dad didn't need any more information than that. "Should be all right. Just go quietly, okay?"

I nodded, then reached up and turned the wheel to open the hatch. I pushed up and peeked outside. The noise of the engines was deafening, and there was hardly any light.

"All clear. Back in a sec," I said. I put my right foot on the back of the main bench seat and pushed myself up and out, on to the roof of the LAV III Stryker Engineer Squad Vehicle. Designed for minesweeping and road clearance, it was squat, solid, armour plated and boasted a mean looking set of guns on the roof; this was state of the art kit. It also had nice comfy couches, which is why we'd chosen to stow away in it for the flight back to England.

The fuselage was literally freezing; the US Army obviously hadn't considered the health and wellbeing of stowaways when they designed the in-flight heating system for the C-17 Globemaster III cargo plane. I clambered down on to the metal floor. The only light came from the small round window in the door to my left. I walked across to it and peered out, careful not to trip on the numerous metal tracks that ran the length of the fuselage. We were above the clouds, and the full moon cast a brilliant, cold light. Our vehicle was at the very back of the plane, its rear hanging just above the ramp, which would be lowered to allow it to drive out when we landed in England. Other vehicles and pallets of supplies and ordnance were queued up behind it in the dark and cold.

I walked up the body of the plane a little bit and unzipped my fly, letting rip against the side of a pallet full of bags of flour. Little bit of flavour for your bread, you bastards. I sighed in relief and smiled as I did the zip back up again. Better.

I turned to walk back to the others and then something hit me in the face and I was flat on my back, seeing stars. Before I could get my bearings I felt someone sit on me, straddling my chest, wrapping their hands around my throat and holding my head against the metal. I looked up to see who had attacked me. All I could see were the whites of his eyes. Dressed entirely in black, and with shoe polish on his face, this guy was practically invisible.

"Is this the way to Business Class?" I asked.

He hit me again and my head made a clanging noise against the floor.

"You're that Limey kid," said the man.

"Limey?" I said, playing for time. "Do people really say Limey? Isn't that a bit out of date now?"

"Where are the others?"

"Others?" Suddenly there was a knife at my throat.

"We were given orders not to kill you," said the man in black. "The general wants that pleasure himself. But hey, he's not here so if I drop you out the back no-one will ever know."

In the confusion of embarkation there was every chance that he wouldn't have heard about any skirmishes that took place, so I said: "No others. Just me. They didn't make it."

"Right," he replied mockingly. "Hey Joe, check around. He must've come out of one of the vehicles."

I couldn't see who he was talking to. It was impossible to know how many of them there were. I wondered what they could have been doing lounging around the unheated fuselage of a cargo plane full of vehicles and supplies, then I registered that his black clothing was a jump suit.

"So you're, like, American parachute ninjas or something?" I asked.

"Or something."

There was a loud thud and a groan from the end of the plane then a floodlight came on, momentarily blinding me. The man atop me rolled sideways and ducked behind a pallet, seamless and silent.

I blinked at the light and realised it was the spot on the top of the Stryker.

"Come on, Lee," shouted my dad. I pulled myself upright and ran for the vehicle, past the stunned body of another man in black. I vaulted up on to the Stryker, where Dad was standing behind the spotlight and mounted gun emplacement, his eye pressed up against the huge sighting lens. "Get inside."

I slid down into the belly of the vehicle, where Tariq was waiting, gun at the ready.

"You couldn't fucking hold it?" he said, witheringly.

"The sights on this thing are great," said Dad loudly. "I mean, I can only see your right foot, but if I..." There was a loud report as he squeezed the trigger, then he ducked back down to join us. "They'll be considering their next move for a minute or two. Lee, how many are there?"

"I don't know," I replied. "I only saw two. I think they're parachutists, and they're blacked up, so I reckon they're dropping from this plane before we land. Advance guard, maybe."

"And we thought it was only kit in here. Bloody hell," said Tariq.

"We don't want to get into a firefight," said Dad. "Pressurised cabin, all sorts of bad things happen."

"But you just shot at him!" I said.

"Calculated risk. Just to make a point. Let's hope he doesn't call my bluff, or things will go wrong very quickly."

A voice echoed down the plane, barely audible above the roar of the engines.

"Hey, Limeys!"

Dad popped his head back up and shouted: "Yeah?"

"Hold on!"

There was a clunk and a whirr of machinery.

"Oh shit," shouted Dad and he ducked back inside the vehicle, pulling the hatch closed behind him. He looked white as a sheet.

"What?" asked Tariq and I, in unison.

But Dad wasn't listening, instead he scrambled past us and into the driver's seat, where he started pressing buttons frantically. Tariq and I followed, taking up positions either side of him, looking down at the various touchscreens which were illuminating one by one as the vehicle powered up.

"What are you doing?" I asked again.

"Got to initialise the CBRN, it's our only chance," he muttered. Tariq and I looked at each other and shrugged. Suddenly the plane lurched to one side and began to descend. The noise from outside the vehicle began to get a lot louder.

"Oh fuck me, no," I whispered as I realised what was happening. The look on Tariq's face told me that he'd worked it out too.

"Got it!" yelled Dad. There was a hiss of compressed air and the sound of bolts locking. "I've turned on the CBRN system. We're airtight and pressurised." He pulled the seatbelt across, strapping himself in.

"Lee, strap yourself into the other seat," he ordered. I sat down and did as I was told. "Tariq, you're going to have to find something to brace yourself against back there. I think I saw some straps you could use. Just lie flat on one of the couches and try not to let go. This is going to be rough."

Tariq nodded wordlessly, and disappeared into the back.

"CBRN?" I asked, trying not to think about what was about to happen.

"Chemical, Biological, Radiological, and Nuclear warfare system," he replied.

"Cool."

The vehicle shook.

"Tariq, you strapped in?" Dad shouted.

"Yeah," came the tremulous reply from the back.

"They must have decided we were too much trouble to flush out," said Dad.

"They're right," I replied.

"Remember that time at Rhyll," said Dad, "when I took you on the rollercoaster?"

"Jesus, do I ever."

"Fifteen people with your sick in their hair. I thought they were going to lynch us. This is going to be much worse."

"Oh, thanks for the..."

The vehicle flew backwards at enormous speed, flinging Dad and I forward against our straps and squeezing the air out of us. Time elongated, and the g-force was overwhelming. I tried to breathe but couldn't force my lungs to inflate. My eyes watered, my ears roared and popped, I would have screamed if I could. Then my stomach flipped and we were falling, weightless. The seat fell away from my arse and the straps dug deep into my shoulders as I was dragged down by the dead weight of the plummeting metal cage that surrounded us. It went on forever until there was an almighty snap as the cords on the 'chutes went taut and our descent slowed. Now the pressure went the opposite way, as the deceleration forced me down into my seat, crunching my spine and pressing my chin down in to my chest as I suddenly felt twenty stone heavier. Eventually we hit our descent speed and returned to normal. I gasped like a fish on dry land, hyperventilating.

I looked across at Dad. He was stunned, but okay.

I craned over to see if Tariq was okay. He was lying on the couch, tied by thick straps designed for holding equipment steady on rough terrain, grinning fit to burst.

"Again! Again!" he shouted, like a demented Tellytubby.

The vehicle rocked from side to side in the winds, making me feel seasick.

Dad unbuckled himself and tried to stand. His legs went from under him, though, and he fell forwards on to the console. "Woah, dizzy," he gasped.

"What are you doing?" I asked.

"Need to see where we're coming down," he wheezed in reply, then he staggered back into the belly of the vehicle, bracing himself against the walls as it swayed.

"Are you mad?" I asked, unbuckling myself and tumbling after him. "You don't know how high we are, whether we're even in breathable air yet. If you go too soon, we'll depressurise. If you go too late, you could be unbuckled when we hit the ground and that would not be good." I grabbed his arm and held him back.

"Lee, we might not even be over land."

"Shit," said Tariq, who hadn't bothered to unstrap himself, and was still lying there. "You mean..."

Dad nodded. "We could hit water and sink like a stone. We could be over the Med or the Channel, I don't know. Or maybe over a mountain range. For all we know, we could hit the top of a snow ridge and tumble all the way down the bloody Eiger."

"And what would we do if we were coming down over the sea or somewhere worse?" I asked. "What good would knowing do us? I doubt this thing has a life raft, or skis. Does it have retractable skis?"

Dad glared at me and then smiled in spite of himself. "No, no skis."

"Shocking lack of foresight, that." Dad held my gaze as I shrugged and said: "All we can do is strap ourselves back in and hope. I didn't come rescue you so you could take a nose dive out of an armoured vehicle at 20,000 feet."

He paused and then nodded. "When did you become the grown-up?" he asked as we strapped ourselves back in.

"Ask Mom," I replied and then instantly wished I hadn't. I avoided his eyes and didn't say another thing.

"All right," said Dad a few minutes later. "We've got lots of parachutes holding us up, and the pallet we're on is slightly cushioned, but it'll still be a hell of a jolt when we land. So be ready." We sat, rocking gently, listening to the wind whistle by outside, feeling the hollowness in our stomachs as we fell.

"Do you reckon..." began Tariq, but he was interrupted.

We hit something but we didn't stop falling. The vehicle spun 180 degrees around its centre axis until we were upside down. Then there was another crash and we spun the other way, facing nose down, still falling. Loud cracks and bangs echoed through the metal structure as we fell, swivelling and spinning wildly.

"Trees!" shouted Dad.

Our stop-start, rollercoaster descent slowed as we crashed down through branches and bowers until finally we came to a halt, swinging, facing downwards at 45 degrees. We all caught our breath. The only sound was the creak of wood from outside.

"Everyone okay?" asked Dad.

Tariq groaned and lifted a thumb. I tried to nod, but my neck hurt in all sorts of interesting new ways. "Yeah," I said. "Nothing two years of intensive physiotherapy wouldn't fix."

"Good." Dad breathed out heavily. "Fuck me, that was a bit drastic wasn't it? Remind me never to do anything like that again. And next time, son, bring a bloody gazunder. Anyway, we're stuck. Which is good."

"Huh?"

"If we'd just hit the ground cold, it would have been the equivalent of falling twelve feet. In a chair. We'd have been lucky not to break our backs."

"Now you tell us," groaned Tariq.

Dad activated the driver's side periscope, but the view was obscured by parachute silk, so he unbuckled himself and clambered down the cabin to the gunner's periscope, which was also blocked. He climbed to the hatch, pulling his knife from its sheath as he did so.

"You both stay here, buckled up. I'll go see what state we're in." The vehicle swung perilously as he moved around in it, making me feel seasick. He opened the hatch and shoved aside a swathe of silk.

"We're in a forest," he said. "Pitch black, no lights, could be anywhere."

He climbed outside and we could hear him scuttling around on the shell of the vehicle. "We're only about six feet off the ground and we seem pretty well braced. I think you should unbuckle and jump down."

Tariq and I unstrapped ourselves, climbed to the edge of the roof and jumped on to a soft bed of pine needles. Dad stayed on the vehicle.

"Get clear," he shouted. "I'm going to cut some of the parachute straps and see if I can get this thing on the ground the right way up."

"Don't be daft," I replied. "If you cut the wrong cord, the Stryker could flip and land on you."

"Just get clear, Lee," he said impatiently.

I knew that tone meant no arguments, so I walked away and watched, nervous as hell, as Dad sawed away at the various parachute cords that were holding the vehicle in a complex swaying web. Each cord gave way with a loud twang, huge amounts of tension being released as they snapped. The vehicle lurched, first one way, then the other, then forwards, then backwards. It was like Dad was playing some vast, lethal game of Kerplunk. Cut the wrong cord and it was all over.

Bit by bit the vehicle came free, swinging more wildly as it hung by fewer threads. Then Dad made a mistake, cut the wrong cord and the whole thing pivoted and pointed nose down. Dad was flung forward and was left hanging off the gun turret. Tariq and I gasped, but Dad pulled himself up the roof until he reached the rear bumper. Reaching up with his knife, he cut the last cord and the vehicle dropped on to its nose. Then it slowly toppled backwards and landed the right way up, flinging Dad off it like a bronco rider on a bad day. He landed in a heap, but he was fine.

He stood up, brushing the dirt and pine needles off him. "Right," he said, "let's get this show on the road!"

We cut the straps that bound the vehicle into the pallet, and disconnected the final straggling parachute cords. Then we climbed inside and Dad booted her up. Even after that insane descent, she started first time. The touchscreens came to life. Dad pored over them for a minute or two and then announced: "It's Bavaria."

"What?" I said, incredulous.

Dad turned around, facing Tariq and me with a big smile on his face.
"It's Bavaria. We're just outside Ingolstadt."

"How the hell do you know that?" I asked.

"The satnav's working!" he replied with a grin. "All right, what's your postcode?"

THE STRYKER WAS designed for road clearance, and Dad drove like a demon, so we made good time. Germany's autobahns and France's highways proved impassable, but the satnav steered us down side roads and country lanes, always heading for our next stop – Calais station and the Channel Tunnel.

A couple of times we encountered roadblocks manned by gangs of marauders, but we kept driving straight through them as the bullets pinged harmlessly off our carapace. I knew that the Americans would have attacked England by now, and the knot of fear and anticipation in my stomach wound tighter with every mile. What would I find when we got to the school? Would it be a smoking wreck, ringed by the impaled corpses of my friends? And if so, how could I ever live with myself? I grew quiet and sullen, eaten up with stress, so it fell to Tariq to pepper our journey with anecdotes and nonsense. Sometimes he managed to get a smile out of me, but not often.

Dad and I didn't talk much, but the silence was less charged than it had been in Iraq. Perhaps he was starting to accept that I was more man than boy now, whatever my age. Or perhaps I was just enjoying being with him, watching him be heroic and confident, enjoying having someone look after me for a change, instead of me bearing all the weight. Either way, it was better. Not right, but at least better.

Eventually, after four days of negotiating our way across Europe, we arrived at the station in Coquelles, near Calais. We knew that the Chunnel might be blocked, but we fancied holding on to the Stryker, and if the tunnel were passable it would be a quick and easy trip. What we didn't reckon on was the welcoming committee.

From my position at the gunner's post, I kept lookout using the periscope as the Stryker nosed its way through the station entrance and on to the concourse. Burnt-out trains stood at the platforms, shattered glass everywhere.

On a bench in the middle of the concourse, a solitary man sat watching us.

"You see him?" I said.

"Uh-huh," replied Dad, slowing to a halt and putting on the handbrake.

"What do you reckon?"

Dad didn't answer, I glanced over my shoulder and saw that he was using his periscope to scan the windows of the buildings that overlooked the concourse.

"What you looking for?" I asked.

"Anything. Keep an eye on the guy. What's he doing?"

I pressed my eye against the periscope and zoomed in.

"He's smiling."

"Like a 'hi guys, good to see you' kind of smile?" asked Tariq, frustrated that he couldn't see what was going on.

I zoomed in closer, until the man's face filled my vision. He was dressed in black and grey combats and was wearing sunglasses. I couldn't see his eyes, but there was a cold malevolence about his smile; something feral yet amused.

"No," I said. "More a 'come into my parlour said the spider to the fly' kind of smile." I described a circle, checking for snipers or traps. I saw nothing, but I wasn't reassured.

"I can see the way to the tunnel," I said. "Should we just drive?"

Dad considered it, and shook his head. "No. I dunno who this bloke is, but he could have booby traps anywhere. The tunnel might be exactly where he wants us."

Before we could decide what to do, the man took the initiative. He got up and walked towards us, stopping just in front of the vehicle. He removed his glasses to reveal jet black eyes.

"Bonjour," he said affably.

Dad stroked the touchscreen and spoke into the mic on his helmet. "Parlez vouz Anglais?" His awkward schoolboy French echoed around the empty concourse and he stroked the screen again, turning down the loudspeakers.

"Ah," said the man in a strong French accent, his eyes full of calculation and surprise. "We thought perhaps some Anglais might come through the tunnel. We were not expecting any to go the other way."

Dad put his hand over his mic. "He said 'we.' Lee, keep looking, he's not alone." Then he took his hand away and replied: "We just want to go home. We've travelled a long way."

"I can see that," said the man. "This is not a British fighting vehicle." It was not a question, which told me that he knew his stuff. Military background, perhaps? "My name is De Falaise," said the man, rather more grandly than seemed appropriate. "My colleagues and I control this station. If you wish to pass, we would expect some form of consideration."

"Here we go," said Tariq.

"What do you have in mind?" asked Dad.

"Information."

"What kind of information?"

"Have you been in contact with Britain since The Cull? By radio perhaps? Can you tell us anything about what is happening on the other side of that tunnel? My friends and I, you see, are thinking of relocating."

I caught a glint, just for an instant, in a window behind us. I thumbed the zoom button and sure enough there was a man in position there; tripod, sniper rifle, telescopic sight. I didn't think he could do us any damage, but there might be more.

"Sniper, three o'clock, in the hotel," I whispered.

Dad covered his mic again. "Get ready, Lee," he whispered back. "When I give the word, fire a warning shot. Just a warning shot, mind. I don't want to start a war."

"'Kay."

Dad took his hand away and spoke again. "No contact. It all went dead long ago."

I couldn't see De Falaise's reaction to this, but I imagined it was either disappointment or disbelief.

"That is what I thought," he said. "Then perhaps we could trade something else. I think, perhaps, I would like your armoured car. I think I would like it very much."

"Fire," said Dad.

I gently squeezed the trigger and the gun mounted on the roof burst into life, spraying heavy rounds around the window where the sniper was poised. I saw him leap backwards, arms raised to protect himself from the chips of stone that were flying into his face. Once he was out of sight I squeezed again, destroying the rifle and taking him out of the game. Then I swivelled my periscope to see how our Frenchman would react. He hadn't moved an inch. Cool customer.

The sound of gunfire reverberated around the empty space, fading away gradually. Only when silence reigned once more did De Falaise speak.

"That is a disappointment," he said. "I was planning on letting you go."

Dad didn't wait to hear what he said next, choosing to slam his foot on to the accelerator and drive straight at De Falaise. But the Frenchman was too fast, diving out of the way to reveal the smoke trail of an approaching rocket-propelled grenade.

"Shit!" yelled Dad, and he yanked the wheel hard right, flinging Tariq and I to the floor. We skidded to a halt sideways and before we could get underway again the grenade hit us broadsides.

To this day, that explosion is the last thing I ever heard in stereo.

It's impossible to describe a noise so loud that it blows out your eardrums. It was like a physical blow; like someone jamming a sharpened pencil in my ear and then wiggling it for a bit as the aftershocks bounced around. I screamed and wrapped my hands around my ears, feeling blood pouring from them. Then all I could hear was a deep throbbing tone, like a dead TV. My sense of balance was gone too. I rolled about on the floor of the vehicle trying to stop everything spinning. I vomited all over myself and I didn't become aware of anything else until Dad sat me up and jabbed a needle in my arm. Then I passed out.

I WAS DEAF. I knew that before I even opened my eyes. I could feel the bandages around my head. I opened my eyes and there was Dad, leaning over me. I was on the couch in the back of the Stryker. Tariq lay on the couch across from me. He also had dried blood on his ears, but wasn't bandaged. Dad, I realised, had been wearing the driver's helmet, which would have protected him from the worst effects of the sound, and Tariq had obviously been hurt, just not as badly as me. So it was just me that got unlucky. Great.

Dad stroked my hair tenderly. I could see his lips moving but all I could hear was that dead TV tone in my right ear. My left ear registered nothing at all.

"I'm deaf," I said. Or at least I think I said it. I may have shouted it, or said "I'm cleft" for all I know. It was weird, knowing I was making sounds but being unable to hear them.

Dad nodded and turned away. I think perhaps he was trying to hide his emotions. After a moment he turned back, and mouthed some words slowly. It took a moment for me to work out what he was saying but eventually I got it.

He was saying: "We came through the tunnel. We're home. England. We made it."

CHAPTER FIFTEEN

JANE

It sounds strange to say it, but I was lucky that I was so badly hurt.

General Blythe was convinced that I was some sort of post-apocalyptic spymistress running covert ops at home and abroad, using specially recruited and trained kids like Lee.

"One boy, about eleven years old we think, single-handedly killed seven of my men during the attack on Salisbury," drawled Blythe in his broad American accent.

"Is he alive?" I said, dreading the answer.

"Oh, yeah. We captured him. He's a tough little nut – the only person I've ever had in my custody who lasted more than fifteen minutes of waterboarding. And of course you know how effective that method is at extracting information."

"No, I don't, you sick fuck. Because I'm not a spy!" I shouted.

"When he did break, he told us a pack of lies that had us chasing our tails for a week. Someone trained him, Miss Crowther. You don't expect me to believe that an eleven-year-old gets that kind of resilience out of nowhere, do you?"

"Believe what you like."

"Thank you, I will. And I believe that you are a player. My first instinct was to kill you. But I need to know the details of all your current ops. Do you have people in Russia, the US?"

"Go to hell," I spat.

"Undoubtedly, Miss Crowther, but hopefully not for a while yet. Having instructed my surgeons to save your life, I find that you are too weak to endure our interrogation techniques. They tell me that a single session on the waterboard would kill you, that you need at least a month of bed rest before undergoing any kind of strenuous activity. I'm not willing to sit around waiting for you to get better, but neither do I want to kill you until I'm absolutely certain you've told us everything you know. What to do, what to do?" He was smiling as he said this, toying with me like the sick sadist he was.

"Ah-ha!" he snapped his fingers and smiled. "Got it! I'll torture your friend. Why didn't I think of it before?"

"What friend?" I tried to make it sound mocking, but my fear was too strong to conceal. Had he got Jack? I hardly knew the boy, but I wouldn't sit back and let him be tortured. And what if the others from the school had got tired of waiting for me to come back? Were all the children and staff being held captive somewhere in the house, the guards taking their time choosing which of them would be first for the rack?

The general nodded to the soldier on the door and he left, returning a moment later pushing a woman. She was chained with one of those American prison chain things that loops from feet to hands to neck, so she could only shuffle, and she had a hessian sack over her head. But I knew instantly who it was. The soldier pulled the bag off to reveal Mrs Atkins, our beloved dinner lady. She had a black eye and a bruised mouth, but she stood defiant, her eyes blazing with fury. Then she noticed me, and her reaction told me everything I needed to know about what kind of shape I was in.

"Dear Lord, Jane, what have they done to you?" she whispered.

"We saved her life," said the general. "You'd better hope she's going to save yours." Then he nodded again, the sack was replaced and Mrs Atkins was led away. As she shuffled away she shouted: "You be strong, love. Don't tell them a thing!" Bless her, but that was the worst thing she could have said, merely confirming in the general's mind that I was hiding big secrets.

"I have a few things I gotta get done back at Salisbury," he said. "So I'm going to fly back there now and give you a night to sleep on it. But midday tomorrow, my men are going to go to work on your friend there, and you're gonna have a front row seat. So you think carefully, Miss Crowther. You think very carefully. Indeed." He rose to leave.

"Where's Rowles?" I asked desperately.

"Who?" he asked as he reached the door.

"The eleven-year-old boy you captured in Salisbury. What, you couldn't even get him to tell you his name?" I laughed. "You need better torturers, General."

He flashed me a look of warning. I didn't want to push this man too far.

"He's fine. We got him locked up. Collateral."

"And the girl?"

"Girl?"

I bit my lip. Stupid.

"I'll get my men to look for a girl. Thank you for the tip."

"And the others? The soldiers who were based there?"

But he just shrugged as if to say "what can you do?" and walked out.

It took me a second to believe it, but I knew deep down that he'd killed them. All of them. The British Army had been routed.

The guard left the room with the general, and I was left alone in the wheelchair. I'd lost Sanders; Rowles and Mrs Atkins were captured; Caroline was missing, and all that faced us was torture and death.

I tried to rise from my wheelchair, to push myself up, walk to the door, but I was too weak. I couldn't even muster enough strength to turn the wheels and push myself to the bed. And so there I sat, defeated, broken and scared, watching the general's ugly military helicopter rise from the field where the children used to play football.

As NIGHT FELL there was a knock on the door. I didn't bother replying, after all I was the prisoner. After a moment, the door was pushed open and I was confronted by a young woman in military fatigues.

She stood in the doorway holding a tray on which rested a steaming plate and a glass of water. The woman seemed unsure about whether to enter or not.

"Miss Crowther, may I come in please?" she asked. Her soft accent, Deep South, made her seem polite and diffident.

"Suit yourself," I muttered.

The woman came in, placed the tray on the small bedside cabinet and switched on the main lights. The soldiers must have refuelled the generator. The woman then pushed my chair to the bed and lifted me out off it with surprising ease.

"You're strong," I said as she wrestled me on to the bed.

"I spend most of my time lifting bodies of one kind or another," she said flatly.

When I was settled and tucked in, she stood over me and offered her hand. "I'm Susan, Sue." I looked at her hand and snorted contemptuously. She withdrew it then sat beside me and lifted the bowl of soup from the tray. "It's beef. You need to keep your strength up. It's going to be a long recovery."

I considered spitting it in her face, but what would have been the point? I opened my mouth and gulped down the broth. We sat there not speaking as I ate the food and drank the water. I studied her. By almost anyone's standards she was unattractive. Her figure was short and square, her hair was muddy brown, and she had a flat nose, receding chin and piggy little eyes. She was flat-out ugly, but her brown eyes were kind and her voice was gentle.

"Is there anything else I can get you?" she asked.

"A gun," I joked.

"Small or large?"

I sniffed. But she just sat there, waiting for my response.

"Small, please."

"Ammunition?"

I laughed. "Oh, loads."

She smiled and nodded. "I'll see what I can do, Miss." Then she stood, collected the tray, and left.

What an odd little encounter that was, I thought, as I closed my eyes and drifted into a haunted sleep.

IT WAS STILL dark when I jolted awake, my heart hammering urgently in my breast. Something had disturbed me. I listened and heard the creak of floorboards outside the door. Someone was creeping about outside. I tried to lift myself, but it was futile; pain ripped through every part of me as I tried to move. All I could do was lie there, waiting to see who it was and what they wanted.

The door cracked open quietly and a shadowy figure stepped inside, pushing the door closed behind them as softly as they could. Then they walked to the bed and stood over me.

It seems odd looking back, and I don't know what I planned to achieve by it, but I pretended to be asleep, squinting up at the person, hoping they'd go away. But they leant down and put their hand on my shoulder and gently shook me. No point pretending now, so I opened my eyes.

"Who...?" I began.

"It's me, Miss. Sue. Please don't make any noise, there isn't a guard outside your door, but they do patrol and I don't want to take the risk. I have a message for you from someone called Lee. He told me to give you his love and to tell you not to worry."

I know it's a cliché, but there's no other way of saying it – my heart leapt. I can't remember what I said, it was probably just a mumble of vowels, I was so amazed.

Sue sat on the edge of my bed and whispered softly. "I was in the courtyard this evening, when I heard someone hissing at me from the bushes. It was a man called Tariq. I knew him when I was stationed in Iraq. It's a long story, but I used to pass messages for him sometimes, to soldiers who weren't happy with the way the general was doing things. My, you could have knocked me down with a feather to see him here!"

She talked with her hands, like a big camp drama queen, her eyes flashed with mimed shock and her mouth formed an O of surprise. "He told me that he's here with Lee and Lee's daddy. Now, they caused quite a rumpus back in Basra before we left, and it seems they stowed away on a plane or in a tank or something. To be honest that bit confused me. But either way, they're here now and they're coming to rescue you!"

She flapped her hands and gave a little bounce of excitement as she said that, almost squealing. I had to smile. Her over the top Southern Belle act was so at odds with the way she looked.

Finally I managed to speak. "Lee's here?" I said in wonder. I'd been so certain I'd never see him again, but he was back. The insane boy had actually flown to Iraq, found his father, taken on the American Army, and made his way home. It beggared belief.

"You betcha!" she said with a huge smile. "He's a little beat up, poor kid, but he's here. Now, if you're still not willing to co-operate with the general by midday tomorrow, then that's when they start torturing your poor friend."

"Is the general coming back to join the fun?" I asked.

"No Miss, I'm told he'll only be returning when you decide to talk. In the meantime, while you're trying to make up your mind, I have the item you requested."

She reached into the pocket of her jacket and produced a snubby little gun.

"It's a Beretta, Miss. I hope that's to your liking?"

"Does it go bang?" I asked, amazed.

"It surely does."

"Then it's fine with me."

"Tariq told me to say that the action will begin shortly before midday, for obvious reasons, and that you are to shoot anybody who comes through that door who doesn't say the code phrase first."

"And the code phrase is...?"

"Finally, someone with balls."

I laughed, remembering Mac's final words. "Yes, it would be." I hesitated, but I had to ask.

"Sue. I must say, you're quite a surprise. You are the last person I would have expected to find in uniform."

"I'm a nurse, Miss. I just help put people back together. And the army pays good. Well, it used to."

"But surely you're taking a terrible risk defying the general like this?"

Sue dipped her head, suddenly serious. "I had a fiancé. He was in supplies and, oh, he was so sweet to me. And so brave. When the general started giving orders to attack the population in Basra, my Josh stood up to him. Led a mutiny. But, well, he didn't realise how far the general would go. Josh was ever so smart but he could be naïve."

"What happened?" I asked softly.

Sue sighed and inclined her head towards the window. "Like the man on the lawn. Josh was the ringleader and so the general made an example of him. After that most people just fell into line. Some went native, joined the Iraqi resistance, but mostly people were too scared of the general, or they agreed with his methods, or they just couldn't break the habit of obeying orders, even when the orders were so wrong."

"And you?"

"I bided my time, made contact with those few remaining soldiers I thought I could trust. Waited for an opportunity. We're not all like the general, Miss. Some of us joined the army because we believed we were doing good, fighting for something right and true. I honestly believe that if we can just remove the general and those closest to him, then things will change for the better."

I gazed at her in wonder. "Sue," I whispered, "you may just be one of the bravest people I've ever met."

She put her hand on mine, looked up at me and smiled sadly. "That's sweet of you to say, Miss. I should go now. But you've got your gun and you know the code phrase, so just sit tight and we'll have you free in two shakes of a lamb's tail."

"Thank you, Sue," I replied, squeezing her huge, strong hand. "See you when the dust settles."

"I hope so, Miss."

She rose and left. She was so softly spoken, so physically unprepossessing, but so brave and kind. I had a new ally and I had hope. But then I remembered what had happened to the last two people who'd helped me – Barker and Sanders. The people who got close to me kept dying.

I just prayed that Sue wouldn't suffer a similar fate.

SOMEONE ELSE BROUGHT me my breakfast, a stony-faced guy who spooned porridge into my mouth without a word. I was strong enough to feed myself now, but I pretended I was still too weak. It might not be much of an advantage, but it was all I could manage.

I watched the sun climb higher, feeling more and more nervous. At quarter to twelve I heard someone shouting outside and an engine revving, then there was an almighty crash, my bed shook, and someone opened fire.

I held the Beretta tightly and took aim at the door. Moments later it was flung open and the soldier who'd brought me breakfast backed into the room. I squeezed the trigger and let him have it.

The gun clicked and jammed, a useless chunk of metal. I tried to unjam it, but I wasn't familiar enough with the mechanism to do anything but make an awful grinding noise.

The soldier, unaware of his lucky escape, kicked the door closed and pulled a huge knife from a sheath in his belt. He ran across to my bed, shoved it away from the wall and got between the bedhead and the wall, leaning over me and placing the knife blade to my throat with one hand as he raised his gun in the other.

"I'm under orders to kill you if we come under attack," he growled.

I heard a voice from outside shout, "Finally, someone with balls."

It was Lee.

I tried to shout a warning but the soldier clapped his hand across my mouth and took aim at the door. I bit the soldier's fingers but he didn't let go.

I saw Lee's unmistakeable silhouette through the smoked glass panel on the door as he pushed it open. Then the glass shattered and he flew backwards, out of sight, as the soldier behind me shot him three times in the chest.

CHAPTER SIXTEEN

LEE

IT WAS A day's drive back to Groombridge. As Dad drove, the nausea gradually subsided and my sense of balance slowly returned. The pain in my head helped take my mind off the crippling fear that everyone would be dead before we arrived.

The emergency medikit that Dad had plundered for the injection yielded lots more painkillers, much stronger than anything you used to be able to buy at a chemist's. I began popping Tylenol 3 like it was going out of fashion.

We stopped to rest for the night in a suburban cul-de-sac outside Tunbridge Wells, breaking into Barrett homes until we found one that wasn't full of corpses. The living room was lined with DVDs and sported an enormous widescreen TV. It looked new but it would never show a picture again.

Dad carefully unwound my bandages and mopped the blood off my ear with water from the tank in the loft. When he'd cleaned me up he put his hands on my cheeks and rested his forehead against mine. "You're going to be okay, I promise."

My left ear was still completely silent, but the dead TV tone in my right ear was subsiding, and I found that I could just about hear Dad if he spoke loudly. I hoped the hearing would recover enough to be functional; I didn't think there'd be that many people left who spoke sign language. Being deaf in this world would be pretty fucking lonely. But I refused to give in to self pity. I had the school to worry about and mistakes to make right.

Dad explained that the Stryker had external fuel tanks which were designed to explode away from the vehicle if ignited. The RPG had hit one of them, hence the unusually big bang, but the defences had held and we'd been able to drive away under heavy fire. Had I been wearing the gunner's helmet my hearing would have been fine; Dad just had a mild ringing in his ears.

Tariq, who had been on the opposite side of the vehicle to the explosion, could still hear a constant ringing in both ears, but he could hear us through the background noise. He joked that he had Kevlar eardrums.

We plundered a store of tinned food that we found in the kitchen; obviously the owners had started panic buying when The Cull started. I wondered what had become of them. I spent the night in a child's bedroom, sleeping underneath a Man Utd duvet surrounded by posters of long-dead sports heroes. Knowing that the morning would confront me with God knew what horrors, my sleep was fitful and disturbed.

We rose with the sun and drove the final leg of our journey in silence. We had prepared all our weapons and I had talked them through the layout of the place as best I could. We left the Stryker in the thick woods north of the grounds and approached the house on foot. We stayed inside the woods, scanning the rear of the building with binoculars. It was still standing, but it was eerily quiet. The gardens are ringed by woods on three sides, so we were able to work our way around, checking the house from all angles. Finally we came around to the front and saw a humvee parked next to Blythe's calling card – an impaled man. The man was wearing British Army gear and I didn't recognise him. So the Yanks had been here, some had stayed, and there'd been a killing. But nothing told me what had happened to Matron and the others. I was frantic with worry.

Then Tariq gave a start and pointed to a female American soldier who was walking into the courtyard.

"I know her, she's a friend," he said. Before either Dad or I could stop him he was off, running around the edge of the woods to get closer. We stayed put, watching from a distance as Tariq got the woman's attention and she ducked into the tree-line. After a few minutes she walked back out and Tariq rejoined us.

"They haven't got the kids," was the first thing he said, and I was overwhelmed with relief. "But they have got your matron and another lady. The lady is in the cellar, the matron is on the first floor in the south wing. She has been very ill and is recuperating."

"How many men?" asked Dad.

"Five, including Sue, and she says one of the others is not happy with things and would probably side with us if she had a word with him." He smiled. "Good odds, yes?"

We retreated and made our plans.

What we didn't know was that our every move was being watched.

I'D ALWAYS ASSUMED that one day Dad would teach me to drive, but I thought it would be in a Ford KA or a Mini; I didn't expect my first driving lesson to be in an armoured minesweeper.

I remembered when he'd taught me how to ride a bike. It had stabilisers on the back but somehow I kept managing to fall off anyway. Dad would pick me up, dust me off, dry my tears, and ask me if I wanted to give up. I sniffed and shook my head, checked my helmet was secure, and got right back on the saddle. Learning to drive an armoured car was much easier; if I made a mistake, it wasn't my knees that got damaged, it was whatever car, tree or house happened to get in our way. It was more fun getting it wrong and crashing in to stuff, but I forced myself to concentrate; every minute I wasted was another minute Matron spent in captivity.

"I don't want you out in the open, Lee," Dad had insisted. "You won't hear if I shout you a warning, or if someone's yelling at you to put down your weapon. Going into battle deaf is a surefire way to get yourself killed. I want you in here, safe."

"I'm not disagreeing with you, Dad. But this isn't your fight. You don't know these people, they're my responsibility."

He shook his head in wonder. "Listen to you. Son, you're sixteen. The only responsibility you should have is passing your GCSEs. And as for no ties, this is your home now. So it's mine too. If you're willing to risk your life for your friends, then so am I. Okay?"

"Okay," I said with a smile. "And thank you."

"Don't mention it. Now, let's get these gear changes sorted."

My Dad. Cool as fuck.

So at 11:45 the next day, at the same moment that I knew Dad and Tariq were approaching the house from the west, I strapped myself in, revved the engine, and drove the Stryker as fast as I could across the moat bridge and straight into the front doors of Groombridge Place. As soon as the vehicle ground to a halt, jammed in the doorway, I unbuckled myself, ran back to the gunner's seat and pressed my eye against the periscope. Didn't take long. Two of them came running down the stairs, guns blazing, and I took care of them sharpish. Wow, I thought, that was easy. Only one left. Dad and Tariq appeared at the end of the entrance hall, so I grabbed my gun, opened the hatch and climbed out to join them.

Sue was close behind them with another soldier, a young African-American guy, thick set and jowly.

"We'll get the woman from the cellar," said Sue. "You get Jane."

They peeled away and the three of us ran up the stairs, guns raised, ready for attack from the landing. None came. We turned right at the top of the wide staircase and followed the landing around to the three doors that led off it. The final one, with its thick frosted glass panels, was where Sue had told us Matron was being held. I ran forward but Dad grabbed my arm and shook his head.

He inched towards the door and shouted the code phrase: "Finally, someone with balls."

There was no reply, so he raised his gun and pushed the door open. There was a series of shots from inside the room, the glass shattered and Dad flew backwards, shot in the chest. He hit the ground hard and slid back against the banister, mouth gaping, blood splattered across his face and hands. His gun fell from his useless hands and he gasped for breath as I heard Matron scream "No!" from inside the room.

Why I reacted the way I did, I don't know. Maybe it was second nature to me now. But I didn't run to help my dad. Even though I was in shock, and screaming in fury and pain, I didn't go to help him. Instead, I took the necessary steps to neutralise the threat first. Just like a proper soldier.

I flung myself forward, rolled on the landing and came up crouching, gun raised, in front of the swinging door. I saw a tall soldier standing behind a bald woman in a bed. Without hesitation I put a bullet right between his eyes, spraying his brains all over the wall. I didn't stay to watch him fall. I threw my gun aside, spun around and grabbed my dad, who was blinking in shock.

I wrapped my arms around him, trying not to look at the gaping holes in his chest and the thick blood pouring from them, staining his combats. He looked up at me and mouthed something I couldn't hear. I leant closer with my good ear, trying to catch the words, but his eyes rolled back in his head and he became limp and unresponsive.

I cradled him, rocking him back and forth, stroking his hair, crying. I don't know what I said, but I was speaking to him, trying to keep him with me, trying to talk him out of dying.

I was aware of a commotion behind me but I ignored it. There were people running up the stairs too, but I didn't spare them a glance.

Then there were hands on me, pulling me away. I kicked and fought, but they were too strong. I looked up and saw that it was Tariq and behind him there was that weird bald woman with the sunken eyes and grey skin. She was in a wheelchair now, shouting orders at Sue. Mrs Atkins stood behind them, her hand to her mouth. Tariq held me there, shouting that I should let them work. But the dead TV tone was louder now, rising in pitch in response to the gunfire.

The soldier I had seen with Sue lifted my dad in his arms and carried him away, Mrs Atkins close behind. Sue followed, going down the stairs backwards, carefully pulling the woman in the wheelchair behind her. When they had disappeared Tariq let me go, to sprawl on the landing in my father's blood.

I felt numb. All I could hear was dead air and static.

JANE

I SAW LEE fly backwards from the door and I screamed. He couldn't be dead. He just couldn't. And then my eyes seemed to play tricks on me, because there he was, shaven-headed and bruised, crouched at the door, shooting the guy behind me and then turning round to grab... who?

A young man stepped between us and reached down to put his hand on Lee's shoulder.

"You!" I shouted. "Come here, get me out of this fucking bed."

The man turned to face me. He had brown skin, black hair and kind brown eyes. This must be Tariq, I thought. He didn't move, stunned, it seemed, by what had happened, unsure which way to turn.

"Quickly," I yelled. "I'm a doctor." That did the trick. He ran into the room, grabbed the wheelchair and pushed it alongside the bed. Then he stood there, hesitating. "What?" I said, exasperated beyond words.

"Um, you're..."

I looked down. I was in my pyjamas.

"Oh for God's sake just pick me up, man."

"Right, yeah, of course."

I could hear a low keening noise coming from the landing as Tariq lifted me from my bed into the wheelchair and pushed me towards the two people on the floor. It was only when I reached the door that I realised who the shot man must be.

"Is that Lee's dad?"

"John, yeah," mumbled the Iraqi.

I heard heavy footsteps on the stairs and then John croaked: "A school. After all that, I buy it in a bloody school," and gasped. Lee bent over his dying father and moaned, a low piteous wail of pure emptiness and grief.

I looked to my left and saw Mrs Atkins, Sue and a Yank soldier racing towards us.

"Sue," I shouted. "You're a nurse, yes?"

"Yeah," she said as she skidded to a halt beside me.

"Who operated on me while I was out? Was it you?"

"No, Doctor Cox, he flew back to the main staging area with the general."

"Shit. But is the OR still in place? Did they strike the OR?"

She looked at me and gasped as she realised what I was suggesting.

"No, it's still there, hooked up to the generator and everything."

"Right, you," I said, pointing to the Yank soldier. "What's your name?"

"Jamal, Ma'am."

"Right, Jamal, pick this man up and take him to the OR now. Sue, wheel me downstairs. We have to work fast if we're going to save him."

Sue blanched. "I'm not qualified to..."

"No, but I am. I'll direct you. Sue, it's his only chance. We can do this."

She had gone white, but she nodded. "Ok," she whispered.

Jamal shoved himself past us and reached down to remove Lee, but Tariq blocked his way with a sneer and did it himself, holding Lee back as we moved away. I so wanted to stop and hold Lee, comfort him, feel the reality that he was back. But there was time for tearful reunions later.

"Sue, wheel me downstairs," I ordered. "We've got work to do."

The operating room that Blythe had used to fix me up had been erected in the kitchen. Ironically, it was the same room I'd used for my fake surgery on the captain who'd been shot here. I tried not to think about what I'd done that day, about the young soldier dying in my arms after I slit his throat. Too much blood on my hands.

A polythene clean-room had been erected using gaffer tape, and there was a makeshift airlock through which you entered the sterile area.

Jamal was standing inside the doorway, still holding John,

looking unsure about what to do when Sue wheeled me in. Mrs Atkins entered behind us.

I saw a rack of scrubs in the corner, a tub of alcohol handwash by the sink and a pile of tissue hats and facemasks beside it.

"Is he still breathing?" I asked as we entered.

Jamal nodded.

"Good. No time for protocol now. Jamal, get him on the operating table then get out again." He did so. "Back upstairs, help the others. Mrs Atkins, you're going to help Sue perform surgery."

She nodded briskly. Did nothing faze her?

"Right, both of you, take your shoes off, scrub up in the sink and get those hats and masks on. Where are the instruments?"

"Over there." Sue pointed to a trolley with a metal tray on top of it. In it rested a collection of surgical instruments, some still covered in blood.

"Shit. I suppose boiling water's out of the question?" I asked. Without a word Mrs Atkins walked behind the polythene sheets and I heard a click. She popped out again. "Kettle's on."

"Then let's get to work."

LEE

I sat on the landing, arms wrapped around my knees, rocking back and forth with my eyes closed, my clothes slick with my father's blood.

I felt a hand on my shoulder but I ignored it. It squeezed, trying to attract my attention. I reached up and batted it away. Then someone put their hand across my mouth. I opened my eyes, ready to shout, but Tariq's nose was an inch from mine and he had his finger to his lips. When he saw that I was with him he held up four fingers and pointed down. I saw past him to Jamal, who stood at the top of the stairs, gun raised, craning across the banister to look down into the entrance hall.

Tariq leaned forward and whispered into my ear.

"Wrong ear," I muttered. He switched.

"Sorry," he said. "At least four coming in the front, probably more out back. It was a trap, Lee. They must have been waiting for us to make a move."

"Dad?"

"In the kitchen. Matron and the others are operating on him now."

"Right, let's go."

"I think we..." he began, but I was already on my feet and moving past him. I lifted my machine gun to my waist with my left hand, took my Browning out with my right, and walked past Tariq and Jamal before they could react. I walked quickly, focused and calm, straight down the stairs, peripherally aware of Tariq running to stop me. As I descended I saw two soldiers moving cautiously through the entrance hall, silently checking the rooms. One of them saw me, but before he could warn his colleague or bring his weapon to bear I opened fire with the machine gun.

The bullets raked across his body, flinging him backwards as I crouched and fired the Browning, taking the other soldier three times in the chest. I stood up and kept moving.

Tariq fell into step beside me.

"They'll have heard that," he said wearily, like he was too tired to be angry.

"Good." I said coldly.

A stream of bullets flew past our heads. I dived down the last three steps, spinning in mid-air and letting off some shots at the shooter in the office door. I missed, but the doorframe splintered, momentarily distracting the gunman. Tariq stepped over me and shot the guy in the head.

I'd hit the hard tiled floor with my bad shoulder but I hardly even noticed the pain. I felt a knot of hatred in my belly as I leapt up. These fuckers had shot my dad and I wasn't going to stop until every last one of them was dead.

"Fucking deathwish Terminator shit," muttered Tariq.

I chambered another round and kept moving without acknowledging his sour disapproval. I thought: this must be what it feels like to be Rowles.

"Stryker," I barked at Jamal, who was halfway down the stairs. He nodded and ran to the vehicle, still jammed in the front door. I heard gunfire but didn't look back as Tariq and I walked into the school, guns raised. Past the staircase was a passage that led to the kitchen and the courtyard beyond it. Just as I was reaching forward to open the door, it swung open. I fired without hesitation, putting four rounds into the stomach of the soldier before me. Tariq opened fire beside me, sending a hail of bullets over the head of the falling soldier, wiping out the two men behind him. They fired back even as his bullets hit, but their shots went wide.

The second door on the right was the kitchen, and I ran inside. I could see a polythene tent. Inside it, Matron was directing Sue from her wheelchair as the nurse leaned over the kitchen table working on Dad.

"Time to go!" I shouted.

"We need two minutes to stabilise him," Jane yelled back.

A burst of gunfire came from behind me.

"No problem," I said, turning and opening fire at the soldiers coming towards me.

So help me, I smiled as I took their lives. Then Tariq and I walked on, looking for more.

JANE

THE THIRD AND final bullet landed with a clang as Sue dropped it into the small metal dish.

"What now?" she asked.

"His left lung's collapsed," I said. "He's drowning in his own blood. We need to aspirate. Have we got a tube of any kind?"

Mrs Atkins stepped across to a metal trolley cluttered with implements. She rifled through it and then waved a piece of clear plastic tube.

"Great. Sue, you need to puncture the lung and shove that in."

Sue took up her scalpel and got to work. I leaned forward so I could shout in John's ear.

"John, John Keegan. I need you to concentrate, John. Focus on my voice. I need you to take a deep breath, okay? Very deep, when I say. Can you do that?"

His eyes flickered and he moaned. I took that as a yes.

"Ready," said Sue, holding the tube, which now stuck out of his side.

"Now, John, breathe deep," I said, willing him to obey.

He gasped, then sucked air in through his mouth. It bubbled and gargled in him, then the tube filled with blood and the lung drained its load on to the floor.

I breathed a big sigh of relief. "Good."

There was the sudden shocking sound of gunfire from somewhere in the building. Sue and I exchanged worried glances, but she shrugged. Not our problem yet.

"What next?" Sue asked.

"Now let's patch and seal. We need some superglue. There's some in a tupperware box under the sink."

The gunfire resumed, louder and closer, as Mrs Atkins retrieved the small tube.

"Now glue the entry wounds together. I've a feeling we're going to be moving him before we're finished."

Sue was a calm and efficient nurse. When all this was done with, if she wanted to stay, I'd train her up as a doctor. We needed all the doctors we could get.

"Done," she said.

"Mrs Atkins, roll him over. Sue, come here."

The door crashed open.

"Time to go," yelled Lee.

"We need two more minutes to stabilise him," I shouted. I think he replied, but it was drowned out by gunfire. Then he was gone.

Mrs Atkins had rolled John on to his side so Sue and I could examine the exit wounds. One in particular bothered me. I reached into it and ran my gloved finger around his insides.

"Shit," I muttered. "Sue, glue the other two but this one you're going to have to make an incision, widen it, then go in and tie off the artery. Can you do that?"

"Yes, Ma'am."

The sound of gunfire was moving around the outside, to the courtyard. It was relentless and heavy; whoever Lee and the others were holding off, there were a lot of them. A sudden explosion blew in the windows and made Sue scream as one wall of the polythene clean-room came free and tumbled to the floor. She recovered her wits quickly and proceeded, her teeth gritted with determination.

She looked up and said "Done" the second Lee and Tariq ran into the room.

"Can we move him?" gasped Lee.

"Yes," I replied. "Sue, can you..." But she already had the wounded man in a fireman's lift.

Tariq leaned out of the door and let off a stream of fire then said: "Now!"

He went first, Sue and John behind, then Mrs Atkins pushing me in the chair, as Lee brought up the rear, firing short bursts to cover our retreat.

We left the corridor and came out into the main entrance hall. The armoured car was still stuck in the doorway, but the gun on top was pointing outside, laying down suppressing fire at the moat bridge.

Tariq climbed up on to the roof, then Sue and he manhandled John through the hatch and down into the car. I could see Sue talking urgently to Tariq as they worked, then she turned and leapt down, running past us all, back into the school.

"Where the hell is she going?" I shouted.

"Tell you later," replied Tariq, his head poking out of the hatch. "Now get in here."

Lee and Mrs Atkins carried me up as Tariq fired past us, and I made an ungainly entrance to the car. Lee was still firing as he closed the hatch above us.

"Go!" he shouted. Tariq put his foot down and tore us free of the doorway, reversing across the bridge, turning, and sending us speeding down the drive.

The Stryker started to clang as bullets raked the shell, but Jamal kept going and eventually the firing faded away in the distance. Once he was sure we were clear, he switched on the satnav and we headed for Fairlawne.

John was laid out on the bench opposite me and as our pursuers fell away I saw that he wasn't breathing. Lee was already performing CPR as Mrs Atkins held his father steady. Lee's face was splattered with blood and tears as he breathed and beat the life back into his dad. Eventually he shouted "Got him," and I saw John's chest rise and fall as he began to breathe again.

SITUATED OUTSIDE THE village of Shipbourne, the Fairlawne estate is a huge area of land once owned by the Cazlet family, horse breeders to the crown. Bought by a member of the Saudi royal family in the eighties, the Palladian house was fully renovated and restored. It even had a swimming pool. In many ways it was a better site for St Mark's than Groombridge – bigger, better equipped and closer to Hildenborough, where we had friends. But we chose Groombridge because of its moat, which we thought made it easier to defend. Now that we'd abandoned our second home in a year to enemy forces, it didn't seem like the smartest choice.

We were able to drive up to the front door without Tariq reporting any signs of life. Good, they'd been following my instructions. Secrecy was the best defence.

As long as we'd evaded pursuit – and Jamal, who'd both been watching the road behind us through the periscope, assured us that we had – then we should be safe, for a time at least.

Lee popped the hatch and climbed out, and a few minutes later a gang of boys had gathered to help me out.

I was home.

John had coped well with the journey. He was still unconscious but he didn't seem to be in any discomfort and his breathing and pulse were strong. When I looked up after checking him over I saw Lee watching me anxiously. Just for an instant I could see the frightened boy hiding behind the brutal façade. I gave him a smile of reassurance.

"He'll be fine," I said. But I was lying. I needed to get him into surgery again as quickly as possible, and this time I wouldn't have Sue to help me.

The boy relaxed, the mask came back down. Lee nodded briskly. "Good. Let's get you both inside."

We'd left my wheelchair behind in our rush to escape, so I made an undignified entrance, carried between Lee and Tariq past a sea of excited children, standing around the main entrance hall. Their murmuring faded away to shocked silence when I passed through. I tried to smile and put a brave face on it, but I was a sallow-cheeked, hollow-eyed wreck. I cursed the staff for not keeping them away. I had planned to clean myself up and make a dignified entrance at dinner; now that was blown to hell. I'd just have to make the best of it, but I knew that morale would suffer.

I couldn't worry about that now, though. I began issuing instructions for the creation of an operating theatre.

CHAPTER SEVENTEEN

LEE

I RUBBED THE sticking plaster that covered the cotton wool patch on the crux of my arm and wondered whether my light-headedness was a result of my ear injury, blood loss following the transfusion, or stress.

The sun was just rising above the horizon as I sat on the grass in the Fairlawne gardens, trying to calm myself and reflect on the events of the last twenty-four hours. So much to take in. Matron had been working on my dad for over half of it, all through the night without a break.

I heard the soft crunch of wheels on gravel approaching from behind. The sound changed as the wheelchair was pushed on to the grass. It came to a halt beside me and I heard someone walking away. I didn't look up, just sat there staring at my feet.

"If you're talking, I can't hear you," I said. "You'll have to speak up, I'm basically deaf."

"I've done all I can," said Jane eventually. "Your blood made all the difference. If he lives through the day, I think he'll be fine. But he's in bad shape."

"I know. And thanks." I looked up at her and smiled.

Her eyes were deep sunken with big brown rings around them and bags beneath. Her hair was all gone, shaved clean, and the left side of her scalp was covered by a large white dressing, which marked the site of her surgery. She was pale and emaciated, gaunt and wrecked, huddled in a wheelchair without even the strength to push herself from place to place.

"Jesus, Matron, you look like shit."

She laughed at me and said: "Look who's talking!"

"I didn't recognise you at first."

"And I thought that your dad was you. He sounds like you. Or you sound like him, whatever. Through the glass, in silhouette, I was sure it was you. When I thought you'd been shot..." She left the sentence hanging.

We sat there in silence for a while, watching the sun rise behind the trees. Then I told her my story, everything that had happened from the moment I'd walked away, all those months ago. She listened patiently and never asked any questions, letting me tell it straight.

When I'd finished she reached down and ran her fingers across my scalp.

"I'm glad you're back, Lee. I missed you."

I didn't meet her eyes, nervous of what I'd see there. I wouldn't admit it to myself, but if I looked up and all I saw was maternal affection, I think that would have been the straw that broke the camel's back. So I kept staring at my shoes, not wanting to know yet what it was she might feel for me. Better to leave it undefined for now. There was still so much to do.

"So where is everyone? What happened here?" I asked. And it was her turn to fill me in. As I listened to her tale I grew more and more angry at myself. Angry and ashamed.

"I should never have left," I said when she finished. "If I'd been here..."

"The same things would have happened, but there'd have been more shooting, probably," she said. "As it is, everyone's safe."

"Not Rowles and Caroline."

"No, not them. We have to decide what we're going to do about that."

"I have a few ideas," I said.

"But look at us, Lee. What chance do we have against Blythe and his army? A crippled matron, a deaf schoolboy and an Iraqi – did he say he was a blogger?"

"Yeah."

"An Iraqi blogger, some guy we hardly know and a man with three bullet holes in him. It's not exactly a task force."

"We have to do something," I insisted.

"Yes, we do. We have to hide. Get ourselves well, build up our strength. Bide our time. Come up with a plan."

"And while we're doing that, they secure their position, terrorise the populace, establish martial law across the south of England. No," I said forcefully. "They have to be stopped now. Because once they start setting up bases across the country they'll be too widely dispersed to fight. Our only chance is to take them all out in one fell swoop, while they're still all collected in the one place."

"Oh well, if that's all it takes," she mocked, "I'll call the mothership and get them to nuke Salisbury Plain from orbit, shall I? I want Rowles and Caroline back as much as you do, more so, probably. But there comes a point where you have to cut your losses. We can't win this one, Lee. We just can't."

I couldn't believe what I was hearing, and I felt the anger rising inside me as she spoke. I stood up and leaned over her.

"What happened to the Matron I knew, huh?" I spat furiously. "The woman who'd do anything to protect the kids in her care; the woman who'd stop at nothing to ensure the safety of others; the woman who stood up to Mac when no-one else would; the woman who showed me what true courage is? What happened to her? You don't even look like her."

I walked away in disgust, knowing even as I did so that I was out of order, being cruel and callous when I should have been kind and caring. But I couldn't help it. I was brim full of fury that had nowhere to go, so I took it out on her.

If she shouted after me, I didn't hear.

JANE

"HERE, TAKE THIS."

The voice made me jump. I hadn't heard anyone approaching. I wiped my eyes and looked up to see Tariq offering me a handkerchief. I smiled gratefully and took it, blowing my runny nose and wiping my eyes as the young Iraqi sat in the spot Lee had vacated a few minutes earlier.

"I saw him walking away," he said gently. "He looked angry."

I nodded.

"He is a very angry boy, I think," he continued. "You should not take whatever he said personally. He is young."

I snorted. "And how old are you, exactly?" I asked, not unkindly.

"Not so much older, it's true. But I grew up in a very different world to Lee. I did not expect freedom, I knew it would be something I had to fight for, and I knew the risks. I saw every day what a world run by bullies looked like. It seems to me to be almost the natural

413

way of things. For Lee, freedom is all he has ever known and now to have it taken away from him, it seems unfair. He is a teenager, too. I know he seems older, and he tries to pretend that he is a man. But he is a boy, still, with a boy's anger and a boy's loneliness. He is trying to be his father, you know? I have fought beside his father for a long time and he is strong, resolute, cunning. But he is not an easy man. He never rests, he is always moving. I do not think he really understands happiness. And Lee is more like his father than he knows."

I was taken aback. Here was this person I didn't know, talking to me like we were old friends. I almost got defensive, said "what do you know?" But I stopped myself. He meant well, I could see that. And what he said was true.

"I thought you were a blogger, not a psychoanalyst," I said with a wry smile.

He nodded sadly. "I think I am now a soldier, Miss Crowther. I think these days we all are, no matter what we may have been before."

"I don't want to be a soldier. Neither does Lee."

"I know. But the truth is, from what I hear of you, that you are both very good at it."

"Ha! Have you looked at the pair of us? We're in bloody pieces."

"But you are still standing." He looked up at the wheelchair, realised his mistake, and actually blushed. "I mean, you know what I mean. Sorry."

I laughed out loud. "Don't worry about it. Look, you may be right but I won't accept it. I'm not a soldier, neither is Lee. We're just normal people trying to get a little peace. That's all. I have to believe that one day we'll be left alone."

He shook his head sadly and said: "Not while General Blythe is in command, you won't. He'll be more convinced than ever that you're a threat now. He doesn't like loose ends. We have two choices: we destroy him or we run."

I was too tired to respond to that stark assessment. He rose and pushed me back towards the main house.

"Come on," he said. "Time for breakfast."

I STILL WASN'T ready to face the school, so we had breakfast in the kitchens. Lee was there, sullenly refusing to meet my eye. He, Jamal, Tariq and I feasted on scrambled eggs with fresh basil, and Mrs Atkins and Justin explained what had happened while I'd been unconscious in the sick bay of the school.

They had returned to Groombridge on their own to make sure it wasn't occupied by another group while the others remained at Fairlawne. Then Sanders, Jack and I rolled up to the door. Sanders insisted that Jack be taken to Fairlawne and kept safe, and Justin took him. Mrs Atkins and Sanders made me as comfortable as they could, but neither of them had medical training and I was in a very bad way. That night the Americans arrived in force. Sanders didn't even try to fight, recognising a lost cause when he saw one. Instead, he changed into civvies and pretended to be a farmer. I'd been in a car crash, he told the soldiers. It might have worked, but unfortunately he used my name as part of the cover story. There was no way he could have known they were looking for me, so why give me a pseudonym?

They started torturing him almost immediately. Mrs Atkins was locked up and I was taken away for emergency surgery. At some point Sanders must have broken enough to tell them he was SAS, but it seemed he'd told them nothing else. The Yanks certainly didn't know about Fairlawne or Jack.

It broke my heart to think what Sanders must have gone through. They didn't kill him for two weeks.

Once the school was secured most of the soldiers had gone back to Salisbury, leaving the school apparently exposed, luring Lee and the others into a trap.

And now the choice that faced us was simple: fight or flight. None of us could make our minds up.

"Run where?" asked Lee. "If what Matron's told us about Operation Motherland is true, Blythe's got overwhelming firepower and resources at his command, not to mention a well-drilled army. First he'll begin by terrorising the local population, like he did in Basra. Then he'll start recruiting and training. It won't be long before he takes control of the whole of southern England."

"We could head for the continent, I suppose," I said. "It might be the best option."

"We stayed and fought in Basra," said Tariq. "And John and I are the only survivors. If we try to fight the Americans it is most likely we will all end up with stakes through our chests. And I would like to avoid that if at all possible."

"Even if we do decide to leave, I won't leave Rowles and Caroline there and that's final," I said firmly. "Tariq, you've no ties here, you're free to go whenever you wish. But I will get those children to safety or die trying."

Tariq held my gaze for a moment then inclined his head, a small gesture of acknowledgment and respect. "Lee?"

Lee stared at me as if from a million miles away, finally acknowledging my presence. I held his gaze and smiled a small, sad smile. His face softened and he nodded.

"Yeah, okay," he said. "I owe Rowles my life several times over. We get him and Caroline out."

"Good," I said. "Then..."

"But that's all," said Lee. "You're right, Jane, we can't win this. I'm not starting a war. I don't care about revenge or justice or any of it. I'll go rescue my friends and then Dad and me are going somewhere far away from all of this. It's not my fight. Not any more."

"Fair enough," I said, hoping that I could persuade him to change his mind but knowing this was not the moment to try. "Tariq?"

The Iraqi sighed heavily and shook his head. "Fucking death wish," he muttered. Then he shrugged. "What the hell. I'm in. Jamal?"

"No, Sir," said the soldier. "I'll be hitting the road in the morning. See if I can't get to London, maybe find a way home."

Lee reached across and shook the American's hand. "Thank you for everything," he said. "And good luck."

"You too." He drained his mug and bid us goodbye.

"So what's the plan?" asked Tariq.

There was a long silence.

"I think we ought to talk to the king," I said. "But first, let's go join the school, shall we?"

LEE

JANE INSISTED ON walking into the dining room but she needed assistance, so I held her arm as she shuffled in.

When the children saw us they all rose to their feet and cheered, clapping their hands, whooping and hollering. Some of the little ones ran forward, arms wide, and I had to help her bend down so she could hug them. Green walked up to me, shook my hand, and told me how glad he was to see me. It was nice to be back amongst friends. When I helped Jane stand up again her eyes were brimming with tears. She waved everyone to sit down and I led her to the high table where she sat to address the school.

"Thank you all, so much," she said, uncharacteristically emotional. She wiped her eyes and laughed. "Sorry. As you can see I've been in the wars a bit since I left. But I'm going to be fine and I'm not going to be leaving the school again any time soon." More cheers. "But we have a problem, and I'm going to let Lee explain it to you."

I stepped to the front of the table and began my story, starting with my arrival in Iraq and leaving nothing out. They were children, but they needed to know what we were up against. Nobody made a sound when I had finished. I then handed the floor back to Jane, who told her tale, bringing the school up to date, omitting only to mention the king, who she had subtly pointed out to me as we entered, sitting comfortably with the senior boys.

"So here's what we're going to do," she said finally. "Lee is going to lead a rescue mission to recover Rowles and Caroline. It's important that you know we would do the same for any and all of you. We won't leave our children behind. But when Lee returns with them – and he will – we don't know what the future may hold. It's not over yet, but we promise we will keep you safe whatever it takes. In the meantime, classes as usual." There were some good natured groans, and breakfast resumed, the hum of conversation rising until it was almost deafening.

"Let's get out of here and go somewhere quieter," said Jane. As we walked to the door she looked over and gave the king a nod. The boy rose and left by another door.

We had plans to make.

"THESE ARE THE petrol tankers," said King Jack, pointing at the large map he'd drawn for us. "There are hundreds of them, all full. Here we have the tanks, here the non-armoured motor vehicles, and here the fire engines and ambulances. To the north is the parade ground, and this whole swathe of buildings is the barracks. Then we've got the shooting ranges here and here, the training ground here, mess, medical centre and MP station. That may be where any prisoners are being held, in the cells. This is the main admin building, so it's probably where the general has his office. Then out further east you've got the houses and flats, accommodation for married couples and officers."

"And what's this?" I asked, pointing to a red cross next to the admin building.

"That is the main entrance to the tunnels. There's another one here," he drew another cross by a firing range. "This one's disguised as a cupboard, so there's a slim chance they don't know about it. If they don't, then it's our way in. I imagine the Americans have blown the main entrance by now. If so, there's a good chance that the prisoners might be down there."

"What was kept down there?" I asked.

Jack hesitated. "I suppose top secret doesn't really mean anything any more, does it?"

"Not really," said Jane.

"The tunnels have got all the really nasty stuff in them," he said. "The weapons of mass destruction."

I hadn't known what to expect when Jane had told me we had the king in our midst, but Jack was a normal kid. He sounded middle class rather than posh, he didn't put on airs and graces at all, and he insisted we call him Jack.

"Thank you for this Jack," I said. "It'll be helpful."

He looked surprised. "But I can show you myself. I mean, I'm coming with you."

"Out of the question," I said curtly.

"But I know the layout better than any of you. I'm the only one who can lead you safely though that place."

"We've got a woman on the inside," I said. "She's going to meet us and take us where we need to go. We don't need you. Anyway, what combat experience have you got?"

"Sanders taught me everything he knew," said the boy defensively.

"But have you ever actually been in a fight?"

"I was there when the Americans attacked."

"That's true, Lee," said Jane. "One of the few things I remember is Jack shooting at them."

"Look," he said. "At the moment it's just you and this Iraqi guy, right?"

"My name's Tariq," said the man standing beside Jack.

"Right, sorry. Tariq. Neither of you know the compound like I do, and you could use the backup."

I shook my head. "No. This is a mission of stealth. In, grab, out. With luck we'll be gone before they realise we were ever there. The more of us there are, the greater the risk of us being detected. And I'll be honest, I don't trust you not to go and do something stupid, like trying to blow the place up."

Our glorious majesty sulked for a moment and then said something which changed my mind.

"There's one very special warehouse down there…" he began. We listened until he'd finished speaking; all of us with our mouths open in astonishment.

"And you know the codes?" I asked incredulously.

He nodded. "Sanders showed me. I persuaded him it was my royal prerogative. I think he thought it was funny."

We were all silent for a moment and then Tariq clapped his hands and said: "Well shit, now we've got a ball game!"

JANE

THAT NIGHT JUSTIN and Tariq helped me to a downstairs room they'd prepared for me. After they'd gone I lay in the cool sheets feeling the soft cotton pillowcase on my naked scalp.

I was too nervous to sleep, unsure of what I felt. My joy at Lee's return, my fears for his safety and that of everyone in the school who I'd unwittingly put into the firing line, the loss of Sanders. It was all too much to process. So I lay there, unable to sleep, until I heard a soft knock at the door.

"Hello?" I said.

The door cracked open and Lee stepped inside. "Hi."

"Hey."

He came and sat on the bed next to me, avoiding my gaze. "I'm sorry. For shouting at you this morning, I mean. That was out of order."

I reached out and squeezed his hand. "Don't worry about it."

"It's just, with Dad and you… I mean, he might die and you look so ill. I just…"

"He's going to be fine. He's had a good day. He's sleeping it off naturally now. He's over the worst."

"I thought I'd lose him, too," he whispered. "Like Mum."

"No. Not today, anyway."

He bowed his head, took a deep breath and said softly: "I killed her."

"Sorry?"

"She was so sick. She couldn't stop crying. It was awful. Then there were the seizures and she started bleeding from everywhere. And I couldn't help. I couldn't do anything for her. I sat there mopping her brow with a wet flannel and telling her it'd be okay. In the end she begged me to kill her, to make the pain stop. She'd never have asked me to do that if it hadn't driven her mad. And when she said that, when she said 'Please kill me,' I stopped crying. Because here was something I could actually do, you know? Here was a way I could help her. So I took a pillow and I smothered her. And you know what? She didn't struggle. She put her hand up and held mine, even as I was using it to choke the life out of her. She held my hand and she squeezed it, just like you're doing now. She was grateful, so it didn't feel like murder. Bates felt like murder, even though I suppose that was a mercy killing too. But Mum? No. 'Cause I loved her so much. She was kind and funny and she used to sing me to sleep when I was little. And when she died I thought, that's it. I've killed the person I loved most in the world, the only person left who loved me. I thought I'd actually killed love and that I was broken now, forever.

"Then I came back to school and found you. And then Dad."

He began to cry great heaving sobs. I pushed myself up and wrapped my arms around him, pulling him down on to the bed beside me. I held him as he wept, stroking his head and shushing him into a deep, silent sleep.

LEE

"Dad, I dunno if you can hear me, but I've got to go. Blythe's got a couple of the kids from the school and Tariq and me are going to get them back. I know what you'd say if you were awake, but if you were in my shoes, you'd do exactly what I'm doing now and you know it.

"I reckon we'll be back in a week or so. By then you'll be up and about, I'm sure, waiting to bite my head off for being so reckless.

"If I don't come back, then you'll be among friends here. Jane will take good care of you, and I want you to take good care of her in return. She's special. You haven't met her yet, but she saved your life and mine. Only she's not as strong as she makes out, sometimes. She's better when she's got someone to lean on. And if I don't come back, that's going to have to be you.

"When you called me from Iraq that time you told me to be strong. For Mum. I didn't let you down. You'll never know how strong I was. Now I need you to be strong for me, and for her. I know you will be. You keep sleeping it off and I'll see you soon. I love you, Dad.

"Bye."

*   *   *

JANE REACHED OUT and took my hand.

"I would ask you not to go, but you wouldn't listen, would you?" she said with a sad smile.

"No. But I came back last time, and I'll be back again. I promise. And this time I'll be staying. I meant it, you know. No more fighting for me. I've had enough. I just want to stay here and look after the school. With you. In mono."

Jane laughed. "How is the other ear?"

"Almost back to normal now. I'd say about 80%."

"That's what you get for trying to be a soldier."

"You can talk, Davros."

"Oi!"

I leaned forward, put my hands on her sunken cheeks and kissed her. Then I rested my forehead on hers and closed my eyes.

"I'll see you soon, Jane."

"You'd better, Lee."

Then I stood up and walked away.

I didn't look back.

CHAPTER EIGHTEEN

LEE

"Anything?" I asked.

"No. Just static," replied Tariq.

"And you're sure you got the frequency right?"

"Of course."

"And the clock's right?"

"She said three every morning. She'll be here, Lee. Relax."

The radio gave two bursts of white noise.

"That's her." Tariq pressed the speak button on the Stryker radio and squawked back four times. There was a pause and then the radio crackled into life.

"That you, Tramp?" It was Sue, whispering.

"Yes. Where are you?"

"South perimeter. There's a firing range by the fence."

"I know where she is," said Jack. "We can be there in five minutes."

"Did you hear that, Lady?"

"Sure did. There are perimeter patrols, so go carefully. I'll be waiting."

"See you soon." Tariq clicked the radio off and we primed our weapons.

We had parked the armoured car in woodland close to the base. Although we'd encountered no patrols or guards of any kind, Blythe had begun stamping his authority on the area.

We'd passed Stonehenge on the way to the base; the ancient stone circle was full of staked soldiers, hundreds of them, lined up in concentric circles, staring at the stars, like an offering to an ancient god.

We had no doubt that we'd suffer a similar fate if we were caught. I used the periscope to scan our surroundings. "All clear," I said. We turned off the interior lights and cracked the hatch, climbing out into the cold night air. It was a dark, moonless night, but Jack was wearing a nightsight Jamal had given us before he left.

Leaving the Stryker behind us, we let Jack take the lead. I didn't know what to make of this boy king. He was an uneasy mix of overconfidence and insecurity. He'd been reticent about his royalty, unwilling to explain how he ended up the ceremonial head of state, at least in the eyes of the British Army. Green told me he'd been eager to blend into the background, unwilling to draw undue attention. Yet here he was leading us into the heart of enemy territory on a mission to rescue two children he'd never met. When I asked him why he had insisted on accompanying us he just said it was his duty. I had no idea how he'd fare in combat, but his knowledge of the base, and the ordnance contained within it, was our ace in the hole.

We reached the edge of the trees, where the cover abruptly ended in a fifty-metre stretch of clear grass. Beyond this stood a high chainlink fence. Crouching down, Jack scanned the buildings for movement. He saw a patrol and gestured for us to retreat back into cover. Hidden by the shadows, we watched the two guards walk past us and disappear past the barracks.

"That's the firing range." Jack pointed to a high brick wall just inside the fence. I reached behind me and pulled the wire cutters from my back pack.

"Stay here," I whispered.

I broke cover and scurried to the fence. Lying on the wet grass, I cut a small hole at the base, wincing at the noise each wire made as it snapped. I pulled back a flap of the fence to make an entrance and waved the other two forward. Once they had crawled inside, I followed and pulled the fence closed again. With any luck, the guards wouldn't notice the hole on their next circuit. Stashing the wire cutters back in my bag, I followed Jack as he led us round the wall at the far end of the firing range to a sandpit where cardboard cut out soldiers stood like silent sentries.

"Psst." It was Sue, standing at the corner of the wall, dressed in black, her face covered in boot polish just like ours. She didn't waste any time. "There are three perimeter patrols and they pass here about every twenty minutes. There are other random patrols wandering the base. They don't have a set pattern, so we have to move carefully.

"Where are they?" I asked.

"The boy is being held in the tunnels under the main building, which is where Blythe works and sleeps."

"How did they get into the tunnels?" asked Jack.

"They blew up the door by the main building," replied Sue.

"And the other door?"

"What other door?"

Jack turned to me and grinned.

"And the girl, Caroline?" I asked.

"They never found any girl," said Sue. "What's the plan?"

Tariq told her and she pursed her lips in surprise. "That's a bit extreme," she said. But she didn't raise any objections.

"This way," said Jack. He led us down the length of the firing range and across a road to a small outbuilding with a big metal door. He punched a code into the keypad beside the door and it clicked open. We hurried inside and pulled the door closed behind us, then crept down the concrete steps into the system of tunnels that lay beneath the base. The walls were concrete, with electric cables and pipes running along them. It smelt of damp. The lights were on.

"Knives only," whispered Tariq, drawing his blade and pushing his gun back over his shoulder. "A shot down here would be heard through the whole tunnel system."

Jack moved quickly and confidently, sure of the way. He led us past endless doors, all locked tight. "Some of these go down to other chambers, some are just offices. The two places we're interested in are at opposite ends of the complex."

"Okay," I said. "Two teams, as discussed. Sue, we're going to get Rowles. Tariq and Jack, rendezvous back at the door we came in by." They nodded. "And if you hear shooting, just run. Don't wait for us, or come to help. Just go."

Tariq took my hand and shook it firmly. "See you soon."

They vanished around a corner and I turned to the small, squat nurse. "Lead on."

She moved with remarkable grace for someone so solid, and we hardly made a sound as we moved deeper into the tunnels. Eventually she held up her hand.

"One more corridor and a left turn," she whispered. "There aren't guards outside the actual cell; they're up top at the door. So we shouldn't meet anyone." I stepped forward and took the lead, knife at the ready.

"Stay here," I said. I walked down the corridor, feeling my nerves giving way to the calm that comes before the kill. I reached the corner and took a quick look. Nobody. I waved Sue forward. She went past me to a nondescript wooden door.

"I lifted this earlier," she said waving a key in the air and then using it to open the door. We entered a small, bare room. All the furniture had been removed, leaving it a cold concrete box. There was no light and the smell was awful. The light that seeped in from the corridor revealed a small figure curled up asleep in the corner, and a bucket in the opposite corner. It was just like the cell where I'd found Dad in Basra. Blythe's bag of tricks was small but effective.

I crouched down and shook the boy's shoulder. He was awake instantly. I don't know what I'd been expecting to find. The Rowles I knew was quiet and brooding, utterly self contained and unemotional. He was so ruthless, so terrifying, that I'd forgotten one simple fact: he was an eleven-year-old boy.

His right eye was horribly bruised, swollen shut. His front teeth were gone, as were his fingernails, and his bare arms were covered in tiny cigarette burns. His one good eye wasn't the cold orb I remembered; instead it was full of fear. Rowles scrambled away from me, trying to hide himself in the corner, burying his head in his arms and keening like a kicked dog.

"My God," breathed Sue.

"Rowles," I said firmly. "Rowles, it's me. It's Lee. We've come to get you out of here."

The ruined child couldn't hear me above his petrified whining. I reached out and put my hand on his shoulder, but he flinched away.

"Rowles," I said, louder this time. "Listen, it's Lee. From school. I've come to take you home."

Still no response. I cursed under my breath. We didn't have time for this. I reached forward and grabbed his head, holding his face up and forcing him to look at me.

"Rowles. Come on. We've got to go home."

His eye focused on me then and widened in surprise. "Home?" he whispered. "Home?"

"Yes, home. Can you stand?" His chin wobbled convulsively as he tried to nod. "Good lad. This is Sue, she's a nurse, she's going to help you."

"Hello sweetheart," said Sue. "You take my hands now." Rowles did so, his animal panic replaced by mute acquiescence. I went back to the door and scanned the corridor. Still quiet. I began to think that maybe we'd get away with this.

I turned back to see Rowles standing up. Sue had wrapped her arms around him and he was huddling into her for warmth, snuffling.

"Rowles, this is important. What happened to Caroline? Is she here?" I asked.

"Doctor," he muttered. "The doctor took her."

"So she's not on the base?" He shook his head.

"This can wait," Sue said sternly.

I nodded. "Okay, let's go."

I led the way back through the silent tunnels. We had to move more slowly, as Rowles was weak and disorientated, but we encountered nobody until we arrived back at the door where Jack and Tariq were waiting for us.

"Any joy?" I asked.

Jack shook his head. "I found and primed them but I couldn't find the remote units anywhere. Sorry."

"It was always a long shot," I said. "Let's not worry about it now. We've got what we came for. Let's get the fuck out of here."

And we did. We didn't meet any guards at all on our way back to the Stryker. I leaned against the cold metal hull of the vehicle and breathed a huge sigh of relief. We'd made it.

I climbed on to the vehicle and opened the hatch, turned to the others, smiled and said, "Let's go home."

And that's when I noticed we were missing someone.

"I won't leave him," I insisted.

"Tariq chose to go back, Lee" said Jack. "He may be planning to detonate. We need to get out of here."

I shook my head. "No. He's gone to get Blythe, and he'll want to do it personally. If I go quickly, I might be able to catch him up. Get everyone inside and batten the hatch. Sue, have you got your radio?" She handed it to me without a word. "I'll call if I can but if I'm not back in an hour, you go without me. Understand?" Sue nodded. I looked across at Rowles. He had stopped whining and was sitting on the bench holding a handgun, staring at it intently, almost caressing it. I fancied I could see a flash of the boy I knew.

"You get him back safe to Fairlawne," I said.

"Lee, it's suicide!" said Jack.

"Just give me the door code," I snapped back. Shaking his head, Jack used a biro to write it on my palm.

Then I grabbed the nightsight and climbed out of the Stryker, back into the darkness.

Why did I go back for Tariq? He'd made the choice to go after Blythe without consulting me. He almost certainly hadn't told me because he didn't want me risking my life too. So we'd not managed to wipe out the Yanks, like we'd hoped, but we'd accomplished our primary mission – rescuing Rowles – and escaped. Going back in was foolhardy and, yes, suicidal. So why did I go after him? I've thought about it a lot and the only answer that I can give is that I wouldn't have been able to face my dad if I hadn't.

I snaked under the fence and ran for cover. My best chance of making it to the main building alive was to use the tunnels again. Jack's door code let me in, and I descended once more into the cool, silent passageways. I retraced my earlier steps to the cell where Rowles had been kept and beyond. Eventually I reached a staircase. This was it, the door by the main building. I looked up and saw that the door had been blown clean off. Now there was just a waist-high wooden barrier. I couldn't see or hear anything at the top, but I knew there would be at least one guard. I drew my knife and steadied my breathing. Time to fight.

I crept up the stairs as softly as I could, ready to throw the knife into the chest of anyone who stepped on to the doorway. But nobody did. When I reached the top I risked a furtive glance outside, left and right. The two guards were already dead, lying in pools of blood by the sides of the doorway. Tariq had been here.

I looked to my left and saw a large brick building with imposing steps at the front leading to double doors. This must be the HQ. My nightsights picked out a tiny movement and I realised the front door was just closing. I should have checked the area, but I didn't want to wait. I took a deep breath and sprinted for the door, expecting a hue and cry at any second. None came, and I vaulted up the steps and through the door as fast as I could, wondering how long my luck could possibly hold.

Not, as it turned out, that long.

A long, carpeted corridor stretched out ahead of me. In the middle of it, Tariq was struggling with an American soldier, trying to get him in a neck lock as the man writhed and tried to shout for aid. Tariq had his forearm jammed into the man's mouth, and was trying not to scream as the soldier bit down. I hurried to his aid, and slid my knife in between the American's ribs, up into his heart. He stiffened and then relaxed into Tariq's arms. We dragged the corpse into a broom cupboard and stashed it.

"We have to go. Now," I whispered urgently, grabbing Tariq's bitten arm.

Tariq shook me off and kept going. "You heard what Sue said, Blythe sleeps in this building. I'm not leaving him alive, Lee."

He began climbing the stairs and I ran after him, grabbing him again.

"Tariq, this is madness. You've seen what he's like. If we go now, we might just make it."

The Iraqi shook his head. "No more running. This ends now. You shouldn't have come after me." He put his hand on my shoulder. "Go, Lee. This is my fight."

This was a different Tariq to the man I'd come to know. The light-hearted geek was gone, replaced by cold fury and suicidal vengeance. Suddenly he made sense. This was a man who would lead a resistance movement, who'd stand his ground no matter what, who'd stage mock executions to terrify enemy combatants into talking. I realised that I hardly knew Tariq at all. The celebrity blogger was the person he had been; this ruthless warrior, the side of himself that he kept carefully hidden, was the person The Cull had fashioned him into.

He turned away and kept climbing the stairs. I stood there for a moment, torn between my loyalty to the man who'd saved my life in Iraq and my duty to Rowles, Jane and Dad. But there was really no choice. I went after him.

The first floor corridor stretched to my left and right. Tariq had turned left, and was standing halfway down, outside the only door that had a chink of light showing around the frame. He drew his gun and opened the door in one swift movement, stepping inside, weapon raised. I padded along to the room, drawing my own gun as I ran. When I entered, I saw Tariq standing with his back to me. I stepped to one side to see who he was aiming his gun at. Sure enough, sat on a large double bed with a book resting on his lap, was General Jonas Blythe.

He was smiling.

"Tariq," I said.

"I know," he replied.

"You're thinking this was far too easy, ain't you, kid?" said the general, still smiling.

"Shoot him and let's go," I urged.

428

There was the sound of doors being flung open and boots stomping down the corridor. Then a cacophony of voices were yelling at us to lay down our weapons, put our hands above our heads and get on our knees. I don't know why they bothered, since they didn't give us time to comply. I felt a rifle butt smash into the backs of my legs and I pitched forward on to the floor.

I'm unsure whether the next sharp crack was Tariq trying to shoot Blythe, or the big heavy thing that cracked my skull and sent me spinning into unconsciousness.

THE FIRST THING I heard was screaming.

I shook my head to clear it, trying to ignore the crippling pain. I was tied into a chair by my wrists and ankles, but I wasn't in a cell or warehouse; I was in an office. Quite a nice one, with lots of wood, and paintings of old battles on the walls. I looked to my left and saw Tariq, also tied up. Blythe was standing in front of him, puffing hard on his cigar, making the tip glow bright orange. Then he stubbed it out on Tariq's naked belly and the Iraqi gritted his teeth, staring at the general in furious defiance, all the muscles in his body straining with the effort of not screaming again.

We were both facing the window, so I could see that it was still dark outside. I scanned the room quickly for a clock and found one on the mantelpiece. Four-fifteen. The others should have driven away by now. That was something at least.

I knew that our chances of survival were nil. I'd overplayed my hand and walked into danger one too many times. There was no cunning plan to rescue us, no force capable of fighting their way in here and overwhelming the entire American Army. The only allies we had for miles were a traumatised child, a boy who would be king, and a nurse. And by now they were driving as fast as they could in the opposite direction. The only thing left was to give them as much time as I could.

"Hey Tariq," I croaked. "I think you were right. I think maybe I do have a death wish." I began to laugh.

The general stepped sideways and punched me full in the face. His enormous fist was like a brick and I felt my nose crack. The momentum knocked the chair over and I toppled to the floor. I lay there and laughed as I spat out the blood.

The general nodded to someone behind me and my chair was uprighted. The general stepped back and sat on the edge of his desk, puffing on his cigar.

"Did you really think our security was that bad?" he asked.

"We hoped," groaned Tariq.

"I'm curious to know how you got into the tunnels. You didn't blow your way in like we did, so you must have had the code. Hook up with some soldiers who escaped?"

"Nah," I said. "Didn't you know? We're spooks! We know everything, don't we Tariq?"

"That's right, 007," said Tariq, following my lead.

"Yeah, top special agents, that's us. I heard you met our shadowy boss, The Matron. Let her slip through your fingers though, didn't you. Loser!"

The general smiled. God, I hated it when he did that.

"It doesn't matter," he said. "I'll have complete control of this whole country within the year."

"Right," I laughed. "Wherever will she hide in this huge and almost entirely empty country, which you intend to rule with a few hundred soldiers? You're right, she hasn't got a chance."

"Yeah," added Tariq. "It's not like me and a bunch of friends managed to evade capture in a city for over a year is it?"

Blythe stood up and walked over to Tariq, leaning forward so that he almost touched noses. "And look at what happened to all of you," whispered the soldier.

"Do you really, seriously, think we're spies?" I said. "I mean, come on. You must have worked it out by now, clever bloke like you."

Blythe turned to me, his face full of barely controlled fury. "I know that you managed to turn my son against me. That's all I need to know."

And there it was, the chink in his armour. In spite of all the coldness and detachment he'd displayed at the time, the murder of David was preying on his conscience.

Tariq noticed it too, and this time he took the lead. "We didn't turn your son, General," he said quietly. "He came to us of his own free will."

"Never," spat Blythe. "My son was a good soldier."

"Your son was a traitor," I said. "And he hated you."

"He approached us," said Tariq. "Said he wanted our help to bring you down."

"Couldn't wait to lock you up and throw away the key."

"Said you were a madman."

"Sadist."

"Psychopath."

"A traitor to everything you'd ever believed in."

"He hated you, General."

"Hated you."

The general roared as he grabbed a pistol from the desk and shot Tariq in the gut and me in the leg.

My vision blurred but I was actually glad. Bleeding out like this would be a hell of a lot easier than being staked or electrocuted. Maybe if I taunted him some more he'd even put a bullet in my head.

I hyperventilated, trying to make the pain subside. I'd been shot in the other leg the year before; I remembered this pain and knew I could master it.

"Don't talk about my boy like that," said the general, his voice full of calm menace.

I looked around and saw that Tariq was fading away. The blood from his gut wound was dripping down his naked torso and soaking into his trousers. His eyes were rolling back in his head.

My leg wound wasn't that bad. It hadn't hit the artery so it wasn't life threatening. I needed Blythe to shoot me again.

"Who, David?" I shouted. "The baby you nursed, the boy you played football with, the man you trained? The man you murdered? The son who loathed and detested everything you stand for? Him?"

The general roared in fury and came at me, pistol whipping me over and over until I blacked out. As the world slipped away, I felt only relief. It was all over. I didn't need to fight any more. My battles were done, my sacrifice made, all my sins paid for. I let the comforting darkness embrace me and I fell into deep, soft, warm oblivion. My last thoughts were of Jane and Dad. I saw them in my mind's eye, standing on the grass outside the original St Mark's. They were holding hands and smiling at me, their faces full of love.

"I'm proud of you, son," said Dad.

"I love, you, Lee," said Jane.

I felt myself floating free of my body.

"Sod this," said the voice in my head, pulling me back to reality. "I'm not having this at all. Pull yourself together, Nine Lives. Don't be such a loser. Wake the fuck up, find a way out of this, and castrate this motherfucker, or I'll come back from the dead and do it my bloody self."

I COULD HEAR a voice. I listened carefully, assuring myself that it was external. The accent was American but the voice was unfamiliar.

I was still tied up, my leg was wet with blood and I hurt all over. My head felt like it was going to burst. I tried to open my eyes but found only one of them would respond; the other was swollen shut.

"...spied her rounding up the children," the voice was saying.

Squinting, one-eyed, through the blood, I saw the general standing by his desk talking to someone I couldn't make out.

"I'm sorry, Sir, I don't understand," he said. "What exactly am I supposed to do with the children we capture?"

"Put 'em on a plane to New York, General. We have need of them here."

I couldn't be sure, but it sounded like the voice was coming from a speaker. Of course – he was on the video link, talking to his bosses in America. But it wasn't the president this time, merely one of his subordinates.

"Let me be clear," said the general. "We're in a position to impose rule of law on this whole island, but the primary objective of our occupation of Britain is to capture all the children and ship them to America?"

"Yes, General."

"May I ask why, Sir?"

"You may not," said the man, smugly. "Those are your orders and you will carry them out. Am I to understand that you have an issue with this directive?"

"I just don't understand, Sir. We've spilt a lot of blood getting to this point. I've done some things... some things I'm not entirely comfortable with. A new beginning, he said. A new American empire, won through force of arms but proceeding in justice. Those were the president's exact words to me, Sir."

"Don't quote the president to me, General."

"But how is that to be achieved by rounding up children?"

"That's not your concern, soldier," barked the man. "I possess information that you do not. There is a bigger picture here and you will play your part. That is your job, General, lest you forget. I am your commander-in-chief and I have given you a direct order that you will obey. Is that clear?"

There was a long silence.

"I said is that clear?" shouted the man.

"Yes, Sir," replied the general quietly.

"Then snap to it, soldier."

I tried to turn my head to see how Tariq was doing, but I got shooting pains in my neck every time I tried, so I gave up. Eventually

I managed to open my good eye fully and I saw the general turning off the video conference.

"Trouble with management?" I asked, my voice sounding weak even to myself.

The general turned to face me, his face troubled and uneasy. "You still alive?"

"My granddad...." I broke off in a fit of coughing that brought blood up into my mouth. I spat it out, took a ragged breath, and went on. "My granddad was a soldier. Major General. He told me an army is only as good as the orders it receives. Who's giving your orders, General? 'Cause from where I'm sitting, it sounds like your boss is a crazy old fucker who might just be the world's biggest paedophile. And if you're taking orders from him, that makes you the world's biggest kiddie pimp. Ask yourself, General, is that what you signed up for?"

Blythe walked over to me and stared into my face, studying me. He was calmer now, his fury spent. "Who the hell are you, boy? The things you do, the way you talk. I can't decide whether you're the bravest soldier I ever met, or some kind of lunatic."

I laughed, but it sounded more like a dying gasp. "I told you, General. I'm just a boy trying to protect my family."

"I think I'm starting to believe you."

"What are you trying to protect, General? What's your endgame?"

"Same as it ever was, son," he said firmly. "Freedom."

"And this is freedom, to you? Torture, massacre, impaling civilians on stakes, burning them alive in football stadiums, killing your own son when he questions your motives. This is your freedom?"

He shook his head, momentarily allowing the doubt and weariness to show on his granite face. "No, son, it isn't."

"So what's this all for?" I yelled. "Why are you following these orders?"

"Because I'm a soldier, it's all I know how to do. It's what I am, a thing that follows orders, no matter what the cost. I don't know how to stop." He paused and then said softly "'I am in blood stepped so far that, should I wade no more, returning were as tedious as go o'er.'"

He stepped back then, shook his head, took his handgun from his desk and raised it so it was pointing right between my eyes.

"I'm sorry, son. Close your eyes."

I shook my head as much as I was able. "No, General. Eyes open."

"So be it."

He squeezed the trigger, the hammer retracted, and I waited for the impact that would end me.

CHAPTER NINETEEN

"Hello? Anybody there?"

The voice crackled out of my left trouser pocket.

The general narrowed his eyes. "Thought you'd come alone." He put the gun down and fished the radio out of my trouser pocket. It was slick with blood, and he wiped it clean on my other trouser leg.

"Lee, Tariq, you there?" It was Jack. I cursed inwardly. So they'd ignored my instructions and waited for us, which meant that now they'd be captured and all of this would have been for nothing.

The general held the radio up to his mouth and pressed the transmit button. "I'm afraid the boys can't come to the phone right now. Can I take a message?"

For a few seconds all we heard was the crackle of static and then Jack said "Good morning, General." He was keeping a cool head. Good. "Are they still alive?"

"The boy is. The Iraqi" – he glanced at Tariq – "is still breathing. Don't know if he'll be doing that for much longer. To whom am I speaking?"

"You're addressing the rightful King of England, General. I rule this country, and you are not welcome here."

What the hell was his game? He should know by now that this was not a man you bluffed. I sat there, powerless to intervene, terrified for my friends. I hoped Jack knew what he was doing.

The general laughed. "Son, you sound about fifteen."

"I'm not the first fifteen-year-old king of England, General. And I won't be the last. I'm calling to give you a simple choice."

Blythe rolled his eyes for me, a moment of theatre. Then, grinning, he said "Your Majesty?"

"Leave now. Get in your planes and go back to America. Or I will

434

destroy you and your army utterly." His voice wavered, betraying his nervousness. He didn't quite pull it off, and the effect was awkward rather than threatening.

For a moment the general was too stunned to respond. Then he began to laugh, a deep, rich, booming laugh. "My God, you Brits really know how to raise your kids!"

"Unlike you, General," I said pointedly. That stopped his laugher abruptly.

He flashed me a look of pure hatred and spoke into the radio again. "How exactly do you propose to destroy me, young Majesty? You've got no army left. I've seen to that."

"He's got me, you bastard." That was Rowles, and he sounded anything but nervous. "And that's all he needs."

Blythe shook his head in wonder. "Son, you may have killed some of my men, but... oh, this whole conversation is ridiculous. Where are you, anyway? I presume Keegan let you out of your cell."

"I'm still in the tunnels, General," said Rowles. "In a big underground warehouse with a large nuclear symbol on the door."

Oh.

Oh fuck.

The general saw my eyes widen in shock. He became cautious, my reaction leading him to believe that maybe this wasn't a bluff. He waved at the soldier standing behind me. "Go," he said curtly, and I heard the man open the door and run down the corridor.

"What do you know about this?" Blythe asked me.

I had to think very carefully about what I said next.

"I know that Rowles is a psychopath who doesn't seem to value his own life at all," I said slowly. "I know that he really, really doesn't like people in uniforms telling him what to do. I know that he's been tortured horribly and that probably hasn't left him in the best frame of mind. Oh, and I know that Jack – that's Your Majesty to you – knows the detonation codes for the nuclear warheads collected by Operation Motherland. The ones in the big underground warehouse with the nuclear symbol on the door."

The radio crackled again. "I can hear your soldiers coming down the tunnel, General," said Rowles. "If anybody tries to enter this warehouse, I'll detonate."

"He will, too," I said. "He has... issues."

Blythe narrowed his eyes, thinking hard. He hit the transmit button. "What do you want, son?"

"I want to kill you," spat Rowles, full of hatred. "With a knife, not a gun. Slowly. I want to cut you up, piece by piece. I want to gouge out your eyes, puncture your eardrums, rip out your tongue, slice off your nose, pull out your nails and teeth and hair, cut off your cock and make you eat it, then very, very slowly push my knife into your brain through your eye socket and stir."

Christ.

"I told you," I said. "Issues."

"I'll settle for blowing you up, though. And your army."

"And your friends, and yourself," said the general.

"If I have to."

"Here's what we want, General." It was Jack again. "We are going to drive to the main gate. You are going to bring Lee and Tariq to us and let us drive away."

"What's to stop the boy blowing us up once you've gone?" asked Blythe. "If he is as suicidal as Keegan says he is."

"Nothing except my word," said Rowles. "All you need to know for certain is that if you don't do as I ask, I'll definitely blow us all to hell."

"It's a good offer, General," I said. "I'm done with fighting. Once I leave here, you'll never see me or any of my friends again. We'll just vanish, and you can get on with doing whatever it is your boss wants done. We won't oppose you, we just want to leave. Probably France, maybe Spain, I dunno. But away. Let us go, you live, everyone's happy."

Through the window behind Blythe I could see a thin line of light appear on the horizon. Dawn was coming.

The door behind me opened and someone began giving a report.

"There is someone in the nuclear warehouse, General," said the soldier I couldn't see. "We've drilled through from the corridor and inserted a mini-cam. The boy is sitting next to one of the warheads, and the cover is off."

"So he could be telling the truth?" asked Blythe.

"Yes, Sir."

"Could a sniper take him out?"

"If we can get someone into the ventilation system we believe we could get sight on the target."

"Do it. I want to be informed the second the shooter's in position. Meanwhile, we play along. Get some men in here to clean these two up."

"Understood, Sir." The soldier stomped away.

The general leant down and picked up Tariq's black shirt, ripping it into strips and using it to gag me. Then he picked up the radio again.

"You don't leave me much choice," he said. "Bring your vehicle to the gates now, we'll have the prisoners."

"We'll be there in a moment," replied Jack, sounding surprised.

A stream of soldiers scurried into the room and I was untied and allowed to stand. I'd lost so much blood from my leg that I momentarily blacked out as I stood up. I was caught and sat back down. A doctor patched my leg up as best he could and helped me into a new pair of trousers. I could hear more frantic activity from where Tariq had been sitting. When I managed to look across all I could see was a wall of soldiers, some kneeling down.

"Just patch them up," growled the general. "No need to do too much. They've only got to make it to the main gate, after that they're not our concern."

Eventually a soldier indicated that they were ready, and they lifted Tariq up on a stretcher. He was pale and unconscious, and his breathing was shallow, but at least he was still alive.

Surrounded by soldiers, their rifles raised, we were marched out of the building and on to the main road that ran to the gate. I was unable to walk properly and had to wrap my arms around the shoulders of two soldiers who helped me. The base looked very different in the early twilight, with soldiers running all over the place; some were streaming down into the tunnels, others were lining up beside trucks ready to ship out.

As we moved towards the main gate I saw the Stryker pull up outside. Its gun turret rotated, pointing straight down the road at us. I smiled at the threat. Nice to have some firepower on our side. Then I heard a deep rumbling sound and a tank rolled into view ahead of us. Its gun turret – so much bigger than the Stryker's – rotated until it was pointing straight at the armoured vehicle, which suddenly seemed kind of puny. The general fell into step beside me and made eye contact, holding my gaze steadily, his deep black eyes, so pitiless and cold.

"I want you to know, son, that I'll be coming for you," he said. "I don't care where you try to hide, here or abroad, I'll find you and your daddy one day. And when I do, I'll fry you both alive, so help me God."

I didn't reply, just kept trying to put one foot in front of the other, gritting my teeth against the pain in my leg and focusing on the means of my escape. I had no idea how this was going to pan out, or what plan Jack and Rowles had concocted. Our original plan – for Tariq and Jack to use a remote detonator to set off the nukes after we'd left - had failed when they couldn't find the remote detonators anywhere. So how was Rowles planning to escape?

We approached the gate and the Stryker's hatch clanged open. Jack's head appeared in the opening and he shouted: "Bring them forward."

The general nodded, the gate was opened, and Tariq and I were carried through. This was the most dangerous moment. If they decided to take this opportunity, they could kill us all with ease. It was only their fear of Rowles that stopped them. If their sniper killed Rowles before we closed the hatch and drove away, we were dead.

The soldiers helped me up and through the hatch, lowering me down so that Jack and Sue could take hold of me and drop me on to one of the benches. Tariq was a dead weight when he was lowered in, but somehow they managed to get him stashed away. When the soldiers had gone, Jack closed the hatch.

"What the hell are you doing?" I yelled. "You were supposed to be miles away by now!"

"Not my idea," said Jack as he applied pressure to Tariq's wound and Sue took the wheel. "It was that bloody kid."

"Rowles?"

"He is a scary ass motherfucker, you know that, right?"

I shook my head, confused. "What did he do?"

"Held me to gunpoint, made me tell him about the nukes and the codes, and then threatened to shoot me if I followed him."

"So what's the plan?" I asked. "I mean, does he have a plan?"

"Not that he told me. I've just been doing as he says."

"Great king you are, letting yourself get bullied by an eleven-year-old."

"He had a gun to my head and knife to my balls," he protested. "And his eyes... that kid is not right in the head."

"He was bad enough before the months of torture," I said, shaking my head. "Let me on the radio."

I shimmied along the bench and Sue handed me the radio handset. "He's on setting three," she said. I adjusted the frequency so I could talk without the Yanks overhearing us.

"Rowles, you there?"

"Hey, Sir. You safe?"

"For now, but what about you?"

"Don't worry about me, Sir. Just drive."

"Don't be fucking ridiculous, Rowles. We came here to rescue you, we're hardly going to bugger off now."

"You'd better, Sir, because I plan on detonating as soon as you're clear."

I bit my lip, thinking furiously. How the hell was I going to get him out of this?

"Listen, they've got a sniper coming for you, through the ventilation system. I don't know how long you've got."

I clicked off the radio. "Can you rig up a remote detonator from scratch?" I asked Jack. "Did anyone teach you that while you were here?"

He shook his head.

"Shit." I pressed the transmit button again. "Okay, Rowles, we're going to have to bluff it out. I want you to find some piece of kit there that you can pretend is a remote detonator. If we can convince them you can set off the bomb from a distance, they'll let you walk away."

There was no reply. "Rowles, you there?"

"Yes, Sir. Sorry, I can hear them coming through the ventilation. I don't think I've got much time. I'm not leaving. If we run, they'll just come after us. I know what they do to people, and I'm not letting anyone else suffer like I did. The only way to be safe is to nuke the lot of them, and that's what I'm going to do. So you need to drive away now, Sir. Get to a safe distance."

I was thinking furiously. I couldn't let him die, I wouldn't. But as I was about to try again to persuade him, the Stryker started to move.

"Sue," I shouted. "What the hell are you doing?"

"You heard the boy," she yelled back. "I'm getting us out of here."

"Dammit, turn us around, that's an order!"

"You're not the boss of me, Lee."

"Jack," I cried, "stop her!" But the boy king just sat there looking scared.

I hit the transmit button again. "Rowles, please, don't detonate, just give yourself up. We'll come back for you again, I promise."

"Sorry, Sir," he replied. "I just..." I heard a sharp crack over the radio and Rowles grunted.

"Rowles? Rowles?"

Blythe's voice cut through the static. "Forget the boy. He's gone. Keep driving, Keegan, 'cause I'm coming for you, and I'm going to kill you all myself. There's nowhere you can hide, son. This land belongs to me now!" Then his voice was muffled as he turned away and barked "Launch the Apaches!"

I felt sick to the pit of my stomach.

Jack looked at me, terrified. "What do we do now?"

"Faster, Sue," I yelled. She didn't reply; she was concentrating too intently, driving like a lunatic, trying to put as much distance as she could between us and our relentless, unstoppable pursuers.

Then the radio crackled again and I heard Rowles whisper, "I am so fucking sick of people in uniforms telling me what to do."

Shit.

I leapt forward to the control panel and shoved Sue to one side, causing the Stryker to veer wildly. As she regained control, I began hitting the touch screen. "Where is it? Where is it?" I shouted in fury until finally I found the button I needed. I stroked the glass panel and heard the CBRN system sealing us in and preparing us for a chemical, biological, radiological or nuclear attack and then...

THE GROUND SHOCK once, violently, throwing us back in our seats. There was a second's pause and then the shockwave hit. Incredible noise, like the Earth itself was roaring in agony. And then the Stryker was flying. Picked up and tossed through the air at the front of the blast wave, a sealed metal can holding four people who were tumbled and thrown, screaming and yelling, crashing into metal surfaces and edges, tossed against each other like rag dolls in a tumble dryer, cooked and deafened and shaken. I felt the awful lurch of freefall in my stomach as the Stryker soared through the air, riding the wavefront, spinning madly, cooking us alive, deafening and blinding us, making our senses reel and spin.

We began to descend and then came an enormous crash as we hit the ground. I smashed, face first, into the metal floor and felt Jack and Tariq flop on top of me. Then we bounced, up again into the air, pitching and yawing and cresting the top of our arc, leaving us floating, momentarily weightless, before we began to fall again and crash again and bounce again. In ever decreasing arcs we leapfrogged across Salisbury Plain for what felt like a lifetime, feeling our bones crack. Eventually we stopped taking to the air and just tumbled along the ground, rolling across the landscape like a kicked toy. First we rolled side over side but then the nose dug in and we pitched across the ground front to back, end over end. It was endless, like the worst fairground ride you could imagine.

But eventually the rear of the Stryker dug into the ground and we gouged a deep scar across the plain, slowing until we stopped with a shattering crash that sent us all flying to the back of the vehicle in a smashing tangle of limbs.

The noise didn't stop when we did, nor the heat. The shockwaves of the explosion, weakened now that its greatest fury was spent but still fierce enough to strip the flesh from the bones of any poor soul caught in its path, swept across our craft, nestled in the soil now, dug in for protection against the onslaught.

But in the end that faded away too. The explosion passed over, leaving us broiled and broken, deaf and burned and shattered, heaps of disarticulated flesh in a hot metal stove, unable to see or speak, barely able to feel.

But alive.

EPILOGUE

JANE

WE SAW THE light in the sky as the nuke obliterated Blythe and his forces. Even though that had been the plan, I knew deep down that something had gone terribly wrong.

When John Keegan left Fairlawne in pursuit of his son, I didn't think I'd ever see him again. Lee should have been back long ago, and John should still have been in bed recovering from his wounds.

I suppose I should have learned by now not to underestimate the Keegan men.

He was gone for two days, but on the morning of the third, he pulled up in a people carrier with the four most broken people I've seen in my life.

I worked on them for two days straight, setting bones, performing transfusions, cauterising wounds, treating burns and stitching them back together. Lee had broken every single rib, punctured a lung and shattered his jaw so badly that I had to wire it up; Jack had broken both arms, legs and collar bones in multiple places; Sue had had both an ear and a hand ripped off; Tariq's guts were a mess.

A few days after the first round of surgery was completed it became clear that some wounds would not heal properly and I had to make the awful decision to amputate.

I removed Tariq's left arm below the shoulder and Jack's left leg just above the knee.

I kept them all in chemically induced comas for two weeks, eventually rousing them one at a time when the medicine ran out. When she regained consciousness, Sue just wasn't there any more.

She could breathe and open her eyes, but she was gone, brain dead apart from the most basic autonomic functions.

I euthanised her as soon as I realised. Another death on my conscience.

John sat beside Lee all day, every day, holding his hand, reading him stories, playing his favourite songs on an old battery-powered CD player. I wanted to sit with Lee too, but I felt I would be intruding. So I busied myself with the day to day running of the school and only allowed myself to sit with my poor damaged boy when his father had fallen asleep. I sat there, stroking Lee's hair, fighting back tears, willing him to pull through.

Then one wet, grey day, John came running to find me. I was teaching a first aid class to a group of juniors when he burst into the room.

"He's awake," he said, and I didn't need telling twice. I ran as fast as I could down to the room we'd put aside for recovery and there was Lee, lying in bed with his eyes open. He mumbled something unintelligible and I felt a rush of fear – what if he was brain damaged? But then I remembered the metal in his jaw.

"Don't try to speak, Lee," I said softly. "Your jaw is wired up to help it repair." I saw the understanding dawn in his eyes and I realised he was still in there.

John hugged me hard, crying into my shoulder saying "thank you, thank you," over and over. I hugged him back, looking down at Lee, knowing that he would live but unsure how he would cope with the long, slow process of recovery and adjustment. Half deaf, crippled, held together with wire and plaster casts; his biggest fight was only just beginning. For Tariq and Jack, too.

But there were no soldiers coming after us, no armies left to do battle with. The land was free of military rule.

We were free.

Free.

THE END

THE MAN WHO
WOULD NOT BE KING

ARTHUR ST JOHN Smith sat at a desk in a bland air-conditioned office, pressed the return key on his keyboard and wondered where it had all gone wrong.

When the viral apocalypse wiped the world clean, he had been kind of excited. The terror, the wet beds and the months of self-imposed quarantine in his pokey flat living off cat food and, eventually, the cat, were a bummer, but he eventually came to see his survival as a grand opportunity to turn things around.

All his life he'd been in search of a calling. He was pretty sure that Data Entry Clerk (Croydon (South) Council) wasn't it, but he didn't know what was.

Maybe his new job as Survivor (End of the World) would lead him to his destiny.

His first foray into the devastated world beyond his front door was the most thrilling thing that had ever happened to him. He pulled on his gloves, stuffed his belt with kitchen knives, and bound his face and head with torn sheets, leaving just a slit for his eyes. Once he worked out that his glasses wouldn't balance on a cloth-swathed nose, he sellotaped them to his bindings and strode from the house, ready to do battle. In his head it was a grand narrative – meek suburban wage-slave reborn as survivalist hunter-gatherer, stalking the ravaged landscape, calm and ruthless, ready to fight looters and feral dogs.

Maybe there was a damsel in distress somewhere, in need of rescuing. He reasoned that such a maiden may have been even more reluctant to emerge than he, so he checked every house on his street, hoping to find a lissom beauty cowering in terror, just waiting for him to hold out his marigold-gloved hand and tell her everything would be all right.

He especially held out hope for number 34, where that mousey woman from the library lived. She had smiled at him once, a year ago, on the tram. It had been a Monday. But in her house, it was the cats that had done the eating. So he struck out into the wider world.

His big mistake, he now knew, had been stealing the car.

Before The Cull, he had walked past the showroom on his way to work and every day, without deviation, he would glance at the car as he walked past. He'd never stop and stare at it, that would be ridiculous, but he snatched glimpses of it out of the corner of his eye and nurtured a hard covetous knot in his stomach at the thought of it.

Once he was sure his road was empty of life, his first thought had been for the car. He strolled down the familiar streets, retracing his old route to work, marvelling at the changes in the landscape.

There was Mr Singh's corner shop where he used to buy his wine gums – two packs every Monday morning, enough to last him a week. The shop had been looted and set on fire; a charred corpse dangled out of the upstairs window.

There was the bus stop where the hoodies congregated. They'd jeered at him once as he walked past. Arthur pictured them dying horribly. He wasn't imaginative enough to conjure anything really gruesome, but the thought of them dying of the plague was satisfying. He chuckled. Served the vicious little bastards right.

There was the primary school. He ignored it; he'd never liked kids.

Finally, there was the showroom. His spirits sank when he saw that the windows were smashed and the cars were all gone. His brogued feet crunched over the glass-strewn tarmac as he explored the wreckage. Nothing there. Out the back, however, he saw a garage locked up with a heavy chain. He paused. Should he?

His colleagues would have described him as bland. Not timid, but not dangerous. But with no-one to tell him off, no social disapprobation to keep him meek and mild, he felt a sudden rush of reckless freedom. Licking his lips in anticipation, he scoured the garages for a crowbar, then returned and jemmied the lock away, opening the garage doors to reveal his heart's desire.

A Lamborghini Murciélago, abandoned with the keys still in the ignition. The dealer must have thought to hide it when he realised things were going to hell.

Half full of petrol, untouched, jet black bonnet gleaming in the sunshine, the car invited him to take it for a spin. It was like some magic gift, so improbable it had to be intended. He looked left and right before he got inside, instinctively wary of discovery. But nobody yelled at him, or took a shot at him. The seat moulded itself to his saggy rear, allowing him to recline in the low slung vehicle. It felt right; it felt like a throne. This car was his now and why not? Didn't he deserve it?

He closed the door and gently, almost reverently, turned the key. The car purred into life. He placed his hands on the steering wheel, considered taking off his rubber gloves so he could feel the real leather, but decided to play it safe, pressed his foot on the clutch and then gently depressed the accelerator, revving the engine. The car growled, roared, came alive around him.

In that plush seat, enveloped in that purring, eager metal beast, he felt a rush of something new and strange.

Power.

He was free and alive and it felt good. He released the handbrake and let her rip, tearing down the Queensway towards Croydon town centre, weaving in between ruined and burnt out wrecks.

This must be what it felt like to be a rock star, he thought. Like Chris de Burgh going smooth at ninety, feeling good to be alive; or Chris Rea, on the road to hell.

His drive lasted for thirty seconds, and now, two months later, as he scrolled down the spreadsheet preparing for another dreary morning of data entry, he looked back on that glorious half-minute and thought that probably it would be the most dramatic thing that had ever happened to him.

Because the men in the yellow hazmat suits had been searching the town for survivors, and he'd ploughed straight into a group of them outside Morrisons.

The ones he didn't kill were not happy with him.

He heard the office door behind him swing open, but he didn't turn to see who it was. No point; he knew already.

"You finished yet, Smith?"

"Ha ha, only just started, Mr Jolly." The fake laugh, perfected years before in the accounts payable department of Croydon (South) Council, came easily to him. It was his defence mechanism, a way of signalling that he wasn't a threat. If he were a pack dog, he'd be bowing his head, lowering his tail and whining.

Jolly was his supervisor, a whinging Wandsworth solicitor who'd landed himself a cushy little number running the bureaucracy in the main refugee camp for Kent. Supercilious, patronising and grey, he was identical in almost every respect to Arthur's boss at the Council.

"Be sure you're done by lunchtime," said Jolly. "The camp commander wants that list pronto."

"No problem, sir, be done in a jiffy."

Arthur's supervisor gave an oleaginous moan of assent and retreated. Arthur sniggered. Camp commander; that sounded gay.

He reminded himself to be grateful. The collectors could have killed him there and then, as he'd sprawled out of the Lamborghini, tearing at his bindings so he could empty the vomit from his mouth.

Instead, they'd thrown him into their van, with the corpses, and driven him here, to the camp. They'd been a bit rough with him at processing, but he was so terrified that he'd offered no resistance at all. Identified as a low level clerical worker, grade 5F, he'd been set to work in the offices, away from the barracks and the experimental wings, where all sorts of unpleasantness was visited on the survivors.

They were trying to find a cure, and they didn't care what it took, or who they hurt in the process. Who they thought they were going to cure, he didn't know and he didn't ask.

Barrett, the man who brought round the tea urn, reckoned that the government and royal family were all holed up in a bunker underneath Buck House, waiting for a cure so they could emerge and lord it over what was left. Arthur didn't really believe that.

Then he noticed the name of the next worksheet: Royal lineage.

He clicked it open and saw a list of all the people in line to the throne. It went through the obvious ones – the princes and princesses, the dukes and duchesses, but then it went further, into minor aristocracy and illegitimate offspring. The first column contained their names, the second their dates of birth, the third their last known addresses. And the fourth contained their blood type.

But when he scrolled all the way down to line 346 he gasped in shock. His hand shook and he felt momentarily dizzy.

Because it was his name. According to this, he was 346th in line to the throne of England. The fourth column contained a note: "Illegitimate offspring; unaware; unsuitable".

In a flash he remembered a snide comment his father had made to his mother over Sunday dinner, years before. Something about dallying with upper class twits. She had blushed.

Gosh.

He scrolled back up and started counting.

There were only eleven O-Neg royals in the list above him.

He sat for a while, jaw hanging open, thinking through the implications of his extraordinary discovery. Then he came to a conclusion, sent the document to the printer, and stood to leave.

Finally, destiny was calling.

THE KING OF England, John Parkinson-Keyes, knew damn well he was in line to the throne, and didn't care who knew it. It was why the boys at his private school had christened him Kinky - a bastardisation of King Keyes.

Not that he minded. He really was kinky and he didn't care who knew that either. Hell, it was practically a prerequisite for the job.

"Prince Andrew," he was fond of confiding to credulous hangers-on, tapping his nose as he did so, "has an entire wardrobe full of gimp suits. And Sophie's a furry!"

He'd nod in the face of their astonishment and then glance knowingly at his empty glass, which they would invariably scurry off and refill for him.

He didn't have hangers-on now, of course. Not after The Cull. Now he had the real thing: slaves. And he didn't need to invent tall tales to get them do what he wanted.

"Where's my bloody dinner?" he yelled at the top of his voice, which echoed around the vaulted wooden ceiling of the huge dining room. There was no response. He drummed his fingers on the table impatiently, then cursed and reached for his shotgun. He'd teach these bloody proles to keep him waiting. He cracked the gun open, checked that it was loaded, then snapped it shut and took casual aim at the door.

"Oi!" he shouted. "Don't make me come and find you."

Again, no reply.

Christ, this was annoying. He was hungry. Resolving to teach that tempting young serving lad a hard, rough lesson in master and servant protocols, he rose from his chair and swaggered in the direction of the kitchens, gun slung over his shoulder.

"Parkin, you little wretch, where are you?" he bellowed as he pushed open the kitchen door.

He never even saw the sword that sliced his head off. Well, not until his head was on the floor, and he blinked up at his toppling, decapitated corpse.

The last thing he saw as his vision went red at the edges was a chubby little man in a grey sweater leaning down and wiggling his fingers in a cheery wave.

"Sorry," said his assassin. "Nothing personal."

King Keyes tried to call for his mummy, but he had no breath with which to cry.

The last thing he thought he heard was the portly swordsman saying: "Three down, eight to go."

THE QUEEN OF England, Barbara Wolfing-Gusset, hungrily scooped cold beans from a can with a silver spoon. The juice dribbled down her chin, but she didn't bother to wipe it off, so it dripped onto the dried blood and vomit that caked her best satin party dress.

She'd been wearing the garish pink frock for two months now, ever since the night of her 19th birthday party. Her parents had suggested that maybe a large gathering of people during a plague pandemic was not the best idea, but she'd silenced them with a particularly haughty glance, and invited practically everyone she'd ever met.

Turnout had been low, but that just meant more champagne for everyone else. Plus, that hatchet-faced cow Tasmin hadn't been around, so Barbara had a clear run at Tommy Bond.

It wasn't fair; it had all been going so well.

Yes, Tommy was looking a little green about the gills, but Barbara had assumed that was the champers, and she'd dragged him away from the ballroom for a quick shagette in the scullery. And quick it was. What a disappointment. Tommy came in about ten seconds flat and, as he did so, his eyes rolled back in his head, he began to spasm, and then he vomited blood all over her, fell to the floor – withdrawing in the process – thrashed about until he cracked his head on the stone step and twitched his last.

Ungrateful bastard.

Barbara finished the beans and tossed the tin into the corner. She swung down from the table she'd been sitting on and headed for the door, aiming a kick at the dog, which was still gnawing on Tommy's straggly bones; she didn't want it to have all the meat, she was still planning on making a stew of her beau when she had a mo.

For now, though, her priority was the next chapter of *In the Fifth at Mallory Towers* and the resolution of the poison pen mystery!

Kicking her way through the remains of her fabulous party – mostly disarticulated bones and dresses stained with bodily fluids now, but still the occasional scrap of discarded wrapping paper and tinsel – Barbara went to the drawing room, humming to herself.

She stopped and stared, her mouth hanging open, when she saw the man silhouetted in the French doors.

"Barbara Wolfing-Gusset?" said the man in a bland Croydon accent.

She nodded.

"Baroness?"

She nodded again.

The man raised his arms and Barbara saw he was holding a shotgun.

As the pellets thudded into her she realised two things. First, that no dry cleaners in the world was going to be able to salvage her best party frock; and second, that she'd never find out who'd written Moira those beastly letters.

The man walked across the room and stood over her as she gasped for air.

"Sorry," he said. Then he turned and walked away.

Barbara pulled herself out of the drawing room, leaving a thick, slick trail behind her. It was agony, but she fought her way back through the hall and into the scullery. After tremendous effort, she reached Tommy's rotting skeleton and rested her head on his ribcage. She closed her eyes and prepared for death.

Then she opened them again and shoved the dog away.

For now.

THE SMOKE CURLED upwards from the embers of the Old Schools. No-one left alive in there, then.

Arthur panned the binoculars left and surveyed the wider ruins. The cultists – at least that's what he assumed they were - had done their job thoroughly, but had made his infinitely more difficult.

The message painted on the wall of the (latest, only recently ascended, blissfully unaware) King's house had directed anyone who was looking for him to his school. He'd obviously felt that it would provide a refuge. Arthur supposed it was a sensible idea; if the boy were safely ensconced in a stable community environment, it would make him far harder for Arthur to pick off. For that reason alone it showed common sense. And anyway, where else was there for the boy to go?

On his way to the school, Arthur had decided he would masquerade as a teacher from a similar institution. Computer

Science; useless now, so unlikely to have to prove his credentials. If he could convince whatever passed for staff that he was legitimate – and damn, wouldn't you know it, he'd not got a copy of his Criminal Record Bureau check on him right now and it was going to be hard to get a replacement wasn't it, ha ha – then he could infiltrate the school, identify the boy and wait for an opportune moment to make his move.

Upon arrival, however, he'd discovered the school under siege by a ferocious band of naked, blood-daubed nutters led by some weirdo in a pinstripe suit and bowler hat. He'd stayed out of sight and let the siege play out to its inevitable conclusion – the complete destruction of the school and everyone in it. He was pretty sure there'd been cannibalism involved, but he'd avoided looking too closely once the gates were breached and the real savagery began.

Now, as he looked at the smouldering ruins of Harrow School, Arthur had difficulty deciding what to do.

If the boy king had made it to the school, he had almost certainly died in the massacre. But what if he'd been waylaid en route? What if he'd never made it here? There were too many variables, and Arthur had to be sure. He couldn't have a pretender turning up and causing trouble once he'd taken the throne.

Then a dreadful thought occurred to him: perhaps the boy had converted – he was pretty sure one or two of the boys had joined the cultists. Blimey, he hoped he wouldn't have to wade into that particular hornet's nest.

No, there was nothing else for it; he'd simply have to rummage around in the debris and entrails in search of identification. He might get lucky.

With a weary sigh, Arthur collapsed the binoculars, put them in the pocket of his coat, and stood up. He felt a slight nervous tingle as he broke cover and walked towards the wreckage. He might already be king, and he might find proof of that fact within the next hour. He could embrace his destiny by lunchtime. He felt lightheaded at the thought of it, and lengthened his stride.

TWO HOURS LATER Arthur sat on a blood-soaked bench feeling deflated and nauseous.

Rifling through the pockets of half burnt – and in some cases half eaten - child corpses was not the best way to spend a morning. But, he told himself, if he was going to be king he had to earn the right, and facing up to difficult realities and making hard decisions was part of the job. Kings needed to be made of stern stuff. He was proud that he hadn't flinched in the face of such horror; he'd only thrown up twice.

But he'd found no proof of identity. A couple of bodies had been identifiable by library cards – held on to for what reason, he wondered? Habit? Some kind of totemic article of faith that one day there would once again be fines for overdue books? – but the majority of the bodies were anonymous.

This was not acceptable. He'd managed to find and eliminate ten obstacles with no doubt at all, but now, at the final hurdle, he was going to have to make a leap of faith. The boy was almost certainly dead but Arthur knew that scintilla of possibility, that maggot of doubt, would gnaw away at him for the duration of his reign. He'd never feel entirely secure upon his throne, he'd always be waiting for the day when the miraculously resurrected boy king, now grown up and riding at the head of an army, would rise up to challenge his rule and topple him from the throne.

Unconsciously, his hand rose to his throat as he contemplated Charles I's fate. Then he clenched as he recalled Edward II's.

No, he had to be sure. There was nothing else for it – he had to find the cultists. If he could talk to the boys who had converted they'd be able to tell him the boy king's fate. It was his final test, the last thing he must do to prove that he was worthy of his own destiny. He understood that.

But it really was going to be a pain in the neck.

THE KING OF England, Jack Bedford, picked his way through the wreckage of his school.

Coming back to school had seemed like such a good idea when the world died. After all, if any school was going to survive The Cull, it would be Harrow, wouldn't it? As it turned out, only a few children thought of returning to school, so the community never had time to reach critical mass before their first big challenge.

When the Blood Hunters had turned up to kill and eat anyone who wouldn't convert to their mad creed, Jack and one of his classmates had escaped the slaughter by sheltering in a huge brick ice house deep in the woods that made up a large part of the school grounds. They'd heard nothing in two days now, so Jack had emerged to scout the area.

He was shocked to see the school reduced to a pile of smouldering embers and a half collapsed stone shell. This was Harrow, for God's sake. Was nothing sacred?

The Old Schools, chosen for a last stand in the event of attack, was still smoking, but he approached anyway. There had been twenty-three other children and one teacher – the Head of English, who had proclaimed himself Headmaster – here when the cultists had arrived. Jack didn't hold out much hope of finding any of them alive, but he could at least bury any remains. There were no bodies here, though; everyone had been taken elsewhere during the bloodletting. Jack scrambled away from the still hot embers, ashamed at the relief he felt.

As he approached the dormitories he caught a whiff of cooking meat and a thick smoky stench of chemicals. He paused, thinking again. The sick feeling in his stomach hardened into a knot of fury and fear. He wanted to run as far as he could from this awful place, but at the same time he wanted to find a gun or a knife or a club, pursue the Blood Hunters and massacre the whole bloody lot of them.

He shook his head and sank to the grass, sitting down and wrapping his arms around his legs, resting his chin on his knees and staring blankly at the smouldering wreckage. Who was he kidding? He was fifteen, his arms were too long for his body and he kept bumping into things. Always the last to be chosen for rugby, Jack was not sporty or physically confident; he was gangly, awkward and beanpole thin. Give him a gun and he'd probably just blow his own foot off. He wasn't going to be massacring anybody, let alone a gang of heavily armed psychotic cannibals.

He sniffed and stuck his lower lip out.

Where could he go now? His family were dead, his school destroyed, the only friend he had left was that interloper Ben, who had remained in the ice house, asleep and unconcerned.

Jack sat there, disconsolate. He had no real friends, no family, no home, and nowhere to go. He was unwashed, hungry, tired and simultaneously terrified and furious.

He realise the simple truth of his life – he was prey, and that was all. A tasty morsel to be eaten up by whichever cult, gang or death squad ran him to ground. The best he could hope for was a squalid few months scratching a life in the wreckage and then a brutal and pointless death.

He felt tears welling up in his eyes.

Then he froze as he heard a noise. He held his breath and willed his heart to slow. There it was again. Sounded like someone behind him and to his left. He heard the faint sound of shifting bricks; someone was walking through the rubble of the Old Schools.

Instinctively realising that he had not been seen, Jack slowly raised his head and turned to look over his shoulder. A freestanding wall blocked the other person from view. He rose to his feet and moved away as quietly as he could, taking cover in the ruins of a classroom, peering out through the hole where a window used to be. He glanced down and noticed that his hands were shaking.

There was a sound of shifting stone and Jack saw the freestanding wall wobble dangerously. The unseen man must have destabilised it by accident. Jack heard him scrabbling to escape, but he misjudged it, because the wall toppled away from Jack with a slow, clumsy grace, and there was a loud cry of alarm and pain mixed in with the sound of crashing brickwork.

Unsure what to do, Jack stood there, stunned, watching the wreckage settled. After the sudden noise, silence fell again, for a moment.

"Oh... bother!" came a voice from inside the rising dust cloud. "Damn and blast and buggeration!"

This did not sound, Jack thought, like the cries of a dangerous killer or a mad cultist. But still he did not move, waiting patiently for the dust to settle so he could see who he was dealing with. It took a minute or so, but eventually a silhouette hardened into the prone form of a chubby little man dressed in a v-neck sweater and a puffy green jacket. He was lying with his feet towards Jack's hiding place, but his legs were buried beneath piles of fallen bricks.

The man was trapped.

THE MAN WATCHING from the tree-line cursed under his breath.

"Don't let me down now, Arthur," he whispered. "Not when we're so close..."

Then he reached into his backpack and pulled out a machine gun. Just in case.

JACK STUDIED THE prone man, trying to work out what to do.

The man didn't have a gun in either of his hands, and his bag had fallen beyond his reach. That left his coat as the only likely place for a weapon to be concealed. As he leaned forward and began trying to dig himself out, the coat fell open and Jack was pretty sure there was nothing heavy in any of the pockets.

Maybe this guy was friendly. He didn't look threatening. But what had he been doing here? Was he a looter, come to pick over the wreckage of his school, or something else?

He considered for a moment and then broke cover. He stood in plain sight but didn't move, waiting for the man to notice him. It took a few moments.

"Oh, hello, I didn't see you there," said the man, momentarily forgetting his predicament. He stopped trying to free himself and leaned backwards.

Jack licked his lips; he had a dreadful case of dry mouth.

"What are you doing here?" asked Jack, warily.

The man paused before replying, and Jack fancied that he could see cogs turning in the guy's head as he worked out his response. Subterfuge was definitely not this guy's strong suit. Jack did not think it would be wise to trust him.

"I'm on a sort of quest," he said.

"For what?"

"Not what, young man. Who."

"All right, for whom are you questing?"

"Oh very good. You must be an Harrovian, such good grammar." The man was eyeing Jack almost hungrily. Jack bit his lip nervously. What was this guy's game?

"I'm Arthur. Is there any chance..?" He waved at his trapped legs and smiled.

Still Jack didn't move.

"I asked you who you were looking for," he said.

"A boy. His name's Jack Bedford." The man's eyes were narrow, gauging Jack's reaction to this news.

And Jack was so astonished that he let a momentary flicker of that surprise show on his face before he said: "Never heard of him."

GOT HIM! THOUGHT Arthur. He either knows the boy or – he looked him up and down; right age, at least – *is* the boy.

Arthur was good at subterfuge, though, and had played his cards close to his chest. There was no reason for this boy not to trust him. Plus, his legs hurt like hell, and might be broken, so he didn't think he presented an obvious threat. If this was the king, he could lure him forward by playing the helpless victim. His reached his right hand down, as subtly as he could manage, and wrapped his fingers around a brick.

"Oh, that's shame," he said. "I've got good news for him. Anyway, first things first, can you please help me free my legs? They really are rather sore."

"What news?"

Oh for god's sake, this boy was skittish.

"I'm sorry, I can only tell that to him. I promised." He was pleased with that last flourish.

The boy considered for a moment and then said "I can take you to Jack. I know where he is."

"You mean he's alive? Oh that's wonderful!" *Now help me move these bricks you snot-nosed whelp.*

He let go of the brick, and the boy moved forward at last, reaching forward to help release him. The poor idiot child had no idea he'd played right into Arthur's hands.

IT DIDN'T TAKE long for Jack to uncover Arthur's legs. He worked in silence, unsure whether he should be doing this. He'd been shocked to hear his own name, and he couldn't pass up the chance that this man might be able to help him in some way. But he didn't trust him.

The best plan he'd been able to come up with was to take Arthur back to the ice house where Ben was waiting. He'd introduce Ben as himself and pull faces at Ben behind the guy's back to get him to play along.

Ben was more confident than he was, good at handling confrontations and problems. If anyone could turn this situation to his advantage, it was Ben. He just had to hope that he was feeling sharp today.

Jack heaved the last brick away and Arthur's legs lay exposed at last. There were spatters of blood on his trousers, but he cautiously flexed his legs and then shakily got to his feet.

"Well fancy that!" he cried. "No bones broken."

Jack also stood up, and kept his distance as Arthur hobbled over to his bag, picked it up, and slung it over his shoulder.

"Right then," he said. "Lead on... sorry, you didn't tell me your name."

"I'm Ben," said Jack.

Arthur reached out a hand, smiling insincerely. "Please to meet you Ben, and thank you for helping me."

Jack reluctantly shook Arthur's clammy, limp hand.

"S'this way," he murmured, and slouched off towards the woods. Arthur followed close behind.

"So, do you know Jack well?" asked the man, feigning small talk.

"He was in my house, but he was in the year below. So not really."

"Then how…?"

"We were just lucky. We'd been sent off to collect some firewood when the cannibals attacked. So we just hid in the ice house until they'd gone."

"Nice lad, is he?"

"Don't you know?"

"Oh no, never met him. I'm just running an errand."

"He's all right, I suppose. Bit annoying when you're cooped up in the dark with him for three days."

"I think maybe everyone is." Arthur gave a short, nasal laugh, which irritated Jack intensely. His fear had largely faded, now he was only curious.

THE ICE HOUSE was a small brick dome with a door that you had to crouch to get through; it looked like a brick igloo, sitting incongruously among the school's woodlands, swathed in ivy, better camouflaged than any pill box.

As soon as it came in sight, Jack stopped.

"Better stay here, let me warn him you're coming," he told Arthur. "He's kind of nervous and he's got a knife. We don't want you to get stabbed do we?"

Arthur gave another of his nervous, snorty laughs. "Heavens, no!"

Jack walked towards the ice house, only just resisting the urge to run. As he stooped to enter, he glanced back over his shoulder and saw Arthur standing where he'd left him. The man smiled and waved.

The ice house smelled of damp leaves and dirt. It was dark inside, only a tiny chink of light penetrated the canopy of ivy that covered the small hole at the apogee of the dome. Designed to keep ice frozen throughout the year in the days before freezers, the majority of the ice house lay under ground; almost immediately you were inside, the ground opened up into a cavernous, brick lined hole. In the half-light, Jack could just about make out the sleeping figure of Ben. He was exactly where Jack had left him, curled up on the carpet of detritus that had accumulated at the bottom of the ice house in the hundred or so years since it had last been used.

Jack scrambled down into the hole and shook the sleeping boy awake.

Spotty, unkempt and decidedly common, Ben Wyman didn't deserve his place at Harrow. The Headmaster had insisted that the school should open its door to any refugee children they dredged up, and Ben had been the first. He claimed to be the middle class son of a school teacher from the local comp, but Jack had his suspicions about that. Ben had been wary of the Harrow boys and the haughty ease with which they carried themselves. He'd not been bullied, exactly, but he was ostracised by the other boys, including Jack. But he'd been appointed Ben's 'shepherd', which meant it was his job to show him the ropes and help him find his feet, so they'd ended up spending a lot of time in each other's company.

Even though Ben didn't much like Jack, and Jack didn't much like Ben, they were both too scared to be alone, so they'd stuck together.

Ben sat up quickly and rubbed his eyes. "What?" he whispered urgently, confused and still half asleep. "What's going on?"

Jack leaned in close and spoke quickly and quietly.

"Ben," he said, pressing his library card into his sleepy friend's hand. "I need you to do me a favour."

ARTHUR'S INCIPIENT EUPHORIA was enough to make him forget the pain in his legs. Even this close to his destiny, he chided himself. His ascent to the throne wasn't supposed to be easy, but he'd been so annoyed at the prospect of having to infiltrate the cultists that he'd felt himself to be unlucky. He realised that the wall had been a warning, a reminder not to be ungrateful. This was a test, he understood that, a baptism of sorts, and it was all to a purpose. Fate had plans for him, but it was not to be taken for granted.

So he stood, chastened, and waited patiently for the boy king to emerge from the ice house. He caressed the revolver in his jacket pocket lovingly. Soon, now.

He cocked his head to one side suddenly alert. The snap of a twig. Slowly, he spun through 360 degrees, scanning the surrounding woods, but saw no movement and heard no other sound. Must have been a deer.

His suspicions were instantly forgotten as he saw two boys emerge from the small brick dome. The king, Jack, was smaller than Ben, but carried himself with a confidence sorely lacking in his friend. It was obvious which of the two was of royal blood. It showed in his bearing as clear as day. Arthur was sure that was how he must look to others and wondered how it could be that no one had ever noticed his inherent regalness while he was working at the council. He decided that people lowly enough to be working in such mindless jobs were too stupid to notice such things.

The two boys stopped in front of him. The king stood slightly closer, his friend hanging back, timid.

"Hi, yeah, I'm Jack," said the boy, grinning as if he'd just said something incredibly clever or funny. "What can I do for you?"

And Arthur froze.

Here it was. The moment of his ascension. He stood there, transfixed by the enormity of what was about to happen.

"You had a message for me, you said?" continued the boy, his brow creasing in puzzlement.

Still Arthur couldn't move or speak. Unconsciously, his eyes widened and his mouth shaped itself into an idiot grin.

"Um, sir?" Now the king looked uncertain, and turned to his friend, pulling a funny face and shrugging.

Arthur withdrew the gun from his pocket, still grinning, and shot the King of England, Jack Bedford, in the head, believing him to be a useless commoner.

All the confidence of the boy standing before him evaporated into terror as he saw his friend fall to the ground, and found himself staring down the barrel of a gun.

Arthur was about to pull the trigger again when he hesitated.

"No," he said to the cowering, whimpering child. "Let's talk first."

THE MAN ARTHUR believed to be the King of England, Ben Wyman, sat on his hands on the soft forest ground and tried to control his bladder. The madman sat opposite him, cross legged, gun in hand, regarding him curiously.

If he looked past the madman, Ben could see Jack's body. He was lying with his eyes open, staring at him in silent reproach.

"I never talked to any of the others, but there's one thing I kept meaning to ask them. Did you feel it?" asked the madman. "The moment you ascended to the throne, I mean. It was about a week ago, at two in the afternoon."

Ben didn't know what the correct answer might be, so he said nothing. Happily, the madman didn't seem to mind.

"I imagine you didn't," he continued. "It's not really your throne. You're not destined to remain king, you see. I am. I'll feel the moment of destiny because I'll make it happen. You were passive. Didn't have the guts to go out and seize your power, not like me. I've proved myself, you understand? Not like you, cowering here in this dungeon, waiting for slaughter."

Still Ben said nothing. All those years in the care home had taught him the value of silence.

Suddenly the madman tutted, as if annoyed with himself. "Why am I wasting time?" he muttered, and raised his gun.

"Yeah, I felt it," said Ben.

The madman paused.

"Kind of like a hot flush, sort of thing," he elaborated.

The gun stayed where it was, neither lowered nor raised.

"Made me feel all kind of powerful and stuff," he added, unsure whether this was what the madman wanted to hear.

"And did you know?" asked the madman, his eyes narrowed, intensely focused on his answer.

"Of course," said Ben. "'Course I knew."

The madman nodded. "Interesting." He stayed sitting there, gun half raised, nodding pensively.

Beneath his right buttock, Ben made a fist, scooping up leaves and dirt, ready to throw them into the nutter's face if the chance presented itself.

"Did the other boys notice it, the change in you?"

"Oh yeah, natch."

"That's good. I'll need that, I think."

Ben cursed inwardly. Why had he agreed to go along with Jack's stupid plan to switch identities? It had seemed funny at the time. Jack was scared of his own shadow, and even though he resented Ben's confidence, he wasn't afraid to use it to his advantage. Just like a toff, thought Ben, not for the first time wondering why he'd thrown his lot in with these spoiled Harrow kids, refusing to admit to himself that he had been so scared of being alone that even a bunch of pampered prats had seemed like an attractive peer group. So he'd tried to adopt the accent and manners of the boys around him; he was good at blending in. He'd even begun to think maybe he'd found a home, until the cultists arrived.

He wondered if there was any point in protesting that he wasn't Jack. Probably not. The madman had killed Jack without a second's thought. Ben knew the only reason he was still alive was because the madman thought he was someone else. If Ben told him the truth, and if he was believed, he'd end up just as dead. Better to play along, to try and find some advantage. That was another thing he'd learned in the care home - if silence doesn't work, keep them talking, sometimes you can deflect them.

"Tell me about the others," asked Ben.

The madman shook his head briefly, forcing his attention back to the here and now.

"Oh, they were nothing, really," he replied. "Spoilt brats. Trustafarians. I should have realised that the lower down the list I got, the better they'd be. You're almost normal, like me. It'll be good to have a normal king, don't you think?"

Ben nodded. "So, let me see if I've got this right," he said cautiously. "I'm King of England, yeah? You're next in line to the throne after me. And you've gone around killing everyone in line before me. Now you've just got to off me and you become king. That about it?"

The madman's eyes narrowed, suspicious again.

"You know that," he said.

Ben nodded. "Oh yeah, just wanted to be absolutely sure we were on the same page." He was gobsmacked; he knew Jack had been posh, but he'd had no idea he was bloody royalty. "So, how many kings have you killed?"

Could he persuade the nutter of the truth - that he'd got the wrong person, that he'd already killed the king and was in fact already the monarch? He cursed himself for speaking without thinking; no, he couldn't, because he'd gone and reinforced the madman's belief that you felt the moment your predecessor died, that becoming king was some sort of massive supernatural head rush.

There was nothing else to do. He was going to have to try and fight this guy. Ben knew he didn't have much of a chance, but if he didn't do something he was going to be shot dead at any moment. And he was damned if he was going down without a fight.

He clenched his handful of dirt and prepared to make his move.

"Kings and queens," corrected the madman. "Ten in all. You'll be number eleven."

Ben ignored the nerves and the insistent pressure on his bladder, and rolled to his right, releasing his arms and flinging the forest mulch into the face of the madman.

"Like fuck I will!" he yelled, and then he was up and running.

*   *   *

ARTHUR WIPED THE muck from his eyes as he rose to his feet. The boy had already vanished into the undergrowth, but he was hardly stealthy and he could clearly hear him blundering away to his left. With a weary sigh, he gave chase. It was his own stupid fault. He should have just shot the boy when he had the chance. Then he would have fulfilled his destiny and ascended to invincibility. As it was, his legs hurt, his eyes stung, he had a stitch from running and he was starting to get really cheesed off. Time to kill the boy and be done with it.

He held tight to his gun as he ran.

BEN KNEW THE madman wasn't far behind him, so he put his head down and concentrated on going as fast as he could. A bullet pinged off a tree right beside him, and he put on an extra burst of speed.

He was so focused on his pursuer that he didn't see the man who stepped out in front of him, only becoming aware of his presence when he ran smack into the heavy log the man was wielding.

He was unconscious before he hit the floor.

ARTHUR SAW THE boy lying on the ground and stopped dead. Had he tripped, or hit his head on a tree? He was pretty sure his hopeful shot hadn't found its mark.

He approached the boy carefully. Maybe he was playing possum, waiting for him to get closer so he could spring some trap. Arthur told himself not to be paranoid; there were no traps here.

Which was why he was so surprised when Mr Jolly stepped out from behind a tree and shot him in the gut.

Arthur stood there for a moment, his face a mask of stunned surprise. Then his gun dropped from his hand and he fell to his knees, clutching his stomach. He remained kneeling as his supervisor from the camp walked towards him shaking his head ruefully.

"And you were so close, Arthur," said Mr Jolly as he approached. "So close."

Arthur didn't understand. He was so shocked and confused that he couldn't even form a question. He just stared, baffled, at the man who had shot him.

Jolly knelt down as well, so he was facing Arthur.

"Of all the people I showed that spreadsheet to, you were the unlikeliest candidate," he said. "I'd almost given up."

Arthur registered that his accent had changed. The glottal stops of his Wandsworth accent had gone, replaced by round, plummy RP.

"I really didn't think you had it in you. The one before you, now he was a go getter. But when he saw his name on the list he just laughed. In all, you were the sixth person whose name I added to the spreadsheet, and by far the least promising. Or so I thought. Just goes to show, doesn't it? You never can tell about people."

"I..." gasped Arthur. "I don't..."

"Understand. Yes, I know. You've gone quite round the twist, haven't you? Poor love. I knew you'd finally lost the plot when you killed that reprehensible parasite Parker. Making him a paper crown, painting it gold, then setting him up in a tableau, in a big chair with a roll of silver foil as a sceptre... well, it was inventive, I'll give you that. But a bit bonkers, don't you think?"

"What are you... doing here?" Arthur was beginning to feel lightheaded, as if the world was spinning around him. Gravity suddenly seemed to be on the blink. He saw spots before his eyes and found it hard to draw breath.

"Oh do keep up, Arthur. I replaced my name on the line of succession with yours. Simple plan, really. Convince someone else that they're the rightful heir, they traipse off and kill everyone who stands in their way, and I sit back, watch the show, then pick off the hapless patsy at the end. That way I only have to kill one idiot, rather than eleven."

Arthur's head swam. Was this another test? Surely what Jolly was saying couldn't be true. No, it had to be a test. It was his destiny to be king. He knew that, more certainly than he'd ever known anything in his life.

"You used me?" he groaned.

"Well of course I did, dear boy. First rule of being king – delegate the nastiest jobs to the most expendable serfs you can lay your hands on. And you, Arthur St John Smith, are the most entirely expendable person I've ever had the good fortune to meet. Plus: murderous, delusional and now, very dead indeed."

ARTHUR LAUGHED.

"Funny," he said, his voice little more than a whisper. "You see, I really am the king. I can feel it. You wouldn't know what I mean, of course. But it's in my blood. Don't you realise who I am?"

"Go on, surprise me."

"I'm the once and future king. Arthur, you see? My name isn't a coincidence. My parents must have known. Don't you realise? This is the moment of England's greatest need and I am come again!"

With that final pronouncement, Arthur's eyes rolled back in his head, he toppled sideways and lay motionless.

THE KING OF England, Jolyon Wakefield-Pugh, tutted affectionately.

"Nutty as a fruitcake," he laughed.

He rose to his feet and turned to deal with the last bit of unfinished business.

But the boy was nowhere to be seen.

"Oh," groaned Jolyon. "Oh bugger."

BEN WAS WOOZY and concussed but he still had enough presence of mind to slip away quietly the moment he regained semi-consciousness. Once he was out of earshot he increased his pace, half falling forwards with every frantic step. He made for the school buildings, which seemed to offer the best chance of cover and safety.

The bump to his head had only made the events of the morning seem even more surreal and dreamlike. Had he really been attacked by two men who thought he was king? Had Jack really been shot down in cold blood right in front of his eyes? Could any of this be real?

He broke cover at the tree-line and made for the ruins of the main building. There was a cellar there where he could hide.

But when he made it to the bricks he lost his footing and fell, sprawling on the ruined masonry. As he lay there he could feel consciousness slipping away again. The fear of death overwhelmed him, and he whimpered "Mum" before succumbing to the darkness.

LIEUTENANT SANDERS, LATE of the SAS, now barracked at Salisbury with the remnants of the British Army, had all but given up hope. Six months spent chasing royalty, and all he'd found were corpses. Each time he found a new one he'd contact his superior officer and break the bad news. And each time he was ordered to go find the next person on the list.

Sanders wasn't much of a monarchist, but he had to concede that a figurehead would be a useful rallying point for the scattered survivors of post-Cull Britain. A heroic king or a stern but comely queen would provide a focal point for patriotism and a sense of allegiance that could help rebuild the nation.

It helped keep the army in line too, if they had someone they could swear an oath to.

So he'd scoured the length and breadth of the British Isles with a list of names and last known addresses, trying to find the rightful monarch. And each time he arrived, they were dead. He wasn't stupid, after the third body he'd realised that someone else was using the same list for a different agenda. A radical republican, maybe?

He skipped to number five on the list, but was too late. Then seven. Again, too late, and the body too long cold. Now he'd jumped to eleven. He had to get ahead of this bastard, whoever he was.

When he got to Harrow he went in cautiously, weapon at the ready. The school was still smoking, and he got a familiar sinking feeling. There was no-one alive here.

But just as he was about to give up and go on to the next name, he caught an impression of movement through the wisps of smoke. Moving cautiously, he stalked his prey.

JOLYON WAKEFIELD-PUGH stood over the unconscious body of the boy he believed to be king and considered his next move.

More specifically: knife, gun or brick?

He eventually plumped for brick, reached down and grabbed one, enjoying its heft and solidity. He raised his right arm, ready to bring the brick crashing down on the boy's skull, ready to seize his destiny.

WITH HIS ARM raised, the man presented a perfect target. Sanders knew nothing of his grievance or motive in wanting the boy dead, but he knew a murderer when he saw one. Martial law gave him the right to take action, and he was not afraid to do so.

He put three rounds into the chest of the King of England, killing him instantly, and he felt satisfied that he had done right.

Then he ran to offer aid to the fallen boy.

Sanders turned him over and felt for a pulse. Strong and steady. He was alive, but he had a nasty head wound that needed some attention. He had a medical kit in his jeep, so he leaned down and grabbed the boy's hands, lifting him into a sitting position, ready to throw him over his shoulder. As he did so, something fell out of the boy's pocket on to the ground.

He let go of the boy's right arm and reached down to pick up the library card.

He read the name on the card.

Then he looked down at the boy.

Then he looked back at the card.

"Well fuck me sideways, Your Majesty," said Sanders, grinning fit to burst. "Pleased to meet you."

He threw the child over his shoulder and walked back to his jeep, singing the Sex Pistols' *God Save The Queen* at the top of his voice.

ARTHUR ST JOHN Smith sat in the bottom of the ice house, pressed hard on his stomach wound and wondered where it had all gone wrong.

He had crawled away from the scene of the shooting, instinctively seeking a quiet sheltered place in which to die, like a mortally wounded cat. Now he sat on the soft carpet of moss and leaves, feeling his life seeping out through his fingers, waiting for the fair folk to come and carry him back to Avalon, to wait for the call to come again.

He knew they would find him. It was only a matter of time. He just had to be patient. His destiny was calling, he could hear it on the wind.

A fox peered in at the doorway, sniffing the air, drawn by something else the wind carried – the enticing tang of fresh blood.

Arthur heaved a stone at it, and it ran away.

For now.

CHILDREN'S
CRUSADE

Original cover art by Mark Harrison

PROLOGUE

CAROLINE OPENED HER good eye and winced. It was hard to divorce the pounding in her head from the shockwaves of the explosion that still reverberated around the small room. The walls were painted white but they glowed orange as the fireball billowed up the street outside.

Even with her head swathed in bandages, her hearing muffled, and her vision clouded by the lingering anaesthetic – not to mention the fact that one of her eyes was healing underneath a thick gauze dressing – Caroline knew instantly what was occurring.

Someone was attacking the base.

The night was warm and the window was open. It rattled in its frame and a wave of hot air pushed the curtains towards the ceiling.

She was lying flat on her back with her hands on her belly and was wearing what felt like a cotton nightdress. The crisp white sheets felt luxurious on her bare calves. It had been so long since she'd felt clean sheets.

She remembered her mother ironing the bed linen in front of the telly, watching *Eastenders* from within a cloud of steam.

The curtains fell back into place and the orange glow faded and began to flicker as fires took hold. Caroline heard the crack of small-arms fire; sporadic at first, then constant and concentrated. Fire and a firefight. She wondered how long it would take for the conflict to reach her room, and what would happen when it did.

She sniffed the air, expecting cordite and smoke, but instead smelled lilies, strong and pungent. She focused on the chest of drawers that sat against the wall directly in front of her. The sense that she was one step sideways from reality was reinforced by the uneasy feeling that the world was somehow flatter. If she never recovered the use of her other eye then things would always be this way; the depth of the world reduced to one smooth surface, like a painting or a television.

On top of the wardrobe stood a large green vase which held about ten flowering lilies, their petals white with streaks of purple and yellow. They were exquisite.

Caroline wondered where Rowles had found them, and smiled at the thought of her best friend.

Then she frowned. Where was he?

Engines now, outside. Deep, throaty roars and the rumble of caterpillar tracks coming closer. Tanks, then. She could not imagine who would have the resources to attack this place, the most heavily defended position in the country, base of operations for the entire British Army.

She licked her lips. Her mouth felt musty and she had a sharp, bitter taste at the back of her throat, like bile or grapefruit. Wondering what the time was, she gently rotated her head until she could see the clock on her bedside table. 10:15. Not so late, but it was already dark outside.

She stroked her belly through her nightshirt, feeling the flat planes of her abdomen and the hollow empty ache inside, a reminder that she had not eaten for at least 24 hours. Then she thought: it might be more than that. How long had she been unconscious? It could be days.

She felt no disquiet at the prospect of having lost time in this nice, clean, envelope-smooth bed. What a nice place to lose time, she thought.

A distant whine grew into a piercing shriek that swept across the outside sky like a banshee. Fighter jet. No, two fighter jets. As they screamed overhead there was a whoosh and a hiss then a series of loud explosions as the planes launched missiles into the most entrenched positions, or eliminated British tanks or buildings.

Her nice warm bed didn't seem a safe place to be, but Caroline did not panic. She was too weak from surgery to lift herself into a sitting position, let alone leave the bed and search for shelter. The knowledge of her helplessness freed her from fear. There is no point, she told herself, being afraid of something you can't change; you will survive or you won't and there's nothing you can do to influence the outcome either way.

A tank ground to a halt beneath her window. She heard a whirr of engines as the turret rotated and the gun was manoeuvred into firing position. Then a moment's pause before her bed shook as the shell was fired.

Now she could smell gunpowder and the tang of hot, oiled metal, but the smell of the lilies was not entirely swamped. She imagined the flowers fighting back against machinery, and winning.

Since the explosion had woken her, Caroline had heard no noises from inside the building where she lay, tucked up safe on the second floor in her convalescent room. Now she heard the unmistakeable clatter of boots on the stairs at the end of the corridor. It was one person, running. Looking for somewhere to hide, perhaps? Or coming for her?

The footsteps got closer, then she heard many more pairs of boots coming up the stairs in pursuit.

Caroline scrunched her toes against the soft, smooth bed sheets in a tactile farewell just as the door to her room burst open.

"Caroline?" It was Rowles. He was breathing hard, on the verge of panic, which was unlike him.

"What's happening?" she said. Or at least that's what she tried to say. Her tongue felt like a lump of meat in her mouth and her lips seemed swollen and heavy. What she actually said was "Wa han," but sweet, faithful Rowles understood her.

"American army," he said, by way of explanation as he closed the door behind him, grabbed a metal-framed canvas chair and shoved it under the door handle. Then he ran to her bedside, leaned over and kissed her on the cheek.

"They may not check too carefully," he whispered.

The door handle rattled immediately. She'd thought he was being optimistic.

The boy she trusted more than anyone else alive crouched down beside her bed with a machine gun aimed at the door. It was cocked and ready to fire. He was defending her with his life, and she felt an overwhelming flood of affection for him. It took a huge effort but she managed to lift her right arm out from under the covers and reach across to stroke his light brown hair. He glanced up at her and she smiled at him. His wide eyes and small freckled nose gave him the face of an angel, but stare deeper into those eyes and there was only pitiless darkness. Hard to believe he was only eleven.

He smiled back and just for a moment his eyes lightened. There was still some feeling in there, after all. She hoped one day she'd hear him laugh. But she didn't think it likely.

She remembered her father laughing at an old repeat of *Morecambe and Wise*, his eyes creased to slits as he literally held his sides and rocked back and forth on the sofa like a laughing policeman at a fairground.

If Rowles was going to die here, she was glad she could die with him. She'd heard Matron refer to them once as Bonnie and Clyde, so it was fitting.

The door ceased rattling and the footsteps clattered away.

A moment later she heard boots descending the stairs.

Rowles stood up and walked around the bed, then pulled the curtain aside a fraction and looked out at the battlefield.

"I don't know why they're attacking, but I think they're winning." There was a huge explosion nearby and he pulled back from the window, shielding his eyes. "It's not safe to stay here. We have to go."

Caroline wanted nothing more than to run away with him, but she would need to be carried, manhandled, pushed in a wheelchair. She was twelve years old and would have described herself as solid, even stocky. Rowles was eleven and thin as a rake. There was no chance. She wanted to tell him to go without her, to save himself and leave her be. But her treacherous mouth wouldn't form the words and, she realised with some surprise, she was too selfish for that. She wanted to be with him, no matter what.

"Wel air," she grunted.

"Good idea. I'll go look for one. Back in a mo."

He pulled the chair away from the handle and cracked open the door. Once he'd assured himself that the corridor was clear he slipped out, pulling the door closed behind him.

Caroline was alone again.

The noises of fighting were moving away now. The building in which she lay was quite near the main gates and she presumed it was their destruction which had signalled the start of the assault and woken her up. Now the fight was moving into the centre of the base. But below her window there was a steady rumble of incoming trucks, tanks and other vehicles as the Americans flooded in to join the fight.

She wondered where Matron was. It was unlike her to leave them alone; she should have been with Rowles, giving orders, taking decisions, making the children feel safe, protected, even loved, with a sly glance or a flash of a smile in the direst of circumstances. Rowles' presence made Caroline feel safe, Matron's made her feel she belonged.

She remembered her older sister's arm around her shoulder at their grandad's funeral, reaching up and taking her hand, feeling her sister squeeze it for comfort.

Footsteps and voices in the corridor. Rowles was no longer alone.

The door opened and a tall man with thick black hair and heavy features entered. He was wearing jeans and a t-shirt, but had an SLR machine gun slung across his chest. She recognised him – he was the doctor who had been there when she regained consciousness after the operation. Jones? Johns? She couldn't recall his name.

Rowles came in behind the man, pushing a wheelchair, then closed the door.

The doctor leaned over her.

"Can you hear me, Caroline?" he asked.

"Yuh."

"Can you move at all?"

She lifted her arm feebly and wiggled her fingers until the effort became too much and the limb flopped back down, useless.

The doctor smiled. It was obviously meant to be reassuring but there was something calculating in his eyes, something which made her withhold trust.

"We're going to lift you into the wheelchair," he said. "It may hurt, but I haven't got any anaesthetic on me, I'm afraid. Then we're going to take the lift down to the rear doors where I've got a jeep waiting. If we move quickly, I think we'll be able to get ourselves away from here before they secure the perimeter." He turned and nodded to Rowles, who wheeled the chair alongside the bed then took Caroline's hand.

She was sad to leave her clean, white cocoon, but the pain in her head as the doctor and Rowles pulled her into a sitting position made it hard to concentrate on anything but staying conscious.

"One, two, three," said the doctor, grunting on "three" as they lifted Caroline out of the bed and into the chair. Once she was sitting again, the pain in her head receded.

Outside, there was a whoosh and then a tremendous explosion directly beneath the window. Bazooka, perhaps? The window finally came off its latch and smashed against the interior wall, showering the now empty bed with shards of glass.

The doctor went to take the handles of the wheelchair, but Rowles stepped behind her. The doctor, looking over her head at Rowles' determined, territorial look – which Caroline could picture clearly, even though she was facing the other way – nodded. He turned and opened the door, then waved for Rowles to follow him.

They moved quickly out of the room and into the corridor, turning left and heading for the grey lift doors twenty metres away. Caroline observed the flat details of the corridor as she rolled past door after door, all closed. They reached the lift and the doctor reached out to press the call button, but before he could make contact the lift pinged, the doors slid open, and an American soldier stood before them, gun levelled straight at the doctor's chest.

The soldier and the doctor stood there for a second, frozen in surprise. But the soldier's reflexes were tuned for combat, and when the moment passed he was quickest. Deciding that he didn't need to waste ammunition, he brought his gun around and smashed the butt across the doctor's face, sending him crashing to the floor, stunned.

Caroline was intrigued by the soldier's uniform. It was a camouflage pattern of light and dark browns. Desert clothes, hardly suitable for warfare on the rolling green plains of England.

The soldier stepped over the prone doctor and relieved him of his weapon. Caroline could tell by the tiny vibrations in her chair that Rowles was still gripping the handles tightly, resisting the temptation to go for the gun that was slung across his back, waiting for the right moment. Perhaps the soldier hadn't even noticed the strap that ran diagonally across the boy's chest. Or perhaps he'd made the same mistake that so many had made before him, ignoring the tiny boy, failing to consider him a threat. If that were the case, Caroline knew he'd soon regret that judgment.

The soldier stood upright and looked down at the two children. He didn't say a word, just held out his arm, lowered his index finger, and rotated it to indicate that they should turn around and go back the way they'd come.

Caroline felt her chair move to the left, beginning to describe a circle, then the chair stopped at about 45 degrees and Rowles stepped back from the handles, grabbed the strap, brought his gun to bear, and fired at the soldier's chest.

There was a dry click as the gun jammed and then another of those moments of stunned surprise as boy and man stood facing each other.

Caroline saw the doctor begin to stir on the floor behind the soldier.

The look of astonishment on the soldier's face faded into amusement and he laughed at Rowles.

Oh dear, thought Caroline, allowing herself a tiny smile. That's not wise.

Rowles launched himself at the soldier with a cry, using his gun as a club, beating the man's chest and arms. The soldier lifted one big hand and swatted the gun aside, then lifted the boy off the ground in a bear hug, pinning his arms to his sides.

The doctor was up on all fours now, shaking his head to clear it. There was a loud scream of engines above as the jets made another pass, and a clatter of boots on the stairs at the far end of the corridor, as the soldiers returned.

"Little boy," said the soldier in a thick Brooklyn accent. "You're feisty, aintcha?"

Grasped tight, his feet off the ground, his arms useless, with no weapon to defend himself, Rowles looked puny and weak compared to the man who held him fast.

But Rowles was not beaten yet. With a feral snarl he bared his teeth, leaned forward, and bit hard into the man's throat.

The soldier staggered back and released his hold on the boy. But Rowles did not fall to the floor. Instead, he wrapped his arms around the soldier's neck and his legs around his waist, and continued biting, gnawing, crunching and savaging the man's throat. He growled as he did so, like a wolf ripping out the throat of a helpless lamb.

Great fists raised and smashed the boy's head again and again and Caroline winced at the soldier's scream of pure agony and terror, but Rowles was limpet tight to the man, impossible to dislodge. The soldier took another step back and lost his footing, tumbling down and smashing his helmet against the floor. Rowles leaped up, pulled the knife from the soldier's leather sheath, grasped it tightly in both hands and brought it down in a mighty arc, straight into his heart. The soldier's legs kicked furiously, but his death throes gave the boy no pause.

Rowles pulled out the knife, cut the gun's strap with one swift slice, freeing the M-16 from the soldier's chest, then turned to the doctor, who had by now regained his feet.

"Quickly," he said. The doctor reached forward, grabbed the handles of Caroline's chair and spun her around, pulling her behind him as he backed into the lift.

The clatter of boots was deafening now. Helmets appeared, rising up the stairs at the far end of the corridor. Rowles, his back to Caroline, fired a short burst at the stairwell, which caused the helmets to vanish from view.

Then the boy turned to look at her. His eyes were pitch black, blood dripped from his face and chin, and when he spoke she could see strands of flesh stuck between his teeth.

She realised in that moment that she loved him more than she had ever loved anyone in her life.

"Run," he said softly, his voice full of regret.

The doctor pressed the button and the doors of the lift began to slide closed. Caroline lifted her arm, reaching out her helpless fingers towards Rowles. Their eyes met and she knew, with absolute certainty, that she would never see him alive again.

Through the tiny crack as the doors closed she caught a glimpse of him turning away from her and running down the corridor. Then there was gunfire and screaming, and the soft buzz of the lift's engine as the metal cage lowered her gently to the ground.

As her eyes filled with tears, she caught a faint hint of lilies on the air.

PART ONE

CHAPTER ONE

"WHEN IS IT acceptable to kill another human being?"

The question hangs there as Green waits for an answer. It takes a moment but eventually a girl three seats back raises her hand.

"Caitlin?"

"When they're trying to kill you, Sir?"

We make them say Sir and Ma'am at St Mark's. Old skool.

Green writes this on the whiteboard. I make a mental note to add whiteboard pens to our scavenging list; we're running short.

"Anyone else?"

More hands go up now that someone else has taken the plunge. Green indicates them one by one, writing their contributions up.

"When someone's trying to kill a friend of yours."

"Or a family member."

"When someone is a murderer."

"Or a rapist."

Green doesn't react any differently to this suggestion, but I shift in my seat, uncomfortable both for him and for myself.

"Or a paedo."

"In a battle, like a war or something."

"As part of an initiation."

Okay, we'd better keep an eye on that one.

"When they're stealing your food or water."

"If they try to take over your home."

"For revenge."

Green turns quickly back to the class. "Who said that? Was that you, Stone?"

The boy nods, unsure if he's about to cop a bollocking.

"Revenge for what, though?" asks Green intently. No-one answers.

The class seems confused. "You see, Stone has hit the heart of the matter. A lot of your suggestions – murderer, rapist, paedophile, thief – wouldn't killing them just be an act of revenge? I mean, the crime's already been committed. You're not going to bring back the murder victim, un-rape someone, un-abuse a child. So why kill the criminal other than for revenge? And if it is revenge, is it a justifiable thing? Is killing for vengeance a crime, or a right?"

Another long pause, then a boy at the back, quite close to me, says: "But in those cases it isn't just revenge, is it, Sir? Coz they might kill again, or rape or abuse or steal. So by killing them you're protecting everybody."

Green claps his hands, pleased. "Yes!" he says forcefully. "But what about prison? If you could lock the person away and thereby protect everyone? Remove the danger, and what purpose does killing the criminal achieve then other than vengeance? So again, is vengeance okay?"

"But there aren't any prisons any more, Sir," responds the boy, warming to the discussion. "And food and water and stuff are hard to get. So it's a question of practicality and resources, isn't it?"

I can tell Green is pleased. This boy is lively and engaged.

"So are we allowed to do things now, after The Cull, that we would have considered immoral beforehand?" demands Green.

"Yes," says the boy firmly. "The world has changed. The morals they had before The Cull are a luxury we just can't afford any more."

"You don't think morality is absolute?" responds Green, who once fired a clip's worth of bullets into an unarmed man and has never displayed a hint of remorse. "That some things are just wrong, no matter what?"

"Do you, Sir?"

Jesus, this boy's, what, fourteen? And before I can help myself I tut inwardly and think 'kids these days.' I smile ruefully at my own reaction. Am I getting old? I notice, as well, that he said 'they.' He was born ten years before The Cull, but already the people who ran the world then are another breed, as ancient and unknowable as the Romans. How quickly we forget.

Green beckons the boy forward. "Come to the front, Stone."

The boy rises and walks down the aisle to the front of the classroom, the other children gently laughing at his discomfort. Green hands the boy a book.

"Turn to page thirteen and read Vindici's speech." The boy begins to read, stumbling over the archaic language at first, but gradually gets the hang of it. I sit, transfixed, until he cries: "Whoe'er knew murder unpaid? Faith, give revenge her due!" and I notice a momentary grimace that flashes across Green's face as the knowledge of his act of vengeance twists in his guts.

I quietly rise from my seat, nod encouragingly at Green, and sneak out of the classroom.

When I was at school, plays like *The Revenger's Tragedy* seemed ancient and irrelevant, hard to understand and full of abstract moral question that meant nothing to us. But these kids? This generation of children who saw everyone they've ever known and loved die slow, painful deaths and then had to survive in a world without law, authority or consequence get that play on a level I never could, and Green – twenty-one now and no longer the uncomfortable, persecuted teenager I first met – has turned into a fine drama teacher; impassioned, encouraging, good with kids. He's also a pacifist now, and refuses to touch a gun under any circumstances.

I'm oddly proud of him. Which, given our personal history, is quite something.

I stand in the hallway and listen to the babble of voices drifting out of the four classrooms that stand adjacent to it. It's a good sound, a hopeful, productive noise. It's learning and debate, friendship and community. And it's rare these days. So very rare.

I glance up at the clock on the wall. 10:36. Of course GMT no longer exists, so the world has reverted to local time – the clocks at St Mark's take their time from the sundial in the garden. I wonder if time, like morality, is absolute. Does GMT still exist somewhere, like those echoes of the big bang that astronomers and physicists were always trying to catch hint of, waiting to be rediscovered and re-established? And if the clock that set GMT is lost, and we someday recreate standard time, what if we're a millisecond out? How would we ever know? I linger in the hallway, surrounded by the murmur of learning, and daydream of a world in which everyone is always a millisecond late.

That's what the security and community of St Mark's allows me, allows all of us – the chance to daydream about the future. I can't imagine that any of the survivors who are stuck out in the cold, scavenging off the scraps of a dead civilisation, ever daydream about anything but the past.

Morning break's at quarter-to, so I decide to swing by the kitchen and grab a cuppa before the place is overrun.

I head deeper into the old house, following the smell of baking to Mrs Atkins' domain. Sourcing ingredients to feed seventy-three children and sixteen adults would have been a pain even before Sainsbury's was looted to extinction, but now it's a full time job for Justin, ample Mrs Atkins' very own Jack Spratt.

He finds it, grows it or barters for it; she cooks it. We've got a thriving market garden that the kids help him maintain, plus a field each of cows, sheep and pigs, not to mention the herds of deer that roam the area. We don't have any vegetarians here. This year we're experimenting with grain crops and corn, but it's early days yet. There's a working windmill in a nearby village but demand is high so we only get a sack every now and then, which makes biscuits and bread a special treat. Our carpentry teacher, Eddie, is working on designs for a windmill of our own, but it's still on the drawing board.

Jamie Oliver would approve of our kitchens – everything's fresh and seasonal, and there isn't a turkey twizzler in sight. But there is a pan of fresh biscuits lying cooling on the sideboard as I walk in, so I snatch one and take a bite before our formidable dinner lady can slap my hand away or hit me over the head with the big brass ladle she's currently using to stir the mutton stew she's preparing for dinner.

"Oi! Make your own, cheeky," says Mrs Atkins as she glares at the crumbs around my mouth.

"Any chance of a cuppa?" I plead. "I fancy dunking. I haven't dunked a biscuit in ages."

"There's the kettle, the Aga's hot, but there's no water."

I grab a bucket from the cupboard, head out to the courtyard and draw some water from the well. It's crystal clear and ice cold. Back in the kitchen I fill the kettle and place it on top of the wood burning stove, which radiates a fierce heat.

"Why so serious?" asks the dinner lady as I warm myself, deep in thought.

"I don't want to lose this," I reply. She looks at me curiously, but I don't elaborate and she takes the hint and returns to her stew.

I make myself a cup of tea and grab another biscuit before heading back to the entrance hall and then up the main stairs.

I push open a door marked No Entry and enter the Ops Room. Most schools have Staff Rooms, but St Mark's is not most schools. Instead of pigeon holes and a coffee area, this room has a map of the British Isles covered in pins, and a notice board thick with accounts of missing children.

I am the first to arrive, so I pull up a chair and sit down, stretch my legs out in front of me and take a sip of my nettle tea. I wince involuntarily. I'd kill for a mug of Typhoo, but we've long since depleted our stocks of tea bags. Now if I want a hot drink my only option is home made herbal infusions. I tut. The Cull has turned us all into new age hippies.

I dunk my biscuit and consider the map.

It is not a standard Ordnance Survey map; it does not show motorways, cities and county boundaries. Instead, it is hand drawn, with huge areas left blank and small handwritten notes that chart the limits of our knowledge. This is a map of the world left behind, a chart of rumours and hearsay, overheard whispers at market day, tales of powerful rulers and legends reborn. It is incomplete and surely inaccurate, but it represents the best intelligence we can gather.

Where a pre-Cull map would have read Salisbury Plain, this one has a small drawing of a mushroom cloud and the word FALLOUT written beneath it in red felt-tip. The areas which used to be called Scotland and Wales now have big question marks over them because although we know there are power struggles going on there, we've no idea who's winning; the area around Nottingham shows a bow and arrow with 'The Hooded Man' written next to it. There are other, smaller pictures and names dotted about – Cleaner Town, Daily Mailonia, The New Republic of the Reborn Briton, Kingdom of Steamies – these are the major players, the mini-empires springing up across the land as alpha males assert their dominance and begin building tribes with which to subjugate, or protect, the survivors.

Beyond the shores of Britain some wag has written 'Here be monsters', but I reckon there are more than enough monsters already ashore.

I cast my glance down to Kent and the big red pin that marks the Fairlawne Estate, new home of St Mark's. There are no major players in this neck of the woods. A spattering of green circles mark the regular markets that have sprung up in the area. Unlike other parts of the country, the home counties have mostly reverted to self-sufficient communities, living off the land, trading with neighbouring villages, literally minding their own beeswax.

The alpha males who tried to set up camp in this neck of the woods were dealt with long ago, leaving room for looser, more organic development.

My eyes track north, to a big black question mark. London. We steer clear of it and, so far as we have been able to ascertain, so does everybody else we have regular contact with. Even the army, back before they were destroyed, were biding their time before wading into that particular cess pit. I think of it as a boil that sooner or later will burst and shower the rest of the country with whichever vile infection it's currently incubating. It disturbs me to be living so close to such a mystery, and I know that sooner or later I'm going to have to lead a team inside the M25. I don't relish the prospect.

I hear the bell ringing for morning break and then there's a cacophony of running feet, shouting, laughing and slamming doors as the kids race to the kitchen for biscuits.

The door behind me swings open. I can tell who it is by the lopsided footsteps.

"Hey Jack," I say, taking another sip of tea, hopeful that if I keep drinking I'll develop a taste for it in the end.

The King of England, Jack Bedford, drags a chair from the side of the room and sits down next to me, heavily. Without a word he leans forward, rolls up his left trouser leg and begins undoing the straps that secure his prosthesis.

"Still chafing?" I ask.

He grunts a confirmation, detaching the fibreglass extension that completes his leg and laying it on the floor. He begins massaging the stump.

"It's not so bad," he says eventually. "But I've been reffing the footie. So, you know, sore."

"Come see me afterwards, I'll give you some balm."

"Thanks."

What he really needs is a custom-made prosthesis, properly calibrated. But the tech is beyond our reach. We scoured every hospital still standing and were lucky to find such a good match. I have no idea what we'll do if it ever breaks.

I like Jack. He's sixteen years old, his face ravaged by acne and his hair thick with grease that no shampoo seems able to shift. He keeps himself to himself, and has watchful eyes and an air of secrecy that I'm not sure anybody else has noticed. Only a select few of us know that he is the hereditary monarch, and we have no intention of telling anybody. Jack seems grateful for the anonymity. Nonetheless he has become part of the inner circle at the school, one of those boys that we adults treat as an equal. He's proven himself brave, loyal and capable.

"Anything new?" he asks.

"Yeah," I reply. "But we'll wait 'til the others get here."

"Fair enough."

The door opens again and Lee and his father, John, enter.

"I don't reckon it's likely," Lee is saying, but his father disagrees.

"Think about it," says John. "We know he likes the ladies, and he's got a violent temper."

"But we've no evidence he ever even knew Lilly," says Lee, taking a seat on my other side.

"Lee, she was his son's girlfriend."

Lee shakes his head. "No, I still reckon it's Weevil."

"Dream on," says John, with a laugh.

Neither Jack nor I have to ask what they're discussing. Our DVD nights have been dominated by season one of *Veronica Mars* for the last two weeks and the whole school is trying to solve the Lilly Kane murder. With the internet consigned to history, no-one can hit Wikipedia and spoil it for everyone else, and I keep the discs locked in the safe so no-one can sneak down at night and skip to the end.

"You'll find out in two episodes time, guys," says Jack with a smile.

"May be a while though," I say. "We're nearly out of petrol for the generator. Can't have any more telly 'til we refuel."

Lee makes a pained face. "You're fucking kidding me. Really?"

I let him squirm for a second then smile. "Nah, telly as usual tonight, eight o'clock for the big finish."

"Bitch," he says, smiling, then he leans forward and kisses me. His jaw gives a little click as he does so, a reminder of the damage he sustained two years ago in the Salisbury explosion. He still has two metal rods holding the bottom of his face together. I kiss him right back.

Lee has just turned eighteen. I am ten years his senior. We've been lovers for six months and he makes me feel like a schoolgirl.

Jack rolls his eyes. "Get a room," he says.

When we break apart I catch John's eye, but his face is a mask, giving nothing away. I am still unsure how he feels about my cradle-snatching antics. Part of me couldn't give a damn whether he approves or not, but he's a colleague and an ally, not to mention my boyfriend's dad, so another part of me craves his approval. He's a hard man to get to know, John Keegan. A hardened veteran of numerous wars, he's seen and done some terrible things. He's undemonstrative but never rude; friendly but never familiar. He's fiercely devoted to his son, and Lee to him, but while they get along well and spend lots of time together fishing, playing football and running, there's a slight reserve to their relationship.

I know that Lee killed his mother – put her out of her misery when the virus was putting her through hell. He still hasn't told John this. I think John suspects and wants to talk to his son about it but has never been able to broach the subject. The secret hovers between them, poisoning the air.

"Where's Tariq?" asks Lee.

"Late as usual," I reply.

The door opens and Tariq strides in, chest out, confident, with a hint of swagger. The Iraqi is twenty years old, with hawkish features, thick black hair, eyes that seem to be permanently amused and a vicious hook where his left hand should be. The first person he makes eye contact with is John, and they share a nod of greeting. Before The Cull Tariq was a young lad in Basra, blogging about corruption and running from the militias. Afterwards, he and John led the resistance to the US occupation. John treats Tariq like another son, and Tariq does anything John asks of him, without question.

Lee and Tariq exchange greetings, but with more reserve. They are friends, and they've saved each other's lives countless times under fire, but Tariq doesn't entirely trust Lee. He thinks he has a death wish that could get everyone killed. I'm worried that he may be right.

Tariq pulls up a chair and sits beside John. The gang's all here.

I take another sip of tea. "Nope," I curse. "No matter how much I try to convince myself otherwise, this is rank." I spit the tea back into the mug and put it down on the floor.

"Okay," I say. "John?"

John gets up, steps to the front of the room and sits on the desk facing us.

"Couple of things," he says briskly in his thick Black Country accent. "We've had a response from the Hooded Man. He's invited an envoy to visit and discuss possible co-operation in the future."

"Do we have any idea who he is yet?" asks Tariq.

John shakes his head. "Haven't even got a name. My guess is that he's ex-military, but I don't know for sure. I did find out one thing though, and you'll like this – the man he deposed, who by all accounts was a vicious son of a bitch, was a Frenchman called De Falaise."

Tariq and Lee are agog. "No fucking way," says Lee, eventually. John just nods.

"Anyone care to fill me in?" asks Jack.

"We had a run in with him on the way back from Iraq. He's the reason I don't hear in stereo any more," says Lee. "Is he dead?" John nods again. "Then this Prince of Thieves guy's fine with me.

Even if he does wear tights. Is there word on that, by the way?" John smiles and shakes his head.

"He's building an army of sorts," John continues. "Calls them Rangers. They're a kind of paramilitary police force and so far they seem to be doing a good job of keeping the peace. But it's still a power base, so there's every chance Hood could turn out to be just as bad as the man he kicked out, just more subtle."

"You still think we should send someone?" I ask.

"Oh yeah, but whoever you send should keep their eyes and ears open. If he's going to be a threat, we need to know. So far he doesn't know our exact location, and I'd like to keep it that way, at least for now."

I turn to the king. "Jack, you fancy a trip?"

He frowns. "Wasn't Robin Hood always fighting the king?"

"First off, he won't know you're the king," says Lee. "And second, no, he was fighting the king's brother. He was loyal to Richard. Did they teach you nothing at King School?"

"I missed the first year of Putting Down Rebellious Peasants."

"Has he been having problems with the snatchers?" I ask, bringing the conversation back on topic.

John shakes his head. "They know about them, but so far they're staying out of Hood's territory. I'd bet money that he's got some of his Rangers trying to track them down, but he's hardly going to tell us details of his operations." He pauses and takes a deep breath. I can tell he's about to deliver bad news.

"The second thing is that there's been another raid. A big one."

"Who?"

"The Steamies."

We're all shocked. The Kingdom of Steamies are a community that's grown up along the length of the old Spa Valley Railway. Their philosophy, handed down by their benevolent but bonkers leader, rejects all electrical power, relying instead on steam engines. It's like stepping back to the nineteenth century when we visit their domain, but most everywhere else is like stepping back to the fourteenth so they're ahead on points.

"How many?" I ask.

"They hit the Steamie settlement at High Rocks. There were eleven children there. All gone. They killed most of their parents in the snatch, too."

"That's a hell of an escalation," says Tariq.

John nods. "They're getting bolder."

"Did you track them?" asks Lee.

"Straight to the M25, same as always."

"Double the patrols," I say. "And enough with the rifles. Issue the machine guns. I'm not taking any chances."

"Done," replies Tariq, who is responsible for perimeter security.

"That all, John?" I ask.

"Yeah, although I still think..."

"We should go after them."

"Sooner or later they're going to find us. I'd rather find them first."

"Duly noted."

There's a moment when I think he's going to challenge me, but he shrugs and resumes his seat. He's older than me, and far more experienced. But this is my school, and he accepts that – some days with better grace than others.

"Tariq?"

Tariq remains in his seat, I wonder whether out of laziness or some complex dynamic of male hierarchy that makes him uncomfortable taking the table his one time leader just vacated.

"I've been to three markets this week," he says. "Sevenoaks, Cranbrook and Crowborough. People are paranoid and there are a lot more guns being carried openly. There was a fight at Crowborough which ended with a man being shot. It was a misunderstanding, it seems. Someone trying to return a lost child got accused of abducting them. Tensions are high. When word of the attack on the Steamies gets out, they'll get higher. I didn't hear of any fresh raids, though."

"Lee?"

I know what he's about to tell everyone, so he turns away from me as he speaks. I stare at the thick line of baldness that runs down the back of his head, betraying the presence of a surgical scar. I bear a similar mark.

"I've been up to Oxford for a few days. A while back we heard of a group that had secured the Bodleian and was trying to start up a university. There are about fifty of them, all ages, scholars and students. The boss is a guy called Pearce – big, musclebound, ex-Para. He's an unlikely Dean of Studies, but from what I could tell he's passionately devoted to what they're doing and more than willing to kill anyone who threatens the project."

"Forces?" asks Jack.

"A team of six; four guys, two women. Hardnosed, well armed. Polite but not welcoming. They let me stay overnight, though, and while I didn't sound them out directly, I'd recommend making an approach."

"Why?" asks Tariq. "They're miles away."

"We're a school," I reply. "Where else would the kids go after they finish their studies with us, but university?"

"There's more," says Lee. "Over dinner, one of Pearce's men offered up some intel on the snatchers. He says they've been increasingly active in East Anglia, and thinks they have a staging post in Thetford."

I rise from my chair. My stomach is full of butterflies because I know that what I am about to do puts everything I have worked to create here at risk. But I've mulled it over long enough. It doesn't really matter who these bastards are or why they're capturing children, they're expanding their area of operations and getting bolder. Sooner or later they're going to learn our location and pay us a visit. I don't intend to sit here waiting for them to arrive.

John's instincts are sound. It's time to take direct action.

"So that's where we're going," I say. "I want everyone out front this time tomorrow, full kit and arms. If these fuckers have a place of business, I think we should pay it a visit." I fold my arms and strike a resolute pose, accidentally kicking over my cold nettle tea as I do so.

"That's gonna stain," says Lee with a smile.

WHEN THE MEETING'S adjourned, the inner circle all head back to their allotted tasks. Lee is working in the garden today, Jack is doing an inventory of the armoury, Tariq is teaching creative writing to a classroom full of impressionable teenage girls who hang on his every word. John teaches PE and survival skills, but has a free day. He stays in his seat until the others have left, then leans forward earnestly.

"Good move, Jane," he says.

"But?"

"I want to set clear chain of command in the field. We've not gone looking for a fight in a long time and I want to be sure everybody knows how things work."

"I've told you before John, in here I'm the boss. But in the field you're in charge."

"And you'll have no trouble taking orders from me?" he asks, slightly dubious.

"None. You're a soldier. I'm a... I dunno what I am. I used to be a doctor, then I was a matron. Now, I suppose I'm a headmistress. Either way, you've more combat experience and training than all the rest of us put together. It's only right that you take charge when we're in action."

He nods, biting his lip. I can sense an unasked question.

"Do you think they're ready?" I ask eventually.

He shrugs. "Your guess is as good as mine," he replies. "Jack's pretty nimble on his leg. He's not going to win any 100 metre sprints, but he'll be fine. Tariq can still shoot straight and the claw's a nasty weapon if needed."

"And Lee?"

He pauses, trying to frame his reply correctly. "The limp's almost imperceptible, his arm doesn't have full movement, but again, it's not a handicap. Physically, I think he's as healed as he's ever going to be."

"But psychologically?"

"He worries me."

"Still? It's been two years since Salisbury."

"But he won't talk about it. Anything that happened between The Cull and Salisbury is off limits."

"And that bothers you?"

"Doesn't it bother you?"

"No," I say firmly. "He wants to move on. I've told you everything I can about what happened during the year Mac was in charge, and Tariq filled you in on events at Salisbury. You know the facts. He was so angry all the time but it's faded now. He's calmer."

"I think that's got more to do with you than anything else," says John eventually. I just smile and he doesn't pursue the point. "Anyway, I want you to keep an especially close eye on him while we're out there. PTSD can manifest in unexpected ways. He's been fine here, it's true, but this is a sheltered environment and somewhere he feels safe. I was worried when he started going on field trips, but they've all gone smoothly. My point is he's not been tested. It's just possible he may fall to pieces the first time someone takes a shot at him. Or worse, see red and fly into danger without a second thought."

"I will, but I think you're worrying over nothing." It's a complete lie. Everything he's just said I've been thinking too. If I could think of a way to keep Lee out of danger, I'd take it. He's earned the break. But he'd be insulted and would insist on coming anyway so in the end it would probably do more harm than good. "Not exactly a crack squad of elite forces are we?" I say with a smile. "A one legged boy, a hook-handed man, a partially deaf limping potential headcase and a matron."

He sits back and crosses his arms. "Took out the whole US Army didn't we? I reckon a bunch of kidnappers won't be too much trouble."

But we both know it's bravado.

"While I've got you alone, John," I say hesitantly. "Are you... I mean... me and Lee... is it?"

"Not my business," he says firmly. "He's 18."

"You don't mind, though?"

"That's irrelevant."

"Not to me."

He sighs heavily and his shoulders sag. For a moment the mask slips and I can see concern on his face. But it's not an unfriendly look.

"Honestly?"

"Honestly."

"All right then," he says. "I think you're gorgeous and clever and the best possible thing that could happen to my son right now."

"I hate to say this again, but... but?"

And then he says something that in one fell swoop fucks me up more than I could have imagined possible.

"Jesus, Jane, you don't half remind me of his mother when she was your age."

He rises from his chair, puts a hand on my shoulder for a moment, then leaves.

I sit there for on my own a long, long time.

God, I could kill a cuppa.

I WORRY ABOUT the perishability of rubber.

We've got a huge great pallet of condoms that we lifted from an abandoned warehouse. I remember when we found them, back on a scavenging trip when Mac was still in charge. I insisted we bring them along. At first Lee got a bit embarrassed – he was fifteen, after all – and then a bit annoyed.

"Why the hell would we want them?" he asked me.

I told him he'd understand eventually. I think he thought I was making fun of him, but I was beginning to worry about a residential school full of teenage boys and girls and the difficulty of stopping them shagging like rabbits every time they were out of a teacher's earshot.

Once I was in charge, I organised sex education classes and then made the condoms available to any child who wanted them. No age limit, no questions asked. Simply put, the alternative was lots of teenage mums. I may favour home births, birthing pools and all that jazz but if there are complications I've not got the kit to deal with them.

In post-Cull England, childbirth was once again almost certain to become a big killer of young women. I felt sure that sooner or later we'd hear of a communal birth centre being set up somewhere; it was inevitable. But until then, I wanted to keep pregnancies to a minimum, and sex ed. and free condoms seemed a pragmatic approach.

We've only had one unwanted pregnancy so far and thankfully the birth was textbook. Sharon from Bournemouth has a little boy called Josh and she's not telling anyone who the father is, although everyone knows it's a spotty little tyke called Adrian.

This baby did something I'd not expected. It drew us all closer together, unified the school. Josh somehow became communal property, raised not by Sharon, although I ensured she remained primary carer, but by the school as a whole.

The first time he crawled was during breakfast. He took off down the aisle between the tables to a huge round of applause and cheers from the assembled kids. Clearly, he's meant for the stage.

It was a special moment.

As the common room fills up for the evening's DVD I think of Josh and the effect he's had on us. What would the school do if he were taken? I don't mean if he died. It would be awful, but we're all familiar with death by now, and another reality of post-Cull England was that infant mortality was going to soar to... well, to the kind of levels seen in pre-Cull Africa. Death happens, you get over it, you move on.

I mean if he was snatched, spirited away, never to be seen again. It doesn't bear thinking about.

I dwell on this for two reasons.

Most importantly because the sell-by date on the condoms has just expired.

But more immediately, because children like Josh have been disappearing from homes and villages across the South-East for the last year or so. At first only a few, then more and more frequently and, after the incident at High Rocks, more violently. Someone is running an organised kidnapping ring and it's kids they're after. Chances are they'll eventually come for St Mark's.

I'm not a mother yet, I may never be. But these kids are all mine, in a way. And if someone's going to come and try to take them away at gunpoint, I'm going to stop them, or die trying.

Protecting them means leaving the school grounds, taking the fight to our as yet anonymous enemy. I've not left the grounds since I arrived here in a wheelchair, broken and battered after my time with the American Army. I don't want to leave. I have a kind of agoraphobia, I suppose. This is my home, my community, and the thought of leaving terrifies me. What if I inadvertently lead the enemy straight here? What if I have to watch Lee, or any of the others, die? I'm not a soldier, I never wanted to be a soldier, but that's what The Cull made of all of us. I've spent the last two peaceful years trying to pretend that my fighting days were behind me. But I was lying to myself.

I start the DVD then I head upstairs to strip and oil my guns.

CHAPTER TWO

THE GUN FELT weird; a mix of familiarity and fear.

I settled into my position, feeling the early winter cold seeping up through my trousers from the damp carpet on the floor of the front bedroom. My gun-shot legs would ache all day after this, like an arthritic pensioner.

I rested my arms on the window sill of the old terraced house, carefully avoiding the few shards of broken glass still sticking up from the crumbling putty, and nestled the stock of the L115A3 sniper rifle in my shoulder, sighting down the barrel.

I'd taken it down the firing range a couple of weeks before, when I'd realised that a fight was inevitable. It had only taken me an hour or so to master it. My skills had not deserted me. It was the same weight as the L96 I had taken from the sniper who'd used it to put a bullet in my left leg four years earlier, but it had a silencer, a better sight, and it fired a higher calibre round – 8.59mm rather than the L96's 7.62mm. Basically, it made it much easier to hit the target, gave a near 100% certainty of killing them if I did, and a much greater chance of staying undetected after taking the shot. It felt like an extension of me, but one that I was not sure I was comfortable with, like how I supposed Tariq must feel about his hook.

I couldn't tell you whether it was fear, cold or anticipation that made my hands shake.

The pre-dawn darkness meant I would be invisible to the two men unless they were to turn their binoculars straight at me and, by some chance, pause to study the dark window for a moment. But right now they were pre-occupied with the strangers who'd just turned up on their doorstep unannounced and offered them five captive children. For the right price, natch.

"Do you have a preference?" I asked softly.

"Nah," replied Tariq, from the window to my right.

"I'll take the one with the beard, then."

"Okay."

It had been two years since I'd held a weapon with intent to kill. It hadn't been a conscious decision to avoid guns, but after Salisbury I'd spent so many months recuperating – learning to walk, to use my arms, to talk again – that target practice had been the last thing on my mind. Two years of nobody shooting at us had helped, too. But if I'm honest, I was wary of the things. I knew that my behaviour during and after Iraq had been erratic. I knew that Tariq was concerned about the risks I had taken, and those I might take again.

I shared his concerns.

"Three, two, one…"

I took a deep breath, held it, squeezed the trigger gently, put a bullet in the guard's heart and splashed his innards across a brick wall. He fell without a sound. I saw my dad catch and lower him to the ground. Then he stood and drew his sidearm. Tariq's shot also found its mark, and his target jerked backwards as the top of his head exploded. Jane flinched in surprise and failed to catch him. He crashed into the wall and slid down, staring up at her in reproach.

"Head shot?" I asked as grabbed my heavy pack. "Flash bastard."

"Sight's high," replied Tariq as we got to our feet and picked our way carefully down the rotten, rickety stairs. We left our sniper rifles behind us. They were no use at close quarters, and if all went according to plan they would be collected for us. We pulled the straps of our SA-80s over our heads as we emerged onto the street. As I did so, I realised that my hands weren't shaking any more.

As we ran down the road, the five kids that Dad and Jane had been escorting were throwing away their handcuffs and pulling guns from under their coats. By the time we reached them, the team was ready.

Dad led the way into the compound.

"WE'RE GOING TO go with a variation of the Trojan horse approach that Jane used a couple of years back," my dad had said, earlier that night. We had huddled around the feeble flame we'd just kindled in the fireplace of an abandoned farmhouse about a mile outside Thetford as he outlined his strategy.

"I had Rowles and Caroline with me then," said Matron, as if pointing out the flaw in his plan.

"There are nine of us this time. The odds are better," he replied, unsure what point she was making.

"You never met Rowles," I said.

Dad rolled his eyes and continued. "Jane and I will escort the younger children to the gate. You kids can stay bundled up in your winter coats, so there'll be plenty of places to hide your weapons. You'll be bound with what will look like handcuffs, but in fact..." He threw pairs of handcuffs to each of the twelve and thirteen year-olds we'd selected for this mission. The five children examined them and smiled one by one as they realised they were plastic toy cuffs, easy to pull apart but good enough to fool an unobservant guard in the half light of early morning.

"Sweet," said one of them – a beanpole boy called Guria who had become de facto leader of the younger group.

"We know they keep two guards at the main gate but if last night was routine, they have no one else on the walls or, as far as we can tell, inside the compound," Dad went on. "They are not expecting to be attacked. Anyway, there's plenty of open ground between the gates and the nearest houses, so they'd see a frontal assault coming in plenty of time to sound the alarm.

"Jane and I will approach with the kids in tow and our hands up. They should assume we've come to sell them and let us approach."

"How do we deal with the guards?" asked Tariq.

"I don't want to get involved in close quarters fighting with the young ones around, so while we keep them talking, you and Lee will have to use the rifles to take them out quickly and quietly. The nearest house will provide a perfect vantage point. I couldn't find any booby traps when I recced the area earlier, so you should be fine."

Tariq and I glanced at each other and nodded. "No problem," we said in unison.

"Once the guards are down, you kids take off the cuffs, get out your guns and scatter to the nearest houses. I don't want you inside the compound, because things could get messy, but if we need to make a quick retreat you can cover our withdrawal. Guria, you know how to use the sniper rifle, so you take up Lee's position."

"Fine," said Guria.

"Jane, Lee and Tariq, you'll come with me, inside."

"And then?" asked Jane.

"Then we improvise."

*   *   *

DAD WENT IN first, Tariq followed, Jane and I brought up the rear.

I watched Jane move as we entered enemy territory, marvelling at the change in her. I'd fought beside Dad and Tariq in Iraq and England, but Jane and I had only fought together once, very briefly, during the siege of the original St Mark's, three years earlier. I knew she was capable and ruthless, but I'd not seen this side of her in a long time, and even then I'd never had a chance to study her in action. I'd become accustomed to seeing the gentler, nurturing, matronly for want of a better word, side of her, during the past couple of years. I had mixed feelings about watching her creep into danger, all stealth and purpose. On one hand, I hated the idea of her being in harm's way. I wanted to protect her and keep her safe. On the other hand, *damn*, it was sexy.

She glanced back at me, perhaps sensing how closely I was watching her. She gave me a quizzical look then a quick, amused smile, as if she was reading my mind.

"Focus," she whispered. Then she turned away, back to the business at hand.

The wooden door in the old brick wall led directly into the playground of what had once been a primary school. We crept across a faded hopscotch cross that seemed to be pointing us to the main building – a solid, Victorian stone box with big, high windows which sat at the centre of a maze of single storey brick extensions built in the 1960s. The only sound was the crunch of gravel beneath our boots and the raucous crowing of a rooster, informing the world that dawn was nearly here. Anyone inside was obviously accustomed to sleeping through his daily performance.

Dad waved us towards a side door. We were still in the middle of the playground, as exposed as we could be, when the door handle turned. Dad didn't hesitate. He ran to the door, still totally silent, and was there with his knife drawn as it swung open to reveal a short, heavy-set man in a black jacket. The man was only half awake, mechanically going through the routine of opening up the building for the morning. He was so focused on his task that he didn't notice Dad's approach until the cold knife point brushed against his cheek. Dad grasped the man's top and pulled him outside the door, letting it swing to. We crowded around our prisoner as his surprise faded, to be replaced by amused defiance.

"How many of you, and how many kids?" whispered Dad as Tariq pulled a sidearm from the man's belt and shoved it into his own.

"Fuck off," replied the man, misjudging the situation entirely. He probably thought he could issue a few vague threats, put on a show of defiance, and then we'd knock him out or tie him up or something.

Dad considered his smug captive for a second, shrugged, and slid his knife between the man's third and fourth ribs, straight into his heart. The man never even had time to be surprised. He was dead before the blade came out again.

"Jesus," whispered Jane, involuntarily.

Dad lowered the body gently to the cold, hard tarmac, then flashed her a sharp look as he wiped his blade.

"Problem?" he mouthed silently.

Jane waited perhaps an instant too long before shaking her head. They held each other's gaze for a second. She looked away first. Dad turned, pulled open the door, and led us inside.

Subconsciously I think I'd been expecting the building to have that familiar school smell, but instead we were greeted by the stench of rotting timber, pervasive damp and unwashed bodies.

We found ourselves in a corridor that stretched to our left and right, ending in double swing doors at each end. Wooden doors with glass panels led into what had once been classrooms. A notice board hung on the wall directly facing us as we entered. It still had water damaged paintings and faded crayon drawings pinned to it.

Jane gently closed the door behind us and Dad led us to the right, towards what had looked like the assembly hall from outside. No matter how softly we trod, the squeak of our boots on the linoleum sounded like a chorus of banshees. I nervously walked backwards at the rear of the group, covering the swing doors at the far end, expecting someone to come crashing through them at any moment, guns blazing.

We crowded around the hall doors. The windows had blankets hanging over them on the inside, so we had no idea what we'd be walking into. There was a heavy metal chain padlocked through the door handles. I took the metal cutters from my backpack and got to work.

"We go in quiet," whispered Dad as I tried in vain to cut through the thick steel quietly. "Jane, stay just inside the door and keep an eye on the corridor. Tariq and I will go right. Lee, you go straight ahead. We fan out. No shooting unless absolutely necessary – there could be children in here."

We all nodded.

I finished cutting and threaded the broken chain off the metal handles, leaving it in a pile on the floor. Dad gently pushed the door open and we crept into the darkness, the squeaks of our boot soles echoing against the rotting wooden climbing frames that lined the far wall.

Blankets had been taped over the huge windows that Jane and I walked past as we moved into the hall, but the first light of dawn sent dim chinks of light through the moth holes and gaps to illuminate a large floor space littered with small grey mounds.

It took me a moment to realise that these were sleeping children, huddled on the cold, hardwood floor under ragged old blankets. There was no sign of any guards.

Dad waved me over to him.

"We've got to move quickly," he said. "The other exit is chained from the outside too, so we're stuck in a cul-de-sac. The second anyone walks down that corridor, we're trapped. You head outside and unchain the fire escape, that way we've got choices."

I turned on my heels and squeaked past Jane, down the corridor and back to the playground. Just as the exterior door swung closed behind me I heard a muffled shout of "Oi, who left the chain off? Jim? You there?"

I paused and considered my options, then drew my knife and crept back to the door, stepping over the cooling body of the guard Dad had killed only minutes before. I crouched down and peered through the glass panel, thick with grime and mildew. I could make out a tall woman walking down the corridor towards the hall. She was bringing a shotgun to bear, beginning to be concerned.

"Jim?" she said again, more quietly, wary and suspicious now.

I waited until she had just passed the door, stood up and grasped the handle. I'd have to be quick about this. I took a deep breath and swung the door open, stepped into the corridor and brought the knife to her throat in one fluid motion. She froze.

"To the hall, slowly," I whispered in her ear. She walked forward without a word. I pressed in hard against her back, feeling her body – warm, tense, slim and muscled. She was as tall as me, with dirty blonde hair, and she really needed a bath.

Jane opened the hall door and ushered us inside. She took the woman's gun away and gestured for her to sit on the floor. I could see children beginning to sit up across the hall, sleepy and confused.

"All yours," I said, and then I headed back outside to complete my task.

The sky was bright grey as I skirted round the outside of the building to the fire escape which was, as predicted, chained from the outside. I didn't bother being quiet this time. I chopped the chain and pulled the door open. It made an awful noise as it opened for the first time in years, but nobody came running.

By now there were children standing up, as Tariq moved quietly through the hall waking them one by one and telling them to wake their friends. There was a susurration of whispers.

The plan had been to take one captive for interrogation, rescue the kids, and try to get out of the compound without the alarm being raised. So far so good. I propped the fire escape open with a chair and ran over to Dad, who was kneeling facing the captured snatcher. Jane was still keeping watch at the door.

"I'll only ask you one more time," Dad said as I drew up beside him. "How many of you are there?

The woman, who I could now see was in her early twenties and had multiple piercings all over her face, clenched her jaw and stared ahead, defiantly. Dad shook his head and turned to me.

"Cuff her and bring her along," he said briskly, then he went to help Tariq muster the kids by the fire exit. I pulled a set of genuine cuffs from my pack.

"Wrists," I said curtly. She held out her arms and gave me a sarcastic smile. I shook my head and indicated for her to turn around. She got up on her knees, shuffled so she was facing the wall, and put her arms behind her back.

I snapped the cuffs closed and used them to drag her to her feet.

There were about twenty children gathered by the door now, each with a blanket pulled tight around their shoulders. As I marched the woman across the hall towards them I could see that the boys and girls ranged in age from toddlers right up to fourteen- or maybe fifteen-year-olds. Every one of them looked hollow cheeked and had dark rings around their eyes where hardship and lack of food had taken its toll, but their eyes all told different stories, speaking of everything from broken defeat to spirited resistance. As I approached, one of them, a slight girl with a scowl on her face, stepped up to my dad.

"Why should we believe you?" she said primly, folding her arms and sticking out her chin. "How do we know you're not just going to sell us yourselves?"

I could see that Dad didn't know how to respond to this. Even though he'd spent two years as a de facto staff member at St Mark's he still wasn't very good at talking to children. He tended to be brusque and uncomfortable around them. He wasn't unkind, but he didn't really understand that kids need to be handled with more sensitivity and patience than, say, a squaddie on a parade ground. He liked kids, he just didn't get them.

Tariq smiled and reached for the gun he had taken from the guard. He handed it to the girl, who took it warily.

"This is the safety," he said, demonstrating. "It's cocked and ready to fire now, so all you need to do is flick the safety off, point and shoot. But not at me, please. Okay?"

The little girl nodded at him in mute, wide-eyed astonishment.

"Good girl. I'm Tariq, by the way."

"Jenni," she whispered. "Pleased to meet you."

"And you!"

"If you've quite finished flirting, can we get a move on?" I said. Dad and I laughed as Jenni blushed bright red.

"Jane, let's go," said Dad.

She ran to join us and we led the children – cold, hungry, holding hands in a long chain, but quiet and co-operative – out of the hall and into the open. Tariq ran to the corner and peered around. He signalled the all clear and we moved as quickly as we could to the playground gate.

"One sound," I whispered to my prisoner, "and I'll slit your throat." Even so, I was surprised she didn't try and raise the alarm.

Dad pushed open the gate and stood watching the school for signs of pursuit as the children filed outside. When they were all out, and the gate was closed behind us, I gave a short laugh of relief.

"We're not clear yet," warned Jane, but I could see she was feeling it too. She smiled at me then ran down the road to get the minibus, which was parked down the side alley. It started first time and she drove quickly to the gate where we loaded the children inside.

When they were all safely stashed I leapt up into the front passenger seat with Dad and pulled the door closed. Just Guria and the other kids to collect, and we'd be on our way.

"Turn the heater on, I'm bloody frozen," I said. But Jane wasn't listening.

"Look," she said softly.

I glanced up and cursed.

Five men were standing in the road ahead of us, motionless, watching, waiting for us to make a move. They were dressed in camouflage gear. Dark green hoods obscured their faces. The outlying two had swords in their hands; the two inside them held strong wooden bows raised with arrows poised to fire. The middle one stood with his bow down, casual. Waiting for us to make the first move.

"And it was all going so well," muttered Tariq, over my shoulder.

CHAPTER THREE

"I'LL HANDLE THIS," says John.

But I've seen the way he handles things, and I'm not prepared to let him screw this up. This calls for diplomacy, not violence.

I'm out of the cab and walking before he can stop me.

The middle of the five men raises his bow, notches an arrow, draws the catgut back slowly and sights on me as I step into the road.

"Put your hands above your head and get on your knees," he shouts.

I put my hands up, but start walking towards them. I figure the last thing they'll be expecting is politeness, so as I approach I smile and say: "Could you keep the noise down, please? We're trying to stage an escape here."

I can see this throws him, and he doesn't try to stop me approaching. I stop about three metres in front of him, hands above my head, ensuring that my body language is as passive as possible. His arrow is still pointing straight at my head, and now the two men either side of him are aiming at the cab of the minibus behind me.

He cocks his head, inviting me to explain.

"At a guess, you're Rangers," I say. "From Nottingham, yes?"

He gives me nothing.

"My name's Jane Crowther, I run a school called St Mark's. You may have heard of us."

The man shakes his head once.

"Right, well, your boss invited me to send an envoy up to you last week. One of my people is talking to you guys in Nottingham right now."

He shrugs; what has this got to do with him?

"I imagine you're here to take down the snatchers and rescue the kids," I continue. "Thing is, we just did that. Or at least, we got the kids out of the building and into the minibus. Most of the snatchers are still inside, asleep. And the longer we stand around here making noise, the greater the chance of them waking up and starting to shoot at us. So can we please, *please* take this discussion elsewhere?"

He considers me carefully, then gives a tiny nod.

"Crossroads. One hour," he says to his men. Then he gestures for me to walk back to the bus. "I'll be right behind you," he growls. His men peel off and begin heading back into the shadows. I turn on my heels, but before I can start walking there's a sharp report, a dull impact, and a grunt. Instinctively, I drop to my knees and draw my weapon. I don't even need to look behind me to realise that the leader of the Rangers is slowly toppling backwards – I felt the spray of blood and brains splash across the back of my neck.

I can see Lee leaping out of the minibus cab while his father jumps across to the driver's seat and prepares to pull away.

But I'm confused. I scan the walls of the primary school and can't see anyone at all. The snatchers must still be in bed or, more likely, reaching sleepily for their guns now they've heard shooting. And then I process the fact that the blood hit the back of my neck. The bullet came from the other end of the road. I drop and roll, coming up facing the other way. I can see two Rangers bolting for cover in the terraced houses on either side of the road, and two more dragging their leader away by his wrists.

I'm totally exposed, a sitting duck, and I still can't see the shooter.

"No! Don't!" shouts Lee as he runs towards me. He dives sideways as an arrow comes whistling past me, meant for him. One of the Rangers is shooting at him.

"Dammit," I yell. "We didn't shoot your boss!"

And then I realise, with a sinking feeling, that we did.

"Guria, you fuckwit, where are you?" yells Lee as he staggers to his feet and scurries for cover.

I see a Ranger take aim at the minibus cab and I have no choice. I send two rounds past his head and force him into the doorway of the nearest house. I've just confirmed to him that we're the enemy. No going back now.

Before I can get to my feet and run to join Lee, there's a snapping noise and gravel spatters my cheek. Someone else is shooting at me. I'll be dead if I stay here another second, so I just get up and run as fast as I can for the nearest doorway, the frame of which splinters as I race through into the rotting terrace. Those bullets are coming from the other direction, which means the snatchers have woken up and decided to join in. I crouch inside the hall of the ruined house, trying to work out what to do.

I've got a kid gone rogue with a sniper rifle, misguidedly trying to protect me. There are at least four highly trained Rangers who now want to kill all of us. And there's an angry group of child-rustlers taking potshots at us from behind a big brick wall. Lee and I are trapped in houses on opposite sides of the street, there are four other armed children cowering in houses somewhere, and worst of all a minibus full of kids is smack bang in the middle of the crossfire. Would the snatchers shoot them rather than let them escape? I hear the engine revving. John isn't sticking around to find out. The minibus goes roaring past the house I'm sheltering in, making a break for it, getting the kids to safety.

The moment they're past I risk leaning out and sending some bullets back towards the snatchers. I get a vague impression of three of them lined along the wall. None of the Rangers are anywhere to be seen. I think only one of them is on this side of the street, which means three others are opposite me, with a clear shot if they want to take it.

There's nothing I can do here except get myself shot. Time to go. I race through the house, past an overturned sofa thick with fungus, through a burnt-out kitchen, out the back door, down the old brick-walled yard, past the shed which used to be an outdoor toilet, and through the gate into the back alley.

Before I can get my bearings I hear the unmistakeable sound of a car crash.

Just for a second I catch myself wondering whether any day has ever gone completely to shit so quickly. But the answer, of course, is yes. Once.

Right – stop, think, prioritise.

Lee can take care of himself. Guria and the other four should have the sense to make their way out of the area, if they can avoid the Rangers. I have to worry about the minibus, because if John's wrapped it round a lamppost they could be injured. That's where I'm needed.

I run down the alleyway, away from the school, towards the ominous sound of a blaring car horn.

As I run, I expect to see a Ranger step out ahead of me, or hear one of the children calling for me to stop, but an eerie silence has fallen, broken only by that horn. The back alley is cobbled, with a gunnel running down the middle of it. I race past countless wooden yard gates, some hang off their hinges but most are still bolted shut. As I reach the far end of the alley I pass a row of garages and then I'm out into the street, skidding to a halt and trying to make it back into the alley without being seen. Because the minibus has driven head first into the grille of an enormous lorry, the first of a convoy of three, all boasting huge spray painted red circles on the side like some kind of logo. The street swarms with angry men carrying big guns.

I finally manage to stop about two feet away from a man who has his back to me. I take a step back; he hasn't heard me. I turn, planning to creep back into cover... and I'm staring down the double barrels of a sawn-off shotgun.

So there I stand, watching the steam from the ruined minibus curling into the air behind the head of this gunman, trying to think of something to say. But he finds his tongue first.

"Well fuck me slowly with a chainsaw," he drawls. "Look who it is."

"Oh great," I say when I've caught my breath. "And I didn't think today could get any worse."

He smiles, turns the gun around and slams the stock into my face.

The world goes black.

CHAPTER FOUR

I ACTUALLY SAW the muzzle flash as Guria took out the Ranger.

He was about halfway down the street, just behind the Rangers, in the top window. I opened the door and ran into the road, ignoring Dad's calls to stay put. I didn't really have a plan; I just wanted to stop Jane being cut to pieces in the inevitable crossfire. As the shot man fell, and Jane ducked, I saw one of the Rangers raise his bow to finish me off. I shouted at him to stop, but he wasn't having it. I dived out of the way and heard an arrow whistle past, far too close for comfort.

I was a dead man if I stayed in the open. I had no choice but to hare over to the nearest house and dive inside, sliding on my stomach over the slime that had accumulated in the once pristine hallway carpet. I stood up feeling soggy and sick. My best chance of ending this was to get to Guria and take over the rifle. He was about fifteen houses up on this side of the road. I glanced back out the door and saw Jane had made it to cover across the road. That was a relief. Then the minibus roared past me, bullets pinging off its roof as the snatchers joined the fight from their compound.

Events were moving too damn fast. I ran out into the alleyway behind the house and raced up to where Guria had been hiding. Somehow I managed to get all the way there before any of the Rangers emerged into the alley to make their own escape. Or maybe they were digging in for a fight.

I reached the kitchen door of what I was reasonably sure was the right house, and brought my SA-80 to bear. Guria was one of us, but this was the first time he'd fired in anger. I had no idea what state he'd be in when I found him, and I wasn't going to let him shoot me dead in a moment of hyper-adrenalised panic.

I grasped the old Bakelite doorknob and pushed. The door had been left locked but the wooden frame was rotting away; the lock fell off and crashed to the kitchen floor as the door opened with a wet smack. So much for stealth. I checked inside but there was nobody there so I stepped in and pushed the door closed behind me.

"Guria," I said, loud but not shouting. "You there?" There was no reply so I made my way through the ground floor to the foot of the stairs. There was a skeleton lying sprawled across the bottom steps, the black stain that had seeped into the carpet around it all that remained to indicate it had ever borne flesh.

I stepped over it and climbed the stairs, which creaked alarmingly. They could go at any minute; this house was not a safe place to be, even without the threat of being shot. In the five years since The Cull, the elements had started to eat away at the infrastructure that civilisation had left behind. The endless persistence of water, probing every crevice and crack, with no houseproud DIYers to hold it at bay with supplies from Homebase, had started gradually eating away the houses and schools, shops and offices, and all the places we'd built to shelter us from the cold. There was no-one still trying to live by scavenging the scraps of what was left behind – it had all been corrupted by time.

I reached the landing and spoke again.

"Guria, you there?"

There was no response from behind the door to the front bedroom, which was pushed to. Had I miscounted, got the wrong house?

I pushed the door and stepped inside.

"Guria?" I said softly.

I heard a crash in the distance and the sound of a car horn.

The boy was crouched at the window, still facing the street, grasping the sniper rifle. I could see he was breathing.

"Guria, you okay?" I stepped forward.

He turned his head, as if finally registering that I was there. He was white as a ghost, pupils dilated, staring into the middle distance. He was in shock.

"Oh, hi Sir," he said, as if from the bottom of a deep well. "I just shot someone."

"I noticed."

"His head kind of went pop."

"Yeah, they do that. Good shot, by the way."

"Like a melon."

"Hmm. Can you pass me the rifle?"

"Oh, do you want a go?" He stood up and turned, holding the rifle out to me.

"No, get away from the window!"

But it was too late. He turned sharply, as if he'd heard something, and then Guria, silhouetted in the window, looked down in puzzlement at the arrow shaft sticking out of his chest.

"Oh," he said, and dropped dead at my feet.

The Rangers weren't our enemy. This was all a horrible misunderstanding. There was no need for this to go any further.

I knew all this.

But I looked at the dead child lying at my feet, with his wide eyes staring at the ceiling as his brain slowly cooled and died, and I felt a hard cold certainty in my chest.

Calmly, I reached down, picked the rifle up and raised it to my shoulder. Keeping three steps back from the window, hidden by the shadows of the room, I raised the powerful sight to my eye and switched through the options until I hit the heat sensor. And there he was, the man who'd shot a thirteen year-old boy who'd been my responsibility.

Lurking in the shadows of the bedroom directly facing me, he had no technology to aid his sniping. He felt confident, secure in the murk.

I took careful aim.

"Not a mercy killing this time, Nine Lives," said the voice in my head that had remained silent for two long years.

"No," I replied out loud; the first time, I think, I ever answered him audibly. I squeezed the trigger, putting a high velocity round through the man's heart. He stayed upright for nearly ten seconds before he crumpled like a discarded puppet.

Confident that the immediate danger was past, I stepped forward and scanned the eerily quiet street. At one end the snatchers were emerging from the schoolyard gate, rifles and shotguns raised, looking bewildered, trying to work out what the fuck had just happened. At the other end the car horn still blared, and I saw a wisp of smoke drifting across the road mouth, evidence of whatever accident Dad had driven into.

There was no sign of any of the other Rangers. I assumed they were all hiding on the same side of the street as me. But the snatchers presented a tempting target. There were five of them now, in plain view.

I sighted on the rearmost. The cold hatred in my chest was still there, lending me an almost supernatural calm.

"Oh this is good. I like this," said the voice.

I counted to three and then caressed the trigger once before letting fly. Within five seconds four of the snatchers were lying on the ground – head shot, chest, chest, head. They lay on the cobbles, blood pooling and mingling, running to the drains. The last one standing was left alone, surrounded by the corpses of his colleagues.

"Let him sweat," said the voice.

I held my fire. The man didn't know what to do. He was waiting for the inevitable kill shot, shaking in terror. A dark stain spread from his crotch as he wet himself. He dropped his gun and raised his hands, staring left and right, desperately trying to find me, as if locating me would allow him to appeal directly for clemency.

It took more than a minute for him to decide to turn his back and run. I let him take two steps before I shot the cobbles at his feet. He stopped and fell to his knees then shuffled around to face down the street towards me again. He was crying, hands pressed together in supplication, his chin wobbling as he screamed for mercy.

I let him go on like this for a minute or two, regarding him dispassionately like I would an ant underneath a magnifying glass on a hot day.

Then I blew his heart out through the back of his chest.

"Phew. I don't know about you, Nine Lives," said the voice in my head. "But I've got a blue steel boner that a cat couldn't scratch."

I smiled; so did I. To my surprise, I was quite glad Mac was talking to me again.

That should have been the first clue that I'd crossed some kind of line.

I went down on one knee and leaned over Guria. I gently closed his eyes and brushed away a lock of hair that had fallen across his face.

"Sorry," I whispered.

My business here was done. I had three more Rangers to hunt down. I got to my feet, turned on my heels and stared straight down the shaft of an arrow, notched and ready to fly.

"Drop it, you sick motherfucker," said the Ranger.

CHAPTER FIVE

THERE'S A HAND shaking me, but I shrug it off and turn over, trying to go back to sleep.

"Jane, you need to wake up." The voice is soft but urgent, and the shaking resumes. I try to swat them away. I hear another voice saying "for God's sake," then feel a sudden sharp sting as someone slaps me across the face. I'm instantly wide awake. My head hurts like hell and there's something wrong with my nose. I don't even need to feel it to know that it's broken again.

I'm lying on a very smelly blanket on what feels like a camp bed. It's cold in here and the bright sun is streaming through the windows straight into my eyes. I take a moment to adjust.

"Welcome back," says Tariq as he bleeds into focus next to me.

The best I can offer as reply is a vague mumble that sounds like a question.

"Back in the compound. The school," says John, behind me. "There was a convoy of snatchers coming to pay a visit here this morning. Reckon they were coming to collect this month's cargo. Three trucks loaded with kids and heavily guarded."

"And muggins here drove into them headfirst."

"I wasn't expecting oncoming traffic," says John. "There's not exactly a major congestion problem these days."

I turn to look at John. Every tiny motion of my head hurts. When he swims into focus I see a huge livid rip across his forehead.

"Ouch," I whisper.

He winces, seemingly more embarrassed than hurt. "Yeah. Steering wheel. Knocked me cold for a while."

"And the kids? Hang on," I say, suddenly outraged. "Was it you who bloody slapped me?"

"They're fine," he says, ignoring my protest. "A bit shaken, but they're back in the main hall while the snatchers try to piece together what happened here. Someone took out all their people. They were lying in front of the gate when we walked in. Sniper, I think."

"Guria? Lee?"

"If I had to guess, I'd say Lee."

"How many?"

"Five."

"Jesus. He shot five of them when we'd already left?"

John nods and somehow manages to resist saying, "I told you so."

"Anyway," he says, and I can tell it's an effort. "We can't worry about him now. Jane, one of the snatchers seemed to recognise you...?"

"Yeah. I met him about three years ago. He was part of a child trafficking ring near the school. I shut them down and took him prisoner. I was going to interrogate him and find out where the kids were going, but Operation bloody Motherland turned up and arrested me instead. They let him go."

By now my eyes have adjusted and I can see we're in what must have once been a classroom. There are a couple more camp beds against the wall and some discarded clothes and tins of food. This must be where three of the snatchers sleep. Slept.

I sit up, trying to ignore the pain in my head. I reach for my sidearm, but of course it's gone. So has the knife in my boot.

"They were pretty thorough," says Tariq, brandishing the stump where his hook should be.

The door opens and two men stand silhouetted against the rising sun. "Miss Crowther. What a surprise."

I recognise him from Olly's compound, the day Operation Motherland turned up and ruined my life. "Hello Bookworm. How's it hanging?"

He steps forward and grabs me by the hair, yanking me to my feet and dragging me from the room. Tariq and John make to intervene, shouting protests, but the other man fires a warning shot over their heads and they stand back.

I am dragged down the corridor towards the main hall and thrown, head first, through the swing doors. I crash to the floor, my vision blurring from the intensity of the migraine. But I don't hit hard wood. Instead, my hands and then my right shoulder crash into something soft, yielding and wet. I recoil, my hands sticky with blood. I've been thrown onto a pile of bodies, six in all.

I make to stand but I feel a boot on my shoulder, pushing me down. Then knees in my back and a hand on the back of my head, pushing my face into the gaping wound in the back of one of the dead snatchers. I gag.

"Who the fuck are you?" says a voice that I don't recognise.

I don't reply. The hand pushes my face deep into the gore. I feel my cheek scraping against a jagged edge of shattered bone. Christ, this guy's got a huge hole in him. That new sniper rifle is vicious.

"I won't ask again."

"I'm Jane Crowther. Pleased to meet you," I say, trying not to get blood in my mouth.

"You're sure this is her?" he asks. "She shut down Olly's supply line?"

"Yes, boss," I hear Bookworm reply.

"So what are you?" asks the man in a thick Scottish accent. "Some kind of vigilante?"

"Just a concerned citizen."

"Who goes around massacring people."

"Who goes around rescuing children from kidnappers."

He snorts, derisively. "We're not kidnappers, miss. We're saving these kids. Aren't we, boys?" There's a chorus of muted giggles, although one guy looks uncomfortable, as if offended.

"Saving them from what?"

"Eternal damnation. Apparently."

"It doesn't do to mock the Abbot, boss," says the uncomfortable one, threateningly. The boss nods, suddenly serious.

"You're right, of course, Jimmy," he says solemnly, then winks at me, humouring his colleague. "Anyway, love, we've got you and your two blokes. How many more of you are there?"

"Enough."

He shoves my head hard into the wound and suddenly I can't breathe, my mouth and nose blocked by soggy meat. He literally rubs my face in it, then lets go and stands back. I fling myself backwards, gasping for air, scrabbling away from the obscene mound of carcasses. I catch a glimpse of the children, huddled in the corner of the hall, watching wide-eyed, before I kneel and throw up, heaving long and hard until there's nothing left and I feel wretched and hollow.

I'm still kneeling there with my eyes closed, trying to quell the stomach spasms, when I hear his voice in my ear, speaking softly.

"Finished?"

I look up at him, and am surprised to see how handsome he is. I spit a potent mix of vomit and blood into his matinee idol blue eyes. He just laughs and backhands me, sending me sprawling.

As I lie there, waiting for a bullet to end me, I hear Bookworm say "I reckon Spider will want to talk to her," and my vision blurs, my blood feels like ice in my veins, my head swims and I begin to tremble.

He's alive.

"What did you say?" I rasp, eventually.

"I said our boss will want to talk to you."

"His name. You said his name."

"Yeah." Bookworm sounds confused.

"What was his fucking name?" I yell.

"Spider," says Movie Idol, curious in spite of himself. If his reaction is anything to go by, I must have gone as white as a sheet.

"Spider," I say. "Spider." And then I can't stop saying his name, it pours out of me in a hysterical flood of jumbled syllables. "Spider. Spider. Spider. Spider. Spider. Spider. Spider. Spider. Spider..."

He slaps me again and I fall silent. I barely even know where I am. All I can see is that face. All I can hear is that voice. All I can feel is the sick ache in my stomach as my brother looks down in surprise at...

"Yes," I say quietly, rising to my feet. "Yes, I think he will want to talk to me. I certainly want to talk to him."

Movie Idol narrows his eyes and smiles. "You got history with the big man?"

I nod.

"Fine, you just bought yourself a ticket to London." He turns to address the gaggle of gunmen. "Put her and the kids in the lorry."

Two guys step forward and herd us towards the fire escape. As I step outside I hear Movie Idol giving a final order.

"Oh, and kill those other two fuckers."

I try to turn and protest, but the tide of children sweeps me out into the playground.

There's nothing I can do.

We're herded through the playground and out the front gate into the street. Two big container lorries are waiting. Both have their rear doors open, revealing hordes of terrified children huddled together for warmth. There are six men with guns standing around the trucks, both preventing the children from running and keeping an eye out for attack. Every one of them is a plum target for a good sniper, but for some reason Lee isn't taking the shot. Suddenly I feel guilty – the only thought I've spared for Lee since the Rangers attacked has been to worry about his mental state; it hasn't occurred to me that he might be lying dead in one of these houses.

I turn to look back at the school, where John and Tariq are being executed, and I curse myself for being such a fool. Who the hell did we think we were to come charging in here and take these guys on? We're... Christ I don't know what we are but we certainly aren't soldiers, or even police. It's ironic that we managed to take out the entire US Army two years ago, but now we've been undone by a bunch of child snatchers in lorries.

Our escorts chivvy us into the back of the foremost lorry. As I step up to the ramp I slip in a pile of what smells like human shit. There are no seats in here, and a couple of buckets sit by the doors, empty but reeking of effluent. This must be the kids' toilets, and they've just emptied them in the street. The smell of unwashed bodies, open toilets and fear is overwhelming.

"Sorry it's a bit cramped," says the snatcher next to me, sarcastically. "But your man wrote off the third lorry, so we've had to shove its cargo into these two."

THE MASS OF kids shuffle up to make room for us new arrivals. Just as I sit down I hear two muffled shots from inside the school.

I sit in that lorry, surrounded by despairing children who I am powerless to help, leaving behind two dead friends and a missing lover, on my way to be reunited with the cruellest sadist I've ever met, and I begin, to my shame, to cry.

As the lorry doors swing shut I catch a glimpse of Bookworm leaving the school, scurrying to the rearmost lorry, waving to his boss at the front to tell him the job is done. Then the doors close with a heavy bang and we're plunged into darkness.

CHAPTER SIX

"I'M NOT YOUR enemy."

The Ranger didn't waver for an instant. "I said drop it."

We stared at each other for a moment, as I considered my options and he got ready to skewer me. I dropped the gun and kicked it over to him.

"Useless at close range anyway," I said.

He looked down at Guria's body and I saw the shock on his face. "But he's…"

"Just a kid. Yeah. Shot him anyway, though, didn't you?"

"Never. Not to kill, anyway. Did he move just before he was hit?"

I nodded.

He flashed me a look I couldn't quite interpret then backed onto the landing and gestured me downstairs.

Five minutes later we were in the kitchen of another house, further down the street, where the Rangers had regrouped. The other four kids were there too, rounded up like I was.

As I entered the house, one of the kids – I think his name was Wallis – said: "Hey, Sir, where's Guria?"

I just shook my head and let my captor push me down on the floor, where I sat cross-legged.

"So they call you Sir, do they, son?" said a tall Irishman who seemed to have taken command. "Fancy yourself a general, do you? Like it when children call you Sir? Make you feel important?" He was barely holding in his anger, leaning down, getting in my face, trying to provoke me.

"No, I just find that it helps maintain classroom discipline."

He pulled back his arm to slap me around the face, but one of his fellows grabbed it and pulled him back. He shook the guy off, but composed himself.

"Two of my friends are dead because of you."

"And one of mine, because of you. Plus, if that car horn is anything to go by, the rest may be in serious trouble." I allowed some of my anger to surface. "We had everything under control here until you fucked it all up, charging in and trying to lay down the fucking law. Who made you judge, jury and executioner?"

"I'm not the one who just gunned down an unarmed man."

"A kidnapper and a murderer. That lot have been stealing children from across the country for months now. They leave communities shattered, adults dead. And what for? Do you know? Do you know where they're taking the kids, what they want them for?"

"No."

"Neither do I. But I doubt it's anything good. So yeah, I shot them. It was the best way to ensure we had a clean getaway. If you hadn't butted in, it wouldn't have been necessary."

"So it's our fault?"

"Stop it!" shouted Wallis all of a sudden. We fell silent and stared at him, almost guiltily. "You're a kind of police, right?" he said to the Ranger, who nodded. "Well so are we, kind of. This is all just stupid. We're on the same side. The kidnappers are the bad guys."

There was a long silence, then the lead Ranger said, as calmly as he could manage, "Why the fuck did you shoot Grier?"

"It was a mistake. The boy with the sniper rifle... it was his first time in the field. He panicked. Must have thought he was buying us a chance to escape."

The Ranger closed his eyes and wearily massaged his temples with his right hand. "So Phil shot him."

"And I shot Phil."

"And these kids?" He gestured to Wallis and the others. "Is this their first time, too?"

I nodded.

"So you're what, an army of children?"

"We're a school, not an army. But we defend ourselves when we have to."

"You really think giving children guns is going to help?"

"Has done so far. You'd be in a US concentration camp by now if it weren't for us, mate."

He shook his head in disbelief. "Twelve-year-olds with sniper rifles. Such a fucking mess."

"Guria was thirteen," said Wallis quietly.

"You know what," I said. "We can sort this out later. Right now I'm more concerned about my friends and the children they were trying to rescue. Can we work together?"

He considerd me carefully for a moment. "What you did, shooting those people in the street. That was not right in the head."

"Then sign me up for psychoanalysis, but do it later, yeah?"

He held my gaze, trying to decide what to do.

"Ferguson, we've got movement in the street," said another Ranger, poking his head into the room.

My interrogator turned to leave, then glanced back at me and nodded, indicating that I should follow.

"But this conversation is not over," he said softly as we walked down the hall to the front room. "Just paused."

"Hang on," I said. "I thought there were only five of you. Two are dead, that leaves you and the two in the kitchen. Where did this guy come from?"

"Josh here was on sniper duty himself, upstairs. But he held his fire until he was sure what was going on. Discipline and experience, see?"

We reached the window and peered through the tatty lace curtains. The children we had loaded into the minibus earlier were walking down the street in a tight huddle. It took a moment for me to work out what was happening, but then I looked closer and made out two men amongst the kids, scanning the houses on either side of the road carefully. They must have seen the bodies at the school gates and this new bunch of snatchers were using the kids as a human shield.

But worse – leading the group were my dad and Tariq. Dad had a nasty gash across his forehead that had soaked his face and jacket with blood; Tariq had Jane slung over his shoulder, an unconscious dead weight.

I heard footsteps in the hall and turned to see yet another Ranger enter.

"The convoy's in the next road," the man reported. "The van drove straight into it. It's a write off, and I think the first lorry is too. They're disentangling them now."

"Thanks," said Ferguson, then he turned to me.

"Those people out front..."

"My dad, my friend and Jane. She's our boss."

He nodded and I could see that he was thinking hard.

"Well, we have to rescue them," I said.

Ferguson regarded me coolly. "Do we? Do we now?"

"For God's sake," I said, but then I took a deep breath and stopped for a moment before continuing as calmly as I could manage. "I've got to assume you came here for the same reason we did – to find out who the snatchers are and where they're taking the kids, right?"

Ferguson nodded.

"Okay, so we want the same thing. Track these guys, shut them down. Now you could try and take this lot, capture a survivor, interrogate them. But how many kids would die in the crossfire? Your only option is to infiltrate and collect intel."

"Go on."

"They're going back to the school. I've been in there. I know the layout. We go in and we eavesdrop."

"And free your people at the same time?"

"If the opportunity presents itself," I said, although I was quite clear in my own mind that I'd rescue them no matter what.

"If this fucker tries to stop you," says Mac, "you'll just have to kill him. His men would never know that it wasn't the snatchers."

The group in the street drew level with our house and paraded past silently. We watched them go, seeing the fear on the children's faces as they were marched down a shooting alley.

"Okay," said Ferguson eventually. "But just you and me. If we don't make it back, my guys will make sure your kids get home."

"Done." I held out my hand. He ignored it and walked past me, checking his weapon and barking orders.

BY THE TIME we'd got to the end of the alley, the snatchers and their hostages had made their way into the school. They made the kids carry in the bodies of the men I'd killed.

The wall that ran across the front of the school compound stretched down the sides too, but I'd glimpsed a wire mesh fence at the rear of the building. Ferguson and I broke cover, scurrying out of the alley and down the side of the school, staying in the shelter of the wall.

When we reached the corner I took out the wire cutters and within moments we had slipped into a playground. We darted from slide to roundabout to climbing frame until we reached the outbuildings.

There was no sign of movement at the rear of the school; everything would be happening in the front playground and the main hall, I guessed. We quietly tried all the doors and windows we could find. They were all locked, but time and neglect were on our side. I pushed one window gently and the whole frame came free and fell into the school. I gasped, waiting for a crash, but there was none. I peered inside and saw that it had landed on a mouldy blue crash mat. Ferguson and I climbed inside and found ourselves in a room full of soft foam wedges, mats and seats.

I clambered over the wet, squishy foam and cracked the door open. There was nobody in the corridor, so I headed into the school proper, with Ferguson close behind me. This part of the building had been left to rot, unlike the area around the main hall, which had obviously been inhabited since The Cull. We moved through the eerie, mildewed corridors, stepping carefully to avoid the lino tiles which had curled upwards and made loud cracking noises if we trod on them. We came to a pair of swing doors and I peered through a frosted glass panel and saw movement very close. It took a moment to work out that there were two men standing just on the other side of the door. It looked like they were guarding a room.

I turned to Ferguson and indicated that he should look. He took my place just as there were sounds of movement in the corridor beyond. I could hear muffled shouts and then a gunshot. In sudden panic I lurched forward, gun at the ready, but he spun and put his hand on my chest and shook his head firmly.

We stood there for a moment, me desperate to see what was going on, he resolutely holding me back. He didn't see my hand slowly move towards the knife in my belt.

He held up his hand, releasing me and whispered: "We go around, through the window."

I considered for a moment, then nodded. So we went back the way we had come, back across the foam and out into the playground. Then we skirted the buildings until we were outside the room that was being guarded. I was surprised how calm I was when we reached it. Someone had been shooting in there, so there was every chance that Dad, Jane or Tariq was lying dead. I felt nothing but a fixed certainty that, even if one of them was dead, my gun and my knife would help me make it better.

I peeked over the window ledge and saw Dad and Tariq sitting on a camp bed, looking grim. I tapped on the glass lightly. Tariq jumped in surprise, but Dad just turned and smiled. They came to the window.

"Brace the frame," I whispered, miming how they should hold the window steady.

They looked confused, but nodded. Then Ferguson and I took up positions at either side of the window and pushed. We were in luck. The frame slowly slid forward and oozed out of the brickwork, entire. Dad and Tariq took the weight, carried it inside and laid it on the bed.

"Where's Jane?" I asked when they returned to the window.

"Just took her to the hall," replied Dad.

I reached into my pack, took out two Brownings and handed them to Dad and Tariq.

"Then let's go get her."

Dad shook his head. "No. There are too many of them." I made to protest, but he waved me quiet. "And there are children in there."

"We can't just let them drive off with her, for fuck's sake."

"We have to," replied Dad firmly.

"You could shoot them all and rescue her yourself," said the voice in my head. I actually considered it for a moment.

"How many men in total?" asked Ferguson.

"Fifteen at least. It's some kind of armed convoy, collecting kids from staging posts like this across the country and shipping them into London."

Ferguson nodded. "They're more organised than we'd thought."

"Then let's kill them all, release the kids and go home."

Dad gave me an exasperated look. "Lee..." but he broke off when we heard voices at the door. Without a word, he and Tariq scuttled to the door and took up positions either side. Ferguson and I ducked down below the window ledge.

I heard the door open then a brief scuffle and a groan, then the door closed again. I looked up to see Tariq holding his gun barrel in the mouth of a spotty little man in a dark green hoodie.

"Sod this," I muttered, and climbed into the room. Ferguson followed me.

I pulled my knife out as soon as my feet hit lino, stepped forward and laid the blade across the captive's throat. Tariq removed the gun.

"You're here to kill us, right?" said Dad.

The terrified man nodded.

Instantly, Dad aimed his gun at the wall and let off two rounds.

"Now strip," he said. The terrified man undid the zip on his hoodie. "Quickly!"

"Good idea," I said, as I began unbuttoning my own coat. "I'll take his place and follow them back."

Dad shook his head. "No way, son. You're coming with me."

"But I'm the right height and build," I protested. "Neither of you are."

Dad looked past me, over my shoulder. "But I am," I heard Ferguson say, in response to my father's piercing gaze.

"Oh come on, we're going to trust this guy over me?"

"Yes," said Dad firmly. "I think your judgment is a little off."

"What the fuck is that supposed to mean?" I replied.

"I think maybe he's seen me," whispered Mac.

But Dad wasn't going to get into this now, and our captive was down to his underpants.

"If I get away with this, I'll stick with them until they reach wherever their base is, then I'll try and sneak away, head back to Nottingham," said Ferguson as he hastily pulled on a crusty pair of smelly combats. "You should join my men in the road and head there yourselves."

"And if you don't come back?" I asked peevishly. "If they rumble you the second you walk out of this room?"

"Then there'll be plenty of guys to take my place."

We heard a distant car horn.

"They're wondering where he is," said Tariq.

Ferguson pulled the hood over his head and headed for the door.

"Head North via Hemel Hempstead," says Dad as Ferguson makes to leave. "Look for us there."

"Will do," he replies.

"Good luck," I said as he turned the handle. He didn't acknowledge me at all.

WE WAITED A minute, but we heard no shots and no commotion. Dad left the room and came back a moment later.

"All clear."

I ran into the playground just in time to see the trucks turning the corner at the end of the road. The engines faded away and silence reigned. Jane was gone.

I stood there for a moment, then I began walking purposefully to the gate. I would find my sniper rifle and go after her. Anyone who got in my way would die. Simple as that.

I felt a hand on my shoulder. I stopped but didn't turn around, afraid of what I might do.

"Lee." It was Dad.

"I'm going after her."

"Like hell you are."

"Don't try and stop me."

"There's a pile of bodies back there with bloody great holes in them."

"So?"

"Was that you?"

"Yes."

"And what threat did they pose to you? You shot them when we'd already left. They were irrelevant."

"They were scumbags who had it coming."

"So you're judge, jury and executioner now?"

"When needs must."

There was a long silence. "You're not going after her and that's final."

I burst out laughing and turned to face him, bringing my gun up until it was pointing right between his eyes.

"Really, Dad? You think you can ground me? What am I, twelve?"

He looked at me with such sadness in his eyes that for a moment I felt a stirring of... panic? Conscience? I ignored it.

"No, you're eighteen. But you're out of control. Your judgment is shot and you're a danger to yourself and to the people around you. I am your commanding officer and you will do as I say."

"Like fuck I..."

His eyes gave no warning, and he moved so fast and with such control that I was disarmed and lying face down on the concrete with his knee in my back before I knew what was happening.

"If I let you run around with a gun, how many more people will die? How long 'til you decide that Tariq's broken one of your rules and has to be taken out? Or me?"

"Not that long, at this rate," I said. It was supposed to be a joke, but nobody was laughing.

"If she's harmed in any way, because you stopped me going after her," I said coldly, "I will kill you."

He considered me for a moment and then turned away.

"The awful thing is," he said softly, "I believe you."

I got to my feet and held out my hand for my gun. He considered me for a moment then handed it back. I shoved it in my waistband and then walked back towards the school.

"You'd better come up with one hell of a rescue plan, Dad," I said over my shoulder as I walked away.

CHAPTER SEVEN

IT'S COLD OUTSIDE, and there's no heating in the lorry, but the huddle of children produces a foul-smelling warmth that at least stops us getting hypothermia. There's no light either. Or seats. Five winters without maintenance have reduced Britain's roads to a long trail of endless potholes through which we splash and spring. So we bounce along in the dark, getting bruised and beaten as we crash into each other, or momentarily lift off then slam to the floor on our bony, undernourished arses.

None of the snatchers got into the back with us, so we're unguarded. But the heavy doors are securely locked from the outside, and even if we could get them open, we're hardly going to jump from a moving vehicle, are we?

I expected a flood of eager questions once the doors closed and we were momentarily unwatched, but these children have been broken. They sit silent and scared, clutching their blankets around their shoulders as if they were some kind of armour. One small boy keeps being shoved against me by the movement of the lorry. I try to talk to him, but he ignores me. Eventually I put my arm around his shoulder and cuddle him in close. At least that way, I reason, we won't bang into each other so much. But his response to my attempt at comforting him is to bite my forearm, hard. I yell and snatch it back. Little beast.

"Hello?" I hear a faint shout from deeper in the bowels of the lorry. "Hello, is that the woman who came to rescue us?" It's a girl.

"Yes," I shout back. "My name's Jane. What's yours?"

There's no reply, but a few moments later I hear vague sounds of commotion and I realise someone is fighting their way through the crowd to get to me.

"Hello? Where are you?" she says again.

"Here," I reply, and I steer her towards me in the darkness until I feel small hands grabbing at my coat. I grasp her hands tightly. I fight down my fears and put on an upbeat façade.

"And what might your name be, young lady?" I say cheerily.

"Jenni," she says, and thrusts a gun into my hands. "They didn't think to search us."

For a moment I'm too surprised to speak, and then I remember Tariq giving her the weapon back in the school hall.

"Oh, Jenni," I say eventually. "You are my kind of girl!"

"Where are they taking us?" she asks. I can hear her trying to be brave.

"I don't know, sweetheart. I don't know anything." But that's a lie. I know Spider. I know what he's capable of.

I shove the gun into my trousers and pull my jacket down over it. They searched me back at the school; they've no reason to do so again.

"Where are you from, Jenni?" I ask.

There's a long silence, and I wonder if she heard me, then she says: "Ipswich."

"And how old are you?"

"Thirteen."

"So you were eight when…"

"Everyone died."

"And how have you lived since then? I mean, who's been looking after you?"

"Mike," she says, as if this explains everything. "But he's dead now." Her matter of factness stops me cold. I don't ask any more questions. She lets me put my arm around her though, and she nestles into my chest. She soon falls asleep. I feel the slow rise and fall of her breathing as we rattle and bounce in the darkness. Eventually I rest my head on hers and I slip into a half-sleep. I have no idea how much times passes until the explosion.

In the enclosed space, the bang is deafening. It comes from the front, from the cab, and the lorry lurches violently to the left. We're flung into each other like some mad rugby scrum and there are cries and screams as the lorry tilts past the tipping point and slams down on its side. The doors at the back buckle and a chink of light breaks in. The lorry is still moving forward, crippled now, and we're bounced and jostled. Loud screams from the bottom of the human pile as children are crushed. The lorry jacknifes on its side and the cargo container sweeps in a wide arc then smashes into something solid. We come to a sudden halt and are all flung against the wall, compressed in an awful smashing of limbs. The doors crash open and children spill out of the container, tumbling helplessly onto tarmac.

There's a moment of stillness as our ears ring and we get our balance, re-orientating ourselves. Then the screaming starts again and there are children yelling for air, and for people to get off them, or just crying in pain as the inevitable broken bones grind against each other.

I've ended up at the top of the pile, so I scramble towards the doors as delicately as I can, but it's impossible. The mass of children heaves and shifts beneath me and I'm thrown off balance, unable to escape.

I hear the crack of small-arms fire over the din. I can't locate where it's coming from, but it redoubles my determination and I ruthlessly scramble back to the top of the pile and out the doors, literally sliding out across the backs of children. I draw my gun as I do so. To my surprise I manage a relatively graceful landing as kids rain down around me, blinking in the sudden, bright afternoon light.

The gunfire is coming from my left. I spin and see the snatchers who've survived the crash, huddled behind the open cab door, firing up at concrete embankment. We're on an A road, in the suburbs of London, at a guess. Beckenham, perhaps? I glance around the container and see that the first lorry is still upright, parked a few hundred metres down the road. It is coming under heavy attack, many rocks and a few bullets pinging off its bonnet and roof. Before I can react, they pull away, cutting their losses, abandoning us.

Which isn't necessarily a bad thing.

The kids are still tumbling out of the lorry, all walking wounded. I briefly search for Jenni, but can't find her in the confusion.

Right, time to take control.

I have no idea who's attacking the convoy. They could be good guys, but they could equally be a rival bunch of snatchers. Until I know, I can't afford to start shooting. I look behind me. There's a side street with a pub on the corner. It's derelict and ruined, but it will have a cellar and that's our best chance of shelter.

"Listen," I shout. "Everyone into the pub. Quickly."

But it's no use. I have no authority here. These kids don't trust me, and why should they? They scatter in all directions, in ones and twos, pure panic. Scurrying for cover or making a break for freedom. I see one duo blindly racing past the snatchers towards the enemy guns. One of them is hit in the crossfire and drops, but the other keeps running and disappears into a tower block.

I feel a hand tugging my coat and I turn to find Jenni pulling me towards the pub.

"Come on," she says urgently. Then she shouts at the kids who are still pouring from the back of the ruined lorry. "Come on! This way!" Thankfully, some of them hear, and once they begin to follow us, the others fall in behind them. Jenni and I begin running towards the pub.

We're about ten metres from the door when a man steps out of the doorway. He's about my height, dressed in tracky pants and a thick, quilted coat topped by a beanie. His face is grimy and hard to make out. In his hands he holds a crowbar. He stands with his legs apart and starts smacking the crowbar into the palm of his left hand like a panto actor in Eastenders pretending to be a hard man. He doesn't slow me down. I level my gun at him as I keep running.

Two more men step out of the shadowy pub interior. They're also dressed in rag-tag looter chic, but while one of them dangles a bicycle chain from his right hand, the other has a gun aimed right back at me. Jenni and I skid to a halt, but the kids behind us are too panicked. They sweep past us and then veer right as they see the menacing figures before us.

Instead of heading into the pub the stampede takes off down the side street, leaderless, lost and running into the territory of god knows what kind of gang. I yell at them to stop, but nobody's listening.

"Leave the kids alone, bitch," shouts the man in the middle over the sound of pattering feet and, I realise, nothing else – the gunfire behind us has stopped.

"She's not one of them," shouts Jenni. "She was a prisoner, like us."

"Then she can drop the gun," replies the man.

I aim it at his head. "And let you take them instead? I don't think so. Stay close Jenni."

I notice that the tide of children is ebbing and that some of them have gathered around us. I glance down briefly and recognise a number of faces from the school. About five of the kids we tried to rescue have rallied to my defence.

"She's telling the truth," pipes up a boy so tiny he can only be about eight. "She tried to help us." I make a mental note to hug the life out of him if we get out of this alive.

"Doesn't matter," comes a loud voice from behind us. "She's still a fucking adult. You can't trust them. Everybody step away from her. NOW."

Such is the authority in this woman's voice that four of the kids peel away and begin running to catch up with their fellow escapees. It's only Jenni and the pipsqueak left.

I turn to face this new player.

In the distance I can see the snatchers lying dead in the road, and between us and them stands a group of ten children. And then I do a quick double take back at the pub doorway and realise that they're not men – they've got the slightly out of proportion, weed-thin tallness of teenage boys.

I look back at the group in front of us. They're all teenagers. Only two have guns, the rest brandish truncheons, chains and even pitchforks. One of the kids with a shotgun, a girl, steps out of the crowd and takes point. She's wearing a brown fur coat tied around the waist with a leather belt; she's got a grey hoodie on underneath the coat and she pulls the hood off, releasing a cascade of greasy red hair.

The sun is behind her so I still can't quite make out her face.

I lower my gun. "I really was a prisoner. I'm not one of the snatchers."

She doesn't reply.

"Honestly, I'm trying to help these children," I plead.

The girl steps forward and suddenly I can make out her face. It takes me a second, but then I gasp in shock.

"Well you took your fucking time," says Caroline.

THE SCARS ON the right side of her face look like the worst case of acne I've ever seen. I remember the cleaner's shotgun blast peppering her with shot, seeing her fall, working all evening to sterilise and dress her wounds. Failing to save her right eye.

I don't know what it looks like under the eye patch she's fashioned from elastic and felt, and I don't ask permission to look.

She's taller but still very solid. She'd be pretty if it weren't for her injuries, and her hair is stunning. I spent so long looking for her; it's hard to believe she's actually standing in front of me.

The last time I saw her she was being taken into the hospital at the Operation Motherland base, Rowles at her side. I had assumed that was where she remained until the nuclear blast. But when Lee had recovered from his injuries enough to be able to communicate again, he told me that she wasn't there. The Americans knew nothing about her. She had vanished from under their noses even as Sanders and I were escaping in the opposite direction.

I spread the word that I was looking for her to all our contacts, but I never heard so much as a whisper. Her trail had gone cold by the time I knew to start looking.

I look at the short, square, scarred pirate Jenny in front of me, gun in hand, defiant, leading an army of children, and I feel a strange sort of pride.

"That's my girl," I whisper.

She hands me a mug of hot milk, which I take thankfully, warming my frozen fingers.

"Fresh water's hard to get here," she explain. "But there's a guy who comes to market with milk once a week, so…"

We're awkward with each other. Not quite sure what to say. We slip into survivalist small talk – where do you get medicine, what do you use for fuel, do you have a generator?

We're sitting on a ragged old sofa in the middle of a huge open plan office. Third floor, centre of the high street. The desks and chairs have been cleared away and the floor is a mad maze of old beds and sofas, with long clear runs where the younger kids race around, burning off the little energy they have.

It's a headquarters, of sorts. There must be thirty or so kids living here; closer to a hundred now we've rounded up most of the escapees from the convoy. My hands ache from all the stitching and splinting I've been performing on the injured from the attack. Medical supplies are non-existent, so I've been using all sorts of dodgy unsterilised kit. The sooner I can get these kids out of here and back to the safety of St Mark's, the better. We have enough supplies there to deal with the imminent avalanche of secondary infections. But for now, the last child has been mended and the majority of them are sleeping it off.

Caroline is the leader here, even though there are older, stronger kids in the mix. There are hulking great teenage boys who take orders from her without question.

It takes a while for me to ask the obvious question. "Where are we?"

"Hammersmith."

"Jesus, that far in? I thought this was Bromley. What's it like in the centre?"

"Church land. We don't go there."

"Church…? Never mind. Tell me later." Small talk exhausted, I lean forward and ask the big question. "What happened, Caroline? Where did you go?"

She looks down for moment then, talking to her shoes, whispers: "Rowles?"

"He died, Caroline. I'm sorry."

She nods once. She knew the answer to the question before she asked it.

"He saved us all," I add. "Little madman took out the entire US army, if you can believe that."

She looks up, amazed. "What?"

I nod, smiling. "Nuked them."

Her mouth falls open in astonishment then she begins to laugh.

"He asked about you," I continue, smiling in spite of myself. "Wanted us to find you, tell you he loved you."

Gradually her laughter subsides and she wipes away a tear that could equally have been caused by hilarity as grief.

"He stayed behind so I could escape," she says eventually. "The surgeon who operated on me came to get me during the attack. Spirited me away from right under their noses."

"Where did he take you?"

"We spent a while in a house somewhere in Bristol, while I recovered. Just the two of us."

"Did he...?"

"Oh yes," she says matter of factly. "But, you know, could have been worse." She registers my look of horror and dismisses it with a scowl. "I'm still alive," she snaps, irritably.

"Okay," I say, eager to move on. "And then?"

"He traded me to a trafficker for a pallet of Pot Noodles and a bag of firelighters."

I stare intently at the floor, unable to meet her gaze. "I should have looked after you better," I say. "I'm so sorry. This is all on me."

I feel her hand on mine and I look up. She's not smiling, but she's not scowling either. "Not your fault. Move on," is all she says. But I'm worried for her. Caroline and Rowles were inseparable for a while. Kindred spirits. Bonnie and Clyde. But while she was brave, strong and ruthless to a fault, she didn't have the emotional detachment of her younger partner in crime. I remember the look on her face, the utter horror, when she accidentally shot a soldier who was trying to help us. Rowles would have shrugged and made some comment about tough luck; Caroline was devastated.

Yet here she is leading an army, battle scarred and hardened and not yet sixteen. I wonder if that vulnerable core has been entirely burnt away.

"I thought you'd died in the nuke," I explain. "It wasn't 'til much later that we discovered you weren't there. We searched high and low for you, I swear."

"I believe you. But once the traffickers had me, I was shipped straight to London."

"You escaped, though. I mean, look at this place. Why not come find me?"

"I was... busy for a year or so. And when I did manage to get away, I didn't escape alone. I had this lot to look after. And a war to fight."

"Against who? Who are these bastards?"

She regards me coolly for a moment then says: "Come with me."

As we walk out into the main street and down to the centre of town, we talk more, filling in the blanks. I tell her how I ended up in the van, about the snatchers and how they killed Lee, John and Tariq; she relates stories of all the times the church have tried to track them down or infiltrate them. There's a streak of ruthlessness to Caroline's tale – moles identified and shot no matter how young they may have been, lethal traps laid at freshly abandoned living spaces. She's been fighting a guerrilla war and she's been fighting dirty. I don't have the right to disapprove – she's kept these kids safe in the face of overwhelming odds – but there's a disquieting element to her stories. I can't decide whether her precautions and her summary justice were always justified or whether she's succumbed to paranoia. I remember how Lee was after the siege of St Mark's; reckless, too quick to fight when a calmer head could have avoided the need. I see a lot of that in Caroline. The sooner I get her back to the school, the better.

It's so long since I've been in a city that I've almost forgotten what it's like to be surrounded by concrete. Everywhere I look is evidence of The Culling Year. Burnt-out cars and buildings, skeletons in the street, a wrecked van, turned on its side. Someone's gone mad with an aerosol too – up and down the high street, in big red letters it reads "whoops apocalypse J" over and over again.

With no council maintenance teams to trim them, the trees are taking over. Tough grass is starting to force its way through the moss-covered tarmac, and foxes stroll blithely down the road eyeing us more with hunger than fear, as if calculating the odds of successfully bring us down and making us their next meal.

As we walk and talk, Caroline notices me watching the foxes. "Keep clear of them and they'll keep clear of you. Otherwise they tend to go for the throat. And if you hear a dog barking, go the other way. Don't let them get your scent. We've managed to trap and eat most of the local packs, but there are still a couple of nasty ones left. We lost a girl to one of them only last week. Seven, she was. Poor love wandered off and tried to play fetch with a Rottweiller."

We cross what would once have been a busy traffic junction and suddenly I realise that we're not alone. I become aware of shadows flitting underneath the overpass, and catch a snatch of raucous laughter somewhere up ahead, echoing through a deserted shopping mall. There are people here, all moving in the same direction as we are. Then we turn a corner and I see our destination: The Hammersmith Apollo. The sign above the entrance still reads "Oct 24/5 Britain's Got Talent Roadshow!"

There's a small market outside, a pathetic collection of scavengers trying to barter remnants and relics for food. But there's precious little of that, just an improvised spit on which rotate a couple of thin looking pigeons. The smell isn't exactly appetising.

Caroline notices my disgust. "I know. You've probably got a big old vegetable garden and a field of sheep, huh?"

I nod.

"I dream about mashed potato," she says wistfully.

"Then why are you still here?"

"Because of him," she says, pointing.

I look up and see a huge mural painted onto the theatre wall. It stretches the entire height of the building and depicts a withered old man in glowing white robes. His balding head is ringed by a red circular halo and his hands are stretched out towards us in a gesture of welcome. Blood drips from his fingers. I suppose it's intended to be beatific, religious, holy. But to me it just looks fucking creepy, because standing around him, gazing up at him in awe and wonder, are a gaggle of children.

"The Abbot," says Caroline. "Come on, it's nearly time for the miracle." She leads me through the market and into the theatre.

Inside is a small wiry man with a little stall selling bags of KP peanuts. I gawp. "I know," says Caroline, registering my amazement. "He's here every time, and no-one knows where he gets them. People have tried following him back to wherever he's got his stockpile, but he's too slippery."

"Hey, thin man," she says cheerily. "Can I get a freebie for my guest here?"

The peanut seller smiles broadly and tosses a packet to me. "Anything for you, sweetheart," he says. Caroline blows him a kiss and we walk through the doors into the auditorium as I pull open the packet and inhale the salty aroma. Yum.

"We rescued his daughter – well, he says she's his daughter – from the snatchers six months back," she offers as explanation.

There's a big screen on the stage and a projector in front of it. A relatively large crowd – fifty or so people – has gathered in front of the stage. I hear the cough and splutter of a generator starting up and settling into its rhythm before the projector comes alive and beams snowstorm static for our amusement.

"So what are we going to see?" I ask through a mouthful of honey roasted heaven.

"Wait and see. It happens at the same time every fortnight," she says, as we take our positions at the edge of the crowd.

The television signal kicks in and we see a graphic of a red circle against a light blue background, and then the show begins. The miracle.

The broadcast is by a group who call themselves the Apostolic Church of the Rediscovered Dawn and they're – wouldn't you know it – American. Their leader is the creepy guy from the mural. An ancient, wizened old vampire who's survived the plague despite being – he claims – AB Positive. He provides a demonstration, mixing his blood with O-Neg taken from two acolytes who sport the dead-eyed grins of happy cultists, then holding it up to the camera as it clumps.

The crowd in the studio Ooh and Aah, gasp and clap, then they start singing some bollocking awful gospel shit. The crowd here, though, aren't quite so sold. I get the impression they're just basking in the glow of the television, reminding themselves of moving pictures and cathode ray tubes. The programme is irrelevant, but watching it evokes families gathered around the national fireplace watching *Big Brother* or *Doctor Who*. Happier, simpler times.

When the song has finished, the Abbot gives a little sermon. About children. It takes a few minutes for the penny to drop, and then I remember what the snatcher had said back in the school, about saving the children's immortal souls.

"Dear God," I whisper, my peanuts momentarily forgotten. "They're shipping them to America."

CHAPTER EIGHT

"AMERICA? YOU HAVE to be shitting me."

"No, honest, man. They got planes flying out of Heathrow and everything."

"But why?"

"New beginning. That's what the churchies say. We're rescuing the kids so they can go out to America and find the Promised Land or something. They've got it easy over there, you know."

"Really?"

"Yeah, still got electricity and supermarkets and all that stuff. So I heard."

"And the nukes?"

"Wiped out the political elite. Left a power vacuum that these Neo-Clergy have filled. And they've got everything just fucking sorted, man. Peace, love, charity, all that jazz."

Tariq looked at me over the top of our prisoner's head and rolled his eyes.

"Listen, pal, I don't know where you're getting your information but I know for a fact that America's political elite is alive and kicking."

"Yeah, 'course you do."

"Saw the president himself two years back, on a live... oh. Oh, holy shit!"

"What?" asked Dad.

"What his aide said about children. Do you remember Tariq?"

"I was bit busy being shot, old chap."

"He said, now let me get this right... 'spied her rounding up the children'. It was the first thing I heard when I came round in Blythe's office."

"Well, that's our boss, isn't it?" said our captive. "Spider. The big man."

"Spider? I thought he was talking about Jane. Spied her. Fuck, I'm an idiot."

"What are you thinking, Lee?"

"Don't you get it? That wasn't the bloody president. That was this Abbot guy pretending to be the president. He had Blythe running round at his beck and call, trying to take control of the UK so he could use the army to round up all the children and ship them out to the States."

"And he must have already had a guy on the ground starting the job," says Tariq. "This Spider bloke."

"Who's assumed control this end now that we've taken the army out of the equation. The president's aide told Blythe there was a bigger picture."

"This isn't a new mess at all, then," said Dad. "It's the same old mess."

"But with less impaling this time around. I hope."

"Yeah," said our captive cheerily. "The big man prefers crucifixion."

I clipped his ear.

"Um... I didn't follow half of that," said the guy who'd assumed control of the Rangers. "Can you start at the beginning?"

"Later," snapped Dad. "First of all, this little sod's going to give us chapter and verse on his boss's operation. Aren't you?"

"You betcha."

"Smart lad."

AN HOUR LATER we were gathered in front of a classroom whiteboard as Dad talked us through a map of London that he'd put together during the interrogation.

"These guys are well armed, very organised and disciplined," he told us. "They've got a whole bunch of ex-special forces types running their operation, and they maintain a clear and functional command structure. The good news for us is that they mainly concern themselves with keeping order in London. The snatchers who operate outside the M25 are basically contractors. They're scavengers and lowlifes who work in teams to assemble kids in a number of compounds like this one, spread around the country. Then they're collected regularly by convoys, each of which is run by one overseer from central command who keeps them in line.

"They don't have complete control of London. South of the river their control is pretty much absolute. There are communities there who are actually giving their kids to these bastards willingly. It's an area of hard core zealots and converts. Pretty much entirely hostile territory.

"North of the river the picture's less clear. It seems the population there is mostly controlled by fear and intimidation, although the battle for hearts and minds is ongoing. There's one major pocket of resistance around Hammersmith where – Lee, you'll like this – a gang of kids who escaped from a transport have set up a liberation army."

I smiled. "Nice."

"But according to our man here, there's a major crackdown planned for next week. They've tried to lure them out into traps or get someone on the inside, but it's never worked. They're going to go in hard and wipe them out."

"Not so nice," murmured Tariq.

"What about their command?" asked one of the Rangers.

"This is where it gets tricky. They've set up home in the Palace of Westminster and turned it into a fortress. Concrete barricades, electric fences, gun towers, searchlights. They've even got a minefield. And this is where their boss lives. Spider."

"What do we know about him?" I asked.

"He holds court from the Speaker's Chair in the House of Commons, but apart from that, nothing. No one except the very top echelon get to see him. But he's got a reputation for being utterly ruthless."

"There's a surprise," I said.

"And he keeps his men happy with a brothel he's set up in – get this – the main chamber of the House of Lords."

"Brothel?"

"Rape camp, really, I guess. A whole bunch of young girls who are at the men's disposal 24/7. He's got huge stockpiles of food and booze too. If you work for him, you eat and drink your fill and fuck any time you feel like it."

"Shit, where do I sign up?" laughed one of the Rangers until his mates gave him death stares. He muttered: "Only joking, geez."

"Twat," said one of his colleagues.

Silence fell as we considered the size of the task before us.

"So," said Tariq eventually. "We invade London, fight our way past a city full of brainwashed religious cultists, take on a private army, storm a massively fortified castle that's defended by highly motivated special forces, and kill this Spider fucker. Then we take a plane, fly to America, rescue all the kids and take down a church that effectively rules a continent."

"That's about the size of it," said Dad.

Tariq sniffed dismissively. "That's the problem with life these days. So few real challenges."

"So here's what we're going to do," Dad continued. "Tariq, you're going back to St Mark's. There's a chance that Jane might tell them where the school is."

"No fucking way," I shouted. "She'd die first."

"They might not let her, Lee."

"She'd never talk."

"We can't take that chance." He stared me down and after a long moment, I nodded. He was right. "Tariq, you go back to the school and put them on a war footing. We've rehearsed it often enough, so you know what to do. But be ready to mobilise, too. We might need you."

"No worries, boss," said Tariq.

"Lee, you're going with our Ranger friends here. Meet up with Jack in Nottingham see if you can persuade the Hooded Man to lend us some troops. We'll need all the help we can get."

"He'll want to talk to you about our dead men, too, I reckon," said one of them, threateningly. Dad was instantly right in his face.

"If anything happens to my boy, there will be a very bloody reckoning in Nottingham. Do I make myself completely clear?"

The Ranger tried to stare him down, but failed. He looked away. "Whatever," he said. But he looked away first. Message received.

"And what about you?" I asked.

"I'm going to Hammersmith," he replied, stepping back. "If there really is an army of kids in there, they don't know an attack is coming. I can warn them and either help get them to safety or, more likely, help them fight. It's where my experience will be most useful. We need all the allies we can get if we're going to pull this off."

I WAS CHECKING the saddle on the spare horse the Rangers were letting me ride when Dad took me to one side.

"What now?" I asked tersely.

He looked at me hard, as father and commander fought it out. "It's been two years since Iraq and Salisbury. You've not been in a fight since. You refuse to talk to anyone about anything that happened.

And now, the first time we go into combat, you shoot six people – one potential ally and five irrelevances who didn't need killing."

"I disagree. They really, really needed killing. But I'm sorry about earlier. I wasn't thinking straight."

"I know. I'm sorry too. But I'm worried about you. You're my son and I love you but to be totally honest you scare me a little bit right now. I think your judgement is off."

"That why you're sending me on the diplomatic mission?"

"No, you were the logical choice. But I can't pretend I'm not glad of that."

"Can I have my weapon back?"

He sighed and handed me the handgun. "Just don't shoot Robin Hood, okay?"

We both sniggered in spite of ourselves. "Now there's a sentence I never thought I'd have to say," he said, smiling.

We both stepped forward and embraced, awkwardly. "Good luck in London," I said. "I'll be at the rendezvous, whether he sends help with me or not."

He hugged me hard then let me go and stepped back.

"Be safe," he said.

I put my foot in the stirrup, swing myself onto the horse and trotted over to join Hood's men.

"We ride fast and we won't be making any concessions. So keep up or get left behind," said their leader.

"Don't you worry about me," I said.

"Oi!" It was Tariq, walking towards me, waving. I pulled the reins and steered my horse across to him.

"You off, then?" he said.

"Yup. See you at the rendezvous."

He nodded then looked up at me, his face for once entirely serious. "She'll be fine, Lee."

"Let me worry about her," I replied. "You just keep the school safe. No matter what."

"Promise. Hey, you'd better hurry up, they're going without you."

I turned to see the Rangers galloping away down the road. I kicked my steed hard and took off after them, riding to beg assistance from a legend.

CHAPTER NINE

"HE WEARS THIS black robe with a big hood. He never takes it off."

"So you never saw his face?"

"No, sorry."

"And his voice?"

"He didn't speak. He just nodded or shook his head when they asked him questions."

I put my hand on the arm of the little boy with the missing ear and say: "Thank you."

He nods and scampers off.

"I told you he wouldn't be much help," says Caroline. We're sitting on one of the sofas, back in the office building she calls home, watching the sun set behind the Lyric Theatre.

"And he's the only one here who's met Spider?"

Caroline nods. "He doesn't leave Parliament, and he doesn't show his face. Why are you so interested, anyway? You'll never get near him."

"Someone said that to me once before, but I got close enough to ensure that he'll remember me for the rest of his life."

Caroline regards me curiously. "So you met this guy before The Cull?"

"I think so. No, I know so. It must be him. It all fits."

"And is he the reason you changed your name and went into hiding?"

I look up, startled. "How...?"

"I heard you and Sanders talking after I was shot. You thought I was asleep. He knows you from before, doesn't he?"

"Yes. And it's *knew*, I'm afraid. He's dead too."

"So..."

"Yes, Spider's the reason I went into witness protection and ended

540

up at St Mark's. But it's a long story and I don't really want to talk about it, if that's okay."

"Whatever. So the school's back up and running?"

"Yeah," I reply, grateful that she isn't pressing the point. "Sixteen staff now, seventy-three kids. It would be more if these bastards weren't spiriting them away."

Caroline stares intently at her hands. I can tell she wants to ask the obvious question but isn't sure how to.

"Yes," I say. "All of you. We've got plenty of room."

She looks up and beams. "There are thirty-four of us. Plus kids we rescued today."

"More the merrier," I say, smiling.

"We'll have to go out and around," she says, excited for the first time today. "Coz south of the river is churchland." She looks up at me and stops short, her smile fading. "There's a 'but' isn't there?"

I nod. "Spider. He and I have unfinished business."

"But... but that's mad. Even if you get in to see him, he's surrounded by a fucking army!"

"Oh, he'll see me, all right. And as for the army. Well, one thing at a time, eh?"

I take out my sidearm and chamber a round.

"You are fucking mental, Miss. If you go and get yourself killed, who's going to get these kids to safety? You owe them... you owe *me* that."

She's right, of course. I do.

I know the sensible thing is to get these kids back to St Mark's, meet up with Lee, try and recruit help from Nottingham and put together a properly formulated plan of action. I know this. But John and Tariq are lying dead in that school, and Lee is missing. For all I know, I could be the only one left of our team, and I'm closer to the heart of this mystery than anyone's yet got.

I can't turn back now.

I shake my head. "Sorry Caroline. I'll give you directions to the school," I say. "If I'm not back in three days, take these kids and go."

I lean forward and hug her tightly but she doesn't respond, shocked at my abandonment. "I'm so glad you're safe, sweetheart," I say. "I can't tell you how glad."

Then I let her go, stand up, and walk out of the building without looking back. I don't want to see the accusation in her gaze. I take a moment to get my bearings then take off down the high street, heading for the Thames. If I walk all night, I can be there by dawn.

*   *   *

IT'S A BITTER NIGHT. Clear sky, full moon. The sun's not down for an hour before there's frost on the ground. I walk down the Thameside path in the half-light, listening to the lap of the waves as the tide drags the river down, slowly exposing the rubble of a thousand demolished warehouses and the rotting timbers of ancient wharfs and jetties.

I went on a walking tour of the Thames once, when I was a medical student at Barts and The London. The guide was an ancient old woman, eighty if she was a day, yet sprightly and funny and with a deep booming voice that always reached me, even when I was at the edge of the crowd.

A hundred and fifty years ago the exposed mudflats of low tide London would be swarming with mudlarks, even at this time of night, she'd told us. Children between the ages of eight and fifteen would swarm down to the edge of the retreating water, sometimes wading hip deep in mud laced with fresh effluent and the occasional bloated corpse, scavenging for lost trinkets and dropped wallets. Mostly, though, they just found lumps of coal which had fallen off the barges that passed up and down the river. They'd collect the coal in sacks and then take it to sell to a local dealer. If they were lucky, they'd earn a penny a day.

150 years of progress, of making sure that children were protected from that kind of existence – in the West, at least – and yet five years after The Cull, I'd just left a hundred and thirty children who were living together in a crumbling building, scavenging for food and clothes, barely better off than mudlarks. Most of them would probably never go to school or university, never learn about history or geography or medicine.

Human nature tells me that there are sweatshops in England now. Somewhere, someone will have rounded up kids to use in makeshift factories. It's inevitable. One day someone will let something slip at a market and we'll follow whispers and rumours and track them down. I know with absolute certainty that if I survive this week, one day I'll kick down the doors of an old warehouse and find a hundred emaciated, pallid children dressed in rags, making matches or shoelaces.

And I'll free them, and feed them and clothe them and teach them.

Right now, we are clinging to the scraps of knowledge and technique left to us by the dead, but when the last person who was over 16 during The Culling Year dies, it will be these children who inherit the ruins. It's vital we protect them. Give them a childhood and an education. If we don't, we'll be responsible for a new dark age.

I tell myself this, examine my motives for staying at St Mark's, rehearse all the arguments I've used to justify what we're doing, all the historical precedents that have spurred me on, all the smiles I've brought to the faces of children who would be dead without my intervention. But all of it, every laugh, every smile, just wilts when I think about the man I am walking towards. My grand mission to save a generation of lost kids was discarded, forgotten and irrelevant the instant I heard that name again.

I keep putting one foot in front of the other, forcing my way through the silent city, finally realising the true power of revenge.

IT'S STILL DARK when I reach the reconstructed Globe Theatre. I'm amazed to see it's still intact, despite a thatched roof that's practically an invitation to arson. I'm walking past when I catch an echo of a voice. Faint at first but then, as I pass the wrought iron gates, distinct. Someone is reciting Shakespeare from inside the theatre, presumably on the stage. I stand and listen for a moment, surprised by the sudden, unexpected evidence of life. It's the only sound in the cold, calm night.

It's a man, young by the sound of it, and he's not following any play that I know. He skips from this to that – a comic monologue, a Hamlet soliloquy, a sonnet. After a few minutes, I sit on a bench and give myself over to this improbable voice. Was he an actor? If I enter the theatre, will I recognise him? "Oh, you played whatshisname, on *The Bill*!" Or is he a young man who'd just been accepted to RADA and was about to begin a career that would make him a star, standing alone on a dark stage in the middle of dead city, dreaming of a world where the sex lives of actors were the talk of every sitting room in the land?

He's good. Emotive. Strong, clear voice. I feel a sudden ache in my chest, and I stifle a sob that seems to have come from nowhere. I sit and listen to King Lear's death speech with tears pouring down my face. I have no idea why I'm crying, but I can't help it. The tears just flow out of me.

And as his medley of Shakespeare's greatest hits continues, this suddenly echoes from inside the wattle and daub walls:

"How couldst thou drain the lifeblood of the child,
To bid the father wipe his eyes withal,
And yet be seen to bear a woman's face?

Women are soft, mild, pitiful, and flexible;
Thou stern, obdurate, flinty, rough, remorseless.
Bid'st thou me rage? Why, now thou hast thy wish.
Wouldst have me weep? Why, now thou hast thy will.
For raging wind blows up incessant showers,
And when the rage allays the rain begins.
These tears are my sweet Rutland's obsequies,
And every drop cries vengeance for his death."

I have no idea what play it's from, but I hold my breath, transfixed, until it's finished. The tears turn to ice on my cheeks. When the final syllable fades I release a long, slow breath and rise from my seat.

I walk on, gun in hand, leaving the anonymous actor behind to conjure the spirits of the dead in an empty auditorium.

I have a job to do.

LAMBETH BRIDGE IS gone. There's just a spur of stone sticking out over the river, like a huge jagged diving board. I walk to the edge and look down into the water, rising now that the tide has turned, swirling and bubbling with the strength of the current. Fall in there, you wouldn't last long.

A corpse floats past, face down.

The sun is just edging over the horizon as I walk past Victoria Tower Gardens and reach the Palace of Westminster, the seat of British democracy. I stand and gaze in astonishment for a moment at the gun towers and fences, the thin strip of what looks like bare earth between the wire enclosures, and the sign that says 'minefield'.

On the grass at the centre of Parliament Square stand three crosses, with rotting corpses nailed to them. Some wag has scrawled INRI on the central spar of the middle crucifix. The victims hang there staring at the Houses of Parliament which now sport a huge red circle painted across the stonework.

The wrought iron fence that encloses the Big Ben end of the building has had gibbets attached to the stone corner posts. Only one is currently occupied, by what looks like a young girl. She is curled into a ball, naked and frozen. There are five heads stuck on to spikes along the length of the fence.

A bullet pings off the tarmac at my feet. I hear a high pitched laugh.

"You only get one warning shot, darling," shouts the gunman who's just appeared in the nearest watchtower. "And that's just coz you're pretty. Normally I just shoot people dead. Saving bullets, you see. Every slug gotta kill. Waste not, want not and all that."

"I want to talk to your boss," I shout back.

"You want to die?"

"My name," I yell, "is Doctor Kate Booker." That name feels strange in my mouth again after so long. "I know Spider from before The Cull. Tell him I'd like a word."

I look down at the red dot that's dancing around my sternum. "Trust me, he'll see me."

The laser sight disappears and I stand there waiting for fifteen minutes or so. Eventually, the large metal gate swings open and the man from the gun tower stands there, waving for me to approach.

I walk over to him slowly, full of confidence. I feel totally calm, but I know the nerves are going to hit soon and I'm trying to be ready for that.

"Follow me," he says, and he leads me across the lawn and into a cavernous hall, its walls made of huge blocks of stone and its massive wooden ceiling so big that it bleeds into shadow. Our footsteps echo as we cross the immense floor, passing plaques that tell us this is where Winston Churchill lay in state, and there is where William Wallace was condemned to death.

We ascend a wide stone staircase then turn left down a long corridor lined with epic pre-Raphaelite paintings. We emerge into a huge circular chamber with an unlit chandelier hanging above us. I remember this space from television, watching MPs stand here justifying themselves to the press. Four white statues stand silent in the gloom as we turn right and walk down another long corridor to two wooden doors.

The building passes in a blur of murals, stained glass, intricate mosaics and elaborately designed floor tiles. I concentrate on putting one foot in front of the other, keeping the lid tight closed on the terror that threatens to bubble up and engulf me. This whole place seems exactly as I would have imagined it pre-Cull. There is no evidence of this being the headquarters of a cult. They've kept the place pristine.

We pass through another chamber and walk past a statue of Churchill, sticking his big round tummy out at me as if it were a challenge. Then we pass through a gothic stone arch that seems shattered and wrecked, walk through some big doors and I find myself standing at the far end of the House of Commons. A very faint hint of orange dawn light seeps through the grimy row of tiny windows that provide the only illumination. Tiers of green leather benches rise to my left and right. Serried wooden balconies loom over the room, lending it the air of an arena, which I suppose it always was.

The doors close behind me, the loud bang as they shut jolts me. I spin around but my guide has gone. I am alone.

The room is totally silent, the backbenches deep in shadow. I walk forward on the lush green carpet, towards the table over which the party leaders used to squabble. I'm sure it has some pompous name – the Debating Oak or something – but I've no idea what it is. There are ornate wooden boxes on either side of the table, and I know these are called the dispatch boxes. Or are they? Weren't they the red cases they used to carry?

Oh, who cares.

It's smaller than I imagined, functional and unimpressive but I still feel as if I've wandered on to a film set. That this room should have survived The Culling Year completely intact is hard to fathom. I know there were riots and mobs, mass burnings and massacres on the streets near here. But I suppose the security forces managed to hold the line long enough for attention to focus elsewhere. I know at least one guy who thinks the Government are still here, hiding in air tight bunkers under the ground, waiting for a cure. But the air in here is dead. This is a museum. No-one will ever argue about defence funding in here again. Thank God.

I hear a faint rustle at the end of the hall ahead of me. A rat maybe? I stare into the shadows. A shape leans forward out of the darkness and – dammit – makes me jump and give a little squeal of surprise. Like a fucking schoolgirl.

It's a figure, dressed entirely in a black robe, hood down, sitting in the tall wooden Speaker's Chair. His face is hidden in the darkness, but I know it's him.

Spider.

I stand there, paralysed.

I'd pictured myself surrounded by his loyal troops, pulling out my gun and shooting him, then being instantly cut down, dying there but not minding.

Or I'd pictured myself being frisked at the gate, handcuffed, brought before him on my knees, forced to beg for mercy. But making my pitch well, securing a position as his official doctor, working my way into his trust and then striking the first time he dropped his guard, just a little.

Or I'd pictured myself held down as he raped me then slit my throat. But this. Alone. Unwatched. Armed.

I reach down and pull out my gun, aiming it straight at the black space where I know his head is.

Neither of us speaks for a long moment.

But he doesn't move. Doesn't ring an alarm or shout for help. Doesn't raise a gun in my direction.

Instead, he laughs. Softly, genuinely. Then he leans back into the shadows, resting his head against the padded chair, waiting for me to make my move.

I step sideways, edging my way towards the gap between the table and the front bench.

"Remember me?" I say. I want to scream in his face, but there's no need to shout. Every whisper carries crystal clear.

No response. I reach the corner of the table and begin walking towards him, gun still aimed true.

"Remember Manchester?" Halfway, now. The outlines of his cloak emerging as I approach and the sunlight strengthens from above.

"Remember my brother?" And, oh, yes, I yelled that. And here comes the anger and the terror and the nerves. My stomach floods with acid, my veins race with adrenaline. My hands shake with the force of it.

But I keep walking.

There's a step at the end, just in front of the chair, and I mount it, shoving the gun under the fold of his hood into the black space.

And there I stand, unsure what to do. He's just sitting there, waiting for death. Where's the catch? What does he know that I don't?

I stand there for nearly a minute, the only sound is our breathing – mine hard and ragged, his soft and calm.

Then he murmurs: "I remember, Kate. I remember it all."

That voice. I feel faint at the sound of it. My arm drops for an instant as I go weak. My knees try to buckle, but I force them to lock again. Raise the gun level.

Then he slowly lifts up his hood and pulls it back, revealing his face.

And suddenly it's eight years ago, I'm a completely different person, and the Chianti is warm on the back of my throat.

PART TWO
KATE

Kate gently lowered herself into the near boiling water, letting her skin adjust to the heat in tiny increments, her lips pursed with the pleasure of pain.

When she was fully submerged, only her head poking up through the bubbles, she lay there for minute or two with her eyes closed and focused on her breathing. She took long, slow, deep breaths and pictured the cares and stresses of her day dissolving out of her into the bathwater. Then, her heart rate slow, her head clear, she stretched out a languid hand for the glass of red wine perched on the windowsill above her. She took a sip and moaned softly in blissful contentment.

It had been an awful, wonderful day. Her first shift at A&E. She'd trained for years in preparation, and had some training yet to complete. But all that study, that sacrifice, the sleepless nights and double shifts, the practical exams and psychological probes, the stuck up consultants, insolent orderlies and endless, endless paperwork, had led her to this day; an afternoon spent dressing a huge abscess on the back of a homeless alcoholic who smelt like he slept in a supermarket skip full of rotting meat.

She was going to have to scrub herself raw to get the stench out. The smoke from her joss stick merged with the steam from the bath. It smelt the way she imagined a hookah pipe would, and it made her feel exotic and elsewhere. Plus, it masked the rank odour that still haunted her nostrils.

The flat was silent. The students upstairs, for all their exuberance, rarely partied until 4am. They were asleep, as was her flat mate Jill, a plain, bookish girl who kept herself to herself, liked early nights and slept with earplugs in. Kate liked being awake when everyone else was asleep. It made her feel secure, confident that no-one was watching or expecting anything of her.

The world was asleep, and Kate felt free as a bird.

When she heard the gentle knock at the front door, she initially thought she must be imagining it. But no, there it was again, louder this time. Her hard-won calm evaporated, but she decided to ignore the intrusive noise. It was probably just some pissed up student who'd got the wrong flat. Just ignore it, she told herself. They'll go away.

The knocking got louder and more insistent. Kate muttered: "La, la, la can't hear you." Then she heard the rattle of the letterbox and her name being whispered through it.

"Kit," said the voice. "Kit, I know you're in there. Open up."

Kate sighed. "For fuck's sake," she cursed under her breath as she lifted herself out of the foam. "What now?" She towelled herself down and pulled on her bathrobe, the moth eaten old silk one with the holes in it, and went to let in her brother, James.

"What bloody time do you..." Her half-angry diatribe died in her throat as she pulled the front door open and saw the woman.

"Thank God," said James. "Help me get her inside."

Kate's brother was not tall – about five foot seven – and the woman dwarfed him. He stood in the cold hallway, holding her up. Her head lolled on his shoulder and her feet dragged across the threshold as he and Kate manhandled the unconscious woman into the flat. James kicked the door closed behind him.

"Bedroom," said Kate.

They gently lowered the unconscious woman onto Kate's bed. Just for a moment, Kate hesitated. She looked at the woman's face in the light and was suddenly taken aback. Despite her height, this was the face of a child. Kate mentally re-categorised her – this wasn't a woman, not quite yet. If she was eighteen, it was only barely. This was a girl; a girl wearing white stilettos, stockings and suspenders, a red basque torn open to reveal her left breast, and nothing else. She had been severely beaten. Her hair was long and blonde, her cheekbones high and her lips full. Kate thought she looked Eastern European.

Her training kicked in. "Call 999," she said as she lifted the girl's eyelids and shone the bedside lamp into them, checking pupil dilation.

"I can't, Sis," said James, who fidgeted nervously at the end of the bed.

"Fine, then I will." Kate lifted the handset from its cradle on her bedside cabinet, but James scurried across and made to grab it from her before she could dial. They struggled for a moment before Kate let the phone go and returned to the girl.

"James, this girl needs a hospital," said Kate, checking the airway for obstructions. "What the hell is going on here? Who is she?"

James was hovering at her shoulder, putting her off.

"For God's sake, sit down and tell me what's going on," she barked as she took the girl's pulse.

He lingered for a moment then went to sit at the foot of the bed, wringing his hands anxiously.

"I'm in trouble, Sis. Really bad."

"Save it," snapped Kate. "The girl." Check skull for evidence of blunt trauma.

"Her name's Lyudmila. She's a prostitute. Kind of."

"Not your type though." Examine limbs and ribs for signs of breakage.

"She's from where I work."

"You're a student. You don't work, you scrounge."

He didn't say anything more except: "Is she going to be okay?"

Kate focused on her patient. When she'd assured herself that the girl was in no immediate danger, she pulled the quilt over her and left her to sleep it off.

She grabbed a pair of jeans and a t-shirt, ushered James out while she dressed, then joined him in the living room. He was boiling the kettle in the kitchenette. She nipped into the bathroom, collected her wine, then returned to the cracked leather sofa, tucked her legs underneath herself and said: "Get your tea. Sit down. Start at the beginning."

James plonked himself down at the other end of the small sofa, cradling the mug and biting his lip. Kate had seen her brother up against it more than once – the time he'd been attacked on the street by gay bashers; the day he was expelled from school – but this twitchy nervous wreck was barely recognisable as her flamboyant, devil-may-care, overconfident younger sibling. As he opened his mouth to speak she had an inkling that everything in her life was about to change. She felt a rush of butterflies in her stomach.

But before James could begin, there was another, louder knock at the door.

"Oh, fuck," he whispered. His face went even paler, his eyes widened with fear and he stared at Kate like he'd just seen a ghost.

"Who is it?" she asked, but he wasn't listening.

"They must have followed me. Oh, fuck, oh, fuck, oh, fuck." He leaned across and grabbed her wrist. "Don't open it. Just stay quiet, maybe they'll go away."

The knocking came again, louder this time.

"James, it's 4am and the lights are on. They know we're here. Who is it?"

"They're looking for her." He pointed to the bedroom.

"Why? What are they going to..."

There was a sudden loud crash from the front door, which rattled on its hinges.

"Fuck!" cried Kate, suddenly, finally, scared.

There was another crash and this time she could hear the wooden door frame begin to splinter.

The door to the second bedroom opened and Jill stood there in her sensible flannelette pjs, rubbing her eyes and digging in her right ear for her earplug.

"What the bloody hell's going on?" she asked sleepily.

Kate leapt up and reached for the phone. "Sod this," she said. "I'm calling the police."

"No, Kate, please," shouted James as he rose to his feet.

Another crash from the door. This time it flew open with a huge crack of shattering wood. All three of them turned to see an enormous man framed in the doorway.

With a square head and haircut to match, the man's shoulders were so wide he had to turn a little bit sideways and stoop to fit through the doorway. His suit was large and baggy, more like a tent, and he lumbered into the room, his eyes narrowed and threatening.

James stepped forward, putting himself in front of Kate and Jill. He hunched his shoulders like a dog that's about to be told off by a pack leader, lowered his head, held out his hands in supplication, and started to beg.

"Petar, mate, I'm sorry. I didn't know what else to do. Nate was out of it and Lyudmila needed help, y'know. At least I didn't go to a hospital, right? Right? I mean, I did good not to go..."

The man raised a huge, ugly paw and backslapped James across the face with such force that he flew sideways, crashing into the sideboard and collapsing to the floor in a dazed heap, the silhouette of the man's hand etched onto his face in livid red.

"Hey," shouted Kate, stepping forward and jutting out her chin defiantly. "You leave my brother alone."

He raised his other hand and gave her the same treatment. It felt like being hit in the face with a girder. It lifted her off her feet and sent her sprawling into the kitchenette, scrabbling for purchase on the lino.

It was the first time in her life that anyone had ever hit her. She sat there, stunned, so surprised and shocked that she had no idea how to react. Out of the corner of her eye she registered Jill stepping backwards into her room and closing the door. The giant ignored her, instead opening the door to Kate's room where the injured girl was still in the bed.

He looked inside, assured himself that she was in there, then turned and walked out. She heard him bark a terse order in a language she did not recognise, and then three men entered the flat. They wore similar suits to the giant, and their faces were hard and cruel, but that wasn't what made Kate cry out in fear.

All three of them were carrying guns.

Kate had never seen a gun before. Not a real one, not up close and personal. She'd seen them on telly, of course, and in news reports about gang violence. She'd been trained what to do if a gun was pulled in the hospital, but there was no panic button here, and no guaranteed minimum response time.

The sight of the small, black, stubby metal objects paralysed her. She knew exactly the damage a bullet could do. Her mind was suddenly filled with images of herself lying on the floor, bleeding out from ruptured arteries, lungs filling with blood, choking on her own fluids, twitching and convulsing as she voided her bowels, wet herself and lost control of her body, dying on a black and white lino floor in a pokey flat with the smell of a tramp in her cooling nostrils.

What the bloody hell had James got her mixed up in?

She instinctively crawled backwards into the corner, as if cramming herself between the MDF cabinets would help. One of the men went into her bedroom, another grabbed James and dragged him to his feet, the third came for her. By the time her reached down to take her arm, Kate was hysterical. She began kicking and screaming, flailing around with her fists and shaking her head wildly. She didn't see what hit her across the temple, but if she'd been able to think about it, she'd have realised it was the handle of the gun. Her head swam, her vision sparkled, she went limp with the sound of James' protests ringing in her ears.

She didn't entirely pass out, though. She remained vaguely aware as the man grabbed her wrists, spun her around and pulled her out of the flat by her ankles. Her head bounced off the doorframe with a horrible thud, scraping the back of her scalp so it bled through her hair; it was thickly matted with blood by the time they reached the lift.

She was thrown into the lift like a sack of rubbish and ended up in a foetal heap in the corner. As the doors slid shut, she finally blacked out.

IN YEARS TO come, Kate would grow accustomed to waking from unconsciousness. The sharp pain in her head that revealed the site of the blow; the dry, metallic taste in her mouth; the shock of bright light; the fear that maybe this time some permanent damage had been done. The most important lesson she learnt, though, was not to panic. To take a moment to assess the damage, establish her capabilities.

The first time she awoke from such an ordeal, she didn't have this experience to draw on, so she sat bolt upright and looked left and right quickly, terrified. The sudden movement caused a spike of agony in her head, her vision blurred, and she slumped back down onto what she realised was a red leather sofa, groaning as the room spun around her. She clutched her hands to her head as if that would stop the wild rotation of the room and make the pain go away. It didn't.

"Here, take these," said a voice above her. She squinted up and saw a man looking down at her. He had a glass of water in one hand and a packet of Nurofen in the other.

Slowly, she sat up and reached out for the medicine, gulping them down hungrily, and draining the glass of water. As she handed back the glass she instinctively opened her mouth to thank the man, but then realised her mistake.

"You're welcome," he said softly, with a smile. She registered an accent, but couldn't place it. Russian, maybe?

Kate wanted to run, to scream, to try and escape, but she guessed she wouldn't get five metres. She leaned back into the comfy sofa and took in her surroundings.

The lighting was low and red. She was in a large room, a hall of some kind. No windows, so possibly a cellar. There were sofas and armchairs dotted around on the thick carpet, arranged in horseshoes with glass tables at their focal points. At the far end was a bar and on either side were raised platforms with metal poles that ran to the ceiling. She was in a strip club. An upmarket one, but not one of the majors. Probably central London. Even through the headache she knew what that implied about the management.

There was one more detail, too – handcuffed to the stripper's poles, sitting on the floor with their hands behind their backs, were

James and Lyudmila. The girl was out for the count, but James was conscious. She couldn't be sure in the half-light, but Kate thought he'd been beaten up.

The man in front of her sat down in an armchair. He placed his arms on the armrests very deliberately, as if arranging himself like a work of art ready for display. His movements were precise and considered, but Kate did not think it was vanity. She got a sense that he was so full of anger or violence that even the simple act of sitting in a chair required titanic effort and conscious control.

This man immediately scared her more than anything else that had happened on this bizarre, awful night.

She forced herself to meet his gaze, but his eyes were lost in shadow. He was middle aged, maybe in his forties. Short hair topped a high forehead above a long, straight nose and sensuous, amused lips. He was not overweight nor musclebound and he wore an expensive, well-tailored suit. He should have been attractive, but there was something cruel about that smile, and his body language screamed danger.

"What is your name?" he asked softly.

"Kate."

"Hello Kate. People call me Spider."

Of course they do, thought Kate. Can't have a criminal mastermind with a name like Steve or Keith. She almost voiced her sarcastic thought, but didn't, possibly because she was surprised to find herself capable of levity. She wondered if maybe she had a concussion, and then mentally chided herself; of course she had a bloody concussion.

"Interesting name," she said. "Where's it from?"

His smile widened. "I am from Serbia."

"Oh."

"Have you ever been?"

Kate shook her head.

"It is the most beautiful country on Earth." He paused and Kate felt herself being appraised. "Maybe one day I will take you."

The way he said it left Kate in no doubt that the double meaning had been intentional. There was a long silence. No sound penetrated this room from outside. All she could hear was her own breathing and the soft hum of ancient aircon.

"What do you do, Kate? I mean, for a living?"

"I'm a student doctor. You?"

"Oh, I do many things. Many things."

"Is this your club?"

He nodded. "And let me say, Kate, that if you ever tire of the medical profession, I am sure we could find a place for you here."

"If Lyudmila's an example of how you treat your staff, I think I'll pass."

"Lyudmila broke the terms of her contract."

"How?"

"She spat."

It took Kate a moment to work out what he meant, but when she did she felt sick to her stomach.

Spider leaned forward, gently intertwining his fingers and placing them on his knees.

"How do you know her?" he asked.

"I don't."

Spider looked puzzled and then surprised. He swore in Serbian and despite the language barrier Kate could tell he was amazed.

"You mean James brought her to you on his own?" he asked, openly astonished.

Kate didn't know what to do. If she said yes, would that make things better or worse? Eventually she nodded.

Spider turned to look at her brother and shouted, "Have you found a spine, Booker? I did not think you ever would."

"She... she was hurt, boss," wheedled James. "And Nate..."

"That useless junkie is gone. He works for the Albanians now."

"I know that, boss. But she was hurt, she needed to be looked after. I didn't know what else to do."

"So you took her to this girl?"

"Yes."

"And how..." Spider broke off and looked sharply back at Kate, then back at James. "Ha! She is your sister. You took Lyudmila to see your sister the doctor."

James hung his head in shame and then gave one short nod.

"Sorry, Sis," he said softly.

Spider turned back to Kate and leaned back in his chair again, once more placing his arms just so.

"I apologise for the way you were treated, Kate. I can see that this situation is not your fault."

"But?"

"But I hope you see that I am now in a very difficult position. The business I run is not, entirely, legitimate. There are people who would like to see me locked up. You have seen my face. You know my name. You can identify some of the men who work for me. You are a problem. I think it would be sensible for me to kill you."

"No! Boss, please!" yelled James.

As Spider rose from his chair, his precise movements made him seem almost robotic. He turned and walked over to James, who cowered on the floor. Spider stood above him on the stage and lashed out with his foot, kicking James hard in the face. It was a sudden, shocking action, an explosion of pent up rage. For an instant Spider's limbs were flexible, his neck was loose, his body fluent and fluid. Then, when the blow had been struck, he stood stock still and kind of settled, his body returning to repose, an act of conscious thought, re-imposing order on the chaos he worked so hard to contain within himself. His momentary loss of complete precision seemed almost not have happened.

He spun on his heels, walked back to Kate, and resumed his seat.

Kate could hear her brother sobbing quietly.

She surprised herself by consciously thinking how much she would like to kill this man.

"Who..." Kate's mouth was too dry to form words. She rubbed the sides of her tongue across her teeth to force some saliva into her mouth, then sluiced the tiny amount of liquid to the back of her throat, swallowing. "Who was Nate?" she asked eventually.

Spider's eyes narrowed, calculating. "He was my doctor."

Even though she'd known what he was going to say, the fact of it chilled Kate to the core. This man needed a doctor on call all the time. Dear God, how many women... how many beatings?

"And he's gone now?" she asked.

Spider nodded.

"Then maybe I can help you. Take his place."

There was a long silence. When Kate had woken up this morning she'd known this would be a life-changing day. But not in her wildest dreams had she envisaged sitting in a strip club at the crack of dawn as a Serbian gangster considered whether to kill her or welcome her to a life of crime.

Spider rose again and walked over to Lyudmila. He stood over the unconscious girl, his back to Kate, for a long moment. He stood so still that you could have mistaken him for a shop window dummy. Then he reached into his jacket and withdrew something that Kate couldn't see.

The shot was deafeningly loud, totally unexpected. Kate screamed in spite of herself. Lyudmila jerked once, but other than that you'd never know that a small piece of metal had just evacuated her head.

James cried out, a howl of horror and shame. Spider turned and walked over to him. His body language had changed again. Now he moved like a hunter, loose limbed and balletic.

Kate didn't have the luxury of going into shock. She leapt up from the sofa and ran over to them. Spider still had his gun in his hand, and he aimed casually at James's head. Kate flung herself between the gun and her brother.

She opened her mouth to speak, to beg for her life and James's. But she looked into Spider's eyes, able to see them properly, up close, for the first time. She instantly realised that it would be hopeless. There was neither pity nor humanity in those eyes. They were the cold, dead orbs of a predator, nothing more.

As she realised there was nothing she could do, Kate felt something inside her change. For the first time, she understood that her life lay entirely in the hands of another person, who would end it or not according to his whim. She was no longer in control of her own fate. Her life as she had known it was over. This realisation lent her a sudden, deep calm.

She looked into those eyes. She did not beg, or plead or cry. She did not try to strike a bargain or make a threat. She did not try to seduce him or attack him. All of those things would have resulted, she knew with absolute certainty, in instant death.

She just said one word, calmly, simply and without emotion.

"Please."

THE BARRISTA SCOOPED the soy milk froth over the coffee with a long spoon, put a heart-shaped flourish in the pattern, then sprinkled it with chocolate.

"Two ninety-five," she said, her Polish accent impossible to miss.

Kate paid. She smiled at the young woman, lifted the two mugs and a small packet of biscuits, then walked back to the table in the corner where her broken brother sat hunched and sniffling. She placed the mug of coffee in front of him and took her seat, facing him across the small round table. Over his shoulder she could see people hurrying to and fro down Villiers Street, popping into Accessorize or Pret, enjoying the bustle and business of their daily lives. She envied their ignorance and felt as if she no longer lived entirely in their world.

Her hands were steady as she lifted the coffee mug to her lips. She was surprised by this, but reasoned that she would probably go into shock in an hour or so, when the adrenaline finally wore off. For now, she felt focused, purposeful yet slightly spaced out, as if she had just begun the long build up to a skull shattering migraine.

James, she could see, was already in shock. She'd been trained to deal with people brought into A&E like this; taught how to treat them while eliciting their story, gathering information to help with diagnosis.

"Start at the beginning," she said, more harshly than she'd intended. It seemed that when it came to her brother, her training didn't help.

James sniffed, wiped his nose on his sleeve and took a sip of coffee. He looked up at her and she winced again at the marks on his face. His left eye was swollen shut, his jaw bulged and bruised, and his front left canine was a gaping, bloody hole. Say what you like about his personality, James had at least always been pretty. He'd always jokingly referred to himself as the lipstick half of any relationship. Certainly his boyfriends had always tended to be square-jawed gym bunnies. Kate suspected his pretty-boy days were over.

"I got into trouble about six months ago," he said, but then he ground to a halt, staring at the table top.

"James." He did not respond. "For God's sake, James, snap out of it. I need to know what you've got me into and I need to know now. Just take it slowly and tell me the whole story from the start."

James reached across and placed his hand on hers, squeezing it tightly and taking a few deep breaths to calm himself. Then he looked up and smiled weakly.

"Okay. But if you tell Gran about this, I'll tell her what you did with Bobby Arnold on your fifteenth birthday."

"You bitch, you wouldn't dare!"

"Try me, toots."

They both laughed, but not for long. James opened the small packet of biscuits and offered one to her. She took one as he dunked his in his coffee.

"I dunno why you do that," she said, screwing up her face in distaste.

"What?"

"Dunking. All you end up with is soggy biscuit mush at the bottom of your coffee. It's gross."

He didn't respond and it soon became apparent that their reservoir of small talk was empty.

"I got in trouble, Sis. Big trouble. About six months ago. It was Phil. You remember Phil?"

Kate remembered Phil, all right. She'd known he was trouble the first time he turned up at the pub that Sunday night. Tall, muscled and totally in love with his own reflection, he was boorish, brash and bullying. James couldn't look at him without doing simpering puppy eyes. Kate thought that was the attraction – Phil had finally found the only person in the world who adored him almost as much as he adored himself. He didn't exactly treat James like shit, he didn't need to. It would have been redundant. James practically lay down on the ground and begged Phil to walk all over him.

Kate loved her brother, but Jesus, his taste in men was worse than hers. Nonetheless, she couldn't work out how Phil would have led her brother to Serbian strippers.

"What, he dragged you to lap dancing clubs?" she asked, incredulously.

"No, don't be daft. Phil's problem was gambling. Spider doesn't just run that strip joint. He's got a casino, super illegal, in one of the arches underneath Waterloo station. High stakes, no IOUs. You know Phil worked for that big accountancy firm, right? Well, his boss took him there one night after work. He'd never have been able to get in there on his own, but once he'd been vouched for, he started going there on his own. A lot. One night he took me along. It was fun, you know? He hit a winning streak and we walked out three grand richer."

"Oh James, tell me you didn't go back on your own?"

"I figured, you know, if Phil could do it…"

"You fucking muppet." Kate shook her head in wonder. "Every time I think you can't get any stupider, you lower the bar."

James stared at the table top again. "Yeah, that's right Kit, let's have another round of 'my little brother, the big gay loser.' That's exactly what we need right now. So fucking helpful." He made to stand.

"Oh, sit down," she said wearily. "Fucking drama queen."

He planted his arse on the seat again, sullen and pouting.

"How much do you owe?"

"A lot."

"How much, James?"

"Twenty-three grand."

"Holy fucking Christ."

"I know, all right. I know. About four months back they grabbed me as I was leaving and took me back to see the boss. I swear, Sis, I thought he was going to shoot me there and then. I… I kind of begged."

"And he offered you a chance to work off the debt, yeah?"

James nodded. "He's into some seriously bad shit."

"No, really?" said Kate, finally starting to feel her cool slipping away. "The guy who just beat us up and shot a girl in the head for no reason at all? You think?"

"He's got the casino and the strip club, but there's more. Lots more."

"Like what?"

"Brothels. Well, not really brothels. More like, dungeons, really."

"What, for S&M?"

"No. Literally prisons where he keeps these girls locked up. They're all underground; railway arches, old sub-basements, places like that. There are about six or seven of them that I've been to and I know there are more. The high-rollers at the casino, and the guys at the strip club who want to spend a little more cash when the doors close, this is where they go."

Kate felt bile rising in her throat.

"You've been there?"

"That's my job. I have to look after some of the girls. Bring them food and stuff. Keep them alive."

"Lyudmila?"

James nodded. "She was new. Arrived last week. These girls, right, they think they're going to get jobs here. There's a whole chain designed to get them to the UK. Guys who go around the villages in the Ukraine and Latvia, Siberia and places like that looking for teenagers. And I mean thirteen up, right? They say they're recruiting for cleaning jobs and hotel waitresses, that kind of thing. The girls pay a fee, or their parents do, and they're shipped over here and then they just… disappear."

"These dungeons…"

"It's not just sex, Sis. And it's not exclusively teenagers. There are young kids, too. And murder rooms. And then…"

Kate had heard enough. "Okay, okay. Shut up. Let me think."

"There was this guy, Nate. He did all the doctoring for them. But he was a junkie and he wasn't reliable, so last week Spider threw him out. Sold him to another gang, like. When Lyudmila got roughed up, I didn't know what to do with Nate gone. I'm so sorry for getting you involved in this, Sis. Really."

"I said enough," Kate snapped. "I need to think. Figure out the angles."

"There aren't any, Kit. This guy, he's smart and ruthless and he's got a fucking army working for him. He even gets a whiff of betrayal and we're dead. Both of us. Just like that. No warning, no second chances. And that's if he's feeling generous. Coz if he's not, we'll end up in one of those dungeons, Sis. And no-one – no-one! – gets out of them alive."

"There's always an angle, James. Always," replied Kate. But she wasn't sure if she believed it, not in this case. The only thing she knew for certain was that her stupid, self-destructive, funny little brother, who she loved more than anything in the world in spite of his manifest flaws, was in trouble and, like she had done all his life, she was going to have to rescue him from himself.

"Get me another coffee, eh. And a chocolate muffin." Kate handed James a tenner and sat staring out of the window as he went to the bar. It took a minute or two for her to realise that she was being watched by the man sitting at the window bar in Pret directly opposite. When their eyes met he smiled and nodded slightly, then finished his coffee, left the shop and walked away.

"Oh, James," she whispered. "What have you done?"

THE NEXT FEW days passed in a blur of A&E shifts and deep, dreamless sleep. Spider had said he would call when he needed her, but her phone didn't ring.

Jill moved out of the flat without warning two days after the invasion. Kate came home from a long shift and found the flat half empty. No note, nothing. Bitch hadn't even left the rent. So Kate dug out the most recent itemised phone bill and called every number she didn't recognise until she reached Jill's Dad, who was not amused to hear of his daughter's midnight flit. He promised Kate that his little girl would be at her door in an hour with the rent in full. She was too, sullen and angry and refusing to speak. She held out an envelope full of cash and the second Kate took it she turned on her heels and stalked away.

"Don't be a stranger," Kate yelled at her retreating back, laughing.

She didn't seen the man who had been watching her, but she was constantly on the lookout for him. She was convinced she'd be seeing him again.

After a week she almost convinced herself it had never happened; that it was business as usual, that she hadn't been beyond the looking glass and seen a girl murdered. But then on Friday, as she sat in her track pants and t-shirt eating Pot Noodle on the sofa, watching *Loose Women* on her day off, there was a sharp knock at the door. She considered not answering, but whoever it was would be able to hear her telly.

The giant stood in the hallway, waiting patiently.

"Boss says you got to come."

"Okay, give me a minute to…"

He reached in and grabbed her wrist.

"Now."

"Okay, Jesus, can I at least get my coat?"

But he was pulling her across the threshold. She tried to grab her keys from the hook on the coat rack before the door closed behind her, but he pulled her too firmly and the door swung shut.

"Fuck, how am I supposed to get back in without my keys, dispshit?" she yelled as he dragged her towards the lift. He stopped dead, turned and looked down at her. He didn't say a word, just stared until she said: "Okay, lead on." He turned again and started walking. Outside the air was chilled and Kate felt goosebumps rising on her bare arms as she was bundled into the back seat of a waiting car with tinted windows.

"Look at the floor," said the giant as they pulled away. Kate did so without question.

They drove for about forty-five minutes. When they pulled up the giant reached across and snapped a sleep mask across her face so she couldn't see a thing. Then she was shoved outside and led across what felt like a cobbled street and into a cold, damp space that she was willing to bet was a railway arch. She was led down steps into a narrow space with dead acoustics and dust in the air. Down a corridor, then left and right and left again, and more steps.

"Mind head," said the giant a moment after she scraped the top of her head on what felt like soft brick. She stooped as she was led down a narrow stone staircase. By now, she knew she was deep underground. Another corridor, still stooping. She felt, then heard a gentle rumble somewhere off to her left. It took a moment to realise it must be a tube train.

Kate heard a key turn in a lock followed by the squeal of old hinges, then she was shoved through a doorway and her sleep mask was ripped off.

She was in a brick-lined cellar, barrel vaulted. Narrow but long, it stretched away, its vanishing point lost in darkness. There was a pervasive smell of damp and a distant sound of running water. An oil heater blazed away by the door, so at least it wasn't cold, but in every other respect it was probably the least healthy place in London. Trying not to think about the horrors of Weil's disease or the agony of hypersensitivity pneumonitis, Kate noted the bed, table and wind up lamp, the bucket in the corner with a tea towel draped over it and, finally, the girl sitting on the chair, dead eyed and listless, sallow cheeked and pale.

Kate turned to the giant, who was bent almost double in the corridor outside.

"People pay to come down here?" she asked, incredulous.

"No," he replied. "She come up for work. Stay here rest of time."

"Okay, well that's got to change. You need to get her out of here now."

"You stop her coughing."

"I can't. Not if she stays down here."

"You stop."

"I told you, I can't. Even if I can alleviate her symptoms, they'll come back if she stays down here."

The giant considered this. "Stop cough. Only need to stop coughing for afternoon. After that..." He shrugged.

Kate sighed. "Okay, I'll need prednisone." The giant looked confused. "Give me a pen, I'll write it down."

He handed her a biro and a receipt. She briefly considered ramming the pen into his throat and trying to make an escape, but dismissed the idea as ludicrous. She scribbled the name of the drug and handed him the piece of paper.

"I come back in hour." He slammed the door closed. Kate was imprisoned.

She stood there for a moment, then the girl on the chair burst into a fit of awful, hoarse coughing that went on for over five minutes. Kate held her shoulders as the spasms wracked her. There were flecks of blood on the girl's lips when she finally finished. Her breathing was ragged and rasping.

"What's your name?" asked Kate.

The girl stared at her, uncomprehending.

"Do you speak English?"

No response. Kate pointed at her chest and said "Kate" then pointed to the girl, who just stared back at her as if she were mad.

"I feel like I'm in a bad Western," muttered Kate. Another ten minutes of trying failed to illicit any response. The girl was in deep shock, nearly comatose. There was no reaching her. Kate explored the depths of the tunnel, but found only rubble and rats. In the end there was nothing to do but wait for the giant to return. The girl had moved to the bed when Kate walked back from the far end of the tunnel. Kate sat next to her and put her arms around her bony shoulders. They sat there like that for a few minutes, then the girl rested her head on Kate's shoulder until she fell asleep and slumped into her lap. Kate sat there, with the head of this sick, lost, broken, doomed girl nestled in her lap. She stroked her lank, greasy hair and cried.

As much as she had been forced to confront brutal reality on the night she met Spider, it was during that long hour in that awful place that Kate changed forever. Parts of her psyche scabbed over and hardened, unexpected resolve made itself known, and the well of her compassion was exposed as deeper than she had ever imagined.

When the giant opened the door and handed her the drugs, it was a different woman who took them from him. Harder, colder, angrier and less afraid.

Kate administered the drugs and told the giant that she had done all she could. The sleep mask was replaced, and she was led away from a girl she was sure would be dead by nightfall.

A tiny part of Kate remained behind in that cellar. The tiny piece of Jane that had been born there left in its stead.

She was driven back to her flat, back to the world she knew. But it felt different. Distant. Changed forever. She walked up to her front door and reached into her pocket for her keys.

"Oh fuck it," she cursed, remembering that she had not had time to grab them. She stood and stared at the door and then stepped back and took a running kick at it. She felt the wood give and heard the sharp crack as it splintered. She kicked it again, and again, then shoulder charged it, yelling as she did so, smashing into the door time after time, hating it, wanting to annihilate it utterly, as if it was mocking her. The facia caved and split before, after one almighty crash, it flew off its top hinge and collapsed inwards.

Kate stood there, breathing hard, teeth clenched, eyes wide, her heart pounding, ignoring the pain in her shoulders and legs. She heard a slight cough to her left and turned to see the old biddy from flat four peering anxiously out of her door.

"What?" snapped Kate. The woman's head disappeared inside and the door was firmly closed.

"Didn't you just pay a lot of money to have that door fixed, Miss Booker?" said a soft voice to her right. She spun, suddenly alarmed. But whereas a week ago she might have given a tiny yelp of surprise and felt a jolt of nerves, now she didn't make a sound and stood ready to fight.

The man from the coffee shop stood there in the corridor. Short for a man, about the same height as Kate, he wore a black leather jacket, white shirt and blue jeans above waxed black Docs. He looked about forty, blond hair slightly receding but not too much, with laugh lines around his mouth, and deep crow's feet framing his blue eyes. Kate's first thought was 'he fancies himself.'

"And who the fuck are you?" she snarled.

He reached into his jacket and pulled out a small leather wallet which he flipped open and held up for her to inspect.

"DI John Cooper. Metropolitan Police. Can we go inside and talk? That is, if we can get the door to close behind us."

HE HELPED HER prop the door back up in its frame and shoved a dining chair up against it to keep it in place, then sat on the sofa as she made him a cuppa.

Her mind was racing as she fumbled with mugs and teabags. She'd been considering going to the police, obviously, but Spider had been clear that James would die very slowly indeed if she did so. He had sources within the police, he said, and he'd know the instant she broke ranks. She had looked at her brother's pitiful, tear-stained face as he crouched on that stage, handcuffed to the stripper's pole, and she'd known that she had no choice. This organisation was big and complicated; there was every chance that Spider was telling the truth, that he did have some bent copper on the take. No, she'd decided that if there was a way out of her situation, she'd have to find it herself.

Nonetheless, she slowed her step ever so slightly every time she passed a police station, and felt a jolt of butterflies at the thought of stepping across the threshold and spilling her guts, of sharing the problem, making it someone else's.

The man on her sofa made her almost as nervous as Spider had. Her first thought was that she had made some stupid rookie mistake, given the game away without meaning to, drawn needless attention somehow. Her second thought was that he could be Spider's enforcer, sent here to warn her to keep her mouth shut.

She wasn't sure which outcome would scare her the most.

She took the two mugs through to the living room, handed one to Cooper and sat in the armchair opposite him, sipping her own. She couldn't think of anything to say, so she sat there as he studied her, waiting for him to make the first move.

"Is that brick dust in your hair? Been on a building site?" he asked, not unkindly. His accent was hard to place. He didn't have the Southern glottal stop or the rounded vowels of the North. He spoke precisely, his words chosen with care and delivered in RP, as if maybe he'd attended a posh school as a boy but had then had the edges knocked off his cut glass vowels by years living below his station.

Kate didn't reply, but she gripped her mug with tight, white knuckles.

"And you've got mould or something very like it smeared down the arm of your sweater." He cocked his head to one side and bit his lip thoughtfully. "Underground then. Maybe a railway arch or a cellar. Somewhere old, wet and crumbly, that's for sure. You smell a bit dampy, if you don't mind me saying."

Still Kate did not say a thing, unsure where he was going with this.

"Could you lead me there, or did they blindfold you?" he asked.

The question was so bluntly put that Kate answered it almost in spite of herself. It seemed he already knew everything anyway.

"Blindfold," she said, her mouth dry. She took another sip of tea.

He nodded. This was the answer he'd been expecting. He considered her carefully for a moment and seemed to come to a decision.

"You are in very deep shit, Miss Booker. These are bad, bad men your brother's got himself, and now you, involved with. I take it you know the basics of their operation?"

Kate nodded once. She thought her face must be as white as a ghost's.

"Then you know that they eat people like you up for breakfast. You'll work for them as long as you are useful, but the first time you make a mistake, or they get suspicious of you in any way, or they just decide that they want someone fresh for their evening's entertainment, you will disappear as completely as if you had never existed."

"Why…" Her mouth was dry again. She took another sip of tea. "Why don't you just arrest them then? Isn't that your job?"

"It's not that simple. This gang doesn't exist in isolation. There's a chain stretching right across Europe. This is a huge operation, involving the police of twelve countries, many of which have police forces that see bribes as a normal part of their pay packet. Plus…" He hesitated.

"Plus?"

"Plus, there's someone in our own force looking out for them. I think. Perhaps. I can't prove it." He looked up at her, momentarily suspicious, as if asking himself why he was telling her all this.

"That's why I've approached you like this, at home. Anyway," he continued. "Recently we had a bit of setback. Our… channel of information dried up."

"Nate, yeah? The doctor?"

Cooper looked shocked, as if he'd been caught out. Then he nodded, a little surprised she'd put a name to their mole so easily. "Loathsome little junkie, but easy to manipulate."

"Oh. I see. You want me to take his place."

Cooper sat back in his chair. "Where did they take you just now? What did you see?"

"Nothing useful. An old underground cellar. Damp, as you say. I could hear tube trains and, I think, a river nearby. But that could be anywhere in London, couldn't it?"

Cooper nodded thoughtfully. "And what did you do there?"

"Listen, my brother…"

"We know all about your brother."

"They told me they'd kill him, if I came to the police."

"Most likely. You too."

"Then what the fuck is with turning up at my front door? If anyone sees you… I mean, what kind of fucking amateur are you?"

Cooper smiled. Kate did not think it was particularly reassuring. "Spider doesn't have the resources to keep you under surveillance. He relies on your fear to keep you in line. You were tailed when you went shopping yesterday, and they had someone in A&E two nights ago pretending to have food poisoning so they could see you at work, but they don't watch you all the time. By now they're becoming confident that you haven't gone to the police. And if you haven't gone yet, chances are you won't."

Kate sat there and suddenly felt ashamed and embarrassed. "I would have," she said. "Eventually, I would have. I've thought about it."

"But your brother."

"He's not the hardest of men. He's weak and stupid and his own worst enemy. But he's my best friend. I've had to look after him his whole life, get him out of trouble, keep him from being bullied. Jesus, the amount of times at school I had to fight his battles for him. I suppose I should have known that something like this was inevitable."

"We can keep him safe."

"Not your job, Mr Cooper. It's mine."

Cooper leaned forward in his chair, clasping his hands together and holding her gaze firmly. "If you help us, Kate, you have my word no harm will come to him."

Although this figure of authority was asking for her help, Kate felt as helpless as she ever had. If she agreed to inform for the police, she'd be placing herself and her brother in terrible danger. But if she said no... she thought of that poor girl in the cellar. Where was she now? Dolled up and drugged up, washed and brushed up and delivered to some hotel room for the pleasure of a banker or drug dealer who'd use her and then hand her back to her captors, dead or alive.

She stared deep into Cooper's eyes, seeking reassurance. He smiled at her, and she felt her resistance crumble.

"Okay, okay. What do I have to do?"

THEY DIDN'T CALL on her for another two weeks. But this time she did not allow herself to pretend that life was normal.

At Cooper's urging, Kate signed up for self defence classes. Each day after work she would spend an hour in a draughty scout hut in Camden learning how to turn an opponent's weight against them, learning simple blocks and combos designed to prevent her from coming to harm and allow her time to run.

They didn't teach her how to collapse a windpipe with a single punch, or how to twist a neck and break it, or the places on the body where the lightest blow could cause the most damage. She was a doctor; that stuff she already knew. But knowing and doing are two different things and she knew she lacked the control to throw those kind of punches. Still, she trained and practised and worked out. The face of the girl from the cellar hovered in front of her as she pounded the treadmill and worked the punchbag.

She would look at herself in the mirror before bed and laugh humourlessly. Who did think she was, Rocky? She was a not very tall young woman, slight and delicate. All the training in the world wouldn't enable her to inflict so much as a single bruise on the giant. But nonetheless, she trained and practised and focused.

If any of those bastards tried to make her the main attraction rather than the attending doctor, she'd let them know what a big mistake they'd made.

Then, one Sunday night as she sat vacantly watching some telly programme that passed through her eyeballs and out the back of her head without touching the sides, there was a knock at her yet-again rebuilt door.

Kate took a moment to slow her heartbeat and take a few deep breaths. She told herself she was in control as she rose and grabbed the bag she had left by the door especially for this occasion. One more deep breath and then she opened the door.

Her brother stood there with a bottle of wine and a box of chocolates.

"Hey, Kit," he said, bashful at disturbing her.

"Oh James, not tonight, eh. I've got an early shift tomorrow."

He shuffled his feet. "Sorry, Sis. I've got no choice."

Suddenly Kate realised that, despite appearances, this was not a social call. "Right. I'll get my coat." She turned away but he put his hand on her arm.

"We don't have to be there for an hour or so. That's why..." He held up the bottle of wine.

Kate sighed, stepped back and ushered him inside. "You know where the glasses are," she told him as she closed the door and put the bag back in its place.

He made small talk at first. "How's the hospital... you met a new bloke yet... going to get another flat mate?" That kind of thing. Kate indulged him until he finally ran out of things to say. At this point he'd normally reach into his seemingly endless collection of anecdotes and start telling dodgy stories about this or that night on the town and the disreputable character he'd hooked up with. It was only when the silence fell that Kate realised she'd not seen James hold court like this for months.

"I'm not much of a sister, am I?" she said.

"What?"

"I should have noticed something was wrong. I should have asked about it."

"Don't be daft. You've been up to your ears with training."

"Still." The silence that fell then seemed like it would swallow them whole, and they stared into their wine glasses.

"James, how does this end for us?"

He looked up and his face said it all.

"Why haven't you gone to the police?" she asked.

He shook his head. "Too scared. Why haven't you?"

"Don't tell him," Cooper had told her two weeks earlier. "No matter what. I know he's your brother and all, but from what I can gather he doesn't seem the kind who could keep a secret."

Kate gave James a look that said 'why do you think?' and he nodded. "Right," he said.

"I have an idea, though," she said. "Something we can do to help ourselves."

"Hit me."

"I've considered it."

She got up, grabbed a notepad and pen from the kitchen counter, and sat down again. "I want you to tell me everything, and I mean absolutely everything that you know about their operation. Dates, times, locations, personnel. Everything."

He looked wary. "For why?"

"Insurance."

"Oh, Sis, that's not..."

"Do you trust me?"

"With my life."

"Then spill."

So he did, until eventually he checked his watch and told her it was time to go.

IT WAS A cold, clear night, cloudless and silent.

The yard was lit by sodium lights mounted high on the posts that marked out the limits of the chain link fence. Huge containers were piled high in blocks, forming a kind of maze. The fleet of articulated lorries that ferried them across Europe and beyond were lined up near the entrance, seeming naked and unwieldy without their cargo. The pungent stink of rotting vegetables and the cry of hungry seagulls betrayed the presence of a tip nearby.

Two portacabins, one on top of the other, sat at the heart of the maze. Their lights were on and Kate could see movement inside as she and James walked towards them.

James didn't knock, he pushed the door open and they stepped into a fug of warm, damp, gas-heater air that smelled of stale coffee and cigarettes.

The giant was sitting on a tatty old armchair which seemed comically small for him. His knees were up around his ears. A group of four crowded around him, sipping coffee from plastic cups and smoking. They were talking and joking in what Kate assumed was Serbian.

Kate was relieved that Spider wasn't present, even though she'd known he wouldn't be. Cooper had told her he normally ran things from Manchester.

The giant unfolded himself and rose as the siblings entered. The men fell silent, watching them with eyes that betrayed only the barest smidgin of interest. Each of them glanced briefly at James and then shifted his attention to Kate, sizing her up and finding her either adequate or wanting, depending upon their taste. One of them smiled at her, revealing crooked yellow teeth. She ignored him.

"You have the medicine?" asked the giant.

Kate held up her bag. He seemed content. He handed James a clipboard and a large manila envelope. Her brother took it without question.

"Come on," he said to Kate, and led her back outside to a set of stairs that led up to the portacabin above. A young man stood outside the door, on guard. He unlocked the door as they ascended and ushered them inside. Kate heard the door lock again once they were in.

The small room held eight women and girls. All were sitting on the floor, crowded around a gas heater, warming their hands. They wore simple, functional clothes and had obviously not washed in days. There was a pungent smell of BO.

"Hello ladies," said James, smiling. Kate was disturbed at how easily he slipped into this role. She wondered how many times he had done this before. "If I can please have your passports and travel documents."

One of the women, the oldest of the bunch, maybe twenty or so, Kate thought, translated James' request to the others, and they each reached into their pockets and produced their passports. Kate thought the meekness with which they did this spoke volumes. These girls were scared. They hadn't admitted it to themselves yet, but they knew, deep down, that something had gone wrong, that they had been fooled, that something awful was about to happen to them.

James collected the passports and visas cheerfully, placing them in the manila envelope. He turned to Kate as he did so. "Best get on with it, Kit," he said.

Kate crouched down and opened her bag. Inside were the syringe needles and ampoules that she had stolen from the hospital. Vitamin shots, wide spectrum antibiotics and, as ordered, mild sedatives. She told the girls to roll up their sleeves. Again the oldest one translated.

"What is that?" she asked.

"Nothing to worry about," Kate lied, feeling a tiny part of her die as she did so. "Just vitamins and stuff. Something to give you a boost. You've had a long trip in that lorry."

The woman was suspicious but there had been that faint air of resignation to her question which betrayed her powerlessness. Kate gave each of the trafficked women a shot.

While she did this James got each woman to stand up as he examined them, scanned a list of outstanding requirements on the clipboard, and decided which of the various distribution points they would be transferred to. The skinny one with the blonde hair was pretty enough for the high rollers, so she'd go to London. The three chubby ones were disposable but functional, they could go to Manchester. There was a special request for a young girl for extraordinary duties. James picked out the redhead, who couldn't have been more than sixteen, for this role.

Kate felt sick as she watched him do this.

James tried to present a cheery front as he consigned these women to their various fates. He knew what he was doing; choosing which ones would be raped, which would be murdered, which would vanish into the cellars, and which in the penthouses. But he didn't want them to know what was going on, so he smiled and joked, even though he knew most of them didn't understand what he was saying.

When the allocation was complete, and the injections had all been administered, James told them it was time for sleep because they would be collected early in the morning. He turned off the light as he left them to snuggle together for warmth on the floor, under ragged duvets.

Kate and he went back downstairs, handed the clipboard to the giant, and waited as he studied it. Eventually, he nodded.

"Good," he said. Then he allocated each of the four men a girl or two to transport. James was also given an assignment, driving to Manchester. Kate was dismissed.

The men left and went up the stairs to collect their by now unconscious cargo. James hung back, drinking coffee with the giant.

"I thought you were driving one of them?" she asked.

James stared at his feet, unable to meet her gaze.

"I am," he said. "But they'll... they'll be a while."

The giant laughed. "This is not real man. Not like girls." He laughed again, as if this was the funniest thing in the whole wide world.

Kate wanted to grind broken glass into his face.

"Can I go?" she asked.

The giant nodded. "Get more medicine. More girls next week," he said, and he waved her aside, dismissing her.

Kate stepped out into the night and walked steadily and carefully until she turned a corner and was out of sight. Then she placed her hands on her knees, bent double, and vomited until there was nothing left to come up.

She wiped her mouth on her sleeve, stood upright, and walked out of the yard in search of a taxi.

* * *

"YOU REALLY SHOULDN'T have gone to all this trouble," said Cooper, with his mouth full. Kate laughed.

"If my Gran knew I was playing host to a Detective Inspector and not feeding him, she'd have a heart attack. She feeds everyone who ever knocks on her door. Doctor, postman, Jehovah's Witness, she doesn't care. Even if I call her and say I'm stopping by after dinner at a fancy restaurant she opens the door and says 'ooh love, you're looking a little peaky, I've done your favourite, corned beef pie!' And she'll sit there and watch me eat it, no matter how full of Sunday lunch or curry I am."

"And you've inherited her compulsion?"

"It what we do oop North, DI Cooper. Just because you Southerners think hospitality begins and ends with a twist of lime in a G and T, doesn't mean we're so stingy."

"Well this pasta is great, thank you. I'm not sure what my boss would say. He might accuse me of taking bribes."

"It's not *that* good."

"I'm a copper, Miss Booker..."

"Kate, please."

"I live on pies, chips and coffee, Kate. You may not believe me, but I used to be lean and toned. It's only since I joined the force that I've got so flabby."

Kate didn't think he was flabby. Fancies himself, she thought again, but not unkindly. Fishing for compliments.

"What did you do before?"

"I was in the army."

"Really? I wouldn't have pegged you as the soldier type. What were you, admin or engineer?"

Cooper hesitated. "Not exactly."

"Man of mystery, huh."

"Something like that."

He finished his bowl of pasta and swilled it down with a gulp of lager. Kate collected their crockery and put the kettle on. Cooper browsed her bookcases while she made coffee. Once he'd taken it, he sat down, the informal air almost, but not entirely, banished. She sat opposite him.

"You gave the girls the injections?" he asked.

Kate nodded.

"How many?"

"Eight. Three for Manchester, two each for London and Birmingham, one for Cardiff."

"Good. We'll track them to their destinations."

"And then do nothing because you're waiting for authorisation." The bitterness in her voice was hard to disguise.

"It won't be long now, I promise." He paused and Kate could tell he was considering whether to tell her something. He put down his cutlery and leaned forward across the table intently. "We're tracking a lorry full of girls at the moment. The Ukrainians, for once, actually tipped us off when it left. So far we've managed to keep track of it all the way to Dusseldorf. If we don't lose it before it gets here, we should have the whole trail mapped out clearly. Then we can wrap it all up in one fell swoop."

"That's brilliant!" said Kate. Cooper looked down at the table.

"But?" she asked, dreading his answer.

"They've decided the south coast ports are getting too dangerous. We think they're coming in via Grimsby and straight to Manchester."

"And that's a problem, why?"

"We don't have anyone on the inside in Manchester." He looked up at her and took a deep breath. "We don't think they have a pet doctor up there yet, though."

"Right," said Kate, not quite following his logic.

"And in the next few days he's got a massive shipment of girls arriving there, the first to go direct, bypassing London."

"Which would mean they'd send for me to help process the girls."

"We hope so, yes."

"And you'd follow me so I could lead you straight to them?"

"That's the general idea."

Kate considered this for a moment. "I'd still be in there when you stormed the place, right?"

Cooper held her gaze firmly. "It's the only way. You'll be away from home so they'll let you sleep the night there, I guess, before driving you back."

"Oh great. That's just what I want, a night stuck in a portacabin with those bastards."

"Which is why we'll take them as soon as you lead us there."

"And how exactly will I do that?"

"You'll need to carry some kind of tracking device."

Kate shook her head firmly. "They frisked me last time. They'd find something like that."

"This will be well disguised. Trust me, they'll have no idea it's there."

"Wait a minute. You'll take them as soon as I get there? You mean I'm going to be in the middle of a police raid?"

"Don't worry. I'll be there and I'll make it my first priority to get you to safety."

Kate did not feel reassured.

"So I should expect to get a phone call in the next couple of days," she said.

"Yeah."

Cooper considered her, biting his lip. "I've still not told my boss about you, you know. I'm keeping you completely off the books. With the operation nearing completion, the risk of a leak from within the Met is too great. I still don't know who Spider's got on the inside and until I do, I'm playing my cards very close to my chest."

"But surely the operation you're proposing is going to require a lot of manpower."

"Yeah. I'm bending the rules a bit there." Kate waited for him to elaborate, but "it's not exactly ethical" was all he said.

"Fuck ethics," said Kate, suddenly impassioned. "If this works, you'll be in a position to shut him down for good."

Cooper smiled. "Let's hope so. As they say in all the good movies: so now we wait."

"However shall we pass the time?"

Cooper looked surprised and Kate cursed inwardly. Too obvious. Inappropriate. Stupid. Damn.

He registered her embarrassment and smiled. "I have an idea or two," he said.

KATE LIFTED HER face out off the blue crash mat and groaned.

"This," she said pointedly, "was not what I had in mind, Detective Inspector Cooper."

Cooper laughed as he bent down and held out a hand. She grabbed it and allowed herself to be helped to her feet.

"Again, Sanders. And stop going easy on her," he said.

"Sir," said the massive, muscled soldier who had just thrown Kate to the floor like she weighed less than a feather pillow. "Now remember what I said, Miss Booker, duck under the attack, grab, pivot and throw."

"Soldier, you're three times the size of me. I don't have to duck under your attack, I just have to stand here and let it pass over my head."

The soldier smiled and held out his great meaty hands, ready to attack once more. Kate sighed and prepared to meet his attack. She placed her feet wide apart and raised her own hands, practically doll like in comparison. "Come on then, let's…"

But he was already moving, and once again Kate didn't manage even the most rudimentary defensive manoeuvre. She was face down on the mat again before the second was out.

"Perhaps we should…"

"No," said Kate firmly as she peeled her face away from the sticky plastic. "Let's go again." She got to her feet. "You really know how to show a girl a good time, Cooper," she said. The policeman just smiled and waved from the bench at the side of the dojo.

Five more attacks, five more humiliations until finally, on the sixth go around, she managed to get a hand to his wrist and a shoulder to his stomach. She tried the lift, but it was like trying to topple a solid granite statue. After straining for a few moments, she gave up and allowed herself to be flattened once more.

"Better," said Sanders. "Anyone not trained would have been thrown by that."

Kate scowled at him. "The men I'm dealing with are ex-Serbian military, Sanders, and one of them is even bigger than you."

Sanders cast a curious glance across at Cooper, who nodded once.

"Right," said the soldier. "In which case, I think we're taking the wrong tack. Tell me, Miss Booker, have you ever fired a gun?"

"She won't be armed, Sanders," said Cooper. "Too dangerous."

"Still, they'll be carrying guns, yeah?" Sanders countered.

Again Cooper nodded.

"Then it can't hurt, can it? Come on, Miss Booker, let's get you kitted up."

Sanders led Kate out of the gym and across a sparse concrete courtyard ringed with old single storey buildings. It was about midday but although Cooper had driven her here some hours before, she still had little clue where exactly here was. It was only when she saw a group of men in the distance, running into woods dressed entirely in black, carrying guns, that the penny dropped.

"Not exactly an engineer," she muttered as she entered the long building that housed one of the SAS firing ranges.

"WHY DID YOU do that?" Kate asked as they pulled out of the driveway, several hours later.

She had been thrown and chased, beaten and bruised, and taught how to shoot a variety of weapons. She had, she reluctantly admitted to herself, rather enjoyed firing guns. The power of it was exciting.

"If anything goes wrong, you could find yourself in the middle of a firefight. It's important you be ready."

"Of course I'm not ready. You think a day like that is all it takes to get me ready for a warzone?"

"No," replied Cooper quietly. "But it's all I could think to do."

Kate blushed, ashamed. "Thank you."

"You're welcome."

"So were you one of them, them, in the army?"

"If I had been, I wouldn't be able to tell you. And if I were to cash in some favours by asking old friends to give you a workover, then it would have to be a very well kept secret indeed if I wanted to avoid having my bollocks cut off and fed to me by big men in balaclavas."

Kate couldn't tell whether he was joking or not. "My lips are sealed," she said.

"Good. But remember what you learned here today. It could save your life."

"You promised me..."

"That nothing could go wrong. I know. And it shouldn't. But there are always factors that can't be foreseen."

"Cooper, can I ask you something?"

He nodded, keeping his eyes on the road.

"Why is my brother really working for Spider?"

"What do you mean?"

"He's a student. He's nothing special. He has no special skills or contacts. There's nothing he can do that one of Spider's normal henchmen can't. I'm a doctor, I understand why I'm useful to him. But James?"

There was a long silence as Cooper kept his eyes on the road. Eventually he said: "Spider is gay. And he likes them pretty."

Kate hadn't thought anything about this business could make her feel any more wretched. She had been wrong.

They drove the rest of the way home in silence. Cooper pulled up outside Kate's building as the clock on the nearby church struck eight.

"Home sweet home," he said.

"Want to come in for a nightcap?"

He turned and looked at her, lips pursed, appraising. "No, Kate. Best if I don't. Maybe once this is all over..."

"Right, yes, of course. I only meant a coffee anyway. I'll see you soon, I guess."

"Definitely."

"Okay, off I go. And thanks for today."

"You're welcome."

FOUR DAYS LATER, Kate was sitting in the back of a Ford Focus on the M1 north. The giant was crammed into the front passenger seat and the yellow toothed man who kept smiling at her was driving. The stereo was playing some awful Euro-pop.

The rain was coming down in sheets and the windscreen wipers were barely able to cope as they weaved in and out of the traffic. She didn't envy anyone who was trying to follow them through this deluge. She resisted the urge to check the mobile phone in her pocket. The transmitter inside was working, Cooper had checked it himself yesterday. All she could achieve by fingering it was to draw attention to it, which was the last thing she wanted.

Somewhere out there in the downpour, Cooper and his team were gathering, ready for the kill. After her visit to Hereford, Kate had a suspicion that she knew what Cooper had meant by 'bending the rules'. She had seen footage of the Iranian Embassy siege. She knew what to expect and she knew what to do. She was pretty sure that she'd be seeing Sanders again by the end of the day and that thought reassured her; he inspired confidence somehow, even more so than Cooper.

Everything was going to be fine, she told herself. This has all been planned by professionals. Nothing can go wrong.

The giant turned in his seat and looked back at her. He held out his hand.

"Give me phone," he said.

"Sorry?" she asked, taken by surprise.

"Phone."

"Why?"

He didn't say anything, just kept his hand held out, impassive.

Kate gulped and reached into her pocket, removing the phone and handing it to him.

"Careful with it, eh. That's top of the range," she joked, trying not to reveal her sudden terror.

The giant wound down the window and tossed the phone out onto the motorway. The window closed with a soft buzz of internal motors.

"What the fuck was that for?" she yelled.

The giant turned again and held up a little black plastic box with a small LED that flashed red. "Boss not like bugs," he said, matter of fact. Then he turned back and returned to staring out at the lorries as they sped past, each carrying a cloud of spray behind it.

Kate sat there knowing with total certainty that she was a dead woman.

Two hours later they pulled up outside a huge Victorian warehouse in Moss Side. Kate knew where they were because the giant had not told her to look at the floor and had not bothered with the sleep mask. That they didn't take such rudimentary precautions confirmed to her that she was not going to be allowed to walk out of wherever they were taking her.

The giant unfolded himself into the street and pulled her door open, ushering her inside the warehouse through big black wooden doors. The rain was still pouring, and the air was saturated with the hoppy aroma of a nearby brewery.

The ground floor was massive and unsegregated. Racks of cheap clothing stretched away on all sides into the gloom. The giant led Kate to the stairs and they went up two storeys. The second floor was also full of cheap clothes, this time in piles on tables, being sorted by a small group of women, Kate guessed Somali but she couldn't be sure. This floor had a wall running across it, and the giant led her to a small door which, incongruously, had a keypad lock. He typed in the code and the door clicked open.

The other side of the door was a different world. Kate walked from a low rent sweatshop into a plush corridor decorated with velvet wallpaper, laid with deep red carpets and decorated with modern art prints and photographs, all soft core, nothing too obvious.

The next door led into a lobby area that felt more like a lounge or a bar. Leather sofas and armchairs dotted the room, ringing small round tables with table lamps on them, casting a soft glow. There was an unmanned bar in the far corner..

"Sit," said the giant without looking at her. She did so as he left by a small door beside the bar, going deeper into this hidden world.

Kate sat there, collecting her thoughts. The transmitter was gone, so all Cooper knew was that she had been taken. He'd have no idea where she was now unless he'd been able to physically keep the car in sight at all times. She figured the torrential rain made that unlikely.

She was on her own. There was no cavalry coming.

Worse than that, Spider would know by now that she had betrayed him. He might react in a number of ways. He could kill her outright, but she thought at the very least he'd want her to examine the new intake first. Alternatively, he could disappear her into his system, send her to some dank cellar or a dungeon somewhere to be kept on ice ready for a client who fancied a girl who'd put up a fight. That seemed most likely. After all, she was a resource he could use to turn a profit.

She told herself to stay calm and clear headed. As long as she was alive, there was a chance she could find a way to alert Cooper.

The wild card here, she knew, was her brother. What might Spider do to him?

She didn't have to wait long for an answer.

The internal door swung open and Spider entered. He was wearing a different but equally well cut suit, this time of dark purple. His face was impassive and he moved with controlled, almost robotic precision. He walked behind the bar without acknowledging her, took a glass from beneath the counter and poured himself a whisky before looking up at Kate.

"Drink?" he said.

Kate considered for a moment before nodding. "Red wine, please."

He took a wine glass down from a shelf and began to open a bottle.

"I thought we had an understanding, Miss Booker," he said as he pulled the cork out with a soft pop.

Kate thought it best to stay silent.

"I thought that you understood the consequences of betrayal," he continued, pouring the wine into the large glass.

"My lieutenant thinks I should give you to him. He thinks it would be fun to rape you while strangling you. Although he enjoys fucking them, I think he does not like women very much. He likes to cut them with the bayonet his grandfather used in the Second World War. He keeps it very sharp." The glass full, he put the bottle down, walked over to Kate and handed her the drink. "Does that sound like an appropriate punishment to you, Miss Booker?" he asked.

She took the glass and had to put it down immediately, as her hands were shaking too badly to hold it steady.

Spider remained standing, looking down on her. "I worry, though, that if I were to let him have his way with you, you would not learn your lesson."

The internal door swung open again and Kate stifled a cry of fear as she saw her brother being led into the room by the giant.

He saw her and smiled. "Hi Kit," he said. Then he registered the fear on her face and the single minded focus with which Spider was regarding her, and his step faltered.

"I think," said Spider quietly, "that a different punishment would be better." He turned to James and smiled. "Hello, Booker."

"Hi Boss," said James, giving the most unconvincing smile Kate had ever seen.

"James, how long have you been working for me?"

"Ooh, six months now, I reckon."

"Six months." Spider nodded. "You have been a good worker."

"Er, Boss," said James, trying not to let his fear show. "What's up?"

"Your sister has betrayed me to the police. She tried to bring a transmitter here with her."

Kate met James' eyes and she saw all the hope vanish in an instant, replaced by total despair. Spider reached into his jacket and pulled out a huge hunting knife, shiny and sharp. He turned and walked over to James and caressed his cheek with the sharp edge, tenderly.

"I like you, James," said Spider.

"I, I like you too, Boss," James stammered.

"You have kept me amused far longer than most lovers, but I don't think you do like me. Not really," replied Spider, who was now standing close to James, pressed up close to him. "I think you are scared of me. And that is how I like it. The one thing my lieutenant and I have in common is that we both know there is no enjoyment to be had from fucking someone who is not scared of you."

Kate found her voice at last. "Stop this. Please," she said, rising to her feet. "He's done nothing wrong. It's me you've got the problem with, Spider. There's no reason to hurt him."

"What do you think, James?" asked the Serbian, standing behind the terrified young man, chin resting on his shoulder, knife pressed up against his temple.

James had nothing to say.

"Do you think I should kill you? Or perhaps your sister?" There was no reply. "Petar wants her. You know what he would do to her."

Tears began to stream down James' cheeks but still he stayed silent.

"You still need me to examine the new shipment of girls," said Kate, desperately.

Spider shook his head. "Once I learnt of your betrayal I diverted that container. To the bottom of a river."

"I'll tell you anything you want to know," said Kate, using the only bargaining chip she had left. "I know the policeman who's running the operation. I can lead you to him."

"Do you mean DI Cooper?" he laughed. "We know all about him. What else you got?"

Kate had nothing else.

"Thought so," said Spider.

Then he pushed the knife through the thin bone plate on the side of James' head, straight into his brain.

SHE DOESN'T REMEMBER *what happened next. All that survives is a sound; a low keening that goes on forever and ever. The second the knife went in, the world went black and her mind stopped creating memories.*

The woman who gradually became aware of her surroundings however many hours later was a different person. Someone as yet unnamed. Someone at whose very core nestled a cold, hard knot of calm determination and resolve. Someone with only one thought in her head.

Vengeance.

THE WORLD CAME to the woman a piece at a time.

First it was the faint smell of burning hops. Then the sound of her own breathing. She floated in a dark void, examining the smell and the sound for a long time before her body began to send back signals that told her she was lying on a bed. Then there was a taste of stale wine and bile. Finally, she opened her eyes.

The world looked... different. The room was monochrome – black walls, white nurse's outfit hanging from the white hook on the inside of the door, shiny grey buckles on the straps that adorned the sturdy black wooden cross, white trolley with black implements strewn across it – whips, dildos, clamps and catheters. But even despite the lack of colour, the woman who awoke on that bed (and was it a waking, truly? Had she been asleep or just comatose? Had she really opened her eyes or had her optic nerves instead rebooted themselves after a long shutdown?) somehow knew that even had the room been painted in fluorescent colours they would have seemed muted.

The way she saw the world had literally changed.

The bed springs creaked as she sat up. She had been expecting a headache, but her head was clear and her senses were sharp. There were no windows in this dark place. The only illumination came from four uplighters, one in each corner of the room.

She stood up and checked the door, knowing it was locked but determined to be thorough. She then turned to assess the room, methodically cataloguing its contents in her mind searching for a means of attack or something she could use to defend herself.

She noted the absence of panic, but did not think it worthy of further examination.

The trolley offered the best hope, but there was nothing there that could be of genuine use. The cat o' nine tails lacked the sharp stones that would have rendered it really painful, and she did not think beating a man around the head with a giant black rubber cock would do anything but provoke laughter.

Perhaps if she pushed the trolley itself at whoever entered, it would unbalance them long enough to give her an opening. But when she tried to move it forwards the wheels squealed alarmingly and refused to move.

She made no further progress before she heard a key turn in the lock. She stepped away from the trolley and into the only really clear area in the centre of the room. If she was going to fight, this was all the space she would have to do it in.

The door opened and the giant stepped inside. The woman who was no longer Kate abandoned all thought of fighting.

He closed the door behind him, not bothering to lock it. He knew there was no way she was getting past him.

She stood there, impassive, as he removed his jacket and hung it on the hook, covering the nurse's outfit. He then removed his shirt, revealing an acreage of tattooed chest that was twice the woman's width from shoulder to shoulder. He hung the shirt over the jacket.

He stepped forward and reached out his huge right hand, wrapping the fingers around her throat and lifting her off the ground with a single outstretched arm. He brought her face close to his as she choked. She felt his warm breath on her cheek as he examined her closely. Then he relaxed his grip and she collapsed in a heap at his feet, gasping for air. He turned his back on her, stepped to the door and removed a huge bayonet from the inside of his hanging jacket.

"Stand," he said. The woman did so.

He stepped forward and inserted the bayonet under the bottom of her t-shirt. He ripped the blade upwards and the cloth parted before it like butter meeting a hot knife. The bayonet was so sharp, she thought, you probably wouldn't realise you'd been stabbed until you looked down and saw the hilt sticking out.

The blunt edge felt cold against her skin as it rushed up from her belly to her throat.

When the t-shirt had been split from waist to neck, it fell off her. She stood in her bra, facing this enormous man, knowing exactly what he intended to do to her, and still she felt no fear.

She remembered the dojo, she recalled the moves she'd been taught in a draughty hut in Camden, and she knew that all that training was useless. If he came at her with some momentum, she could perhaps have used it against him. But the room was too small; he had no need of speed. If he had been smaller, she could have tried to throw him from a standing start, but she hadn't been able to throw Sanders who, big as he was, was slight in comparison.

Her best chance, she realised, was the bayonet.

"Rush a gun, flee a knife," Sanders had told her. "If you run at a person who's trying to shoot you, you force them to fire quickly and without time to aim properly. You have a better chance that they'll miss you than if you turn and run. But a knife is different. It's only lethal in close quarters and once you've got a hand to it, it can move both ways. You'd be amazed how many stab victims are killed with their own blades."

The woman focused all her attention on the blade. This man was too strong to wrestle with, but even so she had a slim chance of turning his weapon against him. To do that she had to know exactly where it was, how it was angled, where it was pointed at all times.

He reached down and unbuckled her belt, pulling it out in one fluid movement, cracking it like a whip, and tossing it over his shoulder into the corner.

He angled the knife down, inserting the point inside the waistband of her jeans, directly below her belly button.

Then something distracted him. A distant rumble. The floor shook briefly. There was a scream somewhere far away. He glanced over his shoulder instinctively, even though the closed door and windowless walls offered no vantage.

When he turned his attention back to the woman he noticed she had taken a step backwards. He looked down and registered that she had something in her right hand. Something long and thin. Something dripping.

He took a step towards her and felt his centre of gravity shift in an unsettling way. There was a soft wet sound and he felt pressure on his foot. He looked down to see his entrails spooling out of his belly and falling to the floor like a coil of steaming, lumpy rope.

Still looking at his feet in wonder he saw a hand enter his field of vision and felt it punch him on the breast. The hand withdrew and he opened his mouth in astonishment as he realised there was a black metal handle sticking out of his chest.

How the fuck had that got there?

He reached down and grabbed the handle, pulling it and exposing the blade of his grandfather's bayonet. It emerged from his heart smoothly, without a sound. The room spun and he felt something hit him on the back of the head. He wasn't conscious long enough to realise that it was the floor.

The woman reached down and took the bayonet from twitching fingers, then stepped over the giant corpse and opened the door. Somewhere in the distance she could hear gunfire.

She walked out of the room, blade in hand, spoiling for a fight.

As she moved down the corridor, she could still hear occasional bursts of gunfire somewhere below and ahead of her. She didn't know how, but Cooper and his men must have found the warehouse. This mean that time was not on her side. She had to find Spider before Cooper did.

The corridor ran the length of the building along its external back wall. Tall metal framed windows ranged to her left, a collection of doors to her right. A quick glance outside told her that it was late evening and she was at least one floor above the lobby bar.

The door at the far end of the corridor burst open and the man with the yellow teeth came running through with a submachine gun in his hands. Without noticing the woman, he turned and entered the first door. The woman heard a girl's scream and then a burst of gunfire.

She began to run. The man stepped back out of the room, the barrel of his gun smoking. He turned to walk towards the next door and then stopped in amazement as he registered a woman in a bra running towards him with teeth bared. It took him a second to react, but he soon brought the gun to bear.

"Rush a gun, flee a knife," the woman muttered to herself as she barrelled forwards. The sound of the shots was deafening in the enclosed corridor, and she felt hot air stream across her right shoulder as the distance closed. Then there was a sharp sting in the same shoulder but she ignored it as she crashed into the gunman, flinging him to the floor. The bayonet clattered out of her hands as they fell. She wrestled with him for a moment and then, realising the madness of this, sat up, straddling him like a lover. Again he took a moment to react to this unexpected move, a moment in which she reached down, grabbed his gun, reversed it and used the butt to send the bones from his nose shrapnelling into his frontal lobe.

She leaned across him, grabbed the bayonet again then stood, blade in one hand, gun in the other. She checked the gun once, recalling Sanders' tuition, recognising the vital parts. She pointed it at the chest of Yellowteeth and squeezed the trigger. A stream of bullets thudded into him.

The woman nodded, satisfied.

She heard a door open behind her and she spun around, raising the weapon. A teenaged girl peered out at her, eyes wide with fear. The woman lowered the weapon.

"You speak English?" she asked.

The girl nodded. The woman handed her the bayonet, and the girl looked at it in wonder.

"Take this," said the woman. "Stick it in any man you meet who's not wearing a uniform. Understand?"

The girl nodded.

"Good, now get everyone in these rooms into the dungeon at the far end. Lock the door. The keys are in the pocket of the dead man you'll find in there. Don't come out until the shooting stops. Can you do that?"

Again the girl nodded. "You've been shot," she whispered.

The woman looked at her shoulder and registered a small hole at the top of her arm. She fingered it, and found the exit wound. The bullet had gone straight through and missed both bones and arteries. She didn't feel any pain, though she knew that would not stay the case for long.

She turned, jumped over the corpse of Yellowteeth and ran out the door. She had wasted enough time.

She emerged onto a darkened dance floor with swing doors at the far right. She ran diagonally across it. As she reached the halfway point the doors swung open and three men ran in. All were in civvies and all carried guns.

Their eyes took a moment to adjust to the darkness, so by the time they realised they were not alone it was too late. The woman sprayed the doorway with bullets and the men jerked and dropped. She kept running, jumped over them and flew out the swing doors, ready to fire.

Behind her, in the corridor where she'd killed Yellowteeth, she heard shattering glass as Cooper's men came in through the windows. So now they were ahead of her and behind her. She gritted her teeth.

She had to get to Spider first.

She ran down an empty staircase keeping the gun aimed at the bottom in case anyone else came running through. There was another soft explosion on the far side of the building as she reached the bottom and turned to find herself facing another corridor and another row of rooms.

These doors were open. One, about halfway along, had a single bloodstained hand stretched across the threshold.

The woman walked down the corridor checking each room for survivors. Despite her focus, she knew she would have to help any wounded girls she found, even if that meant letting Spider escape. But Yellowteeth had been thorough. Each room held at least one dead girl, some as many as three. No-one was to be left alive who could testify against them. No witnesses, no descriptions. The woman reached the end of the corridor with something approximating relief and pushed through into the lobby bar.

A patch of darkness on the carpet was the only evidence that someone had been stabbed in the head here not so long ago.

There was a burst of gunfire from somewhere close, beyond the opposite door, then heavy footsteps on the stairs behind her. She scanned the room in desperation. Had they already captured him? Had the bastard escaped her?

Out of the corner of her eye she caught a glimpse of something that didn't seem right, so she turned and realised that there was another door, slightly ajar, behind the bar. It was flat and featureless, disguised as part of the wall, which was why she had not seen it earlier. She ran to it and pulled it open, squeezing through and closing it firmly behind her. Cooper and his team would probably not see the door on their first pass, especially if they were still encountering resistance. If Spider had come this way, she would be the only person in pursuit for now.

The woman smiled, but it was not like any smile Kate had ever worn.

She scampered down the dark, narrow stairs. A small landing with another discreet door marked the ground floor, then the steps continued down into the cellars. The woman saw a glimmer of light ahead and slowed. He turned the corner at the bottom and found herself in a long, low featureless brick corridor, painted black. There was no light here, but she could make out a fading glow at the far end, betraying the presence of someone fleeing with a torch. She took off in pursuit, catching only vague impressions of rooms off to her left and right, each marked by a low, round arch and some brick steps going down into a chamber. The squalid cellar entrances smelt of blood, shit and fear.

The woman barrelled on through the darkness, turning the corner at the far end to find a dead end and an old metal grille in the floor.

It was still open, and the glow of the receding torch seeped out of it. She did not even look down into the sewers before jumping.

She splashed into cold, lumpy water that came up to her waist. The sewer was a round tube of Victorian brick. The current was strong, swollen by the heavy rains, and the water swirled and eddied, trying to pull her feet out from under her. The floor felt slimy beneath her feet and she knew that if she lost her footing she would be in big trouble.

She held the gun high above her head and waded forward, following the fading light around the curve of the tunnel.

She had only progressed a few metres when she stepped into space, a breach in the sewer floor, like a pothole. She unbalanced and fell backwards, disappearing into the raging torrent and being carried forward at speed. She lost her grip on the gun. Flailing around in the darkness, she broke the surface once, twice, gasping for air as she hurtled along.

For the first time it occurred to her that she might die down here.

She lost all sense of orientation. Down was up, left was right. The water roared in her ears, she saw flashes behind her closed eyes and felt the dizziness of impending unconsciousness.

Then she hit something. Something soft, which fell ahead of her, and then she and this object were tumbling together in the water. Something hard hit her on the side of the head; was that the torch or her gun? Just as she thought she was dead, the water threw her out into a void and she fell, momentarily free, drawing ragged, desperate breaths.

She splashed down into a lake of some sort and fought to the surface. There was no light down here. The torch had gone. She floated there, treading water as it swirled around her, calming herself, listening intently, trying to filter out the sound of the waterfall that had deposited her in what she assumed was some sort of junction.

She had not fallen down into this pit alone. The person she had collided with must be here too, somewhere in the darkness.

"Spider," she shouted. Her voice echoed back to her a hundred times. This chamber was big and arched. "Spider!"

She waited, feeling the fatigue in her legs as they kicked against the tide.

"Miss Booker, you surprise me," came the reply at last, his too calm voice seeming to come at her from every direction.

She turned left and right, trying to get a bearing on the bastard. It was no use; he could have been anywhere.

"If I could see you, I would shoot you," he said, seeming more in control. Had he made it out of the water on to some ledge? He didn't sound like he was swimming any more. "But I suppose I will have to settle for leaving you here to drown. Goodbye, Kate."

'Kate,' thought the woman. 'Who's Kate?'

"I'll find you," she screamed. "No matter where you fucking hide, I'll find you."

"No," came the reply, fainter now, moving away. "I will find you, if you survive the day. Trust me."

"Spider?" she yelled. "Spider!"

But there was no reply, only darkness and water and white noise.

A COUNCIL WORKER found the woman later that night, unconscious, half dead, suffering from hypothermia, washed up on a brick shore half a mile under the city. Her body was swarming with rats. When he managed to wake her, she couldn't tell him her name. Delirious, she muttered incoherently about webs as he radioed for assistance.

TWO MONTHS LATER, a nondescript car drove through a pair of wrought iron gates and down the driveway of a minor public school in Kent. It parked behind the main building and two people, a man and a woman, got out.

He wore a smile that spoke of familiarity and nostalgia. Her face betrayed no emotion at all.

"This way," he said, and walked towards the rear doors, his feet crunching on the gravel.

She did not follow him immediately, pausing to take in her surroundings. The sports fields stretched away ahead of her, bordered on all sides by thick woods, lush green in the summer heat. The sky was blue and the air was clear and smelt of pine needles and fresh water. The only sound came from the soft rustle of the leaves in the gentle wind.

"You coming?"

She turned and trailed after the man, who pushed open the door and entered.

The building was impressive and old, but not as old as some public schools. This was a Victorian edifice, imposing and solid. The inside reflected this, with dark wood panelled walls, tiled floors and portraits of illustrious benefactors with big sideburns hanging on the whitewashed walls.

The man led her deep into the silent building, up a small back staircase once meant for servants, to a small door in the east wing. He opened the door then handed her the keys.

"Welcome home," he said.

"It's not my home, John."

"It is now," said DI Cooper. Then he added, smiling: "Matron."

The woman slapped him playfully on the arm and allowed herself the tiniest grin as she stepped over the threshold into the flat. It was pokey but cosy. An small open fireplace sat in the middle of the far wall, with a flower print sofa and chair in front of it. There was a dresser, a bathroom with an old enamelled bath, a kitchen that barely had standing room for one and a bedroom with a single bed and wardrobe. The woman sighed and walked over to the living room window. The view of the fields and woods, with the thin skein of the river glinting on the horizon, was beautiful. This was a good place; quiet and peaceful, isolated from reality. The outside world would not bother her here.

"Yeah, it'll do," she said eventually, heartened by the green and the sun. It was hard to feel too low on such a gorgeous day. But she knew that looking out of this window on a cold, grey winter's day would be a very different prospect.

She heard a click from the kitchen and the rumble as the kettle began boiling. She stayed at the window until the man tapped her on the shoulder and handed her a mug of strong hot tea. She thanked him and sat on the sofa. He sat opposite, on the armchair, sipping his own brew.

"So this is where you went to school, huh?" she said.

"Yeah. I'm on the alumni committee and everything."

"I thought places like this only turned out lawyers and bankers."

"Oh, no, soldiers too. There's a cadet force here."

"Seriously?"

"Once a week they dress the boys up in uniforms and teach them to shoot things."

A flash of unease passed across the woman's face.

"Don't worry," said the man. "Matrons are exempt. You won't ever have to hold a gun again, Kate."

After a short pause she said: "It's Jane, remember? I'm supposed to be Jane now."

"Sorry, I know. But not forever. Once we catch the bastard you can go back to being Kate again."

The woman did not correct his misapprehension.

"The boys arrive tomorrow," he continued. "Then you'll be up to your elbows in Clearasil, TCP and black eyes."

"Can't wait." Another pause, and then: "Do you have any idea where he is?"

The man shook his head. "If I had to guess, Serbia."

The woman nodded.

"Were there any biscuits in there?" she asked. "I fancy dunking."

WHEN COOPER HAD gone, the woman drew a bath and gently lowered herself into the near boiling water, letting her skin adjust to the heat in tiny increments, her lips pursed with the pleasure of pain.

She floated, weightless, closed her eyes and concentrated on her breathing. She took long, slow, deep breaths and pictured the cares and stresses of her day dissolving out of her into the bathwater.

But there were no cares and stresses to disperse. It felt as if there was nothing in her at all. She was hollow.

The woman considered the emptiness dispassionately, turning it over in her mind as one would a vase or an artefact unearthed at an archaeological dig, feeling its weight and form, assessing it.

"Jane," she said out loud. "Jane Crowther. Matron."

She said the name in different ways, trying different intonations, a question, and answer, a hail, a statement.

"Jane. Jane. Jane."

It felt strange in her mouth. But it felt good on the inside.

Yes. She would be Jane now, the woman decided.

And it was right that she should be empty, she concluded, for that was what a newborn was – a vessel waiting to be filled with new experiences.

The woman who was now Jane ducked her head under the water for a moment and concentrated on the still warmth, the only sound her own heartbeat. Then she pushed her head back up to the air and took her first breath.

PART THREE
LEE

CHAPTER TEN

THE IMPLICATIONS OF what I'm seeing overwhelm me.

I stand there holding the gun, frozen in wonder and horror as the events of eight years ago spool through my head like a movie. Each event, each conversation, is suddenly reinterpreted with new and sinister emphasis.

If this is true, then that means… which means that… in which case…

I stagger back from the Speaker's Chair as if hit, almost losing my footing. I think maybe I let out a cry.

"Surprise," says the man in the cloak.

The sound of his voice brings me back to the here and now. I refocus my attention on him, steadying my wavering hands and aiming the gun right between his eyes.

"Oh, Kate," says John Cooper. "Is that any way to greet an old friend?"

CHAPTER ELEVEN

I WAS A little nervous when I rode into Nottingham.

The castle was impressive and welcoming, although they insisted I leave my gun with them for the duration as apparently no firepower was allowed in the town. Hood had his own band of merry men and there was a family atmosphere that reminded me a little of St Mark's. I had some concerns when I saw the army of Rangers training in the grounds, but those fears were dispelled when I met the man and his entourage. These were obviously good guys, which was a blessed relief.

Jack had been there three days already when I arrived and was fitting in nicely. There was something of the chameleon about Jack. He was good at blending in, finding the right tone to strike in a particular group or environment. In Nottingham he was blokier, more one of the lads than he was back at school. It had worked. He had met Hood a couple of times and been greeted with cautious warmth. As we'd discussed, Jack had proposed an arrangement whereby either of our settlements could, if seriously threatened, send a messenger asking for aid which would be immediately rendered.

Hood seemed open to the idea, but it was still early days. Jack was taken aback when I turned up intending to ask him to deliver on his end of the bargain so quickly.

"I don't know if he'll be up for that. Things aren't exactly quiet around here," Jack told me as we walked around the castle boundary on the day I arrived. "There's some nutty cult on the rise and it's got them a bit spooked. Plus, you know, they had a hard fight against that French geezer so they're cautious about going looking for trouble."

"Geezer? Really, Jack? Geezer?"

"What?" he replied, I thought slightly shiftily.

I laughed. "Was that the commonly accepted term at Harrow for French psychopaths?"

"No," he said, straight faced. "The accepted Harrovian term for a French psychopath was Le Geezer. But, you know, I didn't want to confuse you with the complicated foreign lingo."

"Right."

He gave me a sudden appraising stare, as if trying to work out what I was getting at which, since I was just joking, made me wonder what he thought I was getting at. I shook my head and filed it under the category of 'Jack being odd'.

"Anyway," he went on, "they've got quite a force of Rangers. As you've found, they don't carry guns, just knives, swords, bows and arrows, quarterstaffs. Proper mediaeval stuff."

"So where," I interjected, "did all De Falaise's firepower end up?"

"I asked that, but they're not saying."

"'Cause we could use it, if they'd let us."

Jack shook his head firmly. "No chance. Hood has a thing about modern weapons. If they had an arsenal somewhere, he's either destroyed it or put it somewhere no-one else can find it."

I nodded. "So how many men can he spare us?"

Jack winced. "I don't know if he's willing to spare us any, but I got the impression that the best we could hope for is maybe five or six."

I looked up at the castle walls, where we'd seen at least fifty Rangers being put through their paces. "Fuck, really? That's it?"

"He said he has to make the cult his top priority. Plus..." Jack trailed off, seemingly unsure of what to say next.

"Yes?"

"Well, what happened in Thetford? 'Cause whatever it was, those Rangers you came back with kind of hate your guts."

"Things got complicated."

He waited for me to say more, but I kept my mouth shut. Even I wasn't entirely sure what had happened back at the compound. I kept replaying the moment I killed the begging snatcher, trying to reconstruct what I was thinking at the time, trying to work out whether it was justified. But I came up empty handed time and again. It was like I hadn't been me at all when I pulled the trigger. I was beginning to suspect that I couldn't recall what I'd been feeling because I hadn't felt anything at all. And that scared me.

We rounded a corner and found ourselves back at the castle gates. Jack saw this girl called Sophie who he'd been mooning after, with a total lack of success on his part and no encouragement at all on hers, and took off to resume his charm offensive.

I went to find Hood.

THE LIVING LEGEND was pacing up and down in front of a map of the area which was hanging from the wall of what used to be the visitor's centre.

Courteous yet taciturn, he had a weather-beaten face that spoke of a life outdoors. He seemed uncomfortable inside and every now and then I caught him flashing tiny glances at the walls as if suspicious or resentful of them. I don't think he realised he was doing it.

He indicated that I should take a seat in one of the moulded plastic chairs that were piled up in the corner.

"Tell me about De Falaise?" I asked, substituting curiosity for small talk.

He regarded me coolly. "Like a good war story, do you?" The implication was unspoken but clear.

"My Dad and I had a run in with him, back in France," I explained. "I'm deaf in one ear because of that bastard."

He looked surprised and I admit I felt a little pleased with myself. I got the impression he was not an easy man to surprise. I realised that something about his quiet authority made me want to impress him.

"You were in France?" he asked. "What were you doing there?"

"Making my way home."

"From?"

"Iraq."

Now he was really surprised. I intended to leave it at that, just be enigmatic and cool, but I felt a sudden need to confess. Something about this strange, solid man made me want to unburden myself to him.

Hood pulled up a chair and sat opposite me as I talked, listening without comment as everything that had happened to St Mark's since The Cull poured out of me. The choices, the killing, the monsters and heroes. As I spoke the sun went down until only a solitary candle lit the room, catching the lines on his face until it seemed I was speaking to a statue or a demon. Hood had an amazing quality of stillness. I don't think he even blinked while I spoke, and I spoke for a long, long time. In that quiet, half lit room it was as if there was something not quite natural about him, something more than human. Or maybe something less.

When I had finished – and I was completely honest about what had happened in Thetford – I fell silent and waited nervously for his response. He sat there, impassive, for what felt like a lifetime.

"Have you told your father this? Or Jane?" he asked softly, the voice seeming to come from the very fabric of the building.

"Some of it," I said. "Not all."

He rose from the chair and walked across to me. He laid his hand on my shoulder and looked down into my eyes. There was such compassion in them, but no pity. I felt a lump in my throat and realised I was about to cry.

"You should."

"I..." I found it hard to form feelings, let alone words to express them. "I want..."

"I know what you want, son. But I can't give it to you."

He turned and walked to the door then paused and said, over his shoulder: "You can have a team of men. My very best. They'll be at your disposal from dawn tomorrow."

He half turned and looked back at me through the gloom.

"And Lee, if things go badly, send word if you can," he said. "If it's at all possible, I'll come."

Then he opened the door and left.

I sat in that chair watching the candle flicker against the darkness until the first hint of light crept across the horizon. Then I wiped my eyes and made ready for war.

CHAPTER TWELVE

TARIQ FELT THE frost crunching beneath his feet as he walked across the grass towards the school. The air was crisp and cold but the sky was clear and the sun shone strong but heatless.

He loved this place. All his life he had dreamed of escaping from Basra, of never again seeing dust or sand or dun coloured buildings. This place, with all its rain and greenery, its tall palladian columns and huge windows, was as far away from his birthplace as he could imagine. When he had lain in his bed at night as a boy, this was what he had dreamed of. Another man might have felt a twinge of guilt when he realised that, in some ways, The Cull was the best thing that ever happened to him. But not Tariq. He rarely dwelt on the past and seldom paused to examine his motives or feelings. He lived in the moment and he liked it there right well, thank you very much.

As a teenager he had pictured his future as a journalist in the UK, lobbing perfectly formed gobbets of vitriolic prose at Saddam and the Ba'athists over the internet. But he didn't mourn the loss of his dreams and ambitions. He was a teacher now, and a member of a community that had taken him in and made him part of a family. He would settle for that and count himself lucky.

He'd fight for it, too. Fighting seemed as natural to him as breathing. He had stood in opposition to someone or something his entire life – Saddam, the militants, the Americans. It was only in the last two years that he'd had nothing to fight. Peace had brought its own challenges, though, not least the loss of his lower left arm after the Salisbury explosion. The pain had gone now but he still felt occasional flashes of feeling in his missing fingers, and the stump itched like hell if he wore his hook on hot days.

He raised the artificial limb and flexed the metal claw. It made a soft clicking sound as he did so. The younger kids called him Captain Hook, but he didn't mind that. He'd even play along sometimes, bellowing a piratical "ARRRR!" and chasing them down the corridors as they screamed with terrified delight.

The thought of anyone taking them away and making them slaves caused an old familiar anger to rise inside him. He'd almost missed it.

He pushed open the doors and walked inside. The first person he met was Green. Tariq thought Green was a bit odd. Gawky, with acne scars and floppy blond hair, he was very quiet and reserved in company. But give him a classroom of students or, better still, a gang of people wanting to put on a play or a musical, and he was driven, focused, funny and inspirational; a natural performer. Tariq had assumed he was gay, but recent rumours suggested otherwise. The oddest thing, though, was that he didn't take part in any of the military training exercises. Matron had exempted him, and only him, from all such activities. She'd never told Tariq why. She'd just said: "He's earned it."

Green nodded a greeting as Tariq entered, then smiled in relief as the four kids he'd brought back with him shuffled past in search of baths and bed. But his face fell as he realised no-one else was following on.

"That's it?" he asked.

"Call an assembly, ten minutes, dining hall," replied the Iraqi. "All kids of ten and up. I need to get some food in me first."

He hurried off to the kitchen and left Green to round everyone up.

TARIQ HAD BEEN a leader before, in Basra. Giving orders came easily to him, and he felt no nerves as he stood in front of over forty children and twelve adults.

"Hands up everyone who was at the original school during the battle with the Blood Hunters," he said.

About twenty hands went up.

"And how many were here when we moved from Groombridge?" About thirty.

"And how many of you want to move again?"

There was a murmur of disquiet.

"Because there's a chance we're going to come under attack. And I, for one, am not running and hiding this time!"

He was hoping for a chorus of "Damn straight!" but instead Mrs Armstrong spoke up from the back.

"Why not start at the beginning, eh, love?" she asked. "Tell us where the others are."

Tariq looked down at his audience and shook his head in wonder at his own stupidity. These weren't his fellow rebels from Basra, these were bloody kids, and he had started off like he was a sports coach gearing his team up for a big match. What was he thinking?

So he told them, honestly, without sugar coating it or hiding anything, exactly what had happened and what they had learnt at Thetford.

"We've prepared for a siege, over and over," he said in conclusion. "You all know your roles and positions. My job is to make sure that this place stands firm, no matter what. And with the defences we've got and the strategies we've drilled, anyone who attacks this place is going to find they've bitten off more than they can chew."

He fell silent then, waiting for some kind of response.

"No," came a voice after a moment's silence. It was not shouted, but it was spoken forcefully. It took Tariq a second to realise that it was Green speaking.

"You want to say something?" asked Tariq.

Green got to his feet and gestured to the podium where Tariq stood, asking permission to address the room. Tariq nodded and stepped aside, surprised.

Green cleared his throat and looked at his feet as he prepared to speak. Then he looked up and addressed the room.

"Somewhere in London there's an army of kids fighting a war," he said. "Kids like you and me. Kids who should be here, with us. We've been looking for allies recently, building trade relationships with the Steamies and the rest, and trying to arrange mutual defence pacts with Hood and Hildenborough. We know some of the people we encounter may be hostile or dangerous, but we keep looking for allies who can help us.

"These kids in London don't know it, but they are already our allies. Because they're us. They're you and me and her and them, if we'd never found this place. If Matron hadn't stuck her neck out and fought for us. If Lee hadn't seen off Mac. If Rowles hadn't sacrificed himself to keep us safe.

"If not for their efforts, we would be those kids. Scared, alone, fighting a war against kidnappers. Or worse – shipped to America already, where God knows what would have happened to us.

"And how do we repay the sacrifices our friends have made to keep us safe? We hide here and hope the bad guys don't come looking for us? Well, yeah. Of course Matron and Lee want us to do that. It's natural. They've fought hard to keep us from harm, to create this place for us. They don't want to risk it or lose it. Of course they want us to stay here and protect this perfect haven they've built.

"But the thing is, they've also taught us by their example. And their example teaches us a different lesson.

"It tells us that the only safety worth having is the kind you fight for.

"It tells us that sitting around waiting for other people to look after you is asking for destruction.

"It tells us that protecting people weaker than ourselves is the most important thing we can possibly do with our lives.

"They're out there now, fighting for us. God knows where Matron is, or what's happening to her. Lee's dad has gone to London to try and lead a gang of kids against an army that will almost certainly kick their ass. Lee's gone riding off into potentially hostile territory with a bunch of men who we don't know he can trust.

"And we're supposed to sit here and let them do all this for us because it's what they would want us to do?

"Fuck that.

"Fuck hiding.

"Fuck defences.

"Fuck keeping a low profile.

"If we want to justify what they've done for us, we don't do it by staying here and letting them risk their lives for us again.

"We do it by joining them.

"We do it by fighting for ourselves.

"We do it by going to war.

"We've spent all this time looking for allies to help us, and now we've found some. But they need our help instead.

"So tomorrow, instead of running all the drills we've rehearsed a thousand times, I say we get kitted up, arm ourselves, and take the fight to the enemy. We go to London, we meet up with John and this resistance army in Hammersmith, and we shut these motherfucking nutjobs down and bring those kids here, to safety, where they belong.

"Who's with me?"

Tariq stood, mouth gaping open in astonishment, as the whole room rose as one and began cheering. Green stepped down from the podium and walked across to him.

"They're all yours," he said with a smile.

CHAPTER THIRTEEN

CAROLINE RUBBED THE sleep from her eyes and sat up.

"What?" she mumbled.

"There's a man," said the young boy who had just shaken her awake.

"What kind of man?" she asked, reaching for her jumper.

"Soldier," said the boy.

Caroline was instantly awake. She pulled the jumper over her head, grabbed her jeans and got to her feet.

"Where?"

"He was at the market just now."

"Just now? What time is it?"

"I dunno," shrugged the boy. "Sun's up."

"You know the rules about going to the market on your own," she scolded.

"Didn't go on my own," he pouted. "Went with Jimmy and Emma."

"Who are how old?" she asked, rhetorically. But the boy had stuck out his lower lip and refused to make eye contact.

Caroline shook her head wearily, wondering when she ended up a mother.

"Okay," she said. "So this soldier, why come tell me?"

The boy sulked a little bit more then finally muttered, petulantly: "He was asking about us."

"Did anyone tell him anything?"

The boy shook his head.

Caroline reached down and began secreting her arsenal of knives about her person, then she grabbed her shotgun and ran for the door.

*　　*　　*

THE MAN WAS not very subtle.

It was not uncommon to see people dressed in combat gear, especially these days. But something about the way he wore it told you that it was more than just an affectation. This man was a soldier born and bred; his bearing and body language proclaimed it like a loudhailer. It was something about the way he looked at things. You could see him scanning the environment, calculating routes of ingress and egress, assessing the potential threat of everyone who passed his eye line, turning his body every now and then to make sure his awareness was 360 degrees. He was armed, too, with a machine gun strapped across his chest; his hand was always on it, ready for action.

This man was alert and dangerous.

And looking for her.

She thanked Tom, the potato seller, for allowing her to shelter under his awning as she observed the man, then stepped out into the open square.

The man clocked her instantly, as she'd expected he would. She stood there and deliberately met his gaze, then nodded right, indicating a side street down which she then walked. He followed her a moment later.

They met in the quiet street, surrounded by burned-out cars and looted shops. She had the shotgun raised and ready to fire as he stepped into view.

"Hands down," Caroline said.

He let go of his gun and let his hands fall to his side. Caroline considered shooting him there and then. Even talking to this man was a risk, but after a long moment she decided to let him speak.

"Who are you and why are you looking for me?" she asked.

"My name's John. I heard there was an army of kids here, fighting the snatchers. Is that you?"

He had a Midlands accent, and something about his tone of voice made Caroline feel that perhaps he wasn't the villain she'd been expecting.

"Maybe. Maybe not."

"I'll take that as a yes. Good. I have news for you. And an offer."

"I'm listening."

"At dawn tomorrow you are going to be attacked by the church. They know where you are and they've decided to finish you off."

"How the fuck do you know that?"

"My friends and I captured a bunch of them two days ago. One of them was very talkative."

Caroline digested this information for a moment, then asked: "Offer?"

"I want to help."

"How?"

"I've got a lot of experience of fighting in urban environments. I can help you, teach you how to give them a very memorable welcome."

"My mum always warned me to be careful of things that seem to good to be true," said Caroline. "Why would you do this?"

He shrugged. "Because it's the right thing to do."

Caroline snorted derisively.

"I represent a place, a safe place," said the man, undeterred. "A school actually, where a bunch of us look after kids."

Caroline sneered. "Right," she said. "And that doesn't sound at all creepy." She stared hard at this man, trying to work out if he was telling the truth. Despite her sarcasm, she was surprised to find that her initial instinct was to trust him.

"This school have a name?" she asked.

"St Mark's."

Caroline suddenly felt sick. First Matron and now this guy? This was too much of a coincidence. Matron had gone looking for Spider only yesterday. They must have captured her and tortured her until she told them where Caroline and her kids were hiding.

This guy, Caroline realised, was a church infiltrator.

And she knew how to deal with infiltrators.

"You don't say," said Caroline. "And you run this school, do you?"

"Me and some others."

"What's the name of your Matron?" she asked.

He narrowed his eyes, curious at this unexpected question. "Jane," he said eventually. "Jane Crowther."

"And you are?"

"I told you, I'm John."

"John Keegan?"

The man's face betrayed his surprise and he nodded. Caroline walked forward, 'til the barrel of her shotgun was less than an inch from the soldier's chest.

"Where is she?" she asked.

"What?"

"Where are you holding her?"

"I'm sorry, I don't..."

"Guys!"

Ten teenaged boys stepped out of doorways and from behind cars, carrying their weapons in plain sight, encircling Caroline and the man.

"Take the gun off," she barked.

"Listen, lets rewind a bit, I don't think we..."

"Take. It. OFF!"

He did so, letting it clatter to the tarmac from where it was retrieved by one of the boys, who gripped it excitedly. Caroline saw the realisation flash across the man's face – that he had miscalculated, was outnumbered and surrounded. She followed his eyes as they darted left and right, assessing which of the boys he should go for and which route of escape he should take back to the market. She saw his posture change ever so slightly as he prepared to make a move.

So she stepped forward and brought her knee up hard into the man's bollocks, doubling him over with a whoosh of escaping breath. 'Let's see you make a run for it now,' she thought smugly.

"Jane left here yesterday, heading straight for you bastards," she said.

"No, wait..."

"She told you where we were, didn't she? Jesus, I don't know what you did to her to make her give us up, but I know her. She'd have to be half dead before she told you anything that would lead you to me."

"You've got it wrong..." the man gasped through his pain.

A tall boy stepped forward and cracked the man hard across the head with a truncheon. He crumpled to the ground.

"Don't answer her back, fuckhead," the boy shouted.

"Luke," said Caroline, addressing the boy. "Get back to the others, tell them to pack up and move out. We're not waiting, we're going now."

The boy nodded and ran off down the street.

Caroline knelt down beside the man.

"What was the plan, eh?" she asked. "Infiltrate us, let us think you'd help us fight the church and then lead us into a trap? Box us up and ship us out, problem solved?"

The man looked up at her. "I'm telling you the truth, I just want to help," he said, his voice rough with pain. "How do you know Jane? When was she here?"

"I know her, you bastard, because she's my friend. And she tricked you. That's the best bit. She may have led you right to us, but she fucked you up at the same time."

"I don't…"

"John Keegan's dead, motherfucker. She told me herself." Caroline laughed, but there was no real humour in it. "She told you to pretend to be a dead man because she knew it would tip us off. So you lose, asshole. She was too clever for you."

"No, wait, I see what's happened here…"

Caroline stood up, levelled the shotgun at the man's head, and blew his brains all over the street even as he tried desperately to cling to the cover story she'd so easily seen through.

"Back home, now," she ordered, and the boys took off down the street.

Caroline stayed for a moment, looking at the corpse of the man who'd tried to win her trust. She had a moment's doubt. What if…?

But she shook her head. No.

"Joke's on you, churchman," she said, and then she ran after her friends.

JOHN KEEGAN'S BODY lay in the street until nightfall, when the foxes and the dogs fought over it.

The foxes won, and dragged it hungrily away.

CHAPTER FOURTEEN

"I ALWAYS THOUGHT you kind of fancied me, Kate," says Cooper, after swilling down the last mouthful of turkey with a swig of Chablis. It's the first thing he's said since I entered the room, escorted by two guards, and sat down to dinner.

The spread was impressive and smelt incredible. I considered refusing to eat, sitting there with my arms folded, defiant. But that would have been self defeating. I practically lick the plate clean, despite the nausea that his proximity provokes.

I consider correcting him, telling him I'm Jane now. But I pause for a moment as it occurs to me that the distinction is no longer so clear cut. Not now, not with this man sitting across the table from me.

"I did," I reply. "But I always had really, really crappy taste in men."

"Had?" he asks, amused.

"I've had better luck since the world ended."

"So I gather."

"Excuse me?"

"I heard on the grapevine that you hooked up with my old mate Sanders." He leans back in his chair, smug at my surprise. "Oh, yes, I've been keeping tabs on you, Kate. Or, rather, my friends have."

"The Americans."

He nods. "I couldn't believe it when your alias cropped up. I tried to tell Blythe that he'd got the wrong end of the stick, but he didn't buy it. He was so convinced you were some kind of spook."

I have a fork. If I launch myself at him, I've got a better than even chance of getting it through his eyeball. But he knows that I won't. The reason I can't kill him now is the same reason I couldn't shoot him in the Commons. I need answers. Unfortunately, I don't know how to begin asking the questions.

I can't tell whether he's changed in the last eight years, or whether the version of him I met before The Cull was a carefully constructed act. Is this the real man? He's not that different. Speech patterns and body language are the same. The smile, the eyes, the good natured air of vague sarcasm – it's all exactly the same.

"You have so many questions for me, don't you?" he asks.

I nod.

"Then hit me. I'll fill you in." He dabs his lips with a napkin and pushes his chair back from the table, stretching his legs out and linking his fingers behind the back of his head. The midday sun is streaming through the lead latticed windows along the riverside wall of what used to be the Speaker's Cottage. It casts his face into sharp relief.

I try to form my first question, but I come up blank.

"Let me get you started," he says, smiling, for all the world the image of the genial, helpful friend. "Spider is dead. He died that very day."

The same day I did.

"How?"

"I garrotted him."

"Why?"

"He had outlived his usefulness."

I shake my head. "No, sorry. You have to go farther back."

"The clues are all there. You work it out. The point is that the man who killed your brother is dead."

"But you let me think he was still alive."

"Yes, I did. Listen, your role in leading me to his base of operations in Manchester was invaluable. I'd been trying to get a bead on that place for months. Little bastard wouldn't tell me where it was. That was the problem, really. He'd decided not to trust me any more. Thought he could go it alone, run the business without my help and protection. Or, most importantly, without paying me my cut."

"So you taught him a lesson."

"Just so. The idea was that he would kill you himself. I planted that really obvious bug in the phone, assuming he'd find it and shoot you. How was I to know he'd go and kill your brother instead? That was a shock, I can tell you, to find out you were alive. I couldn't just kill you, not after that. It would have aroused too much suspicion. So I managed to wangle you into witness protection."

"And of course my absence protected you, not me."

"Exactly."

"You must have needed someone else on the payroll, someone at Hereford."

"Natch."

"And another bug besides the one in the phone."

"In your shoe, set to become active after a couple of hours so that it would avoid detection."

I nod, dotting Is and crossing Ts in my head. "So you ran Spider's operation, he was just a front?"

"Uh-huh."

"And now…?"

"Now I don't need a psychopathic Serbian mass murderer as my mouthpiece. There's nobody to stop me running my business just the way I want. I use his name though. It had kudos in certain circles. Even after The Cull, there were people who knew the name. It made things easier."

My mind works furiously, piecing it all together.

Cooper must have met Spider when he was in Serbia with the SAS during the Balkan conflict. Spider was probably already running some kind of organised crime ring, maybe even a trafficking route. Cooper offers him a way into the British market and they go into business together. Then he leaves the army and joins the police, managing eventually to get himself assigned to the case, making sure no-one gets close to his operation. This all works nicely until one day Spider gets cocky and tries to shut him out and run a Manchester 'branch' all on his own. He must be watching Cooper, making sure he isn't followed. That must be a very complicated game of cat and mouse. No matter what Cooper tries, Spider outwits him.

Cooper needs a way in that Spider won't see coming. And then I turn up, eager little lamb, and lead him straight there. Cooper uses a few of his mates from the SAS to storm the warehouse. At least one of them must have been on the take.

(Sanders? No. I dismiss the thought. Couldn't have been.)

God knows how he spun that one, but he must have had some way to get his bosses to swallow it. He shuts the warehouse down and then hides me away in St Mark's where I can't be any threat to anyone.

Cooper sits opposite me, studying my face as I process everything he's told me.

"You're wondering who you can take revenge on now, aren't you, Kate?" he asks. "Spider's dead, and even though I duped you, I was not directly responsible for James' death."

"Indirectly, though. You planted the fucking bug."

He shrugs. "Kate, he was dead the moment he caught Spider's eye and you know it. The bug was an excuse on a particular day. If it hadn't been that, it would have been something else."

He's right. I do know it.

I consider the man sitting before me and I'm confused. Spider was obviously a monster. Everything about him screamed danger – the way he looked at you, the way he moved, the way he spoke. He was a predator, a shark, a psychopath.

But Cooper is different. Kate never had a moment's unease about him. He was jovial and pleasant but inspired confidence. And he still has an easy capability about him. He doesn't seem unhinged or mad, scary or dangerous at all. He seems like a bloke. Just an ordinary bloke.

He thinks of people as goods to be traded, commodities whose profit potential can be realised – but his manner gives no hint of the pitiless void at the heart of him.

"I spent so long fantasising about what I'd do to that man, if I ever had the opportunity," I say.

"I bet you did. But I'm not him."

"No, you're not. You're the man who used me, set me up to be killed and then condemned me to a life ruled by a lie."

"Mea culpa."

"You're also the man who trafficked vulnerable girls into hell."

"That too."

"Why?"

He shrugs. "Because I can," he says, a parody of abashed modesty, like a cocksure young man admitting to sleeping with a friend's girlfriend; he knows it was wrong but he actually also thinks it was kind of cool.

"But surely you must have realised it was wrong?" The words feel foolish and naïve, but I want an answer.

"The world was built on slavery, Kate. How do you think this country got built? Or America? Or Rome or the pyramids or anything lasting? What I did, what I do, is perfectly natural. The slave masters of the past were pillars of the community, members of guilds and lodges, knighted and rich, the toasts of the town. Why shouldn't I be?"

I look at this man I once invited into my bed, and I feel sick to my stomach. Spider may have been a monster, but he wasn't the worst of it. Not by a long shot.

"I never took advantage. It's important you realise that," he continues. "I busted countless drug dealers in my time. They all had one thing in common – they were users too. The ones who didn't get caught, the smart ones, stayed clean. It was the same with me."

"So that makes it all right then?" I am on the verge of shouting. I take a deep breath.

"I trafficked them into the country, I set them up, sourced the clients and took the money," he says, for some reason intent on justifying himself to me. "But never, not once, did I ever take advantage of one of them. That would have left me vulnerable, you see? There was no room for emotional attachments on the job.

"I had a girlfriend. That surprises you, doesn't it? Jenny. Nice woman, worked for HBOS. Thought I was a dull copper, which kept me safe. And her."

It takes me a moment or two to collect my thoughts.

"All right, morality aside, how did you pull this off?" I gesture to the building around us. "How did you end up here?"

CHAPTER FIFTEEN

MY DOUBLE LIFE ran like clockwork after you helped me sort out Spider. I found a new front man, someone else within the organisation. You never met him. He became the new Spider. It became a title rather than a person, which served me well. It made it clear to the new guy that he was disposable, and it allowed me to continue to use the, shall we say *brand awareness* that Spider had created amongst our clients and competitors.

I considered coming down to school and finishing you off, you know.

Really. You were a loose end. I hate loose ends. But in the end I figured it was riskier to break cover than leave you to rot.

Did you enjoy being Matron? What am I saying, of course you did – the world's ended and you're still doing it!

I had a fifteen year plan. Worked it out while I was undercover in Sarajevo, back in the day. I won't bore you with the details, but it worked, was working, would have worked.

Three years to go when the fucking Cull hit. Three years and then I'd have packed my bags and vanished off the face of the Earth. Nice little mansion in South America, I reckoned. Get fat, raise a few kids.

Best laid plans, eh.

They knew a lot earlier than they let on. About the blood type thing. Since I'd been in the army, my medical details were on record. I was contacted when the press were still talking about bird flu. Recalled to Hereford.

There was this soldier, Major General Kennett.

Really? What was your impression of him?

Ha! Yeah, I agree actually. Decent bloke. Capable. Prissy, though. Couldn't make the hard decisions.

He briefed us. Not completely, obviously, but he told us we were immune and that it would get bad enough that there might be a breakdown of public order. We were going to be the last line of defence when the police and regular army were no longer able to cope.

Operation Antibody it was called.

I know. Laughable.

They knew, though; the Government. Makes me wonder how long they'd known by then. What they knew about where it came from.

I've searched this place and Number 10 top to bottom more than once. Nothing. No clue at all. I thought there may be some evidence at the MI5 or MI6 buildings, but all the interesting parts are still sealed up. I don't reckon we'll ever know how it started or where it came from.

Who cares now anyway?

Once I was drafted again, my main concern was the organisation. I kept in touch with my new Spider by phone, trying to maintain control. I got regular reports as things fell apart but eventually I lost touch with them all.

My network was gone, my resources were gone and I began to suspect that the money I had accumulated would soon be worth less than nothing. All that effort, for what?

So we were broken into teams and dispatched across the country to key installations – nuclear power plants, arms depots, local governments, that kind of thing.

I was part of the London team. We were all Regiment or ex-Regiment; the best, you know? Our job was to protect the Government.

At first it was pretty easy. The regular security teams were bloody good. We just shadowed them, learning the ropes. Then when one of them went down, one of us would step into the breach.

They'd done the same in Government, you know. Formed an inner cabinet. The handful of O-Neg MPs, some immune peers and a few other top dogs. They were running things long before the rest of the real cabinet fell ill. It was like the ones who knew they were going to survive just started ignoring the ones who were doomed, as if they were already dead.

Some of my colleagues thought it was callous, but of course it was the sensible, expedient thing to do.

The armed forces were recalled from abroad and the O-Negs were weeded out. That's when the word spread, you know. Someone in the army worked it out and told the press.

Anyway they formed these units of immune men and women. Army, police, fire and medical. All the emergency services. Even the

BBC were sorted out, a core team of broadcasters who could keep a skeleton news service on air until there was no-one left to watch it. But there weren't enough of us to go around, so they had to be concentrated in one place. One safe haven where there would be enough immune people to stick it out until it was all over and retain order and civilisation amongst themselves.

It was a good plan. It's what I would have done. They made one crucial mistake, though. They chose the wrong place to make a stand.

They chose London.

Why do – sorry, *did* – all politicians have such a love affair with London? I never understood it. Obviously what they should have done is taken off for somewhere remote, rural. I actually said this to the PM once.

Sorry? Oh yes, he was immune. I know, what are the odds! Things would have gone very differently if he hadn't been. There'd have been an almighty power struggle. But because he was top dog, and he knew he was going to survive, he was able to lay down the law pretty much unchallenged. He was a subtle fucker, too. Lots of backroom deals went down before the rest of Parliament worked out what was going on.

So, yeah, I told him he should move everyone out to Macynnleth or some other alternative energy centre or something. And it's not as if he didn't think along those lines, 'cause the plans for Operation Motherland were drawn up at around this time, so they knew the advantage of being away from the urban centres, they knew the risk of secondary diseases and riots and all that stuff.

But he was determined that they had to stay put, right here in the Palace of Westminster, barricading themselves in like it was Fort Apache.

"The people need to see that we haven't deserted our posts," is what he told me.

And of course once the news got out about the virus and what it was really doing, the riots began.

I thought I'd seen desperation before, during the siege, but this was a whole other order of magnitude. The savagery of it was...

We set up concrete barricades along Whitehall, blew Westminster Bridge, put up gun emplacements in the cathedral. Put a ring of steel all around Parliament Square and kept them out. Hundreds of thousands of them. It would never have worked in peace time. We'd have been overrun. Tear gas and water cannons, even rubber bullets wouldn't have kept them out.

We had live ammunition, though. And grenades and tanks.

There came a day when it was obvious that we were going to be stormed, that Parliament was going to fall. I was with the PM when he made the call to shut down the BBC. He insisted he had to close them down before we opened fire on the crowds. Didn't want news of the massacre to spread. I thought that was stupid – the more people knew, I reckoned, the better. Spread a little fear, show them we mean business. But he wouldn't have it.

I think he was ashamed of the order he was about to give.

I was given the job of leading the team that flew to White City. There was a tent city outside Television Centre, as if people wanted to be close to some symbol of order and safety. The good old BBC, they'll look after us. You know, I think there was more faith in them than in Government at that point.

They let us in because they thought we'd been sent to protect them. When we ordered them to go off air they refused.

So that's where the massacre began. I must say it was a very odd feeling, kind of surreal, shooting Jeremy Paxman in the head. We took some fire too. God knows where they got guns from, but they put up a good fight. Kate Adie may have been in her sixties, but she shot two of my men. And fucking Andy Hamilton stayed on air on Radio Four the whole time, but we'd cut the lines to the transmitter, so no-one heard his final broadcast. I let him live, actually. He always made me laugh

Once they were down I radioed in and the shooting began back in Whitehall. By the time we got back it was mostly over. There were bodies everywhere. I remember flying over Trafalgar Square and seeing it thick with corpses, like a human carpet.

Sorry? No, not at all. It was necessary. I thought so then and I still think so. Needed to be done.

The problem was that the PM's power base wasn't as strong as we'd thought. There were some people in cabinet who tried to stop him giving the order to open fire. While I was busy at the BBC, these dissenters tried to stage a coup. Some of our guys, SAS bodyguards, joined in. Said they couldn't carry out an order like that.

Wimps.

It was a hell of a fight. By the time we got back, the PM was already dead, killed in the initial confrontation. Despite that, his supporters were winning. The coup was botched and the rebels were executed on the spot.

But the next day something unexpected happened. Kennett turned up with a force of soldiers, and told us that we were under arrest. Following illegal orders, he said. Took some balls, I reckon, for him to stand up to us. There were eighteen of us, entrenched, all Regiment. He knew that we wouldn't just roll over, and he knew he couldn't force us to hand over our weapons. So he basically turned his back on us, threw us out of the army, said we'd all been dishonourably discharged and would not be welcome at Operation Motherland HQ.

Then he buggered off to Salisbury and left us in charge of the wreckage.

The only one who left with them was our mutual friend Sanders. One of the rioters had managed to hit him with a rock while he was on the barricades, so he'd been out of action when the order to fire was given. Lucky bastard had a get out of jail free card. I reckon he'd have opened fire like the rest of them, but later that day he swore to me that he wouldn't have.

You think so? Well, I suppose you got to know him a little better than I did.

Anyway, with the PM dead, most of the cabinet wandering around like headless chickens, and the bleeding hearts executed, I saw my chance and took control. It wasn't hard. I had the most experience of command. I acted like I was the boss and they fell into line.

But Central London was empty. Those left alive fled the centre after the massacre, and the virus was still finishing its work.

I was the ruler of a ghost town.

I didn't have grand ambitions. We fortified our position as thoroughly as we could, gathered up all the food we could find, and waited for the virus to burn itself out. That was a long winter. Quite boring, actually.

By the time spring came I'd worked out a new plan. I divided the city into quadrants and we began clearing it. Emptying the roads of cars, dragging all the bodies to mass pyres, stockpiling fuel and resources. We did that for a whole year, one street at a time. Reclaiming the heart of the city.

The army stayed away. I knew they were collecting weapons from all around the country and building their great depot on the plain, but they didn't want to get involved in London. Kennett left it to us. Probably figured that time would only make him stronger and us weaker. He'd have been right too. I'd consolidated my position but I had no real power base because nobody would come into the centre any more. I think Kennett would probably have come for us eventually, and I'd have been toast. If it wasn't for the American.

I bet you encountered a lot of religious cults in the last few years? I expected the same thing to happen in the outskirts of London, but they all unified behind one preacher. I first heard about the American three years ago. He'd built up quite a following in West London. I found out later that he'd flown into Heathrow and started preaching at the first settlement he found. He taught people how to tune into the broadcasts.

That's right, yeah. The Miracle.

So he gathered a huge following very quickly and then one day he and a gang of his followers walked into my territory and said hello. I think his acolytes were supposed to intimidate us. They were all dressed in army surplus and carrying shotguns.

They nearly wet themselves when they realised who we were.

He didn't, though. He stayed very cool.

So I let him talk. Gave him dinner at Number 10, allowed him make his pitch. I needed allies, after all. He showed me the broadcast and I was impressed. I didn't think this Abbot guy was the new messiah but I could see how people could want to believe he was.

I wasn't convinced they were a real force, though. I mean, a bunch of religious nutters run by a Yank didn't seem like much of a threat to Operation Motherland. But then, after dinner, the Yank took me down into the cellars of Number 10. There was a door down there that I'd not been able to breach. The keypad was still active, run by some distant power source, and I'd had no joy with the code.

But this guy knew it. That's when I really started paying attention. I asked him who he was, but he just smiled. To this day he's never told me, but he must have been CIA, probably based here before The Cull. He knew all sorts of crazy shit, let me tell you.

The bunker down there is pretty extensive, with lots of comms equipment. He took me to an office, which I think was the PM's retreat in the event of a major attack, and said to pick up the red phone on the desk.

I did so, and after a second's silence I heard someone saying my name.

The voice at the end of the phone said he was the president, that he was working with the Abbot, and that they had managed to restore rule of law. He wanted to know if I was the de facto PM so of course I said yes.

Long story short, he had a proposal for me. If I would start exporting children to the US, he would send their army to back me up.

Now, look at this from my position. On one hand, I have a power base but no power, and the British Army knows where I am and is almost certainly getting ready to come and flush me out. On the other, I'm being offered the support of an entire army that will *do as I say* as long as I provide them with the resource they require. Can you think of anyone better suited to round up the kids and ship them abroad? I mean, it's kind of top of my CV, isn't it?

So I told the president about Operation Motherland. Where they were and what they were doing. I told him if he wanted my help, he would have to eliminate them first.

He put me in touch with Blythe in Iraq and the rest you know. I realised that once Kennett was out of the way, I would have to deal with Blythe, but at least initially he'd be on my side. I'd have time to work out a strategy to deal with him.

And then, hallelujah, the Yanks took out Kennett and his forces, but managed to get themselves wiped out in the process. I'm not ashamed to say I did a little jig when I heard about the nuke. Couldn't believe my fucking luck. The biggest single threat to my power base had been neutralised and there was no fallout.

Well, not for me, anyway. Ha ha.

At that point I could have told the president to go fuck himself, but the thing was I kind of enjoyed being back in the trafficking business. It gave me something to do, and it meant that my sphere of influence spread. People started to become afraid of me, to respect me and my forces. Me and the Yank still work together. He takes care of the religious stuff – brainwashing the plebs and spreading the word – while I take care of logistics and manpower.

Pretty much the entire territory inside the M25 is mine now, and soon we'll start moving outside. I actually had your school down as my first port of call. Once I've dealt with a little problem in Hammersmith tomorrow, maybe we'll take a trip there together.

What? Oh, didn't I say?

How do you think the Abbot stays alive? Blood transfusions, Kate. Daily. Fresh, young, healthy blood from universal donors.

He's basically a vampire.

And Britain is his blood bank.

CHAPTER SIXTEEN

"ATTACKING THAT CONVOY had seemed like such a good idea at the time," said Caroline, shaking her head in frustration. "This is like herding cats."

The army that she'd accumulated during the previous year were pretty well drilled. They followed orders and knew when to shut up. The hundred or so kids that they'd released from the convoy, on the other hand, were a gaggle of confused, impulsive, homesick brats with snotty noses and bad attitudes. Trying to smuggle them out of the city without drawing attention would have been hard enough, but doing so while they fought, cried, wandered off or kept nipping into abandoned buildings in search of a bed, was driving her nuts. She had to keep reminding herself not to be to angry. They were hungry and tired, and it was a freezing cold night.

While she mostly managed to keep a lid on her anger, her fear was growing unchecked. They needed to get a move on. It would be dawn in an hour and they weren't far enough away from their old nest yet. The trail would be fresh and easy to follow. The churchies had jeeps and helicopters. It had taken Caroline six hours to move the kids about a mile north; it would take their pursuers two minutes to cover the same distance.

"Luke," she called. The gangly teenage boy who served as her lieutenant was at her side in an instant. He was a year older than her but he was puppy dog loyal and hard as nails. "I want you to take Andrew, Melissa and Lizzie, and scout ahead. Find us somewhere to hole up. Somewhere defensible, okay?"

He nodded, gathered up the other three kids and ran to the end of the road, scanning for activity, then ducking out of sight. They were travelling parallel to the main road out of Hammersmith, using the residential side roads as cover. The idea had been to go north 'til they crossed the M25, then swing west and circle round until they were above Kent before heading south to the school. At this rate, she realised, it would be a death march. She was rapidly coming to the conclusion that they would have to find somewhere safe to stay out of sight while a couple of them made the journey. That way the school could send a lorry to collect the kids. That is, if the school was still there. Caroline was sure that Matron had given up their Hammersmith base, what if she had given up the school too? She dismissed the thought, not because she didn't think it likely, but because there was nothing she could do about it. If the school was gone, she decided, they'd just have to go to ground in the countryside. There'd be plenty of places to disappear.

Those kids who'd been with her for a while were trying to keep the new arrivals quiet as they neared the street corner. Caroline was in front, gun at the ready, when she heard a single shot echo back to her from the road ahead. She spun around waving frantically, indicating for the kids to scatter. Her 'soldiers' immediately began shushing the kids and herding them into the abandoned houses. In one minute the street was empty, the fear of imminent discovery managing what she'd been trying for hours to achieve – keeping the little brats quiet so she could think. She could see the pale faces of her guys at the doorways of the houses they'd taken shelter in, standing guard, waiting for her to make a move.

She gripped the gun tightly and ran to the pavement, pressing herself into the shadows and creeping forward so she could peer round the corner into the next road.

Her heart sank as she saw a pair of dual-cab pickups on the road, their roof-mounted spotlights picking out her four friends, who were down on their knees with their hands behind their backs. Each vehicle carried a team of four heavily armed men, three of whom were advancing with their guns trained on the captives. The road was wide and open, and the cars and kids were in the middle of a huge junction, providing almost no cover. She couldn't get close to them without being seen by the two men who were standing in the open backs of the vehicles, scanning the area for possible attack.

They were too far away for her to hear what the men said when they reached the four kneeling children, but she could tell they were shouting. Andrew was typically defiant and shouted back, which earned him a gun butt in the face and then, once he'd fallen over, a hard kick to the solar plexus.

Caroline clenched the gun tighter, so wanting to blow that fucker's head off but seeing no way to do so without leading them right to the children she was trying to protect. She was about to turn away when first one lookout then the other went rigid and dropped like stones off the sides of the vehicles on to the road. Caroline hadn't heard any shots. What the fuck had just happened?

The men interrogating her friends didn't seem to know either. At first they just looked confused. One of them walked to the nearest car to see what was going on. Just as he rounded the cab he dropped too, silent and instant. Caroline realised they were under attack, but she still had no idea by whom, or how. She was still too far away to approach unseen, even with this distraction. If she made a play, there was still a better than average chance that she'd be cut down. She bit her lip and, fighting down her instinctive desire to wade into the fight, waited to see how this would play out.

The engines of the vehicles revved as the two drivers indicated their desire to leave. The two men still in the open hesitated, unsure, and then ran – one to each cab. Neither of them made it. This time, as the second one fell, Caroline caught a glimpse of something sticking out of his chest. She couldn't be sure at this distance and in this light, but she thought maybe it was an arrow.

The drivers didn't wait another second. They screamed away at speed, racing to escape this silent attacker. One of them made it, but the other began swerving wildly from left to right before smashing straight through the frontage of an old pub, erupting into flames. The archer must have managed to shoot the driver through his windscreen while he was moving. Shit, this guy was good.

The other pickup squealed around a corner and vanished into the night as Caroline broke cover and ran to see how her four friends were doing. Andrew was sitting up, his face a mess of tears and snot. The other three were getting to their feet, mouths open. Caroline went and inspected one of the dead churchies. Sure enough when she rolled him over there was a thin wooden arrow buried deep in his chest. It had been painted black.

"That's mine," said a deep voice behind her and she spun, instinctively raising her weapon as she did so.

Since there were no streetlights, there were few shadows for the archer to step out of. He just sort of materialised out of the darkness. Dressed head to toe in dark green, he held a wooden bow in his right hand. A quiver of arrows stuck up over his left shoulder.

"The beauty of arrows, you see, is that they're recyclable. Shoot a bullet or a cartridge, like the one that shotgun of yours fires, and it's gone forever. But an arrow…" He stepped past her, reached down and yanked the wooden shaft from the dead man's chest. It came out with a soft squelch. "That can be used again."

"Who are you?" asked Melissa, who was now standing behind Caroline.

"My name's Ferguson," said the archer in a thick Irish accent as he wiped his arrow clean on the dead man's jacket. He stood up and slotted it back into his quiver, ready for another day. "I'm a Ranger." He seemed surprised that this pronouncement was greeted with silence. "From Nottingham," he added. And then: "I'm with Hood."

He stared at their blank faces, waiting for the spark of recognition. Nothing.

"I can see we need a better publicist," he said, smiling.

"Thank you," said Andrew, now on his feet.

"You're welcome. You know what would be a good way to thank me? Getting this young lady to stop pointing a shotgun at me."

Everyone stared at Caroline, who held her gun steady. "Hood?" she said. "Robin Hood in Nottingham?" The sarcasm dripped like honey.

"The very same," said the archer.

"Right. And you're, what, one of his Merry Men?"

The archer shook his head "No. I'm one of the Sullen Men. The Merry Men are, you know, merrier than me. They crack more jokes."

Caroline could see her friends smiling, but she didn't follow suit. "Why should I trust you?"

The archer allowed indicated the dead bodies of the churchies that littered the crossroads, the look on his face saying 'you want more proof?'

"Bit convenient, though, isn't it? You just turning up like this, just in time to rescue us from the bad guys. Almost like it was staged."

"Caroline, seriously?" said Luke.

"Think about it, Luke. Perfect way to gain our trust. What if Matron didn't tell them where the school is? This would be a perfect way to infiltrate us and get us to lead them straight there. They've already tried it once, remember."

"He killed them, Caroline," said Melissa.

"Yeah, and wasn't that easy?"

"You think they let him?" Andrew's tone of voice betrayed the incredulity he and all his friends were feeling. Caroline didn't understand why they couldn't see it.

"They're fucking churchies, guys," she said. "Probably think

they're martyrs, seventy-eight virgins waiting for them or something."
She glanced at their shocked faces. "What, you doubt my judgment
now, after everything we've been through? Don't you see this is what
he wants? Turn you against me, let you lead him to the school and
then it'll be a fucking army of snatchers turning up at to carry us off.
We should just kill him and move on."

Luke stepped forward and gently laid his hand on the barrel of
her shotgun. "Too paranoid, Caroline. I don't buy it."

The archer wisely stayed silent, watching Caroline closely, waiting
to see how this would play out.

Caroline clenched her jaw. She could just pull the trigger, finish
this guy regardless. It was the safe thing to do. It was necessary, she
knew that. Why couldn't the others see it? Once he was dead they'd
fall into line, they'd have no choice. Who else was going to shepherd
them to safety? They'd realise eventually that she was right. She
squeezed the trigger gently.

"No!" shouted Luke, pushing the barrel down as the gun went
off. The cloud of lead pellets embedded itself in tarmac. The archer
didn't even flinch.

Caroline spun fast, dropping the gun and drawing a knife from
her belt as she did so. The blade was at Luke's throat before he
could step backwards.

They stood there, frozen, for a long moment. Luke was scared but
defiant, sticking his chest out and staring Caroline down. Eventually
she withdrew the knife and resheathed it.

"Traitor," she spat. Then she turned on her heels and stalked off
into the darkness, away from her friends and the children who were
beginning to emerge from hiding to see what was going on.

She needed to be alone.

FERGUSON FOUND HER an hour later.

The shop downstairs had been looted clean, but the flat above
it, although long abandoned, still had some stuff lying around that
no-one had bothered to cart off. She lay on the double bed, ignoring
the smell of mould, and took another swig from the bottle of whisky
she'd found down the back of the sofa.

She disregarded the soft knock at the front door. It was open
anyway, and she knew it would just be one of her friends come to
coax her back. She already knew she was going to relent, but she
allowed herself the luxury of sulking there in the darkness, knowing

that she was being self-indulgent but needing to be persuaded, needing someone to make explicit how much she was needed and valued.

She didn't look up as someone entered and sat at the foot of the bed. Which is why she was so surprised when they began talking and she realised who it was.

"How long have you been looking after them?" asked the archer.

She thought: I don't recognise your right to ask me that. She didn't reply.

"It's not easy, being a leader," he said. "Managing people, trying not to let them down, making decisions when they're too stupid or lazy to make them for themselves."

"They're not stupid," muttered Caroline. "They're just kids."

"True. But how old are you?"

"Fuck off." She took another swig.

"Not old enough to be drinking that, that's for sure."

"Touch my bottle and I'll slice your fucking hand off."

"Wouldn't dare," he said. "Your deputy told me where you're making for."

"Then he's a blabbermouth twat who deserves everything he gets."

"You kiss your mother with that mouth?"

She looked up, open mouthed, then she threw the bottle at his head. He swatted it away.

"Sorry," he said, seemingly genuine. "It's just something you say, isn't it?"

"Not any more," she growled through gritted teeth.

"No, I s'pose not."

There was a long awkward silence before Caroline said: "What do you fucking want, anyway?"

"This school you're heading for, St Mark's."

"What about it?"

"Luke says their matron was with you. Is that right?"

"Like you don't already know," she muttered darkly.

"Is what he told me correct – did she go to the centre to kill Spider?"

Caroline glowered at him then eventually nodded once.

"And you used to know her? You were at the school?"

Again she nodded.

"Right. Well that's good, because you see I met some of their people. Three guys – Lee, John and Tariq. Do you know them?"

"I knew Lee for a while. Never met his dad or the other one. They're dead, anyway. The snatchers killed them when they captured her."

Ferguson shook his head. "No, they didn't. I was there that day. I was in the other lorry, the one you didn't manage to liberate – good job, by the way. We faked their deaths so I could get inside Spider's organisation."

Caroline shook her head. "No, don't believe you."

"They're still free. By now they should have got word to my boss. We're going to bring these bastards down, Caroline. And you can help us."

"No, Matron said they were dead. She said she knew they were dead."

Ferguson paused, slightly thrown by her insistence. Caroline heard the edge of panic in her voice and tried to damp it down without success.

"I promise you, Caroline, they're alive. The school is safe, and my boss will be sending help. I've been in Westminster for two days. I've mapped the layout, the disposition of their forces, their timetables. Everything. I need to get this information to my people so we can mount an assault..."

"What did he look like?"

"Sorry?"

"John. Lee's Dad. What did he look like?"

"Um, medium height, brown hair and eyes. Strong chin. I dunno, I didn't study him. Why?"

Caroline felt like wetting herself. She tried to rationalise it, to tell herself that no, she had been right, the man she'd killed had definitely been an imposter. But she knew.

Oh, God, she thought. What have I done?

CHAPTER SEVENTEEN

By THE TIME we reached Hemel Hempstead my arse hurt like hell. I'd done plenty of horse riding after The Cull, but not so much since Salisbury. I had shooting pains in both my legs, souvenirs of the times they really were shot, and chafing in places that, thank God, had managed to avoid being shot so far.

I got down from my horse feeling like an old man, walking bow legged and grunting the way oldsters do when they get up from an armchair.

"Behold, the mighty warrior," laughed Jack as I hobbled towards him.

I let my horse loose to graze on the patch of grass by the car park of what used to be the West Herts College.

"Tease me again and I'll shoot you in both legs," I snapped. "See how you like horse riding then."

He patted his steed on the flank and it trotted off to graze alongside its fellows.

The sun was setting. It had been a cold, rain-drenched ride and although the downpour had finally ended, the evening temperature was dropping fast.

"Is it open?" I asked, indicating the double doors that led into the main college building.

Jack nodded.

"We'll sweep it first. Just in case." This was Wilkes, leader of the six Rangers that Hood had gifted us.

Tall and solid, he was a no-nonsense Yorkshireman with ruddy cheeks and jet black hair. He'd hardly spoken to me since we'd been introduced, except to make clear that he and his men were here to help, but they'd do so on their terms and wouldn't be taking any orders from me. I didn't argue. I figured once they met Dad they'd fall into line, recognising the value of having a trained soldier in command.

The five men with him talked and joked amongst themselves, but gave me a wide berth. At least they weren't openly resentful, like the ones who'd ridden with me up from Thetford, so I supposed that was progress of a sort.

I stepped back and let them enter first, with swords drawn. Jack and I stood outside feeling foolish and cold. Five minutes later the door swung open again and one of them ushered us inside.

The college had been trashed, but there was still plenty of wooden furniture for us to chop up for firewood. Within the hour we had a big bonfire in the car park. We gathered round it for warmth and shoved foil-wrapped potatoes into the flames to roast.

No one came to investigate the fire. If there were people still living in the vicinity, they stayed away.

"I thought they'd be here by now," I said as I watched the flames consume a pile of old lab tables. "The snatchers were due to attack the kids in Hammersmith yesterday. If Dad got them out in time, they should be here."

"You think they might be having to fight their way out?" asked Jack.

"Could be," I replied.

"So how long do we wait?"

"We go at dawn, I reckon. If they're besieged, they'll need us."

"Oh, yeah, you eight guys are a hell of a rescue force."

I spun around, startled by this new voice. Tariq stepped into the firelight, gun in hand, smiling broadly.

"Don't move!" came a yell from the other side of the bonfire.

"Relax," I shouted as I got to my feet. "He's with us."

"What happened?" asked Jack, as anxious as I was at seeing Tariq here. "Did they attack the school already?"

Tariq shook his head, then indicated behind him with his hook. I stared into the darkness and realised that he was not alone. About forty children I recognised stepped forward into the orange light. They all wore their camo gear, their faces streaked with shoe polish, their hands full of hardware.

"We decided," said a boy I was shocked to realise was Green, "to bring the fight to them."

"THAT FUCKER SHOT me. Shove a knife in his throat would you, Nine Lives?"

I ignored the voice in my head as I approached Green, who sat on his own at the point where the fire's warmth ceased to give protection against the frost that was settling on the hard ground.

"Hi," I said. "You mind?" I indicated that I'd like to join him, and he waved me forward. I sat down next to him, watching the crowd mingling around the fire.

"You want to know what made me change my mind. Why I picked up a gun again and joined the team," he said. It wasn't a question. "Honestly, I don't know." There was a long pause as he considered.

"Partly it's because I feel like a grown up now," he said. "I know I'm strong enough that no-one could make me do the kind of things Mac made me do when I was part of his team."

"That was what you were afraid of?" I didn't know whether to be insulted or not. Did he really think that Jane or I would ask him to do something he didn't feel okay with?

"You don't know what it was like," he said, staring off into the distance. "You always played things your way, but I liked being a follower. It made me feel safe. It's attractive, you know? Allowing something else to make all the decisions, ceding your free will to someone else."

It wasn't attractive to me. In fact it was baffling. But I'd seen enough cults and armies to know that what Green was describing was more than simply common.

"If you do that," he continued, "then the person who's in control can make you do anything, anything at all, and you never think about the morality of it. You rationalise it away and say that it's their fault. You're just following orders. No blame attaches. It insulates you."

"But you did question it," I pointed out. "You turned on Mac. You shot him dead, mate."

"Not soon enough." He sighed. "But afterwards, when he and the school were gone and we'd relocated, I decided to treat it like a drug. I though I had to go cold turkey. No guns. No power to give orders. No clique or gang. I would be completely independent. That way no-one could ever get their hooks in me again. I couldn't fall off the wagon, be seduced into letting someone else tell me what to do."

"So it wasn't fighting you were afraid of, it was following orders?"

He nodded.

"And you don't feel that way any more?"

"No. I trust you and your Dad, and Jane and Tariq. You're good people. Plus, I know now that it wasn't a drug. I won't have a relapse because I changed when I shot Mac. It's taken me a while to realise it, but I'm a different person now. There's nothing left of the boy I was. His vices aren't mine. His weaknesses, either."

He turned his head and looked me in the eye. "Think back, Lee," he said. "To who you were before The Cull. Is there anything about that person that you recognise when you look in the mirror?"

I shook my head. "No."

"Me neither. I'm a man now," said Green, turning back to the fire. "I know my mind and I know I'm capable of choosing for myself. And right now, I choose to fight. I owe it to Matron, and to all the kids I teach."

"No, really, just stab him would you?" said the voice. "Pious little shit."

"Thank you," I told Green, pretending I didn't hear a dead man whispering in my ear. "I won't betray your trust."

Green smiled into space. "You'd better not," he said.

EVENTUALLY EVERYONE ELSE left to spend the night in the beds at the nearby hospital. I stayed put and watched the fire burn. I knew I should try to sleep, that going into battle tired is suicide. But there was no point even closing my eyes. Ferguson hadn't made contact, Dad was missing and Jane was captured.

I didn't know what to worry about most – my Dad fighting off a besieging army, Jane being tortured by a monster who treated people like dirt on his shoes, or our chances of getting cut to ribbons by landmines and gun towers sometime around teatime the next day. Whichever way I turned, things looked bleak.

As the sun rose I heard the distant engine of a lorry. I grabbed my gun and ran to the main road, careful to stay out of sight as the noise grew louder. A minute or two later a removal lorry, huge and unwieldy, rolled down the road. As it passed I caught a glimpse of the driver and ran out, waving my arms and shouting. He must have seen me in the rear view mirror because the lorry pulled up and Ferguson jumped down from the cab.

I ran to met him.

"Is my Dad with you?" I asked.

He shook his head. "I found the kids, though."

"The ones in Hammersmith?"

He nodded. A girl jumped down from the other side of the cab. Short and stocky, with an eye patch and long red hair, there was something vaguely familiar about her.

"Hi Lee," she said as she walked to Ferguson's side. My face must have betrayed my confusion, because she added: "Caroline."

"Bloody hell," I said, astonished. "We looked for you everywhere."

"I know. Matron told me."

"What?"

"Lee, did you get to Nottingham?" asked Ferguson.

"Um, yeah, there are some of your mates in the hospital. Just down the road on the right." He took off past me to compare notes with his colleagues. Caroline walked to the back doors of the lorry and opened them, revealing a small army of children huddled in the back.

"Caroline," I asked. "Have you seen Jane?"

She nodded, and something about the way the blood drained from her face told me that she did not have good news for me.

CHAPTER EIGHTEEN

"I MEANT TO ask," says Cooper as we walk the corridors of power. "Were your people responsible for taking the plane at Heathrow last week?"

"Someone took a plane?"

He examines my face closely to see if my surprise is genuine. He decides it is, and he nods.

"Yeah, a bloody 747, no less. A woman and a bloke killed a bunch of my guys and flew to New York, leaving me with four months' worth of children backed up at the airport."

"I came here to kill you," I suddenly blurt out, frustrated by small talk.

"No, you came here to kill the man who killed your brother. Your surprise prevented you from killing me. And now I've answered all your questions, you have all the facts at your fingertips. So you have a choice."

"Which is?"

"Join me or die," he says slowly, rolling his eyes, as if explaining something very simple to an idiot.

"But why offer me that choice? Why not just kill me? What makes you think I won't pretend to join up in order to save my life until I can find a way to betray you?"

He sighs and looks up at the ceiling, shaking his head at my obstinacy. "I like you, Kate. Always did. You've got, what do they call it? Pluck, spunk, guts."

"God, you really are a public school boy, aren't you."

"Plus, you know, you're not bad-looking, all told."

"Oh, thanks," I say, then a thought occurs to me. "Christ, you're not saying you want to go steady?"

"Don't be silly. I'd wake up with a knife in my heart."

"Trust me, it wouldn't get that far."

"Pity," he says with a wink, as he walks away. I trail after him as he promenades through his echoing palace, confounded. I just can't work out why I'm still alive.

"This is the central lobby," he says as we enter a huge chamber with four corridors running off it at each point of the compass. A massive chandelier hangs above our heads and statues regard us gnomically from the shadows. "Directly above us is a big tower and in it there's this huge metal contraption, like an engine," says Cooper. "No-one has any idea what it is. You see, when they were building this place they gave the contract for the central heating to a guy who said he had a revolutionary new system that he would install. Once he was done all they had to do was switch it on and voila, nice warm Palace. But when they opened it for use they switched it on and nothing happened. So they called for the guy to come explain and he'd gone. Legged it with the money! So no-one knows if this machine above is a real central heating system that turned out not to work, or a huge fake thingy put there to make the con look good!"

As he talks I realise he's enjoying himself, holding court, having an audience. And then it dawns on me that I haven't seen him speak to anyone since I arrived. He's barked orders, taken reports, had brief conversations about logistical issues, all with his fellow ex-SAS inner circle or the newly recruited chancers and religios. But I've picked up no sense of camaraderie, no friendship, just cold business.

"Jesus fucking Christ," I say as it hits. He turns to look at me.

"What?" he asks.

"You're lonely. That's it, isn't it? It's lonely at the top for the poor slave trader. You don't have any friends, only subordinates and acolytes. You don't want a girlfriend, necessarily. You just want someone to talk to."

He says nothing, but the smile has gone from his face, the mask has dropped and there's a warning in his eyes. He doesn't try to deny it, though.

"So you think I'll just hang out with you while you tell me top Parliament facts, and bitch about how hard it is pimping for a vampire? You think we'll end up buddies? That I'll gradually come to understand, to empathise and commiserate? And how do you see this ending, huh? Will I fall into your arms and soothe away your ennui, finally won over by your dignity and…"

A single, shocking slap to the face silences me. But only for a moment.

"You are fucking deluded, you know that? Look at where we are. Look at what you do. You're the fucking king, Cooper. You don't get to have friends. You get to have subjects. You don't get understanding. If you're lucky, at best you get loyalty, at worst obedience through fear and then betrayal. That's the job, your majesty. Fucking live with it."

I fall silent, breathing hard, furious and defiant.

He waits for a moment, although whether he's waiting for me or him to calm down, I'm not sure.

"You just demonstrated exactly why I want you around, Kate," he says softly, his face full of something like admiration.

"What, 'cause I think you're pitiful?"

"No. Because you kept talking even after I slapped you." He turns on his heels and walks away briskly. "Try anything clever and you'll be shot," he says over his shoulder. "See you at seven sharp for dinner."

So HERE I am, given the run of the Houses of Parliament. I'm not alone, though. I've got a shadow; a bored looking soldier who lurks around corners and watches from a distance in case I try and scale the barbed wire fences, stroll through the minefields or jump into the river... actually, that's not a bad thought.

I gaze out of a first floor window, considering the current of the Thames. I can see it swirl and roil beneath me, strong, tidal and deadly. Freezing cold, too. I dismiss the idea. It would be suicide. I glance at the ornate cornices that decorate the outside, wondering if maybe I could climb down at low tide. But no. Again, suicide.

A rope perhaps? I file that thought away.

I notice a sign directing me to the House of Lords and I figure I may as well take a look. I'm surprised to find a guard on the door. He sits on a chair staring into space, not enough wit even to read a book to pass the time. As I approach I wonder if he's in some kind of coma, but he looks up as I reach for the doors.

"You got the boss's permission to go in there?" he says, his voice a low moan of thoughtless boredom.

"No. Do I need it?"

He purses his lips and shrugs. "Knock yourself out," he says. "The one with the tattoos swings both ways. You clean up after yourself, though. If you damage anything, I mean. I'm not bloody doing it."

I have no idea what he's talking about, but I push open the door and enter the second chamber.

I'm greeted by a young black woman in a short black dress.

I stare at her for a moment, in surprise. Then my gaze moves past her to take in the room beyond. There are about twenty women here, all dressed casually. The upper benches have been made into little nests, with blankets and pillows and piles of clothing. It only takes me a moment to work out what I've walked into.

"Hey Jools, we got fresh blood!" yells the woman in front of me. A short Asian woman steps down from her nest and walks across the floor towards me. All eyes are on me.

Jools stands in front of me, hands on hips, assessing me.

"You a bit scrawny," she says. "They'll feed you up, though. You got a name?"

"Jane. I'm, um, not... Are you the boss here?"

A chorus of cackled laughter makes me blush. "Look behind you, sweetheart," says Jools. I turn and there, written across the doors in white paint is the legend: "We are your lords now. Bow down before us."

"Only boss here is Spider," she says. "But he visits me more than most, so I got his ear, like. You know?"

A woman on the bench behind her laughs and says: "You got his cock, more like!" More laughter from the ranks.

I can't help but assess Cooper's preferred concubine. My height, small hips and breasts but a pretty heart shaped face. A woman, but girlish. Tough though, streetwise.

"So that makes you, what, top dog in the harem?" I ask.

"Summat like that, yeah. So we'll get you a bed sorted then you can tell us your story."

"No," I say hurriedly. "I won't be staying."

She cocks her head and narrows her eyes, all welcome swept away by sudden suspicion.

"That so."

"I'm a doctor," I say, as if that explains anything.

"Shit, I was an MP," comes a voice from somewhere to my left. "Don't make no difference here."

"I mean," I go on, "that I'm here to help. How many of you are there?"

Jools doesn't answer.

"Are you all well? When did you last have a check up?"

"We all clean, if that's what you mean. If we weren't, we'd be in the river."

"That's not..." I'm too uncomfortable to know what to say. I'm out of my depth here.

"How many of you are there?" I ask again.

"Nineteen," says Jools.

"Okay. Thanks. I'll, um, I'll see you around, I guess."

Jools steps forward and gets right in my face, chin up, eyes wide. "Not if I see you first," she says.

I can't get out of there fast enough.

Yet as I walk away from Cooper's rape room, it occurs to me that there are nineteen women in that room, and the ones who haven't gone all Stockholm will be very angry indeed.

I have nineteen potential allies on the inside. It's not much, but it's a start.

THERE IS A special quality behind the eyes which all the men who work for Cooper have. Something cold and dead and hidden. Every one of them has it. The guy following me around Parliament is the same. It makes sense, I suppose; to be the kind of person who treats other people as cattle you must either have to kill some part of you off, or be born without it in the first place.

Whatever that part of a person it is – compassion, empathy, simple kindness – it dies easy. All it takes for it to wither away is peer pressure and time.

"What did you do? I ask him as I open my bedroom door in the morning and find him standing outside, patient as stone. "Before."

He shakes his head, unwilling to discuss it. I don't think he's one of the original SAS team. I wonder who he was, and I wonder what changed him. School teacher who watched his pupils die, perhaps? Accountant who found comfort in ledgers and spreadsheets but feels cut adrift in a world without numerical order? Drug addict forced to go cold turkey? Or just a family man who held his wife and children as they bled out?

He's a pretty nondescript bloke. Not a muscled heavy or a lean military type. He's in his early forties, slight spare tyre around the waist (which testifies to how well they eat here), receding hairline, pallid skin. The threat that he implies comes not from physical strength or bullish machismo; it comes from the way he looks at me as if I were a tiresome detail, a turd laid on new carpet by an eager puppy which has to be cleaned up. Just a bit of business.

What would his pre-Cull self have done if he had known what he would become? Rub his hands in glee or put a rope around his neck and end it all?

What would I have done, had I known who I would become?

I've not slept a wink. All night I've lain in bed staring into the darkness, trying to work out a strategy but I've got nothing.

No-one's coming to rescue me. I guess the kids we brought with us to Thetford may have made it back to the school and told them what happened, but their standing orders are to fortify and defend. There's no-one there with the authority or gumption to attempt a rescue. Anyway, it would be suicide.

Cooper still doesn't know where the school is now. The Yanks will have told him about Groombridge, but they never learned about Fairlawne, so it should be safe.

Unless I tell him. Maybe that's what he'll do – wait until he's bored with me and then torture me to get the location of the school. Rich pickings for him there.

I may have to work out a way to kill myself. But I'm not there yet. Not quite.

CHAPTER NINETEEN

IT DIDN'T TAKE long for Wilkes and Tariq to start arguing.

"I've been trained for this, mate."

"In peace time. I led the resistance against the American Army in Iraq. I have experience that you don't."

"Of getting everyone under your command killed."

"John delegated command to me if he didn't make it."

"You aren't the boss of me, mate."

"I'm not your fucking mate."

And so on until eventually Caroline shouted: "Oh why don't you just whop your cocks out right now and we can see who's biggest?" which made Jack snigger but didn't exactly help.

"Listen," I said to the council of war gathered around the fire. "We all agree we need a clear chain of command. Yes?"

Wilkes, Ferguson, Tariq, Jack and Caroline all nodded. Green just stared into the flames.

"And we all agree that if my dad were here, we'd be happy to let him lead us because of his experience and training?"

Again they all nodded.

"So we should make finding him our first priority. We know he was on his way to Hammersmith to meet up with Caroline. For some reason he never got there. We have to track him down. We can't win this fight without him."

"Lee, we have no idea where he is or what happened to him," said Tariq. "I want to find him as much as you do, but we have no leads and we don't have any more time. Jane is on the inside and God knows what they're doing to her. We have to get her first."

"Don't you think I want her safe?" I countered. "But we have no chance if we keep fighting amongst ourselves like this. We need a strategy and a leader. Dad's the only one we would all agree on."

"We could vote," said Jack.

"What?" asked Wilkes, incredulous.

"He's right," said Caroline. "We could vote. Elect a leader."

"I won't take orders from him," said Tariq, more apologetic than angry.

"Then we don't vote for a leader," continued Jack. "We vote on a plan. Chances are we're going to need to break into at least two forces anyway. As long as each group has a leader who agrees to the plan, we're fine."

"I'm not going into battle with a strategy voted for by children," said Wilkes.

"We may seem like children to you," I said, trying to keep the anger out of my voice, "but between us we've seen more combat than you."

"Do you have a better suggestion for breaking this deadlock?" asked Caroline.

Wilkes considered for a moment, then shook his head. "What do you think, Pat?"

"If we can come up with a plan we all agree on, it sounds sensible to me," said Ferguson.

I leant over and whispered in Jack's ear. "Well done, Your Majesty, you just convened your first Parliament."

WE TOOK THE discussion inside then, to one of the lecture halls of the old college. Ferguson drew a map of the enemy stronghold on the whiteboard. His attention to detail was impressive. He picked out the fences, minefields and gun towers, as well as various internal details such as where the children were being kept, and the location of the Lords' brothel.

There came a point where the level of detail began to disturb me.

"Question," I said as he picked out Spider's sleeping quarters. "How the hell did you get inside, collect all this intel and then get out again without being caught?"

"With great care and a little help."

"From?" I tried not to sound too suspicious, but failed.

"Once the lorries arrived at Westminster I got straight out and ran inside, shouting that I needed the loo. If I'd hung around, they'd have realised I wasn't their man. I'd been in the Palace of Westminster once before, on a tour, so I vaguely knew where I was heading. I made straight for the Lords." He looked expectant, waiting for us to realise something. When none of us did, he said: "The brothel."

"Jesus, Pat," said Wilkes.

"If I'd tried to hang around making sketches and stuff, I'd have been caught," Ferguson explained. "The only chance was to get in and out as quickly as possible. So I went straight to the brothel and told the guard on the door that I was a new recruit and I'd been waiting all week for some loving. He let me in, no problem."

"You sick..." began Caroline.

"Let him finish," said Tariq.

"There's about twenty women in there. Well, women and girls. They have these kind of bunks set up on the benches. Some of them got up and came over to me, but most just lay there hoping I wouldn't pick them out. I pushed the eager ones aside and picked out the youngest and most frightened girl there. I figured maybe the confident ones might not have been exactly trustworthy. The girl led me to a little nook behind the Speaker's Chair where there was a mattress.

"Her name was Tara.

"And there, in total privacy, where no-one would disturb us, I got her to tell me everything she knew about the snatchers' operation. Layout, routines, names – everything. I got lucky picking her; she paid attention.

"When she'd told me all she could, I went out the main doors again. I found an office overlooking the river – luckily it was low tide, so I climbed out and down to the shore."

He noted my look of disbelief.

"I used to be a rock climber, okay?"

I held up my hands. "Ok."

"I was inside for forty minutes at the most. Then I waited 'til nightfall, found an eyrie in one of the buildings on Parliament Square, and spent a day mapping the external defences and noting their patrols.

"Big Ben still chimes, you know. All their scheduling hangs off it.

"Happy?"

I nodded. "Sorry. Force of habit."

"Don't worry about it," he said, and went back to giving us the lowdown.

* * *

IT WAS SUNDOWN again before we all agreed a plan of action. After that there was nothing to do until morning. Tariq came and found me as I lay on a hospital bed, failing to sleep.

"So what do you think?" he asked as he sat on the next bed.

"I think it's a crazy plan, but it just might work!"

"Ha, yeah, reckon that's about it."

"What do you think, Tariq?"

He bit his lower lip and held my gaze. "I think it's the best we can do in the circumstances."

"But…?"

"But I wish John was here. What do you think can have happened to him?"

I shrugged. "God knows. Caroline says he never reached them, so somewhere between Thetford and Hammersmith something went wrong. As soon as we're done with the snatchers, I'm going to retrace his route. For all we know, he could be lying in a ditch with a broken leg or something."

"Why not go now?" asked Tariq. "We can handle the assault. You go find your dad."

I regarded him coolly. "Still don't trust me in a fight, huh? Still trying to get rid of me."

He hesitated a moment, choosing his words carefully. Then he said: "Do you remember when we rescued Jane back at Groombridge, the day John was shot?"

I nodded.

"You were… I don't know what you were like. Those Yanks were shooting at you and just walked towards them like you were bulletproof."

"So?"

"You're not bulletproof, Lee. And neither am I. I stood with you, followed your lead because I had no choice – it was either that or leave you to die. But I was sure we were dead men."

I shook my head, unsure exactly what he was getting at. "We weren't though," I said. "We won that fight."

"God alone knows how. We should have been killed a dozen times over that day. Luck like that doesn't hold, Lee. Sooner or later it runs out. You acted like a mad man. That's fine if it's only your life you're risking. But it was mine too."

"What's your point, Tariq?"

"My point is that tomorrow you're going to lead a team of children into battle against the fucking SAS and I want you to realise that you're not invincible. If you go wading in there like the Terminator, it's not just your life you'll be throwing away."

"Did I ever tell you about Heathcote?" I asked. Tariq shook his head. "He was one of my school mates. The Blood Hunters held him captive during the siege. I took a knife and slit his throat just for a chance to get close to one of the bad guys. Sacrificed him in cold blood. I'd do that a hundred times over if it meant winning."

Tariq stared at me, his face a mask. I couldn't tell if he pitied me or feared what I might do. Then he stood up and walked away without a word.

I lay back down on the bed and closed my eyes, willing myself to sleep.

But the sound of Heathcote's screams, and the hot slick feel of blood between my fingers, kept me awake 'til dawn.

CHAPTER TWENTY

IT BEGAN TO snow heavily as they split their group into three.

The younger kids who had escaped Hammersmith with Caroline were taken back to St Mark's in the removal van, driven by one of the Rangers. They had no place in a battle, and they'd be safe back at the school.

Lee, Jack and Ferguson had taken off on horseback at first light, heading for the Thames, their saddlebags heavy with ordnance.

Everyone else had piled into the three school minibuses Tariq had used to bring the team from St Mark's. They headed west, to Heathrow.

The ranks of Caroline's little army had been swollen by a bunch of the older kids from the convoy they'd attacked. There were nearly fifty of them now. Wilkes, who was in joint charge of this part of the operation alongside Tariq and Green, had insisted that there be an age limit. They'd fought over that for an hour until they'd agreed that any child under thirteen was not to be involved in the fight.

The other bone of contention had been firearms. The team from St Mark's had brought crates of various types of gun with them, and plenty of ammunition. Caroline felt strongly that every child should be given a gun, but no-one agreed with her. Too risky, they said. More chance of them shooting each other than the bad guys.

In the end they'd compromised. Only those kids who'd been trained would carry machine guns and grenades, which meant all the St Mark's lot. Her lot would be allowed handguns if they were sixteen or over. The younger teenagers could have knives, clubs, bats or that kind of thing, and they were to stay behind the kids with guns, as a second wave to mop up stragglers. Wilkes was unhappy with this compromise, but Lee and Jack insisted that the children be allowed to fight. It was, Lee said, their fight in the first place.

Caroline was relieved when Lee left. There was something behind his eyes that she didn't trust. Right up to the moment she met him again she had been unsure what she would say.

"Hi Lee, long time no see. By the way, I executed your dad the other day."

"Wow what a coincidence bumping into you! 'Cause, you see, I bumped into your dad a few days back. Yeah. Blew his brains out."

"Lee, I don't know how to tell you this, but your dad's dead. The churchies got him."

That last one had been her favourite. Blame it on Spider, get Lee fired up for the attack, make it personal. But it turned out he and Matron were together now (and by the way, euw, she was like, ten years older than him) so he had a personal stake in the attack already. Anyway, if she told him that, he'd press her for details and she was sure he'd have worked out she was lying sooner or later. Being caught in a lie like that would be worse than just staying silent.

She told herself that she was being silly, that he was an ally and a friend. But she looked into his eyes and was absolutely certain that if he knew what she'd done, he'd kill her on the spot.

So she'd played dumb, denied all knowledge.

"No, no-one approached us. We left 'cause Matron told us where the school is now and we decided to risk the journey."

She crouched behind the enormous wheel of a 747 on a Heathrow runway, wet through and chilled to the bone, but she counted herself lucky to be there. Lee had believed her and had decided to go looking for his dad only after they'd brought down the snatchers. Plus, he was off with the Rangers leading the other pincer of the attack, so she didn't have to be around him. More importantly still, the other kids who'd witnessed John's death weren't around him either. She'd not yet had a chance to take them to one side and brief them, tell them what had happened, make them swear to keep it secret. She'd have a chance to do that now, though, before they met up with Lee again.

Assuming he didn't die in the coming battle. Which, she realised guiltily, would solve a lot of problems for her. For a moment it occurred to her that if things went her way, she might get the chance to shoot him in the confusion. Friendly fire. No-one would ever know it had been deliberate. She pushed the thought aside, pretending she hadn't had it, shocked at herself.

But she had to admit, it would be convenient.

She banished the thought and focused on the task at hand. In the near distance stood a row of lorries. She counted thirty-four in total. All had the familiar red circle of the church sprayed onto their sides. They were neatly lined up in the shadow of an enormous hangar. This was their target.

Caroline watched Tariq and Wilkes as they ran from car to car through the car park that sat between the taxiway where she crouched, and the hangar.

There was one guard patrolling lazily in front of the huge sliding doors that once allowed airliners in for servicing.

When the two of them were at the very edge of the car park, Wilkes drew back the string on his bow and sent a thin shaft of wood straight through the guard's heart. He dropped without a sound.

He and Tariq broke cover, racing for the small, human-sized door that sat in the middle of the plane-sized one. When they got there they stood on either side of it, ready to deal with anyone who came out. Wilkes waved to Caroline, who in turn waved to the kids and Rangers sheltering behind the concrete wall at the end of the line of planes. As per their orders, they didn't run out. Instead they walked en masse, with Green and two Rangers at their head, older kids at the front, younger ones at the back.

When they reached her, Caroline joined them at the front. The army of children walked towards the hangar, silent and full of purpose. When the whole group stood united, she, Wilkes, Tariq and Green checked their watches and began a countdown. Then Green and Wilkes broke right while Tariq and one of the other Rangers broke left, slipping around the edges of the hangar with five armed kids in tow.

Caroline took up a position beside the door, alongside a Ranger, waving the remaining kids back against the hangar doors. The snow fell silently as they stood there, breath clouding the air, waiting for the exact moment. Eventually, after ten minutes had passed, Caroline raised her right hand and counted down from five with her fingers. When the last finger made a fist, she took hold of her machine gun, stepped back from the hanger door and, in tandem with the Ranger whose name she still hadn't bothered to ask, kicked it open and went in shooting.

The second they burst into the hangar, Caroline realised they'd made a massive mistake. All their planning had been based on the idea that the kids would be sleeping on the cold floor of the cavernous, empty space.

But in the centre of the concrete expanse stood the biggest plane

Caroline had ever seen. A guard was already running up the staircase to the door in its nose. It was the only staircase running up to the plane – the doors at the midpoint and rear of the plane were closed.

Underneath the fuselage, Caroline saw Wilkes, Tariq and their teams bursting in from the two rear doors, similarly amazed at the scale of their miscalculation.

The kids were on the fucking plane.

Caroline was closest to the moveable metal stairs and she put on a burst of speed as she registered the situation, racing to get within firing range before the guard could make it inside the plane and close the door. He had made it as far as the top step before she managed to get a bead on the man, and sent a stream of bullets thudding into him. The guard cried out, spun and toppled down the stairs, a dead weight and an obstacle.

Caroline kept running, aware of the kids streaming into the hangar in her wake.

"Don't let them close the door," came a distant, echoing yell from Tariq.

"Well, dur," she muttered as she raced towards the metal stairs.

As she reached the foot of the stairs she jumped over the still twitching corpse of the guard she had shot and began pounding up towards the door, which began to swing closed ahead of her. The men closing it were well protected behind its bulk, and she'd climbed only a few steps before she realised there was no chance at all of reaching the door in time, or getting a clear shot at the men who were closing it.

She dropped her gun and it swung free on its shoulder strap as she reached into the pocket of her fur coat and pulled out a grenade. She bit the pin and pulled it out with her teeth, never breaking her upwards stride as the gap between door and fuselage narrowed. She took three more steps and then stopped, drew back her arm and threw the grenade as hard as she could towards the tiny gap. It soared through the air and straight through a space merely twice its width.

The door slammed shut amidst a chorus of shouts from inside. There was a loud clang as the door lock was engaged and then immediately disengaged. The door began to swing open again, ever so slowly.

Then the grenade exploded, blowing a huge gaping hole in the side of the plane, sending the door, and various body parts, flying over Caroline's head. The shockwave picked her up and tossed her backwards off the staircase into the freezing cold air high above the concrete floor, which rushed up to greet her as she screamed.

CHAPTER TWENTY-ONE

"THEY BLEW THE bridge because the point where it meets the bank is their weakest spot," said Ferguson.

I panned across with my binoculars to focus on the jagged outcrop of stone that marked the opposite side of the now destroyed Westminster Bridge. I could see immediately what he meant. At the foot of Big Ben there was a patch of open ground between the wall of the Palace and the edge of the bridge accommodating some steps that led down to a tunnel entrance. The tall black fence that ringed the Palace only came up as high as the bridge, which meant that you could get inside by laying a plank of wood across the gap and leaping in. Obviously not an option when the CCTV systems were all working, but now it seemed eminently doable.

"It's called Speaker's Green," explained Ferguson.

"What's that tunnel entrance?" asked Jack.

"Westminster Tube. There are tunnels direct from the station into the Palace and that big building opposite it, the one with the black chimneys. That's Portcullis House where the MPs' offices used to be. There's a tunnel running from there under the road into the Palace as well."

"In which case we should go in underground, through the tube," I said. "They blew the bridge but they didn't blow the tunnels, did they?"

"They didn't need to," the Ranger replied. "Once the pumps shut down, the tube tunnels all flooded. The old rivers that run under the city reclaimed them. If we had scuba gear, maybe, but even then it'd be madness."

"So we go in over the fence there?" asked Jack.

"It's an option, but it's the wrong end of the building," said

Ferguson. "If we go in there we have to travel the whole length of the Palace to get where we're going, which massively increases our chances of discovery. No, our best way in is there. The Lords Library."

He pointed to the opposite end of the Palace, to the huge tower that marked its southernmost point.

"There are only two places where the Palace backs directly onto the river, and that's the towers at either end," he explained. "In between there's a bloody great terrace between the wall and the river. What we have to do is get on the water, moor at the foot of that tower, and climb in one of the windows. It's our best way of getting in undetected."

"I don't know about you, mate, but I'm not Spider-Man," I said. "There's no way in hell I'm going to be able to scale that wall."

"What we need," said Jack, "is one of those grappling hook gun thingys that Batman uses."

"Nah," said Ferguson, smiling. "We can do better than that."

Ten minutes later we climbed down from our vantage point through the ruined interior of St Thomas' Hospital, emerged into a street buried under a thickening carpet of snow, and set off in search of a dinghy.

"WHATEVER YOU DO, don't fall in, okay?" said Ferguson unnecessarily as we climbed into the small inflatable that we'd found in a River Police station half a mile upstream. "The water is freezing and the current is deadly. If you hit the water you're dead, simple as."

"But we're wearing life jackets," I pointed out.

"Don't matter," says the Irishman. "You probably won't be strong enough to swim to the shore. You'll stay afloat, but you'll freeze to death before you hit land."

"I thought Irish people were cheery, optimistic types," said Jack as he climbed carefully into the rubber boat.

"What the fuck ever gave you that idea?" asked the Ranger, untethering the boat and pushing us away from the shore.

"Um, Terry Wogan?"

Ferguson clipped his ear and handed him an oar. "Row, you cheeky sod."

There was no moon, but the world was clothed in white and the sky was still thick with falling snow. The current took us quickly and we floated out into the Thames.

"We can't use the engine, 'cause they'll hear us," explained Ferguson. "And we don't have an anchor, so the hardest thing will be to bring ourselves to a halt long enough to climb out. When I give the signal, you two need to start rowing as hard as you can against the current. Got that?"

Jack and I nodded as Ferguson used his oar to steer us as close to the bank as possible. Although the blizzard was providing us with the best possible cover, there was no point in taking foolish chances; the further out we were, the easier we would be to spot.

I was astonished at how fast we moved, and we were floating alongside Parliament within ten minutes. As we neared the farthest tower, Ferguson gave the signal. Jack and I dipped our oars and began paddling frantically against the tide, trying to slow us down. The Ranger took his bow and notched an arrow. Attached to the shaft was a small metal grappling hook from which trailed a slender nylon rope. Despite all our efforts, we continued to sweep down the river, but Ferguson did not allow himself to be distracted. As we reached the tower he let the arrow fly. It soared away into the white and although we listened, we never heard it land. But the rope didn't tumble back to the water.

He grabbed the end of the rope and looped it through one of the metal rings on the rim of the dinghy and pulled. I sighed with relief as the rope went taut and he pulled us in to the edge of the river, where the dinghy nestled underneath the concrete lip that marked the ground floor of the Palace. He tied it off and Jack and I gasped with relief as we dropped our oars. My arms were burning from the effort of rowing against a current that laughed at my exertions.

We looked up at the blue nylon rope that trailed up into the night sky. The snow was so thick now that the top of the tower was lost to view. The rope seemed to rise up into nowhere. We all pulled on the rubber-coated climbing gloves that Ferguson had looted for us from a sports store on our way into town, and put on the strange climbing pumps which were soft and lacked soles, but had rubber moulding all over, for purchase.

"Climbing in these conditions is extremely dangerous," said Ferguson. "So we'll go in the first window we come to. Take your time, don't hurry, and remember – there's no safety rope, so whatever you do, don't lose your grip."

I handed him the heavy kit bag that was the key to our success. He slung it over his back, took the rope in both hands and launched himself off the dinghy. He scrambled up over the concrete lip in no time at all. We waited until we heard a muffled crack and saw shards of stained glass tumble past us into the water. I gestured for Jack to go first.

He nervously followed Ferguson, but whereas the Irishman had been speedy and confident, Jack was all over the shop. His prosthesis slowed him down, and his fibreglass foot scrabbled uselessly against the wet concrete and he slipped backwards more than once as the nylon rope got wetter and more slippery. Eventually he also disappeared over the concrete lip and the rope went slack indicating that he'd made it inside.

I grabbed the rope and pulled myself up. Every set fracture and old bullet wound protested as I hauled myself skywards, but I focused on doing everything slowly and carefully, and managed a steady, unwavering ascent.

When I crested the concrete rim I saw a gothic arched hole where a stained glass window had nestled. I reached up to grab the window sill and two things happened in quick succession: there was a burst of gunfire from inside the room, and Jack crashed out of the window to my right, flying backwards in a cloud of glass and lead, clutching Ferguson's black kit bag, plummeting soundlessly into snowfall.

I braced my feet against the stone, looped the rope around my left hand, reached into my coat, pulled out my Browning and then pushed up with my legs, propelling my head and shoulders in through the gaping stone window frame, firing as I went.

CHAPTER TWENTY-TWO

CAROLINE HIT THE floor hard with her right shoulder, which made an awful crunching sound. She rolled with the momentum, tumbling like a drunken acrobat.

She screamed as she hit, but it was more battle cry than fear. There was anger in it too, that none of them had reckoned on so obvious a reversal of fortune. That plane was huge and made a perfect billet. Somebody should have worked that out.

When she finally stopped moving and skidded to a halt, she hurt everywhere. She just wanted to lie down, close her eyes and rest for a while. But she did what she always did in moments like this: she asked herself what Rowles would do. As soon as she asked herself that question, she opened her eyes, gritted her teeth, gripped her gun and got the fuck up.

Her shoulder was useless and there was something pulled in her left leg; her hearing was muffled and... woah... her balance was a bit off. But she limped back towards the plane, ignoring the pain.

The kids were pouring up the stairs and through the jagged blackened hole that denoted where the door had been a minute ago. Small circular windows ran the length of the plane on two levels, which meant that this plane was a double decker. The windows along the lower level were lit by the strobe flashes of gunfire; the upper windows revealed blurs of movement but no fighting yet.

She felt a hand on her shoulder and she whirled, gun raised. It was Tariq. He was looking at with concern and his lips were moving.

"Speak up," she said. "Part deaf. Explosion."

"I said are you okay?"

"What do you bloody think? Come on." She turned and kept moving towards the steps. Tariq fell in beside her as Wilkes and the ten kids that had come in the other end streamed past them towards the stairs. Caroline glanced up at Tariq, who waved them past, obviously determined to stick with Caroline.

"I don't need a baby sitter," she said.

"Well I do," he replied, still focused on the stairs ahead. "And you're the designated adult."

Caroline smiled as she swung the gun back up to her hip.

"This plane is huge," she said as they reached the foot of the stairs. The last few kids were disappearing into the belly of the plane above them.

"A380," said Tariq. "Biggest airliner ever made. Lap of luxury."

A huge explosion blew out the rear doors and a man dressed entirely in black and with an Uzi in his hand tumbled backwards out of the resulting gap in the fuselage, arms flailing. He fell onto the concrete head first, his brains and lungs suddenly finding themselves colocated.

"They do know we want some of them alive, don't they?" asked Caroline as she dragged herself up the stairs.

A man appeared in the hole above them, firing back down the body of the plane. Caroline hardly blinked as she squeezed the trigger and cut him down where he stood.

"I don't know, Caroline. Do they?" asked Tariq as she stepped into the plane.

She glanced down at the dead snatcher then looked up at Tariq and made a sad face. "Sorry," she said.

Tariq tutted as he stepped across the jagged metal edge. "Just don't let it happen again."

They turned and walked into the passenger section, guns raised, and all their wisecracks died unspoken as they beheld the carnage before them.

The two aisles were littered with corpses of children and snatchers alike. The air was thick with cordite and the walls and ceilings were sprayed with blood.

Caroline couldn't have told you whether it was her post-explosion balance problem or the sight of that charnel house which caused it, but she turned, bent over and was violently sick.

"FIFTEEN OF OUR children dead," said Tariq as he sat down next to her in the business class compartment an hour later. "Seven of yours, eight of ours. Plus the thirty-two kidnapped kids they blew up in their attempts to escape."

Caroline shook her head in disbelief. "And?"

"Two of the Rangers are down."

"Wilkes?"

"No, he's fine."

"What about captives?"

"Two. Wilkes is just getting started on them. Thought you might want to come along."

Caroline thought about this for a moment and decided that no, she really just wanted to sit here drinking this nice wine she'd found in the galley.

"Drinking before noon?" asked Tariq.

"Unless you have any other painkillers to hand, I'll stick with tried and tested if that's okay with you."

The Iraqi reached out and took the bottle from her. She glared at him, eyes narrowed.

"No, it's not okay," he said sternly. "The only thing worse than a sixteen-year-old girl with a gun and an itchy trigger finger is a *drunk* sixteen-year-old girl with a gun and an itchy trigger finger."

"Jesus," said Caroline as she stood. "Listen to Jeremy fucking Kyle. Fine, I'll lend a hand."

She limped past him and climbed the staircase to the luxury cabins that sat on the floor above.

She pushed open the cabin door and found Wilkes and Green standing over two men sat on the double bed, hands tied behind their backs.

"Have they agreed to help yet?" she asked.

Wilkes shook his head. "Not yet, but they…"

Caroline pulled a kitchen knife from her belt and before the Ranger could stop her, she leaned forward and thrust it deep into the heart of the captive nearest to her. His mouth formed an O of surprise and he let out a strangled gasp, then his eyes rolled back in his head and he slumped against the wall, stone dead.

Caroline pulled out the knife, wiped it on the sleeve of her coat and turned to the other man on the bed.

"We can do this without you, you know," she said calmly. "Your only chance to live another minute is to agree to help us. Otherwise we'll go to plan B. What do you say?"

He nodded in mute horror. Caroline patted his cheek chummily.

"Good man."

As she withdrew her hand she noticed that she'd smeared his face with blood. She pointed to her cheek. "You've got a little spot there," she said, helpfully. Then she walked out, passing Tariq who stood in the doorway, slack jawed.

"Fucking hell. That girl scares me," said Green once he'd got his breath back.

"Oh, I dunno," said Tariq. "I kind of like her."

CAROLINE LIMPED DOWN the stairs. When she reached the bottom she heard heavy footsteps following behind her.

Wilkes emerged and grabbed her arm, pulling her through business class and into the cockpit. He slammed the door and stood before it, arms folded, face red with fury.

Caroline remained composed.

"The last time an adult locked himself in a room with me, I cut out his heart with this knife," she said. "So be aware, if your hand goes anywhere near your zip, you'll lose it. And I don't mean your hand."

Having dragged her in here to give her a piece of his mind, Wilkes found himself momentarily speechless.

"Did you see the body count out there?" he eventually asked.

Caroline nodded.

"Those were children," said the Ranger. "Children! They should never have been put in that position. A battlefield is no place for a child. We can't go forward with this plan, not after this. I'm calling it off. I'm only sorry I didn't do this sooner, then maybe some of those kids would still be alive. But this ends. Now."

"Oh really," replied Caroline, her voice dripping with sarcasm. "Well that's good to know. Pass that message on to the snatchers, would you? Give them a good talking to about it. I'm sure they'll stop the kidnapping then."

"Fighting them is a job for men," said Wilkes.

"No, you sanctimonious fucker, it's a job for boys and girls," yelled Caroline. "It's not grown ups they're kidnapping. It's kids. This is our fight, their fight. Not yours. You're the outsider here." She stabbed him the chest with her index finger, jutting her chin out and shouting in his face. "Since The Cull I've met one – ONE! – adult who hasn't tried to fuck me over. Every other predatory bastard out there thinks I'm either cattle to be bartered for food or a warm body to use and toss away. So don't you fucking dare, Mr High-And-Mighty-Grown-Up-Man, tell me that children have no place in the front line. Because it's you lot who've bloody put us there. And believe me: every adult we meet is going to regret standing by and letting that happen. What does the bible say – the children shall inherit? Well that starts right now and you're either with me or against me. So shut up and help or fuck off out of my way. Because I promise you, if you try and stop me I will kill you dead."

She was breathing hard and furious when she finished her tirade, staring into Wilkes' eyes, all challenge and fire.

He stepped to one side and let her pass without saying a word.

THEY GOT ALL the children off the plane and gathered them together on the hangar floor. Green had done a head count and taken note of all their ages, so again they divided them by age. There were 132 kids under 13 amongst the 298 surviving captives. Green wanted to give one of his rousing speeches, but Tariq shook his head.

"Just let them choose," he said.

So the 166 remaining kids were given a choice to join the fight or leave with the youngsters. 45 of them chose to leave, too traumatised by the massacre they'd just witnessed. They joined the younger kids in two lorries and were sent back to St Mark's, driven to safety by the two surviving Rangers.

A third lorry, driven by one of the older kids, carried the corpses back for burial.

That left 121 new recruits who were again divided by age. 52 of them were over 16, and they were each given a firearm and an hour's group training in the hangar. The rest were set loose in the airport on a mad scavenger hunt for weapons; they returned with an impressive array of metal bars, chains and knives.

The sun was setting when they gathered by the lorries that were painted with the red circles. Wilkes stepped forward and shot the lorries up a bit, making it look as if they'd survived an attack. Then the army of children hid their weapons under their clothes, piled into the containers and got ready for war.

As Tariq watched the kids climb into the containers her felt a tug at his jacket and turned to find a familiar face looking up at him.

"They won't give me a gun," pouted Jenni.

Tariq smiled, glad to see she was still alive. "That's because you're still only thirteen."

"But you gave me a gun before and I managed not to accidentally shoot anybody with it," she said. "Please, Tariq. Pretty please."

He reached into his kit bag and handed her a Browning. "Okay, but don't tell the guy with the bow and arrow, all right?"

The girl went up on tiptoes and kissed Tariq on the cheek. "You're a sweetheart," she said.

The Iraqi was surprised to find himself blushing. Jenni secreted the gun inside her coat, but didn't move to join the other kids in the lorry. She glanced around furtively, as if looking for someone, then pulled him down the side of the lorry, out of sight.

"Listen," she said. "There's something you should know about John Keegan..."

THE SURVIVING SNATCHER was installed behind the driver's seat of the lead vehicle. He was in his mid-thirties, solid and capable looking, dressed in combats. Tariq thought that if he'd had to kill one of the captives, this was the one he'd have killed; the one Caroline stabbed had been snivelling and broken. This one was more composed. The Iraqi sat beside him, knife in his lap.

"Here's what you have to do," he said. "You lead the convoy to Parliament. If we're challenged when we arrive, you say Heathrow came under attack by unknown forces and you managed to escape. All we want to do is get inside the perimeter fence. Once we're in, I swear you'll be free to go. Understand?"

The snatcher nodded and turned the ignition.

They drove through the night, making slow progress down roads clogged with vehicles abandoned by the fleeing masses during The Culling Year.

The snow came down in thick, solid looking flakes, reducing visibility and making the going harder as they progressed. For a while Tariq thought they wouldn't make it, but as the day drew to a close they pulled up outside the tall black metal fence that ringed the Palace of Westminster. Big Ben loomed above them in the blizzard, marking the time as twenty past seven. They were actually a little early but that was okay.

The light was pre-dawn murky and the air was thick with snow as the snatcher honked his horn.

"Remember, once we're in, you can go," said Tariq, knife in hand. "Just don't try anything."

A minute later there was a knock at the window. The driver wound it down.

"What the fuck you doing here, Tel?" asked the guard, shivering despite the thick Puffa jacket he was wearing.

"We had a bit of business, mate," said the snatcher. "Someone attacked us at the airport. Had to evacuate. Let us in, will you? I'm bloody freezing."

"You and me both. All right, put them underground." The guard stepped back and waved them forward.

The gate swung open and the three lorries pulled into the courtyard. The snatcher swung the lorry round and drove down a concrete ramp into the underground car park. He pulled into a bay and switched off the engine. The other two lorries pulled up alongside.

Tariq opened the door and stepped out. He gave the thumbs up to Wilkes, who sat in the cab of the adjacent lorry, looking unenthusiastic.

But Tariq's triumph was short-lived. There was a cacophony of boots as men streamed down the ramp and burst through the interior doors, machine guns in hand.

Tariq stood frozen to the spot as the lorries were encircled by ten very well armed, very angry looking soldiers. The guard from the gate stepped forward and met the snatcher who had driven the lorry, by now out of the cab and running to meet his comrades. He took a gun from the guard and walked up to Tariq, smiling.

"I didn't give the password, dipshit," said the snatcher. "What, you think we're amateurs? We're SAS, pal. And you are really going to regret fucking with us."

CHAPTER TWENTY-THREE

I CAN HEAR Big Ben chiming midnight as I lie in bed, unable to sleep.

I've been given a room in the Speaker's Cottage. It's luxurious, furnished with lovely antiques that have been polished to a fine lustre, and the flock wallpaper feels expensive. The bed is huge and comfy, the eiderdown deep and warm. The window looks out over the river and catches the rising sun in the morning. It's a very nice room indeed.

But it's a gilded cage. Cooper sleeps next door in an even more opulent chamber, and when he escorts me to bed in the evening he locks my door so I cannot sneak out and kill him as he sleeps.

I lie awake listening to the creaks and echoes of this old building as the night cold grips its bones. I can hear Cooper pacing the floor. He's not exactly walking up and down outside – he ranges wider than that – but every few minutes his soft footfalls pass by my room and I hold my breath, listening for the key in the lock. So far he's always kept walking, but this time around he's stopped outside my door.

Silence falls as I lie there, holding my breath, waiting for him to enter or leave. He's been there for five minutes now. What is he doing? Listening at the door? Wrestling with his conscience? Plucking up the courage to come in? The silence lasts so long that I begin to doubt what I heard. Maybe I just didn't hear him leave. He can't have been standing out there, motionless, for so long, can he? That's paranoid.

Yet I feel that just by listening for him I've been drawn into a deadly game of cat and mouse. I consider getting out of bed, creeping to the door and peering out the keyhole. But if he hears me moving around that may catalyse a decision, lead directly to him entering.

So I lie here, listening to the sound that is no sound – the sound of a man trying to decide my fate.

I was surprised when I found the women in the Lords. Not because I didn't realise such a place probably existed – armed men who run internment camps have always kept women for their use, from the comfort women to the women kept alive for 'special duties' in the concentration camps. No, what really surprises me is that Cooper visits them himself. He had been so insistent that he never had any of the women or girls that he trafficked before The Cull. I believe him, too. Now, it seems he no longer feels the need for such restraint. He even has a favourite. I wonder what insight Jools might be able to give me into the real man.

I resolve to go and talk to her again in the morning. My movements around the Palace are not restricted, but I am closely watched and another visit to the Lords risks arousing Cooper's suspicion. Still, I need allies, and those women are the best I can hope for right now.

I hear a sound outside my window, like a sharp crack. The air is thick with snow and all sound is muffled, so I have no idea where it came from or what it was. A drifting boat bumping against the embankment, perhaps?

There are no more sounds and I realise that it distracted me. Has Cooper crept away while I wasn't paying attention?

The silent waiting resumes. Another five minutes pass and I can feel my eyelids starting to droop in spite of myself. Sod this, I think. I'm going to sleep. I turn over, pull the eiderdown up to my cheek, and close my eyes.

The instant I do this I hear a loud banging on the door of the cottage. My eyes snap open. I hear Cooper turn and walk away from my door – so he was still there! – and go to answer. I have a feeling that whatever has occurred may provide an opportunity, so after a second's consideration I jump out of bed and pull on my jeans, jumper and shoes.

I tiptoe to the door, grabbing a glass from the dressing table as I do so, placing it against the thick wood, trying to hear what's going on. It's hopeless, though; all I can hear is the muffled drone of their conversation.

Then there are hurrying footsteps coming my way. I leap backwards as the key is thrust into the lock. I stand in the middle of the floor, fully dressed, no point trying to pretend I was asleep. The door opens and Cooper stands framed there for a moment, surprised to find me up and about. His surprise soon passes.

"Kate, I need your help," he says. "Come with me, please."

Over his shoulder I can see one of his goons standing expectantly in the hallway, machine gun at the ready.

"Help with what?" I ask, not moving.

He pulls a handgun from his waistband. "You'll see," he says. He steps forward, grabs my wrist and pulls me after him.

"Hey!" I protest, but he spins and snarls at me with such menace that I'm momentarily silenced. Even when he slapped me he seemed in control, but in this brief instant I catch a glimpse of a different Cooper – furious, savage and ruthless, almost feral.

'Ah-ha,' I think. '*There* you are!'

He drags me down a small winding back staircase to the ground floor, through a series of carpeted corridors – green carpet, meaning we're in the Commons – then into the corridor that joins Commons to Lords, through the central lobby and up to the closed doors of the Lords itself.

There are six or seven of his soldiers gathered at various vantage points, all with their guns trained on the doors. The air smells of cordite. Unconcerned by the fact that his men are staying in cover, Cooper walks right up to the doors, still pulling me behind him. He stands in front of the doors for a moment then kicks them open and strides into the ornate, high-ceiling chamber.

The women are gathered in a line on the back bench to my left. They're all sitting bolt upright with their hands upon their heads, eyes wide and fearful. In the middle of the room, on the big red cushion they call the woolsack, stands a man in a hoodie with a bow and arrow. The string is taut, the shaft of the arrow aimed straight at Cooper's heart. My mind races. This is one of Hood's Rangers. Have they decided to take Cooper down? Is this the beginning of an assault? I feel a momentary rush of hope but then damp it down. There's no firing from anywhere in the building, no sounds of combat or attack. No, this is one man. Here to deliver a message, maybe?

It occurs to me that it might actually be Hood himself.

Cooper pulls me to his side, wrapping his left arm around my throat and holding his gun to my temple.

"Drop it or she dies," he yells.

The hooded man stands there, unmoved. He doesn't say a word.

Cooper lifts the gun an inch and fires a round just over my head, deafening me and making me yelp in surprise. I inwardly curse myself for being such a wuss. This is the point where I should bite his wrist or stamp on his foot, distract him for a moment and run for it. But there's a small army behind me and only one man ahead.

"I dunno who you think I am, but I have no idea who that woman is. Why should I care if she lives or dies?" The Ranger has a thick Irish accent. Not Hood, then. He's a bit shit, too, 'cause I've never met him before in my life but already I can tell he's bluffing.

Cooper drops the gun so it's pointing at the floor. For a moment I think he's backing down but then, the instant before he fires, I realise what he's about to do.

"No," I shout, but my cry is drowned out by the percussive blast that sends a small lump of lead into my right foot.

I scream in agony and go limp, unable to stand. Cooper's arm is tight around my neck, holding me upright. I begin to choke. As the blood pounds in my ears and my vision blurs I hear a voice shouting:

"All right, all right! We surrender!"

Lee?

CHAPTER TWENTY-FOUR

"I'm sorry about that, Kate," said the man I assumed was Spider as he handed Jane the syringe.

She took it without making eye contact and stuck it into her ankle, depressing the plunger. A few moments later her shoulders relaxed as the morphine did its work.

I knelt on the hard tiled floor of the central lobby with my hands on my head, fingers interlaced. The muzzle of a rifle rested gently on the nape of my neck, ready to end me if Spider gave the order. Ferguson was on his knees next to me in the same predicament. I'd counted seven soldiers in the lobby with us, mostly dressed in black or combats, all heavily armed. I could tell they were proper soldiers, not followers who'd joined after The Cull; something about their bearing and expressions told me they were professionals.

Corridors ran off the circular lobby in four directions, and white statues stood against the walls, regarding us coldly.

Spider was physically unprepossessing. Of slightly less than average height, he had blond hair and blue eyes but lacked Brad Pitt's good looks. He didn't have that quality of madness about him that Mac or David had possessed, nor the world weary doggedness of Blythe. He seemed kind of ordinary.

I didn't doubt he'd have killed Jane, though.

Ordinary, then, but dangerous.

"Do you have a surgeon?" asked Jane through gritted teeth. She sat on a chair against the far wall, white as a sheet.

"I'm afraid not," he replied, seeming genuinely apologetic. "We make do and mend."

Kate grimaced. "Fine," she said. "How about antibiotics?"

"Yes, we have those."

"Good. I want to get over to St Thomas', I can patch myself up there, assuming any of the equipment still works."

"I'll detail one of my men to take you there now." The boss nodded to a soldier to his left, who stepped forward and helped Jane to stand.

She hopped away but just before she left the lobby she turned and said: "Oh, and Cooper?"

Spider, who had been staring at me intently with a nasty smile on his face, looked away.

"Yes, Kate?"

"If you hurt either of them. At all. I will kill you."

He laughed. "Oh, Kate, please. You didn't manage to exact revenge last time. What makes you think you'll manage it this time?" He paused for effect, then said: "Don't worry. They'll still be here when you get back. Probably."

She limped around the corner and Spider turned to us again. He knelt in front of me.

"Five years I've been running things here," he said. "Five years. I have a team of highly trained, heavily armed special forces at my disposal and an army of daft religious nutters out there who think I'm the representative of the Messiah. In all that time I've had plenty of people try to break out of here, but no-one's ever been stupid enough to break in before. Why on God's Earth would you do such a stupid thing?"

"Good question," I answered.

"It wasn't rhetorical," he said, allowing an edge of menace to creep into his voice.

"Should I call you Spider or Cooper?" I asked.

He appeared to consider this seriously. "You can call me Cooper," he said at length.

"Well, Coop, I guess you could say I have a compulsion."

"What would that be, then?"

"I feel compelled to hunt down murderous bastards and wipe them out."

He narrowed his eyes and pursed his lips, considering my admittedly weak bravado.

"And how's that worked out for you?"

"Well, three years ago me and my friends managed to wipe out a cannibal cult that was terrorising the countryside. Not as well armed as you guys, but they were all naked and bathed in fresh human blood, so they were a little scarier, I think."

"Good for you."

"And then, of course, there was the Americans."

"Excuse me?"

"The Americans army invaded a couple of years back. You may have missed the memo."

"No, no, believe me, I got that one."

"They didn't last long."

Cooper barked a sudden laugh and clapped his hands.

"Are you trying to tell me," he said, "that you single-handedly fought off the US Army?"

"Not single-handedly, no. I had an eleven-year-old boy helping me. But essentially, yeah."

"And how did you do that, exactly?"

"We nuked the fuckers."

"You nuked the fuckers."

"Yup."

He stared deep into my eyes. I stared back and smiled.

"You know," he said. "I almost believe you. And this is how you go about killing bad guys, is it? You wander into their bases with some stupid plan and get yourself captured?"

The soldiers standing around us sniggered.

"Um, actually yeah, it kind of is."

And then what do you? Manufacture some miraculous escape? Call in the cavalry? Light the Bat-signal?"

More laughs.

"No, I just wait."

"For?"

"A mistake."

He leaned in close 'til I could feel his hot breath on my face. "I don't make mistakes, kid."

He held my gaze for a moment then asked: "So how do you know Kate? No, wait, let me guess. You're one of the boys from St Mark's, yes?"

I nodded.

"I used to go to school there," he said. Which teachers survived The Cull?"

"Bates and Chambers."

"Didn't know Bates. Liked Chambers, though. Maybe I'll have him over for dinner once I've taken the school."

I shook my head. "Nah, he died a while back."

"Pity. Where is the school now, by the way? I sent a team there last year and it was just a burnt out wreck."

"We're somewhere you'll never find us."

"I could torture you. You'd tell us eventually."

"I was waterboarded in Iraq, pal. Bring it on."

Again he laughs. "Iraq, now? I can't decide if you're a superhero or a fantasist or both. You're certainly entertaining, I'll give you that. Final question: how long have you and Kate been together?"

"If you mean Jane, she's my Matron and that's all."

"She may be Jane when she's at school, but here she's Kate. Trust me on that. And you're lying, but I don't hold it against you. I should probably keep you alive, use the threat of killing you to make her tell me where the school is. But something tells me that you're more dangerous than you seem. So, firing squad at dawn, I reckon."

I just smiled at him. Our part of the plan might have failed, but if Tariq and the others kept to their schedule, they'd be here before dawn. I looked sideways and saw the snow falling through a far off window and bit my lip.

"Dear God, you're amateur," said Cooper as I glanced back at him. "Never played much poker, did you?"

He stood up then and turned to one of his soldiers.

"These two aren't the whole story. There's someone else coming, another attack. They're supposed to be here by dawn, but he's worried they won't make it because of the snow. Spread the word to be ready."

Cooper looked down at me contemptuously. "I used to be a copper, lad. I know all the tells."

He turned to Ferguson. "And you, Green Arrow, what's your story?"

Ferguson didn't say a word, he just stared straight ahead, jaw clenched tight.

"Smart man," said Cooper after a moment's silence. "I'll tell you what I think. I think you're one of these Rangers I've been hearing reports about. I think you've teamed up with these school runts. Quite the little power base. My question is this: is the next attack your lot?"

Ferguson stayed silent.

Cooper clapped his hands once, as if about to sum up at the end of a staff meeting. "Right then. Lock the boy up. Take the man and start chopping bits off him until you find out everything you can about his organisation. When Kate gets back, bring her to me. Double the patrols and issue extra ammunition."

He turned his back on us and walked away.

"I'm off to bed," he said cheerily. "I want to be fresh for the firing squad."

CHAPTER TWENTY-FIVE

CAROLINE FELT LIKE crying.

She'd spent so long fighting these bastards, trying to keep the children safe, trying to avoid ending up exactly where she was now – locked up, weaponless, powerless, cattle waiting to be shipped to the slaughter.

When the lorry had come to a halt she'd given the order for the kids to get their weapons out and be ready. They'd crouched there in the dark waiting for the back of the container to open, ready to pour out and finally take their revenge. But when the doors swung open she found herself staring down the barrels of about fifteen machine guns. She heard gasps and cries of alarm from the children ranged behind her. There was a moment of stillness during which Caroline was sure they were going to open fire, kill them all there and then. But the moment passed and one of the soldiers ordered them to get out one at a time and throw their weapons on the floor as they did so.

Caroline was at the front, so she got down first and tossed her gun on the ground. She was then frisked and sent to stand in the corner where she was covered by two guns. The children in both lorries went through the same procedure until they were all standing together, penned in, surrounded by guns.

She looked for the adults – Tariq, Wilkes, Green – but they were nowhere to be seen. They must have been taken away the second they arrived. She wondered if they'd been shot already. She tried to reassure the other children, but half of them were from St Mark's and didn't know who she was.

"Why should we listen to you?" sulked one boy, and she didn't have an answer for him.

She wanted to tell them that all was not lost, that they were only half the attack and if they just held their nerve Lee, Ferguson and the kid with the limp would be coming to rescue them. But the soldiers could have overheard her, so she kept her mouth shut.

When the last of the children had been unloaded, the soldiers marched them up the stairs into the Palace of Westminster. They went down a narrow corridor lined with heavy wooden doors and were herded into a big room dominated by a series of tables arranged in a square. Each sitting had a computer screen mounted in it, so Caroline reasoned it was some kind of committee room.

When all the children had been crammed inside, one of the soldiers stepped forward to close the door.

"For you, Tommies, ze var is over!" he said as he pulled the door shut. She heard some of his colleagues laugh as the door slammed shut and the lock turned.

She turned to see her army. An hour ago they were a heavily armed bunch of feral kids ready to kill any adult they encountered. Now they were just a bunch of scared, powerless children, jostling for space in a too-small room.

Behind them, huge leaded windows reached to the ceiling. The first light of dawn broke over the buildings that ranged along the opposite bank of the river.

"UM, MILK, TWO sugars," said Tariq. And then, instinctively, without thinking: "Thanks."

Green flashed him an amused look. "Tariq, mate, they're going to kill us. I don't think we should be thanking them for putting sugar in our tea."

Wilkes just glowered.

"Who said anything about killing you?" said the man who entered the room rubbing sleep from his eyes and yawning. He turned to the soldier who was pouring tea for the prisoners. "Bill, did you say we were going to kill them?"

The soldier shook his head. "No, Sir."

"Thought not. Carry on. Oh, and a tiny splash of milk and one sugar for me too, while you're at it. Ta."

The man sat at the head of the conference table and leaned back in his chair, rubbing his hands through his bed hair. He looked at Green. "You're English, right? And you, your accent is... what?"

"I am Iraqi," said Tariq, proudly.

The man nodded. "You have a touch of Black Country in your accent, though. Learned it from squaddies, at a guess. Yes?"

Tariq nodded.

"You can call me Spider, I'm in charge here," said the man as he reached out to take the mug of tea his subordinate was proffering. He stirred it thoughtfully. "You gentlemen would be the second pincer of the St Mark's attack, am I right?"

The three captives sat silently.

"Yes, I am," said Spider. "I noticed that when I said that, you gulped," he nodded at Green, "and you glanced ever so briefly at the table," he pointed at Wilkes. "Dead giveaways."

He took a sip of tea. "So let me fill you in," he said. "Your advance team botched it. One of them is floating out to sea, the other two – Lee and one of your colleagues", he indicated Wilkes, "are in custody as we speak. My men have been torturing the Ranger but he's stayed silent. So far. Master Keegan is languishing in a committee room, contemplating his fate. I intend to have them shot in," he glanced out of the window at the pink light bleeding across the rooftops, "ooh, about half an hour."

The soldier placed mugs of steaming tea in front of the three captive men.

"You three have a chance to avoid being executed," continued Spider. "If, and only if, you answer all of my questions quickly and completely."

Tariq folded his arms and shook his head. "No chance," he said.

"But they're quite simple," replied Spider. "For example, number one: were you really responsible for the destruction of Operation Motherland and the American army at Salisbury?"

"Oh, hang on, wait a minute, I know this one," mugged Tariq, scratching his head, scrunching his eyes up and thinking hard. Eventually he opened his eyes and beamed in triumph. "I know. The answer is: yes we fucking were! How many points do we get? I want lots of points for that one!"

Green stifled a laugh. Wilkes continued to glower.

"And you, funny man, would I be right in thinking you met Lee in Iraq?"

Tariq nodded.

"So, not a fantasist after all," said Spider thoughtfully, sipping his tea. "Good. Next question. I understand your role in this abortion of a plan. Trojan horse, army of children. Very *Lord of the Flies*. But what was the role of Lee and his team? I know your attack was planned for dawn, so what were he and the Ranger going to do during the night? What trap were they planning to spring? Or were they just a diversion in case you couldn't get in the gates?"

Tariq smiled smiling, holding Spider's gaze, giving nothing away. He shook his head slowly.

"Sorry mate," he said. "Don't know that one. Ask me something about movies. I'm good with movie questions."

"All right," said Spider, putting down his tea. "Here's one: you know that moment in the final act of an action movie, when the wisecracking hero gets captured by the bad guy who interrogates him but, realising he's getting nowhere, tells a lackey to kill the supporting character and then leaves the room, enabling the hero to overpower the lackey, escape, and win the day?"

Tariq's smile faltered for a moment, and something behind his eyes changed. Then the smile returned, although it was sadder than before, knowing and resigned. He took a deep breath and nodded.

Spider put his tea down, reached into his trouser pocket, pulled out a handgun, raised it casually, and shot Tariq right between the eyes.

"My question is this," said Spider as the gun smoke drifted across the table. "Why does the bad guy never just shoot the hero himself?"

The Iraqi sat there for a moment, his eyes wide with surprise, the smile still fixed on his frozen face. Then he crumpled forward, his shattered skull hitting the table with a solid crack. Blood pooled around his head as it shook and juddered then eventually lay motionless.

Spider moved his arm slightly to the left so the gun was pointing at Green.

"I'll ask again," he said. "What was their role in your attack?"

Green sat transfixed, staring at his dead friend, tears pooling in his eyes.

Spider reached up and ostentatiously chambered a round.

"Diversion," whispered Green after a moment. "They had a bag of grenades. They were going to set off some explosions at the south end of the complex when the kids came through the gates. Draw your forces away."

Keeping the gun trained on Green, Spider turned his gaze to the soldier by the door.

"We didn't find a bag of grenades, did we Bill?" he asked.

"No," replied the lackey. "But the one who went out the window, he had a big kit bag with him. That was probably it."

Spider lowered the gun and nodded satisfied. "Good," he said.

"Now if only your smartarse friend there had told me that earlier he could have enjoyed, oh, another half an hour of breathing."

Spider stood up and walked to the door. "Put these two in the Moses Room with the boy, then assemble a firing squad on Speaker's Green."

"And the body, Sir?"

Spider glanced at Tariq's corpse absent-mindedly as he walked past. "Oh, toss it in the river."

CHAPTER TWENTY-SIX

I SAT BENEATH the huge fresco of Moses bringing the tablets down from Mount Sinai, and made an accounting of all the ways in which I had fucked things up. It was a pretty impressive list. Dad was missing, Jack was dead, Ferguson and I were prisoners, and Matron had been shot. With our part of the attack prevented and Cooper expecting trouble, there was a very good chance Tariq and Caroline's forces would be wiped out the second they arrived.

It looked like Tariq was right. I would shortly be getting everyone killed.

"Feeling sorry for yourself, Nine Lives?" Mac whispered in my ear. "Don't be pathetic. Take your lumps. This is the third time you've gone strolling into enemy territory. The third time you've baited the bad guy in their lair. How did you think it would end? Did you really think you were invincible? Frankly, I'm surprised he didn't shoot you dead in the Member's Lobby. He looked the type."

I paced the room, ignoring my internal heckler, looking for a way out. But the place was buttoned up tight. There were guards outside and nothing in here I could use.

Eventually I sat down in the chairman's seat at the head of the huge square of tables, put my feet up on the polished desk surface, and tried to sleep.

I couldn't think of anything else to do.

"HOW THE FUCK do you sleep at a time like this?"

The voice startled me awake and I jerked in alarm, unbalancing my seat and toppling myself in a heap on the floor. That such a quality piece of slapstick didn't elicit any laughter was my first clue that things were even worse than I realised. When I'd gathered my wits and looked up to see Green and Wilkes standing over me, I felt a knot of fear solidify in my stomach.

"Surprise," said Wilkes dourly, pulling out a chair and sitting down wearily.

I scrambled to my feet, the implications racing through my head. All my questions died in the face of their presence as one by one the obvious answers presented themselves. In the end there was only one thing left to ask.

"Where's Tariq?"

When Green also took a seat, not meeting my eyes, that answer also became apparent.

"How?" I ask eventually.

"Spider," said Green.

"Short guy? Blond?"

Green nodded.

"His name's Cooper," I said. "Spider's his stage name. Cooper sounds a lot more ordinary, doesn't it? Less menacing, more suburban. Call him Cooper, robs him of some of his power, I reckon."

"Whatever you fucking call him," growled Wilkes through gritted teeth, "he shot your pal in cold blood less than five minutes ago."

"I don't think he likes you," whispered Mac.

"Where are the kids?" I asked.

"No idea," said Green. "They took us away before they opened the lorries. I reckon they've got them locked up somewhere. That's assuming they didn't just leave them in the lorries and drive them back to Heathrow."

I shook my head. "Not in this snow."

"Did you not hear me?" barked Wilkes, red in the face and suddenly furious. "Your friend is dead, Keegan. Does that not register?"

To be honest, it didn't. I'd seen so much death, lost so many friends and comrades, Tariq's death just added a digit to the death count. I didn't think anybody's death could affect me any more. Maybe even Jane's. I knew I'd do anything to save her, but if I imagined her death it left me cold. I knew that whatever happened I'd just carry on living. I didn't think I could be any more damaged than I already was.

"Jack's dead too," I said, as if it were an answer to his question. "We were caught before I even got in the window. He ended up in the river. Did you know he was the rightful King of England?"

"What?" Wilkes looked at me as if I was a madman.

"No really. King John. Honest," I said. "He was being looked after by the military when we met him. He kept it very quiet, though. Didn't want anyone to know. Just wanted to be one of the gang. Someone out there became the monarch earlier tonight. But whoever they are, they'll probably never know."

Wilkes shook his head in disbelief. "You are a bunch of fucking loonies. How the hell did we ever let ourselves get involved with you? I should kill you right now, you little shit."

"Easy," said Green, his voice stern with warning. The sight of this slight teenager telling the burly Ranger to behave was laughable, but such was the authority in Green's voice that Wilkes just clenched his jaw and turned away in disgust, done with the pair of us.

"Ferguson's alive too, in case you were wondering," I said archly. "I think they're torturing him at the moment, trying to get intel on your lot."

Wilkes didn't say a word.

"Fine, you have a good sulk," I said. "Green and I will try and come up with a plan to get us out of here."

Green laughed. "We'd better be quick," he said. "They're assembling a firing squad right now. The guy who marched us here said we'll be dead on the last strike of eight o'clock."

"There's still Jane," I pointed out.

"You saw her?" he asked.

"Yeah, she was here. She got shot by Cooper and went to a hospital to patch herself up. She knew his name, and he called her Kate."

"Kate?"

"Hmm. It's her real name, from before she came to work at St Mark's. She was there under witness protection. And Cooper said he used to be a copper. I wonder."

"You think they knew each other before The Cull?"

I nodded. "It's possible. I didn't get the impression she was a prisoner here. Not like you'd think, anyway. Jane's our ace in the hole. When she gets back, she might be able to influence Cooper somehow. I don't know."

"You're clutching at straws, kid," sneered Wilkes. "We're dead. Simple as."

As if to prove his point, the door to the committee room swung open and a tall soldier stood framed in the entrance.

"Up," he barked.

We all got to our feet and shuffled towards the door.

"Get a fucking move on," shouted the lackey.

As we walked down the long corridor between the Lords and Commons, on our way to be executed, I was surprised to find that I wasn't nervous. I recalled the terror I felt when the Blood Hunters wrapped that noose around my neck and dropped me into space, or the fear when Blythe pulled the lever of the electric chair, or the desperation when I realised Rowles was about to blow us to dust. The urge to live, the fear of death, were strong in me then.

But now I just felt numb, empty, resigned. Maybe even a little relieved. I'd been shot before and it hadn't started to hurt until a good few minutes afterwards. The nice thing about a firing squad is that there aren't any minutes afterwards. I reckoned it'd be a painless death, give or take. And once it was done there'd be no more fighting. I wouldn't have to bury any more friends. I wouldn't have to sit Dad down and explain about Mum.

It's not as if I was looking for an opportunity to die, but I admitted to myself that I wasn't that upset about the prospect of it. Tariq had been wrong, I realised as I walked. I didn't wish for death. I was simply indifferent to it.

We passed through a stone archway out into the cold dawn air. The patch of grass that sat between the walls of the Palace and the edge of Westminster Bridge was almost knee deep in drifted snow. A gaggle of armed men huddled against the wall, smoking cigarettes and gossiping quietly. They fell silent as we processed into the yard.

The man walking with us waved for us to line up against the metal fence, facing Parliament with the river at our left.

We crunched over to the fence and stood there, unsure exactly what to do.

There was an awkward silence as we stood there facing our executioners, who looked everywhere but at us, unwilling to risk meeting our gaze.

"Look at us," shouted Wilkes after a minute that seemed like an hour. "Fucking look at us!"

One by one they obeyed, and as they did so I saw their expressions harden, their faces set. These were not the kind of men to have doubts. When it came to the crunch, they were stone cold.

"Lovely day for a shooting," said Cooper as he strode into the yard. Jane limped behind him, her foot encased in a blue plastic cast. She looked at me and her face crumpled. I'd not seen her cry in so long. I wanted to run to her but I knew I wouldn't get two feet.

"Cooper, please," she said, choking back tears. "I'm begging you, don't do this."

He turned, raised his hand and slapped her hard across the face. She reeled.

"Fucker," I shouted, stepping forward. A stream of bullets thudded into the snow in front of me and I looked left to see one of the soldiers waving me back to the fence.

"I'll do anything you want," begged Jane, trailing forlornly after the man who held our lives in his hands.

He stopped when she said that, a terrible smile creeping across his face. He turned back to her again, slowly this time, full of menace.

"And what, exactly, do you think I want from you, Kate?"

She stepped forward, her red, tear-stained face contorted into a grotesque parody of pleasing. She reached out and stroked his chest.

"I can be anything you want, Cooper," she said. "Anything at all. Just please, don't kill them."

For the first time that day I actually felt an emotion – pure, burning fury. I bit back my protest and clenched my fists, rooted to the spot.

Cooper reached out a hand and stroked Jane's cheek once, gently. Then he leaned forward as if to kiss her, stopped an inch from her lips and said: "Just another whore, then."

He stepped away, turned his back on her and barked an order to his soldiers.

"Put her with the men."

"Sir?" asked the guy who seemed to be second-in-command, surprised by the order.

Quick as lightning, Cooper drew his sidearm and shot the man twice in the chest.

"I said, put her with the others," he yelled as his lackey toppled backwards into the snow.

Another of his men, eyes wide with alarm at his leader's sudden, shocking loss of composure, stepped forward, grabbed Jane's arm, and dragged her over to us.

She took her place alongside me, facing the firing squad. I reached out my hand and our fingers intertwined and grasped tightly.

She leaned over and tried to whisper something to me, but the huge bell in the tower above us began to chime.

The soldiers began to line up.

The first strike of eight o'clock sounded, sonorous and familiar.

They checked their weapons.

The second chime of the hour.

They all flicked off their safety catches.

Third chime.

Cooper bent down and lifted the machine gun from the corpse of the man he'd just shot.

Fourth chime.

He joined the line of executioners.

Fifth chime.

He flicked off his safety catch.

Sixth chime.

He raised his weapon.

Seventh chime.

He shouted "Make ready!"

I turned to Jane and embraced her, clasping her tightly to me, ready for death, eyes closed, ears ringing.

"I love you," I whispered as the clock struck eight.

CHAPTER TWENTY-SEVEN

I BALANCE THE torch on the table then take the scalpel and carefully slice down the side of my shoe, just above the bit where it meets the foam sole. Every tiny movement sends a shock of pain through my foot, so I go slowly. I'm in a small office, sitting in a padded chair, foot up on the table in front of me.

St Thomas' hospital has been pretty much gutted. When The Cull hit, I was safe at St Mark's, riding it out behind thick metal gates in the middle of the countryside. I can't imagine what it must have been like here in a hospital. The flood of sick people, all dying, incurable, hopeless and doomed. The doctors, succumbing themselves one by one but trying to keep the service going as long as possible, filling the beds and trolleys and corridors with sufferers, all hooked up to drips. At some point they must have started euthanising people, adding extra morphine to the intravenous bags, putting people out of their misery. I imagined the final deaths, when there were no more doctors left, the last surviving patients lying here in a building strewn with corpses, feverish and delirious, dying mad and raving.

In our hunt for medicine we came across a small supply room in which sat a skeleton. It wore a white coat and a bottle of pills lay beside its outstretched hand. A doctor or nurse, immune but broken by the horror of it all, retreating into a darkened closet and gulping down pills to make it stop.

I looked at that skeleton and thought that could have been me, if my brother had never got involved with Spider, if I'd completed my medical training, become a doctor. I'd have been on the front line of the hopeless war against the AB virus and it would have killed me, indirectly but inevitably.

I don't allow myself the luxury of envying the corpse in the store room. Instead, I grab a scalpel and blade, a bottle of antiseptic, a needle and thread and some gauze bandages, then I limp across the hall to an office where I can work.

The blood-soaked shoe drops off my foot and hits the floor with a wet slap. The sock follows suit. I'm gritting my teeth in agony as I work, but I stay focused. Lee is alive and I have to get back to him. I'm the only hope he has.

When I heard his voice echo out of the Lords I felt a powerful rush of joy and horror. Joy that he was alive, and horror that he was surrendering to Cooper. I've already lost one man I loved to Cooper's schemes. I refuse to lose another.

In one respect being shot in the foot was a blessing. Had I been upright when I'd heard his voice I'd probably have burst into tears and run into his arms like a teenage girl in a pop video. But I was already crying in pain and I couldn't walk, so that wasn't really an option. I tried to play it cool, not let Cooper see how much I cared for Lee. I treated him like he was just another kid from the school. But I think Cooper knew; I think Lee's reaction to seeing me shot gave the game away.

I probe the small hole in the top of my foot. The bullet had passed straight through, right next to the bones that run to my big toe. Luckily it's not hit any of them, so I'm not going to be crippled. The damage is to flesh and muscle only, so if I can sew it shut, sterilise and bind it, then it should heal all right. If I stay off it for about a month, that is.

As I sew the wound closed I say to my guard through gritted teeth: "I'll need a cast. Go through the store rooms, there should be some somewhere. Hard plastic shell, foam lining, velcro straps, shouldn't be hard to spot."

The guard lingers, unsure.

"Oh, for God's sake, I'm hardly going to be running away, am I? Just fuck off and find me a cast, will you?"

He grunts and leaves. I glance out the window.

The moon is just starting to wane, and the snow is still coming down. We took a jeep across Waterloo Bridge to get to the hospital. The snow was so deep it was hard to drive, and I wonder if we'll find it as easy to get back. I know I've got to hurry. Cooper could be torturing Lee right now.

I splash some more antiseptic on the closed wound and stifle a cry of pain. The morphine's beginning to wear off. No chance of finding any of that here, it will all have been cleared out long ago. I bind my foot tightly and then grit my teeth and try to stand. It feels like someone's shoved a knife through my foot and every time I take so much as a fairy step they twist it savagely. I collapse back into the chair. No use pretending. I'm hobbled. The cast should help, though. Where the fuck is that squaddie?

I hear the door swing at the end of the corridor. Thank fuck for that.

"Did you find one?" I shout. There's no reply, but I hear footsteps crunching in the broken glass and detritus that litters the corridor. They sound strange, as if the person is limping, and each alternate step sounds hard and heavy, like a peg leg pirate. The footsteps get closer until I see a figure come to a halt in the darkness outside the room. Whoever they are, they're too short and slight to be the squaddie. The figure stands there, arms by their side, and I make out a knife hanging from their right hand. I feel a shock of fear. Then I shine the torch on the figure and gasp in surprise.

"Hello, Jane," says Jack.

I FIRE OFF a thousand questions. How did Lee and the others survive Thetford? Where are they all now? He answers me impatiently until my enquiries are exhausted and I ask him to find me a cast for my foot.

"Will this do?" asks the boy king as he appears at the door again a few minutes later, holding a blue foam cast.

"Yes!" I shout, and grab it off him. I gingerly place my foot in it and pull the Velcro straps tight. Once it's secured I stand up, waving away Jack's offer of a helping hand. I take a step and, while it hurts like hell, it's more bearable.

"Thanks, Jack, that's much better."

"You know," he says with a wry smile, "you could just cut it off. I hear they can do wonders with prosthetics these days."

I look down at the piece of table leg and foam that he's gaffer taped to his stump.

"How did it break?" I ask, walking out as I talk. Together we hobble down the corridor, two cripples together, both too proud to join arms for mutual support.

"Lee, this Ranger bloke and me, we're climbing into Parliament, right? Up a rope, from a dinghy on the Thames," he explains. "It's bloody tough going for me, but I manage it. The Ranger, his name's Ferguson, he helps me in through the window. So he turns back to help Lee climb up, and I grab the kit bag. But as I do that, two soldiers come into the room and tell us to put our hands up. Ferguson spins around, fast as you like, and he's just a blur, right, all martial arts and stuff. But one of the guys manages to shoot me. I'm standing right in front of the window and I bring the bag up as a shield, but the bullets shatter my prosthesis, I lose my balance 'cause the bag's so heavy, and I go flying back out the window."

We reach the top of the stairs and finally admit that we need help, so we link arms and begin going down the stairs sideways, like some ridiculous quadrupedal crab.

"I swear, I thought I was dead. But dumb fucking luck, I land flat on my back in the dinghy. The bag knocks all the air out of me and I'm laying there, pinned down and legless, gasping like a guppy. And I can hear shooting from above me, right, so I reckon Lee's gone in the window. I roll the bag off, get my breath back, and try to climb up and help. But it was hard enough when I had the prosthesis; it's fucking hopeless with one leg.

"Eventually the firing stops and I wait for Lee or Ferguson to call down for the bag, but they don't. So I reckon they're dead or captured, yeah?"

"Captured," I say as we pause to catch our breath on a landing. The corpse of my guard lies on the floor beside us, staring at the ceiling in surprise. My torch picks out the dark stain that marks where Jack's knife punctured his heart. "They're not dead yet."

Jack smiles. "Thank fuck for that."

I kneel down and rummage through the dead man's clothes until I find the keys to the jeep. I also take his machine gun, sidearm and a nasty looking knife. Jack and I link arms again and resume our ungainly descent.

"So I figure our mission's a bust," he says. "But I reckon I can still be useful, right, so I untether the dinghy and manage to row to a mooring and haul the bag up onto the embankment up these old stone steps. I figure I can flag down the others and give them the bag."

"Others?"

"Yeah, Tariq, Green and this crazy girl who says she knows you."

"Caroline?"

"Yeah, that's her. They've got this army of kids and they're gonna turn up at dawn, get inside the gates and then storm the place."

I stop dead in amazement and he topples forward, unbalanced, and slips down a few steps before he grabs the railing and manages to stop himself.

"But that's suicide!" I say.

"It wouldn't be if Lee and I had managed to pull off our little plan," he replies, righting himself and flashing me a sour glance.

"Which was?" I ask. "What was in the bag?"

So he tells me what their plan was. I stare at him for upwards of a minute, running it over in my head.

"That," I say eventually, "is fucking genius."

Ten minutes later we hobble out into the snow. My feet sink in it halfway up my shins, and it's still coming down.

"So where did you stash the bag?" I ask as we crunch across to the jeep.

"I was waiting halfway down Whitehall when I saw you being driven past," says Jack. "I just buried the bag in the snow and took off after you. I followed the tyre tracks. Sorry it took me so long. I'm not as light on my feet as I used to be."

"You and me both."

I pull open the driver's side door and clamber in. I tentatively depress the accelerator with my knackered foot. It hurts, but the cast makes it doable. Jack climbs in the other side. I turn the ignition and gun the engine. The wheels spin uselessly in the snow for a few moments and I fear we're going nowhere, but eventually they find purchase and we slip-slide away.

Without the orange streetlights making everything look slightly disco, London seems pristine and beautiful in the moonlit snow as I fight the wheel back to Westminster.

"The snow is our best friend," I say as we come down the Strand past Charing Cross station. "The guard has a little booth by the gate. He's expecting me back, and in this weather he won't be able to make us out properly from where he's sitting. There's a good chance he'll just pop the gates and wave us through."

"You don't want to wait and hook up with Tariq?"

I turn left onto Whitehall.

"Why should we? If we can get inside before they arrive, you can still fulfil your part of the plan. I'll stall Cooper and keep Lee alive until things kick off, then it's every man for himself."

"Here," shouts Jack. I slam on the brakes and we spin through 360 degrees before we stop. Jack lurches out into the snow and walks to the side of the road where he digs out the kit bag and limps back.

He tosses it in the back seat and gets back in. Another wheel spin, another moment of fear, but the four wheel drive doesn't let us down. I turn the jeep back the right way and we head off again. As we approach Big Ben I note the time: ten past seven. There's a faint hint of dawn across the river as we pass the road that runs to the ruins of Westminster Bridge.

A minute later we pull up to the gate. I flash my headlights and honk the horn once.

"Be lazy," I mutter. "Just this once, be lazy." I have the sidearm ready in my hand, just in case.

The gate swings open, pushing a tide of snow away into a thick drift. I send up a prayer to numerous gods, drive through the gate and down the ramp into the underground car park.

I pull into an empty space and switch off the engine.

"You know where you're going?" I ask.

Jack nods, resolute but nervous. "I think so."

"You can do this, Jack," I say. "Everything depends on you now. Go slow, go quiet, but get there. When was the attack scheduled to start?"

"The first strike of eight o'clock."

"Then get moving, and remember: every year the monarch should come to the Lords to make their speech saying how things are going to be different from now on. This is your chance. Make it good."

He nods, grabs the bag, and climbs out. In moments he is lost to the subterranean darkness.

I wait for a moment, gathering my thoughts, preparing. Then I too get out of the vehicle and walk into the Palace of Westminster, knowing there's a good chance I will never walk out again.

I LIMP AS fast as I can to the Speaker's Cottage. There is no guard at the door, and all is silent when I enter. A sudden thought grabs me, so I hobble as softly as I can – not too difficult on this deep carpet – across to Cooper's bedroom door. I take the cold brass doorknob in my hand and turn it ever so slowly. It rotates without a squeak, the door is unlocked. Careless, Cooper. Thought that since I was out of the way and guarded, that he could relax a little.

I push the door open. The well-oiled hinges do not betray me. In the half light I can make out his bed. There, fully clothed above the covers, Cooper snores gently.

I can't believe it can be this easy. I glance over my shoulder, wary of sudden discovery, of a soldier who will leap out of the shadows and shout "fooled you!" But there's nobody. I step forward, drawing the knife from my belt as I do so. Normally I would have gone for my gun, but something in my subconscious diverts my hand to the hard metal blade.

I advance towards the bed. One strike, swift and sudden, and it will all be over. He lies on his side, his right temple presented as if offered to the knife.

I stand above him and raise the blade but before I can strike the door to the cottage clatters open and a soldier bursts into the hallway. Cooper starts up in sudden surprise, woken from deep sleep. He registers me in the darkness. I plunge the knife down with a scream, but the moment had passed. He's too fast for me. He spins sideways and the blade hits the eiderdown, sinking deep into feathers and mattress.

"Freeze!" comes a voice from the doorway. I let go of the knife and slowly raise my arms.

Cooper scrambles across the bed to the other side, where he switches on the bedside lamp. He's genuinely shocked, the first time I've ever seen him on the back foot.

I have no idea where it comes from, but I snarl at him, hissing like a cat, feral, furious and thwarted.

"Kate," says Cooper, panting with sudden exertion. "You are endlessly surprising." He turns to address the soldier in the doorway. "Report."

"We got them, Sir. Two lorries of kids. Armed to the fucking teeth. We've got their leaders downstairs now."

Cooper nods, arranging his clothes, making himself presentable. "Good. Keep Miss Booker here until I return."

He leans forward and picks up the knife. As he does so he notices the guns and wags his finger like a teacher remonstrating with a naughty pupil. He holds out his hands and I pass him the firearms. He shoves the handgun in his trouser pocket.

"I'll deal with you later," he says, then he strides from the room, closing the door behind him as he goes. I throw myself upon the bed, furious at myself for wasting such a golden opportunity.

I sit and stew for twenty minutes, trying to come up with a plan. Now that Tariq's forces are captured, Jack's diversion is the whole of our attack. It's not going to be enough.

If I do manage to slip away when Jack makes his move, I need to know where to go.

Twenty minutes later Cooper returns, smelling of gunpowder.

"What have you done with the children?" I ask the second he enters.

"They're safe, don't worry. They'll be held until the snow clears then we'll just ship them straight back to Heathrow. I must say, your friends are a resourceful bunch. Their plan was a good one, and it almost worked. But my men are better."

He sits on the edge of the bed and throws the handgun onto a dressing table. I see the top slide is retracted, indicating it's been fired. He follows my gaze.

"You really should have told that Iraqi not to be such a smartass," he says by way of explanation.

Oh no. Tariq.

He nods in response to the look on my face, and he taps the spot between his eyes.

I fly at him, fists swinging, teeth bared, but he bats me away as if I were a kitten. I tumble to the floor, my foot burning with agony.

"You know, Kate, I think I made a mistake with you. I thought perhaps we could be friends. I see now that I was naïve."

I spit in his face.

He wipes it away with a sneer. "Your friends are no use to me. The kids I can use. But the adults..." He shrugs. "I think it's time to end this."

He reaches out and grabs my arm, pulling me to my feet. "Follow me," he says and walks out of the rom. I hobble after him. I have to buy some time for Jack.

"What are you going to do?" I shout after him.

"A ten gun salute, I think," he says over his shoulder.

He hurries down the staircase to the front door. I limp in pursuit.

"Why kill them? They're no threat to you now." I know that sounds lame, but even if he pauses for a second to argue with me, it'll be a second gained. He sweeps out the front door, passing a guard from whom he grabs a fresh sidearm.

I trail after him, beginning to beg. He ignores me. He turns a corner and I hear him declaim: "Lovely day for a shooting!"

I follow him outside into the stark white dawn. I see Lee, Green and a Ranger lined up against the fence, a group of armed soldiers opposite them. Oh god, it's a firing squad. My knees momentarily go weak with fear.

"Cooper, please," I say, choking back tears. "I'm begging you, don't do this."

He slaps me, Lee protests and a soldier opens fire. For a sickening moment I think he's shot Lee, but it was just a warning shot.

I'm crying now, pleading with Cooper, barely even conscious of what I'm saying. I step forward and come on to him. I'm sick at myself as I stroke his chest, all the time driven by the voice at the back of my head saying 'just play for time, just play for time'.

Cooper shouts an order then shoots one of his men, and the next thing I know I'm being dragged across to the fence and stood up next to Lee. I reach out and grab his hand.

I lean towards him and whisper: "be ready to run" but my voice is drowned out by Big Ben's insistent chime.

The men line up. Cooper joins them. They raise their guns as the clock counts down the final seconds of our lives.

Where the fuck is Jack?

I turn to Lee and we embrace.

Dear God, I may actually die here.

He whispers something to me, but I can't make it out.

Then my senses explode in fire.

CHAPTER TWENTY-EIGHT

As THE FINAL chime pealed I heard a deafening burst of machine gun fire. I braced for the impact, but there was none.

My ears rang as the shooting got louder. Then I felt a hand on my shoulder.

"Put the woman down and fucking run!" yelled Wilkes above the cacophony.

I opened my eyes, totally confused. Jane was already pulling away, dragging me along the edge of the fence to a stone alcove in the far wall where we could shelter.

I tried to make sense of what was happening. Cooper and his men were ranged along the far edge of the fence, backs to the river, engaged in a fierce firefight with a group of young women who were shooting at them from the covered stone walkway down which we'd been marched minutes earlier.

I glanced ahead and saw a figure beckoning us to a doorway. I thought my mind must be playing tricks on me, because it looked like Jack. Jane pulled me sideways as a stream of bullets whipped past us, cutting a straight line in the old stonework. We scurried through the doorway and behind a stone wall, under cover. Green was already there, gun in hand, raining fire on the pinned down firing squad. Wilkes hurried in after us.

Jack shoved a gun in my hand and smiled at me.

"What the fuck is going on?" I shouted above the din.

"I landed in the dinghy," he shouted back. "I had the bag. Jane got me back in. Voila." He indicated the groups of armed women and beamed.

It takes a minute for the penny to drop. Somehow Jack has pulled it off and completed our mission – he's got the kit bag of guns to the women held captive in the Lords and turned them loose.

Jane turned, popped her head above the parapet and sent a burst of fire towards the bad guys. Then she ducked back under cover, leaned over to me and kissed me long and deep.

We only broke apart when there was a huge explosion from behind us. I peered over into the yard to see the last of Cooper's men pouring through a gap in the wall. They must have blown it open with a handful of grenades so they'd have somewhere to retreat. The snow-covered grass was littered with corpses and red with blood.

I turned to the group that ranged along the walkway.

"Jane, do you know where the kids are being held?"

She shook her head. "One of the committee rooms is all I know."

"We need to find them as fast as we can," I said. "There aren't enough of us to win this, and we're too concentrated. Can you lead us there?" Jane shook her head.

"I know where they are," shouted one of the women Jack had released from the Lords. I waved her over to me. She was gaunt and thin, pretty but tiny and undernourished. She had fire in her eyes, though, and she held the gun firmly and with confidence.

"And you are?"

"Jools," she said. "I heard some noise from one of the rooms we passed on our way here. I reckon the kids are in there."

"Get them out, get them armed," I said.

She nodded and smiled a grim smile that promised horrible death to anyone who got in her way. I decided I liked her.

"Come on girls," she yelled, and she took off at a run. The women streamed after her, free and armed and hungry for vengeance.

Jane pulled herself upright and hobbled into the snow to check the bodies. As she did so I turned to Wilkes and Green.

"Wilkes," I said, "you should find Ferguson, okay? I don't know where they took him, and he's likely to be in a bad way, but they may decide to just finish him off, and we could use him." I noticed he didn't have a gun, so I took one from Jack and handed it to him. He looked at it suspiciously, then nodded to the weapon.

"Fine," he said. "Just don't tell the boss about this, right?"

"Promise," I said, remembering Hood's feelings about firearms.

He took off after the women into the Palace complex.

"You two, with me," I said, then I followed Jane into the snow. Green and Jack followed behind.

"Is Cooper here?" I asked.

Jane shook her head.

"Okay," I said. "We're going after them, through that hole in the wall. Green and I will take point, Jack you follow close behind and take care of Jane."

"I don't need taking care of, Lee," she said, momentarily indignant.

I stepped forward and kissed her nose. "Don't be daft. You've got a fucking hole in your foot."

I raised my gun to my shoulder and moved to one side of the hole in the wall. Green came up close behind me.

"You ready for this, mate?" I said, still unaccustomed to seeing him with a gun in his hand.

"Fuck yes," he said resolutely, which was good enough for me.

I lifted my hand and counted down from three then slipped sideways through the wall into the House of Commons Library tower, gun high, ready for anything.

CAROLINE HEARD THE shooting and the explosions and became frantic. The attack was going ahead after all. They were supposed to be part of it, trapping the bad guys between two pincers and bottling them in. If there was only one wave of attackers, the soldiers would be able to dig in, fight back or escape. There'd be no-one to outflank them.

She began banging on the committee room door and yelling: "We're in here!"

A boy grabbed her shoulder from behind. "What are you doing? Are you trying to get us all killed?"

She swatted him away and kept banging on the door.

"Shut the fuck up!" came a yell from outside. That must be the guard.

"Come in here and make me, dipshit!" she yelled back. Then she turned to the assembled throng behind her and said: "When he opens the door we charge him. There are way too many of us for him to hold off, okay?"

A few children began fighting their way to the back of the crowd, scared now that things had come to a head. But the majority stood ready, nodding and squaring up, ready to run.

Caroline kept yelling until she was cut off by a burst of machine gun fire right outside the door. Something hard slammed into the door and she heard it fall to the ground. Was that the guard?

Moments later the key turned in the lock. Caroline held up her hand to hold the children back, telling them to wait for the right moment.

The door swung open and there, standing over the guard's corpse, were fifteen young women carrying machine guns.

"You lot ready to fight?" asked the woman at the front.

There was a brief pause then the children yelled en masse and poured out of the room looking for something, anything – anyone – to destroy.

The riot had begun.

WILKES ACTED ON instinct. He had no clue where they might have stashed Ferguson, but he figured it would be somewhere underground. He didn't know why, exactly, it just seemed appropriate; you didn't torture people in daylight, it was a dark, subterranean activity.

So he ran through the building, hearing gunfights all around him and a huge screaming furore to his right that sounded like the scariest borstal in the world at playtime, until he found a staircase to run down.

The gun felt odd in his hand. The boss had strict rules about firearms and even though he knew that he would be mad to toss it aside, it felt wrong to be carrying it. Just before he found the staircase he ran past a huge glass case mounted on the wall and stopped to gaze in wonder. Ranged within the display case were five beautiful shiny swords. The plaque underneath read 'Lieutenancy swords'. They must have been used for ceremonial events, like the opening of Parliament. He doubted they were sharp, but he smashed the glass with his elbow and reverently lifted down the big central blade. Its hilt fitted his hand like a glove and the elaborate silver designs that protected the swordsman's hand glittered in the light. He knew the names of each individual metal curlicue like a litany – contre-guard, anneau, pas d'ane, quillon, écusson. He smiled as he felt the weight of the sword against his palm.

He shoved the gun into his pocket – no point throwing it away just yet – grabbed a second sword, and ran down the stairs, a blade in each hand. Cold steel, he decided, felt much better than a firearm.

The cellars were a maze of tiny winding passageways, and Wilkes checked each door, finding pokey offices, store rooms, and finally a bar. The door opened from the inside just as he was reaching for the handle, so he stepped back and raised the blades. One of Cooper's men stood in the doorway, weapon raised, but the sight of a man with two swords took him by surprise. That instant of confusion was all Wilkes needed. He lunged forward, both swords level, and felt both the steel blades slide through the man's clothing and body smoothly and with little resistance.

So they were sharp after all.

The guard went rigid and the machine gun fell from his hands. The two swords were the only thing keeping him upright as blood poured from his mouth and his eyes rolled back in head.

Wilkes executed a perfectly poised fencing retreat, withdrawing the swords in one fluid motion, letting his skewered opponent crash to the floor, then he leapt over the body into the bar.

Here he found Ferguson tied to a chair, his face a mass of bruise and blood, stripped of his shirt, his chest a dot-to-dot of cigarette burns.

He cut through the plastic ties on the ruined Ranger's hands and knelt down so they were face to face, hoping against hope that his friend had not been broken by his ordeal.

Ferguson looked up, swollen eyes full of fury. He asked for water, his voice a faint whisper. Wilkes found a pitcher of water on the bar and gave it to him. Ferguson gulped it down then stood, a trifle unsteadily. He held out his hand and Wilkes passed him his shirt and hoodie. Ferguson dressed himself carefully then looked down at the dead body of his tormentor, machine gun laying beside him ready for use.

Ferguson looked up and held out his hand.

"Sword," he said.

GREEN AND I advanced through the wreckage of the Commons Library. Jane and Jack hobbled after us, covering our rear and sides.

"Remember," I said quietly as we picked our way across the rubble, "his core team were SAS. They know more about close quarter combat than all of us put together. Our only hope is to contain them, pen them in, give them nowhere to run. If this turns into a running fight, they'll pick us off easy."

The explosion had set fires in the old wooden building. Already flames were licking at the bookcases that lined the walls. Huge, heavy, leather bound copies of Hansard began to smoulder.

"This place," said Green, "is going to go up like a candle. We don't need to follow them in there, Lee. We can just stay outside and wait. The fire will force them out."

I looked down the long corridor ahead of me – a shooting gallery if ever I saw one – then back to the burning room. He was right.

"Back outside, now," I yelled, and we retreated to Speaker's Green. Burning pages began to rain down from the walls as we backtracked.

"We need to think this through," I said, turning to Jane. "Do you think he'll stand and fight or run for it?"

"Fight," she said firmly.

"Good, then what we have to do..."

My voice was drowned out by a roar somewhere off to our left. I glanced at the others in confusion then ran through the snow, underneath Big Ben and into the yard. A tide of children was pouring up out of the underground car park. At their head ran Caroline, a machine gun in her hands. The women from the Lords brought up the rear, yelping and whooping and firing in the air.

I tried to wave them down, to prevent them hurtling headlong into the Palace, but there was no stopping them. This wasn't an army, this was a mob and God help anyone who got in their way.

Caroline ran over to me as the mob streamed into the building, screaming and yelling and tearing the place apart, every one of them carrying a club, chain or gun.

"Not quite how we planned it," she said to me, panting and excited. "They left all our weapons in a pile in the car park, so we just collected them."

"We need to come up with a strategy for this, some plan..."

Caroline cut me off with a derisive laugh. "Forget it," she said. "Genie's out of the bottle, Lee."

I stood there, frustrated at the way the situation had slipped out of our hands so quickly.

"Fuck it," said Jack. "Let's follow them." He didn't wait for my assent, he just stomped off. Caroline went with him, Green shrugged as if to say 'what can you do?' and followed suit. I turned to Jane, who was looking anything but excited by this turn of events.

"Problem?" I asked.

Her face clouded. "I don't want anyone getting to him before I do. Cooper's mine," she said. Then she too limped after the others.

I watched her walk awkwardly until she reached the door to the building – ripped off and smashed to pieces.

"I see what you like about her," said the voice in my head. "She's feisty."

Jane stopped and turned to look at me.

"Are you fucking coming, or what?" she shouted.

*   *   *

I WALK THROUGH the Palace of Westminster with Lee at my side, trailing in the wake of the mob.

My foot pounds agonisingly as we shamble through the corridors of power. Everything has been ripped apart. Shattered wood panels litter the carpet, paintings and murals have been smashed and shattered.

The Commons is a scene of total devastation. The plush green leather benches have been slashed and the stuffing lies everywhere, mirroring the snow outside. The Speaker's Chair lies broken next to the upturned debating table. Centuries of tradition reduced to firewood in a few minutes.

A soldier lies sprawled in the middle of the floor. His head has been bashed in with a dispatch box that lies next to him, its lid snapped off. There are two dead children on the stairs that lead up to the back benches. I hurry over and kneel beside them, but they are shot to pieces and beyond help. One, a young girl, is a stranger to me, but I recognise the boy from St Mark's. I close their sightless eyes and stand, gripping my gun tightly, eager for retribution.

The row of grimy windows at the top of the chamber to our left begins to flicker orange as the fire sweeps parallel to us. It won't be long before it reaches this chamber.

We emerge into the Members' Lobby. Marble figures lie on the ground, arms broken, heads smashed off. We pass a group of four kids toppling a statue of some long forgotten administrator, his outstretched finger hectoring and stern; it snaps off as the figure crashes to the tiles.

Ahead there is gunfire and shouting, explosions and screams, and the constant angry roar of children on the rampage.

There are a series of loud reports down the corridor to my right. I spin to see a soldier backing away, firing a handgun as he goes. Then it clicks uselessly, the ammunition exhausted. He throws the weapon at whoever is advancing towards him, then turns to run in my direction. I raise my gun to cut him down but before I can fire a tall figure bursts into the corridor in a flurry of limbs and steel. The soldier raises his arms to protect himself, but the swordsman brings his blade down in a sweeping arc and cleanly severs the man's head from his body. It rolls towards me, the cadaver toppling to the floor behind it. The swordsman stands upright and walks towards us, dripping blade at his side. His face is a mass of bruises.

"Ferguson, is that you?" says Lee.

The figure nods as he reaches us. One of the four kids, finished with the statue now, runs forward and kicks the soldier's severed head as if taking a penalty. It soars into the air and narrowly misses a second sword-bearing Ranger who emerges from the corridor and ducks in alarm as the head flies past, breaking the window on its way out.

"Fucking hell!" swears the Ranger. He turns and shouts at Ferguson. "We're supposed to disable when possible, Ferguson. You know the boss doesn't like us killing if we don't have to."

Ferguson turns and stares at Wilkes who immediately puts his hands up.

"But, you know, do what you feel, pal," he says sheepishly.

The kids laugh and high five the head kicker, then they take off towards the Lords, following the sounds of the fight.

Lee, the two Rangers and I follow on behind.

As we walked through that corridor something strange happened to me. I felt my pulse racing, faster than it had even when I was lined up in front of the firing squad. My hand started spastically clenching and unclenching on the stock of my gun and Mac began to shout at me.

"Come on Nine Lives, what are you doing straggling at the back?" he bellowed. "Fucking get in there. Crack some skulls. Come on, for fuck's sake."

I tried to ignore him but he was too loud, too insistent. The desire to kill grew so strong that I could barely hold myself in check.

"Stay with her," I said to Wilkes. Then I looked at Ferguson as if to say 'You coming?' He nodded once, and we ran ahead, into the fray. I heard Jane shouting at me to be careful, but it barely registered.

We came to the Lords and found the doors smashed open. The noise from inside was indescribable. As we entered we found the mob of children, nearly all of them, I reckon, formed into a circle. Some were standing on the red leather benches to get a better view of the makeshift arena they'd constructed on the floor of the house. They were literally baying for blood, chanting, cheering, jeering and yelling. I fought my way through the crowd to the front edge and found two of Cooper's soldiers – big, burly men in black combats, shaven headed and scary – standing with their backs to each other, circling around and around waiting for the crowd to surge forward and tear them to pieces. They were bleeding, desperate and cornered.

The men were unarmed, and the children had enough weapons between them to gun them down a hundred times, but it seemed the crowd was eager for a more primitive spectacle. They were hurling anything and everything they could find at the men – books, computer equipment, chairs, heavy wooden boxes. The men were, I realised, being stoned to death. I felt a surge of excited bloodlust and ran out into the lobby where I had passed some more shattered statues. I grabbed a heavy, sharp piece of marble and ran back, fighting my way through the crowd to the front again, cradling it in my hands.

The men were batting away the objects that were flying at them, but they couldn't get them all. A gold finial smashed into the face of one of them and he reeled backwards. The children cheered as blood began to pump from his nose. He stopped for a moment and bowed his head, wiping the blood onto his sleeve. I smiled as I stepped forward, raised the heavy stone block, and brought it crashing down on the man's head, feeling his skull crack and crumble beneath it.

"Yeah!" cried Mac. "That's more like it! Kill the bastard!"

The man slumped against me, blood spurting from his head, spraying all over me. I brought the rock down again and again, splashing his brains all over my chest. The children cheered and stamped their feet. The other soldier stepped forward, holding out his hands. I'm unsure whether he was begging for mercy or trying to get me to stop. I brought the stone down one more time and the man collapsed to the floor. I dropped the stone on what was left of his head, drew my gun and shot his colleague in the face. There was a huge cheer from the crowd as the man's head jerked backwards and he toppled to the floor.

I raised my blood drenched arms, gun in hand, and I roared. The crowd echoed my triumph. If I registered the horror in Ferguson's face, Mac's encouragement was enough to make me to ignore it.

"Come on!" I cried.

The crowd of children parted before me then fell into step behind as I ran past the broken golden throne and out the rear doors into the Royal Gallery – a long corridor lined with opulent paintings of heroic military scenes from the nineteenth century. I ran at the head of the mob down that hall towards the doors of the Queen's Robing Room. The doors were slightly ajar, but there seemed to be nobody ahead of us, so I ran headlong toward them.

Only when I was two thirds of the way down the hall, with a hundred screaming children behind me, did the doors suddenly swing open to reveal four men, two standing, two kneeling, machine guns raised. And standing in between them was Cooper, smiling as he saw us approach.

"Fire!" he shouted.

The four machine guns opened up simultaneously.

It turned out I was right – being shot multiple times doesn't really hurt. It's like being punched by someone wearing boxing gloves; you feel the impact in your torso but there's no pain, just a sudden pressure and shocking push backwards as you absorb the momentum of the bullet as it spins into your flesh, tearing and ripping and smashing its way through you.

I hit the tiles hard and slid forward on a tide of my own blood.

All I could hear was gunfire and screaming.

And then, as silence fell inside my head, Mac whispered one word, clear and calm.

"Gotcha."

CHAPTER TWENTY-NINE

I HEAR THE volley of gunfire and the sudden change from yelling to screaming as I pass the threshold of the Lords.

Ahead of me I can see the mass of children pouring past the Queen's chair, waving their weapons in a frenzy. Suddenly the tide turns and they back away and turn to run towards us. The children at the back are taken by surprise and some fall to the ground to be trampled by the mass panic that sweeps over them.

I try to wave them down, to get them to stop and regroup, but they're like a herd of panicked cattle – unthinking and unstoppable. Wilkes pushes me hard, flinging me onto the front bench, saving me from being trampled in the rush.

When the stampede has passed, I pull myself off the bench and see Wilkes picking himself up across from me. We can hear the commotion of the retreating mob behind us, and the groans of the injured and dying ahead.

"Put that bloody knife away and pick up a real weapon," I hiss at Wilkes, annoyed by his sword. He nods reluctantly and pulls a handgun from his pocket with his left hand, although he keeps the sword raised in his right. We advance either side of the throne into the corridor beyond.

The long, wide room is strewn with bodies. The air is thick with smoke so it's hard to make out the far end, where Cooper and his men must be. The light is streaming through the windows behind them, casting their shadows into the smoke, making them seem ghostly.

I turn to Wilkes.

"Find someone, anyone, and go around. Get behind them."

But before he can move there is a cry from the far end and the sounds of a struggle. The shadows dance and writhe in the smoke, there is a brief burst of gunfire, then footsteps on the tiled floor as someone comes running towards us.

"Stay right there!" I yell. The running man stops dead as the smoke begins to clear.

As the scene fades into view I first make out Cooper, standing about a third of the way to us, holding a handgun. He stares at me and snarls, a cornered animal. Then behind him I gradually make out four of his men, kneeling with their fingers laced behind their heads. Standing behind and above them are Green, Jack, Jools and some of the other women from the Lords, who have managed to outflank them.

"You're trapped, Cooper," I say, sighting my gun carefully on his chest. "There's nowhere for you to run. Your army's defeated, your prisoners are freed, your Palace is on fire."

He looks left and right desperately, searching for an escape route, but there is nothing. Then he looks down at his feet, at the dead and dying, and he barks a short, humourless laugh.

Quick as a flash he drops to the floor and grabs one of the shot children, dragging them to him and then pulling the body to the side wall.

I nearly scream as I realise that the bloody mess he's dragging is Lee.

My knees give way and I crash to the floor as I cry out. It sounds like someone else. Surely that scream of anguish can't have come from me?

In a moment Cooper is sitting with his back to the wall, legs wide, with Lee slumped back against his chest as a human shield.

My breath comes in short, ragged gasps and I try to focus through my tears. Lee is still breathing, I can tell that, but he's been shot multiple times, across the chest and abdomen. He is literally soaked in blood from head to toe.

His head lolls back against Cooper's chest and his eyes open, rolling wildly, confused and in shock.

Cooper brings his gun up, presses it against Lee's temple, and stares at me over my dying lover's shoulder.

"He's still alive, Kate," he says, no longer shouting. "There's a chance you could save him. Get him to St Thomas' quickly and you never know."

Lee's eyes focus on me and his face forms a question. Then he looks down at the forty or so dead and dying children that litter the floor before him and his mouth hangs open.

"What did I do?" he whispers as he surveys the carnage. He looks up at me with eyes clouded by tears and blood. "Matron, what did I do?"

I hear myself sob. This isn't the resolute warrior Lee has become. He just sounds like a frightened child.

I take a deep breath and force myself to take control. I slowly rise to my feet.

"Okay," I shout. "If you let him go, I promise you can walk out of here."

"Like fuck he can!" It's Jools, shouting from the far room, bringing her gun to bear on Cooper. "That rat bastard is mine."

"Julia, darling," says Cooper. "I didn't know you cared."

He takes the gun away from Lee's head for an instant and fires a single shot towards the far room. The gun is back at Lee's temple before Jools' lifeless corpse hits the ground. Jack cries out in alarm. There are shouts and screams both ahead and behind me.

Lee's looking left and right, starting to focus, starting to get a sense of his situation.

His eyes focus on the far wall and he seems to study the painting that dominates it. I glance right to see what he's looking at and realise it's a huge representation of the death of Nelson, who lies cradled in Hardy's arms much as Lee lies slumped in Cooper's.

He smiles, and blood bubbles from his lips. Then he turns and looks at me.

For a moment I'm back in Manchester, staring into the eyes of my brother, seeing the realisation of his own death so clear.

Lee mouths words, trying to tell me something, but I can't make out what it is.

I cry out. "No!"

But his awful sad smile widens.

Then he lifts his right hand, grabs Cooper's gun, still tight against his skull, slips his finger inside the trigger guard and pulls.

There is a single shot.

Then many.

CHAPTER THIRTY

THEY COUNTED TWENTY-three dead soldiers, forty-six dead children and three young women in their final sweep of the Palace of Westminster. Plus Lee, of course.

Some of the soldiers' bodies had been horribly mutilated. One had been literally torn apart. Green chose to believe it was the women from the lords who did that, not the children.

He organised teams to recover all of the bodies from the building – all their dead, that is. They left the snatchers to burn, and buried their dead in Parliament Square.

When the mob finally burnt itself out they gathered in the road outside, dazed by what they'd done, slowly coming down like clubbers after a great night out. Green addressed the crowd, telling them about the school, offering a home to all those who wanted to come with him. Anyone who wanted to return to the communities they were snatched from could come back with them too, he promised to arrange safe transport home.

A bunch of the comfort women elected to come with them, but a group of nine children refused to come along, insisting that they could look after themselves, distrustful of all adults even still. He let them go.

The fire spread more slowly than expected, but the entire Parliament complex was ablaze by the time they loaded the remaining children back into the lorries and set off for St Mark's through the snow.

As they reached the edge of the city two of them parted company with the main convoy. Jack led a small team to Heathrow where they spent three busy days siphoning off aircraft fuel, laying charges, planning the biggest explosion since Salisbury. When they pulled out of the airport, they left a huge conflagration behind them.

All the planes burned, the runways a mass of unuseable craters. Nobody would be flying children to the US from there ever again, and neither could the American Church land and start again. In the week that followed, they took care of Gatwick and Luton before returning to St Mark's.

Wilkes and Ferguson, who had taken off back to Nottingham once the battle of Westminster was over, had promised the Rangers would take similar steps at Birmingham, Manchester and Leeds airports. Obviously there were still local and military airfields the church could use, but they agreed this sent a strong message and was worth the effort.

Jane took no part in any of this. She sat silent, comatose, her eyes fixed on some distant point. She let herself be led into one of the lorries, compliant, like a puppet or a doll.

When they got back to the school she took to her bed and stayed there. She would eat when she was fed, sleep when the candle was blown out, wake when they opened her curtains.

But that was all.

It was as if she wasn't even in there anymore.

EPILOGUE

CAROLINE OPENED HER good eye and winced. It was hard to divorce the pounding in her head from the pounding on the door of her small room. The walls glowed orange, lit by the dying embers of the fire that kept ice from forming on the inside of the windows on these long, cold nights.

Even through her hangover, Caroline knew instantly what was occurring.

Someone was having a baby.

"Okay," she shouted wearily. "I'm coming." The hammering stopped and she heard footsteps scurry off down the corridor outside.

She rubbed her head and reached for the glass of water that she always kept on her bedside cabinet. She gulped it all down, wishing there were still such things as aspirin or Nurofen.

"What's going on?" murmured Jack, rolling over and nuzzling into her neck.

"The baby's coming," she whispered. "You go back to sleep."

He mumbled something and rolled back again, pulling the blankets tight to his neck. Within moments he was snoring softly.

Caroline reached across and stroked his hair tenderly before bracing herself and swinging her legs out of the warm cocoon of the bed into the freezing night air. The rug protected her feet from the worst of the cold as she pulled her jeans and sweater on. Her breath misted the air in front of her face as she added central heating to the list of things she would wish for if she ever found a lamp with a genie in it.

She sat back on the edge of the bed, pulled on her slippers, then hurried to the door and emerged into the first floor landing of Fairlawne, the new home of St Mark's.

The school she had returned to six months previously was very different to the one she had left two years before that.

It wasn't just that they were in a different building now; the sudden influx of new children had shifted the balance of the place. The easy cameraderie she remembered from their time at Groombridge was gone. There were new cliques and new gangs, new classes, new troublemakers and new favourites.

New names on the memorial wall, too.

With so many of the adults dead, they had too few staff to deal with the new intake. Although a bunch of the women who had been kept prisoner in Westminster turned out to be naturals, they couldn't replace what the school had lost. Green seemed to be in twenty places at once – breaking up fights, teaching classes, organising the repatriation of rescued kids, tending to the wounded and damaged. He was magnificent, holding the school together almost single-handed.

It felt as if the whole school were in a kind of shock, perhaps from the children's realisation of their own savagery during the battle of Parliament, or perhaps from the loss of so many friends and teachers.

Caroline felt it too. St Mark's was holding its breath, unable to relax, waiting for something to happen.

The winter had been unbelievably long, harsh and fractious. The fireplaces burnt twenty-four hours a day and the snow seemed never ending. They'd had little contact with the other communities they'd befriended. Travel was arduous in those conditions, so they became isolated. The whole school suffered from cabin fever. Tempers were short and food was scarce. There were so many new mouths to feed that the supplies they had laid in were inadequate, so they ended up slaughtering more of their livestock than they could afford. Caroline knew that by the time spring arrived they would have depleted all their meagre resources. They would have to work hard all summer – and pray God it was a good harvest – to lay in enough to see them through another winter.

The rumour had spread that the world was entering a nuclear winter caused by some distant cataclysm; another Chernobyl or a nuclear skirmish. But even as the winter entered its sixth bitter month Caroline was sure spring would come again; the snow would melt, the blossom would appear, the flowers would bloom. They had to.

On one of the very few times the school had been visited by traders from Hildenborough, they heard that the Abbot had made his final broadcast, murdered on air by a Brit. The Church had been defeated at home and abroad. They were safe again.

Even in the cold darkness, some children were congregating on the landing as Caroline hurried to the birthing room, woken by the screams, emerging to see what was going on. She ushered them back to their beds.

She paused of the threshold of the room, disturbed by the noises coming from within.

Ever since she'd arrived here, Caroline had spent at least an hour a day in this room, sitting beside the bed, reading out loud. Mostly Jane Austen, keeping it light. Sometimes, less often, she had just sat and talked. Once she had confessed to the murder of John Keegan and broken down in tears. As she'd cried into the eiderdown she'd felt a hand on her hair, stroking it softly. It was the only sign of understanding she'd had in all that time.

Matron hadn't spoken a word since that day in Westminster.

Now Caroline stood outside Matron's room and heard her screaming her way through labour. It felt odd to hear any noise coming from that mouth.

She stepped inside. Matron was sitting up in the bed, legs splayed, face red, breathing hard. She reached out her hand when she saw Caroline enter, so she stepped forward and held out her hand in turn. Matron grasped it tight and pulled the girl to her side. They stayed like that, hands locked firm, as Mrs Atkins oversaw the birth.

All the noises that Matron vocalised were primal. They were roars and cries and groans and screams. Not one word passed her lips – no fucks or shits or Jesus holy motherfucking Christs.

It was an animal birth.

The baby was born as the first light of dawn crept in the window.

Caroline held the child as Mrs Atkins cut the cord. She gasped in wonder at the tiny, blue screaming thing in her hands. So light and so angry at being removed from the nice warm place that was all it had ever known.

She laid the newborn on Matron's naked chest and pulled the sheets up to protect it from the cold. It fell silent immediately, eyes open, comforted by the warmth of its mother's skin and sound of her heartbeat.

"It's a boy," said Caroline.

Matron looked up at Caroline and smiled through her tears.

"I know," she said. "His name's Lee."

Later, Caroline walked out of the room into the half-lit hallway and told the lingering children the good news before ushering them back to bed.

She walked down the stairs and out the front door to watch the sun creep over the snow covered tree-line. Despite all the losses of the last few years, all the terrible things she had done and had done to her, the hardship of their lives and the endless winter that had enshrouded them for so long, she knew, with absolute certainty, that she was where she belonged, safe and loved.

As her eyes filled with tears, she caught the first faint hint of spring on the air.

THE END

BONUS MATERIAL

SCHOOL'S OUT: THE PITCH

Author's Note: For a brief time prior to launch, Abaddon Books circulated their shared-world bibles widely and encouraged submissions from anyone who wanted to pitch. I sent in three one-page outlines; two for *Pax Britannia* (now the sole domain of the estimable Jon Green) and one for *The Afterblight Chronicles*. Here's the outline for *School's Out*.

SCHOOL'S OUT

"When the plague had finally burned itself out and the dying stopped, the surviving boys and staff gradually drifted, one by one, back to the school. After all, where else was there for us to go?"

AUTUMN TERM: POWER STRUGGLES

At St Bart's College, an exclusive boys-only boarding school in an old stately home in the Pennines, only two teachers and the Matron survive to take care of the remaining pupils. Mr Bates, the PE master, was head of the school's Army Cadet Force, and he takes control, forming the boys into a military unit, mounting a raid on the local TA armoury, running drills and exercises. Bates is a tin pot fascist, and constantly butts heads with Mr Gibbs, the art master, whom he summarily executes one day at breakfast for questioning an order. The sixth form prefects are the 'officers' but they are loyal to MacKillick, a sadistic bully who makes the junior boys' lives a misery. Bates interrupts MacKillick and some of his cohorts engaged in the gang rape of Matron, who had unwisely attempted to discipline him. Bates attempts to intervene, but the boys first disarm and then crucify him, thereby taking control. MacKillick's regime is brutal and punishing, and the junior boys are constantly humiliated and mistreated. Matron is kept locked away for the use of MacKillick's loyal lieutenants. When one boy is sentenced to death by firing squad the fifth formers begin plans to oust him and his cronies from power.

SPRING TERM: THE BLOOD MOAT

MacKillick organises regular scouting parties to hunt and scavenge supplies from surrounding villages and towns. They begin to find evidence that nearby settlements of survivors are being attacked and plundered, but no bodies are ever found. Eventually they encounter another hunting party, smeared from head to toe in blood, hunting for human prey. Two boys are captured, the rest barely escape alive. Sensing the opportunity for a good fight, MacKillick leads a team to track down the culprits. They track the party back to their HQ, an ancient moated manor house. The moat is red with blood - the blood hunters believe that by surrounding themselves with a circle of human blood they will protect themselves from the plague. They have been harvesting the area, draining their captives' blood into the moat, and then eating the remains. MacKillick is forced to stage his first major military campaign – the infiltration of the enemy camp, the extraction of his comrades and perhaps, if he can pull it off, the destruction of the enemy's capacity to retaliate. Unfortunately he reckons without the treachery of his subordinates, and during the rescue attempt they contrive to leave him behind, unarmed, in a cell in the enemy camp.

SUMMER TERM: SIEGE

Having rescued their comrades, though not without cost, the battle weary boys return to the school and attempt to set up a model society run along democratic lines. Fifth former Phil Norton is elected leader, crops are planted and their position is fortified. After a month of relative calm they find themselves besieged by the blood hunters now led by a vengeful, and clearly psychotic, MacKillick, who has slaughtered his way to the head of the tribe. One panicked junior attempts to sneak out at night, but is captured and executed in front of the school when the boys refuse to open the doors. Co-ordinating with a scouting party caught outside the school, Norton organizes simultaneous counter-attacks from within and without, but the fight goes badly and order breaks down, leading to vicious, prolonged, room to room fighting throughout the school. Casualties are heavy, but eventually the schoolboys gain the upper hand, and Norton and MacKillick fight it out man to man in the main school hall. MacKillick wins, breaking Norton's neck, but no sooner has he bellowed his triumph than he is shot dead by the now fully recovered Matron, who assumes control and proves herself to be a far scarier badass than anyone could have expected. Unfortunately, the fighting has started fires, and the school burns to the ground. The remaining boys, led by Matron, set out to find a new home.

BONUS MATERIAL

SCHOOL'S OUT: DELETED PROLOGUE

Author's Note: The initial synopses were well received, and I was asked to provide a more detailed breakdown and a sample chapter for two of them, one of which made the cut. The following extract was part of the pitch for *School's Out*, and it stayed in the book 'til very late in the day, but I eventually decided to cut it. Jon, the editor, was a bit wary of that, but I convinced him. It was fun to write, and helped me establish the tone, but it was the only part of the book not written in the first person by Lee, so it felt out of place. I felt the eventual opening was much stronger because it established the 'voice' of Lee, his age, the setting of the book, and his attitude to authority all within the first few lines.

PROLOGUE

THREE MONTHS AGO

WHEN THE ANTI-PSYCHOTICS finally ran out, Alex began to wonder if rescuing his brother from the asylum had been the wisest move. After all, delusional psychopaths with messiah complexes do not make for the easiest of flat mates. By the time the knife made an appearance, he was pretty confident that he had made a serious mistake.

'Dave, what's the knife for, mate?'

No response. Just the scary eyes, the fixed stare and the knife.

'Dave? Do you, um, want to talk about it?'

Eyes. Stare. Very big knife.

Alex considered his options. He'd seen his brother in the grip of an episode only once, years ago, before he'd been sectioned. It hadn't been pretty.

Since the murders, Dave had been resident at a secure facility just up the road. There, on a daily diet of drugs and group therapy, he'd reverted to the good-natured older brother Alex had always worshipped. He'd seemed so normal again that it had been easy to write the episode off as an isolated incident, just one very bad day from which Dave had long since recovered.

As long as Alex didn't think about the dead girls, then he could pretend everything was fine.

So when the world began to die and Alex realised that Dave would be left alone and helpless, it seemed the most natural thing in the world to go and rescue him from the chaotic, corpse-strewn asylum. He'd plundered the medical facility for the necessary drugs, and supplemented his stock by scavenging local hospitals and chemists. But the supply had run out three days ago, and only then had he paused to consider what he'd do if Dave had a relapse.

Now, confronted by the knife, he finally realised the scale of his error, and he began, ever so slightly at first, to panic.

Dave stood silent in the kitchen, eyes wide, knuckles white as he gripped the carving knife handle tightly, staring at his brother with his head cocked slightly to one side like a curious puppy. There was no expression on his face, no chilling psychopath smile, no deranged leer or snarl of fury. This lack of expression was what scared Alex most of all.

'Dave? Are you all right, mate? Is everything okay?'

No response.

Alex had two choices. He could unload the bags of scavenged food on the kitchen table and make small talk as if nothing was happening, hoping that normal behaviour would snap Dave out of his reverie, or he could bolt and hope that Dave didn't come after him. Neither option appealed.

Dave mumbled something.

'Sorry Dave, what was that?'

Dave mumbled again, and Alex craned forward, trying to make out the words.

'Sorry, what?'

Slowly, menacingly, ever so carefully enunciating his words, Dave replied: 'I said, how was the Shopkeeper's fez?'

Alex bolted.

He dropped the bags to the floor, spun in the doorway and sprinted down the hall to the front door. He reckoned he had about a three-metre lead on Dave. Thank God he'd left the front door open. He sped out the door and turned left down the covered walkway that ran along the front of this floor of the block of flats, heading for the stairs. He reached the top of the stairwell before he realised Dave wasn't behind him.

He stopped to catch his breath, bent over, hands on his knees, gaze fixed on the front door to their flat, hanging open halfway along the walkway. Maybe Dave wouldn't come after him. Maybe he'd misread the situation. Maybe...

Dave walked slowly out of the door and turned to face his brother. The knife was still in his hand. They stood there, staring at each other for what felt like an eternity. And then Dave started running.

Alex pelted down the stairs three at a time, but he knew he was in big trouble. He didn't fancy his chances of making it to the street. Dave had always been the leaner of the two, faster, more agile.

Dave caught up with Alex as he reached the second floor. Alex felt his brother barrel into him from behind and what felt like a fist punching him hard in the kidneys. Before he could even register what was happening he was over the railings, weightless and falling.

The impact knocked all the breath out of him, but somehow it felt soft, as if he'd jumped onto a feather bed rather than fallen twenty feet onto a hard concrete forecourt. He lay there, immobile, knowing that his death was imminent, but too concussed to really care.

He saw his brother emerge from the stairwell and walk slowly over to him.

He saw his brother crouch down beside him, felt him stroking his hair.

He saw his brother reach down and dabble his hand in the pooling blood and smear it across his face.

As his vision faded away, the last thing Alex heard was his beloved, blood-soaked brother mumbling to himself, over and over.

'Safe now. Safe now. Safe now.'

BONUS MATERIAL

PORNOKITSCH INTERVIEWS

Author's Note: The wonderful people at *Pornokitsch. com*, now increasingly known for organising the Kitschies awards, interviewed me twice in 2010 for the *School's Out* trilogy: once in January, to talk about *School's Out* and *Operation Motherland*, and once again in June, when *Children's Crusade* had come out. *Children's Crusade* was later nominated for a Kitschie.

The following are reproduced with their kind permission.

FIRST INTERVIEW

JANUARY 14, 2010

Previously in the *Afterblight* series, readers had been exposed to the Big, Apocalyptic Picture. But, in *School's Out*, you chose to drill down to the disaster's impact on an isolated – essentially inconsequential – location. What lead you to focus like this?

Partly the old dictum of 'write what you know,' partly an deep affection for the original BBC series *Survivors*.

I know about boarding schools and all their little madnesses, as I've suffered in them as both student and teacher - there's an awful lot of autobiography in *School's Out* and a lot of therapeutic bloodletting as I took great pleasure in killing people from my youth!

Also, the thing that worked for me about Survivors was that these were people who were not directly involved in events - they didn't know anything about the plague, they weren't special, they were just ordinary folks trying to deal with the consequences of somebody else's fuck up. That appealed to me. That sense of trying to live through a huge event but not having any sense of the big picture, of what the hell is really going on.

The big question, of course... why kids?

Because they're far more vicious than adults. Crueller, nastier, less predictable and more morally flexible. Just watch kids bullying each other in the playground. It's horrific the way they gang up, scent weakness and strike. I think adults can become monstrous under pressure, but mostly they've had the rough edges smoothed off by experience and it takes a bit more for them to revert. But kids are not fully formed personalities yet, they're still pushing the boundaries of social conventions and trying to define themselves, so they do the most awful things sometimes. And the most wonderful, of course.

Over and above his young age, Lee seems to frequently have bouts of consciousness over his evolution into a killer. This runs contrary to genre conventions, in which a character's progress to lethal competence is generally seen as "advancement." Why can't Lee just accept that he's a badass and run with it?

Because I don't believe those characters. Hardened killers with no conscience are either psychopaths or sociopaths. Guys who kill while being in sound mind and for the 'right' reasons are either very damaged by it, or they wrestle with their conscience a hell of a lot. Even Jack Bauer stops and has a good old cry every now and then.

I read an interview with a British Army sniper last week - a cold, calculating, methodical killer, but definitely one of the good guys. And he's killed many, many very bad men. He seemed to be okay with it, but at the end of the interview he revealed that he hadn't kept score and he didn't actually know how many men he'd killed. And I thought that refusal to keep a tally said a lot about the psychological pressure he must be under. You can't tell me he hasn't had some long, dark nights of the soul.

Lee is, I suppose, like me in so far as I think I would have it in me to kill in those circumstances, but I know that I'd be a bloody wreck before, during and after the act. It just seemed more believable somehow. By the third book, which I'm writing now, the people around him are actually scared of what he might do in a fight, because they reckon his PTSD is so bad he might either flip out and go psycho or, worse, get them all killed. So the better he's getting at killing, the more fucked up he's becoming. That has to come to a head at some point.

Your father (noted folk musician Harvey Andrews) has also written quite a bit on the power of war and violence (albeit in a slightly different creative form). Has that had any influence on your work?

Definitely. I don't see how he couldn't really, as he's the best storyteller I know [**Learn more about his work at *www.harveyandrews.com***]. If you listen to "Soldier," or "Somewhere in the Stars," those songs evoke a strong sense of people caught up in violent times who are kind of bewildered by how they got there and unsure how things got that bad. All they want is to go home and live an ordinary life. And that's exactly who Lee and Jane are.

The key sequence for me in *School's Out* is where Lee says that he just wants to be able to find somewhere quiet and read a book, have a normal day. That's what he's fighting for - the right of people to be left alone to do nice things like play football and bake cakes and stuff. I could never make a hero out of a character who's fighting for power or glory. Those people are monsters.

In the end, I think that even though my Afterblight books are extremely violent, blood and thunder tales, they're essentially anti-violence. Which is having my cake and eating it I suppose. But the characters are all extremely reluctant warriors who want to stop fighting but find the world won't let them. The books don't glory in violence, or at least I hope they don't.

Lee's growing up a bit now, and so are his adventures. Initially he defended the school, but now he's liberated Iraq and defended the British Isles from invasion (from the US, no less). He's accomplished a lot for something that can't even get his driving license yet. How will he top this in *Children's Crusade*?

The first book was very interior and personal, kind of like a horror movie; the second was a big, widescreen war movie. Book three, which will probably be Lee and Jane's last outing for the time being, is hopefully a blend of the two. But it's more Jane's story than Lee's this time around.

Jane has some serious stuff from her past to deal with, so it's an extremely personal mission for her, but there's also a really nasty and powerful enemy to fight, albeit not one quite as OTT as the entire US Army! The bad guys in book one were cannibals, in book two they were warriors, in some ways the villains of book three are the worst of the bunch in that they don't kill you or eat you, but they'll treat you as if you were cattle, totally dehumanising you.

And speaking of growing up... In *Operation Motherland*, I started to see the first inklings of a little something between Lee and "Matron." I suspect the *Daily Mail* would have a fit. Or is this just my sordid imagination?

No, they're a couple by the time book three begins. I hope the *Daily Mail* does have a fit. That would be mission accomplished!

In *Operation Motherland*, you cheekily added a nod to Paul Kane's French mercenaries from *Arrowhead*. Was this a one-off, or can readers expect to see more "cross-overs" coming? Did he know you were doing this? Are there Blighterbrunches where you all sip tea and chart the post-Apocalyptic landscape?

Paul and I have swopped notes extensively. I love his books. I was really pleased to be able to have a new short story at the back of his last one and - first exclusive scoop! - I'm pleased to announce that he's returning the favour by doing an original story for the back of *Children's Crusade*. It's quite the love-in!

In fact, Lee takes a little trip to Nottingham in book three, so the crossover is far more explicit this time. It's a bit tricky in that our timeline doesn't match the publication schedule – *Operation Motherland* is set before *Arrowhead*, but was published after. And *Children's Crusade* is set before *Broken Arrow*, which is already out. So we're leapfrogging each other. In fact I was able to tease the villain for *Broken Arrow* in *Operation Motherland*, though because it wasn't out yet, no-one noticed!

Also, *Children's Crusade* takes place concurrently with *The Culled*, the book that kicked it all off, and if things go according to plan we'll see certain events from that first book in a slightly different light.

School's Out, Operation Motherland, Children's Crusade and... *The Unofficial Guide to Dawson's Creek*? Somewhere in a drawer, is there the first draft of the Cull hitting Capeside, Massachusetts? Who starts the crucifixions first: Dawson or Pacey?

Pacey is Lee, obviously, because of his affair with his teacher in season one. I reckon Dawson would be the first to snap. It'd be snuff movies and all sorts with him. And now I'm picturing Michelle Williams in combats with a gun... sigh...

Red Dawn or *Battle Royale*?

Red Dawn, dude, every time. Lea Thompson with an M16? Hell yeah!

SECOND INTERVIEW

JUNE 02, 2010

As it says on the back cover, *Children's Crusade* is the "third and final year of St Mark's School for Boys." Say it ain't so! Is this truly the final volume of my favourite homicidal schoolkids?

Yes. I like stories that have a beginning, middle and end. I would be wary of revisiting the well too many times and hitting diminishing returns. The day I got the commission for *School's Out*, once I'd finished doing cartwheels, I came up with the basic outline of all three books and knew, before I wrote word one of book one, that I wanted it to be three and only three. Look at how Lost picked up once they decided they were going to end it rather than stringing it out until they were cancelled. Big lesson there.

I don't want to give anything away to our readers, BUT... not everyone makes it through the book. And I won't lie – a few of the deaths really shocked me. As the author, how do you decide who lives and who dies? All that god-like power...

I never write with the explicit intention of shocking the reader - that's a blind alley, a stupid thing for a writer to do, and kind of insulting to the reader. If there are shocks, they happen almost by accident, which is the best way.

I don't want to sound wanky and say 'the characters write themselves!' coz obviously that's untrue and I always sniff derisively when I read an author saying that. But I know what they mean, and I've found with each of the books that there comes a point where it feels like the events of the story are carrying me along with them and

I'm just holding on for grim death, transcribing them. Obviously I'm controlling the story, but it feels like I'm not. It's odd, hard to describe without seeming to be completely up myself, and it's a great feeling.

What I tend to do is plot the book as it would happen if all the heroes' plans worked, then I have the plans go horribly wrong and as the characters improvise to compensate, so do I.

So to answer your question - I really had no fixed idea who would live and who would die. Right up until a character actually breathes their last there's every chance they might make it out alive. In the end, those characters who die were just in the wrong chapter at the wrong time, and paid the price.

Also, I firmly believe that a character's death should be surprising and should hurt the reader. I remember how devastated I was when Tara died on *Buffy*, or Wash bought it in *Serenity*, or Penny died in... hang on... WHEDON!! (shakes fist)

So if a character's death surprises me - and they always kind of do, actually, even as I write them - then hopefully they'll surprise a reader too. And I like the idea that the deaths of my characters knock the reader back. That's satisfying, 'cause it means the characters worked and connected.

Children's Crusade reads like the Afterblight's All-Star Game - with substantial appearances from characters developed by Paul Kane and touching on villains and themes first introduced by Simon Spurrier. We touched on this before, but what's it like working in a world this cooperative? Does Mr Kane mind you killing off a Ranger or two?

Paul picked out the two Rangers who have lead roles in the book and handed them off to me for development. But he did rein me in on their use of firearms and their rule that they should fight to wound, not kill, wherever possible. Also he was kind enough to say that I nailed Robert's character – then gave me a whole slew of notes on what I'd got wrong about the scene where he met Lee :-) So I did rejig things to keep him happy. (Cause, you know, he scares me!)

I always intended to tie book three very closely in with *The Culled*. As time passed and *The Culled* started to seem less immediate I questioned whether it was still wise, but I eventually decided that it added texture and rewarded long-time readers. There's even a very small reference to one of the character from that book in the long flashback in the middle of this one - see if you can spot it.

I should stress, though, that you don't have to have read the other books to enjoy mine, just that it's an added layer if you have.

As the last in the trilogy, *Children's Crusade* might not be the best book for Afterblight virgins. What would you suggest to our readers that want to get into the series?

There's a chronology at the back of *Children's Crusade*. I'd recommend reading them in chronological order, which just co-incidentally means starting with *School's Out*. How about that :-)

Ok. Zombies attack. You can have one weapon, one sidekick and one song for your zombie-slaying soundtrack. Go...

Flamethrower; Felicia Day; *Zippity Doo Dah*.

ABOUT THE AUTHOR

SCOTT ANDREWS has written episode guides, magazine articles, film and book reviews, comics, audio plays for Big Finish, far too many blogs, some poems you will *never* read, and two previous novels for Abaddon.

He lives in a secret base hidden within the grounds of an elite public school which serves as a front for his nefarious schemes to take over the world. His wife and two children indulge him, patiently.

You can contact him at www.eclectica.info, where you'll find all sorts of nonsense.

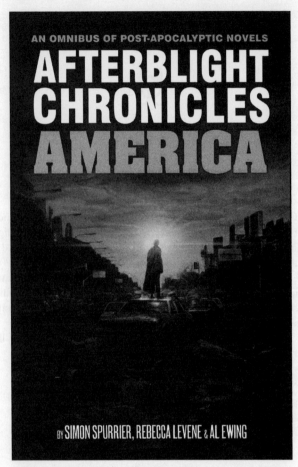

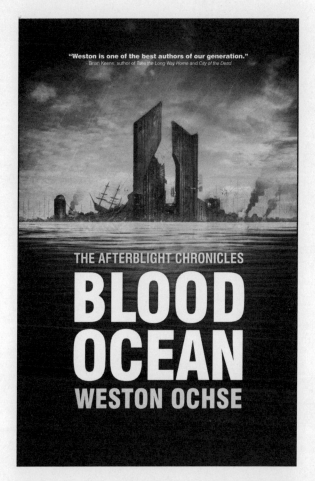